Montana Cowboys

Sandy Sullivan

Montana Cowboys

Erotic Romance

Montana Cowboys Box Set

Copyright © 2018 by Sandy Sullivan

E-book ISBN: 978-1-944122-74-4

First E-book Publication: December 2010

Second E-book Publication: September 2015

First Box Set Publication: June 2018

Cover design by Dawne Dominique

Edited by Ariana Gaynor

All cover art and logo copyright © 2018 by Sandy Sullivan

Dedication

This book is dedicated to my fans. You've stood by me through my changes in publishers and my experimentation with other genres, but it all comes back to the cowboys.
I love you all!

1

**LOVE ME ONCE
LOVE ME TWICE**
Montana Cowboys 1
Sandy Sullivan

Red Rock, Montana
Established 1895

The headlights reflected the white letters on the green sign, bright as day, even though darkness shrouded the countryside. Snow fell in flurries heavy enough to make it difficult to see and stay on the roadway. Deep ruts in the snow gave Natalie Bennington something to follow, so they obviously hadn't plowed the road in a while.

"I never will understand why in the hell they put the sign for town clear out here," she grumbled. "It's still a good five miles in yet." A deep sigh left her lips. "I sure as hell never thought I'd be back here. Fifteen years is a long time to be gone. I can't walk away from Gram though. Not after what she's been through."

The tires spun as she tried to go a little faster.

"Wow. These roads are bad."

Her grip on the steering wheel tightened, turning her knuckles white.

"I haven't really driven in snow in ages, well, nothing like Montana snow anyway."

A small hill loomed in front of her, and she knew if she didn't speed up to some degree, she'd never make it up. With a miniscule amount of pressure on the gas pedal, she started a slow climb.

Halfway up, the tires started to spin, and the back end of the car began to fishtail.

"Oh no." The ditch to her right loomed from the darkness like the gaping holes of hell. "Shit, shit, shit!" Barbed wire fencing stretched from one pole to another just beyond the backside of the trench, and without a doubt, she knew the gully had her name on it. The back of the car slid faster and faster toward the right while she struggled to keep it on the road, to no avail. Seconds later, she heard a dull thud and a loud crack as the rear hit the dirt, slipping into the crevice. The next thing she knew, she was staring through the windshield at the falling snow while the beams from her headlights reflected nothing—only disappeared into inky blackness.

"Now what the hell am I going to do? It's still a hell of a long walk to town, and it's snowing like crazy," she grumbled and slammed her fist against the steering wheel. This trip started out bad and continued worsening the farther she got from "civilization". The truck stops stunk, the food sucked, and the motel beds couldn't have one ounce of padding left in them because she felt every spring and every bulge. The truckers ogled, flirted, and propositioned at each gas station and bathroom stop. In addition, the weather hadn't helped, snowing almost constantly. The highway department closed the interstate for two days—two days of dealing with lonely men and very few women at a motel she wasn't sure didn't rent rooms by the hour, outside Coeur D'Alene, Idaho. Her cell phone battery died earlier in the day, and she'd forgotten her car charger at home.

I should never have come on this trip, but Grandma needs me.

On the verge of tears, she bit her lip and shook her head. She could give into the frustration and aggravation while no one could see her. *One, two, three, four, five.*

Too many times, she reminded her students to count to five before they did anything while angry.

It really doesn't help a whole lot.

Headlights appeared, coming from the direction of town.

"Great! Maybe it's someone who can help me get my damned car out of this hole."

The door handle felt cold under her hand when she tried to pull it and open the heavy panel. Gravity wasn't her friend, even though she pushed with everything she had, it wouldn't budge.

"Hello? Anyone in there?" A deep baritone yelled while he tapped on the window.

"Yes! I can't get the door open."

"Hang on," he said and disappeared for a second.

"Wait! Where are you going? Don't leave me in here. I'll freeze to death."

"I'm not leavin', honey. Hold tight."

The endearment sent a little flutter in her stomach. No one called her honey or darlin'. Then again, this was Montana, home of the gentleman cowboy, where every female was honey, darlin', or sweetheart.

Metal squeaked and groaned, but the driver's side finally opened.

"Hey there. In a bit of a pickle, huh?"

"You could say so, yes."

"Can you crawl out while I hold this open?"

"I think so."

The snow crunched under her boots when her feet touched. The man let the door bang shut behind her.

"Thank you," she said, trying not to slide into the hole behind her.

"You're welcome. How'd you end up in there anyway?"

"My car fishtailed in the snow and in the gap I went. What's it look like?"

"Easy. Just askin'," he replied, pushing his black cowboy hat back on his head.

"Can you help me get it out?"

"Sorry, darlin'. I have four-wheel drive, but it doesn't matter. Your car ain't goin' anywhere. The drive train snapped."

"You're kidding."

"Nope, I saw it in two pieces when I drove up. Are you sure you ain't hurt?"

"I'm fine other than bruised pride."

"Where are you goin' and I'll give you a lift?"

"Into Red Rock. My grandmother's actually."

"You ain't from here are you?"

"Not anymore, why?"

"You used to be?"

"Yes, actually. I was born and raised here until my parents moved us out of town about fifteen years ago. My gram still lives here."

"What's your name?"

She frowned, clamping her lips closed, afraid she already gave out too much information. If the man happened to be a psycho or something, she'd probably already told him enough to find her.

As if he could read her mind, he said, "I'm not some weirdo, just a good 'ole country boy. Born and raised here and trying to help a lady in distress."

"Are you serious? I don't believe you." She cocked her head to the side, studying his features the best she could in the dim light, "My name is Natalie Bennington."

"Nat? The same Nat in the band?"

"No one calls me Nat."

"I did, or should I say *we* use to. Me and Kale anyway."

"Cade Weston?"

"One and the same." He shifted from foot to foot, stomping his feet a couple of times. "You know, I'd love to stand out here and chitchat, but I'm about to freeze to death. The roads are impassible if you don't have chains or four-wheel drive. I'll grab your stuff and take you home."

Once he retrieved her suitcase from her car, she followed him to the passenger side of the truck, and asked, "What are you doing driving in this if the roads are so bad?"

The door opened with a lift of the handle, and she could finally see his face a little—only enough to see the corners of his mouth lift in a smile and a flash of white teeth. She still couldn't see his eyes, but from what she remembered, he had the prettiest baby blues of anyone she knew.

"Shootin' pool and havin' a good time. It is Saturday."

"I should have known."

The wind howled outside the windows, but the heater blast warm air throughout the vehicle. Snow swirled in the beams from the headlights, almost obliterating the view outside.

"Wow. It's really coming down out there," he said, once inside, shutting the door.

When he took his hat off and tossed it onto the back seat, she got a glimpse of the brown locks she remembered. A moment later, he fixed his gaze on her, and she forgot to breathe.

Holy shit!

A five o'clock shadow of whiskers covered his jaw, making him look a little rugged and a whole lot handsome.

He put the truck in drive and slowly pulled around her car.

"They won't tow my car, will they?"

"No. It should be fine until tomorrow. The snow is supposed to stop later tonight, and the plow should be through early."

"I hope they don't bury it."

A warm chuckle left his mouth, sending goose bumps flittering across her arms.

Cade and Kale were two of the most popular boys in school. Somewhat opposites in looks, Cade with brown hair and blue eyes, and Kale with dark brown hair and brown eyes, they kept many a girl twittering behind their hands in hopes of a little attention from one or the other, or both.

"Don't worry. If they do, I have a shovel."

The lights of town came into view a short moment later, but her grandmother's house was still a few miles away. Red Rock, Montana hadn't changed much in the time she'd been gone. A few businesses she remembered were now gone, and a few new ones took their place. Johnny's Gas Station still occupied the corner of Olive and First. A chain store grocery replaced Smith's. The Hometown Feed hadn't moved. Nevertheless, right now, all the doors were closed tight and nothing stirred except the wind and snow.

"What are you doing now, here in Red Rock?" she asked, curious about the man he turned into after school.

"Same thing I've always done. Work horses." A quick glance in her direction had her shivering. "And tryin' to stay out of trouble. Not easy to do in this town sometimes."

What the hell is wrong with me? Yeah, he's gorgeous, but I'm not looking to get into a relationship with anyone, much less someone in Red Rock.

"True. Have you managed to do that so far? Stay out of trouble, I mean."

A wiry smile crossed his mouth. "Not so much. I stole a car a long time ago. Well, I should say we did, Kale and I."

"Wow! Really? You didn't come across so rebellious to me."

"Luckily, the car belonged to a neighbor, and they didn't press charges since it made it back to them in one piece. If I remember right, you left town before I really got into trouble. Where did y'all go anyway?"

"Oregon. My dad got transferred after the plant closed here."

"Must have been hard."

"Yeah. Not easy making new friends at fifteen after you've spent your entire life in a town no bigger than a suburb of Portland." One shoulder lifted in a shrug. "I survived and even made some close friends."

"I heard about your grandfather. I'm sorry."

The sight of him sitting across the truck from her made her wonder what he thought about her all those years ago. "It's okay. He had a good life. Mom and Dad want me to try to convince Grandma to move to Portland with them. I don't think it's happening though. She loves this town."

"How long are you planning on being here?"

"I'm not sure. I took a leave of absence from work."

"What kind of work?"

"Elementary teacher."

A smile spread across his lips when he looked her way again.

"What?"

"It suits you."

"Thanks. I think," she replied with a frown, and he laughed. The warm sound made her shift on the seat, heat curling in her belly and spreading down her legs.

"You never did take compliments very well."

"When did you ever compliment me, Cade Weston? If I remember correctly, neither you nor Kale ever gave me the time of day, much less a compliment."

The lights of her grandmother's house came into view, and he pulled into the driveway, shut the truck off, and said, "Teenage boys don't know how to give compliments, Nat. You've changed since all of us were kids."

"I know, cynical and bitter."

"No, I mean you've turned into a real beauty. I certainly don't see the gangly teenage girl I remember. I'm sure we've all had issues and problems over the span of time."

"Sorry. I didn't mean to dump on you."

"It's okay. Obviously there is some sourness."

"Yeah, well, maybe I'll tell you about it someday. For now, I need to get inside. I'm sure my grandmother is worried sick. Thanks for the lift," she said, pushing open the door. "I guess I'll see you around."

"Probably. I'm always around somewhere," he replied. "Be careful going up those steps. They might be a bit icy."

"Thanks for the warning, but I do remember winters in Montana; very cold, very windy, and not much fun."

"Unless you are sledding down Marshall Hill."

"People still do that?"

"All the time."

"Man. I haven't been sledding in forever." After they moved to Oregon, rarely did her family do anything like sledding together. Her parents fought a lot since her mom hadn't wanted to leave Red Rock and her dad worked all the hours he could get to buy them a house. She shook her head to clear the melancholy thoughts.

Life got lonely for the awkward fifteen-year-old from the hick town in Montana.

Her sister, Andrea, felt the same way, although, much younger than Natalie, friends came much easier to her and fitting in hadn't been such a chore.

"Let me get your suitcase and walk you to the door," he said, opening the drivers' side.

"I can get it."

"I'm trying to be a gentleman here, Nat," he said with a smile. "My parents did raise me to be one, even if I didn't take to it very well sometimes."

Moments later, he stood at her side of the truck and held the door open for her.

When she stepped onto the driveway, her foot slipped, and she grabbed the door of the truck, Cade's arm whipping around her waist to steady her.

"Careful."

Heat spread from where his hand touched, down to her toes, and back up, settling low in her stomach. No man made her react this way, not even Steven; the man she once loved, or thought she had, for over two years before he decided he needed someone younger, prettier, and skinnier. Sure, she wasn't model thin. Her lips had a little natural pout to them, and her legs seemed somewhat long, but overall, she didn't think she was ugly or anything.

"Thanks," she whispered, looking up at his face.

Damn, he's hot. Always was, but I almost forgot about his rugged good looks. And the way he filled out with muscles and bulges in all the right places...yummy.

Her shoulder brushed his chest, and she wondered if he had lots of hair or only a little. The few times she'd seen him and Kale without shirts, they'd been young enough not to have much, but now it made her wonder.

The boys around Red Rock used to swim in the river meandering south of town, and many times, she and a few of her friends would watch from the bridge. Pre-pubescent boys had her all a twitter at fifteen, just like any girl her age. Cade and Kale were some of the cutest boys in school and *everyone* wanted their attention, including her at the time. They'd both been more into the popular girls. The cheerleader types—not the band geek, like her.

"This driveway is pretty slick."

"Grandma probably hasn't had anyone shovel it in a while. It looks like the drifts are pretty high."

"Yeah," he replied, stepping back and grasping her arm with one hand while holding her suitcase in the other. "Take small steps. It'll make it easier to walk on."

Giving him an exasperated glance, she said, "You know, it does snow in Oregon sometimes too."

His lips lifted in a grin. "But this gives me a reason to hold your arm."

Stepping onto the porch, she moved out of his reach as the light flipped on and her grandmother opened the door.

"Natalie Marie? Is that you?"

"Yes, Grandma. It's me."

"Who's with you, honey?"

"Cade Weston, Grandma. He drove me here since it's snowing so badly. I managed to put my car in a ditch outside of town."

"Well, Cade. Come on in and sit a spell where it's warm."

"I would, ma'am, but I'm on my way home. I've got a mare tryin' to foal."

"Nonsense. I'm sure you could use a cup of coffee to warm you. Now get in here. We're lettin' all the heat out."

Cade laughed, and Natalie had to smile when he said, "Yes, ma'am."

"No use arguing, you know."

"Not with your grandmother."

When they stepped inside and shut the door, Cade took off his hat and Natalie got the full affects of his devastating good looks. The jean jacket and T-shirt stretched over his chest like a second skin. Worn blue jeans hugged his lean hips, and pointed-toe cowboy boots completed the picture of the Montana cowboy to a 'T'.

The rough clearing of a throat brought her gaze back to his face as heat flushed her cheeks when she caught his gaze. His lips twitched with mirth when he tried to hold back his grin.

Busted!

"Sit. The couch is comfortable. I have coffee brewing anyway. I figured Natalie would want some when she got here."

"After you," he said, sweeping his arm aside in one of the most gallant gestures she'd ever seen.

Whoa! Wait just a damned minute here. Stop thinking he's some white knight or something — even if the thought of those rough hands and some delicious sex seems really good right now. How long has it been again? Too frickin' long! The last time with Steve even sucked and not literally.

"What have you been up to Cade?" her grandmother asked from the kitchen.

"Not much ma'am. Stayin' out of trouble, or tryin' to."

"How's your wife?"

Well, shit! So much for a hot romp with a sexy cowboy.

"What's her name again, Cade? Cindy, I think," her grandmother continued, oblivious to Natalie's disappointment.

"Uh, we divorced about four years ago, Mrs. Oliver."

Okay, maybe the hot romp with a sexy cowboy isn't out.

"Oh? I'm sorry to hear the news. Natalie never has married. Too busy taking care of other people's kids."

Blue eyes fastened on her and she shifted on the seat.

"Grandma, can we not talk about my lack of marriage please?"

"She did have a steady man for awhile, but Steve was a jerk and a liar," her grandmother told Cade. "I told you from the beginning, but you wouldn't listen to your grandmother. I'm glad you came to your senses before you got into anything permanent." The statement directed at Natalie, making her cheeks fill with heat at her grandmother's words.

A quick breath blew the hair off her forehead and she mouthed 'sorry'.

He reached over and squeezed her fingers. Electricity shot up her arm, sending delicious sensations across her nipples.

Damn it!

Her grandmother handed Cade a cup of coffee, and one to her, before taking a seat in the recliner across from the two of them.

"How long are planning on staying, Natalie?" her grandmother asked.

"I don't know. However long you need me to, Grandma. I took a leave from the school, so I can stay until whenever."

"Well, maybe Cade can take you out to dinner one night so you aren't cooped up here in this house with me all the time. There's no need for you to be here all day, every day. When you call your mother and father, tell them I am *not* moving to Oregon. I'm staying right here in Red Rock."

"Grandma, Cade doesn't have time to worry about ferrying me around town. Besides, it's not as if I'm not a native. And yes, I'll tell Mom and Dad you aren't moving to Oregon."

"Actually, I'm not busy tomorrow. I was going to offer to come over and shovel the driveway for you, Mrs. Oliver, and I'd love to take you out to dinner, Nat. You know, for old time's sake."

"See. He wants to take you out to dinner," her grandmother said with a wink.

"I appreciate the offer, Cade, but I really should spend some time with my grandmother, and I..."

"Nonsense. The handsome gentleman asked you out for dinner. You'll go if I have to push you out the door."

She tipped her head back on her shoulders and laughed. "All right, Grandma. You make it sound like I haven't had a date in forever."

"Only since your scumbag, short-dicked..."

"Grandma!"

"Okay, so I don't know whether he was actually short-dicked or not, but I *know* scumbag fits the bill."

A roar of laughter filled the air, and she glanced at Cade with a grin and a shake of her head.

Cade came to his feet and said, "I really should be getting back to the house. Thank you for the coffee, Mrs. Oliver."

Natalie stood to walk him to the door, ignoring her grandmother's wink when Cade's back turned.

"I'll be over bright and early to shovel the snow."

"It's okay. You really don't need to—"

One finger against her lips stopped her words.

"I want to. Besides, it gives me a reason to see you again."

"You asked me out to dinner, remember?"

"True. Okay, it gives me a reason to see you before five tomorrow evening."

"All right already. Be careful out there, huh?" A quick glance out the door told her the snow had slowed dramatically. "I'm sure the roads are still slick, and if the temperature drops anymore, the snow will ice over."

"I will. Don't forget, this weather is nothing new to me. I'm a born and bred Montana boy. I'll see you in the morning," he replied with a wink. "Sleep well."

She watched him walk to his truck and slide inside as the interior light illuminated his face. The headlights came on, and she could see the outline of his hand lift in a wave before backing out of the driveway and disappearing down the street.

A shiver rolled down her back, and she wasn't quite sure if it came from the look in his eyes when he put his finger against her lips or the frigid air outside.

Cade Weston. High school jock. All around hunk and he wants to take me out to dinner. Who would of thought?

2

"You're taking who out to dinner?" Kale asked on the other end of the phone the next morning.

Cade and Kale remained best friends even after high school and through turbulent marriages on both their parts, but each came to their senses when their wives became lovers. Both women broke the news at dinner one night. They informed their husbands they'd decided they were lesbians and wanted to be together—without the men.

"Natalie Bennington. Remember her from high school?" Cade replied as he pulled on his jeans, T-shirt, and thick socks. He'd planned to be at Mrs. Oliver's first thing this morning, but the sun already started a good trek across the sky before he rolled out of bed. He'd been up half the night with the foaling mare at the barn on his property. The house wasn't complete yet, but the barn and the pasture areas were.

"Yeah, kind of geeky looking band girl. Didn't she have long blonde hair, green eyes, and braces?"

"You got it, but now she's hot! Oh my God, hot!"

"How would you know?"

"She put her car in a ditch outside of town. When I left the bar, heading home, I found her. The drive train busted and the car stopped ass end in the gully. I'm glad she didn't get hurt, but her car wasn't going anywhere, so I took her to her grandmother's."

"Playing the knight in shining armor, huh?"

"I guess, but let me tell you when I saw her face, I about shit, man. Thick hair you could really wrap your hands in, big green eyes with little flecks of gold, and legs that could stop traffic. I'm gettin' hard just thinking about her."

Kale's tolerant chuckle reverberated through the phone line. "So where has she been?"

"Her parents moved to Oregon after the plant closed."

"And she's back here now, why?"

"Remember readin' about Doc Oliver dyin' a week or so ago?"

"Yeah."

"He was her grandfather. I guess she's here to help her grandmother somehow."

"She's not staying long then."

"I don't know for sure. She said she took a leave of absence from her teachin' job."

"A teacher?"

Cade grunted in affirmation. "Elementary."

"Figures. I would have pegged her for the teacher type even way back then. Where are you taking her for dinner?"

"The Millhouse, I think."

"Wow! Going all out, aren't you?"

"I figured what the hell, you know. I haven't taken anyone on a date in months, much less been laid."

"You think she'll go for a little short term fun?"

"Maybe. She hasn't had a steady guy for a while from what her grandmother said. Mrs. Oliver made sure to tell me too."

"Figures."

"I better go, Kale. I told them I'd be over this mornin' to shovel the drive. Two women tryin' to do it didn't sit well with me."

"Okay. Call me later."

Cade hung up the phone, grabbed his truck keys, and slipped on his jacket. Within moments, he pulled in front of Mrs. Oliver's house, noticing first thing—Natalie's car sitting on the street near the mailbox.

"Stubborn woman," he grumbled, shutting his vehicle off and popping open the door. "I would have taken her to the garage to have them tow it here."

The next thing he realized was Natalie standing in the middle of the driveway with a shovel in her hands.

"I told you I would be here, Nat."

Her hand shoved a few wisps of hair out of her face. "Oh, hi, Cade. I know you did, but when you weren't here by ten, I started without you."

"You did a good job, but let me finish it. Women shouldn't be shoveling snow."

One perfectly arched eyebrow shot up. "Excuse me? Are you going all male-chauvinistic on me?"

Oh shit!

"Sorry. I didn't mean it the way it came out. Men are built bulkier and with more muscle mass to handle physical labor better than women."

The shovel made it into a pile of snow and stood upright with a *twang*. Her eyes narrowed, and he wasn't sure if he would make it out of this alive, even if she was damned cute all flustered and pouty.

"Besides," he said, wrapping one arm around her waist and tugging her closer. "What does it hurt to let a man take care of you a little?"

Before he could change his mind, he brushed his lips over hers in a quick kiss then released her.

"Why don't you make some hot coffee? I'll have this done in a minute."

Her lips pressed into a firm, straight line, but lifted in a small smile at his wink.

"All right. Black?"

"Yeah," he replied, slipping his jacket off his shoulders, leaving him in nothing more than his T-shirt. The shoveling would work up a sweat in no time if he left his coat on. A quick glance in her direction, gave him the enticing view of her backside in a nice pair of jeans as she made her way up the stairs.

Damn! She even has a nice ass to go along with everything else.

A honk from a car behind him drew his attention to the street. He almost groaned when he saw the familiar sight of Kale's Chevy.

"Hey bro," Kale said, stepping out of his truck.

"What are you doin' here?"

"Our conversation this morning had me wondering. I figured I'd check out Ms. Natalie myself."

"Great," he said with a groan.

Moments later, Natalie returned with coffee in hand.

"Holy hot damn," Kale whispered only loud enough for Cade to hear.

"Told you."

"Well, well, if it isn't Kale Dunn. What brings you by?" she asked, stopping next to him and handing Cade the cup.

"Cade told me this morning he ran into you and planned to come over and shovel the driveway. I thought I'd be a gentleman and help."

Cade covered his snort with a cough.

"Isn't that sweet? But I really don't think there's enough for two strong, healthy men to do. The drive isn't very big, after all."

"How about I keep you company while Cade shovels then?" Kale asked with an innocent look.

Cade felt like punching him.

"Great! Come on up to the house. I know Gram has more coffee and probably even some of her coffee cake left."

With his mouth hanging open, Cade watched Kale slip and arm around Natalie's shoulder and walk with her to the door.

"Well I'll be a son of a bitch. I'm gonna kill him," he growled under his breath.

It only took him about fifteen minutes of heavy shoveling to clear the driveway, especially after getting pissed at Kale for honing in on Natalie. True, they'd shared a woman or two over the years. Okay, maybe like ten from before they married and after their divorces, but Cade didn't have any idea if Nat would be one of them.

A one-man woman comes to mind with her, but then again, I could be wrong. Maybe she might be up for a little adventure after her lack of relationship lately.

The shovel found a spot next to the garage door before he headed up the porch. A high-pitched, tinkling laughter met his ear when he stopped at the front door. With a quick peek through the curtains, he saw Nat and Kale sitting close together on the couch with her grandmother sitting across from them. The intense uneasiness sweeping through him, didn't sit well. Possessiveness and jealousy weren't new feelings for him. They'd been the primary reaction to the news of his ex-wife's betrayal, but having them for a woman he hardly knew, had him wondering at the reasons.

He lifted his hand, rapping on the door a couple of times.

"Come on in, Cade. You don't have to knock," Natalie said, pushing open the screen. "It didn't take long to shovel the drive at all. It would have taken me a lot longer, I'm sure."

"I don't think it's supposed to snow again for a few days at least. Hopefully it'll stay clear for you for a little while anyway."

"Let me get you a refill on your coffee and you can sit a spell."

"Maybe Cade wants to go to lunch along with you and Kale, Nat. Wouldn't that be nice?" her grandmother said with a twinkle in her eye. His gaze focused on his friend, and Kale mouthed *what* as he returned the scowl.

Nat took his coffee cup into the kitchen, but called out, "I don't know, Gram."

"Nonsense, Natalie. Having two men fight over you seems like a wonderful idea, even to this old lady."

Her face flushed with color when she returned to the living room, hot coffee in hand. Cade figured he'd let her off the hook. Having lunch with her and Kale wasn't in his plans, but making tonight special for her was.

"You know, I'm sure it would be a great time having lunch with you two, but I'll have to pass. I have an appointment I can't get out of early this afternoon, but I'll be here right at five to pick you up for dinner. Sound like a plan?"

"Mmm...sure, Cade," she replied with a frown crinkling the skin between her eyebrows. "Where are we going for dinner? You know, so I know whether to wear a dress or jeans."

"It's a surprise, but wear a dress," he said. "I plan on pamperin' you tonight."

"Oh?"

"Yep." Taking the seat on the other end of the couch, he thought it amusing when she seemed uncomfortable sitting between him and Kale.

If she only knew how much I'd like to sandwich her between the two of us, in other ways.

Little Miss Natalie Bennington definitely had his interest and it appeared she also garnered Kale's. Rather funny actually, in high school, she wasn't his type or Kale's, at all. Cheerleader, blonde, built like a brick shit house, and loose panties fit the description of those making it into their favor. Natalie was the shy girl who stayed away from the football players, preferring to spend her time with the others in the band and those into the science stuff.

"You didn't say how long you planned to stay, Nat," Kale said.

"I really don't know. It depends how long Gram needs me. I don't have anything back in Oregon holding me at the moment, so I can be here for a while if need be."

"Wonderful. I'd really love to get to know the Natalie Bennington you've turned into," Kale replied, brushing his fingers against her shoulder when he put his arm across the back of the couch. Cade clamped his jaw so hard, his teeth hurt. The insane urge to snap Kale's fingers rushed through him.

A heavy sigh left her lips and Cade wondered why.

He finished his coffee and stood. "I'd better get going so I don't miss my appointment. Walk me out?" he asked, taking her hand in his.

"Sure," she replied, coming to her feet.

They walked outside, hand in hand, and he liked the feeling of her warm palm in his.

The smile on her lips and the shy way she dropped her gaze, made him feel like a kid again. Like a first date or something.

I guess it will be in a way. We never dated in school.

"You really don't have to go out of your way tonight, Cade. I know you probably feel cornered into dinner with my grandmother's suggestion and all."

He let go of her hand and wrapped an arm around her waist. "I want to, Natalie. Why can't you believe that? I find you extremely attractive, funny, cute, and I want to see what makes you tick," he whispered, brushing his lips against her ear. When he moved back, her big green eyes drew him in, making him want to feel the softness of her lips under his again. The miniscule brush of their mouths before did nothing but whet his appetite for more. He wanted to stroke the inside of her mouth and feel her return the hot brush of his tongue. He wanted to know what it felt like to have her give herself to him and let need take over.

Seconds later, his mouth hovered over hers—wanting but waiting for her to give him some indication she needed it too.

A slight shift of her weight toward him gave him the answer he sought.

The cell phone in his pocket rang, and he closed his eyes with a groan.

Damn it!

He knew that ring tone—his sister.

Impeccable timing.

"Sorry," he whispered, stepping back and pulling out his cell. "Hi, Elizabeth."

"Hey, Cade. Mom wants to know if you are coming over for lunch today."

"I planned to. Is there a problem?"

"No. She wants you to stop at the store on your way and grab a few things."

"Fine. I'll call you when I get there. Bye, sis." The phone shut with a click. "I guess I'll see you tonight."

Natalie nodded and rubbed her arms.

"I shouldn't keep you out here. It's too cold without a jacket," he said, running his hands over her bare flesh.

"I'm fine. Thanks for shoveling the driveway."

"You're welcome. Anytime." A heavy sigh rushed from between his lips. "I better go before Elizabeth calls back wondering where I am." Not wanting to walk away without feeling her lips, he brushed his mouth over hers, smiling to himself when she lifted up on her toes to meet him halfway.

* * * *

God, he tastes good. I really want more, but here and now is not the place.

"Mmm...you better go," she whispered, after a quick sweep of his lips.

"Yeah. I'll see you in a little while."

"All right. Five o'clock, right?"

He nodded and opened the door to his truck.

Moments later, he waved and pulled away from the curb, heading down the street.

When she turned toward the house, Kale stood at the door, leaning against the frame with his arms over his broad chest and a wicked smile on his lips.

How the hell did this happen? I'm having lunch with Kale and dinner with Cade. I would never have thought in a million years, I'd see either of them on this trip home, and here I am, having meals with them on the same day. This is totally unbelievable and so crazy it's funny.

As she headed toward the house, Kale opened the screen for her. "Ready for lunch?"

"Uh, sure. Let me grab my purse and we can go."

Her shoulder connected with his chest when she brushed by him, sending exciting tingles down her arm.

Whoa! Wait just a damned minute here.

A quick glance into his dark chocolate eyes and she almost forgot where she was going. The two men were such a contrast. Kale with his dark good looks, hot build, hard thighs, and trim waist, could make any woman cream her panties, and then there's Cade, all light brown hair, baby blues hot enough to melt butter, solid chest, and lips so soft, she wasn't sure he even kissed her, and man, could he kiss!

"I...um..."

"Your purse?"

The rush of air against her lips when he spoke had her wondering if his kiss would be any different than Cade's.

"Oh...uh...yeah."

Within a few minutes, he had her seated in his truck and they were driving down the now plowed street, toward town.

"So. What have you been up to since high school?" she asked, curious about the direction of his life.

"School and work. The normal stuff."

"School? You went to college somewhere?"

"Yeah. University of Montana, actually. I got a football scholarship out of high school and got my degree in Architecture."

A laugh bubbled from her lips. "You and Cade always were the stars of the team."

"Kind of hard not to be when I played quarterback and he played tight-end. Didn't you play in the band?"

"Yes, the flute."

"Ah. I remember. The shy band girl."

"I wasn't shy."

"Yeah, you were, Nat. If I even said hi to you, you'd mumble and glance away."

"Neither you or Cade knew I existed. And I'm not sure why both of you are playing with me now." Trepidation slipped down her back. *This is all a game to them. See who can get to the timid, lonely, never been married woman, first.* "You know, I think you should take me back to my grandmother's."

"What? Why?"

"I'm not going to allow you or Cade to amuse yourselves with me. I might never have married, Kale, but I know players when I see them, and you two fit into the category perfectly. I refuse to be the toy you two pull apart."

He stopped the truck on the side of the road, put it in park before he turned toward her, and captured her hand in his.

"Listen, Nat, this has nothing to do with me and Cade wanting to see who can get in your panties first."

A snort left her mouth.

"Really, I'm not." He brought her hand to his mouth and kissed her fingers. "Cade did call me this morning and tell me he rescued you last night, and that I wouldn't believe how hot you'd turned out. Truthfully, I came by because I wanted to see for myself, and I do have to say, you are one gorgeous woman. I can't understand why some lucky guy hasn't snatched you up already."

"You could have any woman you want. Why me?"

"I'm curious. I don't want anything from you, Nat, except to show you a good time. It's only lunch. If nothing else, I only want to talk to you over a nice meal."

After a few minutes of contemplating whether she could believe him or not, she finally agreed. "All right. I'll still have lunch with you, but I'm not looking for a relationship, nor am I looking for a lover."

"Or two?"

"Two? You aren't serious?" she asked, shock zipping down her back. *Two? Two men at once? Maybe he didn't mean it like that. But what if he did?*

"Just a thought, honey," he replied, the wicked grin returning to his face as he pulled the truck onto the road again.

Okay, maybe he did mean it.

When he pulled up in front of The Blue Bonnet Café, she almost laughed. The café had been the hang out for the local kids ever since she could remember. They always giggled at the "grownups" when they came in.

"What's so funny?"

"I can remember hanging out here when we were kids."

"We never hung out here."

"No. You had your little blonde cheerleader types and I had my friends."

"Well, I hope I've out grown looking at only what's on the surface."

Her shoulders lifted in a shrug.

"Come on. They still have the best burgers in town, and I'm starving."

When they headed for the door, he placed his hand at the small of her back. The warmth from his palm did nothing to help her all of the sudden, out of control libido.

This is crazy. Yeah, both of them are drop-dead gorgeous in their own way, but why am I like, ready to drool all over both of them? Why can't I be attracted to one?

"You okay?" he asked, pressing his lips against her ear briefly before she slid into the booth on one side while he took a seat on the other.

"Yeah. I'm fine. This is all a little weird for me."

"Weird how?"

The waitress stopped at the edge of their table and asked for their drink order, stopping their conversation for a moment, but the need to get this out in the open wasn't about to be forestalled. Once their coffee cups were full and each doctored it the way they liked, she said, "Come on, Kale. I'm really not your type or Cade's."

"How do you know our type hasn't changed over the years?"

Okay. I'll play. "What did Cade's wife look like?"

"You remember Cynthia Bishop?"

"Yes, well sort of."

"That's who Cade married."

"See? Blonde, pretty, big boobs."

"And lesbian."

"What? You can't be serious. Really?"

His tempting lips wrapped around the edge of the cup, and he took a healthy drink. "Yes. My wife came from Bozeman. I met her in college, and after we got married, we moved back here. The four of us spent a lot of time together. The two girls became best friends, and more, as time went on. We didn't realize they had taken their relationship into the 'lover' status until one night we were all having dinner at their place and they broke the news they wanted divorces."

"Both of them at the same time?"

"Yeah. When we tried to get out of them what the issues were, they finally confessed they'd become lovers and didn't want us in their lives anymore."

"Wow," she whispered, amazed any woman in her right mind would walk away from either him or Cade, much less for another woman.

"So you see, we've both been burned, and truthfully, I'd love to find a woman I could classify as a real woman. Not one necessarily into shopping at the high-end department stores just because she can, or needs big parties and hanging out with the *in* crowd. I want someone who likes hanging out on Saturday's with me. Maybe watching football even if she doesn't like the game, but wants to because she wants to be near me."

"I can understand your feelings."

The waitress returned for their lunch order, giving her a little time to digest what Kale said. The difficulty came with wrapping her mind around him and Cade's attraction to her. It didn't fit.

"I'll have a cheeseburger and fries, please," she told the waitress.

"The same for me."

"Great. I'll check on you two in a bit."

"Your grandmother seems to be dealing with your grandfather's death pretty well."

"It's not like she didn't know it was coming. He'd been ill for some time, but being a doctor, he wasn't about to get treatment."

"Did he have something specific that caused his death?"

"Yes. He'd been dealing with prostate cancer for a while."

"Well, I'm sorry to hear about his passing. He was a favorite around here."

"I know. It killed my mom to move to Oregon when we did. I didn't really care for it either. Being a sophomore in high school and moving really sucked."

"You must have coped pretty well."

Their food arrived, saving her from commenting on his observation. She didn't think she'd dealt well at all. Yeah, she had a few friends, but not like here in Red Rock. This was home even if it wasn't anymore.

"Did you ever think about coming back here after finishing school?"

"I had to stay there. The cost of college in Oregon played a huge part in my decision to stay, and then, afterwards, the school district close to my parents offered me a lucrative salary to teach."

"Cade said you teach elementary students," he said, popping a French fry in his mouth.

"I do and I love it. The kids are great," she replied, stirring the cream into her coffee after the waitress refilled it. "I never thought of doing anything else."

"They are lucky to have you."

Her gaze caught his, and she cocked her head to the side a little. "I don't understand you at all, Kale."

"What's there to understand?"

"Both you and Cade seem so different from what I remember. It's really hard for me to wrap my mind around it."

He grasped her fingers and squeezed. "We are both simple guys who work hard, play hooky occasionally, still ride horses, sometimes rodeo on the weekends, and hope to find the right woman someday. Nothing more. You're like a breath of fresh air around here. You know in Red Rock, people get on the bus, but they don't get off."

She couldn't help but smile since she knew it to be true for the most part. After her family moved, they did come to visit occasionally, but they never stayed long. Her dad loved Oregon and couldn't wait to get back.

Talk turned to other things like the small place he owned outside of town, some of the children she taught, and the coming Christmas season.

"What's your place like?"

"A typical cattle and horse ranch. I breed and train horses, but I also run some cattle on the property too."

"I imagine it keeps you really busy," she replied, picking at the remaining food on her plate.

"Most of the time. We should be calving and branding soon and that will take up about three weeks of non-stop work. I don't get much sleep during those times, but it's still a couple of months away. When I'm not working the cattle, I've got the horses to keep me busy. Unfortunately, the market for horses unless they are racehorses, isn't much. People aren't riding for pleasure as much these days."

"What about your family, Kale?"

"What about 'em?"

"Do they still live here?"

"Yeah. They own The Double D and are more into cattle than horses these days."

"Cade helps me out there. In fact, he has a small apartment here in town he sleeps in some nights, but for the most part, we share my place. The house on the property is big enough for a whole family with a passel of kids."

"What do you call yours?"

"The Bar KD."

"Your wife didn't take it when you divorced?" A frown scrunched the skin between his eyebrows, and she said, "I'm sorry. It's none of my business."

"Its fine, Nat. No, she didn't take it. She didn't want it. She hated the ranch and everything it stands for. I don't know why she ever agreed to marry me if she felt that way."

"I'm sorry. It must have been really hard."

"It doesn't matter. She got what she wanted, and I'm glad she's not in my life anymore." One French fry slipped between his tempting lips. "What about you? Cade said you were in a long-term relationship."

A heavy sigh left her mouth, and she traced the water droplet on her glass for a moment.

"If you don't want to talk about it, that's fine."

Her gaze caught his, and she felt a shiver roll down her back at the look in his eyes—the look of someone who cares and really wants to know.

After a quick inhale, she said, "I was with Steve for two years. We talked about getting married a time or two, but he never asked really. I never thought there were any problems, until I came home early from a teacher's conference in Seattle. I wanted to surprise him, but he surprised me when I walked into our bedroom and found him in bed—our bed, with another woman."

"I don't understand how people can cheat on each other," Kale replied, pushing his plate away. "I mean, if you don't want to be with your partner anymore, get out of the relationship and move on."

"I know. I never thought about being with someone else while I was with Steve."

"You don't seem to be the type of woman to cheat."

"How would you know, Kale?" she asked with a smile. *Mmm...he wants to know more about me, does he?*

"I don't, but I'd like to. You're a fascinating woman, Natalie Bennington, and I would love to spend more time with you while you're here."

"What about Cade?"

"What about him? You haven't even been on a date with him yet."

"No, but he asked me out first. It's kind of weird to be dating two men."

His eyes twinkled and his lips twitched with a suppressed smile, and she had to wonder what he found so funny.

"Cade and I don't compete for women."

"You don't?"

"Listen, let me take you back to your grandmother's, and we can talk more there."

Okay. Well, that's kind of strange, but whatever, I guess.

Kale paid the bill and escorted her to his truck. The ride back to her grandmother's house seemed almost uncomfortable, although, she wasn't sure why. A song came on the radio, and she hummed along with the tune of Kenny Chesney singing, 'I'd Love To Change Your Name'.

"You know this one?"

"Yeah. I like Kenny Chesney. I have a lot of his CD's."

"I like his stuff too, but George Strait is my favorite."

"Kind of hard to top 'ole King George." A warm laugh left his mouth and she smiled. "You have a nice laugh, Kale."

"Thanks."

They pulled into her grandmother's driveway, and he came around to her side to open the door. His palm appeared in front of her to help her out, and she realized how much she missed the gentlemanly behavior of the Montana cowboy.

"I appreciate you taking me out for lunch. It was very sweet of you," she said, while they walked toward the porch.

"You're welcome. We really need to talk, but I think I'll wait for a better time."

She stopped and said, "Are you sure? You seemed pretty adamant we would talk."

"Yes, I'm sure. It's kind of a weird subject and we really need to be able to discuss it."

The warmth of his hand at the small of her back made her quiver with desire, curling a knot of need in her belly.

When she turned to face him, he cupped her face between his palms and brushed his lips against hers. The softness of his lips took her by surprise, as did the feelings he stirred. Comparing his and Cade's kisses, she realized both were intoxicating in their own way.

"I'd better go even though I don't want to. I would much rather stay and kiss you, but I've got work to do at the ranch." He stepped back and stuffed his hands in his pockets, as if he wasn't sure he could keep them off her. "Can I take you out again on Saturday?"

"I don't know, Kale, I..."

He took her hand in his and brought it to his mouth. The scrape of his whiskers along the back of her hand sent shivers up her arm. Soft lips slipping across her skin's surface and the brush of his tongue made her lips part on a sigh.

"Please?"

The dark brown of his eyes mesmerized her. A small smile graced his mouth, and she heard herself agreeing.

"How about six o'clock? We can have dinner and go dancing or something."

"Six is good," she murmured.

"I'll see you then." Another brush of his lips and he was gone.

3

The knock on the door startled her. *Is it five already?* She jumped to her feet to answer it, smoothing the skirt of her black dress with her hands. Anticipation of the coming dinner date with Cade had her on edge since Kale had dropped her off after lunch. Slick sweat irritated her palms, goose bumps flittered across her arms, and her mouth felt dry. Two hours getting ready for this date did nothing to calm her nerves. She'd tried on everything she brought with her and still couldn't find anything suitable to wear. A quick trip to one of the local boutiques yielded the perfect dress and shoes—never mind the hundred-dollar price tag.

A deep sigh left her lips as she approached the front door and opened it.

The porch light reflected the gleam of gold in Cade's hair, making it almost look like a halo around his head. Angel he wasn't, she decided. Maybe he was hiding little horns underneath because he sure knew how to make her think about hot sex between the sheets.

His black suit jacket fit across his broad shoulders like a second skin, hugging each muscle and bulge of his magnificent body. The stark white shirt made his tan skin appear almost bronze as the collar peeked above the lapels of his coat. One large hand cradled his black Stetson like a baby. Every Montana cowboy loved his cowboy hat. It came with the territory.

His baby blues dilated when they stopped on her face. "Wow," he whispered. The smile spreading across his lips made her feel beautiful and sexy in the strapless black dress she'd chosen. She knew it hugged her curves and emphasized her cleavage. For some reason, she loved the look in his eyes.

"Come in. It'll only take a minute to grab a coat and my purse."

The screen swung out, allowing him to step inside the house.

Natalie turned around only to find her grandmother standing next to the couch, a big smile on her face and a mischievous twinkle in her eye.

"You look very nice. Where are you taking Natalie for dinner?" her grandmother asked.

"It's a surprise." A beautiful bouquet of red roses was clutched tightly in his hand, almost as if loosening his grasp would cause them to disappear. "These are for you."

"Oh my. They're gorgeous, Cade. Thank you," she said, kissing him on the cheek.

His gaze dropped to the floor, and she could have sworn pink flushed his cheeks. "I wasn't sure you liked roses, but they're usually a safe bet for a woman."

"Let me run into the kitchen and put them in water. Then we can go." Quick steps took her into the other room, but she could still hear the conversation going on in the living room.

"It's nice of you to bring flowers," her grandmother said.

"Yeah, well, my parents raised me to be a gentleman and one always brings flowers on the first date," Cade answered, and Natalie smiled. *First date? It sounds like he's planning more than one.*

"Just make sure you have her home by midnight."

"Grandma," Natalie warned from where she stood in the kitchen. "I'm not sixteen."

"I'm kidding, Natalie. Lighten up." The next words had heat crawling up her chest and staining her cheeks a bright red she was sure. "Did you put some condoms in your purse?"

"She did not just say that." Natalie grumbled, pressing her hands to her cheeks.

A roar of laughter from Cade gave her the answer. Her grandmother did indeed mention condoms.

"Don't worry, Nat. I got it covered," Cade replied, making her blush even more.

"I'm going to stay here now, and you two can go out to dinner while I die of humiliation," she yelled from the kitchen.

"No you won't. I've been looking forward to this all day." Cade stopped behind her and put his hands on her shoulders. "We're only teasing, Nat."

"I'm so embarrassed."

He tugged her around to face him and framed her face with his hands. "Don't be. It's not like the thought hasn't crossed my mind from the moment I saw you." Soft, warm lips brushed hers, and she closed her eyes at the sensations ricocheting through her. "Come on. I want to treat you special tonight. Grab your purse and coat. We have reservations."

* * * *

One of the oldest buildings in Red Rock sits on the corner of Main and Smith. The huge stone and steel structure used to be the county courthouse, but now houses The Millhouse Restaurant and Hotel. Cade pulled his truck up to the front and put it into park as a valet came around the driver's side and opened the door.

"May I park this for you, sir?"

"Sure." Cade climbed out and walked to her side. Holding the door open, he extended his palm to help her.

"Wow. When did they convert this?" she asked, taking his hand. Her gaze went up the front façade of the building, amazed at the conversion. Gray stone graced the whole front of the building, and large columns held the top overhang. Huge chandeliers, dripping with crystal accents, graced the ceiling inside the restaurant, were visible through the long windows along the front. Light reflected a multitude of color through the windowpanes and onto the concrete under their feet. Rows of box hedges sat under the windows, and under the canopy of the restaurant, large planters held enormous ferns.

"A few years ago. They made it into a high-class hotel and the best restaurant in town. It's the best food around these parts," Cade replied, tucking her hand into the crook of his arm.

"And expensive too, I bet."

"Don't worry about the cost. It's my treat since I chose to bring you here."

"But—" One finger pressed against her lips, stopping her words.

"No buts," he whispered. A quick brush of his lips against hers and she lost all train of thought. He smiled when he lifted his head and led her inside. Dark red carpet, with white and gold flowers, cradled her heels when they stepped through the gold and glass doors. They stopped next to the podium, of what she assumed was the maître d, and Cade gave his name. Immediately, they received an escort to a cozy table in the corner. Old-fashioned chairs, covered in burgundy brocade with gold accents, sat pushed under the table, and she loved when Cade pulled out the chair for her.

"Thank you," she whispered.

Goose bumps rose on her arms when he brushed his lips against her ear and murmured, "Anythin' for you darlin'."

Crystal goblets and a variety of silverware reflected the lights overhead, and she wondered if she could remember what utensil went with what. The stark white tablecloth looked elegant beyond words, and the feeling of being out of place began to overwhelm her, until Cade squeezed her fingers.

"Have I told you how beautiful you look? You take my breath away."

"I appreciate the sentiment."

"It's the truth."

The waiter stopped next to their table, asking what they wanted to drink, and Cade ordered champagne.

"Trying to get me drunk so you can find out if I really do have condoms in my purse?"

His chuckle warmed her. When he brought her fingers to his lips, kissing each one before sliding his tongue over her palm, it made her want to admit her own wanton thoughts.

"I'm only trying to loosen you up a little."

"If I get any looser, I'll be sliding under the table."

"Um...interesting idea."

Shit!

She retrieved her hand and said, "Shall we decide what to eat?"

The grin on his lips widened.

Open mouth—insert foot.

"What I meant was..."

"It's, okay, Nat. Keep goin', honey. I'm likin' where this is headin'."

Unable to hide the heat in her cheeks, she dropped her gaze to the menu and clamped her mouth shut.

"The sirloin looks good. What would you like?" he asked a few moments later.

"Typical cowboy. Red meat it is."

"Can't help it. Being born and bred on a cattle ranch does that to a man."

"The steak and shrimp sounds good. I really acquired a taste for seafood living in Oregon. The salmon out there is fabulous, and when they bring king crab legs down from Alaska... Wow."

"I don't know how this place will fair in comparison."

"Shrimp is usually a pretty safe bet, even inland," she replied, laying the menu to her left.

Once the waiter had come and gone with their order, their conversation turned to things more personal.

"Kale brought up something when we were having lunch today and I wanted to ask you about it."

A frown appeared on his face and his blue eyes darkened. "Okay. Shoot."

"He said the two of you don't compete for women."

"How did that conversation come about?"

"I told him it felt weird dating both of you, and he said you two didn't compete for women."

"We don't."

"Care to explain?"

"It's not really the type of conversation I'd like to have with you when there are other ears around."

"Oh?"

"The whole thing is rather personal."

"I see," she said, even though she had no clue what he meant. She cleared her throat and took a sip from her champagne. The bubbles tickled her nose, and she had to rub it to calm the sensation. "Kale told me you married Cynthia Bishop."

"Just full of information, wasn't he."

"He also told me how things went down between your wife and his. I can't even imagine it. I'm sorry for both of you. It must have been terrible."

"It wasn't a pleasant time in my life, no. I had no clue anything was wrong. They blindsided both of us," he replied with a frown.

I wonder if he's still pining for her.

"How long were you married?"

"Five years."

"No children?"

A rueful laugh left his mouth. "She never wanted any. The thought of ruining her figure didn't sit well with her at all."

"I don't understand how a woman can not want children."

"You have to think that way. You're a teacher."

"Actually, no I don't. There are several teachers I know who don't want children of their own."

"Really?"

"Yes. They are fine teaching other people's children, but they have no desire to raise any themselves."

"What about you? Do you want children?"

"Someday, when I meet the right man, I'd love to have several. I grew up in a lonely home."

"You had your sister."

"True, but Andrea is quite a bit younger than I am. I love her. Don't get me wrong, but we didn't have the adoring sisterly bond. After we moved to Oregon, I found myself on my own a lot. My parents fought since my mother didn't want to move there in the first place."

"I'm sorry. I can't imagine growin' up in such an environment. My family has always been close, and I have several siblings to prove it."

His grin caught her by surprise and she had to laugh.

The food arrived, and the smell of seared meat made her mouth water. It had been a long time since she'd had the kind of steak you could get in Montana.

"Wow. This looks wonderful."

"I told you they have really good food." He cut into the meat on his plate, popped a piece between his full lips, and moaned in pleasure.

"Do you come here often?"

The water in his glass almost spilled when he grabbed it, washing down the meat with an unhealthy gulp and a rough cough.

"I'm sorry. I didn't mean to make you choke. Are you all right?"

"I'm fine." The words came out in a coarse whisper.

"Are you sure?"

"Yeah. Your question caught me off guard. That's all." His eyes watered and it looked like his nose might run, too.

"Why?" she asked. One small piece of steak slipped between her lips, and she fought a matching moan to his. "Lord, this is good."

"You being here seems so natural. I forget you haven't been here in a long time." He brought the napkin in his lap up to his mouth and wiped the edge of his tempting lips. "I'm actually here all the time, although not as a patron. My family supplies the beef for this place."

"Really? Wow. It must be very lucrative for your parents place then."

"Um, yeah, it is."

Their conversation came to a screeching halt when her cell phone chimed in her purse.

"I'm sorry. I need to see who is calling. It could be my grandmother."

"No problem."

She grabbed her purse from the floor and pulled out the still ringing phone. *Steven? What the hell is he calling for?*

"Somethin' wrong?"

"No. I don't think so anyway." She hit ignore and returned it to her purse.

"Maybe you should have answered it."

"It wasn't someone I care to talk to."

"Oh?"

A frustrated sigh left her lips on a sharp exhale. "It was my ex."

"Ex what?"

"Ex-boyfriend, ex-lover—just ex."

"I see. You mean short-dicked..."

Her hand came up quickly and pressed against his lips, silencing his words. He smiled against her fingers and sucked one into his mouth. Desire, hot and needy, shot down her back, stopping at her throbbing clit.

"Mmm...tastes like chicken," he murmured, releasing her fingers.

A small snort came from her mouth, and she shook her head at his attempts to flirt. *He's damned good at it, too.*

"What?"

"You."

"What about me? Oh, I know. I'm devilishly handsome and built rugged. I have gorgeous eyes. I can rope a steer, herd cattle, ride a horse, two-step with the best of 'em, and make love to you all night long."

A high-pitched laugh bubbled from her mouth as she said, "Not the least bit modest, are you?"

"For you, darlin', I'll be all those things and more." The twinkle in his eyes and the twitch of his lips told her he could and would. All she had to do was ask. The thrill of anticipation danced through her stomach setting it quivering like a thousand butterflies, loose inside. She splayed her hand across her abdomen, wishing it would calm down before she did something stupid, like sleep with him.

* * * *

Once they finished their meal, both laughing at the waiters' suggestion of dessert, Cade paid the tab and escorted her to the podium to retrieve his truck. Getting her alone quickened his pace. The thoughts of holding her next to him, kissing her pouty lips, running his fingers through her hair, and tasting her skin while running his tongue over every inch of her made his cock harden to aching proportions.

"What's the hurry, Cade?" she asked when he whipped the door open on his truck.

"I want some alone time with you," he replied, kissing the tip of her nose. "Problem with that?"

"If it means I get to kiss you again, then nope."

"Definitely, darlin'."

He closed the door behind her and turned away to adjust his cock.

Good God, I need to get between those gorgeous thighs. I haven't been this damned horny in a long time, if ever.

"You know, Kale said you stay at his place a lot," she said when he slipped inside the cab.

"Sometimes. I wouldn't say a lot. I have my own place in town, and my mom maintains my room at the house just in case I ever decide to move back home. Not like it would ever happen. I kind of like my bachelor life."

The lights of town zipped past the windows, the cars thinning out the further they drove. *My apartment in town is nothing more than a bed, a dresser, a couch, and a television. I can't take her there.* He slept there when he did jobs in Red Rock. The other profession under his belt consisted of construction, but building slowed in the winter, leaving him more and more time to work on the home he started on his own property. For some reason, he wanted to show her his space.

"Where are we going?"

"Someplace special," he said, grasping her hand in his. "It's a little ways outside of town though. Do you mind?"

Her eyes twinkled in the lights from the dashboard and she smiled softly. "Not at all. I love that you want to show me something so meaningful to you."

"You're a special woman, Natalie." She frowned, and he wondered why when she stared out the window. "Did I say something wrong?"

When she turned toward him, he could see pain and mistrust in her eyes.

Someone hurt her badly, and right now, I could kill him. He shook his head, staring out the windshield again. *Whoa! Wait just a damned minute here. What the hell am I thinking? The last thing I need is another permanent fixture in my life. A quick romp...yes, but someone stable...no.*

"What are you thinking?" she asked in a mere whisper.

"Me?"

"Yes. You look angry."

"Well, from the look in your eyes, I'd say this ex of yours did a lot of damage."

"How so?"

"You have a wary, distrustful look, but I aim to change your opinion of men. We aren't all like your ex."

They pulled off the road and took a dirt path back several hundred yards until they came upon his partially finished house.

"Wow. Is this yours? You're building it?"

"Yeah. I do construction during the summers, and since it's slow right now, I'm working on this place. Would you like to see? It's not much right now. Just four walls, a roof, and bare studs on the inside, but it's all mine."

"I'd love to."

She reached for the door, but he stilled her hand with his own. "Let me get it."

The soft smile lighting her face did wonderful things to his insides. He moved around the back of the truck, grabbed the flashlight from the large toolbox, and then opened her door.

"We have light."

"A good thing to have out here, in the middle of nowhere, in the pitch darkness," she said. The little giggle to her voice turned to a peal of laughter when he scooped her up in his arms and walked toward the house.

"Put me down."

"Nope. I kind of like holding you, and I don't want you to freeze those pretty little toes."

The wind rustled the branches on the trees overhead and snow flurries fell in a thin veil of white. Once he reached the porch, he let her slide down his body, watching her pupils dilate, and her lips part in invitation. He wasn't sure if he could deny himself, or her, when she leaned toward him. After a mental kick, he pulled the collar of her coat up around her ears, and kissed her nose before taking her hand, entwining their fingers.

"I love the snow. It's one of the things I missed about Montana. It doesn't really snow much in Oregon."

"How about we go sledding on Marshall Hill tomorrow?"

Her face lit up like a Christmas tree. "Really?"

Laughter filled the small grove where the house was built, as they stepped up to the door. "Yes, really."

"You don't have to work tomorrow?"

"I can make time for you, Nat."

"I don't want you to get into trouble or anything, Cade. I mean, it's not that important."

The green of her eyes almost glowed with excitement at the thought of a simple thing like sledding, and he wasn't about to disappoint her. "We'll go and I won't take no for an answer. Now, let me show you my house."

They stepped inside, the smell of pine mixed with caulking, paint, glue and other construction scents, met his nose. She brushed the snow from her coat and looked around even though it was difficult to see.

"Hang on. I have a small generator on the back porch. Let me crank it up and we'll get a little more light and maybe some heat."

"I could do heat," she said, running her hands up and down her arms. *I could make you warm all over.*

He cleared his throat and ducked through the doorway, ignoring the tightening pressure in his groin. She looked too damned cute standing there with her red nose and cold lips, and he wanted nothing more than to warm her in more ways than one.

Two pulls on the generator and it cranked to life. The lamps he left inside the living room came on and spread a glow throughout the room.

"Wow. This is great, Cade," she called from inside. "It's going to be really big."

"Not too big, but enough for a family anyway," he replied, returning to her side. "This is the livin' room, and there's gonna to be a river rock fireplace along the wall over there. Large picture windows will be right here so we can look out over the pasture and watch the horses and cows grazin' in the distance."

"I can picture it. It'll be beautiful," she whispered, and he wondered at the longing in her voice.

Grasping her hand, he led her to where the kitchen would be. "This is the dinin' room, and the kitchen will be against this wall with a window over the sink lookin' outside so you can watch the kids in the backyard.

We'll have a huge farm table so all the extended family can visit for Sunday dinner."

She stepped in front of him and slid her hands inside his coat and around to his back. "It'll be the perfect family home." Her warm breath skimmed over the exposed area of his neck, sending chills down his back. The softness of her lips brushed against the underside of his jaw, and he fought a moan rumbling in his chest.

"Natalie," he whispered.

"Mmm."

"Nat, darlin', we'd freeze to death in here if we so much as…"

"Kiss me, Cade."

He took her face between his palms, and brushed his lips against hers. A soft little moan escaped her mouth, only to be caught by his when he fit their lips together and his tongue swept inside. Their bodies molded like one piece of a puzzle to another. One hand slipped into her hair, tangling in the long strands while the other wrapped around her back, pulling her closer. There would be no mistaking the long, thick erection pressing against her stomach. He ravished her mouth. Stroking, licking, sucking motions had her whimpering in need as her tongue met him touch for touch. The desire to feel her skin outweighed everything inside him, screaming *stop, before this goes too far.* Two fingers unbuttoned the front of her coat. He parted the material and tugged her back in. Breasts pressed flat to his chest. The silky material of her dress did nothing to hide the hard nipples poking him.

Hot and insistent desire sprang to life. Something he hadn't felt in a long time made him pull his mouth from hers and skim over her cheek to her ear.

"God, I want you," he whispered. Her answer came out in a needy whimper. Small nibbles to her ear and the whimper grew. Her coat became a vice as he pushed it off her shoulders, trapping her arms against her body with it. A lick to the spot on her neck, just under her earlobe, and her breathing hitched up a notch. Sensations rushed all his nerve endings, and he groaned as he fought the headlong dash of need to push her to the plywood floor and bury himself inside her sweet heat. He brushed a kiss over her bare shoulder and pulled her coat back into place. Green eyes blinked in confusion. Pouty lips begged him to kiss her again, but he refused to give into unyielding desire in nothing more than a fuck-fest.

"Why did you stop?"

"Because, I don't want to make love to you on a plywood floor. I want you in my bed, not here. You deserve so much more."

She laid her head on his shoulder and buried her nose in his neck. A heavy sigh rushed from her lips. The sweet floral scent of her perfume made him dizzy with desire. Heat scorched him where they touched.

"Take me home with you, Cade," she murmured. Her warm breath singed his skin and tattooed her image on his brain until he couldn't think.

"Wait right here." He quickly returned to the generator, cutting the power to the house. When he returned to the spot he'd left her, she held out her arms, and he scooped her up, holding her close to his chest.

Within moments, he had her inside his truck, speeding down the dirt road toward the highway to town.

I can't take her back to my place. It's not the spot I want to make love to her for the first time. Two fingers scratched his jaw. *But where? Kale's? No. I don't want to share her. Back to the Millhouse? I could get a real nice room there, but man! It seems so cheap doin' that.*

"Cade?" Her soft voice brought him out of his musings to see her wide green eyes staring at him from across the cab of his truck. "You're thinking too much." She unbuckled her belt and slid to the middle of the bench-seat before re-hooking her seatbelt and placing her hand on his thigh. His dick jumped in his pants. A sexy smile played on her lips, and he wondered if she knew exactly what she did to him with her touch. "It doesn't matter where we go... except, not to my grandmother's."

A nervous laugh left his mouth. "I wouldn't even think of goin' there, darlin'. Somehow, I think privacy isn't on your grandmother's agenda, although she sure seems to want us together."

"Don't get your drawers in a bunch, cowboy, she wants me with any-one who doesn't use, abuse, drink, smoke, do drugs..."

"In other words, a nice guy?"

"Yeah. A nice guy. Are there any of those around anymore?"

"I'm one."

"I know and it terrifies me."

"Why?"

"The few nice guys I've been with, I get bored. You know, they say women always go for the bad boy."

"I can be bad too," he admitted with a grin.

A little smile played on her lips, and he wanted to kiss her so bad, he could taste her on his tongue.

"I'm sure you can. After all, you did steal a car when you were younger."

"Damn. I shouldn't have told you, but if it makes me bad enough to get you, then I'm okay with it."

The next thing he realized, they reached her grandmother's street. His heart dropped in his chest when they rounded the corner and a sea of flashing red and blue lights greeted them.

"Grandma?" she whispered, terror clear in her voice.

"Easy, Nat. Let's find out what's going on."

He stopped at the curb and put the truck into park. An ambulance stood nearby and a police car was parked in the driveway. The door opened with a flick of his wrist, and he rushed around her side to help her out so he could be the rock she might need to lean on, depending on what was going on inside the house.

With one arm around her shoulders and the other holding her hand, they headed for the door, but the police officer guarding the entrance refused to let them in.

"Can I help you?" the officer asked.

"I'm her granddaughter. What's going on with my grandmother?" Natalie asked.

"The paramedics are working on her now. I'm not sure what happened. We got a call, but the caller was difficult to understand."

"I need to go inside."

"Of course," the officer replied, tipping his hat. "Cade."

"Arnie."

"You with her?"

"Yeah."

"Go on in. I'm sure they'll need some information or something."

4

"Grandma? What's happening? What's wrong?" Natalie asked, rushing to the side of the gurney.

"I'm fine, honey. Don't worry," her grandmother said, although the words seemed slurred. Her usually bright and cheerful eyes appeared dull and the left one didn't look quite right.

Natalie squeezed her fingers, and the paramedics finished strapping her in.

"We're taking her to Red Rock hospital, if you'd like to follow," one of the paramedics told her and Cade.

"We'll be right behind you," he answered. "Why don't you change real fast, darlin'. I'm sure it's gonna be a long night, and you probably don't want to be hangin' out at the hospital in your dress."

"Is she going to be all right?" she questioned, worry knotting her stomach.

"I don't know, but we'll be there for her no matter what. Now, go on and get changed."

She watched momentarily while they wheeled her grandmother out the door before she rushed upstairs.

T-shirt and jeans. Tennis shoes. Socks. The list of clothing items rattled off in her head when she reached her bedroom and unzipped her dress, flung off her shoes, and ripped the nylons down her legs. *She'll be fine. She has to be. I don't know what I'd do without her.*

When she finally finished dressing, except for her shoes, she headed down the stairs to find Cade pacing the living room like a caged lion—a beautiful, sexy, mountain lion or something. His hands stuffed in his pants pockets, chewing his bottom lip with his teeth.

He's worried about her, too. Gotta love a man who cares about elders.

"Let me get my shoes on and we can go," she said, taking a seat on the couch.

"We'll have to take it easy. It's starting to snow again."

Her gaze ran over him from the tip of his cowboy hat to the pointed-toe boots on his feet. *He really is one of the good guys...with a little bad streak.* She stood, tugging at the bunched up material near her hips for a moment, liking the way his eyes narrowed while watching her.

"Let's go see what's wrong with Grandma," she said, taking his hand and leading him toward the door.

It's a good thing the hospital wasn't far. He had them there within fifteen minutes.

"What do you mean I can't see her?" she demanded.

The clerk behind the desk popped her gum and tapped on the keyboard. "She's being examined, and they won't let you back there right this minute. Take a seat. They'll come get you when you can see her."

"This is ridiculous. That's my grandmother back there."

"I understand. Let me see if I can get one of the nurses to come out and talk to you."

"Easy, Nat. Getting upset isn't goin' to get you anywhere in here," Cade said, pulling her tight against his side.

"I know. I just wish I knew *something.*"

He led her to a couple of chairs in the corner and forced her down on one. "I'll be right back. I'm goin' to find the vendin' machine and get us both some coffee."

"Cade?"

"Yeah?"

"Thanks for being here. I don't know how I would handle this without you."

Warm lips brushed against hers and she sighed. "Anytime, darlin'."

When he walked away, she couldn't help but notice the looks he got from the other women sitting around the waiting room, and she felt a ping of jealousy zip through her.

Jealous? I don't have any reason to be jealous. He's being a friend, nothing more.

"Never mind the way he kissed me earlier," she murmured out loud. "And what about telling him to take me home with him?"

One quick exhale blew the hair off her forehead, and she rubbed her hands up and down her arms.

This is stupid. Getting involved with him is stupid and silly, but ohmigod can the man kiss.

"Get your mind out from between your legs, Natalie. You're grandmother needed you, and you were out getting frisky with Cade Weston."

"Nat?" a familiar voice said from the doorway.

"Kale? What are you doing here?" Her gaze fixed on his familiar chiseled features and the worry in his eyes. He took a seat next to her, taking her hand between his.

"I heard your grandmother's address on the scanner at the house. I went by there, but everyone had left. Her neighbor said they took her away in an ambulance, so here I am. Are you okay?"

"I'm fine, but Gram isn't. I'm not sure yet what the trouble is. They won't let me back there." Accepting his firm reassurance, she leaned into his embrace, absorbing his strength. "I'm so scared."

"It'll be fine, honey. Don't worry," he whispered before he kissed the top of her head.

"What are you doing here?" The growl in Cade's voice took her by surprise.

"Cade," Kale said with an answering grumble.

"Kale."

"Stop it you two," she demanded, moving away from both of them. "We aren't here to start getting possessive. And I'm not going to come between you and your friendship. You two have been friends far too long."

"You aren't," Kale insisted, but she saw the narrowing of Cade's eyes.

"Here's your coffee, Nat. I brought cream and sugar since I wasn't sure how you took yours."

"I appreciate it, Cade. Thanks. I'm sure it's going to be a very long night."

"I'll be right here with you, darlin'. You know that, right?"

"You don't need to stay. I can get a cab home and—"

Two of his fingers pressed to her lips, stopping her words. "I'm stayin'."

She nodded, took his fingers, and entwined them with her own.

"You don't need to stick around, Kale," Cade said.

"What if I want to?"

"Damn it! This is nuts. Knock it off! You aren't going to pull me apart like two dogs fighting over a piece of meat."

"Miss Bennington?" the nurse called from the doorway.

"Yes?"

"You can come back now."

"Thanks." She handed her cup to Cade and said, "You two play nice."

* * * *

"What the hell are you doing here, Kale? Really?" Cade asked, resisting the urge to punch his friend. Stumbling on Kale holding Natalie when he returned with the coffee, threw him for a loop. The feelings rushing headlong across his heart seemed strange, and he wasn't sure he liked it at all.

"I told her and I'll tell you too. I heard her grandmother's address on the scanner, and I got worried. No one was at the house so I came here. I didn't realize you two were still together and you'd be here with her."

"Where else would I be? I had a date with her, remember?"

"I know. I figured you'd have gone home by now. It's going on midnight."

"What? She turns into a pumpkin at midnight?"

Kale ran his fingers through his hair, Cade almost laughed at the hairs sticking up in several directions. "Hell, I don't know. I wasn't sure if you and she might be..."

"Doin' the horizontal mambo?"

"Maybe. Shit, Cade. I know I wouldn't mind gettin' between those thighs, and I know you feel the same way."

"Watch how you're talkin' about Nat."

"You sound almost protective, there buddy. What's up? Yesterday you were all for getting her in the sack and sharing her. Now you're not?"

Right now, he wasn't sure what he felt, but the feelings she stirred out at his house and the protectiveness running rampant through his chest, made him uneasy. "I'm sorry, Kale. I don't know how I feel right now, other than if she needs me, I'll be there for her. She doesn't have any-one here. Her grandmother is her only family, and she doesn't have any friends around these parts anymore."

"You goin' out with her again?"

"Why?"

"I asked her out for next Saturday."

"And?"

"She said yes."

Jealousy reared its ugly head, sending anger and irritation down his back. "I planned on taking her sleddin' tomorrow. She said she hadn't been in a long time."

"Sounds like fun. A little snow, some hot coffee, a little snugglin' by the fire."

"That's the plan," he replied.

"You jealous she said yes to dinner with me, Cade?"

He sipped his coffee and narrowed his gaze on his long time friend. Damn right he was jealous and he didn't like it one bit. Neither of them had ever been attached to the women they shared. It always came with an unwritten law—no deep involvement—just sex. *But Natalie's different.*

"Are you?" Kale repeated. "Because, you know, we had an agreement. No involvement—"

"I know what the damned agreement is, Kale."

"You've fallen for her, haven't you? Already. Head over heels—"

"Shut up, Kale. Just shut up."

"Cade?" Natalie's voice came from a small door to his right.

He put his coffee down on the table and faced her. "What's up, Nat? How is she?"

"They think she'll be okay, but she's had a stroke. Her speech is still slurred a little and her right arm is weak, but she'll survive. She's going to need rehabilitation, and they are going to keep her tonight for observation."

Her eyes sparkled with unshed tears, and he knew she held her emotions in check. *Such a strong woman.*

"Come here, darlin'," he said, opening his arms.

A small, choked sob broke from her lips as she threw herself into his embrace, burying her face against his chest.

"Sshh. Everythin' will be okay. You'll see."

She tipped her back and said, "But what if she never recovers? She won't be able to live by herself anymore. She'll have to go to a nursing home or something. That would kill her, Cade."

"I know," he whispered, brushing the tears from her cheeks. "We'll take it one day at a time. No use gettin' all upset about it right now."

"I thank God, I was here already. What would happen if none of us were around? Yes, she called 911 herself, but at least I'm here to help her recover." A gasp left her lips, and she stepped out of his embrace. "I have to call my parents. They are going to have a fit over this." Her steps took her back and forth in front of the door, and the thumbnail on her right hand disappeared between her lips. "If they find out I wasn't there, my mother will have a cow! I'm supposed to be here helping her and taking care of her, not out on dates with the local bad boys. Crap!"

"Natalie, listen," Kale said, coming to her side. "Your grandmother insisted you go out and have a good time."

"That's right, darlin', she did, and she would have been upset if you stayed at the house," Cade added.

Her hand waved in front of her face, dismissing the arguments they made. "It doesn't matter. My mother will *not* understand."

Cade took her hand and drew her back into his arms. "Listen, you are entitled to have a life too. She can't fault you for it anymore than anyone else."

Both arms went around his waist, and she snuggled up to him. "Thanks. You two are the best friends a girl could have." After a quick hug, she released him and said, "Do you want to come back and see her? You too, Kale. I know she's worried about me, so it will help alleviate her uncertainties if she knows you are both taking care of me."

"If it's all right, I'd like to. I want her to know she doesn't have to worry about you," he replied.

"I'm sure she'd love to see you," Nat said. "Come on."

She took one of his hands and one of Kale's and led them through the doors. The three of them walked hand in hand until they reached one corner of the emergency room. A curtained off area stood to their left, and Natalie called out to her grandmother to make sure they could come in.

"Come on in, honey. I'm decent, well if you call these damned gowns with no back so your ass hangs out for everyone to see, decent."

He couldn't help but smile. Mrs. Oliver's a feisty old bird and nothing would keep her down. "How are you feeling?"

"Like shit. You?"

He shook his head and laughed. "Nothin's gonna keep you down, is it, Mrs. Oliver?"

"Nope. Been around too damned long to let it. Old Doc, God rest his soul, always said, 'There are two theories about arguing with a woman, neither one of them works.' Now, did you two have a good time at dinner? And when did you pick up your other hunk?" her grandmother asked when she noticed Kale standing behind them.

"Grandma, don't worry about how my date went and so you know, Kale came to the hospital when he heard your address on his scanner. He was worried is all." Natalie tucked the sheet under the edge of her until her grandmother swatted at her hands. "You'll have to stay here overnight, the doctor said, so they can watch you for a bit."

"Damn it, Natalie, stop mothering me. I'm a grown woman, and I can take care of myself. And don't be calling your mother and telling her about this. She'll end up flying her ass up here and then I'll have to deal with her too. The wet behind the ears doctor already told me I needed to stay."

"Wet behind the ears, huh?" the very nice looking doctor said as he stepped up next to the bed and smiled.

"Well, yes. You can't be much older than Natalie there is, and she's my granddaughter. How old are you anyway? You married?"

"Grandma! Will you stop trying to play matchmaker for me with every man in Red Rock!"

"I love you, Nat, and I want to see you happy. Besides, I'd love it if you settled down with some nice man here." Her grandmother looked at the doctor again and asked for a second time, "Are you married?"

"Yes, Mrs. Oliver, I am, happily married," the doctor replied, twirling his wedding ring on his left hand.

"Well damn," she grumbled and Cade had to laugh. "You and Kale aren't, young man, so don't be laughing too hard. I'll have you hitched to Nat in no time if you give me half a chance."

"Do you have a gag around here somewhere," Natalie said.

Her grandmother's eyes narrowed. "Have you talked to your mother yet?"

"No, Gram."

"Then don't."

"You know I have to call them and let them know what's happened."

"No you do not, Natalie. They'll just worry and everything is fine. I'm a little weak, but with a little rehabilitation, I'll be like new."

Cade saw Natalie glance at the doctor, and he shook his head. A deep sigh left her lips, and she sat down next to her grandmother. "Gram, listen, I have no doubt with your stubborn nature, you'll do wonderful in rehab, but you have to be ready if you don't regain your strength. What happens then? You won't be able to stay—"

"Don't you dare tell me I'll have to move out of my home. Your grandfather built our house with his bare hands, to raise our children in, and I will be there until the day I die. If I have to hire someone to come in and stay with me, then I will."

"I'll stay with you, Gram. You know that."

"I appreciate the sentiment, Natalie, but you have a life too. You have the children you teach. You can't leave them in a lurch."

"I'm staying and I don't want to hear anymore about it. However long you need me, I'll be here."

Cade liked the sound of that.

A nurse strolled in a few moments later and said, "We'll be taking her upstairs to her room now."

"You go on, honey, and have your men take you on home. There's nothing more you can do here. I'm going to be tucked in and sleep for the rest of the night."

"All right, Gram. I'll come back first thing in the morning to see what they've decided and we'll go from there." She leaned over and kissed her grandmother on the cheek. "Behave yourself, please."

"We have ways of making her behave," the nurse said with a chuckle.

"Don't go getting carried away with the drugs. I don't take anything more than Tylenol for a headache now and then," her grandmother snapped. "Keep them sedatives in your pocket."

"Yes ma'am."

Once the nurse wheeled her grandmother away, Cade took her hand in his and kissed her palm. "Let's get you home and tucked in."

"Thanks Cade. You too, Kale. You've both been lifesavers for me, and I can't thank you enough."

"You're welcome, Nat," Kale replied. "We know you're kind of alone here, even though this is your home away from home."

"You have no idea."

* * * *

The three of them walked out through the waiting room hand-in-hand. Surprised looks and blatant stares followed them out the door. The hostile glances made Natalie shiver.

"Wow. Can we say uncomfortable?"

"Don't worry about those people. They don't know what's goin' on with the three of us, and they're being rude," Cade replied. "It's none of their business, and I personally don't care what people think."

"Me either," Kale added. "I'm going on home. Cade will make sure you get back to your grandmother's safe and sound. I'll check with you later on this week about our date Saturday. Okay?"

"Gosh, Kale. With everything going on, maybe we should rain check?"

"We'll see, honey. No worries."

"Thanks."

"Of course," he said, brushing his lips against hers. "I'll call you in a day or two."

Cade's eyes narrowed into agitated slits and a frown pulled down the corners of his lips.

The two of them had been snapping at each other when they were in the waiting room and she didn't like it. Jealousy came as a hard pill to swallow, and she didn't want to come between two friends.

Silence enveloped her and Cade once they settled into the cab of his truck and headed back to her grandmothers. She'd been all ready to let him take her home to get down and dirty. Now, she wasn't sure what she wanted. Oh, she wanted Cade. No doubt about it, but could she have nothing more than a short-term, quick roll in the hay? It would be so unlike the Natalie anyone knew. Her family wouldn't believe it. Her friends would think she lied because it wasn't the Natalie they know.

A short time later, Cade pulled into her grandmother's driveway, turned off his truck, and came around to her side to hold the door.

"Such a gentleman."

The sexy grin he gave her sent tingles down her arms as he pulled her close and escorted her toward the front.

She fished the key out of her purse, slipped it into the keyhole and opened the door. Paper, plastic, and miscellaneous other objects lay scattered about the living room from when the paramedics work on her grandmother. "What a mess."

"I'll help you pick up. It shouldn't take long. There really isn't too much here."

"You don't have to do—"

The brush of his warm lips over hers stopped her words.

"I want to."

Ten minutes later, the living room was spotless again, and she gave him a silly grin.

"I know it's getting late."

"Yeah, I should probably go," he replied, tucking a curl behind her ear. "I enjoyed spendin' time with you. Thank you for going out to the house with me."

"I loved it, Cade. Thanks for showing me. It'll be beautiful when you're finished."

"I guess our sleddin' date tomorrow is out of the question, huh?"

She nodded and said, "Yeah. I need to be at the hospital first thing so I can find out what the plan is for Gram."

"I'll tell you what. After we get things settled with your grandmother, we'll go sleddin'. It's less crowded around noon anyway." He took her hand and pulled her down on the couch with him. "I need to tell you somethin', Nat."

"You look so serious. It can't be that bad."

His hand slid into her hair, tugging her closer. The brush of his lips against her cheek made her sigh and close her eyes.

"I want to make love to you, Natalie." The feel of his tongue on her earlobe sent shivers down her spine. Tiny nibbles on the soft skin below her ear made her squirm on the couch. His two strong arms wrapped around her, pulling her onto his lap. His thumb brushed over her nipple and she felt it tighten into an aching bundle of nerves. He continued his trek down her neck with his lips as he unbuttoned the front of her blouse and pushed it aside. "Tell me you want this."

"Oh God yes. It's been way too long."

He lifted his head, and stared into her eyes. The blue of his gaze bore into hers while his hands cupped her face. "You're beautiful."

Unable to continue to look at the intensity of his stare, she dropped hers to his lips. Sensual, full, and delicious, she wanted them on her body. Everywhere.

"Kiss me."

"Oh, I plan to, darlin'." He kissed her eyelids. "Here." He kissed her cheeks. "Here." He kissed her nose. "And especially here." His tongue swept across the seam of her lips, coaxing her to open for him. The moan coming from her mouth didn't sound like anything she'd ever heard before—part animalistic and part inhuman, the sound took her by surprise. "You taste good. I could eat you up."

One hand palmed her breast and teased the nipple through her bra. With a quick flick of his fingers, the material parted, and the ache intensified with the look in his eyes. Hunger, raw desire, and need sparkled in the blue depths.

He closed his lips over her nipple, sucking it deep into his mouth.

Her back arched and yearning rushed through her. Red-hot longing spiraled from his suckling straight to her clit. She wanted this man—needed him with everything inside of her.

"Cade, please," she whimpered, threading her fingers in his hair.

"Where's your room?" he asked after lifting his head.

"Up the stairs and to the right. First door."

With a powerful flex of his muscled thighs, he lifted her high in the air and cradled her against his chest. Swift steps took them upstairs and to her temporary bedroom. A small lamp on the bedside table gave her just enough light to see the wicked smile on his lips and the shine of desire in his gaze. He dropped her legs, sliding her down his body. Every rock hard inch of his tempting flesh skimmed over hers. Nipples tightened and ached as they scraped over the material of his dress shirt and jacket.

"You're still dressed," she murmured. Her lips met his whiskered jaw and slipped over the surface. Her tongue circled his ear, her teeth nipping at his earlobe.

"Why, yes I am. We'll have to rectify the situation quickly." One hearty moan spilled from his lips. "If you don't knock it off, this is gonna be a short ride, darlin'. It's been a while."

"We don't want that, now do we?"

"Hell no. I want to love you slow."

"Sounds like a plan to me. By the way? You talk too much."

"You won't hear another peep out of me."

A challenge? I like challenges.

"No?"

He shook his head, and she cocked an eyebrow, letting a wicked grin play across her mouth. The slow unbuttoning of his shirt didn't garner a sound—pushing it and his jacket off his shoulders...nothing.

Oh, I don't think so.

Unbuckling his belt while her teeth nipped at his pecs and grazed his nipples, got her no response, and she smiled.

It's on baby!

His pants and boxers fell to the floor with a slight nudge of her hands. The full length of his cock sprang free, standing tall and proud against his stomach, just begging for her touch—her mouth. A quick peek through her lashes revealed his clenched jaw, the firm line of his lips as he fought the sounds in his throat, blue eyes sparkling like sunlight on the open ocean.

"Do you want to say something?"

The jerking shake of his head gave her the answer.

His fists clenched at his sides. Touching her would give him away, she knew.

She flattened her palm on his chest, slowly sliding it over the valleys and planes of his body. Goose bumps followed the path of her hand, while crisp chest hair tickled her skin. Saliva pooled in her mouth with the need to taste him. Every tempting piece of flesh called her name, urging her to bring her mouth closer still. The path of her lips followed the trail of hair from the center of his chest, across his washboard abs, to the tip of his cock. Pre-cum glistened on the slit. His breathing sounded short and raspy. She dropped to her knees, grasped both of his ass cheeks in her hands, pulling him closer. Musky male, mixed with his arousal, met her nose. She licked her lips, opened her mouth, and took the head of his cock between her lips. The swirl of her tongue around him got the desired response. A hearty moan spilled from between his lips, and he threaded his fingers through her hair.

"God, Nat," he growled.

"Mmm," she hummed against his flesh. His hips rocked toward her, taking up the rhythm of her mouth.

Several shaky breaths later, he said, "Natalie, honey, I don't wanna come in your mouth." He pulled her up in front of him and crushed his lips over hers. His tongue swept inside, tangling with hers in a dance older than time. When he freed his feet of his jeans, he walked her backward toward the bed. The edge hit the back of her knees, and he followed her down in a tangle of arms and legs. Raspy breaths flittered across her cheek and then to her ear.

"You make me crazy."

"Cade, please. I need you to make love to me."

"Oh, I will."

"Now."

"Nope. My turn to play."

Before she knew exactly what he meant, the warmth of his lips slipped down her neck and latched onto her breast. Uncontrollable desire rushed through her. Want for this man. Need for him to make her his, even if it was only for tonight. The rough calluses on his palm chafed her skin when he slid it over her belly. The sensation drove her crazy. His hand nudged her thighs apart. The material of her jeans kept them from skin-to-skin contact, but the pressure of his touch through the barrier of material had her groaning low in her throat.

"We need to get rid of these. I want to feel your skin."

The snap gave way to the insistence of his fingers, and she lifted her hips. He grasped her pants, tugging them down and off her feet. Her silky little thong did nothing to hide anything from his intense gaze.

"These are so sexy," he whispered with his lips against her belly. One finger slipped down the edge of her underwear, between her thighs, and to her pussy. The whimper trapped in her throat escaped on a sigh. Her legs parted and he chuckled softly.

"Do you want me to touch you?"

"Please," she moaned.

"Where, darlin'?"

"My...um..."

"Tell me, honey. I don't know what feels good for you." He moved to between her thighs, and she could feel his warm breath on her pussy. His tongue wet the silky material still guarding her from his touch.

Breath hitched and legs trembled.

"Here?" he asked, sliding two fingers under the elastic.

Talking became impossible. Thoughts fled, except for knowing he now lay between her thighs, and his breath felt heavenly against her goose bumped flesh.

Not waiting for her answer, he stood up, grabbed the edges of her underwear, and slipped them off. Seconds later, the moist pad of his tongue returned.

"Ah God, Cade!"

"Easy, honey," he coaxed.

In none of her previous relationships had her partner done this. Granted, she hadn't been in many. She hadn't lost her virginity until she went to college, and the guys there didn't care. It was all about them and their needs.

Slick and wet. That's what she felt when he licked from slit to clit. A moment later, he stiffened his tongue and toggled her clit.

"So sweet."

Two fingers slid into her pussy, and she thought she'd die. Her whole body tingled. He drove those tempting digits in and out, in and out, sending her to the brink and pushing her over when he flicked her clit with his tongue at the same time.

A hearty moan spilled from her lips when her climax exploded through her belly.

"Cade," she whimpered.

One...two swipes of his tongue and he kissed his way back up her abdomen. Her trembling eased, and she opened her eyes mere slits. The wicked grin on his face made her shake her head.

"What?" he asked.

"You."

"Me? I only did what I thought you wanted, although, you never really said for sure." He looked almost unsure. "You didn't like it?"

"Of course, I did. How can a woman not like that?"

"Just checkin'," he murmured against her lips.

Wanting to feel his tongue deep inside her mouth, she opened for him and moaned when he slipped it inside along hers.

The rock hard length of his erection nudged against her pussy.

He lifted his head and said, "Hold that thought. I need to grab something."

Within seconds, he returned with a condom between his fingers.

"Anticipating?"

"Hopeful."

Her gaze dropped to his chest, and she fiddled with the hair there.

"Nat? You're okay with this, right?"

When she didn't lift her eyes back to his, he put a finger under her chin.

"I...mmm. I don't want you to get the impression I do this all the time. I've only ever been with three men my entire life and—"

The kiss he placed on her lips stopped her words. The brush of his tongue against her lips forced a groan from her mouth. After a few moments of heart-stopping kissing, he lifted his head again.

"Darlin', I don't care how many men you've been with, and no, just because you are willin' to let me love you, doesn't mean I think you're loose. I'm thrilled we're here right now. I've wanted to get you like this since I helped you out of your car out there on the road. Whatever happens after this, we'll take one day at a time."

Her heart lightened with his words. This meant something to him. It had to. How could he love her like this if it didn't?

He tore the condom open with his teeth and rolled it over his impressive erection.

"Open for me, honey."

Both legs went around his waist and he eased inside her pussy.

"You feel like heaven."

She hissed between her teeth.

"Are you all right? I'm not hurtin' you, am I?"

"No. It stings a little. It's been a long time."

"I'll go slow," he whispered. "Even if it kills me."

A soft laugh left her lips. "It's okay now. Fill me up."

The tortured groans spilling from his lips made her smile as he rocked his hips, sliding all the way in. In and out. Torturously slow.

"Cade?"

"Mmm?"

"Faster. Harder."

"Ah hell, darlin'."

His rhythm increased ten-fold. Flesh against flesh. Hot, sweaty, sexy bodies molded together in the pale light of her bedroom, sprawled on the bed she used to sleep in when she came to visit her grandmother as a child.

A quick flip and she straddled him.

"Oh yeah. You remember how to ride, honey?"

She lifted her butt and let his cock slide part way out before she shifted again, sliding him back inside.

"Just like that. Hell yeah. Ride me, babe."

In no time, she set an even pace, bringing them both to the brink. Both of his hands stopped on her hips, as he helped her shift exactly how they both needed to bring them ever higher. She rested her palms on his chest, raking his nipples with her fingernails, enjoying the hiss escaping from his lips.

Heat rushed from her toes, up her legs, spearing through her abdomen. She climaxed on a cry, spilling desire over his cock.

"Yes, yes, yes," he panted, driving his erection into her several more times before finding his own release, her name on his lips.

She collapsed on his upper body until her breath semi returned to normal. His fingers brushed over her back, almost tickling her skin. He rolled them both over so she lay next to him, her head resting on his chest.

Moonlight filtered through the gauzy curtains on the window while his fingers traced a pattern on her arm, causing goose bumps on her flesh.

She didn't want to ask what happens now, but the words hung on the end of her tongue. The biggest question in her mind wasn't what happens between them but what about Kale?

"Spill it, darlin'."

"Huh?"

"I can hear the wheels turning in your mind from here," he said, kissing the top of her head. "I know you've stuff running around in your pretty head, so if you want to talk...let's talk."

"I don't want to talk right now, Cade. But, will you stay? Tonight, I mean. I don't feel like being alone. This house is huge, and I don't like the thought of being here by myself."

"Sure, honey. I'll cuddle up and sleep right here next to you."

"Perfect," she said in almost a purr.

Within moments, she drifted off to sleep with his big body curled around hers, and her hand slack on his abdomen.

5

Grey skies met her eyes through the small opening in the curtains, when Natalie opened them the next morning. The warmth of the arm lying across her abdomen took her by surprise, for a moment, until she remembered Cade spent the night. Memories of their lovemaking rushed back, flushing her body with heat and embarrassment. She never behaved so wantonly with a man before. Begging for his touch, and crying out his name in her climax, just wasn't Natalie Bennington.

"You're thinking too much," he whispered against her ear.

"I didn't know you were awake."

"I kind of figured."

"Listen, Cade. What happened last night—"

"Was magnificent. I'd love to do it over and over with you."

"But I don't normally act like that."

"Good. I'm glad I made you lose control. Natalie, there's nothing wrong with what we did. We're both adults, and because we are, we can do what we want without permission from anyone."

She frowned and huffed out a small puff of air. His fingers grasped her chin, turning her head toward him. Soft blue eyes met hers, melting her irritation like snow on a hot summer day.

"You are a very sexy, beautiful woman."

A small snort left her lips, and she covered her mouth with her hand.

"You don't think so?"

"Put it this way. The last guy I was with, left me for someone younger, skinnier, and prettier."

"He's an idiot."

"You have to say that. We're lying here buck-ass naked together."

"No, I don't, Nat. Hasn't anyone ever told you how pretty you are?"

Her gaze dropped to his chin, but she refused to answer.

"Honey, look at me." When she raised her eyes back to his, he said, "I don't sleep with ugly women."

"Oh my God, Cade. You didn't just say that!"

"It's the truth. Your eyes are a gorgeous green and remind me of the sea. Your breasts fit perfectly in my hands." He palmed her breast and his thumb rasped over the nipple bringing it to an aching point. "You are the same age as me, and I don't feel old, so I guess it means you aren't either."

"Hazel. My eyes aren't green."

"They can be depending on your mood, darlin'."

A hearty laugh spilled from her lips. "Way to bring the heat down a notch, Cade."

The wicked grin on his lips brought a smile to her face.

"I could really use a shower. How about you?" he asked, waggling his eyebrows.

"Somehow I think there's more to this than the need to wash."

"Of course." Two fingers pinched her nipple, and she fought the moan bubbling in her throat. "Getting you naked—"

"I'm already naked, if you hadn't noticed."

"Mmm. Yeah, I kinda did. But I thought more like hot water tricklin' over your breasts, soaping your skin so it's slick to my touch, before bendin' you over and slidin' into your sweet heat from behind."

"Okay. All right. I get the picture. Sex in the shower."

"Not just sex. Sizzlin'..." He licked the seam of her lips. "Scorchin'..." He teased her ear. "Blisterin'..." He nibbled her neck. "Wicked shower sex."

Goose bumps dotted her flesh with every word he spoke. The rich, low growl of his voice with each syllable sent need zipping down her back to settle between her thighs. Her pussy throbbed with the racing of her heart.

"You know you want to," he murmured

She captured her bottom lip between her teeth.

"I promise I'll make you come at least twice."

"Twice?"

"Uh-huh."

Her fingertips tingled with the need to touch, to arouse him like he aroused her, and to make him feel this same unrelenting need to have him buried to the hilt inside her that she felt.

"First one in gets to adjust the temperature!"

In a flash, she jumped from the bed and headed for the bathroom with him on her heels. The sharp squeal coming from her lips surprised her when he scooped her up in his arms and stepped into the shower.

"Now what are you gonna do?"

"I like it hot. What about you?" she asked.

"Oh yeah. The hotter the better."

Steam rolled out of the open shower stall. Her grandfather built an impressive travertine tile shower with multiple showerheads pointing in several different directions. Natalie loved this shower, but sharing it with Cade brought on a whole new meaning.

"This is really cool," he said, checking out the different heads, adjusting each one to spray just right. "Did your grandfather put this in?"

"Yes and I love it."

Cade grabbed the pouf off the ledge along with the lavender scented shower gel. "So this is where the lavender scent comes from."

"Huh?"

"The sweet smell of lavender I've come to associate with you."

"Oh. Yeah. Probably so. I use it all the time and some of the lotion I use on my skin is lavender too."

The messy material foamed with the soap when he squished it several times. The soft slide of the bubbles over her skin, felt like heaven—across her neck and over her breasts. Inching his way from breast to navel and then through the curls at the juncture of her thighs.

"Mmm."

"Feel good?" he asked in a strangled whisper.

She couldn't help but notice his straining cock standing proud against his abdomen.

"You have no idea."

"Turn around and I'll do your back."

Warm spray beat against her chest as he ran the soapy implement over her back with one hand, kneading the muscles of her shoulders with his other.

"Wow. You are really tight."

"Lots of stress lately."

The bubbles disappeared with the spurt from the showerhead, but he continued to work the tight knots.

A soft moan slipped from her lips. His hands wandered down her back, continuing to roll his thumbs over the bumps and valleys of her body until he reach her ass. The next thing she felt was both hands on her breasts, molding the flesh to his palms and rolling the nipples with his fingers. Her head lolled back onto his shoulder. His cock pressed into the crack of her butt.

"Ever had a man in your ass, Nat?"

"No," came out in a moan.

"Want to?"

"Maybe. I've thought about it."

"Not right now, but it's something we'll have to explore."

"You're going to make me into a wanton woman, Cade Weston. No one will recognize me at all."

"And this is a bad thing?" he whispered. The rough pad of his tongue did delicious things to her neck while he continued teasing her nipples. His teeth nipped at her earlobe and one hand skimmed down her belly. "Open for me, darlin'."

Her thighs spread without thought, and she almost screamed as one callused finger slipped over her clit.

"Easy."

"No such thing," she panted. "God it feels good."

A whimper rose to her lips when both hands disappeared and he stepped back. She turned her head, blinking in confusion.

"Sit on the side there." His voice dropped an octave, and he almost sounded like he was having a hard time breathing.

She squeaked when her butt hit the cold tile.

"I'll warm you up in a second, darlin'. Put your butt right on the edge."

She scooted closer. "Yeah, like that." He dropped to his knees, between her legs. "Oh my. So pretty. So pink." Her head fell back against the tile when he licked from slit to clit. A soft moan spilled out of her mouth. Two of his fingers found her pussy and slowly pushed inside. The high-pitched whimper didn't sound like anything she'd heard before. Well, maybe she had. Last night in fact.

His other hand pulled back the hood protecting the tight bundle of nerves. Her butt almost came up off the tile as he toggled her clit quick. The fingers inside her pussy pushed in and out. The whole scene felt surreal and like something out of a porn movie, but she didn't care. Cade brought her to the edge of climax, backed off on his ministrations long enough for her to settle down, and then brought her back up until she hung on by her fingernails. Frustrations made her ball her hands into fists, and then splay her fingers wide as she fought the rise and fall of her passion. She wanted to grip his hair and force him to bring her over the abyss. Desire coiled in her belly. Need zipped from her toes. Warmth spread up her legs, bursting through her pelvis on a scream as cum dripped from her pussy and over his fingers.

He kissed the inside of her thigh, nipped it with his teeth, and licked her clit one last time.

"One."

Heavy eyelids opened to find him grinning at her.

"Climax. I promised at least two."

"Uh, yeah."

She wrapped her hand around his cock and stroked up and down.

His breath hitched and she smiled. *At least he's not immune to my touch.*

"You're killin' me, darlin'. I want inside you so bad, I hurt."

"Then do it. Fill me up."

Her hand guided him to her pussy. Hot water sprayed over his head, running down his chest in rivulets. She took one of his nipples between her lips and sucked. The hard nub beaded against her tongue, and a hearty moan escaped his mouth. The head of his cock slipped a tiny bit inside, and he stopped with a quick inhalation.

"Condom."

His jaw clamped in frustration. The tick in his jaw told of his ability to hold his need in check without slamming into her without regard to protection.

"Are you clean?" she asked, her gaze boring into his.

"Yeah. I got tested a few months ago and I always use a condom."

"Me too. I'm on birth control."

"What are you saying, Nat?"

"Fuck me, Cade. I need you."

His eyes rolled back in his head. "But—" She planted her heels on his butt, pulling him close, pushing his cock deep inside her. "Ah hell," he growled as he grabbed both of her hips and began thrusting.

The feel of his cock sliding in and out of her pussy without the barrier between them, couldn't have felt more amazing. Hot, silky steel rammed home with each plunge. Every slide had her whimpering. Her pussy vibrated with his insistent lovemaking. Legs trembled. Pulses raced.

"Come for me, darlin'."

The rough gravel of his voice sent her over the edge, shattering her into a thousand pieces of sparkling light as she screamed his name.

Seconds later, his own completion reached its peak. His ragged breaths and rapid, jerky thrusts told her he couldn't hold back. She flexed the muscles of her vagina, and he groaned deep in his chest, climaxing on a rush.

"Oh God, Nat," he growled, burying his nose in her neck.

She trailed her fingers down his back while they caught their breath. The water started turning cold and she shivered.

"We need to get out of here before the water turns to ice. Your grandfather obviously didn't have a huge hot water tank."

"I'm sure he never expected his granddaughter to have sex in his shower either."

That got his attention. He groaned as he got to his feet and then pulled her up in front of him.

"You aren't sorry we did this, are you?"

"Sorry? No. Overwhelmed? A little."

"No need to be, honey." He kissed her nose and turned off the water. A big, fluffy towel hung from the rack on the wall within easy reach of his fingers. A moment later, he wrapped her in it and rubbed her down.

Once they were both dry, they went back into the bedroom and silently got dressed.

"Coffee?"

"That would be great," he replied.

"I'll make some while you finish dressing." The door opened with a twist of her hand, and she hurried down the stairs to the kitchen. Images and thoughts flew threw her mind while she filled the pot with water and added the grounds to the basket.

What the hell am I doing? I just had wild sex with Cade, both last night and this morning, but I have a date with Kale on Saturday. I should break the date. She chewed her bottom lip. *But I don't want to. Is it bad of me to want both of them? What would Cade say if he knew I still wanted to date Kale?*

"What are you thinking so hard about?"

"Sorry, I didn't hear you come in," she replied, her cheeks heating with embarrassment.

"Obviously. So are you going to tell me?" he asked. Both arms came around her waist and he pulled her to his chest.

Her gaze dropped to the center of his chest, and she fiddled with one of the buttons on his shirt.

One of his fingers slipped under her chin, forcing her gaze back to his.

"What if I said I still wanted to date Kale?"

* * * *

A fist to the gut would feel about the same. The sheen of tears on her lashes told him she wasn't sure about the whole thing and needed him to reassure her it would be okay.

"Honey, if you want to date Kale and me both, it's fine. We aren't exclusive." He raked his fingers through his hair when he stepped back. "Hell. We haven't done much dating ourselves except dinner last night."

"And sex."

"Yeah, and sex, but I don't want you to get the idea it means we won't see other people." For some reason he wasn't sure he liked that idea much.

"You and Kale seemed at odds last night at the hospital, and I don't want to come between your friendship."

"Let's play it by ear, okay? I know you have a date with Kale on Saturday. Go on your date and have a good time. If you want to have sex with him, go ahead."

Frown lines appeared between her eyebrows. "It wouldn't bother you if I had sex with him?"

I didn't say it wouldn't bother me.

A heavy sigh rushed from between his lips. "I'm not saying I would like it, Nat, but I need to tell you something about me and Kale."

The coffee pot sputtered and spit. "The coffee's done."

"Great. Let's grab a cup and sit down. I want to explain something to you."

She poured two mugs and brought them to the table along with sugar and cream.

"This is great, honey."

"So what is it you need to tell me?"

He took a deep breath and said, "You know Cynthia and Kale's wife left us to be together."

"Yes."

"Before the two of us married our respective wives, there was a time or two where we shared a woman. It's happened since our divorces too, once or twice."

"Shared? I don't think I understand."

"Have you ever heard of a ménage relationship?"

Her bottom lip disappeared between her teeth, and her eyes narrowed. Moments later, those same gorgeous green orbs widened in shock, and her mouth formed a small 'oh'.

"You had sex with her? Both of you? At the same time?"

He nodded and answered, "And there's been more than one."

"Wow," she whispered.

He could see the wheels turning behind those expressive eyes, but he stayed quiet, letting her think through it.

"How many?"

"How many women?"

"Yes."

"There's been ten total over the years. The last one happened a few years ago. It's not like we do it with every woman I date or he dates. The girl has to be open to the possibility, and we kind of try to gauge it if the occasion arises." He brought the coffee cup to his lips and sipped at the hot liquid.

"Have you thought about it with me?"

Coffee flew across the table as he spit the contents of his mouth.

"Gosh! I'm sorry, Cade. I didn't mean to make you choke or anything," she said, slapping him on the back.

"Its fine," he rasped in between coughs. His eyes watered, and he felt like a ten-pound weight was pushing against his chest. *Thought about it? Oh, hell yeah. Thought about it. Dreamed about it. Masturbated thinking about it.*

"Are you sure?"

He held up one hand, coughed twice, and motioned for her to sit back down. "We haven't discussed it in detail, Nat."

"What's that supposed to mean?"

"We've mentioned it to each other. Okay?"

"So you have thought about it between you—talked about it."

"Yeah, Natalie, we have. I really don't want to go into this right now, but —"

"Too bad, Cade Weston. You brought it up. I'm only trying to get answers. Now, I can either talk to Kale or you can be truthful with me."

"Fine."

"I want you to answer my questions truthfully and fully. Is that understood?"

Why he got the feeling this was her teacher persona, he wasn't sure, but all of the sudden, he felt like a high school kid again.

"I've never had sex with two men at the same time, obviously."

"All right."

"How does it work?"

He nervously cleared his throat before he said, "Most of the time, it starts with one guy and the second one joins in. There are a couple of ways it's considered a ménage. The term ménage can classify several types of relationships, but for me and Kale, it's always been the two of us and one woman."

"What's the other types?"

"Multiple women and one man or vice versa."

"Oh." Her lip disappeared between her teeth again. "All right. Go on."

"Normally, the woman has one...um...cock in her pussy and one in her mouth or in her ass." He stood abruptly and refilled his cup. This conversation made him horny as hell, even though they'd had sex not an hour before. He pressed his palm to his throbbing cock. *Down boy.*

"Sounds interesting."

Oh hell! She's actually contemplating this? I would never have thought she'd be game for two on one.

"Let's not jump into this, all right? I mean you and I had sex, yes, but you might not be interested in having sex with Kale."

She tipped her head to the side slightly and smiled. He didn't like that particular smile.

"Maybe. Maybe not. I won't know until I have some alone time with him."

Shit! I don't like where this is going.

The phone rang on the wall, and she got to her feet to answer it.

"Hello?"

Cade took his cup and moved back toward the table.

"Yes, Gram. We'll be on our way in a few minutes. We're having a cup of coffee."

The grimace on her face told him her grandmother figured out something.

"I know I said *we*, Grandma, but I'm not going to elaborate on the phone. We'll be there shortly." A short pause and she rolled her eyes. "Bye, Gram."

"Caught onto the *we* real fast, didn't she."

"Oh yeah. Nothing gets by her." Her cup made it into the sink. "Shall we go?"

"Sure." Several swallows later, he set his cup in the sink next to hers. They moved toward the living room where they dropped their coats the night before. "Can we swing by my apartment? I really need to change into something a little more casual."

Her gaze slid down his dress shirt and across the bulge tenting the front of his pants.

"Of course we can. Tight jeans on you are nice too."

"Wicked woman," he grumbled, but he couldn't help the smile lingering on his lips. *Saucy wench.*

The door closed behind them, and his hand settled on the small of her back as they walked to his truck. Inside the cab, silence surrounded them for the short ride to his apartment.

"Wow. You live here?" she asked as they pulled into the lot. His building actually consisted of an old store in downtown with some of the upstairs converted into apartments.

"Yeah."

"This is great. Where's your place?"

"Second floor. Come on. We'll go through the back. They have a great, old, cage-style elevator we use."

The back door of the building opened into a wide hallway. Bricks lined the walls and tile graced the floors. Wood accents, large potted plants, and gold gilded mirrors completed the picture.

"I thought you made it sound like this place was hardly anything to look at, Cade. It's beautiful in here. I can't wait to see your apartment."

"It's not much. A bachelor pad, if you will. I'm not here a lot."

"Kale said you stay at his place sometimes. Do you have your ménage sex there?"

Hell! This is going to get weird. I can't believe she keeps bringing it up.

"Um. Yeah. Sometimes there. Sometimes here."

He closed the cage on the elevator and up they went. The door to his apartment sat to the left of the landing. Wood paneling covered the walls on this floor, but the same tile lined the floors, and the same large plants and gilded mirrors graced the walls.

It didn't seem like much to him, but the wonderment in her eyes when he opened the door to his place, made him think twice.

"This is yours?"

"Yeah," he replied, trying to see it through her eyes.

His big leather couch took up one wall with a matching recliner on the opposite side of the living room. Heavy wood tables accented the couch and flanked the chair. A large brick fireplace engulfed one whole wall and glass hurricane lamps bordered the edges of the mantle. The state of the art kitchen, with its stainless steel appliances and granite countertops, appeared to the right from the entryway. The big bay window looked over the street below.

She walked to the window and pulled back the white curtain. "You can see everything going on in town from here."

"Yep. More than I want to sometimes."

"This place is fantastic, Cade. I'm glad you showed me," she said, coming back to his side and slipping her arms around his waist.

"Me, too." The brush of her lips against his brought his thoughts right back to getting between her thighs again. "Let me change real quick and we can be gone."

"Maybe I want to watch."

"You do that, darlin' and we'll be here another hour."

"Only an hour?"

"I've created a monster."

Her wild giggle followed him into the bedroom.

A short twenty minutes later, they stood at the door to her grandmothers' room at the hospital, and he had to smile at the sound coming from inside.

"I am *not* taking Xanax. I have no need for a sedative, and you will not force one on me, young man."

"But Mrs. Oliver, the doctor ordered—"

"I don't give a shit what that lame brained, bobble-head, piece of meat in a lab coat thinks. I have all of my mental faculties about me, and I will not bend to his will. Do you understand?"

"Yes ma'am."

Cade fought the grin on his lips, trying to cover it with his hand, but a matching one lingered on Natalie's mouth, too.

"You can tell him to find some other helpless old lady to stuff full of medication, but this one isn't doing it. Not today and not tomorrow!"

Natalie shook her head. "What are we going to do with her?"

"She's going to give them hell at the rehabilitation center."

"I know. Those poor nurses."

A roar of laughter left his mouth before he could stop it.

"Natalie Marie, is that you hanging out there?" her grandmother called.

"Yes, Gram," she replied.

"Well get your butt in here, girl. I want to find out exactly who *we* is."

Natalie glanced at him, tipping her head to indicate he should precede her.

"Oh, no. I'm not going in there alone."

"Chicken."

"Bauk. Bauk."

"Fine. I'll go first." She strolled inside, and he didn't mind the glimpse of her perfect little ass either. "Hi, Gram."

"It's about damned time you got here. What took you so long?" He walked in behind Natalie and her grandmother said, "Oh. I gotcha. How did the springs hold up on your old bed?"

"Grandma! Oh my God. You didn't just say that."

"Well you did, didn't you?"

Natalie's face turned bright pink.

"Never mind. You don't have to answer," she replied with a twinkle in her eyes. "How are you, Cade? How'd you sleep? Oh wait, good I would imagine if the red cheeks of my granddaughter tell me anything."

"Yes, ma'am. Quite well, thanks," he said, laying his hand on Natalie's shoulder. It bothered him when she shrugged out from under his grasp and moved toward her grandmother as if she wanted to get away from him.

"I would appreciate it if you didn't discuss my sex life, Grandma."

"If you didn't want me to know who *we* was, then you shouldn't have brought him with you."

"She's got you there, Nat."

"You aren't helping matters here, Cade," she told him and then turned back to her grandmother. "How are you feeling this morning? You seem irritated."

"I am *irritated.* The stupid, idiotic doctor thinks he can cram drugs down my throat and make me complacent so I won't fight him and his brainless decisions about my care. I want another doctor."

"Gram, no one will take care of you like grandpa did. You have to understand that."

"I know, Natalie, but I'm not going to let them drug me and shove me into some nursing home. I've decided I'm going home."

Natalie opened her mouth to protest, but Mrs. Oliver stopped her in her tracks.

"I've made my decision. I'm stronger today than I was yesterday, and I know my speech isn't quite as slurred. I can walk with a walker and get around some. We will bring in the physical therapist to the house. If you're staying, we can do it all there."

"All right, Gram. I'll take you home and we'll work it out."

Her grandmother patted her hand and said, "I knew you'd see it my way."

Cade shook his head, smiling when her grandmother winked at him.

"Will you stay one more day so they can evaluate your condition?" Natalie asked.

"Evaluate what? I'm fit as a fiddle."

"They'll need to have the physical therapist do some things with you to decide how best to proceed with your rehabilitation. Please stay one more day."

"All right. I guess I can't argue with you about it, but I won't take any drugs. I'm not letting them knock me out."

"Fine, Gram. No drugs to knock you out."

With a bit of a cocky smile, Mrs. Oliver settled against the pillows, asking, "So, was he good?"

Gratefully, he wasn't drinking anything, because, it would have been a repeat of earlier when he spit his coffee across the kitchen. Now, he knew where Natalie got her snarky remarks and her don't-take-no-shit attitude.

"I can't believe you just asked me how good he is in bed."

"Why not? He's a strapping young man. I think he could satisfy you pretty well. In the bed, in the shower, in the kitchen..."

"Enough, already," Natalie grumbled. "I'm not discussing my sex life with you."

Cade didn't think Natalie's face could get any redder. How could he have known the old lady would know where they'd had sex, or she did a damned good job speculating.

"Knock. Knock." All three of them turned towards the door, to see Kale poked his head inside. "Can I come in?"

Oh hell! How much did he hear?

6

"Hi, Kale," Natalie said, shifting her gaze to Cade to gauge his reaction. She didn't like the stiffening of his spine. "Come on in. What are you doing here?"

Kale walked over and kissed her on the cheek.

"I figured I'd come by and see how your grandmother was doin' this mornin'. I didn't expect to see you here." He turned and stared at Cade. "Or you, Cade."

"Kale." The name sounded almost like a growl from Cade when he stepped in front of Kale. "I'm sure you noticed my truck in the lot. There aren't too many trucks with *Weston* on the tailgate."

"I didn't notice."

"Whatever," Cade grumbled.

"Enough you two," she said, stepping between them.

"Oh, let them go, Natalie. I love a good scrapin' between grown men over a woman." Her grandmother rubbed her hands together gleefully and then folded them over her chest. "I think you can take him, Cade."

"Grandma, will you stop encouraging them, please, for God' sake." Natalie put one hand on each of their chests. "You are not going to fight over me."

"We aren't fightin', Nat."

"You would if I let you, so knock it off."

Cade's cell jingled in his pocket. With a scowl and a grumble, he pulled it from his pocket, flipped it open, and growled, "Weston." His eyes narrowed and he turned towards the door to take his call.

"I'm sorry, Kale. I don't know why he's acting so possessive."

"Could be because you slept with him," her grandmother said. Natalie wanted the floor to swallow her whole, or a gag for her grandmother. She couldn't decide which at the moment.

"I see," Kale replied. "Well then."

"Can I talk to you a minute?"

He shrugged and said, "I guess."

"In private?" she asked, taking his hand and pulling him towards the door. "We'll be back in a minute."

"Take your time. I'll keep Cade occupied," her grandmother called as they walked into the hall.

They kept walking until they reached the end of the hall. When she turned to face Kale, her heart dropped into her stomach. Sadness stared back.

"Did you and Cade sleep together?" he asked, but uneasiness rang clear in his voice.

"Yes."

A long sigh escaped his lips and stuffed his hands into the front pockets of his jeans. "I guess there's nothing more to say then."

He started to walk away, but stopped in his tracks when she said, "He said he didn't care if we went out or even if we had sex."

Kale turned back around and gave her a wide-eyed look. "He did?"

"Yes." She took his hand in hers. "What happened between me and Cade just happened. It wasn't planned. But it doesn't mean there is anything permanent, lasting, exclusive, or whatever you want to call it, between us."

"Wow."

"You know what else he told me?"

"No."

"He told me you two share on occasion."

She almost laughed at the choked look on Kale's face. His eyes bugged and he coughed several times. "He did?"

"Yeah. But he also said it had been awhile." She glanced to her left and then to her right. Several doors on patients' room stood open. "I'm not discussing this here, in the middle of the hospital, but you and I need to talk. I know we have a date on Saturday, but I want to talk to you before then. Can we have dinner tonight?"

"Uh, sure. I'm free."

"Good. Now let's go back to the room and see what other kind of chaos my grandmother is starting with Cade."

They walked back into the room in time to hear her grandmother telling Cade the end of the story about how her grandparents met and married. "My daddy hated ole Doc with a passion, and he swore if he ever showed his face at my daddy's place again, he would fill his ass full of buck-shot. It didn't stop Doc though. He walked right up to the house, told my daddy he was takin' me to the next county, and we were gettin' married."

"Sounds like Doc," Cade replied. He turned around, noticing they returned to the room. "Nat, I'm sorry, but I have to go. My foreman called and one of my horses is havin' some trouble. I need to check it out."

"It's fine, Cade. I'm sure Kale will take me home."

His lips firmed into a straight line, and she could tell he didn't like the thought of her alone with Kale at all. *Mmm. Interesting.*

"Of course I will," Kale added. "I'd be happy to."

"See? Everything will be fine."

"I hate to leave you like this, darlin'." The look in his eyes said it bothered him. *So much for not caring if I date Kale.*

"I know you have to go, Cade. I understand. You have business to tend to and you've already spent a lot of time with me." She reached behind his head and brushed her lips over his. The pressure of his mouth felt marvelous, and she hated to stop the kiss, but the audience present made it impossible to do anything more. "Call me tomorrow or something."

"All right." With one last look at Kale, Cade left the room with the soft click of the door closing behind him.

She cleared her throat and turned back toward her grandmother. The mischievous twinkle in her eyes made Natalie nervous. If it's one thing she came to realize since she'd been back in Red Rock, her grandmother wasn't your typical old lady.

"Grandma, butt out," she warned.

"I don't know what you mean, Natalie. I'm not doing anything."

"Well, listen. I need to get going. I have some things to do at my place before our dinner date tonight. Do you want me to take you home?"

"No. It's fine, Kale. I want to visit my grandmother for a bit before I head back to the house."

"I promised Cade I would take you home."

"I'm a big girl. I can call a cab. You go on."

"What time do you want me to pick you up?"

"Five?"

"Sounds perfect." After a quick kiss good-bye, he disappeared too.

"You're having dinner with Kale?"

"Yes, Grandma."

"But you had sex with Cade."

"Yes, I did. But Cade and I aren't exclusive. I've only been back in Red Rock a few days, and I haven't been out of my relationship with Steven very long either."

"Then why did you have sex with him?"

The heavy sigh rushing from her lips sounded hollow, even to her own ears. "Everything would be too difficult and lengthy for me to explain, Gram."

Her grandmother hoisted the head of the bed, settling back against the pillows. "I'm not goin' anywhere. Spill it."

Natalie knew she wouldn't get out of telling her grandmother the entire tale of what happened between her and Cade, but she wasn't about to give her explicit details.

"I'm attracted to Cade. Hell, I'm attracted to Kale too."

"I believe that is rather obvious."

"This whole thing is rather funny, you know? Neither of those two gave me the time of day in high school."

"Go on."

"When Cade helped me out with my car on my way into town, I thought it was only for old time sake. Then he asked me to have dinner with him. I don't know whether Kale asked me for lunch yesterday because Cade asked me on a date first or what. I feel like I'm being torn in two by them. And I don't want to ruin their friendship. I'm afraid this is turning into some kind of competition. Who can get the shy band girl to fall in love with them first?"

"In love?" her grandmother asked with a raised eyebrow.

"I'm not in love with either of them, so don't get your hopes up. I can't seem to get either of them out of my head. Last night just happened. Cade took me to where he's building his house. It's beautiful up there, Gram. He has it set back in the trees with a huge pasture in front. The framework and stuff is already done. He said he was building it for his family."

"Nice."

"Listening to him talk about how his wife would be able to look out the window of the kitchen and watch their children playing in the yard or how they could look out the front and see the cows and horses grazing in the pasture—it made me want to be that woman."

"It sounds like you have feelings for Cade already."

"I don't know, Gram. He's gorgeous, sweet, and smart. Everything a woman could ask for."

"All right then, what about Kale?"

"They are such opposites in looks, and Kale is all those things too."

"But?"

"Nothing. I'm confused. Cade told me he didn't care if I dated Kale or even had sex with him."

Her grandmother frowned and said, "I wouldn't be surprised if he didn't mean it at all."

"I know what you mean." She stood and walked to the window. Cars sped past below her, and she wondered if anyone slowed down to feel the passion in the wind, the rain on their face, or the love of their family these days. If someone asked her a year ago if she'd be standing here in Red Rock, trying to decide over two different men, she would have told them they'd lost their mind. "I read somewhere once that men can have one-night stands or casual sex and it doesn't mean a thing to them, but women are emotional creatures. It's difficult for us to be in a relationship under those circumstances."

"You know I'm here for you, honey, no matter what you decide, whether it be one, both, or neither."

The both part snapped Natalie's head around, staring open mouthed at her grandmother.

"I'm not sure you are aware of this or not, Natalie, but your mother dated two men at the same time."

"She did?"

"Yes. It shocked the entire town. It went on for a while. Almost a year, I think, before she finally settled on your father."

"Great. Now I'll be stirring up old rumors and whispers, when people around here realize the connection of me and my mother."

"You never were one to follow convention, sweetie. Don't start now. If it requires you dating both men to decide which one is better suited to you, then so be it, and to hell with the busybodies in town. They'll find something else to gossip about in no time."

She walked back to the side of the bed and hugged her grandmother. "Thanks, Gram. I love you."

"I love you, too. Now, get you a cab and head back to the house. You've got a date with one handsome man in a few hours."

"I'll be here in the morning to pick you up and take you home. Please, don't give the nurses a hard time."

"Me?" Her grandmother batted her eyes innocently.

"Don't give me your innocent look. I know better." Natalie kissed her on the cheek. "I'll call you later."

"Sure, honey. Have fun tonight."

* * * *

For the next several hours, Natalie paced like a caged animal. She tried on every piece of clothing she owned, but nothing seemed right. Without knowing exactly where they were going for dinner, she had no idea what to wear. Kale seemed more of the laid-back kind versus Cade. The nervous anticipation skipping through her body did nothing to help the situation. She finally decided earlier in the afternoon to forgo going out somewhere and found a couple of steaks in her grandmother's freezer. Food always seemed plentiful in the house. Fresh vegetables, fresh fruit, makings for salad, a couple of potatoes for baking, and dinner would be grand.

Five o'clock arrived with a dong of the doorbell, and she jumped in response.

Her palms felt itchy and damp. The hair on her neck stood and chills rolled down her back.

"This is nuts."

The door opened with a sharp tug of her hand.

"Hi," Kale said. "Can I come in?"

"Please." A quick flick of the lock on the screen and he stood close enough to smell. *Oh Lordy. I love the scent of his cologne. Something spicy and all male.* "Um. I couldn't find anything to wear so I decided to cook for you, if you don't mind."

"Mind? Honey, I haven't had a home cooked meal in ages. No way do I mind a beautiful woman putterin' around the kitchen makin' me food."

"Great. Come on in. You can drop your coat on the sofa. Would you like a beer?"

"Your grandmother keeps beer?"

"No silly. I ran to the corner store and grabbed some," she said with a laugh. "Of course, she could very well be a beer drinker sometimes. Hell, I don't have a clue."

"You didn't get to spend a lot of time with her growing up after you moved, huh?"

"No, and I'm sorry for it now. The last couple of days with her have been fabulous. When I go back to Portland, I'll have to make sure I come for visits often."

"But you'll be staying a while now, right? I mean, with her needing help around here and all."

"I'll be here for a few more weeks anyway. It all depends on how well she does with her rehabilitation. We won't know until she's done it for a week or so."

She grabbed two beers from the refrigerator, popped them open, and handed him one. Their fingers brushed, and her fingertips tingled from the contact. Not quite the same reaction she had to Cade, but interesting, all the same. After a sip of her beer, she motioned for him to follow her back to the living room.

They took seats, side-by-side, on the couch. "I've already got dinner in the oven. I would have grilled, but it's a bit cold out there," she said, running her sweaty palms down the thighs of her jeans.

"Don't go to any trouble on my account," he replied, with a squeeze to her knee.

"No trouble at all. How about a movie? Gram has a pretty decent DVD collection."

"Sure."

"Why don't you pick something and I'll check on dinner. I'll be right back." Her quick escape to the kitchen gave her a moment to think and breathe.

How in the hell am I going to bring up this threesome thing with Kale? I know he mentioned something yesterday during lunch, but since I had the conversation with Cade, everything seems kind of strange.

"You okay in there?"

"Yes. I'll be right out. I'm sticking the potatoes in the microwave." *Breathe, Natalie, breathe.*

After taking care of her tasks in the kitchen, she moved through the doorway to the living room, stopping in her tracks. Kale had turned the lights down low, and with the sun setting so early in the winter, it made quite a romantic picture. A fire burned bright in the fireplace, crackling and popping to the music he put on the stereo. Garth Brooks crooned The Dance softly in the background.

"I decided I didn't want to watch a movie with you right at this moment. But I'd love to dance with you."

"Here?" she asked in a small laugh.

"Of course. At least here, I don't have to worry about other cowboys cutting in because you're the prettiest girl in the place."

"You can compliment me all you want. I don't mind."

Laughter echoed in the room, and he pulled her tight against his chest. "I love it! You're great."

He took her right hand in his left, allowing his other hand to skim down to her lower back. The soft music continued to play and she lost herself in the feel of being in his arms.

"This is nice."

"Mmm. I think so too," he murmured, brushing his lips against her ear.

"Kale," she whispered.

"Hmm."

"We need to talk."

"Yeah, I know."

"Cade and I talked—"

The ping of the microwave interrupted her trail of thoughts.

"I think that's the potatoes," he said.

"It is," she replied, stepping out of his embrace. "The steaks should be about done too. Would you set the table?"

"Sure."

The warmth of his hand at the small of her back, sent tingles down her legs. When they reached the cupboards, she grabbed place settings for two and handed him everything he needed to set the table. A low whistle came from his lips to the tune on the stereo as he set the plates and silverware out.

She pulled the meat from the oven, the potatoes from the microwave, and the vegetables from the stovetop. "Why don't you grab the plates and we'll fix them over here."

Plates in hand, they moved back toward the table together. He set his down and held her chair.

"Thanks."

"You're welcome."

"You know, it's funny. Men in Oregon don't do those kinds of things."

"Things?"

"Hold doors, pull out a lady's chair...you know gentlemanly things."

"See. You should move back to Red Rock so you can be treated like the lady you are." His smile devastated her control. Dimples peeked out of his cheeks, she hadn't really noticed before. The five o'clock shadow coating his jaw line tempted her to touch, to feel the scrape of his whiskers against her fingertips, and to lose herself in his lips on her hand.

"If it were only that easy."

"You can live where ever you want, Nat."

"At the rate I'm going, I'll be here a while. I'm not sure how my grandmother is going to do here in the house." She folded the napkin in her lap. "Luckily, they already turned one of the downstairs rooms into a bedroom when grandpa was sick."

"Have you talked to your mom about all of this?" he asked. His tempting lips wrapped around the beer bottle when he took a long draw.

"No and I probably won't. She's going to be majorly pissed at me about it, but my grandmother doesn't want me to call her, and I feel it's her choice, not mine."

"Your grandma is a hoot."

A hearty chuckle left her lips. "You aren't telling me anything I haven't figured out. I never know what will come out of her mouth next."

Watching his face, she wasn't sure what to make of the looks passing over it. At the point of her mentioning talking to Cade, he appeared annoyed.

"I really didn't want to bring this up during dinner, but I need to get this off my chest."

His gaze dropped to her breasts, and she cleared her throat to bring his attention back to her face. "I didn't mean those."

"Sorry," he said with a sheepish grin. "Can't help it. They are rather nice."

"The girls' thank you, but we need to talk seriously here."

"All right." The fork full of potato disappeared between his lips, way-laying her thoughts for a moment.

"Cade and I talked about the two of you sharing."

"Sharing what?"

"Don't act like you have no idea what I'm talking about, Kale. Sharing a woman."

The frown on his face did nothing to alleviate her uneasiness.

"What exactly did Cade tell you?"

"You've done it ten times—sometimes at your house and sometimes at his apartment—a few of times before you both married, and a couple times since the divorces. But it's always with the acknowledgment and consent of the woman involved."

A heavy sigh left his lips in a rush and she smiled. He apparently didn't like this conversation much.

"Sounds like he explained things pretty well."

She nodded. "Yes, he did. I want to hear your side of things and if you two talked about having said type of relationship with me."

"You?"

"Yes, me, Kale. Don't look so surprised. I'm not a complete idiot. I know men talk, and if you two have done it before, then I want to know if you discussed doing it with me."

The look on his face was almost funny, as his cheeks flushed with color.

"You're embarrassed."

"A little." He jumped to his feet, pacing the kitchen floor. "I'm not the type of man to talk to a woman about bedding her." His fingers cut a path through his hair. "You told me earlier, you and Cade already had sex."

"Yes, we did. Last night and this morning."

"Twice?"

She looked away for a second then focused back on his face. "Well, yes. He spent the night last night and it happened."

"Shit."

"It doesn't matter, Kale. The issue I'm having right now is my attraction to both of you. Handsome doesn't come close to describing you two. Either of you can have your choice of women, I'm sure, and I am beyond thrilled to think you are attracted to me."

"Why wouldn't we be, Nat? You are beautiful, sexy, smart, and sweet. You're the type of woman every man wants to come home to after a hard day's work."

"Thank you. But you are avoiding my questions."

His fingers trailed through his hair again, leaving several strands sticking up, and she wondered why she felt the need to smooth them back into place.

"All right, yes. Cade and I discussed it right after he found you out on the road. The next morning, in fact. Neither of us really went into detail."

"How do you feel about sharing?"

"If the woman is accepting to it, then I'm good with it. It can be an amazing experience for her, but also for the guys involved."

"Cade described to me how it works."

"Thank God," he murmured, and she couldn't help but smile. *Poor guy.* He seemed so uncomfortable talking about this; it almost made her want to let it go. *Almost.*

"How would you feel about me having sex with both of you?"

"Do you want to have sex with me?"

"I don't really know, Kale. We haven't had much time together, you know, getting close, cuddling and all."

"Have you had time to do those kinds of things with Cade?"

"Things just happened with Cade. He showed me his house, and he's been a rock for me with my grandmother. We came back here after all the turmoil from yesterday and things heated up from there. Now, I want to spend time with you and find out if this attraction I feel can lead to something more."

"I'd like that too."

"Good. Come finish your dinner. I didn't mean to cause an issue while we were eating. I'm comfortable with you, Kale, and if nothing else, I think we could have a really good friendship."

He grimaced and shuttered.

"What?" she asked.

"The *friendship* word."

The laughter bubbling from her lips sounded more like the Natalie she knew. Serious conversations like this weren't part of her personality, but she felt it needed saying. "I didn't mean it. I swear!" She held up both hands in surrender as giggles still filled the room. He grabbed both of her hands in his and kissed her quickly.

"Good. Let's finish this fabulous meal then we can watch a movie, go out for drinks, dance, or whatever. Anything you want to do, but it has to afford me the opportunity to wrap my arms around you and get close. I want the same chance you gave Cade."

Kale kept the conversation light, making her laugh the rest of the meal. Serious didn't fit the description of his personality at all. She did remember him being more of the class clown when she lived here during her childhood. Joking around and never taking things too seriously was his specialty.

"You remember Mrs. Baxter, right?"

"The English teacher?"

"Yeah. You probably didn't know it, but she started dating the football coach."

"Mr. Alexander? You're kidding me, right? Those two couldn't be more opposite. She was, um, what's the word I want? Frumpy, I guess, and he was the handsome jock. He had all the female students panting after him, even if most of us in school were jail-bait for him."

"Guess what? They're married now."

"You're kidding? Really? Wow!"

He nodded. "I believe they had a baby a couple years back, too."

"I would never have pictured those two together."

"Me either, but I guess it goes back to opposites attract sometimes."

"What about you? Do you want kids someday?"

"Yeah, I'd like to have a couple anyway. My ex never wanted kids. I didn't realize it until after we'd already been married a year and I mentioned it to her. You would have thought I'd asked her to carry an alien inside her or something. She freaked."

"To each his own, I guess."

"Do you want kids, Nat?"

"Of course. I'd love to have several, but I need a husband first. I don't believe in having a child until there is a loving relationship to bring them in to. I've seen way too many one-parent households with my students. It's a major struggle for the children and the parents." She grabbed their plates and took them to the sink. "Let me quickly wash these and we can take our drinks into the living room."

"Let me help."

"Really?"

"Sure. My mother did raise me to help around the house. I even cook sometimes."

Both hands planted on her hips she tapped her toe. "I thought you said you hadn't had a home cooked meal in ages."

"Oops. Busted." He shrugged and laughed. "I meant, by a beautiful woman. I do cook for myself, but it's not the same." His lips brushed her nose and he pulled her close. "Mad at me?"

"No."

"Good. Can I kiss you now?"

"Do you want to?"

"More than anything on Earth right now."

The warmth of his breath on her face had her toes curling in her shoes. The wicked little smile on his mouth made her heart skip a beat. When he brought his lips closer, hers started to tingle in anticipation. He'd kissed her before, but not an all consuming, passionate, melt-your-panties kind of kiss and that is what she wanted.

One hand slid into her hair. The other held the side of her face. He nibbled at the sides of her lips, sweeping his tongue over the seam of her mouth, before plunging inside when she moaned. Both of her hands went around his neck, and she tilted her head to fit their mouths together better. Tongues explored the insides of each other's mouths, licking, entwining, and stroking. Each diving and retreating.

His hands slipped down her back, tugging her close enough her breasts brushed his chest as her nipples tightened. He tasted good—damn good.

When he finally sighed and pulled away, she wanted to chase him down and bring him back.

"Some kiss," he murmured, pressing his forehead against hers.

"Yeah."

With a rough clearing of his throat, he took her hand and pulled her toward the couch. "Do you want to stay here, or do you want to go out somewhere? The honky-tonk down the street has a live band tonight."

The phone on the end table jingled, and she frowned. "I wonder who that is." Her grandmother didn't own anything close to being high-tech, so no caller ID. "Hello?"

"Hey, Nat."

She glanced at Kale and replied, "Hi, Cade."

7

"Is everything okay over there?" Cade asked and she had to shake her head.

"Of course. Why wouldn't it be?"

"I wanted to check in with you. Is Kale there?"

"Yes, Cade, he is. We're sitting here on the couch."

"Doin' what?"

"None of your business, mister."

"Well, I—"

"Give me the phone a sec," Kale said, taking the receiver from her hand. "Cade? I didn't butt in with your time with Natalie, so quit butting into mine."

She smiled, shaking her head and glancing down at her hands where they lay in her lap.

"She's in perfectly good hands with me, and put it this way, I won't do anything you didn't do. Nighty-night." He shut off the phone, stood up, and unplugged it from the wall. "The hospital has your cell phone number right?"

"Yes."

"Good. Cade doesn't, does he?"

The laughter in her chest just about burst free. "No."

"Perfect."

"You." She chuckled. "Unplugged." The giggle turned into a full-blown laugh. "The phone."

One of his eyebrows shot up and she couldn't help it. Her stomach hurt from laughing and she doubled over.

"I didn't think it was that funny."

"I'm sorry, Kale," she gasped. "It's not. But the jealousy on your face is."

"Jealous? I'm not jealous. I've never been jealous of Cade."

When her giggles finally calmed, she said, "How do you feel knowing I had sex with Cade before you?"

"Before? Are you saying you plan to have sex with me?"

"Answer my question."

"All right, yeah. It bugs me some, but I'm willing to forget about it. But you have to be willing to give me the same chances."

"I'm here with you tonight aren't I?"

"Yeah."

"Then you have the same chances he had. You can woo me, love me, and sweep me off my feet, too. I have to warn you though. You have your work cut out for you."

"Why?"

"Sit down and I'll tell you about some of my past relationships."

"Okay."

Once he took his place next to her on the couch, she said, "I dated my ex for a couple of years. His name is Steven. He's the father of one of my students—well, he used to be. I haven't had his daughter in my class in two years."

"Awkward."

"At first, yes. He asked me to dinner, and I tried to explain to him I didn't date my students' parents."

"Persistent, wasn't he?"

"Very much so. I finally agreed to have dinner with him. One thing led to another, and we ended up sleeping together the first night, which I don't normally do."

"But you slept with Cade last night on your first date."

"Thanks for reminding me."

"Sorry."

"Anyway, he became my whole world. I loved his daughter as if she was my own. We moved in together, and I thought everything in my life had come together. I loved my job. I loved him, and I thought he loved me, until I went to a conference in Seattle. The conference ended earlier than expected, so I came home a day before he expected me. I wanted to surprise him, but I got the surprise of my life when I walked in on him with another woman, in our bed."

"Wow."

"Yeah."

"What did he say?"

"He didn't make excuses. He said he had wanted out of the relationship for a while. I wasn't what he wanted in a wife."

"What the hell did he want?"

"Someone younger, skinner, and prettier. The woman in our bed was a new partner in his law firm. She recently joined them straight out of law school."

"He's an idiot."

A dry chuckle left her mouth. "Cade said the same thing."

"We agree on one thing then." He kissed her nose. "I think you are a very special woman, Natalie, and I'm thrilled to be here with you tonight. If something happens between us, then so be it. I'm not pushing. Would I like to make love to you? You're damned straight, but it'll happen when and where we choose and not before."

"I appreciate you giving me time."

A frown crossed his face. "Are you going to sleep with Cade again?"

"He doesn't know it yet, but no. I need to figure out what is between you and me, and me and him, before I sleep with him again. It's not fair to put that kind of pressure on a budding relationship."

"I'm glad to hear you say those words." He wrapped one arm around her shoulders and pulled her to his side. "I don't want to have to kill my best friend."

"Oh, stop it, will you," she said, punching him in the side.

"Ouch."

"Pleeaassee. I did not hurt you."

"My pride," he pouted then laughed. "Shall we watch a movie or go to the bar?"

"How about we go to the bar for a little while then come back here and watch a movie. It's still early."

"Sounds good to me." He brought her to her feet with him, shooing her to get her purse and a coat.

Snow fell in big flakes, coating their hair and jackets. The bar was only three blocks from her grandmother's house, and since it wasn't too frigid outside, they decided to walk. Hand-in-hand, they strolled down the sidewalk, taking in the sights. Christmas lights adorned almost every house. Big, inflated Santa Claus', twinkling lights of every color, nativity scenes in every size and shape, and some decorations so elaborate, they took your breath away, graced yard after yard. Christmas happened to be her favorite holiday. She frowned as she wondered if grandma would even decorate this year with grandpa gone.

"What do you want for Christmas?" Kale asked, bringing her thoughts back to him.

"Oh, I don't know. I love the holidays. It's my favorite time of year. I love to decorate, bake, and have a big family dinner on Christmas Day. You know all those family type things."

He tugged her close to his side. "Sounds like a great Christmas to me. I hope you'll still be here."

"I probably will with everything going on, and I really don't have anything to go back to Oregon for, except my parents and sister."

"All the more reason to stay here."

Within fifteen minutes, they stood outside the big double doors of the Saddle Club as loud music waved and ebbed every time the doors opened.

"Shall we?" Kale asked, holding one for her.

The band's attempt at God Bless The Broken Road by Rascal Flatts wasn't too bad, but it wasn't like the original either.

"They aren't terrible, huh?" hollering over the music as he nodded toward the stage.

"Not terrible, no, but the original band is much better."

The soft chuckle next to her ear sent shivers down her back. "I'm sure they are, but those big bands, like Rascal Flatts, don't come to Red Rock."

"Maybe someday they will."

"Let's dance," he said, pulling her toward the dance floor.

Several sets of eyes followed their path, making the hair on her arms stand on end. Kale put both hands on her hips and pulled her in close. She laid one on his chest while the other went around his neck.

"Damn, I love the way you smell," he murmured, his lips pressing to the soft skin beneath her ear.

"Lavender."

"Mmm."

"Cade and I—" His head came up so fast, he about knocked her unconscious, and she immediately apologized. "I'm sorry, Kale. I didn't mean to bring him up while with you."

Two fingers pressed against her lips. "Shh. Don't worry about it. You spent most of today with him. It's understandable to relate things that happened today with his presence."

She kissed his fingers then pulled them away from her mouth. "It's not fair to you. I promise, I won't bring him up again tonight. All right?"

The beat changed into a two-step with a fast rhythm, keeping them scooting across the floor. Kale twirled her and brought her back into his arms as he set their steps into motion. The bass guitar and the beat of the drums, thumped to the beat of her heart. Sweat tickled along her scalp. It had been some time since she danced like this, and the exertion had her breathing a little hard, or was it the man holding her?

"You're a pretty good dancer."

"Even two-steppin'? I haven't done this in ages."

"They don't two-step in Oregon?"

"Not much. You can find a few country bars, but not too many, and I'm not usually the bar-hopper type. I do like a beer now and again though, and the atmosphere of the honky-tonk is kinda cool sometimes."

"My kind of girl."

She bit the inside of her lip as his words seeped in. The uneasiness she felt in continuing to encourage this thing with Kale, made her feel like a heel. *Decisions. Decisions.* Choosing between the two of them got harder and harder with each passing day and every moment spent with them. Maybe it would be better if she went back to Oregon. If her grandmother had a live in caregiver, she wouldn't need to stay. Her ordinary, lonely life back home awaited her, but somehow, the thought wasn't comforting at all.

"You're thinking too hard," he whispered in her ear.

"Sorry."

"What's the frown for?"

"Can we sit? Or maybe it would be better if we went back to my grandmother's house."

"If you'd rather, its fine with me," he replied as they stopped dancing.

"Yeah. I think so. I think some alone time would be good."

"I'm all for alone time." A small chuckle left his mouth before he leaned down, brushing his lips against hers. "Let's go."

A few moments later, they stepped outside to see the snow coming down in a heavy blanket of white.

"Wow. It's really snowing now."

"How about I call a cab to take us back to the house?"

"No, let's walk. It's not very far," she replied, taking his hand and pulling him into the snow. "Besides, it makes it better to warm up when we get back. A nice fire, a little hot chocolate or coffee, soft music, and some snuggle time."

"Sounds like the perfect way to warm up after a walk in the snow. Besides, by then, my hands will be like icicles, and I'll need somewhere to warm them up. Along your hot body comes to mind."

"Hot, huh?"

"Oh hell yeah," he said with a wicked grin. He tucked her hand in the crook of his elbow as a saucy whistle left his lips. She couldn't help the smile on her mouth. His easygoing personality and take no shit attitude seemed to be just what she needed right now.

Once they reached the house, she unlocked the door and flipped the light on. "How about you build the fire back up and I'll get the coffee started. I think there's even some apple pie in the refrigerator."

"Apple pie? With ice cream?"

She shook her head, smiling at his little boy enthusiasm. "Yes, with ice cream."

"You gotta a deal, babe."

With the coffee finished and the pie dished up, she balanced the plates in one hand and the mugs in the other as she pushed the swinging door between the kitchen and living room with her butt. The crackle and pop of the fire seemed cheerful and bright. Kale had returned to the couch, but when she came through the door, he jumped to his feet to help her.

"Let me get those," he said, grabbing the coffee mugs.

"Great fire."

"It helps having good kindling and dry wood."

"I can imagine. I don't know the last time I had a real fire. My parents' place has a gas fireplace."

"Gas is for sissies."

Her laugh sounded dry and brittle. "Yeah. It's not the same as a log fire."

"With the snow falling outside, a warm cup of coffee, and some awesome apple pie? I'm in heaven here."

She kicked off her shoes and tucked her feet underneath her. "How's the pie taste?" The groan and satisfied smile on his mouth gave her the answer. "I guess that means good?"

"I haven't had pie this good since I went home last."

"How long ago was that?" she asked, slipping a bite into her mouth.

"Two days ago."

She laughed so hard, the plate jiggled in her fingers. "You are so busted. I'm so going to call your mother." The frown lines settling between his eyebrows and the fake frown on his lips made her laugh harder. "Typical man. Afraid of his mother."

"You're damned right. My father knows who tows the line in their home and it's not him," he replied with a deep chuckle. The sound sent shivers down her arms. She loved his laugh.

"So tell me. What kind of woman are you looking for?"

"Well, let's see. My ex came from money, and she expected us to live as her parents did. She didn't quite get that it takes time to establish one's self and have money coming in regularly. I had the jobs, but they weren't steady. I supplemented our income with breaking horses. She hated the lifestyle, hated living so far out of town. I didn't want to hobnob with the social circles in Red Rock and she did."

"I find myself more of a homebody, too. I like going to movies sometimes, at the theatre, or going out for coffee because I can, but it's not a normal thing. I don't go out a lot," she replied.

"I would love to find a woman who is comfortable with herself enough not to worry about going to the store without makeup on, someone happy in jeans and a t-shirt, who likes riding horses, dancing, and enjoys going to barbeques. A woman that doesn't mind if I hang out with the guys sometimes and can find happiness in the little things—the laughter of a child, the snow falling, the wind in the trees, the sparkle of the sun on the lake, or the freedom of the wild horses running across the open plains."

"You are a hopeless romantic, Kale."

His cheeks flushed pink, and he dropped his gaze to the pie in his hands.

"You're blushing."

"I can't help it. I don't take compliments well. Never have."

The warmth of his skin under her palm felt good. The crisp, dark hair on his forearm, tickled her hand. "Well let me tell you. You're one special guy."

"Special enough you could fall in love with?"

* * * *

What the hell am I doin'? Scaring the hell out of her, that's what! Disgusted with himself over his behavior, he slid his plate onto the coffee table and grasped her hand in his.

"I'm sorry, Natalie. I shouldn't have said something so personal or pressure you in such a way. It's not fair to you." Her hair felt like silk between his fingers when he tucked a stray curl behind her ear.

"No, it's not, Kale. I'm having a hard enough time dating both of you, but I forgive you. You are kind of at a disadvantage since Cade and I already had sex."

"Thanks for bringing that up."

"Crap. I'm sorry now. I shouldn't have brought it up again."

"I know he's already made love to you, and I want to more than anything in the world, but I think we need to take some time to get to know each other better. Rushing isn't my style. Of course, I don't have six months to woo you either."

"Six months?"

"Yeah. I don't sleep with a lady unless I've known her for a few months." The softness of her skin under his fingers made him want to stroke every inch of her, from the top of her head to the toes on her feet. Desire raced down his back, settling in his balls.

"Really?"

"I'm not much into one-night stands, Nat. It's not the way I am. Some guys can sleep with a woman without any kind of emotional ties—not me. I need to feel something for her before I sleep with her."

"I've heard men can have sex without emotion where women tend to need the emotional closeness."

"I'm fine with kissing you and holding you right now. Don't mistake it for not wanting you beneath me." Their eyes met and held. The green of her gaze appeared intense, hot, and full of emotion. "I want nothing more than to feel your heat wrapped around me, but I'll wait for the right time."

And for some reason, I don't want to discuss a threesome including Cade right at this moment. The thought irritates the hell out of me.

"How about a movie? I picked one out earlier and popped it into the DVD player, but since we ended up doing something different, I left it alone."

"Sounds like a great idea to me. What did you pick?" she asked, snuggling into his arms and throwing one leg over his.

"Die Hard."

She sat up with a start, her eyes wide with shock. "My grandmother had Die Hard?"

The look on her face made him laugh. "Yes, she did. Every last one of them too. We could have a Die Hard marathon tonight."

"There's what? Four of them, right?"

"Yep."

"At approximately two hours each, so that makes eight hours of movies with no pee breaks, no food breaks—um, I think I'll pass."

"All right. How about two of them tonight. It's six thirty now and four hours of movies would make it ten thirty."

"Sounds good, but I'm going to need sustenance. I'll have to check the kitchen for snacks."

"We had dinner about an hour ago, besides the pie and ice cream, so I should be good for a bit. How about we watch the first one and then worry about snacks."

"Works for me," she replied, snuggling into his arms again as he switched on the television and DVD player.

The roar of the opening credits filled the room with sound drowning out anything and everything but the hum. Action flicks were his favorite, like any guy he knew. Chick flicks tied women in knots, but he did give into those occasionally, depending on the woman. For Nat, he would watch a chick flick.

A soft lavender smell reached his nose, and he inhaled her scent, holding it inside, and savoring it for a while. Stray strands of her hair tickled the underside of his chin. The pillow softness of her breast molded to his chest where she lay against his side. Her hand rested on his stomach and he fought the groan rumbling inside. If she moved her hand just a little, she would brush against the achy fullness behind the fly of his jeans. The need to have her cup his cock and stroke it about drove him insane. Her warm thigh pressed against his. His fingers slipped from her shoulder, down her arm, and back. The silkiness of her skin made him ache to taste and take pleasure in everything about her.

"You okay?" she murmured.

The warmth of her breath skipped over his skin. He wanted her lips. Everywhere. He cleared his throat and squeaked, "Uh. Yeah."

"You don't sound okay," she replied, tipping her head back.

"I'm fine. The smell of your hair is driving me crazy. That's all." Her tongue peeked out and slipped over the surface of her lips. "You're killing me here."

The smile creeping across her mouth looked almost wicked. *Did women do wicked smiles?* He didn't know, but decided hers qualified.

Her hand pressed to his chest, and she scooted back so they were nose to nose. "I want your mouth."

"Where?"

"Here," she whispered, tapping one finger to her lips. "Knock my socks off."

The growl coming from his mouth didn't sound like anything he'd heard before, but it definitely sounded possessive, and he didn't care. Kissing her could be his downfall—throwing in the towel—giving up the goose, or all of the above. He couldn't help himself. Tasting her became a priority as he lowered his mouth to hers.

The soft groan came from one of them, but he couldn't tell who. It seemed to float between them, passing back and forth from her mouth to his. Her tongue tentatively touched his lips and he opened for her with a moan. Women didn't usually come on to him, and he found it refreshing for Natalie to pursue him to some degree. He knew she needed to see the differences between him and Cade—feel what it was like to kiss him, make love with him. Finding out if the attraction burning between them could hold a candle to what she shared with his best friend became imperative.

The kiss deepened with a small tilt of her head. His fingers threaded into the tendrils of her hair and held her in place. Her lips were soft and felt perfect under his. She shifted so she lay across his lap, but never broke the kiss. Chest to breast. His cock stiff and aching as it pressed into her hip. He wanted to cup her breast in his palm and rake his thumb across her nipple, but he refused to give into his desire and hers. Pushing her would be a mistake. Giving into her would be a death-null.

He lifted his head and stared into the pools of green. "Nat, honey, we need to stop this."

"Why?"

His forehead met hers as he fought the urge to throw caution into the wind. "I don't want you to make love with me only because you are comparing me and Cade."

"But I'm—"

The brush of his lips stopped her words.

"You had sex with Cade last night and this morning. I want us to get to know each other better before it happens between us. Can you understand?"

She didn't look happy, but she nodded and scooted back.

Great going! Now she'll feel like shit for coming onto me.

"Please, don't feel bad, Natalie. It has nothing to do with my attraction to you. If I thought it would be you and me, without Cade between us, I'd throw you over my shoulder and haul your ass upstairs right now." He grasped her hand, pressing it to his aching erection. "Can you feel how badly I want you?"

"Either that or you've got one hell of a big rock in your pocket."

Loud laughter took the tension down a notch or two. "I know where you get your sense of humor, but God woman. I can see I have to watch everything I say for fear you'll turn it around and bite me on the ass with it."

Her eyes sparkled and danced with mirth. "Bite your ass? Uh-huh. Sounds like fun."

"I'm not saying another word." The zipping motion across his lips made her laugh.

"Let's enjoy the movie, and we'll leave the heavy petting and necking for another date."

He nodded, but didn't reply as he continued pressing his lips tight together.

One eyebrow shot up in a saucy I-don't-think-so look right before she twisted and straddle his hips. She was right where he wanted her, even if he refused to tell her so. Her teeth nipped at his lips, and he fought the smile trying to break free. Her tongue snaked out, licking the seam, but he refused to open. Changing her direction of attack, she slid her lips over his cheek until she reached his ear. Teeth nipped at his earlobe then sucked it between her lips. Still, he refused to utter a sound. He never realized how sensitive the skin below his ear was until she bit it softly before continuing her trek down his neck. The collar of his shirt gave way to the insistent push of her nose.

When the hell did she work the buttons loose on my shirt?

Before he knew it, the material parted, and her fingers began working his left nipple. She pinched and pulled on the responsive nub while biting and licking his neck and shoulder. The hot, insistent throb in his balls drove a whimper from in his chest to his throat, but he refused to release it.

"Talk?"

He shook his head.

"Oh, you are so screwed, buddy."

If only she meant what she said.

She pushed the material off his shoulders, continuing her journey down his chest until her lips closed over his right nipple.

His eyes rolled back and his head lolled against the back of the couch.

Damn, she likes to bite!

Her teeth scraped the hardened bud and desire clenched at his balls. His fingertips itched to pull her head tighter against him, but he refused to give into the yearning. His hands curled into fists. He wouldn't give into the feelings she stirred unless she made the first move. This sure felt like the first move to him.

The jingle of her cell phone interrupted her play.

"Shit."

"What?"

"Nothing I did made you talk, but my cell phone ringing did? Wow."

The phone rang again.

"Ignore it."

"I can't. It's my mother."

8

The phone continued ringing while she hunted for her purse. "Damn it! Where the hell did I put it?"

"On the end table," Kale replied while buttoning his shirt.

She fumbled with the latch, scrambling to grab it before it went to voicemail. "Hi, Mom."

"What took you so long to answer the phone?"

"I...um...I'm busy."

"Where's your grandmother? And why isn't anyone answering the home phone?"

Shit! Kale unplugged it.

"How do I say this without you yelling at me?"

"What's wrong? What happened? Spill it, Natalie Marie."

"Calm down, Mom. Grandma is fine, but she's in the hospital."

"Hospital? What the hell is going on over there?"

"It appears she had a small stroke."

"I'll be there tomorrow," her mother said, almost shouting into the phone.

"No, Mom. Grandma doesn't want you here. That's the reason I didn't call you. She wouldn't let me. She's doing fine. The hospital is releasing her tomorrow to come home."

"Home. How can she go home, Natalie, if she had a stroke?"

"It's not serious. She's a little weak on one side, but I'm staying, and we are going to have a physical therapist come in and work with her here at the house." She rolled her eyes as she glanced at Kale. With clothing back in place, he almost looked perturbed. His irritated steps took him back and forth in front of the fireplace while he raked his fingers through his hair.

"Well, tell your grandmother I don't care if she doesn't want me there. I'll be on the first plane in the morning. You'll need to pick me up at the airport. I'll call you when I know what time."

Great! This is just what I need, my mother hovering.

"Mom, really. You don't need to come. Everything is fine here. I'm taking care of grandma."

"Exactly what happened? Did she fall or anything, complain of weakness?"

Natalie bit her lip and tried to think of something to say that wouldn't give her away.

"What aren't you tell me, Natalie?"

"I wasn't exactly here when it happened, Mom."

"You weren't there? What in the hell are you doing? You went there with specific instructions to help your grandmother finalize everything and bring her back here to live with us. God, can you do anything right?"

"Thanks, Mother. I really appreciate the support. I'm sorry I let you down. Do whatever you want because obviously I can't measure up to your standards." With a soft whimper and a tear streaking down her cheek, she snapped the phone shut with an irritated click.

"Come here, honey," Kale said, wrapping his arms around her and pulling her to his chest.

She buried her face against his shoulder and cried like a baby. Her mother rarely got to her these days, but sometimes, she couldn't help thinking how much of a bitch she could be.

"Shh. It's fine. Whatever she said to upset you can't be bad enough to cry over." His strong hands moved over her back, soothing her and bringing her tears to a stop.

"It doesn't matter, Kale. I'll never be good enough for her."

The callused pad of his thumb wiped away the remaining tears from her cheek. "Why do you think that?"

Two steps back and her legs hit the couch before she sat down, crossing her arms over her chest. "It's always been clear. I wasn't the boy she wanted. For Andrea, it didn't matter. She was the second born. The first born had to be a son, which obviously, I'm not."

The couch sunk when he took the seat next to her, pulling her into his embrace. "You are definitely good enough. Don't let her negative attitude bring you down. You're a beautiful, intelligent, sexy woman and any man would be thrilled to call you his own. Your mother will come around eventually."

"I doubt it, but thank you for saying such nice things."

"If I didn't believe they were true, I wouldn't say them." One finger under her chin brought her face around so their eyes met. The chocolate brown of his, sparkled in the firelight.

"I think you should go, Kale. I'm sorry. I'm not real good company right now," she whispered, afraid he would try kissing her again. Her hands rubbed up and down her arms.

"If you want me to, Nat, I'll go."

With a stiff nod of her head, she gave him her answer. It would be better if she were alone tonight after the dressing down her mother gave her. If her mother would indeed be flying into Red Rock tomorrow, she needed her strength to deal with her, and right now, her heart wasn't into figuring out her feelings for Kale or Cade.

"Can I see you again?" he asked as he stood.

"Of course."

"How about Saturday still, since this one was an unexpected date?"

"All right. Dinner and a movie?"

"Sure. I'll pick you up about six?"

"Sounds perfect. See you then."

"Do you have some way of getting to the hospital to pick up your grandmother?"

"Yes. Her car is here and I have the keys. I'm all set."

"Good. Call me tomorrow once you two are back here, safe and sound. I want to know you're okay. These roads can be tricky."

"Even though I haven't lived here in a while, Kale, I have driven in snow."

"Oh yeah, when?"

"I used to ski Mount Hood every winter."

"With plowed and sanded roads leading right up to the ski area, I presume."

"Well, yes."

"Not the same as driving around here and you know it. Just be careful, babe. I don't want you in the hospital, too."

"I will, but I'll call you when we get back here."

"Good. Walk me out?"

"Sure," she replied, taking his hand in hers.

The snow had stopped, except for an occasional flake here and there, but a good quarter of an inch covered the ground. Her boots crunched in the snow with each step. No Christmas lights decorated her grandmother's home this year, and she made a mental note to ask about putting some up. Lights always made the season seem more real to her.

Kale wrapped both arms around her, tugging her close. "Can I kiss you good-night?"

"I'd like it if you did. Things kind of got interrupted in there."

"Yes they did, but I'm glad they did. You definitely had my attention and things were moving pretty fast."

Heat crawled up her neck and splashed across her cheeks.

"No need for embarrassment, Natalie. I was enjoying myself with the attention, but we already discussed waiting to make love."

"I know, but you threw the challenge out there, and I'm not the type of girl to back down from a challenge."

"I gathered that," he replied, chuckling softly.

Seconds later, she parted her lips to accept his kiss. Man, did the guy know how to kiss. Is it a prerequisite to being a hunk? Knowing how to kiss a girl out of her panties?

His tongue snaked inside her mouth, stroking along her tongue and fueling the fire. A soft moan left her lips as she tipped her head to take more. After several moments of light-your-underwear-on-fire kissing, he lifted his head, kissed her nose, and stepped back.

"I'll talk to you tomorrow."

"Uh, yeah. Tomorrow."

"Sleep well," he said, blowing her a final kiss.

When his truck backed out of the driveway and disappeared down the street, she sighed, shaking her head. Time. Time to think and analyze these feelings would be a great idea.

"A hot bath, lots of bubbles, and a hot romance novel. Mmm. Sounds like a perfect way to unwind from all of this and relax."

Back inside the house, she plugged the phone back into the wall, turned off her cell phone, and headed up the stairs. The bathroom she and Cade made love in that morning also held a huge tub, big enough for at least two people. Lavender bubble bath, hot water, a big fluffy towel, clean pajamas, and she had it made.

A soft sigh escaped her lips as she sank into the hot water. Long, hot soaks were not a pleasure she often affords herself, but what the hell. She didn't have anywhere to be right now. No man to worry about, no papers to grade, and no television shows to miss, so an extended warm bath could be the ticket necessary to focus.

Grandma is going to be so pissed if Mom shows up tomorrow, but I have a gut feeling she will. She never knows when to butt out and leave people alone. The groans spilling from her mouth sounded almost animalistic. Muscles relaxed. Her arms felt heavy and her eyes closed.

"I think she's more than open to the idea, Kale." Cade's voice boomed off the walls in the bathroom.

"Maybe. We didn't get a chance to discuss it earlier," Kale answered.

"Well I did and she seemed totally fascinated by it." Cade's lips brushed hers. "Natalie, honey, do you want us?"

She moaned, shifting in the water.

"I take it that's a yes," Kale replied.

Two naked bodies slipped into the bath with her, splashing water over the sides of the tub. Cade's hand palmed her right breast and Kale's took her left.

"So round. So perfect," Cade whispered in her ear. "We're gonna make love to you, Natalie. Both at the same time. I want your perfect round ass and Kale wants inside your hot little pussy."

Her nipples pulled tight under their fingers. Cade raked his thumb over the sensitive tip, and Kale rolled the other between his finger and thumb. Her back arched and she whimpered in need.

Cade's fingers abandoned her breast and skimmed down her belly to slide between her legs. "Open for me, darlin'."

Thighs parted. Whimpers rose and fell from her mouth uncontrollably as the two men brought her higher and higher. Kale's lips closed over her nipple. His teeth and tongue did delicious things, sending desire zinging from the tip to her clit. Cade pushed two fingers into her pussy. "Oh yeah. Hot and slick."

Desire spiked hard. "Oh God!"

"Tell us what you want, Nat," Kale murmured in between tonguing her nipple.

"I want both of you inside me. Please."

Kale leaned against the tub, grabbed her hips, and pulled her so she straddled him. One swift plunge sheathed him deep inside her, causing her to throw her head back and groan. "Yes."

"My turn, darlin'," Cade said, moving between Kale's slightly bent legs.

"Cade," she moaned.

"What, honey?"

"Now, please." His cock bumped against her tight back hole.

"Easy. You said you've never had a man there before."

"I don't care. I want you inside me."

Kale shifted his hips, sliding in and out several times, fucking her hard.

"Easy Kale. Let me in man."

"Hurry up. I'm about to blow here."

Cade pulled her ass cheeks apart and slid two fingers inside. She whimpered and pushed against his hand. "You like that?"

"God, yes. More. I need more." His fingers disappeared and the head of his cock brushed at her entrance. "Please, Cade."

A sharp, loud ringing brought her upright in the tub.

"Holy shit! I was dreaming?"

The phone rang again and she almost cried. There would be no satisfying the sexual frustration running through her body without the help of a man or maybe two.

"Hello?" she groaned into the phone, hoping it wasn't her mother again or her grandmother.

"Nat, darlin'. Are you okay?" Cade asked on the other end.

"Cade," she breathed. "Thank God you weren't my mother."

"You sound out of breath. Did I interrupt something? Is Kale still there?"

"The only thing you interrupted was my bath, and no, he isn't here. He went home about an hour ago."

"I almost came over there. You weren't answering the phone, and I don't have your cell number."

"Everything is fine, Cade. You don't need to come over here."

"What if I said I wanted to?"

Maybe I should. I mean, I know he could take care of this problem I have now, but I told Kale I wouldn't until he had a chance with me too.

"I would like nothing more than for you to come over here, Cade—"

"Great! I'll be right there."

"But no."

"No?" The surprise in his voice almost made her laugh.

"No. You shouldn't come over here. There's nothing you can do for me right now. I'm going to get out of the tub..." He groaned deep into the phone. "And get ready for bed. Alone."

"Ever had phone sex?"

"Excuse me?"

"Phone sex, Nat. You know. We talk. You make yourself come and I do the same. Are you game?"

"Seriously?"

"Yeah. Why not? Even if we did have sex earlier today, you just talking makes me hotter than hell."

"I am horny," she murmured, drying off.

"Why? Kale?"

"Actually, yes and no. I've been over that for a while, but I had one really great dream while I was in the bathtub."

"A dream, huh."

"Yep."

"Care to tell me about it?"

"Let's just say you and Kale were both in it."

"Oh?"

"Uh, yeah. And remember how you told me about how you two work a threesome?"

He replied in a choked, "Yes."

"Put it this way, I have a really vivid imagination."

"Aw, fuck."

"Mmm. Yeah, you could put it like that."

"Are you sure you don't want me to come over?"

"I'm sure, but I think the phone sex thing could take care of my problem and maybe yours."

"What are you wearin'?"

"Nothing."

The low growl through the phone made her smile. "You?"

"Right now? Jeans and boxers, but give me a second." The shuffle, zip, and whoosh of his clothes were loud on her end of the phone. "Okay. Now, nothin'."

"I need to go into my room. Hang on a sec." She unplugged the bathtub, wrapped the towel around her, and moved toward her room. "Do I need my vibrator?"

"Depends."

"On?"

"Do you think I can make you come with my voice?"

"I think I'll skip the vibrator and make you work for it, stud."

"Oh, honey, you asked for it." He cleared his throat, dropping his voice an octave. "Are you stretched out on your bed?"

"Uh-huh."

"Take your right hand and move it over your right breast."

A soft moan left her lips when she did as instructed.

"Roll your nipple between your fingers like I want to do. Can you feel it? Feel my fingers."

"Yeah," she breathed.

"Wet your other fingers with your tongue then swirl it around your other nipple. That's my tongue, darlin', swirlin', and lickin' at the pretty little pink nub."

"God, Cade. You're pretty good at this."

His chuckle on the phone brought her down a notch.

"My hand is sliding down your belly to part those full, pink lips."

Her breath hitched.

"Swirl your finger around your clit."

"Mmm," she hummed.

"Perfect, darlin'."

"Are you coming along with me, Cade?"

"Oh, you know it. My cock is so hard, I could pound nails with it right now."

"Stroke it for me. Feel my warm hand wrapped around you, sliding up and down."

"Toggle your clit for me, honey." Cream slid between her ass cheeks. "Are you wet, Nat?"

"Definitely." She captured a little of the silky wetness, using it to lubricate her ministrations on her clit. "It feels like your tongue."

"My, my. Naughty girl."

Rasping breaths in the phone matched hers. She knew he bordered right there with her. Her motions quickened. Pressure increased. Her legs tingled with the pressure to come.

"I'm gonna come, Cade. Come with me."

"I'm right there, darlin'. Fuck, this is so hot."

Pleasure rushed up her legs and burst through her pelvis on a flash of need so strong, she cried out and heard his answering moans in her ear. Several moments of rasping breathing told her he needed a minute to return to normal, too.

"Was it good for you?" she asked with a giggle.

The warm chuckle told her the whole scenario didn't bother him at all and she needed that—needed to know he was okay with out of the ordinary, because, her life, at the moment, seemed anything but ordinary.

"So do you want to tell me about your dream?"

"Not unless you plan on getting me off again over the phone."

"I don't think so. I'm wiped and I need a shower. It's been quite a while since I've had phone sex."

"Feeling old, Mr. Weston?" she asked

"Hell no. You make me feel like I could do anything, darlin', includin' keepin' you well satisfied in the bedroom."

"I hate to say good-bye," she whispered, feeling the loss of him already.

"I know, but you should probably get some sleep. I'm sure you need to be at the hospital bright and early in the mornin'. If you aren't, your grandmother will flag down some trucker and hitch a ride home."

"Yes, she would, but I've got other things on my mind too. My mother will probably be flying in tomorrow."

"Your mother? Why?"

"She called earlier and I couldn't help but tell her about Gram. She came all unglued and said she would be on the first plane out of Portland and would be here some time tomorrow."

"Your grandmother isn't gonna like that at all."

"You aren't telling me something I don't know, but my mother won't listen to me. I tried to tell her."

"It'll be okay. The two of them will have to hash it out between them, and I wouldn't bet on your mother winning."

She laughed and rubbed her nose. "No. I'd bet on my grandmother any day of the week."

"You're a lot like her, you know."

"My grandmother?"

"Yes. You've got her spirit and spunkiness."

"I appreciate the sentiment."

"You're welcome. Now, I'm goin' to head to the shower. You get some sleep."

"Yes, sir."

"I kind of like it when you talk all submissive."

"Don't get use to it." The laughter in the phone had her shaking her head. "Good-night, Cade."

"Night, darlin'."

* * * *

The sun rose bright and early the next morning. Blue skies peeked through the thin layer of clouds, and for now, it appeared there wouldn't be any new snow today.

Natalie got up early, showered, dressed, and grabbed two cups of strong coffee before heading to the hospital to pick up her grandmother. The old Buick sitting in the garage had to be something out of the nineteen-eighties, but she knew her grandmother loved the old car. Thankfully, the town plowed the roads after last night's snow.

"Good morning, Gram," she said, breezing through the door with a smile on her face.

"What's so good about it?"

"I see you're in a wonderful humor this morning," she replied, kissing her grandmother on the cheek. "No handsome male nurse to give you a bath?"

"*Hrmph.*"

"You're speechless? That's a first."

Her grandmother stuck out her tongue and Natalie laughed. "Don't get your panties in a wad, granddaughter. Speechless, I'll never be."

"I believe you, Gram. So what's the issue already?"

"Your mother."

"Oh shit."

"Yeah, oh shit. She called bright and early to inform me she would be flying in today to take care of me. I don't need her here and I don't want her here."

"I know, Gram. I'm sorry. I didn't have much choice but to tell her what happened. She called the house last night and wanted to talk to you."

Her grandmother patted her hand. "No worries, honey, I'll take care of her. I may be old, but I sure in the hell ain't dead yet, and she's not about to take over my life. I know she left you with specific instructions on what to do while here. I don't have any plans to allow anyone to bully me into leaving my home."

"Mom doesn't stand a chance, does she?"

"Hell no. I raised her and I know what to do with her. If she doesn't like it, she can get her ass back on a plane and go right back to Oregon."

She couldn't help but smile. Her grandmother had more spunk and grit than a lot of people she knew. "Has the doctor been in yet to discharge you?"

"If he had, do you think I'd still be sitting here in this flimsy thing they call clothing?"

"No, Grandma, I imagine you wouldn't be. You would already be dressed and sitting downstairs, tapping your foot."

"You're damned right I would."

"What did the physical therapist say?"

"Read it yourself," she replied, waving toward the packet of information on her tray table.

Natalie picked up the paperwork and scanned it. Three times a week with the in-home physical therapist and exercises to do on her own. The percentage of weakness on her right side didn't seem too bad, but she wasn't a medical professional.

"Are you prepared to do these exercises everyday like they suggest?"

"If it means your mother not coming, of course."

"You know you can't avoid it. She's coming whether you want her to or not."

"And we'll go rounds when she gets here. You can count on that, because I don't want her here."

"Hopefully, she won't stay long."

"How about if she turns around and goes back on the same damned plane she comes here on?"

"Somehow, I don't think she will, Gram."

"What do you think she'll say when she finds out your dating two men? Oh, by the way, how did the date go with Kale last night? Anymore hot sex?"

"I'm not discussing it with you," she replied, taking the chair across from the bed.

"Oh, come on, Nat. Let an old lady live vicariously through you."

"You'll survive, Gram and no, I did *not* have sex with Kale last night." *I'm not about to tell her I had phone sex with Cade.*

"Well, damn it girl! You had the perfect opportunity."

"Can you imagine what my mother would say finding out I'm dating two men, much less, if I had sex with both of them?"

"It's none of her business, Natalie. You're a grown woman, and you can make your own decisions on who you want to see and who you want to sleep with."

"I know, but she's so controlling. She loved Steven. She had a huge fit when she found out I broke it off with him. It didn't matter to her I caught him in bed with someone else."

"And we both know my opinion of him."

She laughed and shook her head. "Yes, Gram, we do."

Both eyebrows shot up almost to her hairline. "Your mother expected you to stay with dick-wad even after he screwed another woman in your bed?"

"Yes. She told me it must have been a mistake and men have those kinds of weaknesses. I needed to forgive him and seek counseling."

"Counseling, my ass! The man cheated on you. There is no excuse for that kind of behavior in a relationship. Never once did your grandfather ever look at another woman, much less, have sex with someone else in our bed."

"The relationship you had with grandpa is the kind of loving connection I want with my husband. I'm not going to settle for less. I refuse to be complacent in a marriage."

"Good for you, honey. The right man is out there for you. He may not be Cade or Kale, but you'll find him, if you don't settle. Never settle for anything except the real thing."

She captured her bottom lip between her teeth.

"Spill it, Natalie. You're holding out on me," her grandmother said, crossing her arms over her chest.

"Don't tell Mom I told you, but my dad cheated."

"Your dad had an affair with another woman?"

"Yes. Several years ago, I believe, but she smoothed it over, forgave him and everything."

"And?"

"He still cheats on her, but she chooses to ignore it now."

"Wait until she gets here. I'm going to kick her ass for her!"

"Well, good morning ladies. How are we this morning?" Doctor Bridges said as he came through the door. "Ready to go home, Mrs. Oliver?"

"Damn right and it's about time you got your ass off the golf course and got me out of here." Her grandmother flipped the covers off her legs and threw them both over the side of the bed. "Get me my walkin' papers and we'll be on our way."

"You know it will take a few minutes, Gram, so calm down."

"She's right, Mrs. Oliver. I've written the orders for your discharge, but it will take a bit for the nurses to get the paperwork ready. Sit back and relax for a bit."

"They can get up off their lazy butts and get it done. I know they are all sittin' around the nurses' station gossiping about who you are sleeping with this week, Doctor Bridges."

The man coughed and looked at her, but she only shrugged.

"I'll...um...see what I can do to hurry them along," he replied, walking backwards toward the door.

"You do that and I'll get dressed. Get my clothes out of the closet there, Natalie. I want out of this place."

"I know you do, Gram. Hang on and let me help you."

"I'm not an invalid."

"Yes, ma'am, I know."

She prayed they would hurry with the paperwork. Her grandmother wouldn't be patient long. By the time she dressed and tied her shoes, the nurse came through the door with her discharge papers.

"You don't need to go through all of it, miss, I know what it says."

"Mrs. Oliver. I am required by law to go over this paperwork with you and make sure you understand the instructions. I have to sign my name to it saying you understand. Would you like me to put my license on the line?"

"No. I guess not, but hurry up."

In no time, they had her bundled up and inside the old Buick.

"Be careful, Natalie. I don't want you to wreck my car."

"I will, Gram."

"Go slower."

"Grandma, I know how to drive."

"I realize you do, but this is my car, and no one has driven my car since your grandpa got sick."

With a shake of her head, they drove out of the parking lot and started down the main street. If she kept the conversation going, maybe her grandmother wouldn't harp on her about her driving. In no time, they were pulling into the driveway at the house.

"I wonder whose car is sitting on the street. I don't recognize it," her grandmother said as Natalie turned off the ignition.

"I'm not sure."

Seconds later, they found out when Natalie's mother came barreling out the drivers' side door, yelling at the top of her lungs. "Natalie Marie! You're supposed to be here taking care of your grandmother, not dating half the eligible bachelors in Red Rock and sleeping with the other half."

9

"Oh hell," Natalie groaned. "I thought she wasn't coming until later?"

"Obviously not," her grandmother replied.

"Hello to you too, Mother."

"Don't hello me, young lady. I've got words for you."

"Butt the hell out, Marie. She's done nothing wrong. The only thing she's done while she's been here is take care of me and have a little fun."

"A little fun? A lot more fun than she needs to be having. She should be on the phone with Steven, trying to work things out, not dating who-ever takes her fancy," Marie said, standing with her hands on her hips and tapping her toe.

"Steven is an asshole. And we aren't discussing this in the driveway." Her grandmother took her arm and said, "Help me inside, honey."

"Get her things from the backseat, Mother."

"Wha—"

"You heard her, Marie. Get my things from the backseat while she helps me into the house."

"Well, I never."

"I imagine that's part of your problem," her grandmother replied and Natalie chuckled softly. "If you had some good sex once in a while, you wouldn't be so uptight."

The chuckled turned into a full-blown laugh at her mother's expense.

Once in the house, she helped her grandmother sit on the couch and moved toward the kitchen to make coffee, giving her something to do with her hands, other than strangle her mother, but she could still hear the banter in the other room.

"You need to mind your own business, Mother."

"To hell you say. Natalie is having a good time while she's here, and I see not a damned thing wrong with it."

"She wasn't sent here to have a good time."

"No, she was sent here to wrap me in a straight-jacket if necessary and cart my ass back to Oregon."

A minute or two of silence followed her grandmother's words, and Natalie could imagine her mother's mouth opening and closing like a guppy. The whole scenario made her giggle. God, it felt good to laugh. It had been a while since she'd felt like laughing.

"I'm not going back to Oregon, Marie. I'm completely competent, so trying to say I'm not, won't work. I know every attorney and judge in this town, and there isn't a one who will say I can't take care of myself. You might as well get your ass back on the plane and go back to your low-life of a husband."

"Low-life? What are you talking about, Mother?"

"Natalie told me about Gerald cheating on you. If you are stupid enough to stay with him when he's screwing around with whatever bimbo catches his fancy this week, then you aren't the woman I raised you to be."

Shit! She wasn't supposed to say anything.

"You are a beautiful woman, and you shouldn't be treated like you have no brain-cells in your head. You're intelligent, caring, and have a wonderful heart for those less fortunate than you. Quit letting him take advantage of you, Marie. He dragged you away from your family. Had you hold up in the god-forsaken suburb of Portland. Pushed you into living a life you didn't want and forcing your children to live a life away from God's country. This is where you belong, not in Oregon."

Silence met her ears as she strained to hear anything her mother said to her grandmother's accusations.

"Mom, I'm sorry. You're right."

"Halleluiah and praise the Lord."

Natalie grabbed three cups of coffee, and the cream and sugar. Her eyes welled with her grandmother's speech, and it broke her heart to know her mother suffered for her and Andrea. Never had her mother said a word about being miserable, but since her grandmother pointed out the facts, she could see it plain as the nose on her face.

"Anyone want coffee?"

Marie silently wiped her eyes, and nodded while her grandmother took one of the mugs from Natalie's hands.

The jingle of the telephone on the end table brought her head around to stare at it and wonder who might be calling now.

"Aren't you going to answer it?" Marie asked as she set her cup down on the coffee table.

"Uh, yeah." Natalie grabbed the phone and said, "Hello?"

"Hey, darlin'."

"Hi, Cade."

One of her grandmother's perfectly painted on eyebrows shot up in a wide arch and a huge smile spread across her face. "Invite that hunk on over here."

Natalie shook her head no and narrowed her eyes on her grandmother.

"I take it your grandmother is home safe and sound."

"Um...yeah and my mother is here."

"Oh great. I bet it's a nice family reunion," he replied.

"Uh, no," she told him into the phone. "Gram, I'm going to take this in the other room."

"Oh?" her mother asked, her fingernails tapping on the edge of the ceramic mug. "Why not talk in here, Natalie?"

"I'm not talking to Cade in front of you, Mother. This is a personal call." She spun on her heels and moved toward the kitchen. When she picked up the receiver she said, "You can hang up, Gram."

"Damn it. I thought I was quiet enough you wouldn't hear me," her grandmother replied with a laugh. The hanging up of the receiver clicked in her ear.

"So your mom is there, huh?"

"Yes, unfortunately. She's already started in."

"About?"

"Evidently, my mother got wind of my dating while I've been here."

"Oh. Not good."

"Yeah. I've already received the raised voice and 'how could you' talk, and she hasn't been here an hour yet."

"I called because I wanted to see if you would like to go sledding day after tomorrow. Since your grandmother is home now and your mother is there to help, you could sneak away for a couple of hours."

"I don't know, Cade. It's probably not a good idea. I don't need to give my mother anything else to lecture me about."

"The snow should be perfect—all fluffy from the snowfall last night and it's supposed to snow again tomorrow, but be clear the next day. Great sledding weather. The sun should be out and it's not supposed to be frigid cold. I would love to keep you warm though."

"All right, I tell you what. Pick me up at ten. We need to talk anyway."

"Talk? That's not exactly what I had in mind."

"I know it's not, but we need to anyway."

"Great. See you then," she replied.

He softly said goodbye and she hung up the phone.

"So Cade's coming over, huh?" her grandmother asked from the living room.

A heavy sigh escaped her lips, and she dropped her head back. "Eavesdropper!" she yelled with a laugh.

"What can I say? You talk loud."

"Not that loud, old lady!"

"Natalie Marie!" her mother exclaimed.

"Oh give it up, Mom. Grandma and I are two of a kind."

Her grandmother let out a roaring laugh, and Natalie had to smile. It was good to hear.

"Sledding?" her grandmother asked. "Sounds like fun."

"I haven't been sledding in ages. I go skiing sometimes, but never sledding."

"It'll be good for you then. Cade's a nice man."

"Yes, he is, Gram." She took a seat next to her grandmother and asked, "What shall we have for dinner tonight?"

"A nice, big, juicy steak sounds wonderful."

"I'm sure the doctor recommended dietary changes with your stroke."

"I'm not changing my diet to suit his idea of what the hell I should eat."

"Grandma, be serious please. You know you'll have to cut back on the red meat and work on your cholesterol levels. He gave you several prescriptions to help with those things, but you need to make changes too. Exercise and eating right are important to your recovery." Natalie bent closer to her ear. "And you don't want Mom sticking around any longer than necessary, do you?"

"Oh, hell no!" her grandmother exclaimed. "She can go back to Oregon any time, and don't let the door hit you in the ass on the way out, Marie."

"Mother, I know you don't want me here. You've made that perfectly clear, but—"

"But you don't give a shit what I want or whether I need you here or not. Natalie and I were doing just fine without you."

"Natalie wasn't even here when you had your stroke. She was out with some *cowboy* from Red Rock who only wants to get in her underwear," Marie snapped.

Natalie watched grandmother's eyes narrow and her face pull into an angry glare.

"My granddaughter's behavior is none of your business. I told her to go out and have a good time. You are the idiot who is trying to get her to go back to dick-wad. Leave her alone and let her do what she wants to do. I don't need a damned babysitter."

Natalie let out a high-pitched whistle, immediately stopping the verbal battle waging between the two. "Enough already. Mom, what I do is none of your business. If I want to date while I'm here, then I will. I am *not* going back to Steven under any circumstances. Finding him in our bed with another woman sealed the deal for me and there's no going back. Grandma, you need to keep your blood pressure down and stop getting so worked up over things Mom says. You know the two of you can't agree on anything these days."

Both women sheepishly apologized.

"Much better. Mom, why don't you go shopping or something since you obviously plan to stay for a few days, or whatever. I'm going to fix some lunch and then go upstairs to work on some lesson plans I started for the children back home, since I'm not sure when I'm going to teach again for right now. Gram, why don't you go and take a quick nap, and I'll wake you when lunch is ready." Her mother got to her feet, disappearing upstairs without another word. "Come on, Gram, I'll help you into the room down here."

"You're a wonderful woman, Natalie. Have I ever told you that?"

"Thanks, Gram. I love you, and I hope you know I'd never leave you here alone to deal with all of this."

"I know, sweetie, and I love you too. I want you to be happy and find the one man you can love without a second thought."

"I'll find him someday. You just need to stop playing matchmaker."

"No can do, honey. It's in the blood."

"Ah shit!"

* * * *

The next two days with her grandmother and mother at each other's throats at every turn had her on edge. The constant bickering and snapping made her want to pull her hair out by the roots, she hoped the sledding trip with Cade would help smooth those exposed nerves.

Around ten, Cade's truck pulled in the driveway, and her mother cocked an eyebrow when she headed for the door.

"Come on in," she said, pushing open the screen.

He leaned down and brushed her lips with his. The quick inhalation of breath from her mother made her head turn, but the wide-eyed look on her mother's face had her wondering what was going on and why did she look like she'd seen a ghost.

"Mitchell?"

"Uh, no. Mom, this is Cade—"

"Weston," her mother finished for her.

Her mother's face went pasty white, and she sat down in her chair with a thud. "I-I'm sorry. You look exactly like your father, I would assume."

"Mom, do you know Cade's father?"

"You could say so, Natalie. I dated him."

"You what? You dated Cade's father?" she asked, shock reverberating through her. "When?"

"In high-school. I was born and raised here remember? Mitchell, Gerald, and I all went to school together."

Shit! Is Cade's father the 'other man' grandmother mentioned?

The gentleman in Cade wouldn't allow her mother not to at least make his acquaintance. With hat in hand, he stopped next to her chair, holding out his hand. "It's nice to meet you, Mrs. Bennington."

"Yes, you too, young man. I assume your father is well? I haven't seen him in several years."

"He's doin' fine, ma'am."

"Tell him hello for me when you see him again, will you?"

"Of course, ma'am. I'm sure he'll be glad to hear from you."

"Uh, Gram? If you don't need me for a bit, Cade is taking me sledding."

"Very nice," her grandmother replied. "I'm sure you'll have fun sitting between those hard thighs."

Natalie gave up trying to figure out what her grandmother would say next, but the shocked looked on her mother's face was worth any price. "Let me get my coat and we'll go."

"Make sure you put some condoms in your purse, Nat," her grandmother called, and she just shook her head.

"Yes, Grandma."

As Cade followed her down the hall, she could hear her mother asking, "Are those two sleeping together?"

God, Gram, don't...

"Of course, they are, Marie. Good grief; what the hell do you think young people do these days, go out for soda's?"

Ah, hell! "Gram, please!"

"You go on, honey, and have a good time. Don't worry about your mother and me. We'll get pizza for dinner. Cade, you bring her back when you're done."

Heat crawled up her neck, and she turned to find him standing behind her. She couldn't help it. A huge smile spread across her lips, and she buried her face in his shoulder. Her shoulders shook while she tried to calm her laughter. She didn't have to see the look on her mother's face to know her penciled eyebrows were riding her hairline and her lips were pursing in a permanent soured expression.

"It's fine, honey. I love your grandmother. She's a hoot. And I think she's about the funniest person I've been around in a long time."

She raised her head to find his big, baby blues staring right into her eyes. "Good. I love her too. She means the world to me and I can't imagine leaving her."

Did I just say that? I don't want to leave Red Rock?

"I'm glad to hear it. Maybe it means you'll stick around permanently," he replied before kissing her quickly then grabbing her coat to hold it for her.

"I...uh."

"No more talk of staying here, for now. Today, we enjoy the snow and each other. Okay?"

"Sure."

"We'll see you ladies later," he called, ushering her toward the door.

"Wrap that rascal, Cade," her grandmother called, and Natalie about died right there on the spot.

"Got it covered, Mrs. Oliver." His warm chuckled fueled the burn on her cheeks.

"Will you stop, please? You're encouraging her," she whispered out of the side of her mouth. She couldn't stop her own laugh though. "Bye, Gram. Bye, Mom."

"Have a good time, Natalie," her mother replied.

"Oh, and Nat?"

"Yes, Gram."

"The bench seat in his truck might look like fun, but really, a nice soft bed is better. He's a big guy and I'm sure he needs the room."

"Let's go, please. She's killing me here." Natalie giggled. Gasping for breath between laughs, she waved over her shoulder and walked outside.

Snow glistened in the sunlight like diamonds on a blanket of white. She'd almost forgotten how beautiful Montana winters were, but Cade planned to remind her with this sledding trip. They drove to Marshall Hill and found a place to park. Several of the school children apparently skipped school today since the hill seemed crowded.

"Wow. There are lots of people here."

"Not really. This isn't much. You should see it on weekends."

"I can imagine."

Once they stood outside of his truck, he took her gloved hand in his, grabbed the sled from the back, and they started their trek up the hill. It really wasn't a huge rise, but if she remembered correctly, the sledding on it was great—swift and clean. No rocks or trees to worry about and it leveled into an open field.

"Do you want to go down alone?" Cade asked.

"I kind of like grandma's suggestion of being between those hard thighs."

"You sure know how to crank up the heat."

She felt totally wicked. "Heat? You want heat?" Her hand slipped between them and cradled his cock through his jeans. "Oh yeah. Hot and hard."

"You're a wicked woman, Natalie Bennington." He leaned down and nipped at her earlobe. "I want to get you alone so bad, I ache. How about we skip the sleddin' and go back to my apartment?"

Two steps back and she grinned. "Nope. You promised me sledding and sledding is what we're going to do. Saddle up, big boy. Ride 'em hard."

"You're a witch," he growled.

The wicked giggle coming from her lips almost sounded witchy too.

Cade set the sled down and climbed on. "Come on, honey. You wanted between these thighs. You got it."

Her breathing hitched, and her lips dried just thinking of climbing between his legs and wiggling her butt against his cock. The dream from the night before came back in a sharp picture. He was about to slide his hard length into her ass when the phone woke her from it. Now, the images seemed real, causing her nipples to bead into hard nubs.

"You comin'?"

Not yet.

"Mmm. I'd love to."

His eyebrow arched and his lips twitched. One finger crooked in invitation as his smile widened. "Right here, honey."

She crawled onto the sled, slipping between his thighs, wiggling her butt backward until she felt his cock pushing against her ass.

"I want to fuck you there so bad," he growled in her ear. "Tight." He licked her neck. "Hot." Her pussy throbbed as blood rushed in, and she moaned.

"Hey, mister! Move it! Some of the rest of us what to slide down too," a small boy, about ten, yelled, drawing their attention.

"I guess we should get moving, huh?"

"I'm movin' all right," he murmured, grinding his cock against her ass.

"Sledding, Cade, sledding."

"Oh, yeah, right," he replied with a chuckle. He pushed them off the hill, and tucked both booted feet in next to hers. Cold wind rushed passed her exposed ears, stinging her unprotected cheeks. Nothing could compare to the thrill of sliding down the hill at breakneck speed with one of the most gorgeous guys she knew snuggling against her back.

When they reached the bottom, she laughed out loud, jumped to her feet and yelled, "Let's go again!"

The smile on his lips took her breath away when he joined her in laughter. "Okay." He grabbed her hand and they headed back up the hill.

Over an hour later, exhaustion set in. It had been a long time since she'd done this much climbing and walking. "Wow. I'm beat."

"I can imagine. We've been down the hill probably fifty times."

"Not that many," she replied. "Twenty."

"Nope. I'm sure it's at least fifty."

"I need something warm to drink. How about we hit the diner in town and get some coffee."

"Sure. I could use some lunch. I'm gettin' kind of hungry."

"Is it lunch time?" A quick glance at her watch confirmed what she already suspected. "Wow. I didn't realize it was so late. Maybe we should go by the house and check on Gram."

"Why don't you call her? I'm sure everything is fine or your mother would have called you."

"All right. I'll call her while we walk back to the truck."

"Perfect," he replied, tucking her hand in his.

The phone rang in her ear soon after she dialed.

"Hello?"

"Hi, Gram. How are you?"

"I'm fine, honey. How's sledding?"

"It's been great, but now we're heading into town for some coffee and lunch. Can we bring you anything? Are you okay?"

"We're fine. Don't interrupt your fun. Have a good time and don't worry about being home for dinner. I'm sure you'll need some snuggle time to warm up certain parts."

She couldn't help rolling her eyes, and Cade mouthed 'what', but she shook her head in answer.

"I'll be home after while, Gram. Don't kill Mom while I'm out, all right?"

"Of course not, Nat. I only gagged her and tied her up in the basement until you get home."

"You did not!" Her grandmother laughed hysterically. "Please tell me you are kidding, Grandma."

"I'm kidding, Natalie. I've got her tied to the bed in the guest room. Have a good time and I'll see you later." The phone went dead with a click in her ear, and she fought the urge to call back. She stared at the phone for a second, debating.

Cade took the phone from her fingers, stuffing it into her pocket. "She's fine, Nat. Your grandmother is kidding."

"I'm not so sure." She giggled. "My mother is a handful when she wants to be."

"Your grandmother can handle your mother and twenty Marines along with her."

"Very true."

"Let's get lunch and we can swing by the house afterwards," he said, opening the door to the truck.

"All right." Her stomach growled. "I am kind of hungry."

Within minutes, they parked at the diner and took a booth in the back. The waitress came by their table, asking what they wanted to drink.

"Coffee, please," Natalie said, rubbing her cold fingers together.

The woman gave Cade a frown when he took Natalie's hands between his and stroked them over her freezing digits.

"Make it two, Audrey."

"Sure, Cade. I'll be right back."

"Someone you know?" Natalie asked.

"Audrey? Sure. She grew up here too. Why?"

"The dirty look I got."

"What dirty look?"

"When she comes back, you'll see it."

Audrey returned a few minutes later with their coffee and took their order. The anger Natalie saw on the woman's face gave her pause. *Obviously, Audrey has a thing for Cade.*

When she finally walked away, Natalie asked, "Did you ever date her?"

"No."

"Well, she must want you to, by the look in her eyes."

He took a small sip of his coffee and said, "What look?"

"The one that told me she'd meet me in the parking lot on some dark, rainy night to beat the shit out of me, if given the chance."

"You're imaging things, Nat. I have never given her the impression I would be interested in dating her."

"She wants you to though."

Cade grasped her hand in his, squeezing her fingers. "I don't want her. I want you. On the couch, in my bed, in the shower, on the countertop—"

"Enough! You're making me blush."

"I want to make you hot."

"Um, that, too."

"Then I'm doing a good job?"

"An excellent job."

"Will you come back to my place so we can take care of our little heater problem?"

"I can't."

"Can't?"

The tentative shake of her head made him frown.

"Why not?"

"I promised Kale I wouldn't have sex with you again until he's had a chance."

"Chance at what?"

"To woo me, or whatever you want to call it."

"You told me you didn't have sex with him last night."

"I didn't."

"But you had phone sex with me."

"Well, yes, but that's different. It wasn't real sex. I can't have real sex with you again."

"We can have phone sex then?"

She looked at the ceiling and shook her head. "I'll have to clear it with Kale."

"Clear it with Kale? This is ridiculous, Natalie. If we want to have sex, then we should be able to have sex," his voice started to rise, drawing several pairs of eyes to them.

"Please, keep your voice down. I don't really want the whole damned town to know about us."

"They already know about us, Natalie. Watch." He stood and turned toward the crowd. "Folks! Most of you know who I am, but many of you don't know this beautiful lady." His hand swept to her, and she wanted to crawl under the table.

"Cade, please."

"This is Natalie Bennington, and she and I are dating. In fact, we've had sex." Hands clapped and several gentlemen in the place gave him thumbs up.

"Damn it, Cade! I'm walking out of here right now unless you sit back down." She knew her face had to be flaming red, and she wanted to kill him right now.

He slid back into the booth and sipped from his cup.

"How could you do that? You've completely embarrassed me in front of the whole town. I do not believe you!" She made up her mind swiftly, grabbing her purse and sliding out of the booth. "You can eat by yourself, and don't bother to call or come over, because I don't want to see you again."

Tears burned her eyelids, but she didn't care. She had to get out of there and fast.

"Natalie!" he yelled behind her. "Natalie!"

She kept right on moving until she rounded the next corner and saw a cab sitting next to the curb. The door came open with a tug of her hand, and she rattled off her grandmother's address. "Quickly, please."

"Yes, ma'am," the driver responded, flipping the car into drive.

She glanced over her shoulder to see Cade sliding to a stop at the corner then throwing his hands in the air. Tears fell and a sad sob escaped her lips. *I thought he really cared about me, but all he's interested in is showing off in front of everyone. I'll never be able to face anyone in this town again.*

Moments later, her grandmother's house came into view, and the cab pulled to a stop at the curb.

"Five fifty, ma'am."

After paying the driver, she slipped out the door, slamming it behind her. The wetness on her cheeks felt cold, but her heart felt colder. Caring meant getting hurt. How in the hell she came to care about Cade in such a short time, she didn't know, but she didn't like it.

When she walked inside the house, her grandmother asked, "Where's Cade?"

"Still at the diner I would imagine, where I left his happy ass."

"Oops. What did the big jerk do, honey?" Tears started again and she couldn't stop them. "Come here, Nat. Grandma will make it better."

"Where's Mom?"

"Upstairs ruffling through things, just to be annoying."

She slid into her grandmother's embrace and laid her head on her lap as she did when she was a little girl. The scratch of her polyester pants felt rough against her cheek. The gnarled fingers of her favorite person in the world, stroked through her hair, easing the tension and heartache.

"It sucks to love sometimes," her grandmother whispered.

"I don't love him."

"Oh, honey, yes you do, or you wouldn't be so upset right now."

"I can't fall in love with someone inside of a week, Gram. It's not done that way."

"The heart doesn't always follow logic, Natalie."

"But what about Kale?"

"What about him? You don't sound like you care for him the way you care for Cade."

"I feel like I need to give Kale a chance, Gram. I've only been out with him once, and I haven't slept with him."

"Do you want to?"

"I think so." She captured her bottom lip between her teeth, pondering the thought. Did she really want to have sex with Kale? Did she crave his touch as she did Cade's? No, but it felt right to have Kale touch her. "Yes, I'm pretty sure I do. I haven't been with many men in my lifetime, and I sure don't want to settle with one unless I'm positive I don't want anyone else." She pushed herself up and stared into her grandmother's knowing eyes. "What am I thinking, Gram? It's not like Cade has proposed or anything."

"Then have a good time, honey. There's nothing wrong with making sure one or the other of them is the right man for you. Maybe neither is, but you won't know until you give it a chance to develop and bloom." Her grandmother wiped the remaining tears from her cheek.

"You're right. I'm going to ignore Cade for now and focus on Kale."

"What did Cade do to piss you off?"

"He stood in front of everyone at the diner and told them we were dating."

"There's nothin' wrong with that."

"It wouldn't have bothered me at all, but he made sure to mention we had sex too."

"Dumb-ass."

The chuckle spilling from her lips, made her heart feel lighter. "Typical male is more like it. Overbearing, boastful, arrogant—" The jingle of the phone interrupted her words. She grabbed the phone off the end table and handed it to her grandmother. "If it's Cade, I don't want to talk to him."

"You should tell him why you're pissed."

"He knows. Trust me."

Her grandmother answered the phone, winking at her as she said, "Sorry, Cade. Natalie doesn't want to talk to you right now." The nod of her grandmother's head and the smile on her lips, made Natalie giggle. "Sounds like you screwed up royally, boy. You should know better than to get all full of yourself and shoot your mouth off in front of a crowd." She could hear the low murmur of his voice even though she couldn't hear the words. "I don't think you're good enough for her." The tone got louder, and his words more high-pitched. "It doesn't matter what you want, young man. You need to prove to her you're worthy of her love. The stunt you pulled today tells her you aren't. From what she told me, it was immature, cold, and stupid of you. Get used to being alone if you are going to act in such a manner all the time." More loud noises and a few cuss words came through the phone. "Well, she's already called Kale, and he's planning on filling the hole you created. Suck it up, boy, and get a life." Her grandmother didn't wait for him to say another word before hanging up the phone.

"Oh my, Gram! He's going to be so pissed off."

"Who cares? He needs to understand, pulling shit like that is completely unacceptable behavior for a grown man. I can understand a teenage boy doing something so asinine, but he's old enough to know better."

"Very true."

"Stick to your guns, Natalie, and go out with Kale. If nothin' else, it will teach Cade a lesson he won't readily forget. He'll know he can't push you around or act childish in the future."

"I love you, Gram."

"I love you too, girl. I hope you find the happiness you deserve. You know, I would love for you to find a handsome, down home, country boy and settle right here in Red Rock, but I understand you need to do what is best for you."

"I know. I'm not sure one of the men you described exists though."

"Oh, he exists, all right. You just have to find the one right for you. Right now, you have two following you around like puppies on a string. Work it girl, work it!" her grandmother replied, swinging her hips and pumping her fists.

Natalie laughed so hard, her stomach hurt.

"My, my. Aren't we having fun down here," Marie said, coming down the stairs. "What's so funny?"

"Gram was just giving me some man advice."

"Oh?"

"Yeah."

Her mother arched an eyebrow, waiting.

"Don't worry about it, Mom. Cade did something stupid while we were out. Typical man behavior anyway, and I took a cab back here."

"What did he do?"

"Bragged."

"I don't understand," her mother replied, sitting in the recliner across the room.

"It doesn't matter, Mom. He knows he's in deep shit, and Gram gave him a thing or two to think about, so it's over for now." Natalie rose to her feet. "I need to make a phone call, so I'll be in the kitchen."

She dialed Kale's number and waited. Moments later, his gruff voice answered, making her smile. "Hi."

"Hi, Nat. What's up, babe?"

"Not much. I wanted to talk to you for a minute. Are we still on for Saturday?"

"Of course. Why wouldn't we be?"

"I wasn't sure if maybe Cade called you."

"If he did, I didn't get it. I've been in the barn all mornin'. You caught me comin' in for a bite to eat. Was there somethin' specific he might be calling about?"

"Um. No. I told him a little while ago, I didn't want to see him again."

A deep, choking cough sounded on the other end of the line.

"Are you all right, Kale?"

"I'm surprised is all," he squeaked and coughed again. "Man, he must have really screwed up."

"You could say so, yes, but I didn't call to discuss Cade."

"What did you call for then, Natalie?"

"I want to come out to your place tonight, and I want you to make love to me."

10

"Excuse me?" Kale asked, his voice high.

"I want you to make love to me."

"I-uh."

"What's wrong, Kale? Don't you want to?" She hadn't contemplated that he might have changed his mind.

"Well, of course, I do, Natalie, but I thought we agreed to wait until we knew each other better."

"I've decided I know you well enough."

"I don't know what to say."

"Say yes and I'll see you this evening," she said, hoping he wouldn't say no. She needed to do this to make sure her feelings for Cade were real.

"All right. I'll pick you up around six. Work for you?"

"Perfect. See you then." She hung up the phone and turned around to find her mother leaning against the counter. "Hi, Mom." *Shit. How much did she hear?*

"I think we need to talk, Natalie."

"Talk? About what?"

"You dating two men and obviously sleeping with both of them."

"I'm not sleeping with both of them...yet."

"Sit down, honey."

After glancing at the seriousness on her mother's face, she took a seat at the kitchen table. The same table she baked cookies with her grandmother on, did her homework on when her parents were at work, and the same table she had dinner with Kale on.

"Your grandmother informed me she told you about me dating two men in high-school."

"Yes, she did and I don't see a problem with doing that."

"Good. It appears you are taking the same path, to a degree, and a very strange one."

"I don't understand."

"One of the men I dated was Mitchell Weston. The other was your father, Gerald."

"So you chose Daddy over Mr. Weston."

"Not really, no."

"You didn't?"

"I had to marry your father because I was pregnant with you. But I never stopped loving Mitchell." Her mother stood and walked to the window. Natalie wondered what her mother saw—life how it might be if she'd held out for the love she wanted, or maybe the miserable existence she now lived. "I had been dating Mitchell for some time. Your father expressed an interest in me, and Mitchell had become distant. I wanted to make Mitchell jealous and to express his love for me, other than a high school crush."

"So you dated both men."

Her mother nodded and continued, "Your father and I went out several times. Mitchell and I had a huge fight over me seeing your father, but he still refused to tell me he loved me. I felt crushed and alone. Your father comforted me. I liked him, but I wasn't in love with him. We had sex once and you were conceived."

"You had to marry Dad then."

"I guess you could say that yes."

Trepidation rolled down her back as she thought about one possibly sickening thought. "Please, tell me I'm not Cade's sister."

A dry, non-humorous chuckle left her mother's lips. "No, Natalie. You are your father's daughter. Mitchell and I had never made love. I wanted to save myself for our wedding night. The wedding that never came."

Natalie stood, stepped behind her mother, and wrapped her arms around her from behind. "Oh, Mom. I'm so sorry."

"Seeing Cade today brought back all those memories. He looks exactly like his father—the same blue eyes, proud chin, and muscular build." A heavy sigh left her lips. "I found out a piece of information later on that made the whole thing make sense. Mitchell received acceptance to a college out of state. He knew I couldn't go with him, and he didn't want to leave me alone in Red Rock. He thought pushing me away would be the best thing. Mitchell and Gerald were both a year older than me and I still had to finish high school."

"He really did love you."

"Apparently, but by then, I had you and my marriage to your father. I gave my word to love, honor, and cherish until death us do part."

"Is that why you won't leave him, even though he continues cheating on you?"

"Yes. Unless he asks me for a divorce, I'll never leave him."

"Wow."

Her mother turned, and Natalie could see the terrible sadness in her eyes. "I don't want you caught in the same mistakes I made. Make sure you love the one you choose."

"I thought you wanted me with Steven?"

"I didn't realize how miserable you really were with him. When you told me you caught him cheating on you, it was as if my whole life came back to slap me in the face. I couldn't see past my own guilt to realize you needed out. Forgive me?"

"Of course, Mom. I love you."

"I love you, too, Natalie, and I'm sorry I've made such an unhappy family life for you."

"It's fine. I wish we hadn't moved from Red Rock though."

"We had to."

"I know. The plant closed."

"It wasn't only the plant closing. If we had stayed here, I would have thrown everything away to be with Mitchell again." They took their seats at the table, and her mother grasped her hand between hers.

"Seriously?"

"Yes. Right before we left, he and I talked. That's when I found out all the other things, and he admitted he loved me, but he had a wife and children, too, by then. He wouldn't leave them. The vows exchanged with Callindra meant everything to him, and he wouldn't break them."

"Mr. Weston sounds like an honorable man."

The sad smile on her mother's lips, almost made her cry. "You only know the half of it. But I didn't come in here to go into details about my mistakes. You seem to care for Cade."

"I'm not sure, Mom. We're great together, but then he pulled the stupid stunt today. It made me realize I don't really know him at all."

"Mmm," her mother hummed. "I understand you are dating Kale Dunn? I don't believe I know his family."

"Kale and Cade were best friends in school. They remembered me. After Cade rescued me the night I drove in, they've both been paying a lot of attention to me. Things happened between Cade and me the other day, but I haven't had sex with Kale. I plan to rectify the situation this evening."

"Are you sure you really want to?"

"Yes. I may not go through with it, but I need to know. Things started to heat up last night, about the time you called."

"I'm sorry I interrupted you."

"No big deal, Mom. Kale didn't want to take our relationship any further right then, but I was kind of in the middle of teasing him. He's going to pick me up around six. We'll have dinner and go from there. I need to figure out the feelings I have for both of them. I'm attracted to each of them in a different way and it's driving me crazy."

"Follow your heart, Natalie. It won't steer you wrong."

Her mother got up from her seat, kissed her cheek, and walked into the living room, leaving her alone in the kitchen with her thoughts.

* * * *

Six o'clock came and went, no Kale.

What the hell is going on? He's a no show?

No call. No nothing. She tried calling his house, but no answer.

"I don't believe this. I've been stood up."

"You never know. There could be a problem at his place, Nat. Give it some time," her mother replied, absently flipping through television channels.

"Time, my ass! I'm going upstairs to take a bath. He can go to hell," she grumbled and turned toward the stairs.

The doorbell rang and she glanced at the door. *Do I want to answer it knowing it's probably Kale, or do I want to ignore it and climb into a hot bath?*

"Oh hell." The door opened with a tug of her hand on the knob. "What?" she snapped.

No response. There wasn't anyone on the other side of the screen. *Ookay.*

She popped the screen door open and stuck her head outside. The screen was pulled from her grasp and a startled shriek slipped from her lips when Cade grabbed her arm, bent at the waist, and hoisting her over his shoulder. She wasn't sure, but she thought she could hear her grandmother's amused cackle coming from inside the house.

"Go get her boys!" Now that was definitely her grandmother.

"Go Kale," Cade yelled, taking off at a dead run toward his truck.

"Put me down, Cade!"

His hand came down hard on her ass cheek. "Hush."

Within moments, he stuffed her inside his truck, climbed in beside her and slammed the door. Kale sat on the other side, sandwiching her between the two of them.

"Move it, Cade, before her mother calls the cops," Kale growled, checking the mirrors.

Cade cranked the engine, shoved the vehicle in drive and squealed the tires as they took off down the street.

"What in the hell do you think you two are doing?" she snapped, while desperately trying to hide the smile on her lips.

"Kidnapping you. What does it look like?" Kale replied.

"You were supposed to pick me up two hours ago."

"I know, babe, but Cade and I came up with this plan instead."

"And what exactly is *this plan* you two concocted, and how does it involve me?"

"We're taking you back to Kale's so we can have a conversation about us."

"Us?" she asked, not sure she wanted to know what they meant by 'us'.

"You, me, and Kale, darlin'."

"After what you pulled earlier, Cade, there is no you and me."

"You're wrong."

"Wrong am I? How do you explain the fact that I called Kale and told him I wanted to come over to his place tonight, and I wanted him to make love to me? Hmm?"

"You didn't fuckin' tell me she said that, Kale," Cade growled, slowing down for a light.

"I figured it all came back to her wanting both of us, Cade."

"Don't talk like I'm not here, damn it!" she yelled. "This is my decision. Not yours."

"Do you want both of us, Natalie?" Kale asked, taking her hand between his.

"I don't know what I want, but you two bullying me into this little rendezvous isn't going to help make up my mind."

The next turn and they were driving down a long, dirt driveway with a large ranch house in the distance. She assumed this was Kale's home.

A large white two story home with a porch wrapping around three sides reflected the florescent light from the barn. Lights burned in the front windows in an inviting gesture to visit. The large structure behind the house looked like the typical Montana barn with huge doors and painted bright red. The pasture to the side of the house held several horses—their gleaming coats a sharp contrast to the white snow beneath their hooves.

"Wow. Nice place."

"Thanks."

She glanced at Cade from of the corner of her eye and asked, "Are you going to let me walk in or are you going to do the caveman thing and drag me by my hair?"

"Don't tempt me," Cade replied, and she stuck her tongue out at him.

Kale opened his door and held out his hand, but she ignored him. He was in as much trouble as Cade for pulling this stunt.

The huge front door mocked her with its inviting oak door when she stepped onto the porch.

"Allow me," Kale said, opening it for her to enter.

"Don't get all gentlemanly on me now, Kale."

"Have a seat, Nat," Cade said with a sweep of his hand.

She took a seat on the couch, and the two of them sat across from her in the matching recliners. Kale's place looked like a typical ranch home. Open living room with leather furniture and wood accented tables gracing the middle, and a huge rock fireplace took up one whole wall. The dining room stood to her left, but remained empty since he lived alone, she assumed. The kitchen looked like something out of a chef show, like Paula Deen or something, with its stainless steel appliances and shiny granite countertops. When she glanced back at her two hosts, her palms started sweating and itching. Having two gorgeous men focus on her might be how wet dreams are made, but she wasn't sure about it right at this moment.

"So what's this all about?" she asked, sliding her palms down her pant legs.

"I told you in the truck...us," Cade replied.

"Care to elaborate on the *us* part?"

"You were furious at me after lunch this afternoon—"

"An understatement, to be sure."

"What I did is inexcusable and I'm sorry. I tried apologizing when I called, but your grandmother chewed my ass."

"I know. I heard."

"Then Kale called me and told me what you said. Well, most of it, anyway."

The scowl he gave Kale, almost made her smile. He obviously didn't like the idea of her sleeping with his friend, no matter what he said before.

"He didn't mention you telling him you wanted him to make love to you."

"What difference does it make?"

"It makes a lot of difference, Nat. I care about you a lot and I'm not sure how I feel about you sleepin' with Kale."

"You told me you didn't care."

"I was wrong. All right? I do care."

"Do we really have to discuss this in front of Kale?"

"Yes. He's part of this. There is a burn between you. It's very apparent to me, but I can't be in a serious relationship with you until you figure out how to extinguish it."

"You're awfully quiet, Kale. What do you think of all this?" she asked, staring into his brown eyes.

"I want you, Natalie. I've never made any excuses or tried to deny it, but if you are serious about Cade, I'll back off."

"What if I said, I want both of you?"

You could hear a pin drop in the eerie stillness settling over the room. The air grew thick with the tension zinging from her to Cade, then from her to Kale. She waited with bated breath for either of them to say something...anything.

"Are you sure?" Cade asked.

"I want to know what it feels like to be loved by both of you at the same time. Then, maybe, I can decide how I want to play this. I know a threesome type relationship can't work, or should I say, won't work in this town. It's too small and with my job as an elementary teacher, it would be impossible. But if you two are willing, just this once, then I'm game."

"I want to be perfectly clear on this, babe. You want Cade and I to both make love to you, at the same time?" Kale stared across the expanse of the living room, a hopeful look on his face. When she glanced at Cade, he wore almost the exact expression, and she almost laughed.

"Yes."

Both of them sprang off the recliners in a matter of seconds and immediately took the seats of either side of her—Cade on her right and Kale on her left sandwiching her between them.

"You'll have to help me out here, guys. I don't have a clue what I'm doing."

"We'll take care of it, darlin'. Don't worry," Cade growled, his voice deep and sexy. His nose nuzzled against her ear and his warm breath sent shivers down her arms. She closed her eyes and parted her lips.

Kale turned toward her so his chest cradled her shoulder and arm. She pulled her hand back, gasping when it brushed his erection.

"All for you, babe." He took her hand, pressing it hard against his long, thick shaft. "God, I want you so bad, I hurt."

"Tell us what you want, Nat," Cade said, one hand cupping her breast as his thumb rasped over her nipple, making it tighten painfully.

She whimpered low in her throat and pushed her breast further into his hand.

"Good?"

"Yes," she breathed.

"Let's get this shirt off," Kale added, starting to unbutton her shirt.

Moments later, both men peeled the silk from her shoulders, leaving her in only her lacy bra.

"Nice," Cade told her. "But it needs to come off too. I want to feel your sexy, pink nipple puckering hard against my tongue."

Kale unsnapped the back of her bra when she leaned forward, and both men pulled a strap off her arms.

"Oh, man," Kale hissed. "I don't think I've ever seen something so perfect." He palmed her left breast, molding it to his touch. "So gorgeous." He pinched her nipple between his thumb and forefinger, and she almost came off the couch as desire zipped from the tip of her breast to her clit. The rough pad of Cade's tongue flicked at her right nipple. The moans spilling from her lips sounded low and coarse. Her head fell back against the couch, and she looked at the two men through her lashes. Cade's light brown hair was such a contrast to Kale's dark locks. Both were amazing, kind, loving, and melt-your-panties sexy. Both had calluses upon calluses on their hands from hard, every day work...honest work, and she'd never felt anything more enticing than two sets of hands on her skin.

Kale brought her face to his and slanted his mouth over hers. His tongue slipped over the seam of her lips, asking permission to invade the dark cavern of her mouth. When she parted her lips for him, he dove inside, sweeping away any and all thought. Every whimper and groan captured in the exchange of tongues.

"Holy hell, that is totally hot watching him kiss you," Cade groaned against her neck.

Hot breath flittered over her cheek as Kale moved toward her ear. Teeth nipped at her earlobe, and she tipped her head to give him better access to the skin of her throat.

Cade's mouth moved to her breast and he sucked the hard tip deep into his mouth. A tortured whimper escaped as he tongued her nipple.

Fingers pulled at the snap near her waist. She didn't know who they belonged to and she didn't care. Cade's mouth disappeared and she bit her lip to keep from calling him back.

The zipper on her jeans came down with a tug, and she heard Cade murmur, "Lift your hips, darlin'."

Cool air hit her skin as her pants and underwear came off her legs. Goose bumps flittered over her flesh, but she wasn't sure if it was from the sharp inhalation of breath from Cade or from the cooler temperatures of the room.

"Open for me, honey. I'm gonna eat you up," Cade said, dropping to his knees between her parted thighs. Two warm hands grasped her hips and tugged her to the edge of the couch cushion. "Oh yeah. Pink, pouty, and perfect."

She couldn't help but laugh at his words.

"What?" he asked, staring up at her. His blue eyes sparkled in the lamplight and a little smile twitched at his lips.

"Nothing."

His face disappeared between her legs, and she groaned when his tongue licked from her slit to the tip of her clit. *Good Lord, I love it when he does that.*

Kale's mouth moved down her chest, capturing the tight nipple in his mouth.

"Ah, God," she moaned and arched her back. With Cade's tongue doing wicked things to her clit and Kale's mouth sucking her nipple it wouldn't take long for her to crawl off the ledge of climax. Her hands balled into fists at her sides as wave after wave of sensations bombarded her body. Need spiked hard and her legs trembled. Whimpers she couldn't hide slipped from her lips.

Cade slipped two fingers knuckle deep into her pussy, and she almost slipped off the couch while she fought the climax hovering just out of reach.

"Easy, babe," Kale whispered. His thumb and forefinger rolled her right nipple while his mouth recaptured her left.

Heat crawled from her toes and burst through her pelvis as she felt everything centering on the mouth sucking her clit and Kale's ministrations on her breasts. Cade's tongue captured the cream sliding from her pussy as he hummed his appreciation against her flesh.

"Oh yeah," Kale groaned while continuing to roll her nipple. "I can't wait to get between those gorgeous thighs."

"I'm thinking you two have too many clothes on," she said, trying to bring her breathing under control.

"Mmm. Me, too," Cade replied. First, his t-shirt hit the floor, then his jeans. Within seconds, he stood in front of her, hard, ready, and oh-so-delicious.

"Your turn," she told Kale. "I wanna see what I've been missing." Kale chuckled and stripped to bare skin, her mouth watering at the sight. "Damn." She scooted closer and wrapped her hand around his girth.

Kale threw his head back and growled low in his throat, with an answering groan coming from Cade.

"Ain't nothin' hotter than watching your woman stroke another guy's cock, but just this once."

"Your woman?" she asked even though she continued to stroke Kale's cock.

"Damn right," Cade demanded. "We'll settle that tomorrow. Tonight is all for you. We are going to make you come so hard, you'll see stars."

Kale removed her hand and took a seat back on the couch. "Now, babe, suck me."

"Demanding. I like it," she chuckled as she grasped him in her hand and scooted closer.

"Wait," Cade said. "On your knees, darlin'. I'm gonna play."

On her hands and knees, with her mouth hovering over Kale's cock, she would be open to Cade's probing fingers. A position she knew she would love.

A cold dollop of lube hit her ass. "Shit! Did you have that stuff in the freezer or what?"

"Sorry, honey. I'll warm it up real fast," Cade replied, sliding a large smear down the crack of her butt and into her tight hole.

"Mmm," she hummed as she took Kale's cock into her mouth and Cade slipped a finger into her ass. Pressure built inside her pussy, making it throb with need.

Cade's tongue danced up her spine as he continued to probe and prepare her for his penetration. Even if she never had a man there, she read enough about it to know there would be some pain, but hopefully some intense pleasure too.

Her head bobbed up and down with each passing stroke over Kale's rock hard erection. His hands fisted in her hair, guiding her to what he liked, teaching her how to please him. Even though they both said this night was for her, she wanted to make sure she pleasured them well, too.

Small kisses and tiny nips accompanied Cade's pass over her back. Shivers raced down her spine with each flick of his tongue and slide of his lips.

Kale's breathing became ragged and sharp. She curled her hand around his balls, stroking and rolling them in her hand, bringing a tortured whimper to his lips. His shaft hardened and pre-cum glistened on the tip when he pulled himself from her mouth. "I wanna come in your hot pussy, babe."

"You ready, darlin'?" Cade asked, turning her around to face him.

She nodded her head once and said, "Tell me what to do."

"Kale, why don't you lay on the floor near the fireplace, and she can straddle you while I slide into her tight ass."

"Sounds like a plan to me," Kale said, moving to the floor and spreading himself out like a sacrificial Thanksgiving dinner. "Ride me, Nat. I want your sweet heat surrounding me."

"Both of you have condoms, right?"

Kale reached into the small drawer of the coffee table and pull out two foil packages. One sailed across the table at Cade, and Kale tore the other open with his teeth.

She trembled in anticipation. Hot, delicious sensations spiraled through her, settling low in her belly.

"Come to me, Natalie," Kale coaxed with a wicked sparkle in his eyes and a come-hither crook of his finger.

Lips parched when her mouth suddenly went dry as she watched Kale, and then Cade, roll the slippery latex over their impressive lengths. Kale's cock was a miniscule bit thicker than Cade's, but Cade's seemed longer, and for a moment, she panicked at the thought of having him inside her ass.

Cade licked her neck and whispered in her ear as if he knew her thoughts and reservations. "It'll fit, darlin'. I won't hurt you. All you have to do is say stop if you don't like it, but I'm thinkin' you're gonna love this."

After a quick, fortifying breath, she scooted across the floor and straddled Kale's hips. He captured the back of her head and pulled her lips to his. The crush of her breasts against his chest did luscious things to her nipples, and she moaned low in her throat. His tongue brushed the seam of her lips, coaxing her mouth to open for him. Tongues danced, entwined and dueled as both speared and retreated. Kale's hand grasped her hips, positioning her exactly where he wanted her. His rock hard erection bumped at the entrance of her pussy and slid in until only the head lay penetrating her folds.

She tore her mouth from his and lifted herself to take him the rest of the way. With a slow, easy slide, the full length of his cock penetrated deep inside her pussy.

"Oh, God," she breathed.

"Ah, hell yeah," he groaned. His legs trembled beneath her and his hands tightened their grip on her hips.

A quick glance at Cade revealed him palming his own cock, a look of pure bliss on his face. Her pussy twitched and pulsed. He obviously enjoyed watching her fuck Kale. "Are you joining us?"

"Right now, darlin'," he replied, moving behind her. "Lean over Kale's chest." Doing as instructed, he opened her ass cheeks, and she could have sworn she heard an almost animalistic growl from his lips. The whole thing made her feel sexy and beautiful. Colder lube landed on her crack, and she sucked in a ragged breath when Cade eased two fingers inside her tight hole. A low hiss escaped her mouth at the penetration and stretching of her ass. "This will help make it easier."

With each movement of his fingers, the vibrations of need spiked higher and higher. Kale rolled his hips, shoving his cock in and out of her pussy in a slow rhythmic motion meant to ease her into Cade's access.

"Oh yeah. Perfect," Cade murmured when she started pushing back against his hand.

"Please."

"Please what, princess?" Kale asked moments before closing his lips over one nipple.

"Cade! Do it, please. I need you."

The head of his cock paused at her entrance and then, slowly eased inside, passing the tight ring of muscles.

"Easy, darlin'."

"Oh, God! It burns."

"I know, honey. It'll pass in a second. I'll go slow."

He continued to push with unhurried firmness, pausing when she hissed at the burn, then moving more and more, until she completely encased him.

"Holy hell," he growled with his lips against her back. "You are so damned tight, honey. I don't know how long I can last."

After a quick kiss to the back of her neck, he must have moved, so he held himself upright because the angle changed and shoved his cock in so far, she could feel the crisp hair at his groin against her butt.

"So full," she sighed.

"You all right, princess?" Kale asked, watching her face for a reaction.

"Perfect, but now you two need to move. I need this. I want it right now."

The tortured sound coming from Cade seemed echoed by Kale as the two of them found a rhythm of movement to bring her to the peak of ecstasy within moments. Heat exploded through her pelvis, making her pussy cream, coating Kale's cock, lubricating his movements. Her pussy quivered and clamped down on the cock riding so deep inside her, she thought for sure he touched her womb.

"Yes, yes, yes," Cade panted behind her with each thrust of his hips. "You are so damned hot and you feel so perfect."

If she thought the first peak of climax blew her mind, the second burst of hot, explosive feelings rupturing inside her, blasted the first climax right out of the water. Stars burst behind her eyelids, and her pussy and ass clamped down on the steely flesh of the two men giving her pleasure. The cry from her mouth didn't sound like any sound she could think of, but she didn't want to think—only feel. They continued riding her hard until first, Kale's groan of completion, and then Cade's echoed in the silence of the living room.

"Are you all right, darlin'?" Cade asked after slowly withdrawing his now semi-erect cock from her ass.

"Mmm. Yeah," she whispered as she lay sprawled across Kale's chest.

"I don't know, Cade. I think that sounded almost like a purr."

"A purr of contentment, I'm thinkin'."

"You think too much, Cade," she grumbled, already half asleep.

"I've got a great idea. Let's all head upstairs to my room, and we can snuggle the rest of the night."

"I don't want to move," she told them.

"I'll carry you," Cade replied, pulling her from Kale's embrace and scooping her up in his arms.

A contented sigh left her mouth and she snuggled to his chest. "Hurry. It's getting chilly now that we aren't creating heat."

"We can always create more," he whispered with a chuckle. He took the steps two at a time even carrying her weight. The muscles of his six-pack abdomen bunched and rolled with each step.

"I don't think so. You two wiped me out," she answered. She nipped at his chest with her teeth and he yelped. "Don't piss me off, mister. I bite." Her laugh turned into a shriek when he dropped her in the middle of the bed.

"Quit hogging the bed, Nat. Move your ass over in the middle." Kale chuckled and whipped the blankets back on the king size bed.

She quickly snuggled into the warm blankets and waited for the two men to get into position. Cade wrapped an arm around her shoulders and pulled her to his side so her head lay on his chest.

"Perfect," he murmured, kissing the top of her head.

Kale's warm body found her back, and he lay one hand across her abdomen, before he placed a kiss her to her shoulder. "Sleep, princess. All will be worked out in the morning."

Her eyes grew heavy with the warm maleness surrounding her, and she drifted off to sleep.

11

Morning came way too early for Natalie. The warmth at her back and the crisp hair under her cheek told her the experiences of the night before weren't a naughty dream. She really had sex with both Cade and Kale at the same time. The soreness between her legs reminded her of the wild ride they had taken, but she knew it would be a onetime only thing.

"Mornin', darlin'," Cade whispered against her hair.

She tipped her head back and stared into his baby blues. "Morning. I guess it wasn't a dream, huh."

His amused chuckle made her smile. "Nope. Not unless you high jacked me and took me along for the ride." His eyebrows crunched as he frowned. "We need to talk, Nat."

"I know, but can I get some coffee first? I'm not good at negotiations without coffee."

"Negotiations? Is that how you see us? Something we have to work on terms about?"

"Look, Cade," she said, pushing herself into a sitting position. "Up until you kidnapped me from my grandmother's, I didn't want to see you again. Remember? Which, by the way, I will have words with her about, since I know damned well she was involved."

"Keep it down you two. Someone is trying to sleep here."

"To hell with you, Kale Dunn!" she yelled as she scooted off the bed and threw on a t-shirt she found on the floor.

"What did I do?" he grumbled.

"You're guilty too. Both of you. Drag me out here against my will when all I wanted was to figure out whether I really do love you Cade Weston or whether I—"

"Love me?" Cade asked, grabbing her hand and tugging her closer. "You love me, Nat?"

"No, I mean yes, I mean, I don't know, Cade." She inhaled quickly and blew it out in a rush. "I think so. You drive me crazy when we're together, but I can't get you out of my head. I dream about you at night. I want to be near you all the time. I'm jealous when you talk to other women. These are all new things for me. I've never felt like this before and it scares me to death." The soft click of the bathroom door made her realize Kale left. "We shouldn't be discussing this here. This is Kale's home."

Kale poked his head out of the bathroom and said, "No. It's fine. Go right ahead, princess. I know what you and I had wasn't anything compared to what you just described you feel for Cade and I'm thrilled for you two. I hope someday I can find a woman like you who feels those same things for me."

"I do love you, Kale, but only as a friend. Thanks for last night."

"You're welcome, babe. My pleasure. Now get on with it you two. A man needs his privacy." The beaming smile he gave her told her he was completely okay with the way things turned out. Another click and the door closed.

Cade stood and grabbed his jeans from the floor. Kale thoughtfully grabbed all their clothes from the living room while he carried Natalie upstairs the night before. After snapping and zipping himself into his pants, he sat down on the bed and rubbed his palms down his thighs.

"Natalie, darlin'. God, I wish I knew what to say."

Great. I'm in love with a man who doesn't love me. Why am I not surprised things turned out like this. I mean come on! I've been back in Red Rock two weeks, and I'm thinking I love him? This is nuts. She found her clothes and pulled them on with jerking motions. *I need to go home. Back to Oregon. The time spent with him is too much. I can't handle this. I don't want to. I want my simple, nonexistence back where no one pays any attention to me. I have my cat and my lonely life.* A choking sob broke from her lips and a single tear slid down her cheek, but she wiped it away in angry motions.

"It's fine, Cade. I understand. I mean we only got reacquainted a few short weeks ago. I can't possibly think how you would come to care for me in that short amount of time. It's ludicrous."

He grabbed her hand and pulled her down on his lap. "Don't put words in my mouth, honey. I didn't say I didn't care about you. I didn't say I didn't love you, because I do."

"You what?"

"I love you, Natalie Bennington. You've become my whole world and I don't want to return to feeling alone. I made Kale help me kidnap you last night because I couldn't bear the thought of you mad at me. What I said yesterday was completely uncalled for, and I've been kicking my own ass for being so stupid. Your laughter brightens my day. Your smile warms my heart. I want you to stay in Red Rock with me."

"Stay?"

"Yes. Will you marry me, Nat? Marry me and stay with me in my unfinished house up in the middle of nowhere?" The warm chuckle from his lips had her heart singing. "Raise babies with me? And love me until the end of my days?"

She wrapped her arms around his neck and buried her nose against his throat. His unique scent filled her senses and the love she felt for this man, overflowed her heart. "Yes to all those things, Cade. I love you so much. I can't imagine my life without you in it."

The tears returned, but this time they were happy tears. She couldn't believe the man of her dreams had been right here in Red Rock the whole time.

Home. She'd finally come home.

Epilogue

The high-pitched wail of a baby's cry echoed in the clearing, and Cade couldn't help but smile. His first-born. His son.

"Well, Daddy. How does it feel?" Kale asked, pounding him on the back.

"You have no idea."

"I think it's fabulous. My two best friends' have a child together, and I couldn't be happier for you, Cade. When are you two going to have another one so you have a matching set?"

"Ask Nat. I doubt after the fifteen hours of labor she endured, she'll let me near her for a while."

"Yes, well I'm sure, given time, she'll let you back into your bed and not make you sleep on the couch anymore."

"It's about time you figured out how that thing between your legs works, Cade Weston," Mrs. Oliver said from the rocking chair on the porch. "You and Natalie have been married two years now."

He smiled and shook his head before bending down and kissing her on the cheek. "I love you too, Gram."

"God, I hate when you get all mushy on me. I have to keep you in line, you know." Her eyes sparkled as a playful grin spread across her face, and she winked.

The door opened and Marie stepped out carrying a blanket wrapped bundle. "Do you want to see your son now that's he's all cleaned up? The mid-wife is working on Natalie, so it'll be a minute before I suggest you go back in there."

Marie handed him the baby and he pulled back the soft wool from his son's face. "Hey there, little guy? You gave your momma a hell of a night, huh." The baby blinked several times and opened his eyes. "I'm not sure if you're gonna have my blue eyes or your momma's green ones, but your hair is definitely light like hers."

"What did you and Natalie decide to name him, Cade?" Marie asked, taking the seat next to her mother.

"Alan Mitchell Weston."

"It's a beautiful name, and I'm sure your father will be thrilled you've given your son his grandfather's name," Marie said. "I forgot to tell you how sorry I am about your mother's death. I can't imagine the pain your father is going through."

He swallowed hard, fighting the tears of sorrow along with the tears of happiness at the birth of his child. His mother would never get to hold her grandchild in her arms now and it made him very angry. A drunk driver hit her two months ago when she headed home from town. Lucky for her, she died instantly and didn't suffer, but the man who hit her would if Cade had any say in the matter.

"Thank you, Marie. It's been really rough on all of us. I thought for a bit during the whole thing, Natalie might go into labor early, but this little guy..." He kissed the baby's forehead. "Managed to stay put until it was time." The baby started to squirm and screw up his face. "Mmm. I think he needs his mama."

The group chuckled when the baby let out a piercing scream, and Cade hurried into the house to find his wife.

Natalie lay propped up in the bed, dosing quietly when he walked in, but her eyes opened and a beautiful smile graced her face as he approached the bed.

"How are my two favorite men?"

"This favorite man needs a kiss," Cade replied, bending down to brush his lips over hers. The kiss went on for several minutes, and he had to pull himself away to keep from ravishing her right then. "This favorite man needs food I'm thinkin'."

"There you go with your thinking again," she replied with a laugh. "Here. Let me have him. He probably needs to nurse."

Cade's cock twitched in his pants when she dropped the edge of her nightgown and positioned the baby at her breast with a soft 'oh' when he latched on.

"It'll take a bit of getting used to, Natalie, but you'll be a pro in no time," the mid-wife said. "I'll check on you in a day or two. If you have any trouble, call me."

"Thanks, Leslie. You've been a dream."

"You made it easy. Get some rest."

The soft click of the door signaled her departure and he pulled up a chair next to the bed. "How are you feeling, darlin'?"

"Sore and exhausted, but I'm thrilled our baby is healthy."

"Me, too." His fingers danced down her arm and he watched in fascination as the goose bumps rose in their wake. He loved how responsive her body was to his touch.

"What's wrong?" she asked entwining their fingers.

"I'm just sad my mom couldn't be here. I know how much she looked forward to holding her grandchild."

"I'm sorry, Cade, but I'm sure she's watching over us from above and will be at God's elbow looking out for our children while they grow."

He nodded and said, "You know her favorite time of the day always used to be sunrise. She loved to get up bright and early and wait for the sun to creep over the horizon. She used to tell me it made her feel close to God."

"I'm thrilled our son decided to make his entrance into the world as the sun came up over the hills this morning. He's his grandmother's special baby."

"I love you, Natalie Weston."

"I love you too, Cade. May God bless us with many more just like this one," she said, brushing her fingers down the baby's cheek.

"From your mouth to God's ears, my love."

The End

1

BEFORE THE NIGHT IS OVER
Montana Cowboys 2
Sandy Sullivan

Kale Dunn watched with amusement and then admiration, as the red-haired woman stomped through the throng of people inside the Saddle Club and headed straight for the unsuspecting guy standing next to the pool table. Kale's mouth flopped open when she pulled back her fist and decked the guy, dropping him to the floor.

"Holy shit! Did you see that?" he asked the guy sitting next to him at the bar.

"What?"

"The red head over there just decked Jeff Cox."

"Really? Where?"

"By the pool table," he replied before he grabbed his beer bottle from the bar and moved toward the ruckus.

The woman struggled against the arms holding her as she let out a string of cuss words with enough color to make a sailor blush. "You son of a bitch! Get up, Jeff. You fucking coward!" she yelled. Her intended target still sat on the floor rubbing his chin.

"Calm down, Laurel," Jeff said.

"Calm down my ass!" She pulled one arm free. "If you are such a man, why the hell don't you face me? You beat up on my little sister until she's black and blue, and then you come down here and pick up some other chick. You're nothing but a fucking pussy!"

"It's none of your business what Elizabeth and I do at home."

"Bullshit! She's my sister and you will *not* lay a hand on her again. I'll kill you myself before I let you hurt her anymore."

Kale's admiration grew by leaps and bounds when he heard her words. Only a coward of a man would hit a woman. Unfortunately, he knew the guy and he had to get involved.

Red curls framed her face and spilled down her back in a cascading wave of fire. Black jeans hugged her hips and a white tank top curled around her breasts like a lover's hand. Shit kicker boots sliced through the air as she tried to worm her way free of the two men holding her. Long legs outlined by the tight jeans and a taut butt ripe as two perfectly formed cantaloupes, had his palms itching to cup the mounds just to see if they felt good in his hands.

Kale controlled his laughter, but he couldn't stop the twitching of his lips. One petite five-foot-three woman took down a six-foot man with one punch. Her knuckles probably throbbed and burned from the impact, but she didn't seem to notice.

"What seems to be the trouble here?" Kale asked, coming to stand between the woman and Jeff, who had just picked himself up off the floor.

"Who the hell are you?" she asked, irritation clear in her tone.

Sapphire blue eyes spit fire at him and he wondered if he really should get in the middle of this, but he couldn't help it. She intrigued him beyond her dazzling looks and take-no-shit attitude.

"Kale Dunn. You?"

"Laurel Hayes," she snarled, her gaze focused on the man behind him. "You don't need to get involved in this, Mr. Dunn. This is between me and ass-wipe there."

"I disagree. You see, Mr. Cox is my employee."

"You own the Bar KD?" Her gaze fixed on him finally and his heart slammed against his ribs. *Damn, she's got pretty eyes to go along with the knock-out body.*

"Yes, ma'am. I can't let you go around beatin' up my guys. I need him to ride tomorrow," Kale replied as he tried to hide his amusement. He nodded to the guys holding her to release her. Wrong move. She immediately lunged at Jeff again, so Kale grabbed her around the waist and hauled her up against his chest. With a sharp jab, her elbow connected with his jaw and they both tumbled to the floor. The air left his lungs in a whoosh when all one hundred twenty pounds of her landed on top of him.

"Let go," she spat, twisting and turning in his arms. Her butt rubbed against his groin, immediately bringing his dick to attention.

"Sorry, babe. No can do. But if you don't stop squirming like that, we'll be doin' our own little dance in the front seat of my truck."

A cold shower wouldn't have brought such a quick response as she immediately stopped moving. Air rushed from between her lips in rapid, panting puffs, making her chest heave and push against his arm.

"Are you gonna behave, Red?"

"Fine," she ground out between clenched teeth. "And don't call me Red. I hate it."

Releasing a low grunt, he rolled over so she lay beneath him and then brought them both to their feet without letting her out of his arms. His job of wrestling cattle all day came in handy some times.

Kale faced Jeff and said, "I do believe you should be goin' home, Jeff, before Red here gets loose and takes you down again. I expect to see you in my office first thing tomorrow morning. Pack your gear before you come."

"Pack my gear?"

"Yep. You're done at the Bar KD. Find another outfit to work for. I'll have your check ready."

"You'll pay for this, Laurel," Jeff snarled as he snatched his hat off the floor and moved toward the door.

Kale watched his employee stomp through the crowd and bang the door hard against the wall as he left. The crowd around them dissipated now that the fun had waned.

Laurel stood in the circle of his arms with the curve of her ass cradling his erection. The faint smell of sweet pea wrapped around his senses and he fought the urge to bury his nose in the slope of her neck.

"You can let go now," she said. "There isn't anyone else here I want to kill."

He eased his arm from around her just in case she decided to hit some-one else and she stepped out of his embrace, leaving a cold, empty space. When she turned to face him, the sight of her hair in wild disarray, her eyes sparkling with anger, and her lips pursed in a pout, made his heart pound and blood rush to his ears. It had been a while since any woman turned him on like this so fast.

"Can I buy you a beer?"

"No thanks. I need to take care of my sister." She turned to leave, but glanced back over her shoulder. "Thank you for firing him. I'm sure my sister won't be happy about him being unemployed. It will probably cause more issues, but I'm glad to see there's a man willing to take a stand on spousal abuse."

Not willing to let her go quite so quickly, he said, "You need to take care of those knuckles, too. Put some ice on them at least." He lifted her hand and inspected the torn skin, fighting the urge to kiss them. "Has he been doin' it for a while?"

"I don't know. I haven't been here very long," she replied, pulling her hand out of his grasp.

"I didn't think you looked familiar. I know pretty much everyone in this town." *And I sure would have remembered you.*

"Homeboy, huh?"

"Yep. Born and raised right here in Red Rock. Is your sister the only reason you're here?"

"Yeah. For the most part." Her lips pressed together in a firm line like she had already said too much. "Well, good night." She tipped her head and walked toward the door.

The sway of her hips beneath her jeans made his dick jump to attention again and he stifled the groan rumbling in his chest. He downed the rest of his beer and set the bottle on the bar. The night came to a screeching halt with her departure and he figured he might as well go on home.

"This is pathetic. A Saturday night and I'm going home alone," he grumbled out loud. Warm Montana air hit his face when he stepped outside. June in this neck of the woods meant heat, mosquitoes, and lots of hard work on his place. Relaxation came with a price for the owner of a cattle ranch and since he didn't have a woman to go home to, he had hoped to find a willing lady at the bar. One red-haired spitfire took care of taking anyone else home. The mood was gone.

His truck sat parked near the back of the lot like so many others in this area. If you didn't own a truck, you weren't a real cowboy. With a turn of the key, the diesel engine growled to life like a panther stalking his prey. Sweat stuck his hair to his head when he took off his hat and tossed it onto the seat next to him.

Several trucks and cars cruised the main street into town and he pulled right in with them. Going home didn't feel right. The darkness of the night, the brightness of the stars overhead, and the warmth of the June evening made him restless. *I could go out and visit Cade and Natalie, I guess.* He glanced at the clock. Ten o'clock. *Nah. It's too late to be buggin' them. They've got the new baby and all.*

The bright lights of the local diner called to him. His shoulder lifted in a shrug and he pulled his truck into an open parking spot. Maybe a couple of his buddies would be hanging around and he could shoot the shit for a little while.

A bell tinkled when he pulled on the glass panel, announcing his arrival to everyone in the place. At least a half-dozen people lifted their hands in greeting as he made his way down the linoleum path to a booth. He stopped and chatted with a few, slapped a few more on the back and then slid onto the bench seat.

"I can't believe you got him fired," a female voice said.

"I didn't do it, Elizabeth. Jeff's boss happened to be at the bar."

His keen hearing tuned into the conversation and he realized the women sitting behind him probably included Red.

"How could you have hit him, Laurel?"

"After he hit you? I'd say it was pretty damned easy."

The sniffing sound coming from the other booth told him Jeff's wife was crying on her sister's shoulder.

"He has no right to hit you. Only a lowlife coward hits women."

"You know nothing about our life, Laurel. You moved here what? Two weeks ago?"

"What is your point, Elizabeth? I'm not going to sit back and watch while he beats the hell out of you until one day he takes it too far."

The waitress approached his table, distracting him for a moment. "Hey, Kale. What's it gonna be?"

"Coffee and how about a piece of apple pie?"

"Ice cream?"

"Of course. Is there any other way?" he asked with a chuckle.

"Nope," she replied and smiled. "I'll be right back."

The conversation behind him caught his attention again.

"You should go on back to Los Angeles, Laurel. I don't think Red Rock is the place for you. This is a small backward town. We have our own way of handling things and a woman punching out a man in the bar isn't it."

"Are you telling me to leave?"

"No, but you need to butt out."

"I'm a cop. I can't turn my back on domestic abuse whether it involves someone I know or not."

A cop? That would explain her taking Jeff down with one punch. He sipped from the coffee cup in front of him and listened.

"Why don't you come with me back to L.A., Elizabeth? You know I only moved here to be near you with all the stuff he's been doing, but I'll forget my job and stuff here if it means keeping you safe."

"I'm not leaving my husband. I love him."

Red's voice rose in anger. "Even after he beat the shit out of you? Wake up, sister. This type of relationship isn't normal."

"It is what it is."

"You are driving me nuts!" Red exclaimed, drawing attention from a few of the diner patrons when several sets of eyes turned in their direction.

"I'm going home."

The booth wiggled against his back with the movement from the woman behind him.

"Elizabeth, please. At least stay with me tonight."

"No. I need to see my husband."

The blonde woman rushed past him and he heard Red yell her name.
"Here's your pie, Kale."

"Thanks, Jen."

The woman in the next booth sighed and he debated on whether to let her know he sat nearby. Deciding it would be best to make his presence known, he turned around.

"Hi, Red."

One perfectly arched eyebrow shot up and her eyes narrowed. "Are you purposely trying to annoy me?"

"Mind if I join you?" he asked, sliding out of the booth with coffee cup in one hand and pie plate in the other.

"Yes."

"Too bad," he replied, sitting down at the table with her. "You really need to learn to curb your temper."

Her lips pressed together in a firm line and he had the insane urge to kiss the daylights out of her until she moaned and molded those perfect breasts against his chest.

"What business is it of yours?"

A forkful of pie reached his lips and when he opened his mouth, her gaze focused on his lips. Hers parted and he figured she had no idea her breathing had sped up, but the rapid rise and fall of her chest told him.

Interesting. Maybe this won't be such a bad night after all.

"I would hate to see you get into trouble. Being a cop, I'm sure you carry handcuffs and a gun."

"Yeah."

"And I'm sure you know exactly how to use them."

"I would hope so."

"There are other ways to get back at your brother-in-law."

"Go on."

"I can't go into detail here. Too many ears."

"What do you suggest?"

"We could go somewhere more private."

A hearty laugh left her lips and she tossed a silky strand of gorgeous hair over her shoulder. "Do I look stupid? I don't even know you. Why would I go anywhere with you?"

"You can trust me."

"I wasn't born yesterday, Mr. Dunn."

"Kale."

"All right, Kale." She leaned against the back of the booth and rested one elbow on the seat. The nonchalant posture did nothing to calm his libido when her shirt pulled tight over those incredible breasts and her nipples puckered enough he could clearly see them through her shirt and bra. "Let me assure you, being a cop in Los Angeles comes with a certain amount of common sense and going anywhere with a stranger is at the bottom of the common sense list."

"Anyone in this diner would vouch for me," he replied with a wave of his hand to indicate the patrons.

"I'm sure they would since you told me at the bar, you were born and raised here."

"It's not like I plan on taking advantage of you without your permission."

"So you plan on taking advantage of me with my permission?"

"It wouldn't hurt my feelin's, darlin'. You are a beautiful woman, after all."

One half of her lips lifted in a smile and his dick jumped to attention. *God, she can turn me inside out with nothing more than a grin.*

"Don't beat around the bush, Kale. If you want to take me home and fuck my brains out, just say it."

He crooked a finger and she leaned close. "I want to take you home and fuck your brains out, Red."

She grabbed the digit in front of her and sucked it between her lips. Her tongue wrapped around the end and he'd never felt anything like it before. White hot desire zinged from the end of his finger straight to his dick. Her pupils dilated, almost encompassing the blue of her irises. His breathing sped up and he panted like a steam locomotive. She dipped her finger into the ice cream on his plate and lifted it to his lips. Unable to fight the urges rushing through him, he sucked it between his lips and nibbled on the tip. Ice cream melted on his tongue and mixed with the salt of her skin—sweet and potent enough to draw his balls up tight against his groin and make his dick strain for release.

After a couple more licks and a nibble or two on his finger, she released it from her mouth and smiled. "Your offer is mighty tempting, but—"

"But?"

"You know, I wish I would have met you sooner. I have a very important appointment in the morning in Boise, with my doctor."

"Doctor?" he asked, frowning.

"Yeah. You see I'm going in for a sex change operation next week." She slid out of the booth and left him sitting there with his mouth hanging open.

* * * *

Laurel reached her car and glanced back through the window to see Kale still sitting where she left him. The roar of laughter coming from her mouth, bounced off the building and she couldn't help but shake her head. If he really believed that, she had some ocean front property in Arizona for him. She rolled her eyes and chuckled as she started her car and backed out of the parking spot.

"Men are so gullible some times."

The drive back to her apartment gave her time to think. This thing with Elizabeth and Jeff was problem and she wasn't quite sure how to handle it. The cop in her wanted to turn him in and make him do time, but she also knew the system. A slap on the wrist, a fine, and nothing more, would be his punishment. If Elizabeth didn't press charges, nothing would happen at all and it sure didn't appear her sister had any inclination of going through with prosecution.

Her thoughts drifted back to the disturbingly sexy, Kale Dunn. The inky black hair curling around his ears and against the back of his neck made her shiver and her fingertips tingle. His black Stetson blended with those curls, giving him a mystifying and mysterious look. His chocolate colored eyes melted her insides like butter under the hot June sun the moment she had locked gazes with him at the bar. Dark-haired, dark-eyed men always got to her in a special way. The steel band of his arm around her waist when he stopped her from going after Jeff again made her think of a horse being corralled. Tied and bound to the hard body behind her, she could only wiggle and squirm in his embrace. His words about doing a dance in the front seat of his truck brought imagines better left hidden in her soul.

She pulled into the apartment complex and looked up at her apartment window. Darkness shrouded the front of the building, but the lone light in the small window made her smile. If anything could make her feel better, it had to be the thought of her daughter. Kimberly, or Kimmy as she called her, was two-feet of bouncing blonde curls, big blue eyes and the sweetest dimples any mother could ask for. At three years old her daughter could wrap any person, man or woman, around her little finger with nothing more than those dimples. Laurel frowned. Unfortunately, the same trait making her daughter so cute came with the reminder of Kimmy's father, Dennis Morgan. The one mistake she would admit to—falling in love with another woman's husband.

Laurel pulled her gun out of the glove box, popped out the clip, and pushed the door open on her car. A quick glance around told her the parking lot seemed quiet and deserted, but it didn't mean she let her guard down. Too many times, she had seen the same scenario. A dark parking lot, a woman alone, and a man who wanted something she wouldn't be willing to give.

Grabbing the leather jacket she'd left in the car, she slipped over her arms and onto her shoulders, concealing the weapon in the back waistband of her jeans. It bothered her to be unarmed. Being a detective in Los Angeles brought out the wariness in her nature. There, no one seemed safe even with someone you knew. She'd always had to be on her toes, aware of everything around her, but here? Things seem slow, laid back, and peaceful. *Boring.*

"Why the hell did I ever leave?" she grumbled as she made her way up the two flights of stairs to her apartment door. Keys in hand, she slipped one into the lock, pushed the door open and called, "Teresa?"

"Hey, Laurel. You're home early. When you told me you were going to the Saddle Club, I figured you would probably be gone all night,"

Teresa replied from her spot on the sofa. The elderly woman reminded her of her grandmother, with her graying hair, and small reading glasses perched on the edge of her nose. A huge ball of yarn sat in the small bag at Teresa's feet while her fingers worked the crochet hook in and out of the wad she cradled in her hands.

Laurel wasn't one to knit, crochet or any of the other womanly things. The hard edge to her personality came from growing up fast and taking life by the horns. Never mind the standoffish way her parents raised her and her sister.

Her keys slid across the smooth surface of the coffee table when she tossed them and rid herself of her jacket. She walked down the hall to her room to store her weapon as she called over her shoulder, "I wasn't there to socialize." Once the gun was tucked into her nightstand drawer, she ran her fingers through her hair and sighed. Her shoulders knotted with tension, she rolled her head from side to side to relieve some of the pressure. The knuckles on her right hand burned. Glancing at the torn skin, she knew she'd have to take Kale's advice and clean them up. *Ice would be in order, too.*

"Did Kimmy behave?" she asked when she made it back into the living room. The place would do for now, but if she planned on staying in Red Rock for any length of time she would need a bigger one. A yard, a dog, white picket fence—Laurel snorted. Yeah, like that would ever happen especially in this podunk town with nothing but cowboys and jerks. *Cowboys aren't bad. Kale is obviously a cowboy.* Laurel jerked her head from side to side to dislodge the thoughts of the distracting man.

"She was a doll, of course."

"Got you fooled too, does she?" she asked with a chuckle. She knew her daughter well. The little pixie of a girl turned into a hellion when she didn't get what she wanted.

"You're her mother. You know her better than everyone else, but she's a little angel when she's with me."

Laurel shook her head and looked at the toe of her boots. Kimberly might be blonde and blue-eyed, but she had her mother's red-headed temper. It was one of the reasons she became a cop. She needed something to tame the temper that ran hot at times, like tonight when she'd decked Jeff. *Not that he didn't deserve it, the fucking asshole.*

Her mind wandered back to the other unnerving man she'd met tonight and she felt her temper calm. *Odd. Very few things cool my temper.*

Red, he'd called her. The nickname drove her crazy normally, but somehow when he'd said it, her body went on high alert. The rock hard bulk of his chest pressed against her back when he had grabbed her made her thoughts go haywire for a moment. Those kinds of muscles and the rough calluses on his hands didn't come from a gym. A man only got those from hard physical labor. At the time, she could have taken him down too, if she had wanted to, but he wasn't her target. The asshole of a brother-in-law made her temper burn and rational thought disappear.

"Thanks for watching her for me, Teresa. How much do I owe you?"

"Nothin', honey. You can buy me lunch one day. You weren't gone more than a couple of hours."

"Are you sure?" Laurel asked. Taking advantage of her neighbors didn't sit well with her.

"Positive," Teresa replied and then kissed Laurel on the cheek. "I'll see you tomorrow. Are you working?"

"Yeah. I'm on the midnight shift. I hate changing jobs for that reason alone. Starting at the bottom of the seniority rung sucks."

"I'm sure you'll be up on day shift in no time."

Laurel didn't think so. Usually, in these small towns like this, no one ever left the police force, which meant she would be on the night shift until she died if she stayed here. "Yeah, well, we shall see. Thanks again for watching Kimmy," she said when Teresa opened the door to leave.

"No problem, honey. Is your sister watching her while you work?"

Fuck! I totally forgot about Elizabeth watching Kimmy. There is no way in hell I'll leave my daughter over there with them. "Yeah, she was, but I can't take her over there anymore. Would you mind watching her for me tomorrow night? I swear I'll find a regular sitter, but I can't on short notice especially working nights."

Teresa patted her arm and said, "Of course, Laurel. Knock on my door about fifteen minutes before you leave, and I'll sleep over here on your couch. No need for her to be taken out of her bed."

"You're a lifesaver, Teresa. Thank you."

"You're welcome. I'll see you tomorrow."

Laurel closed the door behind her friend and dead-bolted it. *A hot bath sounds wonderful right now. Kimmy's asleep, thank goodness. I can relax amongst some bubbles and let my mind wander a bit.* A pair of dark, yummy chocolate brown eyes flashed in her mind and she grumbled under her breath. *I do* not *need to be thinking about Kale Dunn even if he is downright gorgeous.*

The light flipped on with the pressure of her fingers on the switch. Florescent lighting glared from the cheap fixture over the mirror and she wished she had some candles to burn. A bath with candlelight always made her feel more relaxed. "Oh well."

Hot water sprayed from the spigot in a rush. She plugged the tub, sprinkled in some bath bubbles and stripped out of her clothing. With her long, thick, red hair twisted into a bun behind her head and secured with a clip, she slipped beneath the water with a heavy sigh. Water continued to run, slowly creeping up over her flat stomach and encircling her breasts, leaving only the barest peek of her nipples exposed. The handles shut off with a little heaviness from her toes. Rarely did she get a moment alone with a young daughter to support and no husband around.

Her thoughts drifted to Kimberly's father. Their first meeting came back so clear, her heart ached and tears burned her eyes at the sorrow and grief still holding her in its claws years later. Would she ever be able to move beyond her love for Dennis? She didn't know, but she hadn't so far.

"Cadet Hayes?" he snapped, going through the roll call.

"Yes?"

His gaze drilled into her when it stopped on her face. "You will answer yes sir when spoken to, cadet." One eyebrow shot up as his gaze swept over her from head to toe.

"Yes, sir," she replied, unnerved by the heat of his perusal.

He continued calling off names, but his attention returned to her time and time again during the first day and every day afterwards.

Later in the evening he'd been checking the barracks and passed her in the hall. Without turning around, she kept moving until he barked, "Cadet?"

"Yes, sir."

"I suggest you learn quickly who to trust and who not to trust in this academy."

"Sir?"

"There are those inside who would love to see you drown, Miss Hayes. Take heed of my warning," he said and then disappeared.

The days drew on and as a raw police academy cadet, she tried damned hard to make it through the school to prove to her parents she could do it. Dennis had been an instructor at the academy and when she had started to falter on the physical fitness part of the training, he bolstered her courage and became her mentor. They had spent hours together after the regular day, jogging, doing pushups and pull-ups, and running the obstacle course over and over until her time surpassed anyone else in the class. Their relationship became personal once she graduated and was assigned to the same precinct he transferred to after their class made it through.

Tears slid down her cheek as she continued into the past to the day her world stopped.

The call came in bank robbery in progress and she'd been one of the first on the scene. Moments later, several more police cars arrived including Dennis, while she ducked behind the door of her cruiser. "Dennis!" she screamed when the bullets pinged against the metal of her car. Her gaze continued to search for her lover and a moment of panic ran through her. *Please let him be okay. Please, please, please.*

"Stay down, Laurel!" he yelled back from two cars away.

Ten cop cars surrounded the building, but nothing seemed to be able to stop the two bank robbers as they continued the barrage of bullets.

Laurel didn't realize her left shoulder was visible to the men shooting until she felt the searing heat of a bullet when it passed through the muscle. Blood oozed from the wound in her upper arm and rolled down her blue uniform. "Fuck!" she yelled and ducked back behind the car.

"Laurel?"

"I'm hit," she called.

"Damn it!" she heard moments before she saw Dennis scramble out from behind his car and try to work toward her.

"No! Stay there!"

A choking sob broke from her lips as the vision of Dennis' eyes widening when the stray slug hit him on the left side of his head and he slumped to the ground in an ever widening pool of blood.

"Dennis! Oh, my God, Dennis!"

The SWAT team arrived and the bombardment of bullets from the gunman ceased. The robbers were apprehended and the moment she could safely leave her hiding spot, she dropped to her knees next to Dennis and cradled his head on her lap. Tears scorched a path down her cheeks while she sobbed and stroked his hair. She refused to let go until the paramedics and her fellow officers peeled her away from his side.

Her life had come to a screeching halt with the death of her lover. However, nothing prepared for the funeral and coming face to face with Mrs. Dennis Morgan or the realization she now carried a married man's child.

2

"Mommy?" Kimberly's small voice brought Laurel back from the crushing sorrow she felt. Dennis' death three years prior still hurt. Nothing had been the same since. Her parents turned their back on her when they found out she was pregnant with his child and the fact of his marriage came to light. Dennis kept the details of his marriage well hidden and no one believed she didn't have a clue.

"Come on in, baby. I'm in the bathroom." Kimberly's light blue eyes peeked around the edge of the doorframe. "What's wrong? Did you have a bad dream?"

Kimberly's blonde curls bounced as she nodded and her bottom lip stuck out.

"Hang on, sweetie, and mommy will get out of the bathtub. Okay?"

The little girl nodded again and her thumb disappeared between her little pouty lips.

Laurel drug her body out of the tub and dried off quickly. Once she tugged it on, the threadbare T-shirt floated over her head and covered her body to upper thighs. Her boxer shorts covered all the essential parts down below. *Man. Is this sexy or what? If only Kale could see me now, he'd run for the nearest door.*

"Can I seep wif you?" Kimmy whined.

"Sure pumpkin. Let's get this bathwater emptied."

The slow sucking sounds of the water disappearing down the drain reminded Laurel of how her life had went from bad to worse. After Dennis' death and the particulars of her torrid affair were made public, Laurel had transferred to the homicide department and made detective. With no one to support her and her parents disowning her, she fought for everything she had and then some. Los Angeles was a rough town and being a homicide detective in Pasadena, kept her busy, until she got the call from Elizabeth.

"Come on sweetie. Let's hit the hay." Normally, she didn't let Kimberly sleep in the same bed, but tonight she needed the comfort of her little body snuggled up against her. Her child's limitless love and soft, warm hugs, kept her sane.

Laurel flipped the comforter down toward the bottom of the bed and set Kimberly on the bottom sheet. Her daughter scooted to the middle and Laurel took her spot as the little girl curled into her side and sighed.

"I wuv you, Mommy."

"I love you too, baby girl," Laurel whispered and then kissed the top of Kimmy's head. "Go to sleep." Kimmy's soft breathing and the occasional sucking sound lulled Laurel into a dreamy state. Moonlight bounced on the ceiling with every rustle of the curtains on the window as they moved back and forth in the breeze. She trailed her fingers through her daughter's curls, but she frowned when her thoughts drifted to Elizabeth.

After her sister's call and the subsequent visit to her home, Laurel's anger spiked high at the bruises already forming on Elizabeth's cheek. She had taken off to the bar to face down her brother-in-law and give him a little of the treatment he'd inflicted on her sister. The plan hadn't included running into the devilishly handsome Kale Dunn, owner of the Bar KD and Jeff's boss.

"Former boss," she murmured out loud. "And too damned handsome for my sanity."

The exchange in the diner came back to her mind and she smiled. Lust burned bright in his eyes when she sucked his finger into her mouth. Desire ran hot and explosive between them. Unfortunately, there wasn't anything to do about it. Finding a bedmate, lover, husband or whatever, wasn't in the cards for her. The love she carried for Dennis still burned in her soul, but he was gone and had never really been available in the first place.

"Why didn't you tell me, Dennis?" she asked the empty room. "I loved you." Burning pain seared her heart and a tear slid from the corner of her eye into the hair at her temple. Grief had been her constant companion over the last three years, but now she angrily wiped the tears away. "No more. I'm done with all of this. I don't need a man in my life other than an occasional romp between the sheets. I'll take care of Kimberly on my own."

She sighed, closed her eyes, and abandoned the thoughts running through her mind and let sleep overcome her body. Tomorrow would be a long day.

* * * *

Kale wasn't looking forward to dealing with Jeff this morning, but it had to be done. A man who abused his wife wasn't welcome on his place. Drunk or just stupid—it didn't matter. The man had struck a woman.

An irritated knock sounded on his office door and Kale knew it was showtime.

"Come in."

"Kale," Jeff said.

"Have a seat," he replied, noticing Jeff carried his saddle, chaps, bridle, and rope. "You can leave your gear right there."

Jeff dropped everything and approached the desk. "Listen, Kale—"

He held up a hand to stop Jeff's words. "There's no explanation you can give me to change my mind."

"It wasn't like she made it out to be."

"Did you or did you not strike your wife?"

"Well, yeah, but we were arguing about me going out with the guys and—"

Kale held up his hand. "There is no excuse for hitting a woman under any circumstances." The drawer slide open with a tug of his fingers, and he grabbed the check he had already made out for Jeff's final wages. "Take it. I don't want you on my land again."

"Son of a bitch," Jeff cussed under his breath. "Laurel will pay for this."

Kale narrowed his gaze on the man and spat, "You touch her and I will personally put your ass in the hospital. Do I make myself clear?"

"What do you care? She's nothing to you."

"It doesn't matter what she is or isn't to me. If you so much as grab her arm, I'll break yours."

Jeff folded the check and stuffed it into his pocket. The look on the man's face told Kale he contemplated whether the threat was an idle one.

The door shut behind him and Kale let out a long, slow breath and raked his fingers through his hair. How he got caught up in this whole messy affair, he wasn't sure, but it appeared he got himself smack ass in the middle of it whether he wanted to be or not.

No time for reflection now. The cattle in the north pasture wouldn't bring themselves up for branding and the men waited. He pushed to his feet, grabbed his Stetson and sighed. Snapping blue eyes and a saucy smile flashed in front of him and right then, he swore to himself he would get that sassy red-head beneath him sooner or later and he preferred soon.

Over twenty men sat saddled and ready to ride when he made his way around the backside of the barn. At times they took ATVs but it was much easier to roust some of the stubborn ones from the brush on a horseback.

"Hey, boss," his foreman said with a tip of his hat.

"Everyone here?"

"Yeah, except for Jeff."

"He won't be joining us."

"Oh?" the man asked with a questioning raise of his eyebrows.

"I fired him this morning." He swung up into the saddle and said, "Enough said. Let's ride, boys."

Several hours later, the sun hung low in the western sky in a spray of orange, reds, yellows, and blues. Sweat trickled down Kale's back and chest as the last of the calves had Bar KD burned into their flesh. A good day's work he figured. A hard day's work, but it felt good.

Two of the hands put the equipment away while several others cleaned up the shoot and got ready to call it quits.

Kale noticed several buzzards circling above the ridge to his left and narrowed his eyes. "Are we missing any cattle?"

"Not that I know of, why?"

"Buzzards," he replied, tipping his chin toward where several of the birds swooped and dove. "I'm gonna ride up and take a look."

Two of the ranch hands agreed to go with him in case they might need to help an injured animal.

His horse took off at a fast clip with only a nudge of his spurs, beguiling the weariness and fatigue surrounded both horse and rider.

Something didn't feel right, but he couldn't quite put his finger on it. It wasn't unusual for them to lose a calf during this time. Those types of things came with ranch life. They weren't terribly far from the main house and although buzzards were very bold birds, they scattered quickly when faced with intruders.

The thunder of pounding hooves scared the birds hovering near the solitary lump. The only thing even remotely close came in the form of the scattered scrub brush so common for this area. A small line shack on the other side of the hill would be the single sign of civilization except for the main ranch house.

Kale dismounted from his horse and tied the reins of the skittish animal to one of the bushes. "Easy boy. What's got you all riled up?" he asked the horse, watching carefully as the animal danced around and snorted even under his usually calming hand.

Seth stepped down from his saddle and secured his horse next to Kale's before moving off toward the pile of whatever they'd come to check out.

"Shit! Uh, Kale? Fuck man," Seth cursed, stumbling back and holding his stomach.

"What is it?"

"It's...it's a woman."

"What? You can't be serious," Kale said, walking to where he could see the form taking shape the closer he got. "Oh, hell. Jesus Christ!" He moved further away and fought the bile threatening to spew all over the ground near his feet.

"Are you fucking serious?" Rick said from his vantage point still atop his horse. "It's like a body?"

"Yeah," Seth replied, moving back near his horse.

Seconds later, Kale heard the distinctive sounds of retching and he fought the urge to follow suit. "Grab the extra blanket from behind my saddle, Rick, so I can cover her."

"Hell, no. I ain't gettin' nowhere near a dead body."

"Get me the fuckin' blanket, man. She's already been through enough from what I can tell. And grab my cell from my saddlebag. I need to get the sheriff out here," Kale snarled, trying to breathe through his nose to keep from puking.

Rick grabbed the things he asked for and sidestepped closer, keeping plenty of distance between him and the woman. He nervously handed the blanket and phone to Kale and then shot like a bullet back to his horse.

"Pussy," Kale grumbled, taking several breaths to calm his stomach before he approached the woman.

Long blonde hair fanned out around her head, but he couldn't tell much else about her. Her face was black and blue with multiple bruises, obliterating her features to almost unrecognizable. The remnants of a pink halter top clung to her waist after it apparently had been ripped from her body and the same scattered bruises covered her upper torso. A miniscule denim skirt bunched around her hips revealed the lack of underwear and the odd angle of her legs told him she'd probably been raped before she was killed. Absently, Kale wondered if he knew her.

"I'm so sorry, darlin'. God, who could have done this to you?" he asked out loud as he covered her and stepped back. Wiping the moisture gathering at the edges of his eyes with his hand, he sniffed and flipped open his cell phone.

* * * *

Two hours later, the place swarmed with police and after he'd answered so many questions he couldn't remember his own name, they released him. The two hands who rode into the mess with him were finally released, too, and the three of them trotted back toward the house together.

"What do you say we hit the bar, Kale?" Seth asked.

"Sure. I could use a beer or two, but I need to shower first. I stink."

The three of them laughed. The same funk clung to their clothes and skin. Cattle mixed with burnt hair, sweat, dirt and sunshine.

"The Saddle Club in, say an hour?"

"Great," Kale replied swinging down from his saddle. "I'll see you guys there."

The other two disappeared as Kale walked his horse toward the barn.

Lights flicked on from the front of the large structure while the sun set behind the hills. Dust flittered through the air when he opened the barn door and led his horse inside. Metal rungs for tethering hung from a post, letting him slip the horse's tack from its body. This gave him the freedom to brush down the horse after a hard day under the saddle. Any cowboy's top priority meant taking care of his horse.

"I bet it'll feel good to get out from under all this stuff, huh, boy."

The gelding nickered softly and hung his head.

"We'll get you fixed up here in a second and leave you some nice feed and soft hay for the night."

After a quick brushing and rub down, he led the animal into the stall and then latched the door behind him. He swiped the Stetson from his head and then wiped the sweat clinging to his brow. Scorching sun had beat down on their heads and their backs all day and he felt every trail of grime and sweat on his body. *A hot shower and a cold beer is what I need right now and maybe a willin' woman.* Weary steps took his equally tired body toward the house. Between the backbreaking work on the ranch and keeping up with his architecture business, it was a wonder he had time for anything else.

A hearty groan spilled from his lips as the pounding jets of the shower relaxed the tight muscles of his back. Within moments, the spraying water trickled over his naked chest and slid down between his legs.

What I wouldn't give for a woman's hands kneading the knots out of my shoulders.

Women came fairly easy to him most days, but lately there hadn't been any worth pursuing past one night in his bed. He had no one to blame but himself. The forced abstinence of his existence made him frown.

Work had become his entire life over the last couple of years and he didn't like it. All of his bed partners lately left him feeling cold and alone.

Marriage? He snorted. After his ex-wife became a lesbian, his manhood shriveled up and hid. How is a man supposed to feel when his wife leaves him for another woman?

Natalie came to mind. The last real relationship he could recall being in was with her and it really wasn't a relationship at all. One night of hot ménage sex two years ago between him, her, and his best friend Cade, had ended real quick when she blurted out her love for Cade. He didn't begrudge his two best friends. They were perfect for each other and now they'd started their own branch of the family tree, but God, he wanted a woman like her—soft, warm, pretty, good-hearted, and caring. She hadn't plucked at his heart strings really, but she had kept his attention for a short time. Come to think of it, none of the women around Red Rock held his attention for long.

Big blue eyes and fiery red hair flashed behind his mind's eye. *Okay. Laurel caught my eye the minute she stomped across the bar. Would all her passion and fire translate into a wild romp between the sheets? Man, what I wouldn't give to find out.*

Kale shook his head and grabbed the bottle of shampoo from the shelf. The almost see-through liquid filled his hand with a splurt before he scrubbed his scalp clean. Bubbles traveled in rivulets down his chest and abdomen until all the soap was gone. Next came the clean, spicy scent of the soap while he scrubbed all the sweat and grime from his body. With all the soap gone, he rinsed a final time and shut off the water.

A few moments later, he walked into his room with a towel wrapped around his hips. Jeans, T-shirt, and long-sleeved western shirt, and he would be ready to hit the bar. The shower did wonders for his achy, weary body, and now he was ready to party.

Maybe Laurel will show up again. "Get over it. She wasn't interested with the proposition in the diner, and she probably wouldn't be interested tonight either."

He stomped his feet into his boots, adjusted his belt around his waist, and slipped on his Stetson. Truck keys in hand, he opened the front door and then close it behind him.

Moonlight slashed across the ground in silvery streaks, lighting his way to the truck sitting off to the left of the house. Within seconds, he was bouncing down the dirt driveway toward the highway.

George Straight's voice crooned over the radio and he remembered the conversation he had with Natalie about their favorite country singers, right here in this truck. His heart ached for the closeness of a woman who would understand him—Kale Dunn, architect, and cowboy.

The lights of the Saddle Club flashed off and on as he got closer. Tons of trucks and cars of every make and model crowded the parking lot and he wondered at first, where he would be able to park until a spot opened up off to the left. He caught sight of a local Red Rock cop car sitting near the back and questioned whether it might be Laurel.

"Stupid. You have no idea what her schedule is or even what department she works in for crying out loud," he grumbled, popping open his door and then slamming it behind him.

"Hey, Kale," a cute blonde woman yelled from two cars over.

"Hi, Mitzi."

"You come to party tonight, hunky man?"

He rolled his eyes and nodded. "For a little while anyway."

"Save me a dance, would ya?"

"Sure, babe. Catch me inside."

The ebb and flow of the music made his ears ring with each person passing through the double doors. He stepped inside and glanced around trying to find the guys only to see them standing near the pool table while a couple of them played.

"Boss," James yelled, waving from his spot next the wall.

Kale stopped the waitress as she wandered by and told her to bring the group another round on him.

"Anything going on?" Kale asked, reaching the group.

"Nah. It's still early though. I'm sure more people will show up soon," James replied. "Someone in particular you're lookin' for?"

"Nope." The waitress arrived with several beer bottles. "Let's relax and have a good time, gentlemen. We worked hard today."

"Hey. We heard about the woman's body y'all found up on the hill," James said.

"Yeah. Not a pretty picture," Kale replied. "The whole thing sucks because now I'm a damned suspect in a fucking murder investigation." A round of affirmative nods and murmurs echoed around the group as each one took a long sip off the beer in their hands.

Kale felt a hand slide across his left butt cheek and then fingers hook into his belt loop. When he turned to find out who was being so bold, he couldn't believe his eyes.

* * * *

"God, I hate patrol. I should be doing detective work, not this shit of rolling around town looking for drunks, fights, and speeders," Laurel grumbled as she took a left at the stop sign. "I'm a homicide detective for crying out loud."

Streetlamps beamed a warm golden glow across the blackness of the pavement. Sweat rolled down her back and between her breasts from the heat of the summer night. Teenage kids hovered near the corners of downtown and she debated on whether to stop and see what they were up to, but then she remember she wasn't in Los Angeles anymore. Red Rock, Montana didn't have the gangs and violence of the west coast. Kids here didn't carry guns unless it was a hunting rifle in the back window of their truck.

Pop. Pop. Pop.

She went on high alert at what sounded like gunfire. The patrol car did a complete one-eighty when she cranked the steering wheel to the left. Her foot hit the gas and she pushed the cruiser to top speed until she reached the corner where the kids had been standing before. All she could think of was one of those teenagers lying bloody in the street.

The corner came into view and the kids stood around in a circle.

Flashing lights and screeching tires brought their attention to her when she careened to a stop near them and jumped out of her car.

"Everyone all right?"

"No," one answered.

"Let me through," she said and the kids parted like the Red Sea.

Sitting on the ground near a low wall covered in kudzu vine was a young man about fifteen holding his hand at the wrist.

"What happened?" she asked, dropping into a squat next to him. A quick once over of his body revealed a wound to his hand.

The boy's face scrunched in pain and she could tell he fought the tears shimmering in his eyes. "Who are you?"

"I'm Officer Hayes. Are you hurt anywhere else?"

"Just my hand."

"What happened?"

"Firecrackers. I didn't let go soon enough."

Laurel grabbed the microphone at her shoulder. "Dispatch, this is car twelve. I need an ambulance at the corner of Mission and Fourth. I've got a kid with burns to his left hand from a firecracker."

Thank God it wasn't gunfire like I originally thought. Firecrackers are one thing. Gunfire usually means someone is dead.

"What's your name son?"

"Matt Weston."

"Well, Matt. It looks like you've got some pretty good burns on your hand, but I'm sure it will heal in no time." She glanced around at the group of teens and narrowed her gaze. "All of you know better than to play with firecrackers, right?"

"Yes, ma'am, but—" one of the others said.

"No, buts. Fireworks are dangerous and your friend here is paying the price for being careless. It could have been worse. He could have lost his hand altogether." The wail of a siren coming closer caught her attention. "The ambulance will take care of you. Want me to call your parents and let them know what's going on?"

"Yeah. You can use my cell phone. It's in the front pocket of my jeans."

"I'll get it," said another friend. The kid dug into Matt's pocket and retrieved the phone. "Here."

Laurel flipped open the phone and found home on the contacts list as the paramedic unit stopped near the curb. "It'll be fine, Matt. Don't worry."

"My mom is going to be so pissed," Matt replied.

The paramedics pulled out their equipment and approached the group. "What have we got officer?"

"This is Matt Weston. He and his friends had some firecrackers and one exploded a little too close to his hand. I'm going to call his parents."

"Thanks," the paramedic said, even while his gaze swept over her from head to toe and a look of interest appeared in his eyes. "You must be new around here."

"Yeah," was her only reply before she stepped to the side and hit talk on the kid's cell phone.

"Hello?"

"Can I speak to the mother or father of Matt Weston please?"

"This is his mother."

"Mrs. Weston, my name is Officer Hayes and I'm here with your son. There's been an accident."

"What? Oh my God! Is he okay? Where?"

"Mrs. Weston, calm down. He's fine, but he's got some burns to the left hand. Some kids were playing with fireworks and one exploded too close. The paramedics are working on him now and they'll be taking him to the emergency room at Red Rock Hospital to be evaluated. You can meet him there."

"Thank you, officer. We'll be there in a few minutes."

The phone clicked in her ear and Laurel pulled it away to stare at it a minute. She shook her head and moved back toward the paramedics, leaving the phone on Matt's abdomen. "His parents will meet you at the hospital."

"Thanks. Officer?" the guy who'd given her the once over asked, hinting for her name.

"Hayes," she supplied. He wasn't bad looking. Short blond hair, green eyes and muscled all in the right places. *Cute.*

"Do you have a first name, Officer Hayes?" he asked.

She hesitated for a moment. "Laurel."

"Nice to meet you, Laurel. I'm Chance Dalton."

"Dalton!" his buddy snapped. "You can do your flirting later. We've got a kid we need to get to the hospital."

"See ya around, Laurel."

"Probably not."

Chance winked and grinned from ear to ear as they lifted the stretcher and wheeled Matt to the ambulance.

Laurel rolled her eyes and headed for the patrol car to do the paperwork. The flashing blue lights were shut off with a flick of the switch as she settled behind the wheel.

The growl of a diesel engine caught her attention. She lifted her head just in time to see a big Chevy truck run a red light.

Tossing the clipboard onto the seat next to her, she turned on her blue lights again and pulled away from the curb. With her foot hard on the pedal, she quickly gained on the truck, waiting until it pulled over to the side of the road. She radioed into dispatch her whereabouts and the situation before she got out of the car.

There appeared to be a man behind the wheel with a black cowboy hat on. *Not like every man in the area doesn't wear a hat around here.*

Stepping up to the driver's side door, she tapped on the window and indicated for the man to roll the window down.

"Do you know why I pulled you over, sir?"

"Laurel?"

She looked into the cab of the truck and sighed. "Mr. Dunn." *Great. Running into Kale like this, isn't going to be good.* "Can I see your license and registration please?"

Kale shut the truck off and popped the driver's side door.

"Stay in your vehicle, Mr. Dunn."

"Come on, Laurel. It's me, Kale. What's the problem?"

"I know who you are, but I'm also on duty. I need your license and registration," she replied, stepping back and dropping her palm on the butt of the gun at her hip.

"Fine," he growled, leaning over to the glove compartment and pulling out some papers. Next came his wallet from his back pocket. "Here."

"I'll be right back." She walked back to the cruiser, arguing with herself over calling in his information. She really didn't know anything about him at all other than he owned a good size ranch outside of town and he had the most delicious mouth she'd ever seen on a man—a mouth she'd fantasized about half the night.

Procedure said she had to call it in. "Dispatch. Run this license plate please." After she called off the numbers, she waited for the results to come as she watched Kale tap his fingers on the edge of the driver's side window. Long and lean, those fingers could do wonderful things to her body if she'd take him up on his offer. *I bet the calluses I felt last night, would feel really nice on my skin.*

"Car twelve?"

"Go ahead dispatch."

"License clear. Belongs to Kale Anthony Dunn." The dispatcher went on to rattle off his address which matched his driver's license and Laurel tuned out the rest of the information while she checked out his height, weight, eye color and birth date. *Mmm. Thirty-two, huh. With a birthday coming up. Interesting.* A pause in the dispatcher's voice brought her attention back to the situation at hand. "Ten-four."

She grabbed her ticket book, opened her door, and walked toward his truck.

"Are you really going to give me a ticket, Laurel?" he asked, pushing the door open and hooking his boots on the running board.

"You ran the light, Kale."

"I didn't see it."

"Likely excuse. Not like I haven't heard that one at least a hundred times," she replied, scratching out the information on the paper she had over the top of the ticket. "It's Saturday night and there are several teenagers running around town. You could have easily T-boned someone at the intersection. Where are you headed in such a hurry?"

"Home."

"Alone?" The question spilled from her mouth before she could stop it and she mentally kicked herself for asking.

One eyebrow shot up and a wicked grin spread across his mouth. "Yes, alone. Care to join me?"

"I'm on duty."

"What time do you get off?"

"Seven in the morning."

"Well damn."

She handed him the folded piece of paper. "I'm letting you off with a warning. Next time, be more careful." Before he could read the paper, she spun on her heel and retreated to her car.

After she got behind the wheel, she risked a glance at the back of his truck only to see him adjust his side mirror so she could see his face. He tipped his hat and blew her a kiss. The piece of paper she'd given him flashed in the mirror, clearly showing where she'd written her phone number in big bold letters with a pair of lips hanging from the five at the end.

3

"What a sassy red-head," Kale said out loud after he pulled away from the curb. A hearty chuckle left his mouth as he continued down the road toward his place with thoughts of getting her naked and panting beneath him came to mind. "Oh, yeah. Soon, all that fiery temper and smart mouth will be begging and calling my name when she comes around me." He glanced at the paper with her number on it lying on the seat next to him and smiled. "And here I thought going home alone again tonight sucked after I ran into Natalie and Cade at the bar. Leave it to Natalie to run her hand over my ass right there in the bar in front of her husband and everyone."

It had been fantastic to see them out and about. Since their son was born a few months ago, he knew they hadn't been able to have much alone time.

After she'd goosed his butt, he got them into one of the empty booths and they chatted for a while about the baby, their house, what he'd been up to and his lack of female companionship. Naturally, Natalie started in with the matchmaking thing again. God love her, but she needed to leave well enough alone.

"You need a woman, Kale."

"No, I don't, Nat."

"Yes, you do. A nice girl to come home to after you've been out working on the ranch all day. A home-cooked meal, a few kids running around your big house. A son you can teach to do all those things you do with the cattle and horses." Natalie had gone on and on about a friend of hers and then another friend while he leaned back in the booth and rested his arm across the back of the vinyl. Cade held her hand while she continued to talk, but would shoot him a "be patient" grin every few minutes. Kale had come to the conclusion his buddy was pussy-whipped.

Kale shook his head when his attention returned to the road in front of him. "I can't see Red being the nice girl to come home to. Staying home cooking and cleaning didn't fit her personality. If Natalie gets wind of my interest in Laurel, I'd never live it down." He glanced at Laurel's number again on the seat. When she'd slipped the piece of paper toward him and walked away all kind of thoughts raced across his mind. After he had opened it and realized it held her number and an open invitation to call her, his thoughts went haywire. Hot sweaty sex, his lips dancing over her exquisitely soft skin, his fingers trailing over her mound and dipping between her pussy lips to find her drenched and ready for him, all came into sharp focus. His cock ached for her kind of lovin'.

"All right. Thinking about her right now is bad unless I want to go home and jack off with her on my mind again."

The long dirt driveway to his house came into view. The two story ranch style house, with its wraparound porch was home. He thanked his lucky stars every day for his ex-wife's hatred of the place. It kept her from taking it in their divorce.

He parked his truck to the left side and climbed out of the cab. The dry hot air of the Montana night washed across his skin and ruffled the slight curl of his hair near his neck. The inky blackness of the sky gave him the perfect view of the stars. Nothing could compare to the Montana sky at night. One lone shooting star zipped across the black canvas and disappeared into the dark horizon. Coyotes yipped in the distance. Cattle bawled to each other in an answering call to their young. Winter would be upon them before they knew it and the long days of checking cattle, making sure they had feed and keeping the water from icing over, stretched into oblivion. Snow season here meant more work.

Why the hell did I ever decide to be a rancher? "Because it's in your blood and your heart," he said knowing the answer before he had even thought the question. He'd tried to do something different when he went off to college and got a degree in architecture, but the wide open plains and the jagged mountain ranges, called him home shortly after graduation. The hopes and dreams of a young married man with his beautiful wife in tow, rested in the pastures of his home.

The moment Judy saw the place, she despised it. He managed to convince her to give it a shot for a year, hoping she would fall in love with the house and the land. She hadn't. The only good thing to come of her move to Montana, in her eyes, came from her friendship and subsequent love affair with Cade's wife, Cynthia.

Kale walked inside the house and shut the door behind him. Silence met his ears. The same silence crept in on him every night of every day of the week and he hated it. He stopped at the stereo system against the wall and flipped on the radio. Any noise would do right now.

"I should have taken the brunette at the bar up on her offer to go home with me. I'd rather it be Laurel here, but hell, this alone shit is gettin' old," he grumbled moving toward the kitchen for a beer from the fridge. "At least I would be getting laid right now instead of sittin' here drinking alone." With a twist of his wrist, he popped off the cap and tipped the bottle to his lips. Cold, malty liquid slid down his throat and quenched the dryness.

He took a seat on the leather couch, grabbed the remote, and flipped on the television. Channel after channel yielded nothing but old movies, news, or boring sitcoms. The radio in the background wanted to play country tunes about being alone or losing the one you loved.

Kale toed off his boots and stretched out on the couch. A crinkling sound caught his attention and he pulled the folded piece of paper out of his pocket. Staring at the bold numbers and the pair of lips dangling from the five, he wondered if it was her home number or her cell. He smiled and ran his thumb over the drawing, thinking about her tempting full lips, her sparkling blue eyes and the full head of red hair cascading down her back like it was at the bar the other night. It wasn't flaming red or orange like some red-heads he'd seen. Nope. Laurel's hair looked soft and alive with every movement she made—every strand caught the light and reflected it back in a brilliance of strawberry and gold. His fingers itched like crazy to run through her tresses and wrap his hands in them while she sucked his cock deep into her mouth.

Unable to stop himself, he grabbed his cell and dialed the number.

"Hello?" The sleepy murmur coming over the phone didn't sound like Laurel at all.

"I'm sorry. I think I have the wrong number," he said and hit end. "Well that was pretty stupid, you dumbass. You obviously woke up someone in her house." The clock on his cell phone read two-thirty. "Shit. It's fucking two in the morning. No wonder whoever answered was sleeping. Well no use sittin' here gettin' all worked up." He stood, shut off the television and stereo, and quickly finished his beer before walking up the stairs to his bedroom.

* * * *

The bong of the doorbell brought Kale upright in bed with a confused blink. "Who in the hell is at the door at—" He glanced at the clock on the nightstand. "At seven fucking thirty on a Sunday?"

He grumbled and cussed some more, while he tugged on a pair of sweatpants and stumbled down the stairs as the bell went off again.

"Yeah. I'm comin'." He yanked open the door and growled, "What?"

Blue police uniform and red hair caught his attention moments before she turned around and slid her sunglasses down her nose with one finger. "I-uh. I'm sorry, Kale, but I realized after I stopped you last night, I still had your driver's license." Her gaze swept over him from head to toe and interest sparkled in the blue depths. "Did I wake you?"

"Uh, yeah."

"I was on my way home and I figured I'd drop this off." She had his driver's license sandwiched between two fingers.

He hadn't even noticed the missing license last night. Once she'd handed him her phone number and waltzed back to her car, his mind hadn't been on the missing license or registration. Her tight ass, those blue pants, and whether she'd let him use her handcuffs on the bed's headboard cluttered his mind all the way to the ranch.

"Care for some coffee now that I'm awake?" he asked, taking the piece of plastic from her fingers after he pushed the screen open.

"If you're sure I'm not keeping you up," she said, sweeping through the doorway.

The scent of lemon followed her into the house and his thoughts drifted to her last words. *Keeping me up isn't a problem, darlin'.*

He walked behind her toward the kitchen. "The coffee will be ready in a few minutes. How did the rest of your shift go?"

"Good. Not much trouble at all."

"Nothin' like Los Angeles, I imagine."

"Not even close. Most shifts, I worked at least one homicide a day out there. Here it's traffic stops, kids with firecrackers, a cow loose on Rancher John's property—you know." She shrugged.

"I bet Red Rock is kind of boring for you then," he replied, hitting the start button on the coffee maker and returning to the living room.

The open floor plan of the house kept things flowing between the rooms, making it much easier to keep up the conversation.

"No, not really. It's kinda nice actually," she said from the spot she'd taken up near the bay window. "You've got a beautiful view from here. Is all of the pasture back there your land?"

"Yes," he murmured near her ear.

She spun around to face him, startled by the closeness of his voice. Her gaze swept from his eyes, over his bare torso and down his abdomen. No way she could miss the morning wood he sported. The moment he'd opened the door to find her standing on his porch, his dick jumped to attention in a full raging hard-on.

"Let me go throw a T-shirt on," he said, stepping back, hoping the distance would give him a little breathing room.

"Don't get dressed on my account," she replied in a breathless whisper as she moved close and tipped her head back.

The strawberry pink of her lips parted and her eyes sparkled in the bright morning light. Her fingertips seared the skin of his chest like a hot branding iron.

"Laurel," he murmured. "You're playin' with fire, darlin'."

Lips brushed his chest and he stifled a groan. "I need the heat, Kale. It's been a long time for me."

He wrapped his hand in her long, red hair and tugged her close so he could pull her mouth to his. The touch of her lips burned him clear to the center of his soul. Tongues mated and danced, from her mouth to his and back. She tasted of peppermint, chocolate, and woman. The rough material of her uniform rubbed over his skin, abrading his nipples, and bringing them to aching points. Both of her hands went up around his shoulders and behind his neck as she angled her mouth against his and swallowed the moan he released. The twin shirttails slid from her waistband with a tug of his fingers. The need to feel her skin—every inch of the creamy flesh he'd seen the other day—drove him past rational thought. His lips left hers to blaze a trail over her cheek to the tempting flesh of her ear. He nibbled and licked as his fingers worked the buttons of her shirt until it parted under his hands.

"So soft," he murmured, trailing his tongue down her neck. Sharp, short pants rasped through the air when he lifted his mouth from her skin.

The shirt fell to the floor at their feet followed quickly by her bra. Gorgeous, rosy nipples met his gaze. Full breasts—just enough to fill his hands, took his breath away. "Damn you're gorgeous, honey."

The buckle at her waist clinked and rattled when he unfastened it. Fortunately, she left her heavy belt, gun and assorted cop paraphernalia in the car.

"Let me," she murmured, jerking the belt until it fell loose at her waist and her pants dropped to the floor.

Black lace panties caught his eye and he smiled. "Nice."

"Not my usual work attire. You got lucky."

"Lucky is my middle name where you're concerned, darlin'." The thumb on each hand slipped beneath the edges of that sexy underwear and peeled them down her hips. They pooled with the growing pile of her clothes.

"Lord have mercy. You are a sight for sore eyes, honey." His lips trailed across her chest, stopped to suck a pert nipple between his lips, and continued down her flat abdomen until his nose stopped at her pubic bone. "Open." Her thighs quivered under his hands when she spread her legs. "Lean back on the arm of the chair behind you." Pink, blood engorged pussy lips met his gaze, driving him insane with the need to taste her.

Juices glistened on the outer aspect of the treasure he sought. The scent of her arousal surrounded him as he inhaled and rubbed his whiskered cheek over her inner thigh, knowing he would be leaving whisker burn on spots he hoped he'd see again. He slipped her legs over his shoulders and braced his hands on her hips. One swipe of his tongue on her clit and more thick cream spilled from her pussy as a desperate moan left her lips.

"Do that again," she murmured.

He glanced up to see her head thrown back, glossy red hair spilling down, and her eyes closed in rapture.

"My pleasure." He hummed against the hood covering her clit and then nipped at the skin.

Stiffening his tongue, he dipped between her outer pussy lips to dive into the soaking channel of her sex and then slipped up and over her clit. Several swipes of his tongue and she trembled like a leaf in a tornado. Her whole body shook, revealing her need for him whether she would admit it or.

"Oh, God," she whispered.

He did it over and over until endless whimpers spilled from her mouth and her thighs clamped around his ears. Faster, he worked his tongue until concentrating only on her clit and she came apart with a scream of his name. Thick cream coated his tongue while he continued to stroke her until the very last spasm calmed.

"Wow."

The slow glide of his tongue over the inside of her leg made her whimper, so he did it again.

"Kale."

"Hmm?" he murmured against her skin as he looked up into those amazing blue eyes.

"I need more."

"More?"

"Yeah. More of you," she replied, pushing him back and bringing her legs together. "My turn. Get rid of those sweats."

"Yes, ma'am," he said with a smile as he stood. A low whoosh of material was the only sound outside of rapid breathing and pounding hearts.

"Oh, my," she whispered, wrapping her hand around his girth. "Is this all for me?"

"All yours, darlin'. I've been dying to get inside you."

She dropped to her knees, grasped his butt cheeks in hers hands and encircled the head of his cock with her lips.

"Holy fuck, Laurel. God, that's good," he groaned.

"Mmm."

The vibrations of her hum sent tingles from the tip of his dick to the crack of his ass and back. Her mouth opened and she swept the entire length between her lips until he felt the back of her throat. The slick, wet heat had white hot need racing down his spine to center in his balls. He wrapped both hands in her hair and kneaded her scalp with his fingers while she sucked. Each pull of her mouth had him on edge. The ebb and flow of her lips and tongue drew his need to an explosive peak until he forced her to stop, giving him time to focus and push his climax back down to bearable before he came in her mouth.

"I want to come in your hot, wet pussy, honey," he said, forcing her to stand.

"You didn't like it?"

"Hell yeah, I liked it, but I'd rather be inside you when I blow."

Her bottom lip disappeared between her teeth and she stared at the floor a second and then peeked at him through her lashes. "You do have a condom, right? Because I didn't think to bring one. This wasn't exactly planned."

He snapped his fingers and said, "I'll be right back. They're in the bedroom."

"Want me to follow?" she asked, flipping one of those luscious, long red strands over her shoulder.

"If you'd like, but I'm thinkin' I want you bent over the chair with your pretty ass in the air."

Blue eyes sparkled with mischief. "A little dominant are we?"

"We'll have to do this more than once for you to find out," he replied before he disappeared up the stairs, moving at top speed for a man with a raging hard-on. Within moments he'd grabbed a condom from his nightstand, slipped it on with a tortured groan, and headed back downstairs.

She leaned against the leather chair with her feet crossed at the ankles, staring out the window at the sun while it made its path across the morning sky. The same golden light reflected off the waves of red flowing over her shoulders and it made him stop and stare for a moment.

The smile on her lips when she turned to face him snapped him out of his reverie and forced his feet to move again.

Once he stood in front of her, she ran her hands over his chest and said, "Damn, aren't you a sight. All muscles and ridges, bulges and hardness all rolled up into one."

"I could eat you up, lady."

"Do it then, cowboy."

Their mouths met and fused. Hearty moans filled the air again as their tongues dueled and sparred while his hands danced over her flesh. Soft yet tough. The enigma of Laurel flashed through his mind, but he pushed it away. Now wasn't the time to try to figure her out. Now was the time for him to love her and make her his, even if only for one day.

Dragging his mouth from hers, he skimmed over her cheek, down her chest and sucked her left nipple into his mouth. Soft whimpers escaped her lips and she wrapped her legs around the back of his, drawing him closer. His right hand found her other nipple and rolled it between his thumb and first finger. The whimpers grew louder. He flicked her tight bud with his tongue and circled it with the tip to drive her desire higher. The whimpers turned to moans and a shifting of her ass on the arm of the chair.

Letting his right hand slipped down her abdomen, he trailed his fingers through the dampness between her thighs and drove two fingers knuckle deep into her pussy. Tremors raced down her body with each stroke.

"Kale, please," she pleaded.

He removed his fingers much to her dislike from the groans spilling from her lips, but it turned into a sigh when he eased the head of his cock into her heat.

"You feel incredible." He moaned, grasping her hips with both hands.

She nipped at his chest with her teeth then soothed the bite with a kiss. The rough pad of her wet tongue over his nipple sent his hips rocking, and he found himself totally engulfed inside her.

"Oh, yes. Perfect," she purred. "Now rock them hips, cowboy. Ride me hard."

Unable to stop the careening of their lovemaking, he slammed his pelvis against hers as she wrapped her feet behind him and panted. "Yes, yes, yes." Her pussy quivered around him with each thrust, sucking him in and leading him to the edge with her. She shattered in her climax with his name on her lips, shoving him into the endless abyss of sexual gratification right along with her.

Their breathing slowed and the air-conditioning sent goose bumps flittering along her arms. They both groaned when he pulled his semi-erect cock from her warmth.

"Stay for a while, Laurel."

"I can't, Kale," she said, dropping her legs to the floor and looking from side to side. "I have to get home." She grabbed her clothes and slipped on her sexy underwear and then her bra.

"Why? I can show you the inside of my shower. My big bed upstairs. And maybe a few more interesting positions I know." He trailed his fingers down her arm and watched in fascination as the goose bumps returned.

"I spent all night on duty. I need to sleep for a few hours."

"You can sleep here and I can wake you later for a few more rounds of wild sex. Do you have to work tonight?"

"No, but—"

"Then stay with me today. I'd like to show you my place."

She yanked on her shirt and buttoned the front. "I'm not a cowgirl, Kale. I've never ridden a horse. I don't know anything about ranches. I hate blowing dirt and dust." She tucked her shirt in her trousers. "I don't like cows except on a plate."

"Do you like endless blue skies?" He tucked a curl of her hair behind her ear. "Water so clear, you can see the bottom of the deepest pool?" He trailed his fingers over her cheekbone and lost himself a little in her eyes. "Soft fur across your palm?" The need to feel her lips under his drove him to kiss her softly. "Stay, Laurel," he whispered against her lips.

"I can't," she murmured without opening her eyes. "I have a child at home who needs her mother."

* * * *

Laurel slowly opened her eyes waiting for the reaction she knew would be there. The shock, the realization she had a child, the disappointment and finally the shut down, but it never came and nothing could have surprised her more than the open acceptance in Kale's face.

"Does she look like you?"

"Well, I...uh...mmm," she stammered. "No, actually. She looks more like her father than me." Her gaze swept down his still buck-ass naked form. "You probably should get rid of the condom and put your clothes back on."

Moving toward a small bathroom off the kitchen, he disappeared for a moment and she contemplated leaving. *That would probably be really rude. I mean, we did just have wild sex.*

Within moments, he walked back out with his sweatpants firmly in place. Grabbing two mugs from the cupboard over the sink, he poured the coffee and asked, "Cream or sugar?"

"Both."

"Sit for a bit and let's talk," he said, nodding to the chairs at the dining room table. "I'd like to get to know you a little."

Great! He's an after sex talker.

"Not much to tell, Kale. You already know most of it."

"I don't, really. All I know is you moved here a few weeks ago from Los Angeles in a plea from your sister because her husband is beating on her." He set the cups on the table and pushed one toward her. "You're a cop."

"Homicide detective."

"Excuse me, homicide detective and street patrolwoman here since we rarely have homicides." His cute butt met the soft chair across from her. "I now know you have a daughter. How old is she?"

"Three."

"Were you married?"

"No," she replied, pressing her lips together. He didn't need all the juicy details of her affair with Dennis and his death. She sipped some of the hot liquid hoping to forestall any more questions.

"Where were you born and raised?"

"Listen, Kale, I'd love to sit here and shoot the shit with you, but I really need to get home." She stood and flipped her hair over her shoulder. "Thanks for everything and I guess I'll see you around."

"Thanks for everything?" he repeated with a raised eyebrow.

Oh shit.

"Yeah. I mean—"

"Don't bother, Laurel." Both eyebrows now dipped between his eyes as a frown clouded his face. "I'm glad I could accommodate your sexual needs this morning and thanks for bringing my license by. I could have gotten in real trouble from a *cop* for not having it on me." He headed for the front door and whipped it open with a growl. "See you around."

It slammed behind her, hard enough to rattle the glass panes. A weary sigh left her lips as she walked toward her car. *Man, I really screwed that up. I should apologize. I hadn't planned on coming here and having sex with the man.*

"Right. You didn't purposely keep his driver's license last night after you stopped him so you could see him again," she argued with herself. "Yeah, well, maybe. But I didn't plan on having sex with him. If he hadn't shown up at the door wearing nothing more than a pair of sweatpants, I wouldn't have been tempted beyond control to fuck the man."

The door opened with a tug on the handle. She slipped inside and pulled it close with a resounding *bang*. Her forehead met the steering wheel and for a split second, she thought about beating her head against the hard plastic. With a heavy sigh, she lifted her head and thrust the key into the ignition, starting the car.

Silence and guilt rode her hard on the way back to her apartment.

Meaningless sex wasn't on the top of her list of things to do on a regular basis even if it had been a very long time. Fortunately for her, Kale knew exactly how to make her body sing for his without any guidance from her except a whimper or a moan. *The man is good, I'll give him that.* It had been ages since a man made her come with his mouth. Not since Dennis.

Thinking about Kimmy's father would be a really bad thing right about now, but she couldn't stop it when her mind wandered back to the day of his funeral. They'd had plans for dinner later in the evening and her heart burst with love for him. That night she'd planned to tell him those three little words she had never before uttered to any man, but she never got the chance.

Her company issued blue police uniform hid the bandage on her arm from her own bullet wound and her badge held the black ribbon in memory of a fallen comrade. Unable to participate in the service itself, the emptiness and loss almost consumed her.

His parents would be there and maybe his two brothers and she wanted to make a good impression on his family. Dennis hadn't introduced her to any of them yet, but she knew she would have to make their acquaintance today. They needed to know how sorry she was for her part in his death. Grief, anger, guilt and pity played a huge part in her need for closure.

The group stood near his coffin, surrounded by officers from the police force. Soft whimpers and hiccups of women crying caught Laurel's attention and tears pooled in her own eyes.

Laurel approached the casket, steeling herself to see the man she loved with all her heart, lying inside. Her knees almost buckled when she saw his face.

It's not Dennis. It can't be. He looks so pale—so lifeless.

Tears streaked down her cheeks and she gripped the edges of the coffin for a moment. She wanted to touch him, but she couldn't bring herself to brush her fingers over his skin. The white rose she clutched in her fingers would have to do as she laid it over his chest and said her goodbyes.

When she turned to face his family, she pulled her shoulders back and moved toward them.

"Mr. and Mrs. Morgan. I'm truly sorry for your loss."

"Thank you. Did you work with Dennis?" his mother asked.

"Yes, ma'am. I'm Laurel Hayes."

The elderly couple looked at each other and then back to her. "Laurel?" his father asked.

"Yes, sir. I know we've never met, but I was very close to Dennis. I'm sure he's mentioned me a time or two."

"Actually, no he hadn't," his father snapped. "We didn't know about you until two days ago when we were going through his papers."

Taken aback by his father's irritated tone, she said, "Well, I'm sure he had intentions of us meeting. We had been seeing each other for several months and had grown quite close."

His father said, "There is someone you should meet, Laurel." He stepped back and indicated another young woman sitting in the chair behind where they stood. "This is Anita. Mrs. Dennis Morgan."

"Wha—" The words trailed off as her gaze darted back and forth between his parents and the woman silently weeping in the chair. "Mrs. Dennis Morgan?"

"His wife."

Spots appeared before her eyes and her whole body flushed. Sweat popped out on her forehead and passing out seemed to be a real possibility at the moment. One of her police buddies rushed to her side and slid his arm around her waist. "His wife? He's married?"

The young woman stood and moved toward her. Laurel took a tentative step back.

"I'm sorry, Laurel. Dennis and I were having problems. I knew he'd found someone else although he never mentioned you by name. We didn't know about your existence until we went through his journal."

"Oh, my God," Laurel whispered. "I have...I have to go."

She'd rushed out of the funeral without a backward glance, tears streaming down her cheeks at his betrayal, the loss of his love and the untold truths hovering between them.

The unborn life snuggled in her womb would never know his or her father, nor would they know his parents. Love blossomed in her heart for the baby she carried, but she would protect Dennis' child with her very last breath and she knew that meant keeping it hidden from his family.

Laurel stopped the car and sighed. The memories of those days right after Dennis' funeral were the hardest for her to bear. Once the little life inside her began to kick and her abdomen started to expand, her life changed. Kimberly became everything to her. She ate, drank, slept and breathed her daughter—never giving into the needs of her own. In fact, Kale was the first man in over three years to make her feel like a woman again—a woman with desires.

"Enough feeling sorry for myself. I screwed up with Kale and I'll have to find some way to make it right. I really could use a friend in this town besides the few neighbors living next door." When she reached the door to her apartment, she unlocked it and pushed it open silently.

"Mommy!" Kimberly yelled, rushing into her arms.

"Hey baby girl. You're up early."

"You're late," Teresa said with a smile.

"I know. I'm sorry. I had an errand to run before I came home."

One of Teresa's eyebrows rose in question and Laurel felt heat crawl up her chest, across her neck and infuse her face.

Teresa stepped close and sniffed.

Shit.

She tried to discretely inhale the scent on her shirt. Sure enough, Kale's cologne clung to her uniform shirt—a mixture of something spicy and all male.

"You smell good, Mommy."

"Did you eat breakfast?" Laurel asked, trying to take to the attention off the smell.

"She just sat down before you came in. I made coffee if you'd like some," Teresa answered, taking Kimberly from her arms. "Why don't you shower and change and I'll keep her occupied with breakfast until you're done."

"You are a saint," she replied. "I'll be back in a few minutes."

"Do you need me to watch her for a few hours while you get some rest?"

"Would you? I hate to ask. You've been so kind to watch her for me, but I'm really beat. I could use a couple of hours of sleep this morning so I can keep up with her this afternoon."

"Of course, Laurel. You know I'll help you any way I can. What you are doing for your sister is more than you should have to. I know you want to drag that no-good husband of hers out and beat the tar out of him, but she won't let you."

"I wish she would leave him."

"It's not so easy when you're on the receiving end of the fist."

"Have you been in an abusive relationship, Teresa?"

"Yes."

"I'm sorry. I don't mean to pry," Laurel replied. "I'll be back in a few minutes."

"Take your time, honey. We'll talk after your nap."

Laurel nodded with a weary sigh. The night had started to catch up with her. No sleep yesterday, before she went to work, the long boring night of patrol except for stopping Kale and the kid with the firecracker, a rousing bout of sex with Kale and not going to bed yet, equaled exhaustion. *Why does it all come back to him?*

Hot, steamy water quickly fogged up the mirror when she turned on the shower. She stripped off her uniform, but brought the shirt to her nose for a moment and then kicked herself for her whimsical behavior.

"Get over it, Laurel. He might be good for some raunchy sex now and again, but nothing else. You aren't here in the middle of nowhere Montana to hook up with some hot-ass cowboy, even if he's the next best thing to peanut butter toast. Besides, who says he's interested in anything beyond sex?" she asked herself as she stepped into the stream. "I'm certainly not."

The soothing pound of the stream against her head and down her shoulders eased the tight muscles and the racing thoughts of Kale she tried hard to ignore.

She quickly soaped her body and rinsed away the bubbles. The skin between her thighs felt tender from sex with Kale when she ran the washcloth down there. "It has been a long time."

With a twist of her wrist, the shower shut off and she grabbed the dark blue towel hanging from the bar. Rough polyester material scrapped along her flesh as she dried herself and then slipped on an old T-shirt and clean underwear. She grabbed her brush and once it made passed through her hair without tangling, she set it back down and walked into her bedroom. The queen-sized bed looked like heaven on a cloud. She couldn't remember being so tired. The clock on the bedside table read nine in big, red numbers. *I should be able to sleep a few hours. Thank God for Teresa.* Laurel set the alarm for noon, snuggled down beneath the sheet and comforter and was asleep before her head hit the pillow.

* * * *

The steady *beep, beep, beep* of her alarm clock pulled her from one of the sexiest dreams she'd had in a while and of course, it involved the one man she thought might be more than she could handle—Kale.

She groaned softly, smacked the alarm clock to shut off the annoying sound and hauled herself upright in the bed. Her long red hair fell forward, covering her face as she dropped her chin toward her chest to loosen the tight muscles of her neck. Four hours wasn't enough, but it would have to do today. Kimmy needed her.

Thank God, she had a couple of days off.

A timid knock on her bedroom door announced the arrival of her daughter.

"Come on in, baby girl. I'm up."

The door flew up and her bouncing, blonde-headed bundle of energy jumped on the bed and pounced next to her.

"You wake?"

"Yeah. Where's Teresa?"

"In livin' room."

"Have you had lunch?"

"Yes, she has," Teresa answered from the doorway. "I'm sure you didn't get enough sleep and I wish I didn't have an appointment this afternoon or I would watch her longer."

Laurel brushed the curls from Kimmy's forehead and kissed her. Kimberly leapt into her arms when she stood and opened them. "It's fine. I'm thankful for what I got. I'll be able to sleep tonight since I'm off a few days."

"I need to get going. I made some fresh coffee in the kitchen. I'll see you later," Teresa said.

"All right. Thanks again."

"No problem. You behave yourself, Kimmy."

"Bye, Resa." One chubby hand waved at their friend.

"What shall we do today, baby girl, huh?"

"Park."

"You want to go to the park for a while?"

Kimberly's blonde tresses bounced when she nodded and a huge smile lit up her face, showing off her dimples to perfection.

"Okay. Let me get dressed, have a little coffee and then we'll go." She walked with Kimmy on her hip into her daughter's bedroom and set her on the floor. "You play with your babies for a little bit while I wake up."

"You wake, Mommy," her daughter responded with her hands on her hips.

"Not really," Laurel whispered and ruffled Kimberly's hair. She headed back into the bedroom for jeans, socks and shoes and then to the kitchen and the fortifying brew waiting. Moments later, she sank down on the couch and sipped the hot liquid. "Nectar of the gods."

Flashes of her dream zipped across her mind and she moaned softly. The whole thing had started with her standing in the middle of what appeared to be a huge barn. Her naked form gleamed in the florescent lighting of the arena. Both hands were shackled in her handcuffs behind her back. Desire rushed in her ears. She didn't know how she'd gotten there, but she knew Kale was close by. She could feel him.

Moments later, she felt his hot breath on the back of her neck.

"Kale," she whispered and shivered.

"You're so beautiful like this, Laurel. You want a man who will take control sometimes, don't you."

"No."

"Liar," he murmured, brushing his lips against her shoulder. "You're hair is like fire. So alive." His fingers tangled in the tresses and tugged her head to the side, baring her neck for his touch.

The moan bubbling from her lips echoed in the large room.

Both of his hands cupped her breasts from behind and she arched her back. "I love how responsive you are to my touch."

"Open these cuffs, Kale."

"Nope."

"I want my hands on you."

"This is my party, Laurel."

He moved around to the front of her and she could finally see his face. His chocolate brown eyes glittered in the light overhead. The dark hair on his head begged for her fingers to smooth it back into place. Her palms itched to smooth over the rugged plains of his chest.

"On your knees, darlin'."

Soft dirt cradled her as she dropped in front of him. The scent of his arousal met her nose when she inhaled. Need seeped from her pussy to coat her lips in preparation for him to fuck her.

The belt buckle at his waist tinkled in the silence surrounding them when he unbuckled it. Two fingers slipped the button on his jeans loose and then pulled the zipper down.

She licked her lips as her mouth watered.

Denim pooled at his ankles and included his boxer briefs amongst the clothing. His cock curled against his abdomen, bobbing like it was begging her to taste.

"Suck me, honey. I want to feel the back of your throat and I want to see your sassy mouth filled with me."

A whimper spilled from somewhere deep inside her.

His hands wrapped in her hair, urging her to take him with minuscule pressure on her scalp. She took him inside her mouth, wrapping her tongue around him while he moaned above her.

"God, honey," he whispered.

Her head bobbed several times, up and down, as she sucked. She'd rather wrap her hand around him or caress his balls, but the taste and feel of him in her mouth made her wet and needy. His controlling her movements by applying pressure to her scalp had her on the verge of coming.

"Mommy?"

Her eyes popped open with the pressure of Kimberly's hands on her legs and heat flushed her cheeks with the vivid picture of her dream tickling the back of her mind. *I need to get the disturbingly handsome cowboy out of my thoughts.*

"Sorry, baby. Are you ready to go to the park?"

"Yes."

She sighed and set the coffee cup on the table. Hopefully, this trip to the park will wear Kimmy out. "Get your shoes." After Kimberly raced down the hall, Laurel slipped on her own shoes and socks.

"Let me grab my keys, sweetie," she said when Kimberly came barreling out of her room with her shoes on the wrong feet. "Wait. We need to fix those sneakers, pumpkin."

Once her daughter's shoes were on right, she grabbed her purse, keys and a hat for both of them. Her skin freckled while Kimberly's burned in the sunshine.

The park sat only a few blocks from her apartment and the walk would do her good. The cobwebs from her dream and subsequent regression on the couch, still lingered beneath the surface and she prayed the walk would help.

Her daughter skipped along beside her as they stayed on the cement sidewalks and watched the cars and trucks zip past. The day had grown warmer from early this morning. The sun beat down on her head, heating her scalp even though she wore a hat, sending sweat trickling down her back from under her hair. Red Rock boasted a smaller population and very little in the way of excitement for the locals. Laurel kind of like the hometown atmosphere and the laidback feel. Los Angeles had been a hell hole and one she was glad she didn't have to raise Kimberly in.

What the hell? I'm not planning on put down roots in this little town.

I'm here for Elizabeth and nothing more. Red Rock, Montana is not my choice of permanent homestead.

They reached the park and Kimberly ran to the jungle gym while she took a seat on the bench to watch. Several children rushed in and out of the apparatus, sliding down the slides, crawling across the monkey bars and laughing while they played. Three women sat at a picnic table not far away. Their conversation got plenty loud enough and Laurel could hear every word.

"What's the latest gossip, Julie?" the dark-haired woman asked her friend. "You always seemed to know exactly what's going on in this town."

"Let's see. Did you hear about the woman who decked Jeff Cox the other night at the Saddle Club?"

"A woman hit Jeff? I hadn't heard about that, but I'm sure he deserved it. He's had a heavy hand for a long time. I've seen his wife sporting bruises where there shouldn't be, even if they get into a little rough sex," a pretty blonde said as she played with the straw in her cup.

The rough, annoying squeaking sound grated on Laurel's nerves when the girl pushed the straw in and out of the lid.

"Well, the woman took him to the ground with one punch. I've heard she's the new cop in town."

Laurel pulled the cap down on her forehead to shield her face. Having any of these women recognize her would be a bad thing right about now. A reputation as being a badass cop in a little town like this wouldn't help matters with her sister. Elizabeth would take the brunt of gossip and stares more than she already had to.

"And Kale Dunn got into the middle of the fray," the last woman added.

She tilted her head and listened closer when his name spilled into the conversation.

"Kale? Why him?"

"Jeff used to work for him."

"Used to?"

"He got fired right then and there."

"Wow, but I'm not really surprised. Kale is the type of man who stands up for a woman. Remember a couple of years ago when he and Cade Weston were both dating Natalie?"

"Oh yeah. I heard there was some interesting stuff going on between the three of them."

"Like?"

Laurel saw the apparent leader of the group look around her and then lower her voice, but she could still hear every word.

"A threesome."

"Threesome?" one of the others squeaked.

"Keep your voice down, Missy," the blonde snapped. "She's talking about the two men and Natalie having sex. Together. At the same time."

"No shit! Really?" Missy replied.

Heat seeped through Laurel's veins while she listened. Blood rushed in her ears and a quiver spread through her belly. Her thoughts went haywire when she imagined Kale and another mysterious man pleasuring her at the same time. Threesome's weren't something she'd ever experienced, but if Kale was involved, she might jump at the chance—then again, maybe not.

"Cade and Kale had the reputation for sharing a woman in the past. Why wouldn't they share Natalie?"

"But Cade is married to her now. Wouldn't that be kind of weird, Jan?"

"Like I know. It's not like it was me," Jan snapped.

"You sound a bit jealous," the third woman said.

"Hell yes, I'm jealous," Jan replied, while she fanned her face like she'd overheated. "Those two are about the hottest thing around here."

"You're married, Jan."

"I may be married, but I ain't dead, Candace. Kale is still a fine looking man and single."

Yes, he is.

"Mommy!" Kimmy yelled from the top of the slide, waving madly and then sliding down.

The three women finally seemed to notice her sitting not far away and focused their icy stares on her. She lifted her hand in a small wave before she stood and walked toward her daughter.

When she reached Kimberly, she said, "Let's go play on the swing, okay?"

"Kay."

Kimmy took her hand and they walked toward another part of the park, away from the steely-eyed women still watching them.

The plastic of the swing seared through the butt of her jeans. "Wow." Laurel wiggled her butt on the seat and then settled down, pulling Kimmy into her lap and pushing against the ground to set into motion.

Off in the distance, a fairly handsome blond man threw a baseball to his young son, who appeared to be about Kimberly's age. The tightness in Laurel's chest made her realize how much of Kimberly's life her father would miss. The influence of a man in her life wouldn't be there, unless she got married or found a steady man. The day would come when Kimberly would ask questions and her stomach clenched at the thought.

"Mommy," Kimberly said, smacking her small hand against Laurel's cheek.

"What, sweetie?"

"Go for walk." The little girl jumped down once Laurel stopped the swing.

"Where?"

Kimberly pointed to a jogging path the led back into the woods and wrapped around the back of the park before it came back out on the other side of the skateboard ramps. They had taken the path several times and Kimberly loved to pick up bugs and anything else that moved, along the path.

"All right, pumpkin, but once we come back around; we need to head for home."

The pout on her daughter's face almost made her laugh, but she smiled and took Kimmy's hand. There would be no dealing with the rambunctious three year old later on, if she didn't wear her out some before they went back to the apartment.

Leaves rustled above their heads and the canopy of filtered sunlight kept the heat to a minimum down the asphalt path. Kimberly ran ahead several feet and picked up a rock. It skipped off into the bushes surrounding the path with a toss of her hand.

"Don't go too far," she yelled as Kimberly skipped around the bend of the trail and out of sight for a moment. Laurel picked up the pace and rounded the corner. The little girl had stopped not far off the trail near a bush and stood looking down at something on the ground. "You know better than to run ahead, sweetie," Laurel scolded as got closer. "What'cha got there?"

The sight meeting her gaze sent Laurel into cop mode—an uncovered tennis shoe attached to a foot, leg and probably the rest of what looked like a woman's body, under the covering of some compost.

"Move back over here, Kimberly," she snapped in a non-nonsense tone while she reached into her pocket for her cell phone.

Within moments, blaring of sirens sounded in the distance. Cops came from everywhere. She hadn't realized there were so many police on the force in the small town of Red Rock, especially on day shift, when probably ten cops arrived on the scene.

The chief of police arrived first. His large, burly body unfolded from the front seat of his cruiser and Laurel winced. *Great. Just the person I need to see today.*

"Officer Hayes. What have we got?"

"My daughter and I were walking along the path, sir, when I noticed her looking at something off the side. No one touched anything, but there appears to be a body under the compost to the right side. I saw the bottom of the shoe first and up to the knee of one leg."

The man's black eyes pinned her for a moment while he seemed to contemplate something. "Didn't you work homicide in Los Angeles?"

Laurel shivered with excitement at the question. *Maybe this might work into me being able to use my skills after all.* "Yes, sir."

"Do you have someone who can watch your daughter while you dig into this? I'm not sure you heard, Officer Hayes, but we got a report of another body yesterday, outside of town on one of the large ranches. I'm hoping this isn't a serial killer type situation. This could get mighty ugly if we don't get to the bottom of this quickly."

Damn.

"No sir. I hadn't heard about that." She chewed her bottom lip for a moment. "My neighbor usually watches her for me, but she's at an appointment."

"If you can't, I'll assign it to someone else." He turned to head back to his car.

"Wait! Sir, please. Let me see what I can do. Give me twenty minutes while the guys section this off with tape and see if there are any witnesses around. All right?"

"Twenty minutes," the chief replied, his voice gruff and to the point.

Who can I get to watch Kimmy? I don't know anyone except Teresa and Elizabeth, but I can't trust my sister if her husband is around.

Laurel reached for her cell and dialed her sister's number. Jeff answered and she hung up before saying a word.

Think, Laurel.

She paced back and forth near the cruiser sitting in the parking lot. One of the officers had put Kimmy in the back and gave her a cookie from his lunch.

"You okay, Laurel?" Jim asked.

"Yeah, Jim. Thanks for asking." She tapped her finger absently on the cell phone while she tried to think of someone to watch her daughter.

Moments later, her cell phone vibrated in her hand. Glancing at the numbers, she wondered who it could be since not too many people had her number and this one looked local.

"Hello?"

"Laurel?"

"Yes, who's this?"

"It's Kale."

I gave him my home number, not my cell.

"How did you get this number?"

"You have it on your answering machine at home and you gave me that number last night, remember?"

Crap. I forgot about putting it on the answering machine. "Um, yeah. What can I do for you?"

"I want to talk about what happened this morning. Can I buy you dinner?"

The ability to talk disappeared while she chewed her lips and contemplated seeing him again. He wanted to know more about her and her life. The thought terrified her and she wasn't ready to give into the temptation of Kale Dunn for anything other than sex—not yet.

Hesitation and avoidance had to be clear in her voice when she said, "Um, I can't tonight. I'm working."

"I thought you told me you were off tonight?"

"I was, but something has come up and the department needs me. I'm in the middle of trying to figure out where I can find someone to watch my daughter for me." Back and forth she walked, not paying attention to the hurry of feet or the blare of police radios. "I'm sorry, Kale. I really can't talk now."

"I'll do it."

"What?"

"I'll watch your daughter for a few hours."

"You can't be serious."

"Why not?"

"How much experience do you have watching a three year old?" The pause on the line answered her question. "I appreciate you volunteering, but I think you would be so out of your league with her. I'd probably find you sitting in one of your dining room chairs with one of those ropes you cowboys use, wrapped around you, when I got back."

A warm chuckle reached her ear through the phone line. She closed her eyes at the sound, reliving it and their rendezvous from this morning, in her mind.

"All right. I'll tell you what. Let me make a phone call and see if a friend of mine would be willing to watch her for you. She's great with kids."

"She?" Jealousy raced down Laurel's back and she chided herself.

"Yeah. Natalie is married to my best friend and she's an elementary teacher. Let me call her real quick and I'll call you back in a few minutes."

Natalie? Isn't that the name of the woman I heard the ladies at the picnic table talking about?

"Red?"

"Sorry. My mind drifted there for a minute." She inhaled a steadying breath and said, "Okay. I would appreciate any help. I'm at wits end here. The lady who normally sits for me has an appointment and I can't ask my sister. Jeff's home and I won't let Kimmy go over there."

"I'm sure it will be fine, but I'll call you back."

"Thanks, Kale," she murmured, her heart thumping loud in her ears.

"Talk to you in a minute or two."

The phone disconnected with a click and she flipped hers shut. Thoughts zipped across her mind even as she tried to corral them. *Who is this Natalie to Kale? Those women mentioned Kale and someone named Cade. Should I ask? Hell no! He would get the impression I'm jealous or something.*

"Did you find someone to watch your daughter?" Jim asked as she wandered back to his patrol car.

"I'm not sure."

"You better figure it out soon. The chief is getting antsy."

"I know. I'm waiting for a phone call from someone."

Her cell phone vibrated in her hand and the screen showed the same number Kale called from earlier.

"Hello?"

"Hey, Red." The nickname had started to grow on her especially coming from Kale's lips. "Nat said she would watch your daughter for you. I'll have to pick her up and take her out to their house though. Her son is down for a nap right now and Cade isn't home at the moment."

A heavy sigh left her lips as she glanced at Kimmy still sitting in the patrol car while she chatted like a magpie to Jim. "All right. I don't have a choice I guess."

"Where are you and I'll come and get her."

"No, meet me at my apartment. I need to get her car seat out of my car and I'm at the park on Fourth."

"It'll take me about ten minutes to get there anyway. Can you get home before then?"

"Yeah. No problem." The address of her apartment complex rolled off her tongue. "Apartment two-ten."

"Great. I'll see you in a few."

Once he hung up, she told Kimmy to stay there with Jim for another minute and walked to where the chief stood talking with two officers.

"Officer Hayes. What's the verdict?"

"I'll be able to investigate, sir. I've got a friend coming over to pick up my daughter, but I need to go back to my apartment and get her a few things. Will it be all right if I come back in say an hour?"

The chief stuffed his hands in his trouser pockets and rolled back on his heels as he squinted at her. Trepidation rolled down her back. The look on his face didn't bode well, but she was probably the most experienced officer on their force with homicide investigation.

"One hour. I expect you back here before two."

"Yes sir."

Not wasting any time, Laurel gathered up Kimberly and walked back to her apartment to get ready for Kale.

"Hey baby girl, I need you to be a big girl for mommy, okay? I have a friend coming over to pick you up and take you somewhere to stay while mommy works for a few hours." Kimberly's lip came out in a pout and Laurel felt like a heel. Today should have been their day together, but here she was pawning her daughter off some strangers. "I promise we will do something special tomorrow, all right? We'll go for ice cream."

Kimmy nodded, but Laurel knew she wasn't happy.

"Let's get you some clean clothes and a few of your toys packed in your backpack."

The two of them went into her daughter's room hand-in-hand and she let Kimmy pick out which toys she wanted to take, along with a pair of clean clothes and pajamas, just in case she would be later than she thought.

Several minutes later, she heard a knock on the door. Her stomach flipped over itself knowing Kale stood on the other side. Wiping sweaty palms down her pant legs, she tried to calm her shaking hands before she opened the door.

Blowing out a ragged breath, she pulled open the wooden panel and plastered a smile on her face so he wouldn't know how nervous she felt facing him again this soon.

Damn, he looks good. Brown eyes twinkled and the smile she knew could turn her upside down graced his lips.

"Hi."

"Hi. Come on in," she replied, waving him inside with a sweep of her hand. "Can I get you something to drink?"

"No thanks. I'm fine."

You certainly are.

She cleared her throat and shut the front door before she turned and faced him. "Um. Have a seat."

"Nice place."

"Thanks. It's not much, but we don't need a lot."

Moments later, her little blue-eyed blonde, came rushing into the living room and wrapped her arms around her leg.

"This is Kimberly," she said, glancing down at her daughter and then up at Kale.

He got down on his haunches at her feet so he was about Kimberly's height. "Hi pretty girl. I'm Kale."

Kimmy hid her face behind Laurel's leg, but peeked out and stuck her thumb in her mouth. Laurel got down on her knees and wrapped her arm around her daughter's waist.

"Baby girl, this is Kale. He's a friend of mine. He's going to take you somewhere to stay while mommy works, but I'll come and get you later on today. Okay?"

Blonde curls bounced when her daughter shook her head.

"Kimmy, listen," Kale said, running his big hand down the little girl's back. "You'll have fun where I'm taking you. My friend is going to watch you and she has a couple more kids over there today for you to play with."

"Oh?" Laurel asked, confused because he hadn't mentioned other children.

"Nat invited a couple of her friends over who have kids about Kimberly's age so she would have someone to play with."

"She didn't have to do that."

"I know, but it's the way Natalie is. You'll like her."

I doubt it if she's had sex with you.

"And Kimmy? Natalie has horses and two big dogs for you to play with."

"Doggie?" Kimmy asked in her little, tentative voice.

"Do you like dogs?" Kale asked, eyeing Laurel with his questioning glance.

"We haven't had one, but one of our neighbors in Los Angeles had a couple."

"She's not afraid of them, is she?"

A snort left her mouth. Kimberly wasn't afraid of anything. "No. She loves animals."

"Good." He stood and pulled his keys from his pocket. "Shall we get her car seat and stuff?"

"Yeah. I'll grab her bag and be right back. We can walk out together and get her seat out of my car." She returned a few moments later with Kimberly's backpack. "All set."

"Great." Kale reached for the door handle, swung open the door and held it for her and Kimmy.

Laurel locked up everything tight and took her daughter's hand to walk down the stairs, fully aware of the devastatingly handsome man bringing up the rear and probably checking out her ass at the same time. A quick glance over her shoulder confirmed her suspicions when she caught Kale's gaze resting on her backside.

"What?" he asked innocently with his beguiling smile.

She rolled her eyes and kept walking. They reached her car and she unlocked it to grab Kimberly's seat. Kale took it from her hands and they moved toward his truck.

After the seat was buckled in and Kimmy had been strapped into the seat, she kissed her daughter and stepped back.

"Do I get one, too?" Kale asked with his little boy pouty look.

"No," she snapped a little too harshly.

"Don't be such a hardass, Laurel, but then again, I didn't mind your ass this morning."

A strand of red hair drifted across her cheek and she watched as he captured it with his fingers to tuck it behind her ear. The smallest touch of his hands made her tremble and wish things could be different. "Look, Kale. I appreciate you doing this for me and I'm thankful to your friend for watching her. But let me get something straight. What happened earlier was a mistake."

One dark manly eyebrow shot up. "Mistake?"

"Yes. Nothing good can come of any kind of relationship between us. I'm not looking—"

He pressed a finger against her lips and stopped her words.

"I'm not looking for a relationship, Laurel. I asked questions about you this morning because I'm not the type of guy who hooks up with a woman, has sex with her and then moves on without even knowing her name. You are fascinating, sexy-as-hell and I'd like to get to know you a little better before we have sex again."

She brushed his hand away from her mouth and said, "Again?"

The rough pad of two of his fingers trailed down her cheek and the warmth of his breath flittered against her lips. "Yes, again. You frustrated me this morning with your evasive answers, but it doesn't mean I don't want you. I'm far from finished with you."

Her gaze skimmed down his chest and came to rest on the bulge behind his fly. She knew what it felt like to have him buried inside her and God help her; she wanted it again and again. A callused finger under her chin brought her gaze back to his face.

"Call me when you're done doing whatever it is you need to do this afternoon and we'll go out and pick up your daughter together."

He brushed his lips over hers in a soft, non-demanding kiss that left her wanting a lot more.

5

Kale slipped into the cab of his truck and glanced at the blonde tike in her car seat. Even if Laurel didn't think she looked like her mother, he could see the devilish glint in those blue eyes and the wrap-your-heart-around-my-finger smile on the kid's lips.

"Shall we go find you some other kids to play with, Kimmy?"

Twin dimples peeked out of her cheeks when she smiled and his heart was gone. Both of her feet bobbed up and down while she bounced in her car seat. "Yes!"

He laughed at her enthusiastic bobbing and knew Natalie would be in heaven with this little bit of a girl at her house. "Well, you obviously know that word rather well, huh?"

The truck turned over with a twist of the key and when he glanced in the rearview mirror, the worried look on Laurel's face tore his heart in two. The love shining in her eyes for her daughter spoke volumes to Kale's spirit and he knew he had to be careful or she would have him roped and tied in no time at all.

Fifteen minutes later, he pulled into Natalie and Cade's place on the outskirts of town. The quaint wood trimmed, white house sat back off the road surrounded by pasture. Cade had built this place himself over time almost like he knew Natalie would be sharing it with him.

"Doggie!" Kimberly squealed when the dogs ran up to the side of the truck barking their fool heads off.

Kale slipped out of the driver's side and walked around to get Kimberly out of the car seat.

"Hey," Natalie said, coming up behind him.

"Hey, Nat."

"So this is your girlfriend's daughter?"

He spun around and saw the teasing glint in her eyes and the saucy grin on her lips. "Laurel isn't my girlfriend," he replied, pulling open the door on the passenger side. "She's a friend." Once the car seat was unbuckled, he lifted Kimberly from the truck and set her on the ground.

"Doggie!" the little girl screamed and ran toward the big white dog sitting on his butt with his tongue lolling out of his mouth.

Kale knew the dog wouldn't hurt Laurel's daughter except maybe to lick her to death.

"Just a friend, huh?" Natalie teased, stopping next to him and cocking her head before she reached up and wiped something from his lip. Holding her thumb up for his inspection revealed a smear of strawberry colored lipstick. "Have you slept with her?"

"None of your business."

"Never mind. You just told me the answer."

A heavy sigh rushed from between his lips and he glanced at the barn in the distance.

"How long have you known her and why didn't you tell me about her when we caught you at the bar the other night?"

"It's not like anything is going on, Natalie. She moved to town not long ago and I met her at the bar about a few days ago."

"A bar fly?"

The snort from his mouth made her smile. "Not even close. Laurel is a cop."

"Really. Interesting."

"Are you going to be all right watching Kimberly? She's not going to be too much trouble is she?" he asked, scuffing the ground with the tip of his boot.

"Please, Kale," she huffed and rolled her eyes. "I take care of twenty-five six year olds every day. Karen and Audrey should be here soon with Jacob and Anna so she'll have some other kids to play with."

"How's my godson by the way?" he asked while he kept an eye on Kimberly running around the yard chasing Natalie and Cade's white German shepherd.

"Getting big. You need to come out for dinner next week or something. You haven't been out for a while."

"I know. Things are getting busy at my place and I'm down a man now."

"Oh?"

"Yeah. I had to fire one of my guys the other day."

"Fire him, why?"

"Seems he's been heavy-handed with his wife and it's something I won't tolerate."

"How did you hear about it?"

He scuffed his boot in the dirt again, debating on how much to tell Natalie since it all came back around to Laurel and his friend sure didn't need to grab onto anything else to do with Red.

"Fess up, Kale. You're keeping something from me. I can tell. I've known you way too long."

"All right, fine. The night I met Kimmy's mom, she came into the bar and decked Jeff Cox. It seems he had been beatin' on his wife who is Laurel's sister. Laurel took matters into her own hands, came to the bar and laid Jeff out on the floor."

Her eyes widened and she put her hands on her hips. "Seriously? She hit him?"

"Not only did she hit him, but she dropped him with one punch."

"Wow."

"Yeah. Anyway, I told him I wanted to see him in the mornin' and to bring his gear. He was done on my place."

A white truck rumbled down the driveway toward the house.

"Must be Karen and Audrey."

"I'll leave you to your friends then. I've got a few things to do at my place, but when Laurel calls me, I'll call you and let you know when we'll be coming by to pick up Kimberly."

"Did she say what was going on?"

"No and I didn't pry. It's not my business, but I know it had to do with police work," he replied, pulling out his truck key. "Thanks again for watching her, Nat. You're the best."

"Remember that when I bug you for more details later on. And I'm really looking forward to meeting Laurel."

"Great," he grumbled, pulling his cowboy hat down lower on his forehead.

"I heard you."

"Good."

She kissed him on the cheek and then turned to wait for her friends to unload from the car. The other two women waved and he raised his hand to wave back.

Climbing into his truck, he sat for a moment and watched Natalie while she greeted her friends and then chased Kimberly down to take her into the house. He often wondered if Natalie felt any self-conscious issues having to do with him, but her attitude when they were around each other didn't let on anything was amiss. The one and only time the two of them had sex was when he and Cade had a threesome with her. The friendship between her, him and Cade might seem weird to some people, especially if they knew about what happened. Not like he told anyone, but he knew people talked.

Natalie had returned to Red Rock to help care for her grandmother after her grandfather passed away a couple of years ago and to convince the older woman to return to Oregon with her. Mrs. Oliver wouldn't hear of leaving her home and Kale had to smile. Natalie's grandmother was an independent, don't-take-no-shit-from-nobody type woman and she wasn't about to leave her home. She had even encouraged him and Cade to date Natalie while she visited, but Natalie only had eyes for Cade. From the beginning, band geek turned gorgeous woman had wound his friend around her pinky finger. He only hoped someday he could find a woman like her to complete his life.

Several minutes later, he pulled up next to the porch on his house and stared at the front. The ranch meant everything to him. The land, the ranch hands, the cattle and horses—all of it completed him like nothing else could. Ranch life came naturally. He'd grown up on a cattle ranch along with his two brothers and three sisters. Up at dawn to feed, water and clean stalls, became his life from the time he could walk. His parents had instilled hard, honest work would get you ahead in this life, but it didn't guarantee happiness.

From the time he could think for himself, he wanted out of Red Rock. A life in the big city. A life with a beautiful wife, two point five kids, white picket fence and an SUV in the driveway was his dream, so off to college he went for his degree in architecture. He found the beautiful wife and the house in the suburbs, but those things didn't bring him peace. Life on the open plains of Montana called him home.

This house, his house and land gave him peace, but his wife had hated it from the time they had set foot in Montana. The only thing making it tolerable for her came from her friendship with Cade's first wife. Kale had hope someday Judy would love their home like he did, but she hadn't.

The crowning glory came when Judy and Cynthia dropped the mother of all bombshells on top of his and Cade's head one night at dinner. The two women had taken their relationship beyond friendship into lover status. Betrayal, shock, and duplicity played over in his mind like a bad black and white movie, in the days following their declaration.

He recognized it now for what it was, God's way of taking care of him and bringing him back to the life he should never have left.

"If I can find the right woman to share it with, this would all be worth the heartache, time, sweat and hard work," he grumbled as he slipped out of the cab and slammed the door.

Sunlight streaked across the living room floor when he walked into the house. The huge windows overlooking the pasture out back, gave him a bird's eye view of the cattle and horses grazing in the distance. The huge rock fireplace gracing one wall, could heat the whole house in the dead of winter, but right now it stood black and empty.

Retrieving his cell phone from his pocket, he laid it on the island in the kitchen, and grabbed a mug for some coffee from the cupboard. There would always be something needing done on the five-hundred acres he owned, but for now he wanted to relax and think. With coffee cup in hand, he walked into the living room and took a seat in one of the recliners.

At thirty-two years old, it was high time he settled down. His mom had started hounding him about finding another wife—one who would compliment him and help him run his place—a local girl. Trouble with her theory, there wasn't a local girl he cared to look twice at after a night in his bed. Not one of them could hold his interest or his thoughts. *Except Laurel.*

"She doesn't count. She's not a local girl," he said out loud before he took two healthy sips of the strong brew in his cup. "Cowgirl she isn't. She said so herself." *But damn does she look good in a pair of jeans.* "A pair of jeans doesn't the cowgirl make," he rationalized even if he could think of nothing more than peeling the denim off her hips. Thoughts of the sexy underwear she'd been wearing this morning, made his cock swell behind the fly of his pants. "Shit. I don't need to get all horny right this minute."

With a quiet half growl, he stood and walked into the kitchen to place his cup in the sink. A little hard, sweaty work would get his mind off the temptation of daydreaming about one red-headed siren. One little kiss and she'd turned him upside down and inside out.

Thank God for the mind numbing routine of shoveling horse shit and dirty hay into a wheelbarrow. Sweat dripped down his back, plastering the white T-shirt to his skin. The scent of horse droppings, dust and dirt filtered to his nose, but it was a gratifying smell. It meant the world to him because each horse, heifer and calf on the property belonged to him, lock, stock and barrel.

The sound of a diesel truck pulling in outside caught his attention and he wondered who it could be since he wasn't expecting anyone. He set the shovel against the wall, grabbed his hat from the nail and walked toward the door, tugging the gloves off his hands as he moved.

"Hey, Kale."

"Cade. What are you doing here? Nat said you were out of town."

"You talked to my wife?" Cade asked, stopping in front of him.

Kale nodded and pulled his Stetson lower to shade his eyes from the glare of the sun. "Yeah, earlier. Went out to your place about an hour ago."

"Oh?"

"She's doing me a favor and watching a kid for me." One blond eyebrow shot up to Cade's hairline and Kale almost laughed. "She's not mine. She belongs to a woman I know." Both eyebrows shot up and he did laugh at Cade's expression. "There's nothin' goin' on. The lady is a cop and she had to pull an extra shift or something this afternoon and her regular sitter wasn't available."

"Uh-huh."

"Knock it off. I met her in the bar about a few days ago when she decked one of my guys for beating on his wife."

Cade folded his arms over his chest and braced his back against the fence. He obviously wasn't going anywhere until he told him everything.

"Her name is Laurel and he moved her not long ago at the urging of her sister. You know Jeff Cox?"

"Yeah, isn't he one of your guys?"

"Used to be. I fired him."

"Go on," Cade said, pushing his hat back on his head.

Kale knew he should leave out certain parts of what had happened between him and Laurel, but he and Cade had known each other since high school. They slept in the same bed as young boys, made love to several women together when they got older, got drunk together, puke together—hell they had done everything together.

"Let's get something to drink. It's hotter than hell out here and I'm sweatin' like a pig," he said, walking toward the house.

Once they were settled inside, a beer clutched in their fists and a ball game on television for background noise, he told Cade everything from seeing Laurel come into the bar, punching out her brother-in-law to making love to her right there in his living room this morning.

The silly grin on Cade's face had him scowling. "What?"

"You got it bad, man."

"Got what bad?"

"You're halfway in love with this woman already, brother."

"Hell no. I don't need a woman who can't ride, clean stalls or thinks the only thing a heifer is good for is on a plate."

Cade tipped the bottle to his lips and took a long drink before he leveled his penetrating blue gaze on him. "Trust me. Your heart doesn't always listen to the practical side of things. How do you think I fell in love with Natalie so fast, huh?"

"Well, I—"

Cade held up one hand. "All it took was one kiss and one look from those big green eyes and she had my heart in her palm to do whatever she wanted."

"Laurel's got blue eyes and a body wet dreams are made of," he murmured in reply.

"See what I mean? You're in deep my man."

"You aren't helping matters, Cade. You are supposed to be talking me out of this, not encouraging it."

"I would love to see you happy like me and Nat." After another sip of his beer, Cade said, "So, when do we get to meet this mystery woman?"

"This afternoon or evening actually. I told her to come by here when she's done and we would drive out to your place to pick up Kimmy together." The bottle clanked on the coffee table when he set it down. "You should see her little girl. Blonde bouncing curls, her momma's blue eyes and dimples in both cheeks when she smiles."

"You are so done, buddy," Cade said with a deep chuckle. "Listen to yourself."

He wasn't sure he liked the look on his friends face. It had *matchmaker* written all over it. Cade thought since he and Natalie were happily married, everyone should be.

"It doesn't matter. Laurel doesn't want to stay here. She's a cop. Red Rock is like the last frontier especially for a big city homicide detective. Right now, she's doing street duty and I'm sure it's driving her nuts."

"Homicide, huh?"

"Yeah, in Los Angeles no less."

"She moved here from L.A.?"

"Yep," he replied, picking up his bottle again and picking at the label.

"Wow. That's a huge change."

His cell phone jingled in his pocket and he set the beer on the table again to retrieve it. The screen read Laurel. A quick glance at Cade and he knew he didn't want to answer it in front of his friend. "I'll be right back," he said as he stood and walked into the kitchen. "Hey."

"Hi. How's Kimmy doing?"

"She's fine, Laurel. When I left her at Natalie's, she had corralled the dog and he was kissing all over her face as she squealed in delight."

"You left her there?"

The concern in her voice made him panic a little. "Natalie knows kids, honey, I don't. I didn't think I needed to stick around, but if you want me to go back out there, I will."

The sigh coming through the phone told him of her frustration. "No, it's fine. I would have rather met them before she went out there, but this whole thing wasn't planned."

"Exactly what's going on? Did someone call in sick or something?"

"I can't really say, Kale. It's confidential right now, but let's just say I'm doing an investigation."

"All right. Any idea when you'll be done?" he asked, pacing the kitchen and running his fingers through his hair.

"It'll be a few hours yet. Hopefully we can wrap up most of this before it gets dark."

"Drive on out here to my place when you're done and we'll go get Kimmy together."

"Sounds like a plan. I'll call you when I'm driving in your direction."

"Good. Be careful, Red, and I'll see you after while."

"I will and Kale?"

"Yeah, darlin'."

"Thanks."

The phone clicked in his ear. He stared at the screen on his phone for a minute before he shut it. He shook his head and walked back into the living room only to find Cade with a shit-eatin' grin on his face. "Knock it the hell off, Cade."

"I didn't say a word, bro."

"You didn't have to. The look on your face says it all."

"I better get home." Cade stood and set his beer bottle on the coffee table. "I wanted to stop for a bit on my way in since I came from this side of town, to see what you were up to. You need to come out for dinner."

"Nat already invited me for next week."

"Bring Laurel."

He started to shake his head, but Cade just smiled, grabbed his hat from where he dropped it when they came inside and walked toward the door. "See you in a little while."

"Yeah," he replied taking another sip of his own beer while he contemplated Cade's words a little more than he should.

* * * *

Sunlight began to fade behind the mountains in the distance as Laurel pulled up to Kale's house. The two-story brick home with its huge wraparound porch and big windows spoke of attention to detail. The care he paid to his home spoke volumes about the man. Everything was freshly painted. The house, the fence and the barn showed no signs of peeling paint or neglect of any sort.

Horses and cattle grazed in the waning light, but she could still make out the various colors of the animals and wondered how much of the land around his home belonged to him. She'd never known anyone to own this size of a spread. Residence of Los Angeles and the outlying areas hardly had enough yard to call it a yard. The condo she rented out there barely had any grass for Kimmy to play on and she always prayed someday she would be able to move to somewhere that had room for her to run.

The moment she turned the engine off on her car, the door opened and Kale stepped out onto the porch. Tall, built, rugged and looking too damned gorgeous for her peace of mind, the man could make her almost think of staying here permanently. "Forget it, Laurel," she told herself. "Red Rock, Montana isn't a place for you."

"Hey, Red," Kale said as she stepped out of the car and walked toward the door.

"I thought I told you not to call me Red."

"Sorry, darlin'. I can't help it. It fits you."

She rolled her eyes at the same time he leaned over and kissed her on the cheek.

"I hope the day wasn't too bad."

"Not really. It was great to do some investigative work instead of patrol."

"Come on in and sit for a bit before we go out and pick up Kimmy. I talked to Nat and Cade a few minutes ago and they had just sat down to eat dinner."

The warmth of his hand at the small of her back sent heat straight through to her pussy. God, you would think she hadn't had sex in ages instead of this morning, the way she reacted to his touch.

"Would you like a beer?"

"Sure," she replied with a soft sigh when his hand disappeared.

He returned a few moments later and handed her a long-neck bottle of beer with the top already popped. The beer tasted malty and cold as it slid down her throat—two things she needed right at the moment to calm the heat racing through her blood.

She swiped the remaining liquid on her lips with her tongue and had to fight the moan lingering in her mouth at the lust-filled look on Kale's face.

"Stop looking at me like that," she whispered, swallowing again.

"Like what?" he growled.

Her gaze zipped from his chocolate colored eyes, down his chest and stopped on the outline of his cock behind the fly of his jeans. *Damn it! This isn't good.* "Like you want to eat me alive."

"I do. I haven't made excuses nor have I denied being attracted to you, Laurel."

"I know, but us getting involved is a bad idea."

"How?" he asked, stopping next to her and tucking a curl behind her ear.

"I'm not staying here."

"I'm aware of your temporary need to be in Red Rock." His fingers slipped behind her neck and gently pulled her closer. "I don't want a relationship. I have a very clear cut image of the woman I want to share my life with and—"

"And I'm not it."

"Don't put words in my mouth, Red. If you want to put somethin' in there, I can think of one thing I wouldn't mind on my tongue."

His voice trailed off to a murmur as his mouth took possession of hers and she couldn't think of a better word for what he did with his lips. In fact, conscious thought disappeared with the warm, soft slide of his tongue over her lower lip. Unable to stop herself, she opened for him and groaned deep in her throat when he trapped her against his chest and deepened the kiss. Her hands went up around his neck of their own accord and she pressed her breasts to the hard plains of his chest. Both of his palms gripped her ass and lifted her so her pussy lined up perfectly with his cock. The next thing she knew, he set her down on the edge of a huge bed and followed her down with his body.

"I'm gonna make you scream my name, Red."

The rough pad of his tongue slipped down her neck and across her collarbone. Sharp nips of his teeth on her skin sent shivers down her spine and cream spilled from her pussy when he soothed the stings with flicks of his tongue. His palm cupped her breast, kneading it with his fingers and shaping it to fit perfectly in the hand.

Her breaths came out in jagged puffs of air and she didn't think she'd breathe right again until he stopped the torture of her body.

"Kale," she murmured.

Two of his fingers popped the buttons down the front of her shirt open with such deft precision, but she didn't want to think about how many women he'd done the same thing to.

I bet he did with Natalie. The thought of him making love to the faceless woman was like a cold shower.

"Kale, stop."

The buttons of her shirt were already parted and her bra no longer cupped her breasts. His lips closed over one pert nipple and sucked. The edges of his teeth scraped across the turgid peak and she couldn't stop the groan in her throat.

"Stop?" he asked, raking the shadow of whiskers on his cheek over tight bud.

She licked her lips and forced the words through her suddenly dry lips and across her non-cooperative tongue. "Yes."

His brown eyes sparkled in the last rays of sunlight filtering through the curtains when he lifted his head. "You want me to stop?"

A repeat of the words wouldn't come this time, but she nodded instead.

He slowly moved away from her and pulled her bra back down. "I'm sorry. I won't force you—ever."

"I know you wouldn't, it's just..."

"What? Why did you ask me to stop? I thought you wanted it as bad as I do." He grasped her hand and pressed it to his erection. "Can't you tell how much I want you? I know you enjoyed this morning, too, even if we had a bit of a disagreement."

She captured her bottom lip between her teeth and sighed before she dropped her hand from his cock. "I won't deny I like it, Kale. I told you before. It's been a long time for me."

"How long, Laurel?"

The answer hung on the end of her tongue for a moment. "Since I got pregnant with Kimmy."

"Where is her father now?"

God, she didn't want to answer him, but she knew he wouldn't let it go this time. The last thing she wanted was pity from Kale. After several hard swallows to clear the lump lodging itself in her throat, she whispered, "Dead."

"I'm sorry."

"Don't."

He pulled away from her and she wiped angrily at the tears on her cheeks as she sat up and straightened her clothes. Crying for Dennis made her feel weak and used.

Kale leaned over and kissed her cheeks, taking the wetness away with his lips, but they kept falling. A broken sob escaped her mouth and he gathered her to his chest, rocking her back and forth. No words were spoken while he comforted her. She clung to his chest, wetting his shirt, for some time.

When there were no more tears, she sat up and sniffed. A tissue was thrust into her hand and she murmured a quiet thank you. She couldn't meet his searching gaze—didn't want to see the pity in his eyes, but one finger under her chin forced her face up.

"Tell me."

Every minute detail of her time with Dennis from when they got together during her academy training, to the day he died, poured from her lips. Kale never said a word the whole time she talked. How he knew she needed to talk about it, she didn't know, but she thanked her lucky stars for this proud, gorgeous cowboy with his soft side.

What will I do when it's over and I go back to Los Angeles?

6

Kale wiped at the remaining tears on Laurel's face with his thumb, then tucked a stray strand of her red hair behind her ear while she gave him a watery chuckle.

"Better?"

A quick nod gave him his answer. "I'm sorry. I've known you a matter of days and here I am blubbering all over your shirt, asking you to watch my three-year-old daughter—"

"Hey, it's what friends are for, right? Besides, my shirt needed to be laundered anyway."

The chuckle spilling from her lips sounded like a choked sob.

"You didn't bring me in here and worked half my clothes off so I could cry all over you."

"Not exactly, no. I would rather be buried deep inside you right now, but I got the feeling you never took the time to grieve for him. You loved him, right?"

"Yes, I loved him and no, I didn't grieve for him. After I found out about his wife at the funeral, I couldn't do anything but bury my feelings —bury everything. Then when I found out about Kimmy, I didn't know what else to do."

"What about your parents?"

"They turned their back on me. Having a child out of wedlock was bad enough, but finding out the child I carried belonged to a married man...well let's just say it wasn't pleasant."

"Your parents are very old-fashioned, I assume."

"Very. My father is a minister. Good God, if he and my mother found out you and I had sex and barely knew each other?" An exaggerated shutter ran through her body.

"I tell you what. Why don't we put this round of sex on hold? I don't think you're quite up to enjoying it right now and we should probably get out to Nat and Cade's to pick up Kimmy. Otherwise, they might want to keep her permanently."

"She kind of does that to a person," she said with a sniff, a nod and a slight smile.

"Those dimples are what do it. I'm telling you, she can wrap anyone and everyone around her little finger with those."

"You're a goner, Kale Dunn. Caught by a blonde three year old."

He liked her teasing him much better than hers tears. A woman crying about did him in. The heat of a blush crept up his neck and he dropped his gaze to her chest. He wasn't about to tell her the facts. He wanted more from one saucy red-head than he'd ever wanted from any woman. "We should get going," he said, standing and adjusting his still rock-hard erection behind his fly. It wouldn't do to show up at Cade's sportin' wood.

"Yeah, you're right," she replied smoothing her hands down the thigh of her jeans.

"Did you eat?"

A wicked gleam sparkled in her eyes and he silently groaned.

"Food. You know, dinner?"

"Nope. I came right from the crime scene over here."

"Crime scene?"

"I guess I can tell you a little. It will hit the papers tomorrow, I'm sure and it'll be big news in a little town like Red Rock. I'll tell you in the truck on our way over to get Kimmy."

Several moments later, she sat on the passenger side of his pickup and explained.

"Kimmy and I were at the park earlier and she ran ahead of me down the back path through the woods that comes out near the parking lot. When I caught up with her, she was standing off the side looking at something."

"What was it?"

"A body."

"Like someone sleeping or something?"

"No, Kale, a dead body. A young woman actually. Kimberly didn't see the whole thing, thank goodness. She only saw a foot and part of the woman's leg before I got her out of there and called it in."

"Wow. That's weird. Did they tell you I found a woman's body up on the rise on my property?"

"No, they didn't mention it to me, but I haven't received the whole briefing yet. I'll have to check with the chief and find out what's up."

"I'm sure they think I'm a suspect. The body was on my land after all."

"Yeah, not good." She shook her head. "Since I did homicide investigations in Los Angeles, the chief of police asked if I would work on the investigation. Of course, I jumped at the chance. But I didn't have anyone to watch Kimmy since Teresa had an appointment." She reached over and squeezed his thigh. "Thank you for coming to my rescue. I didn't know what to do."

"You're welcome, but you really need to thank Natalie."

Laurel frowned, turned her head and gazed out the windshield. Even in the darkness of the truck, he could see worry lines around her mouth as her lips pulled down at the edges.

"Somethin' wrong?"

A sharp shake of her head told him no, but he'd come to read her to some degree and he wasn't about to take no for an answer—not from her and not when she seemed upset.

"Come on, Laurel. There's somethin' on your mind, so spill it."

Several moments of uncomfortable silence stretched between them and he wasn't sure she would answer until she faced him again.

"All right. I overheard a conversation at the playground between some women and I need to know if what they said is true."

"Shoot."

"Have you had sex with Natalie?"

She couldn't have shocked him more if she'd asked him if he liked men. "Well, I...mmm."

"Never mind, Kale. You answered my question."

"Why do you want to know?"

"I'm not holding anything against you or Natalie. I mean we don't have anything going on between us besides friends. I needed to know so I knew how to take her when I see her."

He pulled the truck over on the side of the road, put it in park and shut off the engine. "Listen, Laurel. I suppose since we are spendin' time together and gettin' to know each other, you have a right to know. Yes, I had sex with Natalie once over two years ago. It's never mentioned between me, Cade or Natalie. It's somethin' that happened, but it's in our past."

"What happened?" she asked, her voice barely above a whisper.

Unsnapping his seatbelt, he shifted around so he faced her. "You have to understand somethin'. The three of us had a past. Nat went to school with me and Cade until her family moved when she was fifteen. She came back to Red Rock to help her grandmother right after her grandfather passed away. Originally, the plan was for her to get her Gram to go back to Oregon, but Mrs. Oliver wasn't about to move from her home. Cade and I were both attracted to Nat when we saw her again, so she dated us both for a few weeks. Cade said somethin' stupid in front of a bunch of people at the diner and she got really mad. She called me and told me she wanted to have sex with me."

"Seriously?"

"Well, she and I had gone out once or twice and Cade pissed her off. He'd told her before he didn't care whether she dated me or even had sex with me, which wasn't the truth. The poor sap had already pretty much fallen in love with her."

"But you weren't?"

He shook his head. "Not even close. Yes, I was attracted to her, but Cade fell head-over-heels fast. Anyway, I made a date with her for the sex romp she wanted, but when I got off the phone, I called Cade and told him what she'd said. We came up with a plan to kidnap her and bring her out here to my place so he could talk to her."

"And you ended up having sex with her?"

Silence stretch for several uncomfortable seconds before he continued, "Cade and I have shared women in the past. Natalie knew that and she was intrigued, I guess. I'm not quite sure how it all started, but we ended up sharin' her."

"Mmm."

"What?"

She tilted her head to the side as a wicked little grin spread across her face. "A ménage huh."

"Yeah, but like I said, it only happened the one time. He asked her to marry him shortly afterward. It wasn't like we wanted to try to make it a permanent thing."

Laurel grasped his hand and squeezed. "Thank you for telling me. I appreciate your honesty."

"I'll never be anythin' but honest with you, Laurel. I think it is one of the paramount things in a relationship."

"We aren't in a relationship, Kale."

"Do you want to be?"

* * * *

Do I want to be in a relationship with him? I can't! I'm not staying here. Plus, he's a suspect in a murder investigation. This is too strange and something I shouldn't be getting into. What if he's the killer? This could be like a Ted Bundy thing and I could be next on the list. Her heart thumped hard but her cop instincts started to kick in. *No. That's just ridiculous. I don't believe he's a killer. I'll just have to set out to prove it. I can't seriously be attracted to a serial killer.*

"I like you, Kale."

"But."

"I don't plan on staying in Red Rock. Can we scratch an itch once in a while? Sure. I'm good with that. Besides, I can't see myself with anyone on a permanent basis. I've tried it and it doesn't work."

"Let's just take things one day at a time and see what happens. Shall we?"

She shrugged and looked out the windshield at the dark night. Stars twinkled above them like diamonds on black velvet. The sky in Montana was so clear, you could see for miles and miles. The air, even at night, held a crispness you couldn't find anywhere else.

The engine roared to life and they pulled back out onto the road. Within minutes, they turned down a dirt lane and she could see glowing lights of a house in the distance.

"Cade built this place with his bare hands. He works construction, but not so much anymore. With Natalie and their son, it keeps him busy running the home place, too."

"Wow. It's beautiful."

"Thanks," he replied with a small grin. "I drew the plans for him."

"Really? You're an architect on top of running a successful cattle and horse ranch?"

He shrugged. "It's what I went to school for to start with. Becomin' an architect was my ticket out of Red Rock."

"So what brought you back?"

"All of this," he replied with a sweep of his hand. "The openness of Montana. The beautiful mountains. The winter air that nips at your nose with the cold. The prairies in the summer with all the wildflowers in bloom. Nothing can compare. I tried the city life with the wife and two point five kids. It didn't work for me."

"You had a wife and kids?"

"Yes to the wife, no to the kids, until the wife decided she'd rather be with someone else. Turned out the someone else was Cade's first wife, Cynthia."

Whoa! "She turned into a lesbian?"

"Yeah. Great for a guy's ego, huh?"

"She's an idiot to give you up."

A sexy little smile lit up his face and she mentally kicked herself for saying the thought running through her head.

"Thank you."

"Well, I—"

The light on the porch flipped on and a tall, handsome blond guy, stepped out. "Are you coming in or are you going to sit out there all night?"

"I guess that's our queue," Kale replied, opening his door.

The warmth of his hand at the small of her back felt comforting and right for some reason, as they made their way up to the house.

"Hi, there. You must be Laurel," Cade said holding out his hand. "I've heard a lot about you."

She glanced at Kale and the deep blush staining his cheeks, told her he'd probably spilled every detail to his friend.

"Cade, this is Laurel. Laurel this is my best friend, Cade."

"Nice to meet you finally," Cade replied.

"You too. I've heard a lot about you and your wife, too."

"All good, I hope."

"Of course. I don't think Kale can say a bad thing about anyone."

"You haven't heard him talk about his ex then," Cade said with a chuckle. "Come on in and meet Nat and our son. She's watching television with Kimberly and Alan."

The first step into the two story ranch made Laurel suck in a sharp breath. The interior of the house was gorgeous. Huge window in the front, let in the natural sunlight during the daylight hours, but also gave them an unobstructed view of the pastures. The western motif of the furniture and accents, gave it a homey feel—a welcoming feel. The open floor plan allowed entertaining in the living room while cooking in the kitchen. Solid granite countertops and solid oak cabinets with beautiful brass handles and pulls complimented the layout of the kitchen to perfection.

"Mommy!" Kimberly screamed, running toward her with her arms outstretched.

Laurel bent down and scooped Kimberly up in her arms, while she peppered kisses over her daughter's face and neck. "Were you a good girl?"

Blonde curls bobbed with her nod, but Laurel glanced at over her shoulder to lock her gaze on Natalie. It's no wonder Kale had been attracted to the other woman. She was stunning. Her green eyes sparkled with life and love when they stopped on her husband. Her blonde hair floated around her shoulders in waves and shimmered with a life of its own, when the light in the room bounced off the curls. Laurel cursed the red mop of hair on her head as she tucked an unruly curl behind her ear.

"You must be, Laurel. I'm Natalie."

"Nice to meet you," Laurel replied, holding out her hand. "I can't thank you enough for watching Kimberly for me."

"Oh, nonsense. She's a doll. I had a couple of friends bring their kids over for her to play with. Alan wouldn't be much fun since he's only a few months old." The bundle in her arms started to squirm and make squeaking noises. "That's my alarm. I think it's time for little man here, to go to bed. Have a seat you two. I'm sure my neglectful husband can find a beer or something in the fridge while I put him down."

The issues she had with Kale and Natalie almost vanished the moment Natalie's gaze stopped on Cade. The love between the two people shone bright for anyone to see if they bothered to look. Laurel still felt a bit self-conscious, knowing she wasn't a skinny woman. Muscle she'd built on her body from the constant demands of her job, turned off a lot of men, but the wide hips and small belly from Kimberly's birth, she just couldn't get rid of. It didn't matter. Being model thin and gorgeous wasn't in her genes.

"Of course. Sorry, darlin'," Cade replied and then kissed her.

The kiss went on for several moments and Laurel felt heat crawling up her neck watching them getting lost in each other.

"All right, you two. You do have company," Kale teased, nudging Cade.

Natalie smirked when she and Cade parted. "You're just jealous, Kale, but I'm sure Laurel could help you out. You have to be nice to her and show her how much of a gentleman you can be. Otherwise, she might kick your butt to the curb."

Laurel couldn't help but smile. Even though she wanted to hate Natalie for her relationship with Kale, she really liked her quick wit and sassy mouth. The comfort level Natalie had with both men made Laurel a little jealous and she wondered if she would ever find a relationship like the three of them shared. *Do I even want a friendship like they have?*

"You okay?" Kale whispered next to her ear while she watched Nat head down the hall.

Shivers skittered down her arms as the warmth of his breath heated her sensitive skin. "Yeah. We probably shouldn't stay long. I'm not sure how long Kimmy will behave."

"We'll stay until you say it's time to go."

"Have a seat you two," Cade said, nodding toward the couch.

She walked to the couch and sat with Kimberly on her lap. Kale took the seat next to her and pressed his hard thigh against hers. A moment later, Kimmy wiggled down and went back to watching cartoons on the television, leaving her sitting alone with Kale's warmth seeping through her jeans. His arm snaked behind her and when his fingers started dancing along her shoulder, she bit the inside of her lip to keep the moan trapped in her throat from spilling out.

"Kale said you are a police officer, Laurel," Cade said handing them each a beer and taking a seat across from them.

"Yeah. I did several years in Los Angeles before moving here."

"I bet Red Rock is pretty borin' compared to the craziness of the west coast."

"It's quite a bit slower, true, but I like it."

"Do you plan to settle here permanently?" Cade asked before he took a sip of his beer.

"I'm not sure. I moved here to help my sister, but she's not taking my advice on getting rid of her no good husband."

A soft chuckle came from Cade's lips. "I heard about you deckin' the guy in the bar."

"Damn, Kale! Did you have to tell everyone?" she snapped, irritated with him for spilling her family secrets. If she wanted everyone in the county to know, she'd tell them herself.

"I heard it from more than just Kale, Laurel, so don't be upset with him. This is a very small town and gossip spreads fast."

She glanced at Kale and then ducked her head to hide the embarrassing blush on her cheeks. Getting mad at him didn't serve a purpose except keeping her from giving into her attraction to him. The soft trail of fingers brought her attention back to the disturbing presence beside her. He could tie her into knots with nothing more than a brush of his fingers. She would have to apologize to him when they got back to his place.

"Oh, by the way, Laurel. Thank you for what you did for my nephew the other night."

"Your nephew?"

"Yes. Matt Weston with the firecracker?"

"I knew your name sounded familiar. How's he doing?"

"He'll be fine, but he won't be sittin' on his ass for a while. His momma tanned his hide good. Not to mention what his daddy done."

The image his words put into her mind, made her smile. Small town ranch America, had very basic ideas on how to raise a family. Tight reins on their children came natural for the ranch owner and his family. It was the reason she'd been surprised those kids were hanging around so late in the evening.

"He won't be hangin' with his friends for a while either. I think his parents grounded him for about a year or so."

The three of them chuckled and Laurel shook her head.

Natalie returned to the living room and took a seat on her husband's lap. "Have you two been boring poor Laurel with your stories again?"

"Us? Boring? Never." Kale snickered.

One eyebrow shot up over Natalie's left eye when she leveled her gaze on Kale and Laurel couldn't help but laugh.

"You can't believe a word these two say, Laurel. Trust me. I've known both of them way too long."

"You believe I love you, right?" Cade asked, his eyes wide with feigned shock.

"Okay. There is one thing I believe, but that's about it. You two love to embellish things."

"Wait a minute, woman. You were gone for several years. You don't know everything," Cade protested even though his fingers caressed her arm from shoulder to elbow and back.

"And I've got both of you two pegged. Don't forget, husband of mine, I've been around you two for the last couple of years and you haven't changed since high school. I could tell Laurel all kinds of stories about you two."

Both she and Natalie laughed at the look on Cade and Kale's faces. The little boy pout on both of their mouths was just too cute.

Kimberly came over and climbed up in Laurel's lap, stuck her thumb into her mouth and laid her head on her shoulder. "I think we should probably go, Kale. Kimmy's getting tired."

"No problem, darlin'," he replied, coming to his feet.

"Thank you again for watching her for me, Natalie. How much do I owe you?"

Natalie looked at Cade and then Kale before she answered, "Owe me? You don't owe me anything, Laurel. I was just helping out a friend."

"Are you sure?"

"Of course."

"Thanks again then. You have no idea how much I appreciate it."

"We should get these two to watch the kids one day so you and I can hit the spa and do lunch. It would be great. I haven't had a chance for a girl's only day since Alan was born," Natalie said as she stood and Cade came to his feet too.

"Um. Sure," Laurel replied, not quite sure what to make of Natalie's overtures of friendship. Women in Los Angeles didn't do those kinds of things unless they'd known each other for years.

"Great. Call me when you get a day off and we'll head into Billings before the snow hits. Trust me, after winter gets here, you don't want to go anywhere."

"I can imagine."

"Do you want me to take Kimmy?" Kale asked.

Laurel wasn't sure what to make of the homey, family feelings she got when Kale acted so much like a father, it scared her. "No, it's fine. I've got her." She turned to Natalie and Cade and said, "Thank you again."

"You are more than welcome, Laurel. Come out anytime and if you are in a spot without a sitter, call me," Natalie replied, slipping her arm around Cade's waist. "We're on summer break at school so I'm free."

"I will."

When they reached the side of Kale's truck, he opened the door and Laurel slipped Kimmy into her car seat sitting behind the passenger seat.

Within moments, they were on the highway headed back for town. The radio played a soft country tune she hadn't heard before. In Los Angeles, she heard everything from punk rock, to hip-hop, to rap. She wondered if anyone in Montana listened to anything besides country, although, she kind of liked the change. Country had a much nicer sound and you could at least understand the words. She tapped her foot to the beat of the music and saw Kale shift his glance down to the floorboard and a small smile spread across his face.

"What?"

"Do you want me to turn it up?"

"No. I can hear it and…" She looked back at Kimmy who had fallen sound asleep in her car seat. "Kimmy's asleep. I don't want to wake her. She can be a bear when she's woken up."

Kale laughed and she smiled. She liked his laugh, almost as much as his kiss and she really liked his kisses. His touch did wonderful things to her, too.

All right! Enough of those thoughts.

A few minutes later, they pulled down the long dirt road leading to his house and she sighed, wanting to escape his disturbing presence, but then again, she wanted him to hold her like he had earlier.

"I probably have something in the house we can whip up to eat. I'm gettin' kind of hungry. How about you?" he asked as he stopped the truck.

"Yeah, I'm hungry, too, but I really should get Kimmy home. We've been out all day."

"Why don't we put her down on the couch, grab some food and then you can run home? She probably won't even wake up when you take her out of the car seat."

"Maybe. Sometimes she sleeps so sound, an atomic bomb could go off and she wouldn't wake up, but other times, she wakes up at the slightest noise."

He squeezed her fingers and brought them to his lips for a light kiss, before he said, "Good. It's settled then. A little food will do us both good."

"I'm sure I could do without a meal or two. My activity level hasn't been what it should be."

One dark eyebrow shot up and a sexy little grin spread across his lips. "You look fabulous, but I'm sure I could help with a little exercise if you'd like."

"Do you think of anything beside sex, horses, cattle, and sex?" she asked, scooping Kimberly up in her arms and walking toward his house.

"Not when you're close by," he replied, placing his hand at the small of her back and brushing his lips against her cheek.

The gentlemanly contact of his palm radiated heat through her middle and down her legs. Damn, the man's touch had her thinking about hot sweaty sex and he did nothing more than guide her into the house.

Kale flipped on the lights and walked into the kitchen while she placed Kimberly on the couch. A handmade quilt lay over the back of the leather sofa. Laurel lifted it with one hand and softly spread it over her daughter. The multiple-colored pattern caught her eye as she smoothed her hand over the material, imagining someone so lovingly stitching it together.

"My grandmother made it," Kale murmured, coming to her side.

"It's beautiful, Kale. I can't imagine the time and care she put into sewing it together."

With a simple shrug of his shoulder, he said, "It's something she loves doing."

"I've never learned," she replied in a hushed tone, damning her upbringing that never included those small, domestic things. She could cook some, sew small things like buttons on, keep her house semi-clean, but she didn't bake unless it came from a box, didn't quilt or crochet and all of the sudden, felt completely useless as a woman.

"I'm sure she would teach you if you'd like to learn."

"She lives here?"

"In Red Rock, yes. She lives with my parents on their place outside of town."

Grasping her hand in his, he lifted it to his lips and brushed a kissed over her palm. All ten toes curled in her shoes and the errant organ lying deep inside her chest, sped up to a pounding rhythm. The dark chocolate of his eyes looked straight into her soul and she wondered what he saw, the worthless woman when it came to anything domestic or the loving mother and good friend she tried so hard to be. Several black curls fell over his forehead and she couldn't resist the urge to push them back into place. She lifted the hand he didn't have in his grasp and pushed the hair back. The silky strand slipped through her fingers, tickling her hand.

His lips lifted in a small smile against her palm and his warmth of his breath over her skin, sent goose bumps flittering up her arms.

"Cold?" he whispered.

"No."

With a small tug, he pulled her into his arms and wrapped them around her like he'd never let go, if she'd only ask, but she couldn't—wouldn't.

"Have I told you how much I love all this red hair?" he asked, entwining his fingers in the strands lying over her shoulder.

Her lips parted but she shook her head.

He lifted a handful of her hair to his nose and inhaled. "Sweet pea."

"How'd you know?"

"It's one of my favorite fragrances. I have some planted on the side of the house."

The question rolled off her tongue in an awed murmur. "You garden?"

"A little," he replied in a low whisper. "I do plant flowers in the spring."

"You'll have to show me."

"Anytime, Red." He stepped back, took her hand and led her into the kitchen. Both of his hands grasped her by the hips and hoisted her up onto the granite countertop of the island. After a quick kiss to her lips, he said, "What would you like to eat?"

I know what I want him to eat.

She roughly cleared her throat, trying without success to block the racing thoughts in her mind. "A sandwich is fine."

"Okay. I've got ham, roast beef and turkey."

"Roast beef would be great."

"Beer or soda?"

"A beer would be good right now, but I probably should drink soda or whatever since I have to drive home."

One dark eyebrow shot up as the words rolled from his perfectly kissable lips. "You can always stay here." He stepped between her splayed thighs, bringing his erection in hot contact with her already weeping pussy, even though their clothing still separated skin from skin. "You know I want you, don't you?"

Every muscle in her body went on high alert when his hands grasped her hips and pulled her closer, centimeter by agonizing centimeter.

Kale wasn't a small man by any means and with her sitting on the countertop; they were in perfect alignment for some soul-shattering, orgasmic sex if she would just say yes.

Talking became impossible between her now parched lips. Her tongue swept out and attempted to wet the surface.

The scorching heat coming from his eyes did nothing to cool her off. When his head dipped and he captured her lips in a spell-binding melt-your-panties-kiss, she was lost. His tongue swept along the seam of her lips asking for her to open herself to him, give herself to him and ride the wave of desire he created every time she stood within a hundred yards of the devilishly handsome cowboy. With a tortured sigh, she complied and then whimpered when his tongue dove between her lips.

Tongues explored each other's mouths with each sweeping touch—stabbing and retreating, dancing together like they'd done it their whole lives.

One palm cupped her right breast and she moaned into his mouth. His thumb rasped over the hardened nub and even through her shirt, she could feel the pressure of his finger.

His lips moved from her mouth, across her cheek and stopped at her ear. Rasping breaths and wicked slide of his tongue sent shivers down her spine and fire through her belly.

"Please stay, Laurel," he murmured against her neck.

Sinful nips of his teeth soothed by the hot, wet licks and the scrape of his whiskers over her flesh left her barely able to think past the rush of desire in her ears.

"Food?" she asked, pulling herself together for a split second to try to bring the situation back under control.

He pulled away from her to stare into her eyes as longing raged in his gaze and confusion rippled across his face with a dip of his dark eyebrows.

"Huh?"

"Roast beef sandwich?"

The rush of need cooled slightly when his lips lifted into a devilish grin and he stepped back. "All right. I'll feed you," he replied, with a small chuckle.

Remaining on her perch, she watched while Kale whistled a soft tune and made sandwiches like a pro. Roast beef piled high, lettuce, tomato, cheese on a hoagie roll, completed the delicious looking delicacy of dinner he prepared.

"Your food awaits m'lady."

"Oh, aren't we the gallant one," she replied, taking the hand he offered to help her down.

With plates in hand, he indicated with a nod of his dark head to the dining room table. After they had taken seats across from each other, they ate in comfortable silence, which astonished Laurel. The feelings this amazing man stirred, made her think of hearth and home, two kids, maybe three, a dog and a white picket fence. Something totally foreign to the liberated woman she thought herself to be.

Moments later, her cell phone vibrated and she wondered who it could be. There weren't too many people who had her phone number.

"Sorry," she murmured, pulling her phone from her pocket and moving toward the window for some privacy.

"It's fine," Kale replied, taking another bite of his sandwich.

"Hello?"

"Officer Hayes? This is central dispatch. The chief needs to speak to you immediately."

"All right. Can you put him on?"

"Yes, ma'am. Hold the line."

After several seconds of silence, a deep, rugged voice said, "Officer Hayes, this is the chief. We have a problem."

"Problem, sir?"

"We've found another victim."

7

Kale watched Laurel snap the phone shut and rub her hand across her face. "Somethin' wrong, darlin'?"

"Yeah. I have to go out again."

"What's goin' on?"

"I can't say specifically, but it's police business and it has to do with the woman we found earlier." She glanced at Kimmy still asleep on the couch. "God, I hate waking her up."

"Leave her here. She'll be fine."

"I can't expect you to watch her for the night, Kale. I should take her home since I have no idea when I'll be back."

He stopped in front of her and took her face between his hands. "She probably won't even wake up, Laurel." Brushing his lips across hers, he groaned as she leaned into his embrace and he wrapped his hands around her back to deepen the kiss. His tongue swept inside her mouth and she brought her hands up around his neck. Her breast pressed into his chest and his cock tightened painfully behind the fly of his jeans. This wanting her and not having her was getting to him.

Pulling his mouth from hers, he whispered, "Go on and do what you need to do. We'll be here waiting for you."

The blue of her eyes softened and darkened to a deep sea blue. "Are you sure?"

"Yeah. Call me later if you can. If not, I'll see you whenever they let you go for the night." A frown pulled down the corners of her mouth and he fought the urge to kiss her again. "Don't let them work you all night, sweetheart. You need sleep, too."

"I know, but this kind of stuff gets my adrenaline rushing. I'll be wide awake for hours now."

"Maybe when you come back, we can put some of it to good use in my big bed."

A small grin little the corners of her lips. "Maybe." She picked up her purse and pulled out her keys. "Call my cell if you have any problems. If she wakes up or you need me for anything."

"We'll be fine until you get back."

Laurel glanced once more at her daughter and the love in her eyes made his chest ache.

"Come on. I'll walk you out to your car."

She shook her head and smiled. "Bad idea. You would probably kiss me again and it would take me another ten minutes to get out of here."

Her fingertips brushed over his lips. The groan rumbling in his chest slipped free, much to hear amusement. "You do that on purpose."

"Not me." Reaching behind him, she wrapped her hands in his hair and pulled his head down to meet her lips. Long before he was ready for it to be, the kiss ended and she slipped out the door.

"There isn't any way in hell I'm going to get some sleep now. I might as well get some work done," he said out loud, raking his hand through his hair. Letting his hand drifted down to his cock, he pressed hard against the erection, hoping to calm it down.

Cold shower?

"I can't do that. If Kimmy wakes up she'll be scared enough already being in a strange house."

Shaking his head and cussing under his breath about one fiery red-head and her too damned kissable lips, he walked down the hall to his office to grab something to work on while he waited. Hopefully, she wouldn't be too long. Otherwise it would be a long night.

* * * *

Sweat dripped in Laurel's eyes as she bent over the prone body of a young, twenty-something woman lying under a tree and half covered with compost. She wiped her forehead with the back of her arm and grumbled under her breath at the stifling heat, thinking she shouldn't be this uncomfortable since she used to live in Los Angeles and the summers there sucked.

With a heavy sigh, she sat back on her haunches and looked at the scene surrounding her. *This is getting crazy. To have a serial killer on the loose in Red Rock? Or are these women's deaths not even related?* Experience and the condition of the body pegged the woman's time of death approximately three hours ago. *It clears Kale of any wrong doing in this particular death since he spent the last couple of hours with me. But what about the others?*

"Hey, Laurel."

Looking up, she noticed one of her fellow officers walking toward her with a forensic kit in his hands. Silently, she compared him to Kale and found him lacking severely. Mike was tall like Kale, but he didn't have the bulk across his chest from hard physical labor the way Kale did, he didn't have the dreamy, smooth chocolate colored eyes like Kale and Mike's blond locks didn't do it for her. She shook her head, wishing the disturbing fascination she had for Kale away so she could concentrate on the case. "Hey, Mike. Are you working this with me?"

"Apparently. Chief called me and told me to come out here and help you."

"Ever done homicide work before?"

"Are you kidding? This is Red Rock, Montana. Population twenty thousand during the rodeo."

Laurel laughed. "True, but you didn't answer my question."

"Nope. I've only seen a dead body twice and those were both in the morgue."

"All right. Let me tell you one thing. Don't touch anything without asking me first. If we screw up any of the evidence, it could mean a conviction for a killer or an acquittal."

"No problem, boss." He glanced at the body and shuddered. "Are you sure it's homicide?"

"No. It's not my call to make that determination—it's the coroners. We just gather the evidence and process it for clues. He decides what she died from."

"Do you think this one is related to the one we found earlier?"

"I'm not sure, but it looks like it's a possibility. Both bodies were found in similar locations and in similar conditions." She tipped her head to the side and studied her newest partner. "Are you from around here, Mike?"

"Yep. Born and raised Montana boy. Why?"

"You might be able to help me since I'm not."

She fired off multiple questions toward Mike until he raised his hands in surrender. "Easy, Laurel. I can't answer your questions that fast."

"Sorry. I talk fast when I'm excited."

He scrunched up his face and she laughed. "This shit gets you off?"

"I wouldn't go that far, but yeah, it excites me. Why do you think I worked homicide in Los Angeles."

"I'd heard talk about you working out there, but I wasn't sure if it was true. I guess this answers my questions."

For the next couple hours, they worked in compatible silence, only to have it broken now and then when Mike asked her a question. The man's work seemed to be flawless and he made sure he didn't do anything to compromise the case. Except his tendency to glance in her direction when he thought she wasn't looking drove her up the wall.

Laurel stood and stretched her back. "I think we're done for now, Mike. We'll have to wait until they move her to finish the rest."

"Okay. How about we get some coffee and take a break?"

"You go ahead. I want to get to the ground under her when they move the body."

One of the guys who worked with the coroner had been hanging around for the last couple of hours, propped against a large tree several feet away. With a quick nod, the man started in her direction.

"You ready now?"

"Yes. She's all yours."

Mike stood beside her until they loaded up the woman and put her on their transport cart. The moment they cleared the scene, Laurel pulled the light from her belt so she could focus on the immediate spot under the woman's body.

"What are you looking for?" Mike asked, dropping down beside her.

"I'm not sure, but I'll know it when I see it."

Within moments, she located something she had a gut feeling would be important to the case and solving how this girl ended up here dead.

A huge grin spread across her face when she pulled out her tweezers, lifted the specimen from beneath the thin layer of leaves and dirt before dropping it into the plastic bag she held.

"What the hell is it?"

"I don't know, but my gut tells me it's important."

The massive high rushing through her veins had her running on pure adrenaline while she continued to sift through the leaves one by one, hoping to find more evidence. Mike took the other side of the resting place of the body and slowly moved things around. They gathered up one or two more things that were possibly related to the woman's death, tucking them away in separate plastic bag, until the entire area had been sifted through.

Blowing her bangs from her forehead with a swift exhale, Laurel stood and shifted from foot to foot, trying to bring some blood flow back into her lower limbs. Daylight had begun to filter through the trees to the east and she cussed under her breath. The last thing she wanted to do was be here through the night. Unclipping her cell phone from her waist, she glanced at the screen. No calls from Kale. Hoping that meant Kimmy hadn't awakened during the night, she fastened the phone back in the clip and brushed the dirt from her jeans.

"I think we've done all we can do, Mike. I'm calling it a day. I've been up for twenty-four hours at least, and I need to sleep."

"Yeah, I'm pretty beat, too. You'll let me know what else I need to do, right?"

"You got it. I'm headed to the prescient to drop this evidence off and then I'm going to go pick up my daughter. I'll see you at the office tomorrow morning. I'm telling the chief I need twenty-fours off."

Mike laughed and said, "You do that, Red."

Her gaze narrowed on him and she spat, "Don't call me, Red. I don't like it."

Mike raised his hands in surrender and took two steps back. "Sorry, Laurel. I won't do it again."

"Good. Then we understand each other." Laurel spun on her heel, pulled her keys from her pocket and walked toward where she'd left her car parked. Snapping at Mike about the nickname sounded stupid when she thought about it now, but she couldn't help it. No one called her Red—except Kale.

Forty-five minutes later, she pulled up in front of Kale's house and shut off her car. Exhaustion had started to settle into her shoulders and she sighed, rubbing the back of her neck and rotating her head, trying to loosen the muscles. She'd opened the files on the cases and compared notes on each to those on the current victim when she stopped at the police station. The bodies were found in similar condition. Badly beaten and raped. Kale had an alibi for each time of death including the one on his ranch. The patrons and the owner of the bar placed him there at the approximate time of death for the victim on his ranch. The second woman—the one she and Kimmy found—he'd spent the morning with her having sex in his living room. He couldn't possibly be the killer with all these airtight alibis. Relief washed through her at the realization. At least she didn't doubt him now. But who was behind the murders?

She slipped from the car and shut the door, hoping she could get Kimmy and go home.

Shit. I don't know if Teresa is doing anything or not. Hopefully she'll be able to watch Kimberly.

Not sure if Kale was awake yet since the sun had barely risen over the horizon, Laurel twisted the door handle and pushed it open. The soft *snick* sounded loud to her ears when she shut it behind her and walked toward the living room.

A smile drifted across her face when she stopped at the end of the couch and took in the adorable scene in front of her.

Kale lay on his back with one arm over his head and his dark eyelashes caressing his cheeks. Kimberly's blonde curls were spread over the arm around her back and she lay snuggled to his side, her head on his chest and her thumb in her mouth.

Tears burned the back of Laurel's eyelids at the scene before her. Never had any man burrowed his way into her heart with one small gesture. Her daughter was her life and to have a man she barely knew jump into help her with Kimmy—well it screamed *keeper* to her heart.

Making her way to his side, she leaned over and brushed her lips over his. The thick lashes lifted when she stood up and a smile that would light the darkest days, lit up his face.

"Hey," he murmured and stretched. "What times is it?"

"Too damned early." She glanced at her watch and said, "Six-thirty."

"Mmm." Kale looked down and smoothed his hand over Kimberly's curls. "She woke up a few hours ago, but went back to sleep pretty easily."

"Snuggled up to you—I have no doubt." *I wish it had been me.*

His brown-eyed gaze slid over her from the top of her head to the tips of her shoes. "You look like shit, darlin'."

"Thanks, Kale," she replied with a chuckle.

"Did you just get here?"

"Yeah. It took all night to process stuff and I'm beat."

"You look like it."

Kimmy yawned and opened her eyes.

"Hey, baby."

"Mommy," Kimmy said, brushing the curls from out of her face. "I'm hungry."

"Big surprise," Laurel replied, scooping her daughter up in her arms. "I'll get you some cereal when we get home." A heavy sigh left her lips as her gaze stopped on Kale. "Thanks for taking care of her for me."

"My pleasure, darlin'. Anytime."

"Be careful of saying something like that. You haven't had to deal with little Miss Hellion on her bad days."

Frown lines crinkled the skin between his eyes. "You need to sleep. Is your neighbor home to watch her for you?"

"I don't know. I couldn't call her. It's too early."

Kimmy scrambled out of Laurel's arms and Kale sat up before tugging Laurel down to his side.

"You shouldn't be drivin'. You'll fall asleep at the wheel. Stay here and sleep for a few hours and then go on home. I can watch Kimmy for a bit longer. No big deal."

"I couldn't ask—" Her words stopped with the pressure of his finger to her lips.

"You didn't ask, darlin'. I offered." Kale stood and walked into the kitchen. Grabbing a bowl, spoon and a box of cereal from the cupboard, she smiled as he made breakfast for her daughter. The whole scene seemed so domestic, it felt right. "Up you go, honey," he said, putting Kimberly on the chair. "Eat your breakfast and I'm going to put mommy to bed."

To bed? Wow. I like the sound of that.

"Your turn."

With a small tug on her hand, he pulled Laurel to her feet and started down the hall, past the two guest rooms until they reached his bedroom. He stopped at the end of his bed and whispered, "Stay right there." Drawers opened and closed while he searched for something. "Ah-ha." A white T-shirt appeared in his hands. He turned around and walked back to her side. "This should work. Take off your clothes."

Laurel's hands trembled as she grabbed the bottom of her shirt and lifted it over her head. Heat glowed in his eyes while she unhooked her bra and let it slid down her arms.

"Touch me," she murmured, dropping the material to the floor. Heat sizzled between them like a sultry summer night in the South. Her pussy wept with need and her nipples tightened into hard little nubs.

"No."

"No?"

"If I do, you'll never get to sleep and though it's great for a man's ego to have a woman pass out after coming so hard she sees stars, it's not good to have her fall asleep while he's making love to her." The smile on his lips looked wistful and patient. "I would love to lay you out on my bed, kiss you from your sleepy eyes to those cute toes, but right now, you need sleep and I need to keep an eye on Kimmy." He slipped the cotton material over her head and pulled it down. The edges of the hem reached to mid-thigh. "You look better in my shirt than I do."

"Please. I'm swimming in this thing," she replied, glancing down.

His left eyebrow quirked and the smile lingering on his lips grew bigger. "But I envy the material clinging to those fabulous breasts and caressing your amazing thighs."

The calluses on his index finger felt rough, but wonderful against her cheek as he traced a path from the corner of her eye to her jaw and then around behind her neck. He pulled her gently toward him and brushed his lips over hers so softly, she wasn't sure he'd even kissed her.

Without taking the kiss deeper, he stepped back, pulled the covers down on his bed and gently nudged her under the covers. "Sleep. I'll wake you up after bit and we'll go from there."

Exhaustion tugged at the edges of her mind. It had been a long time since she'd been this tired. "Don't let me sleep too long. Okay? I can't take up your whole day watching Kimmy."

Need and something else swam in his eyes. "Go to sleep. We'll deal with everything later." After a small kiss to her forehead, he silently walked into the hall and shut the door behind him.

* * * *

Kale returned to the kitchen for coffee and to check on Kimmy. The little girl shoveled cereal into her mouth and spilled bits and pieces on the table. "Slow down, honey. You'll choke."

The wide, toothy, cereal-filled grin she gave him melted his heart. Laurel's words came back to his mind and he smiled. The cute little blonde had wrapped the organ around her finger without even trying.

"Okay. Coffee and then we'll figure out what we are going to do today while your mommy rests. Sound like a plan?"

Kimmy's curls bounced as she nodded and shoveled more cereal in her mouth.

"Done?" he asked several moments later, noticing the cereal had disappeared and only milk remained in her bowl.

Kimberly jumped down from the chair and ran to the back sliding glass door. "Outside."

"Not yet, sweetie pea. We need to get your shoes and socks back on and I need my boots," he said, sliding his cup into the sink.

"Outside!" she shouted, giving him a glimpse of the hellion Laurel mentioned.

"Whoa! Hold your drawers on little girl. Shoes and socks first," he said, grabbing her tiny sneakers from the coffee table. "Come here and we'll put these on."

Within seconds of having footwear in place, the two of them walked out the backdoor. Kale followed quickly as Kimmy took off at a dead run for a three year old, toward the barn and the chickens roaming the ground. Irritated squawks, flying feathers and little girl giggles rang true in the early morning light. The sounds of a happy child made Kale wish he had some of his own, although not with his ex. *Thank God, we never had any.* A shudder rolled down his back at the thought of a child between him and Judy. The fight he would have had on his hands during the divorce and subsequent issues of co-parenting with the bitch surely would have soured any thoughts of other children. A pleasant notion of a child between him and Laurel washed away the acid thoughts of his ex.

"Enough of that. Good God! Laurel isn't looking for any kind of relationship with me or anyone else." He raked his fingers through his hair and followed Kimberly with his gaze. "The last thing I need is to think of any kind of relationship with her. Great sex? Yeah, I'm all for it, but a relationship? No way. She doesn't even want to stay here in Red Rock."

Kale planted his butt on the fence rail and watched the little girl. When she got tired of chasing the chickens, he picked her up, planted her on his hip and headed for the barn. Squeals and giggles almost broke his eardrums as they got closer to the horses.

"Horsie?"

"Yep. Want to ride?"

Twin dimples peeked out of her cheeks with her big smile and his heart melted into a gooey puddle.

One of her blonde curls wrapped around his finger when he pushed some of her hair out of her face. "Someday some poor fella isn't going to know what to do when you flash those dimples at him. He's gonna gush all over himself just to get close to you."

"Horsie!" she squealed and Kale laughed.

"Okay, okay." Sitting her on a bale of hay, he said, "Stay there and don't move."

He grabbed a halter from the nail on the wall and slipped it over the head of his gentlest mare. Knowing he didn't have a saddle small enough for her, he decided to put a regular sized one on and let her ride in front of him. "You know, if your momma sticks around, I'm going to have to buy a saddle your size so you can ride by yourself. I'll even teach you how to ride. How does that sound?"

Her high-pitched giggles and clapping of her small hands made him shake his head. *Girl's.*

Once the mare was saddled, he put Kimmy on the back of the horse, told her to hold on and led the animal out into the sunshine. He led her around the yard a few times while she laughed.

"You're a natural, honey. Look at you!"

With thoughts of checking the fences and cattle on his mind, he tossed the reins over the mare's head, slid his foot into the stirrup and hoisted himself up in the saddle behind Kimmy.

"How about we get a little work done while your momma is sleepin'?"

"Go horsie," she said, rocking in the saddle.

"A regular horsewoman you'll turn out to be," Kale said with a laugh as he wrapped one arm around her small body and nudged the mare into a trot.

For over two hours, they rode the fence line checking for breaks, stopping by the water troughs to make sure the cattle had plenty and just enjoying the scenery—well he did anyway. Kimmy chattered like a magpie with every movement she saw and all he could do was laugh and be amazed at the energy one three-year-old had.

Deciding to cut the time in the saddle short today, he turned the horse around and headed back for the house. Kimberly's chatter had slowed down a little bit so he figure she might be getting tired.

"We can go back to the house, get you a bath and sit and watch cartoons. Maybe I can get some of the work done on the project I have going since I didn't get any done last night."

"Cartoons?"

"Yep. You like cartoons?"

She nodded and smiled as she peeked over her shoulder at him.

"What are we gonna do for clean clothes though, huh?" Contemplating the newest development, he mulled over in his mind how to get Kimberly some clean clothes and probably Laurel too, even though Laurel could run around in his T-shirt and her underwear and he'd be happy as a clam. "I bet your momma's keys are in her purse. We could run over to your house, get you both some clean clothes and bring them back to my house. Then she wouldn't have any reason to have to run home right away." He looked down at the blonde head in front of him. "What do you think, little pixie?"

When they reached the barn, he dismounted and then pulled Kimmy down to set her on her feet. One of the tame barn cats rubbed against her legs and she squealed in delight.

"Good grief, girl. We need to tone down those squeals or I won't have any eardrums left before the end of the day."

Kimmy laughed and chased the cat toward the door with her arms outstretched.

Several minutes later, Kale had the mare unsaddle, brushed down and turned out so he went to find the little scamp, hoping she hadn't gone far.

Walking out into the blinding summer sun, he glanced around, but didn't see her. "Kimmy?" Around the back of the barn—nothing. "Kimberly!" he yelled, starting to panic when he couldn't locate her right away. "Fuck! The pool." Taking off at a dead run, he skidded around the corner of the house and came to a dead halt. A roar of laughter burst from his lips as the terror calmed and relief took its place. Sitting in the middle of the mud hole he made almost daily for the pigs, sat Kimberly with mud from the tip of her blonde, now dirty brown curls, to the tips of her once white tennis shoes.

The pigs grunted and sniffed at her, but did nothing to the intruder in their midst.

"You are bound and determined to get me into trouble with your momma, aren't you little girl."

White teeth flashed amongst the dirt caked on her face when she smiled and clapped her hands, slinging mud everywhere.

"All right little one. Come out of there."

She shook her head and smiled again.

"You're gonna make me come in there after you, aren't you."

After a heavy sigh and a grin heavenward, he stepped into the pen and waded in after her. By the time he got them both near the backdoor, not only did she have mud caked on every surface of her body, but so did he.

"Off with those clothes, missy. We need to throw both of our clothes in the washer," he said, pulling her top off over her head and tugging her pants down but left her underwear since they didn't appear worse for wear. Shucking his boots, socks, jeans and shirt, he grabbed everything up in a pile, herded Kimmy into the living room and plopped her down in front of the television while he put the clothes in the washer and went to find clean ones for himself and a shirt for Kimmy to wear.

Quietly, he pushed open the door to his room and glanced at Laurel sound asleep in his big bed. Her red hair reflected spun gold amongst the strands as the sunlight filtered in through the drawn blinds. Her hands were tucked up under the side of her face and her long eyelashes rested on her cheeks. She looked so peaceful and beautiful lying with her head on his pillow, he had the insane urge to keep her there forever.

With a quick shake of his head, he grabbed clean clothes, a T-shirt for Kimmy and Laurel's dirty clothes from the floor. He had to wash theirs anyway; he might as well do hers, too.

He returned to the living room after pulling on his and dropping the dirty clothes in the washer, to find Kimmy engrossed in the cartoons, but he had to get her into the bathtub.

"All right my little mud pie maker. Let's get you cleaned up," he said, taking her hand and heading for the spare bathroom off the hall. Luckily, the mud didn't reach anything but his clothes so he didn't have to shower too. "Bubbles?" he asked, grabbing an old bottle of bubble bath from when one of his nieces had been over.

"Bubbles!" she yelled.

"Sshh. We don't want to wake Mommy."

"Sshh," she repeated and covered her mouth with her hand as she giggled.

Once he had the tub partly filled and enough bubbles to probably cover Kimmy up, he helped her into the tub and let her splash. He glanced into the mirror and was surprised at the sparkle of life in his eyes at the girlish laughter coming from the tub. It had been a long time since anyone had him laughing the way the two Hayes girls did.

What would it be like to have her and Laurel in his life all the time? To have this cute button of a girl call him Daddy? To have Laurel in his bed every night?

"Not a good thing to be contemplatin'."

He parked his butt on the toilet lid to watch Kimmy while she sat in the tub. His nieces had left a few toys over at his house the last time they were there, so she had a few things to play with.

His thoughts drifted to things he shouldn't be thinking about, but he couldn't help himself. The saucy red-head had wormed her way under his skin and he couldn't seem to get her out or want to, for that matter. He liked having her in his life and he loved being between her thighs even if it hadn't been often enough.

"Okay, little girl. Let's get you washed up," he said, coming to his feet and grabbing the shampoo bottle off the shelf.

When he had her cleaned up and dressed in one of his smaller T-shirts, he put her back down on the floor in front of the television and walked to the dining room table where he'd spread out the plans he was working on. He hoped the work would take his mind of the gorgeous woman sleeping in his bed at the moment, but he didn't hold out much optimism. She seemed to be a major distraction in his life these days and he'd only known her a short time. What would she do to his once orderly existence if she became a permanent part of it?

"Probably give me one hell of a wild ride for the rest of my days," he grumbled good-naturedly to himself.

"Color," Kimmy said, climbing up on the chair.

"You want to color?"

Handing her a blank piece of paper and some spare crayons he kept for his nieces, he smiled as Kimberly's tongue came out of her mouth and she studied her masterpiece. After several minutes, she grinned and handed him the paper.

"Well, what have we here? You've drawn a mighty pretty picture, little lady."

"Horsie."

"Ah. So you've made a picture of the horse we rode today, huh? Very nice. Want to put it on the refrigerator?"

She hopped down from her chair and followed him into the kitchen. A few small magnets hung to the door—advertisements from local businesses he bought supplies from, the pizza place in town and the diner he frequented since he hated eating alone.

"Where shall we put it?"

"There," she said, point to smack dab center of the bottom door.

Once he proudly hung her picture, she whirled around and walked back into the living room, plopping down in front of the television again. He smiled and went back to his plans on the table, but he found himself watching the sweet little girl more than working on his drawings.

The washer beeped indicating the clothes had finished their cycle, drawing him from his musings.

He hadn't realized how much work kids were until he'd gotten involved with Laurel and Kimberly and he wondered how she did it alone—working full time and taking care of her daughter. Moments later, he had the clothes in the dryer and returned to the living room, but instead of going back to his work, he sat on the couch and stared out into the yard behind the house.

Melancholy thoughts drifted through his mind. He'd originally built the house with a wife and children in mind, but when things fell apart with Judy, it became a lonely existence. Yes, he had his hired hands, friends like Cade and Natalie, his parents, and his siblings along with their passel of kids, but all in all, the house seemed barren without the laughter of a family.

The pat of a small hand on his cheek brought him back to the little girl occupying his space.

"Hungry."

Kale glanced at his watch and scowled. *Noon already?*

"Let's get some lunch then, huh?" He stood and followed his little charge into the kitchen.

Detouring at the sound of the buzzer on the dryer, he walked toward the laundry room to retrieve the clothes and get Kimmy dressed before Laurel woke up. Plus, Laurel's clothes would be nice and clean, too. After he got Kimberly dressed, she parked in one of the chairs at his table, swinging her little legs back and forth.

"What do you feed a three year old anyway?" he asked himself as he stared into the bare refrigerator. "We have mayo, God only knows how old sandwich meat." He sniffed the meat and wrinkled his nose, eliciting a giggle from his audience at the table. "We aren't eating that." Next stop the cupboard, which didn't yield much more than the refrigerator. "Hmm. I tell you what. Let me get my boots on and we'll run to the store. We can get something for lunch and maybe some food for dinner," he said, shutting the freezer once he checked there too. "We can barbeque and maybe keep your momma here for a few more hours."

Within a few minutes, he had Kimmy buckled into her car seat and was driving down the driveway toward town. The local grocery had given way to progress a few years ago and now their little town got their very own super grocery store.

Kale pulled into a spot, got Kimmy out and into a cart and walked toward the door. The wide-eyed stares and raised eyebrows brought a frown to his face. Not one to worry about what others thought, he shook it off and pushed the cart down the meat aisle.

"Well, if it isn't Kale Dunn. Who's the kid?"

Narrowing his eyes, he glared at the busty blonde standing next to his cart. "None of your business, Michelle."

"Wow, aren't we the protective one." Michelle eyed Kimberly before she gave him a tolerant smile. "You haven't called me in awhile, sugar. I've missed you."

"I've been busy."

"I see," she said, staring at Kimberly again. "She can't be yours, Kale. She's too blonde and blue eyed."

"What if she is?"

"I'd be asking where you've been hiding her," Michelle said, tapping her fingernail to her lips. "Doesn't matter. I still want you even if you have a kid."

"No, Michelle, you don't want me. You want my bank account."

Painted fingernails ran down the buttons on his shirt. "Not true, lover. I want all of you. Every muscled, tantalizing inch buried deep—"

He put a hand over her mouth to stop her words before Kimberly and everyone in the store heard her. "Knock it off," he hissed. "You've got some nerve, you know. You're screwing half the county yet you think I'm going to play along, well guess what, doll, I'm not interested. Find some other guy to use up and discard. I'm done."

Throwing one of the packages of steaks in the basket, he pushed the cart on down the aisle and around the corner. Kimberly patted the white knuckled grip he held onto the basket and smiled up at him.

"I think we need to get you home, darlin'. You're probably starvin' by now," he said and then kissed the top of her head. Several more items made it into the basket. Hot dogs, buns, lunch meat, peanut butter and jelly, and anything else he could think of to feed a kid, while he kept a keen eye out for Michelle. He wouldn't put it past her to cause a scene again to get his attention.

8

Late afternoon sunlight streamed through the window, pulling Laurel from her wickedly sexy dreams of Kale and what his lips could do to her. Opening her eyes, she glanced around the room, confused for a moment until she remembered him forcing her to sleep in his bed.

His bed.

She rolled over, stretched like a contented cat and then pulled his pillow to her face. The scent of male and the faint odor of his cologne buried in the soft cotton of the pillowcase warmed something inside her she thought dead and buried with Dennis.

Stupid. Getting tangled up with Kale is really stupid.

"Even if tangled and sweaty is what I want, I'll only get hurt in the long run," she grumbled as she sat up on the side of the bed and brushed her tousled hair out of her face.

Visions of how she'd found him and Kimberly this morning, sound asleep on the couch, drifted across her mind. He'd taken her daughter and cared for her like his own. How many men would do such a thing? Very few, she knew. One of the thoughts she never contemplated during her pregnancy or any time since Kimberly's birth was how Dennis would have reacted when he found out she'd gotten pregnant. Dennis had told her he loved her—swore he wanted to spend the rest of his life with her. They'd talked marriage, babies, white picket fences and SUV's, but never once did he let on he already had a wife.

Betrayal and anger slashed through her heart. He might not have lied outright, but he'd lied by omission nonetheless. How could he have done that if he'd loved her?

"Maybe I don't know what love is? Maybe I need to just worry about me and Kimberly and to hell with men." Leave things the way they are with Kale. Sex and nothing else. No entanglements, no worrying about whether he cared about her and Kimberly, or whether they had any kind of future together.

"Future?" She released a small snort and stood to retrieve her clothes. *No clothes? What the hell? I know they were on the floor when I went to sleep.* The long cotton T-shirt covering her essentials would have to do until she could figure out what happened to the rest of her things. The soft material caressed her thighs and her breasts like she wanted Kale to do with his hands. Damn, the man had nice hands, nice lips, nice eyes...she shook her head to clear her wayward thoughts. Going in that direction would lead to other things and right now, she needed to keep her mind clear and her thoughts away from getting him in the bed with her.

Glancing at the red numbers on the alarm clock next to the bed, she cussed under her breath at the stubborn-assed cowboy in the other room, for letting her sleep so late. Rarely did she sleep a full eight hours, but he must have thought she needed to. "I could have sworn I told him not to let me sleep too late."

You were exhausted though.

"It doesn't matter. Kimberly is my first priority, sleep comes second."

Maybe he wants to take care of you for a change.

"Take care of me? I don't need anyone to take care of me."

What makes you so sure?

"I've been taking care of myself for several years."

And you are doing such a fine damned job of it; you decked your brother-in-law for beating up on your sister. Makes sense, Laurel.

"Shut up. Just shut up," she grumbled at her inner voice who loved to argue in her head.

The door to his bedroom creaked open as she tugged on it and stepped into the hall.

"I bet Kimberly has him eating out of the palm of her hand."

The pitter-patter of her feet as she followed the long corridor toward the living room, didn't display the annoyance running down her back in a sufficient amount. When she walked into the front hall and looked across the space, she caught the devilishly handsome cowboy doing something she never thought she'd see—cooking.

"Hey, darlin'. Did you sleep well?" he asked, catching sight of her from near the center island.

"Why'd you let me sleep so long? It's going on three in the afternoon," she said, making sure the irritation could be heard clearly in her voice.

"You obviously needed it, Laurel, or you wouldn't have slept like a dead person. I checked on you a couple of times—even kissed you and you didn't move." He sipped from a spoon and then stirred whatever was in the pot, again, not giving her the satisfaction of a reaction to her bad-tempered snit. "You hungry?"

"Starving."

His warm chuckle sent goose bumps skittering down her arms.

"By the way, where are my clothes? I could have sworn I left them on the floor in your room."

"You did. I washed them."

"You did laundry?"

The raised eyebrow over his left eye and the smile twitching at his oh-so-kissable lips, had heat pooling in her belly and racing down her legs.

"I had to. Your daughter decided to make mud pies in the pig pen earlier."

"She did?"

"Yep. Sneaky little thing took off after she and I came back from checking fences. I thought she was chasing the cat from the barn, but when I found her, she had mud from the top of her head to the tips of her tennis shoes."

Laurel couldn't help the smile she felt drifting across her mouth at the picture. "I should have told you to watch her close. She likes to chase things and get into everything."

His shoulder lifted in a nonchalant shrug as he set the spoon on the counter. "No harm done except maybe the pigs are a little put out."

His steps brought him toward her with a sexy roll of his hips and his eyes held a determined gleam she wasn't sure she wanted to interrupt. Every inch of dominating gorgeous male, tugged at her insides coiling tight like a spring ready to let loose with nothing more than a single tough of his callused hand. Goose bumps rose on her arms again and a shiver raced down her back, the closer he got. By the time he stood in front of her, her belly quivered and her breathing came in rapid pants. Heat spiraled through her veins on a rush, stopping and centering low in her middle. One finger slid down her cheek as his musky male scent surrounded her. Her tongue swiped over her now parched lips. "What's for supper?"

"You?" he asked, dropping his voice to a low purr.

Her pussy clenched and cream slid out of her to moisten her panties in a wickedly erotic way. "Somehow I don't think that will satisfy the hunger making my stomach growl. It would satisfy something else though."

"Later?"

The question and heat in his gaze reminded her of each time he kissed her, touched any place on her body and heaven help her, when he made her scream as she climaxed right there in his living room. *Had it only been a few short days ago? God, it seems like I've known him forever.*

"Maybe." The purr of her voice didn't sound anything like a sound she'd heard from her lips before. *Damn, he's turning me inside out.*

The softness of his lips nibbling at the corner of hers had a moan bubbling in her throat. His hands roamed her back and pulled her hips tighter against his pelvis. The hard erection he sported behind the fly of his jeans haywired her brain and made her think of hot, sweaty sex, long languishing kisses and explosive orgasms.

"Save those thoughts for later, darlin'. Food is ready," he grumbled as his lips whispered over her neck all too briefly before he stepped back and gave her one of his devastating smiles.

"You're rotten and way too tempting for my sanity," she grumbled, earning a wicked chuckle from him. The television blasted cartoons from multiple speakers imbedded somewhere in the walls and she glanced around for her daughter. "Where's Kimmy?"

"Lying on the floor over there," he said, nodding toward the television.

Laurel scooted a little closer to the back of the couch and caught a glimpse of her normally squirmy three year old, engrossed in the slap-stick of the cartoon show.

"I take it you don't let her watch cartoons much."

"Not a lot, but it's fine."

Kale moved around the kitchen like a pro, grabbing dishes and silverware and setting the table for three.

"Can I help?"

"Nope. I got it." His hot gaze slipped over her bare legs and she shifted from foot to foot as chills popped up on her arms. "I love those gorgeous legs, darlin', but you might want to put somethin' more on for dinner."

Deciding to light a little fire under him and keep the lust smoldering in those pools of chocolate brown, she sauntered close enough her breasts brushed against his rock hard chest, and whispered over his lips, "I don't know where my clothes are, cowboy, since someone swiped them from the bedroom."

With a rough clearing of his throat and a few difficult appearing swallows, he replied, "I'll get 'em."

She glanced down, ran one finger over his erection strained the front of his jeans and grinned.

"Witch," he growled and stepped away. His ass leaving looked just as yummy as the front view coming back. He returned with her blouse and jeans freshly washed, dried and *ironed?*

"You ironed my jeans?"

"It's the cowboy way, babe. Creased and pressed."

The I'm-gonna-eat-you-up grin on his lips tempted her beyond endurance to sample from his delectable mouth. Slipping one hand behind his head, she tugged until his searing lips settled over hers. She gasped, giving him access to the inside and allowing his tongue to dive between her parted lips. The invasion had her moaning her delight and tipping her head to fit everything together like two puzzle pieces. Each wicked stroke drove passion beyond control, beyond want and into blistering need.

The brush of his mouth along her jaw to her ear spiked her desire hard as he found the sensitive spot just below and licked. Searing heat from his callused palms radiated down her legs when he gripped her ass cheeks and yanked her up against his chest. All she wanted to do was melt into him and let him do whatever he wanted.

A small hand smacked against her bare leg, dragging the thoughts of hot sweaty sex between the sheets with this devastatingly handsome cowboy, to the pixy face of her daughter. *Shit!*

"Uh, hi baby."

Kimberly held up her arms for Laurel to pick her up.

"I'll get supper on," Kale said, his voice raspy and deep with passion as he moved away.

She bent down and scooped up Kimberly in her arms and asked, "Want to come with me so I can get dressed, babydoll?"

Her daughter nodded and buried her face in Laurel's neck. She felt like shit, ignoring Kimmy like that. Damn the man could make her forget everything and everyone except him and his sexy-ass body.

Moments later, she slipped into the bathroom and closed the door behind them, shutting out the temptation of Kale and the wicked thoughts of his hot mouth trailing wetness all over her.

* * * *

The soft click of the bathroom door brought Kale out of the sex-induced fog he'd been in since Laurel walked out of the bedroom in nothing more than his T-shirt. God, she'd been delectable, willing and scorching hot when he'd touched her.

He raked his hand through his hair and exhaled a frustrated sigh. The sexy red-head twisted him six ways to Sunday and she knew it too. There wasn't a damned thing he could do about it or wanted to do about it either—except fuck her until they both couldn't breathe. Remembering her slick pussy wrapped around him the one and only time he had managed to make her think of him and nothing else, zipped across his thoughts, driving his need for her higher. What he would give to feel it again.

Within moments, supper was laid out on the table and he'd placed a couple of phone books on one chair for Kimmy to sit on so she could reach the table. He stood at the refrigerator pouring himself a glass of milk when he heard the bathroom door open and glanced over his shoulder. The take-no-shit cop had replaced the delectable woman from the top of her tight ponytail to the tips of her toes even if she now wore pressed jeans. The small smile he let drift over his mouth made her eyes narrow as she walked toward him with Kimmy on her hip.

"Supper's on. What would you like to drink?"

"Milk or water is fine for me and Kimmy."

He nodded and said, "Have a seat. I made one chair up for her."

"I see that. Thank you."

After they'd both taken a chair and started eating, he wondered at her quietness. Her sassy mouth had been all over him not thirty minutes before and now she seemed subdued and almost embarrassed by her behavior.

"You okay?"

"Yeah, why?"

"You seem too quiet."

Her shoulders lifted in a shrug, but her eyes didn't meet his. "Just thinking."

"Of?"

When her gaze came up to meet his, he frowned at the distance in her eyes. "I'm sorry about before."

"Sorry?"

"Yeah. I shouldn't have come on to you in such a manner. It's not who I am, Kale."

"Who are you then, Laurel? I thought you were a sexy, smart, funny, gorgeous woman who I'm extremely attracted to and you make me hotter than hel...a furnace when you're close to me," he replied, taking her hand in his and bringing it to his lips.

The soft sigh escaping from her mouth sounded almost forlorn.

She pushed the bowl from in front of her and pulled her hand from his grasp. "I don't want you to get the wrong impression about me—about us."

"What impression are you talking about?"

"The notion there could be something more between you and I than casual sex." She jumped to her feet, pushing the chair back an irritating *scrape* to the tile floor and walked to the windows facing out toward the backyard.

He moved behind her and placed his hands on her shoulders, kneading the knotted muscles with his thumbs until she sagged against his chest. "Let's take this one day at a time. Shall we? I know you aren't lookin' for a relationship and I'm not sure I am either, but I do like havin' you as a friend and I don't want to lose it for anythin'."

"A friend?"

"Friends with benefits then," he whispered next to her ear and felt the shudder roll through her. "I'm more than mildly attracted to you, Laurel, if you hadn't noticed earlier and I'm pretty sure you feel the same way. Where it goes from here, I don't know and I don't think you do either. There isn't anythin' wrong with us spending time together."

The stiffening of her body beguiled the softness of the woman he knew existed. "I can't love anyone else besides Dennis, Kale. He was everything to me."

"Even if he lied?"

She spun around and glared. "He didn't lie."

Bringing one finger to her cheek, he let it slide down and then traced her ear with it. "He didn't tell you he was married."

"N-no, but—"

He pressed his finger to her lips stopped the flow of words. He captured her gaze with his, making sure she understood what he said. She probably didn't want to hear it, but he needed to say it. "It doesn't matter. Unless you are willing to let someone else into your heart, there's no way anyone can compete with his memory. You've made him into someone you wanted him to be in your mind, not the man he really was. He led you on, using you but never giving himself to you like a man should if they are in love with you." Tears sparkled on her lashes and he brushed a small kiss to her nose. "I can't offer you love—not yet, but I can offer you me. I'm nothing more than a hardworking, simple man who finds you drop-dead sexy and loves spending time with you in and out of the sack."

A small smile and soft chuckle made him want to scoop her up and snuggle her on his lap. Her wandering hands had his dick harder behind the fly of his jeans even though he'd hardly softened at all while she'd been in the bathroom. Her touch drove him crazy, but he would wait until she came to him of her own free will without coercion and without the ghost of Dennis between them.

He took her hand and led her back to the dining room table. Kimberly had already climbed down and now sat in front of the television again. Grabbing the dishes from the table, he walked into the kitchen to wash them, but Laurel had already started some hot water and was splashing dish soap in sink.

"I'll wash if you dry," she said, glancing at him through her lashes. "I don't know where everything goes."

"Sure, darlin'. Then how about we find a nice movie to watch until Kimmy is ready to go to sleep." The frown on her face had him asking, "What?"

"I should get on home. Not that I don't appreciate you watching her for me, but we've been here all day. You let me sleep in your bed, for goodness sake."

"I wish I could have been in there with you," he replied sweeping his finger over her lips and then capturing them with his. "Mmm. I love the way you taste." He shifted to her ear and nipped at her earlobe. "I'm not gonna beg, Laurel. Stay or don't. It's up to you."

They finished the dishes without another word, although he had things on the tip of his tongue to tell her like how he wished she would let the memory of her ex-lover go. How he wanted her in his bed and in his life, but he wasn't going to push her. How he loved her little girl and how much she was coming to mean to him in such a short time, it scared the hell out of him. The image of her and Kimberly living with him here, in his home, day by day, year to year, giving him a son or more sweet little girls, hearth and home, Christmas' in front of the fireplace with their children's faces lit up, having his family over for Sunday supper's...

"Kale?"

Damn it! Pull your head out man. She said she didn't want a relationship.

"Sorry. I kind of spaced out there for a minute."

"Yeah, I noticed," she replied with a sad smile.

The phone on the counter rang and he frowned at it. He almost didn't want to answer it and ruin this time with Laurel. When he glanced at the caller ID, he rolled his eyes. Natalie.

He hit the talk button and brought the receiver to his ear. "Hey, Nat. What's up?"

"Hey, handsome. How about you come over for dinner on Sunday and bring Laurel and Kimmy?"

"I don't know. I'll have to ask."

"Grandma and Mom will be here."

"You're going to subject poor Laurel to your grandmother? You are a mean woman, Natalie Weston."

The wicked laugh on the other end of the phone had him shaking his head.

"She's not that bad, Kale. Grandma just has a wicked sense of humor and a mouth without any kind of filter."

"You aren't kiddin' there, honey. She's a hoot. Hang on a second and I'll ask Laurel since she's standing right here."

"She's still at your house? Mmm."

"Knock it off, Nat." He pulled the phone from his ear and said, "Natalie and Cade are inviting you, me and Kimmy to their place on Sunday for supper. Would you like to go?"

Laurel captured her upper lip between her teeth and chewed it for a moment.

"Don't feel pressured, darlin'. It's only supper." The relief and uncertainty reflected in her eyes tore at his heart. "Listen, Nat, I'll let you know in a day or two."

"Sure, Kale. Tell Laurel and Kimmy hello for me and I'll talk to you later. Bye." The phone clicked in his ear.

"If you want to think about it, that's fine. If you don't want to go, it's okay too."

"You know, I really like Natalie and I thought I wouldn't."

"Why?"

She shook her head and dropped her gaze. With one finger under her chin, he brought her face up so he could look into her eyes.

"Tell me."

"I-I need to go," she said, stepping away from him.

Apparently she wasn't ready to give into what he saw in her eyes. Jealousy lit up her gaze when she looked at him and he wondered what else she hid deep inside.

Laurel slipped on her socks and shoes and gathered her and Kimberly's things.

"When can I see you again?"

Her bottom lip disappeared between her teeth and her eyes held a wary look.

"I don't know, Kale. I need some time."

"Time to what, Laurel? To run away from what's going on between us because if that's the case, forget it darlin'. I'm not letting you."

"There's nothing going on between us, Kale."

"Yeah?"

"Yeah," she replied, before she disappeared out the door, Kimmy on her hip and tears glistening on her lashes.

9

"Stupid, stupid, stupid," Laurel chanted as she retrieved the car seat from Kale's porch and slipped Kimmy into it. She wished she had someone to talk to—a girlfriend or someone who might understand all of the crazy things running through her mind and her heart.

As the lights of Kale's house disappeared in her rearview mirror, the tightness in her chest didn't. The feelings of wanting him to hold her and make things better didn't either. The tears burning her eyelids wouldn't go away and she considered flipping a u-turn in the middle of town to return to his house and back to his arms.

"Not an option, Laurel," she said out loud. "Yes, he wants you. Yes, you are attracted to him and he is to you, but it can't go anywhere."

But you want it to.

"No—no, I don't."

Yes, you do. You want him to be the man of your dreams. You want him to force Dennis from your mind and your heart.

The darkness of the parking lot in front of her apartment complex did nothing to calm her nerves when she pulled in several minutes later. Headlights reflected off the front of the building and revealed someone sitting on her steps. She shut off the engine and turned off the lights. "I don't need this right now."

She removed Kimmy from her seat and walked toward the front as her sister stood and wobbled like she was drunk. "Sis?"

"Laurel? Help me," her sister whispered and slid to the ground.

"Teresa!" Laurel screamed as she put Kimberly down and screamed her neighbor's name again.

"My goodness. What's all the ruckus?"

"Call nine-one-one."

"Oh Lordy," Teresa said before disappearing back into her apartment.

Several minutes later, she came back out with a blanket and a cool wash cloth.

"They should be here shortly, Laurel. Here. Put this over her so she doesn't get chilled. What happened?"

"Her fucking dumbass husband. God, I could kill him right now!" She glanced sideways and realized Kimmy stood next to the wall with tears in her eyes. "Can you take her upstairs while we wait for the ambulance? She doesn't need to see this."

"Sure, honey."

The wail of a siren could be heard in the distance about the time Elizabeth said her name. "Laurel?"

"What happened?"

"Jeff."

Rage swept through Laurel so fast, she shook. "Did he do this? Are you telling me he beat the shit out of you?"

"Yes."

"Don't say anything else, Elizabeth. Let the police handle it."

"You are the police."

"I'm not on duty and I can't handle a case where I'm personally involved, but when they ask and they will ask, you'd better tell them the truth," she insisted as the ambulance screeched to a stop in the parking lot.

"What's the problem?" the paramedic said as he dropped his bag and his partner brought up the rear with a stretcher. Unfortunately, she recognized him right away from her issue with Cade's nephew. Chance Dalton. "Well, well. Officer Hayes."

"This is my sister. She's been beaten by her husband and needs treatment, Mr. Dalton."

He snapped back like he'd been smacked, his eyes narrowing and his cheeks flushing with anger.

"Not a problem, Officer. Let me take a look."

While the paramedics worked on Elizabeth and got her on the stretcher, Laurel trembled so hard her teeth rattled. Her fingernails dug into her palms as she fought for control and tried to dissipate the red haze in her vision. The thought of doing bodily damage to Jeff fed her anger to the point she wanted to hurt him—bad.

"Are you coming, Officer Hayes?" Chance snapped.

"I'll be right behind you."

He slammed the door to the back of the ambulance shut, scowled at her and then slid inside the cab. They took off with a scream of the siren and a bark of tires.

Breathe. In and out.

"You go on, honey. I'll watch Kimmy. You stay with your sister until she gets discharged," Teresa said, coming down the stairs with Kimberly in her arms.

"I'm sorry, babydoll," Laurel said, brushing her daughter's hair back off her forehead. "I'll be home soon."

Kimberly nodded, stuck her thumb in her mouth and put her head on Teresa's shoulder.

"You're a lifesaver, Teresa."

The ride to the hospital gave her a moment to think and time to calm down. It wouldn't do Elizabeth any good if she lost her temper and killed her sister's husband. As it was, the asshole could have pressed charges against her for hitting him at the bar. She wasn't surprised he hadn't, really. The man didn't have any balls.

Laurel parked her car and took a deep breath. The hospital would handle it. They had to report it just like she had to if she suspected abuse. Unfortunately, they wouldn't or couldn't do anything unless Elizabeth pressed charges and this time, she would if Laurel had anything to say about it.

She walked into the waiting room and approached the glass window.

"Can I help you?" the woman behind the desk asked.

"They brought my sister in a little bit ago. An assault. I want to see her."

"Let me call back there and find out if it's okay."

Laurel tapped her foot impatiently while she watched the woman talk on the phone for several minutes. The woman kept glancing at her fretfully and she had to wonder what the deal was.

"I'm sorry, but I can't let you back there."

"What do you mean, you can't let me in? She's my sister," Laurel snarled at the receptionist sitting behind the desk.

"I'm sorry, ma'am, but the patient has requested no visitors except her husband."

"No fucking way! The man beat the hell out of her!"

"Laurel?"

She spun around to find the last person she needed to see, but the only person she wanted there. "Kale," she whispered, throwing herself against his chest and wrapping her arms around his neck.

"God," he murmured in her hair. "It scared the hell out of me when I heard your address on the scanner."

Kisses rained over the crown on her head and she fought the tears threatening to fall down her cheeks.

"What's going on?" he asked, pushing her back so he could look into her eyes. The small sniffles she wasn't able to hold in made his eyes narrow and search her face. "Is it Kimmy? Is she hurt? Please tell me she's not hurt."

"She's fine. It's Elizabeth."

"Your sister?"

She nodded stiffly and pushed a strand of hair behind her ear. "When I pulled into the parking lot of my apartment, she was sitting on the steps. She lost consciousness. He could have killed her, Kale."

"Easy, darlin'."

"She won't let me go in with her. If I'm not there, she won't tell—she won't press charges. I know her."

"Honey, there isn't anything you can do. She's an adult. She can make those decisions for herself," he said.

The anger returned in full force as she pushed against his chest, forcing him to let her go. "Then I'll take care of the problem for her." Her steps took her toward the door and her car. The police revolver in her glove box called to her.

Go blow the fucker's brains all over the wall.

"Laurel, wait. Come on." Kale followed her outside and around the side of her car. "You can't do that, sugar," he said, taking her keys from her hand like he knew exactly what she'd planned. "Think of Kimmy. If you shot him, you would go to jail and no one would be there to take care of her."

Kimberly meant everything and what he said was true.

"What am I going to do, Kale? Eventually, he will kill her."

"You can't do anythin', darlin', unless she wants you to," he replied, wrapping his arms around her. "All you can do is be there for her and hope she comes to her senses."

"How can a man beat on a woman like that?" she asked, looking into the deep brown of his eyes—wanting—no needing him to reassure her not all men were animals.

"I don't know, Laurel. I wish I did. I've seen it a few times myself and I don't understand it from either side."

Silence enveloped them for several minutes while she battled the demon on her shoulder telling her to take matters into her own hands and the angel in the form of a rugged cowboy, keeping her calm.

The calluses on his fingers along her jaw had her thinking of something besides killing her brother-in-law and she fought with herself over whether she should take solace in his arms. Her heart won out. "Come home with me, Kale." His eyes asked the question she wasn't ready to answer, except only for now. She needed him tonight. "Please?"

"Sure."

"Let me tell the receptionist I'm leaving so they can get a message to Elizabeth since she won't see me."

"I'll come in with you."

"I'm okay, Kale."

"I want to be there for you, Laurel," he told her as he grasped her hand and entwined their fingers.

She nodded and walked inside the hospital with him by her side.

They returned to her apartment with Kale following behind her car in his truck. She didn't know what she planned, but the need for him to hold her tonight and chase away the demons, ruled everything.

She quickly unlocked the door, but the chain held so it would only open part way.

"Laurel?"

"Hey, Teresa. Yeah, it's me and a...friend."

The door closed and the chain slid back.

She glanced at Kale and felt the heat from a blush creeping up her cheeks. *I'm blushing? Seriously?*

"How is your sister?" Teresa asked when they stepped inside.

Laurel scowled. "I don't know. She refused to let me in once I got there."

"No."

"Yes and the only person they told me she'd let back there was dick-wad."

"I'm sorry, honey," Teresa replied, patting her shoulder. "I know how much you want to help her."

"Teresa, this is Kale Dunn. Kale this is Teresa, my friend, savior and neighbor."

"Nice to meet you handsome," Teresa replied.

Red crept up Kale's neck and splashed across his cheeks at the compliment. "Nice to meet you, too, Teresa. Thank you for helping Laurel so much."

"Oh, it's my pleasure. I'd do more if I could." One painted on eyebrow arched over her right eye and a little grin played on her lips. "I'm gonna go on home now. You two have fun and just remember, these here walls are a bit thin so keep down the moans and groans. You do have a supply of condoms, right?"

Her wicked little cackle had Laurel smiling for the first time in what seemed like days and Kale roaring in laughter.

"Teresa!"

"What? I'm thinking of you, honey. I mean you're gonna have this hunk of a man in your bed tonight, right? Be prepared, I always say. Have fun you two," she said before she disappeared out the door with a very final snap of the latch.

"You'll have to excuse her."

"Why's that? I like her."

Laurel shook her head, glancing at the tips of her tennis shoes. "You would. She's got such take-no-shit attitude."

"Wait until you meet Natalie's grandmother. Oh my, she's a hoot. If we go out there on Sunday, you'll meet her. She definitely gave me and Cade the what for when we were dating Natalie."

The image of Cade making love with Natalie flashed across her mind and jealousy zipped down her spine. *I can't be jealous. To have those feelings means I care more than I'm willing to admit.*

"What's wrong, darlin'?" he asked, pulling her into his arms.

"Nothing."

"Uh-uh. Spill it."

She licked her lips and ran her finger over the front of his T-shirt. His fingers under her chin brought her face up and he looked deep in her eyes.

"There's no need to be jealous of what happened between me and Natalie. It will never happen again."

"I'm not," she murmured, but she knew he could see the lie in her gaze.

"I'm a one woman man, Laurel. If you and I are together, there will be no one else."

"If?"

"Are you saying you want there to be an us?"

"I don't know what I want, Kale, except you in my bed tonight. Don't ask me what happens afterwards."

"If it's all you can give me for now, I'll take it."

All of the sudden his lips and his hands were everywhere. His kiss wasn't soft and coaxing, but hard and demanding. Both of his hands tightened in her hair and tipped her head as he slipped his tongue between her parted lips when she gasped. He commanded her acceptance and dominated her body with each stroke of his tongue. Her nipples tightened into almost painful knots of need. Her pussy wept with want and desire, readying her for the eventual completion of the teasing and touching they'd done over the last few days.

One of his palms cupped her breast through her shirt and teased the hardened nub with soft touches.

"God, I need you," he growled when he lifted his head.

The heat in his gaze scorched her skin as if he'd touched her with a branding iron. Chills ran down her arms and her whole body trembled.

"Do what you will, Kale. I want this. I want you." After what she hoped appeared to be a teasing look, she took his hand in hers and led them down the hall to her room. When the door closed behind them, she reached for him and wrapped her hand behind his head to coax his mouth to hers.

His tongue swept inside, stroking hers, rubbing over the ridges on the roof of her mouth, along the sides of her cheeks, and tangling again with her tongue in the age old erotic dance of lovers. His hands cupped her ass and yanked her up against his chest. When his lips left her mouth to slide over her cheek, she moaned deep in her throat and arched her neck, giving herself over to him in every way a woman can.

"So good," she whispered, loving the feel of this man in her arms.

The softness of his lips along the column of her throat and the scrape of his whiskered cheek over her skin felt like heaven and hell at the same time—heaven from the wicked nips of his teeth and hell from the torturous slow lick of his tongue. She wanted it, all of it.

Planting her hands on his shoulders, she pushed back, forcing him to abandon her neck. The question in his eyes had her reassuring him. "Nothing's wrong. I just want to feel your skin against mine. Take the shirt off," she said, tugging at the hem.

"You first."

They raced to see who could get naked the fastest and Kale won by a long shot as he gave her a heart-stopping grin and flipped his boot across the room. The primitive growl he released sent heat spiraling through her belly and cream dampening her panties. "Let me help you with those," he said, hooking the edges of her underwear with his thumbs and peeling them down her legs. "Oh my. What have we here?"

The rough pad of his tongue danced over her abdomen. A soft moan escaped her mouth and she threaded her fingers through his dark hair. Her belly clenched and her skin quivered when he nipped at the skin and then soothed the bite with soft licks.

He followed her on his knees as she took two steps back toward the bed and sank down on the comforter.

"Spread your legs," he murmured against the inside of her thigh. "Mmm. Wet." One finger slid up the slit. "Hot." Two fingers dipped slowly into her pussy and she shivered at the sensations bombarding her —warm and flush then spikes of need crawling under her flesh. "Mine." His mouth fastened on her clit and sucked it between his lips while those two delicious fingers worked her pussy with a magnificent thrusting motion that sent every nerve ending into overload. Her climax smacked her like a tidal wave coming out of nowhere, bowling over her and washing away anything resembling conscious thought.

"One," he whispered, continuing to slowly lick her clit until the tremors stopped.

"One?" she asked, peeling her eyelids open to stare into the sparkling depths of brown.

"Climax. We'll be working on at least three tonight."

"Holy shit," she whispered, as he stood and waved for her to scoot back on the bed. Her gaze fixed on his face and then slid down his broad chest, across his six-pack abs and followed the dark trail of hair that eventually blended with the crisp ones surrounding his cock. Long, thick and glistening with pre-cum, she licked her lips in anticipation of tasting every part of his magnificent cock tonight.

"You didn't plan on sleepin', did you?" he questioned with a devilish glint in his eyes as he climbed into the bed beside her.

She shook her head and laid one hand on the hard plains of his chest. "I slept all damned day, thanks to one stubborn cowboy."

"Good, because I have an insatiable appetite for one fiery red-head who has been driving me absolutely fucking crazy for days."

Scorching wet lips fastened on her nipple. Electricity zipped from the tip of her breast to her clit, awakening the sleeping giant of her desire.

His fingers plucked and rolled the neglected tip while he sucked the one beneath his lips, deep into his mouth. The steely hardness of his erection bumped against her leg and she reached down to wrap her hand around his girth. He released the nipple his fingers had been teasing, to forestall her hand and trap her wrist.

"I want to touch you." Her voice a small whimper of escalating feelings.

Releasing her breast with a teasing lick, he said, "You'll get your turn after I'm done torturing you a bit. Now leave those hands above your head or I'll find something to bind them."

The gleam in his almost black eyes told her he'd love to tie her up.

"I know you have handcuffs around here somewhere."

Her dream from before came rushing back with stark clarity and her cheeks heated.

"Mmm. I get the impression you might like being restrained a little." His finger traced the seam of her lips, back and forth, taking the dampness and spreading it over the surface. "Are you wet just thinking about it?"

She bit the inside of her mouth to keep the moan from slipping out.

Those delicious fingers skimmed down her torso and then dipped between her pussy lips to spread the cream he found, over the throbbing nub and swirling it until she raised her hips off the bed.

"Oh my yes. You are definitely wet and slick."

His thumb flicked over her clit while two fingers slid deep inside her pussy, tearing the trapped moan from her mouth and a plea from her lips. "Kale, please."

"Tell me what you want."

The hard pecs of his chest met her eyes when she dropped gaze. Asking for what she wanted during sex didn't come easy. Her mother had been a prude when it came to anything between a man and a woman, but also passed those thoughts and feelings on to her. They never talked about sex —never mentioned anything accept to tell her she'd find the perfect man to take care of her and she would give him children, keep his house and do his entertaining for him. Sex would be something she'd tolerate, not enjoy. The first time with Kale hadn't been planned. Remembering how he'd taken her to new heights of awareness, brought heat to her cheeks.

Suck it up and tell him.

"Talk to me, Laurel," he whispered, trailing his fingers down her cheek and his lips over her ear.

"I...uh."

"Fast or slow. Deep or shallow. I need to know what will make it fantastic for you." His gaze met hers and she wanted to shrink back and not expose herself to him anymore. "Huh-uh," he murmured when she tried to turn away.

"I want," she squeaked and then cleared her throat. "You."

"Not a problem, darlin'. How?"

"Inside me. Deep, hard and fast."

The crinkled of a condom wrapped broke the sound of harsh breathing as he quickly sheathed himself and moved between her legs. No soft thrust this time. He buried himself balls deep in one firm snap of his hips.

"Oh, God," she whimpered.

"You okay?"

"Yeah. Feels..."

"Feels?"

"Fantastic. Please."

He took her legs in his firm grasp and draped them over his forearms. The change in position forced him even deeper. His cock slid in and out with each thrust of his hips and each slow rotation of his pelvis.

"Lord, you feel good, darlin'." Two more thrusts. "Tighten those pussy muscles. Yeah, like that."

She lifted her buttocks and moaned. The slow, torturous movement of his plunges was about to drive her insane. Her pussy muscles trembled with the need to feel the friction of his cock. "Faster," she said.

"Nope. My way this time. I want to feel every quiver and every clench of your sweet pussy, baby." Three more slow pushes.

"God, Kale, please," she begged.

She caught his gaze and the passion in his eyes drove hers higher. Sweat clung to his upper lip and the muscles of his neck stood out under the strain of holding back. She shifted up onto her hands and latched onto his nipple with her lips. The soft growl he released egged her on. She nipped at the tip and he lost all control, dropping her legs and pulling them around his hips. She locked her ankles and titled her pelvis up to take everything he wanted to give her—every inch of his impressive cock deep inside. Heat coiled unfathomably low in her middle and raced down her legs. Her toes curled and a deep, satisfying groan slipped from her mouth as she panted, "Yes, yes, yes," with each snap of his hips and each slam of his cock.

"Squeeze me, darlin'. Clamp down and come for me, Laurel. Milk everything I have."

She couldn't stop the wave of her climax from stripping her bare and leaving her heart out there for him to take or leave. Each plunge of his cock took a little more until he slammed deep and took her soul.

Once the tremors stopped, he gathered her in his arms, tucking her close to his side and sighed heavily—like a contented man. He rolled the condom off and dropped it on the waste basket next to her bed before settling back down and relaxing under her hands.

His heart thumped beneath her cheek for several minutes while their bodies cooled. She trailed her fingers through the hair on his chest and traced the line down his abdomen to the head of his cock.

A low grumbling growl rumbled deep under her face.

"You're going to be the death of me woman."

"Are you not up for more? I thought you told me we weren't going to sleep tonight."

His cock twitched under her fingers and she smiled against his chest, then nipped at the flat copper disc.

"Oh, I'm up for more, especially with you."

* * * *

Her hand wrapped around his painfully swelling cock, stroking up and down in slow torment. The little witch knew exactly what she did to him. Her saucy smile and wicked peek through her lashes at him, made him hard enough to pound nails with his dick. *God, she's gorgeous with all*

*her red hair falling around her shoulders, a blush on her pale skin and my
little purple love bites on her breasts. Did she even realize they were there?*

"What are you grinning about sexy man?"

"You," he murmured, threading his fingers through her hair and
wrapping one curl around her nipple.

"Me? What did I do?"

"It's not what you've done. It's what I plan on you doin' before the
night is over. Suckin' me, lickin' me, and ridin' me."

"Mmm. I like your way of thinking, Mr. Dunn. Which shall I do
first?" she asked trailing her lips over his chest and inching her way down
his abdomen. "Lick?" The rough pad of her tongue slid over him from
root to tip. "Suck?" She took the straining head of his cock between her
lips and sucked just the tip before she swirled her tongue around and
around, driving his desire to almost explosive levels. Her hand dipped between his legs and cradled his balls in between her fingers, rolling them,
stroking them and driving him crazy. The hum in her throat reverberated
down his straining shaft and exploded in his nuts.

"Sweet Jesus, Laurel."

Her mouth swallowed every inch of his cock until he felt the back
of her throat. The swallowing motions about drove him over the brink
before he could tamp it down. His toes curled and his legs shook.

"Enough, woman. Grab the condom from the nightstand."

"Oh. Strawberry? Can I put it on?"

"Only if you don't torment me anymore."

"You are no fun at all, Kale, but I want to do one more thing."

He groaned, but nodded—not able to tell her no to anything she
wanted to do to him.

"It's not that bad. You'll like it. I swear."

She placed the condom in her mouth and slowly rolled it down
his shaft.

Holy fuck!

Once she had it in place, she gave him a wicked grin and a saucy
wink as she straddled his hips and took him to the root of his dick, deep
inside her.

She tossed her hair behind her and arched her back. A low purr erupted from her lips when she leaned forward and rocked her hips.

The glide of her pussy over his cock sent shock waves down his spine and a rush of blood in his ears. Grasping her hips, he helped her angle her pussy to give them both the best friction possible.

"Oh yeah. Perfect."

He spread his legs and pulled his heels up to give him more leverage and allow him to meet her down thrust with one up plunge of his own. Leaving her hips, he grasped her breasts and kneaded the firm flesh. God, he loved her tits. Perfectly shaped and the ideal size for his palms. He pinched her nipples until she groaned and sped up the pace.

Her pussy vibrated around his cock as her climax built. The tightening of his balls felt like a rubber band pulling taut, ready to snap his resolve to nothing with each rock of her hips.

The skin of her abdomen quivered beneath the slow glide of his hand. When his thumb found her clit and started to stroke, she through her head back and whimpered.

"Please. Fuck me hard, Kale. Help me."

"Hold yourself up a little. Yeah, perfect," he said.

He pumped his hips as her pussy clamped down on his cock, squeezing until he thought he would lose his mind. She screamed his name when she came hard.

She folded like an accordion onto his chest, breathing hard enough to ruffle the fine hair around his nipple.

"Wow."

"Yeah, but we aren't done yet."

"No?"

He trailed his finger to the pucker of her ass. "Ever had a man here?"

"Once."

"Did you like it?"

She stared into his eyes and a slow smile spread across her lips. He dipped one finger into the hole and she pushed her ass against his hand.

"I take it you did."

"Yes, but I could never get..."

"Don't say it, Laurel. Don't bring him between us right now."

"I'm sorry," she whispered, dropping her gaze.

He put one finger under her chin and lifted her face so he could look into her eyes. "It's okay, honey. I want this to be only you and me, though. No one else."

"So do I, Kale."

"Do you?"

"Yes. He's my past and I need to look at my future. I'm tired of guarding my heart and not letting myself get close to anyone. Let me say one thing. Dennis never wanted anal sex. Period. I want you there. Love me like you mean it, even if it's only for tonight."

With a quick flex of his hips, he had her on her back and hovered above her. "Do you have something for lubrication around here?"

"Um, there's KY in the drawer of my nightstand."

Mmm...interesting.

He reached over and pulled the tube from the drawer and also the dildo he found.

Her chest flushed red hot and her cheeks blushed almost as red as her hair.

"Wha...what are you going to do with that?"

"You'll see. Roll over onto your stomach and spread your thighs wide."

Once she lay on her belly, he flicked on the vibrator and gently ran it over her pussy lips.

"Oh God." A soft moan slipped from her lips.

"Like it?"

"Oh yeah. Don't stop."

Her hips lifted and wiggled with each pass of the plastic tip over her clit. His balls ached and his cock throbbed. The need to bury himself in her ass, drove him to the brink of crazy, but the need to make it good for her forestalled any thoughts of taking his own pleasure before she was mindless with need. When he thought she held onto the brink of sanity by her fingernails, he slipped the vibrator deep into her pussy.

The high keen of her voice when she screamed his name, told him she'd gone over the edge at least once and damn did it sound like heaven to his ears.

Her breath came out in hard pants as he bent over her back.

"Lift your hips, honey," he said pulling the condom over his erection and lubing it up nice and slick.

"Fuck."

"That's the plan, darlin." The low bubble of laughter from her mouth, made him smile. "Easy," he crooned, bumping the stiff head of his cock against her back hole.

The soft hiss of pain from her lips made him take it slow and steady as he eased himself into her tight passage.

"Jesus, you are so tight."

"It's been a long time and with the vibrator still in my pussy, it makes it so much tighter, I'm sure."

"Feels like heaven."

When she relaxed and pushed her ass back against him, he drove the rest of the way inside with a hearty groan.

"Let me know when I can move," he murmured next to her ear.

After several long seconds, she slowed her breathing and spread her thighs further apart. "Now, Kale. Fuck me hard. God, I need this. I need you."

He lifted his chest and grasped her hips with both hands. The slow rock of his pelvis drove his cock deep inside her ass. He almost lost control when she reached between her thighs, pulled the vibrator partially out and started fucking her pussy with it. Matching his rhythm stroke for stroke drove him to the edge of the abyss.

"Holy hell," he growled, his ball drawing up tight against his groin in preparation to blow his load.

"Yes, yes, yes!"

Her pussy clamped down and her ass contracted around his dick, forcing his own climax to burst from his balls and out the end of his cock, to stretch the condom to overflowing proportions.

He dropped his head onto her shoulder and pulled deep breaths into his lungs.

"Oh my God."

"Yeah. You could say that again."

The soft laugh brought a smile to his lips. After several moments, his breathing slowed and he pulled his semi-erect cock from her ass. He picked up the still buzzing vibrator from the bed and walked into the bathroom to dispose of the condom and get something to clean them both off with.

When he returned he slowly rolled her over and then ran the warm wash cloth between her legs.

The deep sigh she released pulled at his heart strings.

"Are you sure you don't know how to ride a horse? You seemed like a natural when you were ridin' my hips there, darlin'."

The little snort from her lips made him chuckle.

After he finished, he dropped the washcloth back in the bathroom and then returned to slide beneath the sheet next to her. She rolled into his side, tucked her head on his chest and placed her hand low on his abdomen, while he trailed his fingers up and down her spine, loving the softness of her skin and the silkiness of her hair between his fingers. God, he loved her hair, loved her tits, loved her eyes—fuck. He loved her. He was so screwed.

10

"Kale?" Laurel whispered, trying to hold onto the closeness, but he shifted and seemed to draw away from her.

"Yeah?"

"What's wrong?"

"Nothin'. Why?"

"You're so quiet. It's not like you," she said.

He seemed distance somehow.

"You wore me out woman."

"Sorry. You're probably tired."

"A little. It's hard work keeping up with Kimmy."

"Tell me about it." She giggled and then sobered. "Stay with me tonight."

"I thought you'd never ask, darlin'."

Within moments, he snored softly next to her while she laid her head on his chest and breathed him in. Flashes of him with Kimberly zipped across her mind and she frowned. He seemed to have wormed his way into a special place in her life whether she wanted him there or not.

Want him there? Are you serious? You want him all right, but how much? Are you willing to give him your heart or are you going to walk away from the best thing that's happened to you?

She needed to think and couldn't do it lying next to his hard body, or feeling his warm breath ruffling the baby fine hairs at her temple. Without waking him, she slipped from the bed, threw on a pair of shorts, a T-shirt and walked to the door. A quick glance at his sleeping form revealed he hadn't moved, so she quietly stepped out into the hall.

She paced back and forth in front of the window in the living room as she chewed on her fingernail.

"What the hell am I going to do?" she asked out loud, hoping someone would tell her or at least give her a clue. "If this keeps up, I'll be in love with him before the weeks is out."

Aren't you halfway there already?

God, she hated her inner voice at times and this was one of them. She didn't need her heart battling with her head right now.

The jingle of her cell phone in her purse stopped her pacing.

"Who the hell is calling me at this time of night?" She grabbed her purse and shifted stuff around until she found it in the bottom and flipped it open. "Hello?"

"Laurel?"

"Jeff? Why are you calling me?"

"Shit, Laurel. I think I went too far."

"What's going on Jeff? What have you done?"

"It's...it's Elizabeth. She's not moving."

"Call nine-one-one you dipshit and I'll be there in ten minutes." She clicked the phone shut and cussed a blue streak as she threw the phone back into her purse. "Motherfucker. I'm going to seriously hurt him." Slipping on her flip-flops still lying under the coffee table, she grabbed her purse and car keys.

"I'll leave Kale a note so if he wakes up he'll know where I went. He'll stay with Kimmy until I get back."

After scrawling a message, she left it next to the coffee pot hoping he'd find it there first. She pulled the door shut on the apartment and headed down the stairs to her car. The parking lot seemed darker than usual. She realized the light near the back of the pavement seemed to have burnt out. The hair on the back of her neck stood up. She glanced from left to right, trying to figure out what seemed different. Gravel crunched under a boot behind her and she spun around just in time to see the bulk of a man swing his arm before it connected with her jaw.

The low growl of the voice penetrated the buzzing in her head. "You little bitch. You think you're so damned smart."

A boot connected with her ribs and she rolled into a ball to protect her middle as pain exploded in her right side, forcing out a whimper.

A low chuckle escaped from the man's mouth. The sound sent chills down her back, right before he hit her again and everything went black.

* * * *

Elizabeth whimpered and pressed her knuckles to her lips to hold the sound in. If she let him know she watched, he'd kill her for sure.

She's your sister for God's sake. Help her! She would never let something happen to you like this.

"I...I can't."

He picked up Laurel and tossed her in the back seat of the car, slid into the front and within moments, he drove out of the driveway.

The terror rushing through Elizabeth finally gave way to love. Laurel loved her. She'd always come, always been there for her every time Jeff hurt her. Leaving Laurel to fend for herself wasn't what a sister should do.

"I'll follow and then call the police once I know where he's taking her."

She started the car and slowly pulled out behind him. If he saw someone following him, he might just killed Laurel and be done with it. Keeping track of Laurel's car, wouldn't be a problem. The multitude of stickers on the back, made it stand out like a beacon. Everything from Disney decals to save a horse, ride a cowboy was plastered across the bumper.

They drove for several miles until they came to a park on the outskirts of town sitting off near the local lake. The car pulled into the deserted parking lot and Elizabeth pulled over on the other side of the road. Apparently Laurel had regained consciousness, but still seemed out of it when she saw him push her sister in front of him and she staggered, holding her head with one hand. Once they'd disappeared into the dense growth of trees, Elizabeth slid out of the car and headed toward Laurel's car.

"Please let it be open. Please let it be open."

She tugged on the handle and prayed. The door opened with a soft click and Elizabeth hoped Laurel's purse and cell phone were in the car. Jeff never let her have a cell phone of her own, afraid she'd be able to call for help or maybe another man would start calling her. She didn't know his reasoning, but he seemed crazy jealous of anyone even talking to her. Not her sister, not her parents...no one.

No purse and no cell phone.

"Damn it," she whispered reverently. "Now what the hell am I going to do?"

The open glove box caught her attention and she noticed the butt of Laurel's service revolver buried under the multitude of papers.

Her gun? But, I don't know how to shoot a gun.

"She needs me. Even if I don't know how to shoot it, maybe I can get it to her so she can protect herself."

Elizabeth pulled the gun from the glove box and wrapped her hand around the butt of the pistol. After she softly closed the door, she tried to keep her steps light as she followed in the direction they'd gone.

Several moments later, she heard voices in the distance.

"You just can't keep your fucking nose out of anything, can you Laurel?"

"I'm not letting you hurt Elizabeth anymore, Jeff. She needs to leave you, you son of a bitch."

"She'll never leave me. She loves me, the crazy bitch. She likes the pain. You should feel her pussy clench around my fingers as I take my belt to her ass until she's welted and bloody."

"I'll kill you before I let you hurt her again."

"It doesn't matter, Laurel. They'll find your body back here in the woods, just like those other two worthless bitches, when I'm done with you."

"Other two?" Laurel asked and Elizabeth crept closer.

What the hell is he talking about?

"You know. You found one of them. They were nothing. Barfly's. But they fessed up a nice piece of ass before I beat the hell out of 'em."

"You killed those girls?" Laurel questioned as she leaned heavily against a tree.

"Yep, but it doesn't matter if you know or not because you aren't leaving here alive either. I'm going to enjoy whipping the fight out of you before you die." He grabbed Laurel's hair, spun her around and plastered her front against the tree trunk. The clink of a chain sounded loud in the dimness of the forest, but not loud enough to attract anyone else's attention even if anyone were around this late at night.

Elizabeth was frozen with fear as she watched her husband tie her sister to the tree. Laurel continued to talk, but Jeff obviously wasn't listening to her.

"You won't get away with this, Jeff. Kale is at my apartment. He'll be looking for me soon."

"So, you're fucking my old boss, huh? No wonder he fired me. You were blowing him all along, weren't you?"

"Does it matter? He'll still be looking for me and when he realized what you've done, he'll kill you with his bare hands."

"Kale's a pussy," he snarled, continuing to tie Laurel to the tree until he seemed satisfied she couldn't get free. Once he finished, he stepped back and grabbed something off the ground.

No, no, no. He's got the whip.

Elizabeth knew the sting of the whip by heart. It seemed to be one of her husband's favorite toys to use on her.

As he stepped back and cracked it a couple of times, Elizabeth stepped out of the shadows. He wasn't going to hurt, Laurel. He could do what he wanted to her, but not her sister.

"Jeff," she said softly, hoping to catch his attention.

He quickly spun around at the sound of her voice.

"Elizabeth? What are you doing here?"

"I followed you after you hit Laurel at her apartment. You aren't going to hurt her. I won't let you."

The crazy laughter coming from his mouth sent chills down her back.

"You? You can't stop me. I'm tired of her getting in the middle of things between us, Elizabeth. The fucking cops are asking way too many questions after your trip to the emergency room. I can't have them snooping around."

She stepped closer and put her body between Laurel and him. "You won't hurt her."

"Get out of the way, bitch. I'll take care of you after I'm done with her."

"I heard what you said about those other women, Jeff. You killed them? How could you do such a thing? I know you like to punish me when I'm bad. I understand that, but kill someone?"

"Shut up, Elizabeth. Just shut up."

She pulled Laurel's revolver out from behind her back and pointed it at her husband. "I'm going to untie her. You stay there."

He took a step towards her.

"I said, stay there."

"You don't know how to shoot a gun, Elizabeth. Give it to me and we'll forget this ever happened. All right, sweetheart? You know I love you."

Her hand wavered.

"Don't listen to him, Elizabeth. He's fucking crazy. He's going to kill me and probably you too, now."

"He's my husband, Laurel," she whispered, tears welling in her eyes. "I love him."

"Elizabeth please," Laurel begged as she wiggled her hands trying to get one free. "Step back here towards me and untie me."

"Give me the gun, Elizabeth," he said and then jumped toward her, knocking the gun from her hand. He brought his fist back and punched her hard, throwing her back away from the gun and into the pile of leaves. "You sniveling bitch!" His voice roared in the darkness, bouncing off the trees and she covered her ears as tears rolled down her cheeks.

I've failed. He's going to kill us both before this nightmare ends.

Jeff picked up the gun and moved toward Laurel. "I thought I'd beat the shit out of you before I killed you, but now that your lovely sister has given me your weapon to use, I think I'll just blow your brains out and be done with you." The butt of the pistol rested against Laurel's temple and all of his attention seemed focused on her.

No, no, no. Elizabeth's hands moved around in the pile of leaves next to her and closed around a heavy branch. *I have to stop this. I have to save Laurel.* She picked up the heavy tree limb, slowly got to her feet and swung it at Jeff's head. The sickening thud as it connected with his skull, broke the silence of the forest around them and he slipped to the ground.

The blank expression in his open eyes told her he wouldn't hurt either of them again.

"Oh, God. Oh God," Elizabeth said and then pressed her knuckles to her lips. "What have I done?"

"Elizabeth!" Laurel snapped. "Untie me, now!"

Her fingers shook as she worked the chains and ropes loose to let her sister free. "I'm sorry, Laurel. God, I'm so sorry."

When the bonds fell away, Laurel grabbed her shoulders and hugged her so tight, she thought she might break some ribs.

"Listen to me, Elizabeth. There is nothing to be sorry for, honey. You saved me—saved us both. He won't hurt anyone every again." Laurel wrapped an arm around her shoulders and they walked back towards her car to retrieve the cell phone she'd dropped on the floor.

Within moments, the wail of sirens broke the silence and the flash of blue and red lights lit up the night.

* * * *

The high-pitch ring of the phone on the nightstand brought Kale upright in the bed. He looked around confused for a moment, trying to figure out where he was. The phone rang again and he reached over to grab it.

Where the hell is Laurel?

"Hello," he croaked into the phone.

"Kale?"

"Laurel? What the hell? Why are you calling your own phone? Where are you?"

"I need you," she choked out and then cleared her throat. "Knock on Teresa's door and have her watch Kimmy. I'm at the park on Oak Street on the other side of town."

"Tell me what's going on," he said, pulling on his pants and shirt.

"I...I can't over the phone."

"Do I hear sirens?"

"Yes."

"Are you all right?"

"I'm okay."

"That's not what I asked, Laurel. Are you all right?"

"I will be when you get here."

He slipped on his socks and boots, then grabbed for his keys. "I'll be there shortly. Stay there." God, he wanted to say I love you, so badly his teeth ached from grinding them together.

Two quick raps on the door to Teresa's apartment and she called, "Who's there?"

"It's me, Kale. Laurel's friend." Teresa opened the door with a sleepy-eyed blink. "Can you come over and watch Kimmy for a bit. I'm not sure what's going on, but Laurel just called and she's on the other side of town."

"Oh, Lord. I hope she's okay," Teresa said, coming out into the hall and following him into Laurel's apartment.

"I think she's fine. I need to get over there and find out what's going on. I'll call when I can."

Taking the steps two at a time, he raced to his truck, cranked the engine and popped it into gear hardly a second after his butt hit the seat.

"She's all right. She said she's all right." The chant sounded hollow, but it was all he had until he held her again.

Ten minutes later, he whipped into the parking lot of the park. Cop cars were everywhere. Blue and red lights flashed, bouncing color off the trees and scant buildings nearby. He was out of the truck before it even stopped; running toward where she stood with her sister huddled in a blanket.

"Laurel?"

"Kale! Oh, God, Kale," she whispered, tears welling in her eyes as she dropped the blanket and threw herself into his arms.

"God, baby, what happened? I don't understand," he said, brushing the hair back from her face and noticing the bruise forming on her jaw and cheek. "What the fuck?"

"Jeff."

"Elizabeth's husband, Jeff?"

"Yeah. I got out of the bed because I needed to think. He called telling me Elizabeth wasn't moving. I grabbed my keys to go to her house and see what was going on, but he jumped me in the parking lot of the complex, knocked me out and drove me here. Apparently, Elizabeth had followed him and then followed us here."

"I'll kill him with my bare hands," he growled, pushing her back and searching the area for the son of a bitch. Death wouldn't be enough for the man.

"No need. He's dead."

"Dead?"

"Yeah, he was going to shoot me and Elizabeth. She hit him with a tree branch."

Kale shook with rage so strong he fought to keep it under control. Luckily, the man was already dead. "I wish I'd been here, darlin'." He softly stroked his fingers over her face. "I didn't protect you."

"He could have hurt you or Kimberly. I couldn't have handled it if he had. It's bad enough he hurt Elizabeth, but I would lose my mind if he hurt you." Her whole body shook with tremors.

Smoothing both hands down her back and up to her shoulders, she slowly calmed and leaned into his embrace. Her warm breath skipped over his neck with each exhalation. Her hands held him tight against her like she thought he might disappear. He wasn't going anywhere—not now—not ever.

"Officer Hayes," the chief said, stopping at her side.

"Yes?"

"We'll need a formal statement, but the information you've already given us is enough for tonight. You and your sister are free to go. She has to stay in the area though until the official investigation is concluded."

"I'm taking them both back to Laurel's apartment for now and then they'll be at my place out on Crescent Highway." He pulled out a business card and handed to the chief. "If you need to reach me."

"Much obliged, Kale. Take care of those two. They've had a rough night."

He piled Laurel and Elizabeth into his truck and drove them back to Laurel's apartment. They packed up a sleepy Kimberly, some clothes for both of them and bid Teresa goodbye, telling her where they could be reached.

"They need to be away from here tonight," he told Teresa.

"You take care of those girls, Kale." She laid her hand on his cheek and whispered, "She's lucky to have such a man as you in love with her."

"Thanks, Teresa. You've been a godsend."

When the lights of his place came into view fifteen minutes later, he released the breath he hadn't been aware of holding. Laurel was tucked into his side in the middle of the seat with Elizabeth silently staring out the window on the passenger side and Kimberly behind them.

He took them all into the house, showed Elizabeth the guestroom, and tucked Kimberly onto the couch with her blanket. Once they were settled, he picked Laurel up in his arms and strode up the stairs to his room.

"Kale, I don't think—"

"Don't think right now, darlin'. I need to hold you. I could have lost you tonight and the thought scares the hell out of me."

Bringing them both down on top of the covers on his bed, he pulled her to his side and tried to calm the tremors of his body.

"Do you hurt anywhere?" he asked, once she laid her head on his chest and sighed.

"Besides my jaw, my face, my arms, my legs and every other part of my body...no."

"How about a hot shower?"

"No, I just want you to hold me."

The warm drop of her tears soaked through the cotton of his shirt.

"Don't cry, honey."

"I can't help it, Kale. I wanted to kill him. If I would have been able to get my gun from Elizabeth, I would have shot him."

"I know."

"He killed those girls."

"Girls?"

"Yeah. The three murders I've been investigating. He told me he killed them."

"I'm so sorry."

One hand snaked under the hem of his T-shirt as she pushed the material up his chest.

"Laurel, honey, you're hurt."

"I don't care, Kale. I need you to make love to me. Make the memories go away even for a little while. Please."

"I can't tell you no even if I should," he replied, sitting up and stripping his shirt off over his head. He quickly stood and dropped his jeans to the floor, grabbed a condom from the nightstand and laid it on the top. By the time he had his clothes off, Laurel already lay naked across the quilt on his bed. "This is gonna be slow and easy."

He cupped her face between his palms, careful not to put too much pressure on the spots where Jeff had hit her and took her lips. The slow glide of his tongue over her lips made his cock sit up and take notice, not that it hadn't already noticed every curve and every crevice of the gorgeous woman in his bed. She groaned and flicked her tongue against his. Unable to stop the wave of desire rushing him headlong into claiming her, he pushed his tongue into the warm cavern of her mouth and rolled them over so she lay sprawled on his chest.

He pulled his mouth from hers, opened his eyes and whispered, "This way you control everythin' so I don't hurt you."

"You would never hurt me, Kale. I know that."

She kissed her way down his chest, stopping to flick his nipple with her tongue and then nip at the tip with her teeth. He grabbed her upper arms to forestall her movements. There would be no way she could take him in her mouth with her jaw bruised and banged up.

"What?"

"Come up here. Put your hands on the headboard and spread those gorgeous thighs."

He scooted down so she straddled his face, grasped her hips in both hands and then licked from slit to clit.

"Oh, God."

"Good?"

"Oh yes. Don't stop, please."

He stiffened his tongue and wiggled it between her pussy lips. A low moan told him she enjoyed the touch. Several flicks of his tongue on her clit and she shuddered above him. He drove two fingers deep into her pussy and concentrated on the hard little nub until she screamed his name and flooded his mouth with her sweet juice. Her breath came out in short, hard pants as he pulled her down next to him.

"Better?"

"A little, but I need you inside me. Fill me up, Kale." He went to grab the condom from the nightstand, but she stalled his hand. "I'm clean. I haven't been with anyone besides you since Dennis. I need to feel every inch of you without barriers. Please?"

"If you're sure."

"I've never been more sure of anything in my life as being with you."

She crawled over his chest, straddled his hips and sank down slowly until he was buried balls deep in her sweet pussy.

"Ride me, baby."

"Oh, yeah. So good." Her fingers plucked at his nipples and he cradled her hips with his hands to help her move.

The hot wet sheath of her pussy caressed his dick like velvet with each rock of her hips. He could feel each ripple of her vagina and each shudder of her body. It felt like heaven without the barrier between them. Skin to skin, heart to heart.

Within moments, she sped up her movements against him and he could feel her pussy quiver and clamp down as her climax approached.

"Come for me, darlin'," he whispered, rolling her nipples between his fingers and lifting his pelvis so he could give her the maximum depth.

"Kale," she screamed, throwing back her head and arching her back when her climax hit.

"Perfect. So perfect," he said, slamming into her several more times until semen shot out of the end of his dick and he groaned in satisfaction.

"God, we're good together," she murmured, lying on his chest several minutes later.

"Yes, we are."

"You know, tonight taught me something."

"Yeah?"

"Yes. To take what I want without worrying about what the future might bring. To take a chance again." She pushed off his chest and stared down into his face with those gorgeous eyes. "I love you, Kale. I know I said I didn't want a relationship and that I could never love anyone besides Dennis, but I was wrong. I need you in my life, in my bed and in my heart."

"Thank the Lord."

"Why?"

"Because I realized tonight I love you and I don't want to you live without you. I need you—you and Kimmy. You mean everything to me."

With a happy sigh, she laid back down on his chest.

He threaded their fingers together and kissed the tips. "Marry me?"

She glanced up and tears sparkled on her lashes. "You want to marry me?"

"Of course, I do. I want to live the rest of my life with you. Raise babies with you. Teach you how to ride a horse and be a rancher's wife."

"But you're an architect," she replied with a giggle.

"Rancher or architect, it doesn't matter. I need you with me—always."

Her head went back down on his chest and he held his breath as he waited for her answer.

"I would love to marry you and do all those things you mentioned, although I'm not sure about the horse thing."

"You bumper sticker on your car says save a horse, ride a cowboy. How about now?"

"Only if you swear to teach Kimmy how to ride a horse, not a cowboy, before she's eighteen."

"I'll have the shotgun ready, darlin.'"

Epilogue

"Enough with all the mushy stuff, Kale. Let's get on with the weddin', young man. This old woman has an appointment this afternoon," Mrs. Oliver said, from her spot in the front of the church pews.

The rest of the guest laughed, but he only had eyes for his wife. "Hold your bloomers on, Mrs. O. I've got a wife to kiss."

Kimberly bounced on the pew from her spot next to Natalie and Cade.

"You better do a hell of a lot more than kiss her, but save it for the honeymoon. I expect me some adopted great grandbabies soon since Natalie and Cade seemed to have forgotten how it's done."

The snort from Cade and the giggle coming from Natalie had Kale rolling his eyes.

He couldn't help but laugh. God, he loved Natalie's grandmother. The woman kept them all on their toes every minute they were around her.

It had taken eight months of planning to get this far and he wasn't about to rush through it.

"I love you, Red," he said, cupping her face between his palms.

"I love you, too."

"Kiss, kiss, kiss," Kimmy said as she jumped up and down on the floor. Cade kept one hand on the back of her dress to keep her from running amok.

It hadn't been a huge wedding—just the right size. His family, Natalie and Cade, and her sister along with the few friends she'd made in town during the last eight months of living with him. Laurel didn't want a big wedding anyway, she'd said, and he wanted to give her everything.

"Shall we do as our daughter wants?" he asked, watching her eyes light up with love.

"Oh, I don't know, Mr. Dunn," she replied, coyly dropping her gaze to his chest and then glancing up through her lashes.

"No?"

"I'm going to do what I want." She dropped her voice to a mere whisper. "Lick you. Suck you and drive you insane since you've done nothing but tease me for the last week telling me we can't have sex until after the wedding."

He released a low growl and yanked her up against his chest. He cupped her ass cheek with one hand, while the other tangled in her loose strands of hair down her back. He brushed his lips over hers and then drove his tongue between her lips.

"Yeah, baby! Whoot! Whoot! Whoot!" Mrs. Oliver shouted from her spot in the pews.

He couldn't hold back his roar of laughter no matter how tempting his red-headed wife looked in her finery and how much he wanted to bend her over the pulpit. Laurel laughed right along with him. After a much too quick kiss, he released her and tucked her hand through the crook of his arm.

"May I present, Mr. and Mrs. Kale Dunn," the preacher said.

He glanced at Laurel and then looked out over the group of friends and family in front of them. "You're gonna get your wish earlier than you probably anticipated, Mrs. Oliver."

With a crook of his finger, he signaled Kimberly to come to them and scooped her up in his arms.

"Now?" she asked.

He gave her a smile and nodded.

"Mommy has a baby in her tummy!"

The End

1

TWO FOR THE PRICE OF ONE
Montana Cowboys 3
Sandy Sullivan

Emma Weston tapped her fingers on the steering wheel of her old truck and sang along to the song on her radio. Singing wasn't her thing, but she loved many of the country bands, their songs and the singers. Man, did she love the singers. The gorgeous guy hanging on her wall at home, Brandon Tucker, was her favorite. She'd give about anything to meet him. Every wet dream she'd ever had centered on his gorgeous body.

Her cell phone interrupted her daydreams of said hunk—Brandon Tucker's voice sang "The Love of My Life," which happened to be her absolute favorite, as the call from Becky came in.

She hit the talk button on the phone sitting in the plastic cup holder attached to her dashboard and asked, "Hey, Bec. What's up?"

"You're going to the rodeo this weekend, right?"

"Yeah," she said, glancing in her rearview mirror out of habit. Her dad constantly scolded her about being aware of her surroundings. You never knew when a stray cow, horse, goat, or some other farm animal might wander into the road. Life in rural Montana came with all kinds of accidents involving animals. "I'm ridin' remember?"

"I forgot. You know how scattered brained I am sometimes," Becky answered.

Emma laughed. "I know, but I love you anyway, Bec." She and Becky had been best friends since kindergarten. "Are you working the beer stand with me?"

"Yeah. Seth asked me to fill in."

"I don't know why you two don't just start datin' and get it over with. You've been moonin' over each other for a year now."

"I can't, Em, you know that. He's too old for me. My daddy would have a cow."

"He's only a few years older than you," she said, giving Becky the same speech she'd already given her over and over regarding the very sexy Seth Reardon who owned the local honky-tonk. "We're both in our mid-twenties, and Seth is in his early thirties."

"It seems kind of weird though."

"Oh, I don't think it is at all. Just don't think of him being older. I mean, look at me. If I could rope Brandon Tucker, I'd be there in a heartbeat, and he's five years older than me."

"Not even a comparison, Em. He's gorgeous, rich, hot, and one of the biggest country music stars to hit the stage in years. He may even be bigger than George."

"No one is bigger than George, but Brandon has it all goin' on. I mean, if I could have ten minutes— Holy fuck!"

The screech of tires as Emma yanked on the steering wheel of her truck and slammed on the brakes echoed along the lonely stretch of highway between her parents' place and town. The crunch of metal and the hiss of her radiator when the fluid inside gushed from the cracked engine rang in her ears as she shook her head and peered out the windshield.

"Emma? Emma, talk to me." Becky's almost hysterical voice came out of the plastic container, now on the floorboard.

"I'm okay, Becky. Do me a favor though and call the police, and have them come out to... Shit. I'm not even sure what intersection I'm at."

"They'll find you. Don't worry. I'll call right now. You were on your way to town from your parents', right?"

"Yeah."

"Hang tight. They'll be there soon."

"Thanks, Bec," Emma replied, listening while the phone disconnected when Becky hung up.

Emma hit the snap on her seat belt to unhook it and then pulled the handle on her door while she pushed against it, trying to get herself out of the truck. It groaned and creaked like a little old man's bones when he tried to stand up, but it finally opened, and she crawled out.

Shielding her eyes from the glare of the Montana sun in the middle of August, she saw the front end of a massive brown and black bus with fancy scrolling on the side smashed into the front of her pickup. "Crap. Dad will kill me for this."

"Are you all right?"

Emma turned around quickly only to have spots form in front of her eyes and her head begin to spin.

"Whoa. Easy there, darlin'."

The deep, rich, smooth as silk voice and the feel of strong hands cupping her elbow to hold her steady had her looking up into a set of dark brown eyes framed by the longest eyelashes she'd ever seen. Only one person she knew had those pretty eyes, and he graced the wall of her bedroom. Collar-length dark hair, windblown by the rustling prairie gusts, wide chest with mouthwatering muscles straining his black T-shirt, trim hips holding up the low-riding jeans, and dusty cowboy boots— holy shit!

"Brandon Tucker?"

"Never mind who I am, honey. You're bleedin' from the cut on your head," the man replied, pulling a handkerchief from his back pocket and pressing it to her forehead. "Hold this on there a minute. It'll help stop the blood."

"What the hell is goin' on here?" an angry voice said from several feet away. "Damn it, Beau."

"Beau?" she asked, totally confused as the second man came storming in their direction from near the door of the bus.

Wait a damn minute here. There are two of them? No way! Two Brandon Tuckers?

"Sorry, darlin'," the first man replied before pushing her down on the bumper of her truck. "Stay there a minute while I deal with him." He walked back toward the agitated man and said, "Knock it off, Brandon. It was an accident. I didn't see the stop sign."

The two men moved toward the front of the vehicles, but Emma could still hear the angry voices.

"An accident? Fuck! Look at the front of the bus. Shit, shit, shit. This is gonna take days to fix, and we're out in the middle of bumfuck Montana, Beau. How do you suppose we're going to get this fixed in time for me to be in South Dakota next week, huh? I have a show to do."

"I realize that, Brandon. Stop acting like the spoiled star and listen to me for a minute. There's nothin' we can do about it right at the moment. They're gonna have to tow both of these into town, and we'll deal with it after we talk to a mechanic."

"We don't have a body shop big enough to handle a bus, but we aren't far from Billings. You could possibly have them tow it there," she said as she stopped next to them and held out her hand. "I'm Emma Weston, and if I'm not mistaken, one of you is Brandon Tucker. Care to explain to me why there are two of you? Or am I seeing double because of the crack in my skull."

"Brandon, quit being a jerk. She's hurt for cryin' out loud," Beau snapped and then turned back toward her. "Sorry, honey. You really should be sittin' down or somethin'. Concussions can really suck. I know. I've had a few."

"Thanks, but I'm fine. Now, explain why there are two of you."

"It's not common knowledge, but yes, there are two of us. We're twins," Beau replied, running his hand through his dark hair.

"Identical?"

"Well, duh." The smart remark came from Brandon as he leaned against the bus and crossed his arms over his chest.

She glared at him and then turned her attention back to the first guy.

"I'm Beau, and you're correct. He's Brandon Tucker."

"*The* Brandon Tucker?"

"Well, d..." Brandon started, but snapped his mouth shut when Beau glared.

"It's nice to meet you, Emma. I wish it had been under better circumstances," Beau said, taking her hand between his. "How's your head?"

Emma could hear the distant blare of police sirens getting closer, telling her several cop cars or at least one car and an ambulance were close. "It hurts, but it'll be fine." She glanced over her shoulder as one of the police cars skidded to a stop, followed by two more. *Damn. The entire Red Rock police force is out here. All three of them.* "I'll take your handkerchief home and wash it for you. It's got blood all over it."

The police officer jumped out of his car and slid to a halt at her side. "Emma? Are you all right?"

Great. I do not *need the overprotective, whinny Alex right now.* "I'm fine, Alex. Just a bump on the head."

"I'm calling an ambulance. You need to get checked out at the doctor."

"No. I don't want to go to the hospital."

"Your daddy will have my hide if you don't get checked out, Emma. I'd rather keep it, if you know what I mean."

"I'll deal with my dad, Alex."

"What happened, anyway?" Alex asked, shoving his sunglass up on top of his head.

Emma tried not to giggle at the sight, but with Alex's premature balding, the sunglasses made him look like a beetle with his eyes on top of his head. He really was a nice guy, and he'd had a crush on her since high school. Unfortunately, she couldn't even think of him in any sort of a romantic way. He would always be Alex the tuba player from band.

She glanced again at the two gorgeous hunks standing nearby with their hands in the pockets of their rugged jeans and T-shirts molded to identical sculpted chests. Never in her life had she thought she'd have a chance to meet Brandon Tucker, and here she stood with two of them. *Two? How come I've never heard of him having an identical twin brother? I know everything about Brandon Tucker, from the size of his shoes to the brand of underwear he wears.*

Beau caught her gaze with his, and the sexy little twitch of his lips as a small smile spread across his face made her blush and go hot all over. Blood rushed to her head, and she felt woozy again, but this time she wasn't sure if it was from the bump or the hot look from Beau.

Next, she took in his brother. *The* Brandon Tucker. The one man who tantalized her dreams at night with wet kisses, hot licks, and the oh-so-gorgeous body. So far, Brandon's attitude left something to be desired. He definitely acted like the spoiled music artist as she listened to him talk to the police officer taking his statement.

"I really think this whole accident is her fault, officer. She couldn't have been paying much attention if she missed a vehicle the size of this bus. I mean, she ran right into us."

"Excuse me?" she said, moving closer when she heard his words. "You ran the stop sign. I don't have a stop sign on my side of the road, buster."

"She's right, Brandon."

"Shut up, Beau. Let me handle this."

"Don't you tell him to shut up, you overbearing, think you know it all, spoiled pain in the ass. Just because you're a country music star doesn't mean shit out here. I live in this town, and your money and your fame aren't going to get you anywhere." Indignation raced through her blood at Brandon's high-handed attitude.

Beau's lips twitched as he stepped back to watch. Emma wasn't sure how she felt about him letting her do all the standing up to his brother, but right now, she didn't care.

"Listen here," the officer said, but backed off when Emma got right in Brandon's face.

The CD player in her truck started playing, for no apparent reason, and what else came on? Brandon's newest CD.

"A fan?" Brandon mocked, one eyebrow cocked arrogantly over his left eye as he stood nose-to-nose with her.

"Not anymore," she snarled and then walked to the side of her truck. With the window down, she crawled inside, popped the disc from the player, and walked back to Brandon's side. "See this?"

"Yeah," he growled.

The cocky grin on his face disappeared when she snapped the disc in half, pulled her arm back, and flung the pieces into the nearest wheat field.

* * * *

Emma Weston had him, Beau Tucker, tied up in knots the moment she crawled out of her wrecked truck. Her soft, singsong voice wrapped itself around his nuts and squeezed, reminding him exactly how long it had been since he'd found a woman worth fucking—not some buckle bunny and not some music groupie, but a real, honest-to-goodness woman.

When she'd come out of nowhere and he'd hit her truck with his brother's bus, he'd been scared to death someone in the vehicle might be badly hurt. Thank goodness she wasn't. The wound on her head might need a stitch or two, but she was walking, talking, and cussing with the best of them. Standing at probably five foot six or so, she would fit right nicely against his six foot frame. Her willowy body, long brown hair, and big blue eyes left him wondering exactly what she'd look like in nothing but a sexy thong.

"Fan or not, Brandon Tucker, you're a jerk," she snapped and then turned on her heel to walked toward Beau. "I'm sorry, Beau. Is he always like that?"

He shrugged and said, "It depends. I'm used to it, I guess." A quick glance at his brother revealed his narrowed eyes resting on Emma. "I think he had a bit too much to drink last night after the show we did in Idaho. He's probably hung over."

"Hung over or not, it's no excuse for being rude."

Hoping he'd have a chance to get to know Emma better, and knowing Brandon would be a part of anything they started, he said, "Give him a chance, Emma. He's really a nice guy most of the time."

"Hmrph."

A short laugh burst from his lips when Emma made the little pouty sound and folded her arms. "You're cute when you pout."

"I'm not pouting."

Before he could stop himself, he smoothed his thumb over her bottom lip and said, "Yes, you are."

Her pretty blue eyes dilated, and her breathing sped up, making her tempting breasts rise and fall with each breath. By her reaction to his touch, he could almost believe she felt the attraction between them too, and for once he realized it wasn't Brandon she wanted this time. Whenever he met a woman he had to wonder if she actually wanted him, or if it was because he looked just like his brother, the infamous Brandon Tucker. With his brother's attitude sometimes, you would think Brandon was the older of the two of them by ten minutes and not him.

Unfortunately for him, Brandon got the voice and Beau got shit. Well he shouldn't say that, really, since he also got the rugged good-looks, dark brown eyes, nice smile, and hard body like his brother. Except Beau turned out to be the nice guy, and Brandon had turned into the spoiled star as women threw themselves at him, begging for attention. Brandon used them and tossed them away like yesterday's garbage most of the time. His brother's behavior bothered Beau. Women meant more to him than a passing one night stand, even if he hadn't found the one girl he wanted to spend the rest of his life with.

Born and raised on a ranch in eastern Montana, they both knew the meaning of hard work, long days, and pushing horns. From an early age, Brandon stood out amongst the crowd. He'd started singing at rodeos, fairs, competitions, and anywhere else he could find an audience. Beau'd tagged along with his brother, managing Brandon's money and his career, and keeping him out of fistfights with jealous boyfriends. Today, he'd had been behind the wheel of the bus due to their driver's having a family emergency back home.

"I'm real sorry about the accident, Emma," he murmured, wishing he could pull her in closer and feel her lips under his.

"It's okay," she whispered, her breathing shallow and her face flushed with what he hoped might be excitement and curiosity. Her tongue came out to lick her lips, catching the pad of his thumb in the process and sending white hot need straight to his dick.

The rough clearing of a throat brought his attention back from where he'd been drowning in Emma's eyes.

"I've called the tow truck, Emma," Alex said, stopping next to them.

Beau wanted to hurt Alex for interrupting the charged moment between him and Emma. The need and desire swimming in Emma's gaze fascinated him.

"Thanks, Alex," she replied, breaking contact with Beau and stepping back. "Can I use your phone so I can call my dad?"

"Here. Use mine, Emma," Beau said, pulling the phone from his pocket. "It's the least I can do."

"Thanks. I'd use mine, but it's buried on the floor of my truck somewhere. I was talking to Becky when the accident happened."

"You were on your phone?" Alex asked, narrowing his eyes. "You know it's illegal to be on your phone."

"I had her on speaker, Alex, so it wasn't illegal. I wasn't texting or anything. I don't do that."

"I'll have to put it in my report though."

Her eyes narrowed, and Beau hid his smile. "Well, make sure you qualify it with all the facts."

"I will, but you know your insurance company might have problems with it."

"It wasn't my fault, Alex. Beau admitted he didn't see the stop sign."

"Here," Beau said, showing her how to operate his phone with a touch to the screen. "Now you can dial regular."

"Thanks again," she said before she moved away.

Several moments later, he could hear her trying to explain to someone on the other end.

"No, I'm fine, Dad. There isn't any need for you to come out here. They'll be towing the truck into town in a few minutes. The tow truck just got here."

A lapse in conversation made him wonder what her father said on the other end, but Beau's attention drifted away the moment her eyes met his. *Pull your head out, man. She's just another babe—and I hope to hell she's nowhere near jailbait, but with women these days, a guy has to be careful.*

Beau shook his head and walked over to the tow truck driver to see about getting the bus towed into town or somewhere they could get it looked at. Brandon had abandoned the party for the inside of the bus the moment the police officer finished with his statement, leaving Beau to deal with everything. *Figures.*

"So. Are you going to be able to tow the bus, too?" Beau asked the driver as he hooked up Emma's truck.

"Nope." The man wasn't forthcoming with information, and he continually glanced Emma's way.

"Do you know Emma?" Beau asked when he saw the man look at her again.

That got the driver's attention. "Yeah. Known her since she was a little girl. Why? You know her?"

Beau shrugged and said, "Only since I hit her truck."

"You were drivin'?"

"Yes. How bad are the damages to hers?"

The man squinted and then spit a string of tobacco juice at the ground, almost hitting the tip of Beau's boot. "Bad enough her daddy's gonna have a few words for ya. The drive train's probably busted, and the radiator and engine are cracked, if I had my guess, by the fluid on the ground under it. I'd say several thousand dollars in damage. You're just damned lucky she ain't hurt. You don't want to mess with the Weston bunch. I'm kinda surprised her brother Cade ain't out here yet." They both looked behind the bus as a large diesel pickup came screeching to a halt on the road behind them. "Spoke too soon."

"Emma Leanne Weston!" the man driving the truck shouted the moment he cleared the door.

"Aw shit," Emma said, walking back toward Beau. "Here's your phone back. Thanks." She turned back around and met the guy halfway. "Chill, Cade. I'm fine." The man wrapped her in a hug and then stepped back.

"Are you sure you're okay?"

"It's just a bump on the head. I suppose Daddy sent you out here."

"Of course. I was on my way back to my place when he called me on my cell." The man she called Cade glanced over her shoulder and locked his gaze on Beau before he glanced back down at his sister, frowning. "What the hell did you do, Emma? You couldn't hit somethin' smaller like a stop sign. You had to hit a bus?"

Beau took the moment to approach the pair, noticing the similarities in their coloring. They shared the same hair color and penetrating blue eyes. "Hi. Um, listen. It wasn't her fault. I ran the sign. I just didn't see it."

Cade looked at him and then back at Emma. "He looks awful familiar. Isn't he the guy you have plastered all over the walls of your bedroom?"

The look on Emma's face almost had Beau laughing. Color bloomed on her cheeks and spread down her neck. Surely there weren't that many shades of red.

"Actually, no, I wouldn't be the guy. Name's Beau Tucker," he said, holding out his hand. "The guy on her wall is probably my brother Brandon. We're twins. He's the singer. I'm the bus driver. At least today I am."

Shoulders back and eyes narrowed, Cade gave Beau the once over and then pushed his hat back on his head and held out his hand. "Nice to meet you, Beau. I'm Cade Weston, Emma's older brother."

"Did you have to embarrass me, Cade? Jesus. I have one damn poster," she snapped throwing up her hands. "You can tell Gabrielle and Dad I'm fine, and I'll be home after they finishing towing the truck in."

"No can do, sis. If I go back there without you, I'll never hear the end of it. I won't even be able to hide at my house, because Nat will harp on me about it too."

"God, I love my sister-in-law," Emma said with a chuckle.

The cell phone in Cade's pocket rang. "Excuse me a sec." He opened it and held it to his ear. "Yeah, I know. I've already told her."

The murmurs on the other end of the conversation sounded like an irritated mother to Beau. He knew all about them, since he dealt with his own parents. Whenever Brandon's face got plastered all over the tabloids about this escapade or that, Beau got to explain it and make excuses for his twin's reckless behavior. Their folks didn't seem to understand Brandon was a big boy and could take care of himself.

"Well, there is a bus involved, Dad." Cade rolled his eyes. "No, not a school bus or anything like that. It's actually a musician's tour bus." A few more murmurs and he said, "All right. I'll ask, but I can't make any promises. They might be busy or on their way somewhere. Bye, Dad."

"Don't tell me," Emma grumbled.

"You know Gabrielle, Em," Cade replied and turned toward Beau.

"My Dad is requesting your presence at the home place for dinner. It's the least we can do, since you've been inconvenienced by this whole thing."

Excitement zipped down Beau's back and settled in his balls. He could actually spend a little more time with Emma if he and Brandon took the invitation. Brandon would kill him, but right now, he didn't care. "I accept on behalf of myself and my brother. We'd love to have dinner with your family. Plus, it would give me a chance to apologize to your father about getting his daughter into an accident."

Emma glanced at him and frowned, although her eyes blazed with heat. Maybe he read her wrong. Maybe she wasn't attracted to him like he thought. He cocked an eyebrow and then glanced down at her chest. Nope, no mistaking the tips of her nipples poking out. Lucky for him, his dick had calmed down a little since he'd stood so close to her, but if she didn't stop looking at him like she wanted to eat him alive, it wouldn't take long for it to rear its head and point right at her.

"Can I talk to you a second?" she asked, taking his arm and pulling him along until they stopped several feet away from the crowd.

"Is there somethin' wrong, darlin'?"

"Listen, you don't have to come out to my dad's place. He likes to get all friendly and stuff."

"But I'd like to."

"Why?" she asked, putting both hands on her hips.

"I'd like to spend a little more time with you. You know, get to know you a little better. I know we didn't meet under the best circumstances, but maybe fate stepped in."

She stepped back and put her hand up to her throat. "I...You...Really?"

"Yeah, really. I'd like to find out what makes you tick. What better place than at your family's house?"

The door to the bus opened, and Beau rolled his eyes. *Great. Just what I need—Brandon out here again.*

"Beau, can I talk to you a minute?"

"Stay right here, Emma. I'll be right back."

They moved several feet away, and he could tell Brandon was gonna blow. He'd probably heard Cade issue the invitation even from inside the bus, since they'd had the side windows open while they drove.

"I'm *not* going to anyone's house for dinner, Beau. I want to find a decent hotel in this shithole town, drink until I'm numb, and then pass out."

"You mean like you do every night?"

"What's it you? You get paid to keep everything straight."

"Maybe I'm tired of being your pansy, Brandon, and digging your ass out of a jam every time we stop somewhere and you get an itch for some pretty thing in the front row. Personally, I don't care whether you go out to Emma's dad's place or not. I'm going, once we get the bus settled. It's getting too late to be doing anything this evening anyway, and it would be a nice reminder of home, having dinner with an ordinary family. I bet they'd even treat you like you were normal, Brandon, and not some high class musician."

He pushed past Brandon, but stopped a few feet away and turned back to face his brother when it dawned on him why Brandon didn't want to go out there. "I get it. This whole not wanting to go out there is because Emma isn't fawning over you and kissing your ass. In fact, she's so pissed at the way you've been acting, she broke one of your CD's and tossed it into the field over there. It's got your goat that you just lost a fan, and you don't know how to handle it, much less the fact she's gorgeous. You're attracted to her too, aren't you? We're usually attracted to the same type of woman, and I bet this is no different."

Brandon rushed to his side and hissed, "All right, fine. She's hot. Okay? And I don't like her drooling all over you and not me. I'm the star here, and it should be me she's gettin' all hot and bothered over, not you. I saw the way she got all gooey when you brushed your thumb over her lip."

"You know what, Brandon? You're an ass and a jerk, just like she said. Maybe she likes nice guys instead of assholes. I aim to find out, whether you come along or not. But let me warn you, if you do go out there with me for dinner, you better take a step or two back and remember how our parents raised us. Lose the megastar attitude and at least pretend to be a nice guy for a change." Without waiting for a reply from his open-mouthed brother, he walked back to Emma and Cade and said, "Why don't you give me the address, and once we get the bus settled, I'll take a cab out there."

"Is Brandon coming?" Emma asked, and Beau wondered why.

"I don't know."

"Yes, I'm coming, and thank you for the invitation," Brandon replied, walking back to where they stood near the back of the bus. "And I promise to behave," Brandon replied with a smile.

Emma scowled, and one dark eyebrow shot up. Her apparent irritation with Brandon made Beau feel much better. Maybe he wouldn't have to compete against his brother for a woman's affection this time. Maybe Emma didn't really want Brandon after all.

"It's settled then. We'll catch a cab and—" Beau said.

"Nonsense," Cade replied. "I'll take everyone into town, and then once everything is settled, we can all ride out to my parents' place together. I'll call Nat and have her meet us there with Alan."

"Beau, why don't you ride with the tow truck driver now that the bigger rig is here to take the bus into town? I'll ride in with Cade and Emma," Brandon said with a satisfied smirk.

Beau wanted to punch him. "But I—"

"You need to handle all the details, brother. You know more about those kinds of issues than I do. Of course, we'll be right behind you, right Cade?"

The arrogant asshole attitude Brandon wore like a suit jacket, shined brightly for all to see as Brandon shoved Beau out of the way and situated himself in close contact with the beautiful Emma.

"Uh, yeah," Cade said with a frown and a strange look as he ushered Emma towards his truck.

"Don't, Brandon."

"What?" Brandon asked, with a wide-eyed innocent look Beau didn't believe for a second.

"Just don't, or I'll kick your ass," Beau snarled. He spun on his heel and headed for the front of the bus.

2

Emma watched, openmouthed, as Brandon charmed every one of her sisters during dinner. If she didn't know better, she would have sworn Brandon and Beau had switched personalities in the time it took for them to get the bus situated, and for Cade to drive them all back to the home place.

From the moment they'd stepped into the house, Beau had snarled and snapped, while Brandon smiled and suckered every female in the house into loving him. In another words, he turned into the Brandon Tucker Emma fantasized about with every breath she'd taken since he'd burst onto the country music scene some five years before.

With a shake of her head, she pulled open the sliding glass door between the living room and the back yard and stepped out into the night's cooler air. Orange streaks painted the evening sky while the sun fought gallantly against the coming darkness. She loved Montana evenings in the summer. They always seemed so romantic—given you were spending them with the right person. For Emma, the right person had yet to come along, but she couldn't wait to find him.

Outside lights flicked on as the sun disappeared, bathing the backyard in a soft blue glow. Tonight's full moon and the clear night sky would make an awesome backdrop for a couple of lovers. "Yeah, right," she murmured.

"Emma?"

She spun around to find one of Tucker brothers headed in her direction. From this distance, she couldn't tell whether Brandon or Beau had stepped outside. Earlier, she'd noticed they both wore distinctive and different colognes, making it easy for her to know who was who if they were standing close enough, since she didn't know them very well...yet.

"Brandon. What are you doing out here?" She tipped her chin up and folded her arms over her chest. "I'm sure the other women of my family will miss your company."

"Will you mind if I go back inside?" he asked, stepping close enough to touch.

The warmth of his breath on her face made her shiver, and she didn't like her reaction at all. "What do you care?"

"I care. You're a very beautiful woman, Emma." One finger skimmed down her cheek and then slipped along her jaw.

With a sharp jerk, she pulled her face away from his touch. "Don't play games with me, Brandon. I'm not fooled by your change in personalities. You were a total jerk at the accident."

"I know, and I wanted to apologize to you. I don't usually act so arrogant."

She didn't believe him for a second and the small snort she released told him so. His earlier behavior screamed arrogance and righteousness.

"I see you don't believe me."

"I didn't say that."

"You didn't have to. I could see it in your eyes."

Her body went into overload when he stepped close again. Goosebumps rose on her arms, and a shiver raced down her spine as the spice of his cologne wrapped around her senses and the warmth of his skin called to her.

"You have beautiful eyes. They remind me of a crystal clear lake." His fingers slipped down her cheek in a soft caress. "I wonder—do they go dark like sapphires when you're aroused beyond rational thought?"

His voice trailed off into a whisper, and his mouth came close enough that if she leaned in, she could feel the firmness of his lips and find out if her fantasy Brandon was anything like the real thing. Did she dare? He'd be gone in a heartbeat when the bus got fixed, but what if she let herself pretend he could fall in love with her? What about Beau?

"Your lips look so soft, Emma. I need to taste you."

Her eyes slowly closed as he nibbled at the corners of her lips and then trailed kisses back toward her ear. His teeth nipped at the soft skin of her neck, sending her thoughts scattering to the wind.

The moment his mouth brushed hers, she couldn't think—couldn't breathe. Everything revolved around his lips and his oh-so-wicked tongue as it pushed into her mouth, demanding she give in to her desire. Without thought her arms went up around his neck, and she returned his kiss lick for lick, nip for nip, and sigh for sigh. Brandon the fantasy and Brandon the real man merged into one. She could no more resist him than she could go without breathing.

The feel of his hand skimming up under her shirt and then cupping her breast drove a whimper from deep inside her to the surface of her lips. The calluses on his fingers from playing the guitar were rough and exhilarating at the same time. A soft mewl escaped her mouth when he lifted his head.

"That's it, darlin'. Give in. You know you want me," he murmured as his lips trailed down her neck.

"Can't do it, can you Brandon?"

Beau's voice, coming from her right, slammed into her like a cold rain —bitter and freezing. Desire cleared like a fog bank cut by the early sun, and she stepped back out of Brandon's arms to face a very angry Beau.

"Beau, listen—" she started, but he cut her off.

"Don't, Emma. It's fine. I'm sorry I read more into the attraction I felt for you. I thought you might have really liked me for me, and not because I'm Brandon Tucker's twin."

Irritated beyond belief, she tried again to make him listen. "No, Beau, you don't understand. Let me explain."

"I do. Really. We go through this a lot, don't we Brandon?" he asked his brother, while Brandon just shrugged and examined the fingernails of his left hand.

"You what?" she snapped. Anger filled her when she realized the whole thing was a game between them. See who could get the girl to give up her panties the quickest. "This is like a game to you two. Is that it? I'm some kind of a fuckin' conquest?"

"Emma, listen," Beau said, stepping closer with his hand outstretched, but she backed away.

"No, you listen. Get out! Both of you. I don't fuckin' care how you get back to town, and I don't want to see either of you ever—and I do mean ever—again." She took two steps toward the door, but Beau grabbed her arm and spun her around. With her temper in full flare, she balled up her fist and connected with Beau's jaw, dropping him to the ground. *Don't touch me,*" she snarled.

Just as she reached the door to the house, Cade came outside and said, "Everythin' okay?"

"No, it's not okay. I want those two out of our house."

"What happened, Emma?"

"Nothin'. Leave me alone. Just get them out of here." Before she could stop them, tears streaked down her cheeks. How could they do this to her? Megastars didn't care about anyone but themselves, and apparently twin brothers didn't either. The lifestyle of a country star must have rubbed off on Beau too.

The moment she reached her bedroom, she threw herself across the comforter on her bed and sobbed. She'd really thought Beau might have been different, and when Brandon had actually started acting like a normal human being, she thought she'd been wrong about him too.

"Emma?"

"I don't want company," Emma mumbled into the blanket.

She felt a warm hand on her hair and the mattress sinking under her as Natalie sat down next to her.

"Honey, I'm sorry things turned out this way."

Wiping the tears from her cheeks, she whispered, "It doesn't matter, Nat. Neither of them are worth the tears."

"So why are you crying so hard?"

"Because I actually was stupid enough to think they might have been different."

"They?"

She turned her head and looked up at her sister-in-law. "Can I ask you a question?"

"Sure, honey."

After a fortifying breath, she asked, "How did things go down with Cade and Kale? I know you dated both of them for a bit."

Natalie bit her lip and slid into the chair next to the bed. "I'm not sure if you really should hear about it." The worried expression on Natalie's face gave Emma pause. Maybe she shouldn't pry. After all, Natalie was married to her brother, and Kale had found his own love with Laurel. "Will you answer a question for me first?"

"Sure."

"Are you thinking you like both of them?"

Emma sat up on the bed, looked up into the gorgeous face of Brandon Tucker on her wall, and sighed as she wiped the tears from her cheeks. "Yeah. It's wrong though. I shouldn't be attracted to both of them."

"Why not? It's kind of hard not to be when they are identical twins."

With a shrug of her shoulders, she said, "But Beau is completely different, or at least I thought he was. He seemed so nice when he helped me out at the accident. Brandon was such a jerk out there, but when he got here, he turned into the guy I always fantasized about—sweet, charming, and hot enough to melt butter."

"You want to tell me what happened outside?"

"Brandon kissed me."

"And?"

"I totally lost myself in him, Nat. I didn't hear anything around me. Nothing penetrated the blood rushing in my ears, except when Beau came outside. The way Beau sounded..." She shook her head. "I felt dirty and used."

"Why?"

"They made it out to be like some kind of competition between them. Who could get in the girl's panties first or somethin'."

"Mmm."

"So please, tell me what happened between you, Cade, and Kale."

Natalie took one of her hands and said, "I came out here to help my gram after grandpa died. I know you've heard about how I ended up in a ditch, and Cade came to my rescue."

"Yeah."

"Well, apparently he told Kale about how he'd run into me, so Kale came over to see for himself. I ended up having lunch with Kale and dinner with Cade."

"Wow," Emma whispered. "You have to tell me. I've heard rumors, you know, around town, but I didn't want to pry."

"The rumors I had sex with both of them?" Natalie asked, pink staining her cheeks as she looked down at her hands for a moment.

"Um...yeah. But it wasn't like at the same time or anything, right?" she asked, totally in awe that someone sweet and grounded like Natalie would date two such different men.

When Natalie lifted her gaze, Emma could see the sparkle in her eyes at the mention of having sex with the two men. "It's true, and yes, it was at the same time."

Shocked and dismayed to find out the rumors she'd heard were true, Emma asked, "Seriously?"

"It wasn't planned or anything, Emma. Cade and I had a huge fight earlier in the day. I was desperate to make your brother pay for his big mouth. The attraction I felt for Kale wasn't anything like I felt for Cade, but saying I was pissed would be an understatement. Your brother had insisted he didn't care if I dated them both, or even had sex with them both."

"He actually said that?"

"Yes. Anyway, I told Kale I wanted to have sex with him, and he agreed. He told me he'd pick me up. Well, when he showed up, both he and Cade were there. They pretty much kidnapped me and took me out to Kale's place. The thought of having both of them together intrigued me, so I asked them if they would, since they'd shared before, and they agreed."

"How was it?"

"Intense, but afterwards I realized I loved Cade, and what had happened wouldn't happen again. Now Kale is happily married to Laurel and has a great family with Kimmy and their new baby, Cody."

"It's not uncomfortable around Kale?"

"No. We're all best friends, including Laurel."

"Does she know about what happened?"

"Yes, and it's something we just don't discuss. It's in our past, and it's not like we ever planned to make it a permanent threesome."

Emma's gaze searched out the poster again. Brandon's kisses outside had turned her inside out, but she wondered if Beau's would do the same thing. The feelings Beau had aroused when they stood so close together out by the bus said yes, but without actually kissing him, she'd never know. Certainly the desire the two of them created in her seemed far more intense than anything she'd ever felt before with any other man.

"I can see those wheels turning, Emma. What are you thinking?"

"I'm not sure. I know how Brandon's kiss affected me, but I haven't kissed Beau."

"You could get burned badly if you're thinking what I think you are."

"I know," she whispered. "And I truly wish I wasn't contemplating having sex with both of them. It's a once in a lifetime opportunity. I hate to think they're competing for me like two little boys fightin' over a toy. If we do this as a threesome, I think it would take the competition thing right out of the equation."

* * * *

The hotel room door banged against the wall as Beau stormed inside and Brandon followed closed behind.

"Fuck!" Beau snarled, tossing his bag onto the couch.

"Easy, Beau," Brandon said, hoping his brother wasn't going to do something stupid like put a hole in the wall.

"Screw you, Brandon. You aren't the one standing here with a god-damn golf ball-sized bruise on your jaw."

"She packs quite a punch." He threw his suitcase on one of the beds and reclined back against the headboard. Emma Weston intrigued him. She didn't fit into the mold of fangirl and she didn't bow to his charms or throw herself at his feet begging for his attention. The attraction definitely sizzled between them. No doubt there, but she wasn't sure what to do with it. He knew what he wanted to do. A quick fling would be right up his alley. But Beau wanted her too. Maybe he should step aside and let Beau have a chance at her? Be the kind a caring brother for a change.

"How did I let you screw this up so bad?"

"Listen, Beau. I'm sorry. Okay? I did instigate the kiss, but I wasn't prepared for the effect of it when she laid it on me."

"Wasn't prepared? How can you not be prepared, Brandon?" Beau threw up his hands and paced like a caged lion. "You've got girls fawning all over you, throwing their bras up on stage, half stripping next to the bus to get a piece of you and all you can say is, 'I wasn't prepared'?"

"Emma threw me for a loop, Beau. She's not like the other women I run into." He rubbed his chin. Women usually came along easy—too easy most of the time, if he were honest with himself—but Emma made him *feel*. His heart raced, and his palms felt clammy when she stood near. And when he'd kissed her? Oh hell! His brain had refused to function and his body had gone into overload, shunting all the blood to his dick in an instant. At first it seemed to be the normal reaction he had around a gorgeous woman, but the longer the kiss went on, the harder it was to think beyond the feel of her lips under his and how perfectly her breast fit into his hand. He shook his head to free himself from the fog of desire and said, "How many fans of mine do you know would tell me off like she did, break my CD, and toss it into the field?"

"Not many," Beau agreed, his features still stone cold. "But I should never have made it sound like we were competing for her."

"We usually do."

"And you usually end up with them," Beau grumbled. "But she's different—special."

"Neither of us knows her at all, Beau. How can you say she's special?" Brandon had never heard Beau talk like this about a woman, and it had him a little worried. Yeah, it would be great to get a little piece while they were stuck in Montana, but falling for a woman wasn't in his plans. He needed Beau with him, and if his brother got tied up in knots over a female, it could certainly through a wrench into their immediate future.

Beau grabbed a beer from the six-pack they'd bought at the local market, popped the top, and slumped into the chair by the window. "I wish I knew." Beau opened his mouth to take a swallow and glared at

Brandon. "Damn this hurts. I'm gonna need some ice on it pretty soon, or I won't be able to open my mouth at all tomorrow."

"So what are we gonna do to get back into Miss Emma's good graces, huh?" Brandon asked, lacing his fingers over his stomach.

"We?"

"She wants us both, Beau."

Beau frowned and took another swallow. "How would you know?"

"I kissed her, remember?"

"Don't remind me, asshole."

Brandon sat up on the side of the bed and dangled his hands between his knees as he glanced over at his brother. "You're just sore because I got to her first, but I have a feelin' you'll get your chance."

"Oh yeah?"

"Yeah. I think she's confused. I mean come on, Beau. We've shared a woman or two—"

"One or two or twenty."

Brandon grinned and shrugged at the small smile on Beau's lips. It didn't matter how many they'd shared in the past, he wanted to share Emma. "She responded to me, but she did to you too—out by the bus. I saw the way she melted under your touch."

"Yeah, but I didn't have my lips all over her and my hand on her tit," Beau snapped.

"I didn't mean for it to go that far so fast. It just happened, but I'm not gonna apologize for it, because it was damn nice. Fit perfectly in my palm."

"Fuck, Brandon. Stop already. I'm gettin' hard thinkin' about her," Beau replied, adjusting his cock in his jeans.

"Makes two of us then."

"So what are we gonna do about it?"

"Hell, I don't know." He grabbed a beer and popped it open. "We could always kidnap her. You know, take her on the road for a couple of weeks."

Beau looked at him like he'd lost his mind, and yeah, he probably had. "You aren't serious, are you?"

"No, I guess not, but it's a thought. I mean, she used to be a fan. She'd probably have a great time on the road."

"Oh yeah. Watching how many women throw themselves at us. Goin' from place to place, barely stoppin' to eat." Beau took another healthy drink. "Somehow I don't think she'd be too thrilled."

"But that's our life, Beau, and I won't apologize for it."

"It doesn't mean she'd like it."

Beau frowned, and Brandon started to worry. He knew Beau was getting tired of the road life. They'd talked a lot about settling down, buying some property and finding a good woman, but neither one had found anyone he wanted to settle down with. "What are you thinkin', Beau?"

His brother downed the rest of his beer and stared at the can, twisting it into a mashed mess of aluminum. "I don't know, Brandon. I'm gettin' tired of this life, but we always agreed I'd be there for you, no matter what happened or how long it took for you to reach your dreams."

Brandon took several sips of his beer, contemplating what life had given him. From early on, he'd been able to sing. He'd always been told the baritone of his voice gave women goose bumps, and he'd played on it, using it to get any woman he wanted. After he broke into country music, he'd lived the high life. Money and fame brought things he'd only dreamed of as a kid.

Their parents weren't rich by any means, but they did all right, and with what he pulled in now, he tried to take care of them for a change by having Beau send them money. He glanced at Beau and shook his head. He couldn't imagine being in this life without his twin next to him. Lately, he'd started thinking about what Beau had given up to be with him on the road all the time. Beau hadn't mentioned his dreams recently, and maybe it was time for Brandon to ask. Red Rock seemed to be a town where they might be able to sit for a few weeks and relax. If Emma Weston came into the picture while they were here, then so much the better.

"What about your dreams, Beau?"

"I don't have any." Beau jumped to his feet, tossed the can in the trash, and began to pace.

Brandon watched as Beau paced from the door to the bathroom and back. "Sure you do. I know you do. You wanted to get some land and raise cattle, like Mom and Dad. Find you a pretty woman, settle down and have a passel of kids."

"One problem, brother. There isn't a pretty woman who wants to settle down with me anywhere around here and we aren't done with your career yet."

Silence stretched between them for several moments, but their thoughts were so in tune, they didn't have to speak to understand each other, or at least for each to have some idea of what the other thought. Brandon knew he surprised his brother when he said, "You know what? I think we need to take a break."

"A break?"

"Yeah. The bus is down for at least two weeks according to the mechanic here in town. Let's cancel the four shows we've got coming up. We can reschedule them. I know we planned on stopping by Mom and Dad's on our way through, but I think it's important for us to stay here."

"And do what?" Beau asked, clearly puzzled by Brandon's wish to spend some time in Red Rock.

"Stay here. Find out more about this little town. There's a woman worth pursing right here, and we both want her."

"You've sure changed your tune from this morning, when you called it a town in the middle of bumfuck Montana." Beau's eyes narrowed, like he wasn't sure if Brandon was serious or not. "What if she doesn't want us?"

Not want us? Is he serious? "Are you crazy?" he asked, wondering if his brother had really gone over the edge. The challenge of one Emma Weston called to his blood, and he knew Beau felt it too.

"She may be attracted to both of us, Brandon, but do you seriously think she'd be interested in dating us both to decide if she might want one of us?"

Brandon let a sly smile lift the corners of his mouth before he said, "Who says she has to choose?"

3

Emma glanced across the street to check for oncoming traffic and then made a beeline from one side of Main Street to the other as she headed for the diner. Her plan today included lunch with Becky and then heading out to the rodeo grounds to get things set up for the weekend. She knew exactly where the two guys taking up a lot of her thoughts were staying, and she wanted to get the work she'd volunteered to do out at the rodeo done so she could focus the rest of her evening on them.

"Emma Weston."

Shit. "Uh, hi Laurel."

"You know better than to cut across the street," Laurel said, from where she leaned against her patrol car. Laurel wasn't tall for a woman at five and a half feet tall, but she had the muscles to back up her police work. Her red hair and dark blue eyes caught the attention of several men in town, but her temper was all redhead when she got pissed off.

"Sorry, Officer. Won't happen again." Unfortunately, her innocent act wouldn't work on Laurel. She'd been around Red Rock too long to be fooled by it. Laurel had moved to town a few years earlier to help her sister with an abusive husband and ended up married to Cade's best friend, Kale. Laurel was usually cool, but very bossy when it came to police stuff.

"Uh-huh," Laurel replied with a cheeky grin. "Where are you off to so fast?"

"Lunch at the diner with Becky before we head out to the fairgrounds. Are you on patrol all day?"

"Yeah." Laurel lifted her sunglasses from her eyes and gave Emma a once-over.

"What?"

"You're wearing that?"

Emma looked down, taking in the white tank top molded to her breasts, the skinny jeans showing off the soft swell of her butt, and the cowboy boots made of the softest leather available on her feet. "What's wrong with my outfit?"

"Plan on ropin' you a man, girl?"

She couldn't stop the little smile on her lips. "Maybe. One or two."

"Two, huh? Sounds like the story I got from Elizabeth might have some merit to it."

"What story? I'm gonna kick her ass for her. I don't care if she is my sister, she needs to butt out."

"Whoa, honey. I'm sure she didn't mean anything by it," Laurel said, placing her hand on Emma's shoulder and squeezing lightly. "She's worried about you."

"There's nothin' to be worried about." She pulled her shoulders back and stuck out her chin with a stubborn tilt. "I'm only out for a little fun while two of the most gorgeous men I know are in town. Once they leave, it'll be back to another small town Saturday night."

The look Laurel gave her said Laurel really didn't believe a word Emma said, but would stand by her, no matter what happened in the end. "Just don't lose your heart, Emma."

"In a few days? Ain't gonna happen, Laurel."

"You comin', Emma?" Becky yelled from the diner doorway.

"Be right there." She turned back toward Laurel and gave her a hug. "Thanks for the advice, but everythin' will be fine. I don't have any intention of losin' anythin' to Brandon or Beau Tucker other than a few hours of my time."

"I hope you're right. Be careful, huh?"

"Always. Catch ya later, Officer." She kissed Laurel on the cheek and turned toward the diner. A moment later, she slid into a booth across from Becky. "Wow, it's warm out there today."

"It sure is. I'm already sweatin' down between my boobs, and I ain't even gotten started yet."

The two of them shared everything—boyfriends, periods, dates, sex and men. Not necessarily in that order. Emma knew she could tell Becky anything, and she usually did—but right now the embarrassment of being attracted to both men made her feel like she needed to keep Brandon and Beau a secret.

"What happened with your accident the other day? I heard you hit a bus."

"I didn't hit them, they hit me, but yeah, it wasn't pretty. Screwed up my truck pretty bad."

"Whose fault?"

The waitress returned with their drinks, and Emma took a sip before she answered. "The driver of the bus. He didn't see the stop sign."

"Wow."

"I'm glad I wasn't hurt, and no one on the bus was, either."

"I saw the bus at the garage earlier today."

Crap.

"Why didn't you tell me the bus belonged to Brandon Tucker, Emma? I thought we shared everything. And then I find out from your sister, for goodness' sake, that you had him at your house last night for dinner."

"Well, I..."

"Hey, Emma."

Holy hell! Emma didn't even have to look to see who stood at the edge of the booth. If Becky's round eyes and slack jaw hadn't told her, the tingle down Emma's arm from his touch would have.

"Brandon." She looked behind her, spotting the bruise on his jaw, and stammered, "S—sorry, Beau. I thought..." *Damn it. They aren't wearing cologne today.*

"It's okay, darlin'. Happens all the time." The smile on his face made her leery. She'd been so pissed at the two of them the night before, she didn't understand how she could look at him now and only think about finding out if Beau's kiss would do the same thing to her that Brandon's did.

She bit her lip and dropped her gaze to the middle of his chest. The blue T-shirt stretched across the expanse of muscle and the jeans riding low on his hips had blood rushing in her ears and liquid gushing from her pussy.

"Wait! There are two of them?" Becky said, her voice almost a squeal.

"Mind if we join you?" Brandon asked, walking up behind Beau.

"Sure. Of course," Becky replied, before Emma could say a word.

Beau sat down beside her and Brandon slid into the booth next to Becky, who sat there with her mouth open.

"Becky, close," she told her, indicating with her hand that Becky should shut her mouth.

"But it's Brandon Tucker and..." She looked at Beau. "And Brandon Tucker."

"Becky, this is Beau Tucker. He and Brandon are twins," she replied, indicating the pair. "Guys, this is my best friend, Becky."

"Nice to meet you, Becky," Beau said, holding out his hand.

Becky took it and blushed to the roots of her red hair when Beau brought it to his lips and kissed the back of her hand. The green-eyed monster of jealousy reared its ugly head, and Emma had to fight it down with a swift mental talking to. Unfortunately, it got twice as bad when Brandon did the same thing.

Emma cleared her throat and said, "What are you two doing here this time of day? Don't you, like, stay up all night and sleep all day?"

"We do normally stay up pretty late, but we had to talk to the mechanic at the garage this morning," Beau replied.

"When did they say the bus would be fixed?" she asked. "I know you've got shows to do the next couple of weeks."

"Oh yeah. Total fangirl over there," Becky said, ignoring the glare she shot her way. "She knows every stop you have on your schedule between now and Christmas."

"I'm flattered," Brandon replied, giving Emma a dimpled grin.

Emma completely forgot to think, breathe, or swallow. *If these two turn on the major charm, I'm so totally screwed.*

The waitress came back to their table to take their order, and both men made themselves at home, ordering lunch and drinks while they kept up the conversation with Becky.

Emma felt lost. Yeah, she'd planned to flirt and make sure they knew she'd forgiven them for what happened last night, simply because she had plans to use them a little herself. Why not? Two gorgeous men seemed interested in her, and even if they would only be around for a few days, she planned to use and abuse them just like they'd planned to do to her. She hadn't planned on jealousy rearing its ugly head when they flirted with Becky.

After their food arrived, Beau asked, "So what are you two beautiful ladies up to this afternoon?"

"We have to help set up tables and stuff at the beer tent for the rodeo tomorrow."

"There's going to be a rodeo this weekend?" Beau asked, giving his brother a strange look that Emma couldn't quite decipher. Brandon shrugged and shook his head slightly.

"Yeah. It's a huge deal here. Founder's Day and all, but they're donating all the proceeds of this year's rodeo," Becky answered.

"To what?" Brandon asked, stuffing a french-fry in his mouth.

"There's a local family who has some really crazy hospital bills to pay. Their daughter has a brain tumor and needs treatment, but they don't have the money to have it done right now. We're raising money for them," Emma said.

Brandon and Beau looked at each other, and then Brandon pushed his plate away.

"Aren't you hungry?" she asked.

"Not really. I...um. I'm full."

Emma didn't think it had anything to do with his being full. The sadness in his eyes made her wonder what kind of tragedy these two shared.

She shrugged and kept talking. "Anyway, all the proceeds from admission and the sales at the beer tent are for them. Everyone thinks there will be a huge crowd."

"Who owns the beer tent?"

"A guy named Seth Reardon. He owns the honky-tonk up on the corner of Fifth and Onion."

"Onion?" The chuckle coming from Beau's mouth focused Emma's attention on his full, oh-so-kissable lips, and she had the insane urge to lean over and lock her lips on his.

She cleared her throat instead. "Yeah, Onion Street. They didn't get real creative when they named some of our streets."

Brandon stood and looked toward the counter for a moment. "Listen, we'll catch you girls later, okay? I have an errand I need to run, but give Beau the directions out to the fairground, Emma, and we'll help you and Becky set up."

"Seriously?" she asked, not sure if he was joking or what. "Brandon Tucker, mega country star, help us set up chairs and tables?"

"Yes, seriously. I'm no stranger to hard work. I had to set up band equipment plenty of times before I had a road crew." Brandon signaled the waitress for the check and handed her a hundred dollar bill. "Keep the change, honey."

Beau got to his feet and then leaned over to tuck a piece of hair behind Emma's ear. The whole world narrowed to his face, his eyes, and his smile. "We'll see you in a bit, darlin'." He leaned over and brushed his lips against hers lightly, leaving her mouth tingling, her nipples taut, and her pussy screaming for attention.

"Hello? Emma?" Becky waved a hand in front of her eyes, bringing Emma back from her fog enough to realize the two guys had left.

"Huh, what?"

"I lost you there for a minute—or should I say several? The second he kissed you, everything disappeared for you."

"Damn. Am I that obvious?"

"Uh, yeah. Duh. You've been half in love with Brandon Tucker from the moment you laid eyes on him. And now? To have a twin brother too? How in the hell will you ever choose?"

"Who says I plan to choose?" she asked, with a cheeky grin and wicked thoughts running through her mind.

* * * *

An hour later, Emma and Becky arrived at the fairgrounds and headed for the beer tent. Seth already had guys moving in and out with cartloads of kegs, barrels, and plywood for the temporary bar, along with plastic chairs and a few tables so people could sit and mingle. The makeshift Boots and Spurs would be open for business when the sun went down. The rodeo didn't start tonight, but one of the local bands always played, giving everyone a chance to unwind after the long work week, sip some beers, and visit with friends.

Emma glanced toward the back of the tent and caught Seth giving Becky a look hot enough to set the tent ablaze while Becky set up tables and chairs near the front of the tent. Those two were so attracted to each other, the room popped with the electrical current they gave off, but both seemed too damned stubborn to break the barrier they'd erected between them. *Maybe I'll play matchmaker a little tonight.*

"Hey, Seth," she said, moving close to where he stood.

Seth Reardon could set a few hearts to skipping with his rugged good looks, hard body, and striking green eyes. He was homegrown Montana boy to the core. Born and raised right there in Red Rock, he'd had several girls all over him in high school, but he was very shy around women. Clumsy and awkward in school, he'd quickly earned a reputation as a geek. Shortly after graduation, he'd gotten contacts, worked out at the local gym, and beefed himself up. When his daddy had died several years ago, he'd inherited the local honky-tonk, and ran it with an iron fist—but he never seemed to find the right girl.

"Hi, Emma. How are you?" he replied, never taking his gaze off Becky.

"I'm fine, but Becky isn't."

"What's wrong with Becky? She isn't sick is she?" The look of concern in his eyes told Emma he cared for her friend...a lot.

"Yeah."

"Well, she needs to go on home then and get some rest. Being out here in this heat probably isn't helping. I'll tell her right now."

"Easy, Seth. She's not sick as in nauseated or whatever. She's heartsick."

"Heartsick. What the hell is that? Some new thing?"

"Since you came along, yeah."

"You're confusing me, Emma. Either she's sick or she's not. Which is it?" Seth tapped his food impatiently and folded his arms across his chest.

"Are you completely blind, Seth Reardon?" she asked, throwing her arms up and scowling.

"I have no idea what you're talking about, Emma."

"The two of you are half in love with each other, but all you do is give each other scorching looks across the room."

"I've tried, Emma. She won't go out with me. She says we can't be anything but friends."

"And do you know why she thinks that?"

"No," he replied, tapping another keg and avoiding Emma's gaze.

"She thinks you're too old for her."

His eyes narrowed, and he snorted softly. "I am not. We aren't more than a few years apart."

"Five, to be exact, but who's counting?" Emma shrugged her shoulders and laid a hand on his arm. "You need to convince her age doesn't mean anything. You two are perfect for each other, but if you don't speak up, she's gonna find someone else."

The sinfully smooth voice of Brandon—or was it Beau?—interrupted her conversation. "No flirtin' with the boss, darlin'."

She spun around and came face to face with both Tucker men. *Damn it. These two are too luscious for my sanity.*

"Hey you two. Have you met Seth?"

"Uh...yeah. Sort of," Beau replied. "Nice to see you again."

"Sort of?"

"We met him earlier, Emma, when we went by the bar to talk to him," Brandon added.

"It's great of you to do this, Brandon. It's going to be phenomenal. I already have someone working on flyers and stuff, since we don't have a lot of time to get the word out," Seth said, wiping his hands on a towel. "We already have a makeshift stage the band tonight will use. If you have a couple of amplifiers, we'll be all set.

"I've already let my fan club president know so she can spread the word too. Fans are great for letting each other in on what's goin' on. I wish we had the whole band, but acoustic will have to do."

"Okay, wait a minute. What are you two talkin' about?" she asked, totally confused as her gaze went from Seth to Brandon and then to Beau.

Beau took her hand and brought it to his lips. "Brandon is gonna do an acoustic show here tomorrow in the beer tent to raise money for the little girl's family you told us about earlier."

"Really? That's like... Wow," she whispered. Her heart swelled with awe for these two men who'd blown into her life like a tornado, bowling her over and twisting her up until she didn't know who she was anymore. "Whose idea was this?"

"Brandon's initially, but Seth jumped on it when we talked to him at the bar," Beau replied. "We've spent the last couple of hours getting things together and trying to let everyone know."

Overwhelmed with gratitude, she hugged Beau and then Brandon. "This is amazing. I can't believe you're doing this for someone you don't even know."

Brandon said, "I could tell it was important to you by the way you talked about it at the diner. It's the least I can do, and it's not a big deal, really."

"Yes, it is Brandon. You have no idea how much this will mean to them. And Charlene is a fan of yours, so it will be so much sweeter for her."

"Cool. Then she should have front row seats," Beau said.

"Along with my number one fan," Brandon added, brushing his lips against her cheek. "If you're still my fan."

"It's gonna take a little more convincing, I'm thinkin'," she whispered in his ear then bit the lobe. "But you're on the right track."

"Okay, enough of all this. We've got work to do," Becky shouted from the corner of the tent. "I thought you two came here to work?"

"Yeah, yeah," Beau replied. "Show me where the pack mules are gatherin' and I'll put my back into it." He slapped his brother on the shoulder, pulled him out of Emma's embrace, and pushed him off toward the group of men moving equipment, but not before he glanced over his shoulder and gave her a playful wink.

Fighting the urge to sigh, she leaned against the beer keg and licked her lips.

"If that isn't the look of a woman wantin' a couple of hunky men, I don't know what is." Becky said, walking up beside her.

"Yeah, well. It takes more than just wantin' to get some, Becky."

"Don't I know it," Becky replied, pulling out a chair and sitting down as she watched Seth moving around behind the bar.

Emma pulled out a chair and sat next to her. "You know, I talked to Seth a bit before Beau and Brandon came in, and he wants to take you out."

"I know."

"You know? How come you won't go out with him, then?"

"I told you, Emma. He's too old for me."

"I've never heard anything so crazy in my life."

"You don't understand. I dream of him all the time. Hell, I go to sleep at night thinking about him after I've used my vibrator. I'd give anything to have his hands on me." Becky sighed and placed her elbow on the table. "Why the hell do you think I help him out when he asks me to? It isn't for the money."

"Then what's stopping you, Becky?" she asked, and then waved her hand in dismissal when Becky started to object. "Besides the age thing, because that's just an excuse and you know it." Emma watched her friend pick at a crack on the table without looking her in the eyes. "You can tell me, Becky. We've been friends forever, and you know I'll never judge you."

When Becky lifted her gaze, Emma saw tears swimming in her eyes. "He's Jewish, Emma. My father raised me Baptist, and he'd never, ever let me date a man not of the Baptist faith."

"But...but you aren't really even a practicing Baptist."

"I know, but my father would never give me his blessing to date a man outside of our faith. You know how old fashioned he is."

"God, Bec. I wish I knew what to say." Emma's heart bled for her friend. Although she'd never been in love, she couldn't imagine not having the blessing of her father, her brothers, and her sisters when she did find the man she wanted to spend the rest of her life with.

"There's nothing to say, Emma. I'll never know the feel of his hands on my skin, the taste of his kiss, or how it would feel to have him make love to me. I can't go against my father. He would disown me, and if things didn't work out with Seth, I would have no one."

"You'd have me and my family. You know that. None of us would turn our backs on you."

"Thank you," she whispered, squeezing Emma's hand. "We need to get back to work. There are still lots of chairs and things to get set up before the crowd shows up later."

Without another word between them, they walked back outside to grab more chairs, but Emma couldn't quite get her friend's dilemma out of her mind. There had to be a way to help Seth and Becky get together, and she needed to figure out how.

She'd grabbed one of the huge empty trash cans and took it around behind the tent to start picking up the mountain of miscellaneous garbage from the bar set up when she was grabbed around the waist and hauled up against a rock-hard chest.

4

Scared out of her mind, Emma elbowed the hard body behind her and reared her head back, smashing the man in the nose.

"Fuck!"

She quickly spun around at the sound of the man's voice and dropped to her knees beside him. "Oh my God! Beau, I'm so sorry. You scared the hell out of me. Are you all right?"

"Hell no, woman! You probably broke my nose to go along with the damn bruise I still have on my jaw." He tipped his head back as bright red blood dripped from his nostril and pinched the bridge of his nose. "A guy needs to be careful around you, or he could get hurt."

"Wait right here, I'll get some napkins." Cussing under her breath, she rushed into the tent, grabbed a handful of paper napkins from the table, and ran back outside. "I'm sorry, Beau, really. I didn't mean—"

"Its fine, Emma. I know I startled you, but damn, woman," he said, his speech garbled by the paper.

"Here. Let me see." She removed the wad under his nose, but he still continued to bleed. "I'm gonna to get some ice for you to put on the bridge of your nose. It'll stop the bleedin' better."

When she rushed back inside the tent, Brandon asked what the fuss was all about. She reassured him everything would be fine before she ran back out again with the ice in a towel. Beau had moved to a picnic table nearby and leaned back against the edge.

"Lay this on there," she said, placing the ice on his face and then leaning over to kiss the spot she'd bruised earlier. "I guess I should stay away from you. It seems all I do is hurt you."

"Not on your life. I'll take my chances if it means holding you, Emma. Just warn a guy, would ya?"

"Well, you shouldn't have grabbed me."

"Yeah, I kind of gathered you don't like bein' startled."

"Cade taught me how to defend myself. You got to be my test dummy."

"Great. Now I'm a dummy." Beau sat up with a small grin on his lips, wiped the remaining blood from his face, and set the ice down on the table. "I think it's quit."

Unable to stop herself, she brushed her lips against his for a moment, tasting what she'd been dying to since the moment she laid eyes on him.

The moment she lifted her head, he said, "I think I might need another one. You know, for medicinal purposes."

Grinning like the cat that ate the canary, she scooted closer and pressed her mouth over his. The moment their lips touched, her body caught fire from the tips of her toes to the roots of her hair. A soft moan broke the stillness of the evening, but she didn't quite know if it came from him or from her. Her arms went up around his neck, and she tilted her head as his tongue dove between her lips to slide along hers. How could two men look so much alike but kiss so differently and taste so good? Beau's hands did a slow crawl down her spine and then cupped her hips. Moments later, she found herself straddling his hips, kissing him like the sun wouldn't come up in the morning if she didn't give in to these feelings he stirred.

Warmth covered her back and a second set of lips found the edge of her earlobe, sending her desire skyrocketing out of control. Teeth nipped, and a tongue played along the skin of her neck while she continued to kiss Beau. Having two men touching, licking, nipping, and focusing solely on her desire had her groaning in frustration the moment Beau's mouth released hers.

"Don't stop."

"We can't continue this out here, honey. Too many eyes," Brandon whispered in her ear.

The evening air sent shivers down her back when Brandon stepped back and helped her scoot from Beau's lap. When she glanced down, there was no mistaking the bulge in his jeans.

"You do this to me, darlin'. You drive me nuts," he growled, taking her hand and pressing it to his cock.

Startled by the fierceness in his words and the strength of his touch, she backed up a step, only to run into the solid body of Brandon behind her. She couldn't deny the hard press of his cock into the crack of her ass, nor the cream spilling from her pussy to coat her silky underwear.

"We both want you, Emma. Are you up for some hard lovin'?" Brandon asked, his hands running up and down her arms.

"W-what do you have in mind?"

Brandon swept her hair back from her neck and pressed a kiss to the soft spot just below her earlobe. "Ever had a man in your ass, honey?"

"N-no."

"Do you want to?"

"Oh God, yes." Heat swept over her cheeks at the admission of such a naughty thing. Anal sex? Good girls didn't give in to such torrid fantasies, did they? "I mean, I've thought about it and I...I'm curious."

"How about after we're done here tonight, you come back to the hotel with us? Nothin' has to happen you don't want, but between me and Beau, we can make your every fantasy a reality."

She sucked in a ragged breath and slowly blew it out in a small attempt to calm her racing heart. Could she really let both Brandon and Beau make love to her? *Make love, hell! It would be down and dirty sex and nothing more.* It would be a dream come true to have Brandon Tucker in her bed—and now that she knew there were two of them, the whole dream might be double the fun.

"What's it gonna be, darlin'?" Beau asked, standing in front of her and running his thumb over her bottom lip.

"Can I think about it?"

"Sure," Brandon replied, and Beau nodded. "We still have some work to do around here to get set up for tomorrow. Plus, I hear there's gonna be dancin' and drinkin' in a while."

"Yeah, there is. It's kind of a small party before the town gets flooded with tourists for the rodeo and all hell breaks loose tomorrow. I need to ask a question though." She licked her lips and took a deep breath. "Have you two done this before? Shared a girl I mean."

"A time or two," Beau answered. "You okay with that?"

"Does it matter? I mean, what you've done in the past, or what you'll do after you leave Red Rock doesn't matter a hill of beans to me. This is only for the here and now. No long term. No promises."

The looks passing between the twins gave her pause. Understanding and acceptance reflected in their eyes, but another, deeper emotion flickered for a moment and then disappeared. They wanted a quick down and dirty affair before they moved onto the next town. Didn't they?

She stepped from between them and headed for the tent. Thoughts danced in her mind and her body tingled with the promise in their words, but could she really have sex with both men?

* * * *

As the two of them watched her walk away, Beau couldn't believe how things were transpiring. The plan was to spend more time with Emma before they left, but he really hadn't been sure if she'd go for it. Yeah, the attraction and fire burned between the three of them. He felt it and he knew Brandon did too. If someone had told him he and Brandon would have a chance at one dark-haired, blue-eyed beauty last night, he'd have told them they'd lost their mind. The way she'd cussed at them and thrown them out of her house, he'd figured they'd blown their chance at anything with her without a whole lot of groveling.

"You think she'll go for it?" he asked Brandon.

"By the way she responded to being sandwiched between us, I'd say yeah. The whole thought of it intrigues her."

"Thinking about it has me hard enough to pound nails with my dick."

"Yeah. You and be both, brother," Brandon replied, pressing his hand down on his dick to try to relieve some of the pressure. "I want inside her ass so bad, I could come in my jeans right now."

"I bet her pussy tastes sweet. I want to eat her until she comes all over my face."

"We keep talkin' like this, Beau, and we'll both be headed for the bathroom to jack off."

"I know."

Brandon looked at his face and asked, "What the hell happened to your nose, anyhow?"

"Our little spitfire head-butted me," he replied, gingerly fingering the bridge of his nose.

"No shit!"

"Yeah. I followed her out here and grabbed her around the waist. I guess she didn't realize it was me, so she smashed her head into my nose. Damn near broke it."

"You're a walkin' wreck there, brother dear. You think you'll be up to makin' our little lady scream?" Brandon asked, slapping him on the back as they headed for the tent.

"Give me two minutes between those thighs, and she'll be more than screamin'."

"Yeah, yeah. I'll believe it when I see it."

"Is that a challenge, Brandon? See who can make her scream first or loudest?"

"Oh, I'm up for it. What'cha bettin'?"

"If I get her to come first with my name on her lips, you owe me one whole day alone with her."

Brandon rubbed his chin and grinned. "And if I make her come first screamin' *Brandon*, then I get one whole day alone with her."

They shook hands and Beau smiled. "You're on brother."

"But we can't tell Emma we're bettin' like this. She'll be pissed."

"Yeah. It'll be our secret."

When they reached the flap in the tent and walked inside, Beau's gaze automatically sought out the woman who had them both on edge. Emma stood at the back of the tent behind the beer taps, talking with Becky. As if she could feel his gaze, she turned to face them and smiled so sweetly, he wanted to grab her right then and run back to the hotel room. He needed to think of something else besides how hot she looked, how soft her hair had been when he'd held onto it while he kissed her, how luscious her lips tasted, and how nice her breast would feel in his palm. Going caveman on her wouldn't be the best move on his part, but damn! If she didn't quit looking at him like she wanted to eat him alive, he wouldn't be able to control himself much longer.

Think of somethin' man—anything besides her right now. Yeah, ridin' herd, stayin' on a bull for the full eight seconds, stackin' hay at our parents' place. Oh hell, this isn't workin' at all!

Several guys walked in with band equipment to set up for their show in about an hour, so he figured he'd help them. Maybe he'd stay so busy, he'd forget about Emma—for oh, about thirty seconds.

The sound of her laughter brought his attention back to her—not like it had strayed much anyway. Whether she laughed, moaned, sighed, or growled, he wanted to hear each sound as he made love to her.

Made love? Seriously? I'm gettin' in way over my head here. Hell, I've only know her two days. I need to think of this like it will actually be. Fuckin'. Having sex. Doin' the horizontal mambo. Boinkin' her. Drilling her ass. Eatin' her out and findin' out exactly how sweet her cunt is. Okay. Yeah. Better. He glanced at her and caught her gaze on him—her eyes blazing blue, her nipples hard points against her tank top, and a little press of her thighs together telling him she was turned on too. *Oh shit! I'm so screwed.*

* * * *

People flooded into the fairgrounds by the truckload. Cars, pickups, four-wheelers, and every other type of transportation one could think of found a spot to park. The annual Founder's Day rodeo was winding up for an all-out party. Tonight would be the opening dance, the beer fest where the locals could come and have some fun before the craziness started in the morning.

"Wow. What a crowd already," Becky said, manning the beer tap on the right side of the makeshift bar.

"Yeah. I hope the tips are good tonight. I could use the cash," Emma responded from the other end.

"Oh, please, Emma—you always rake it in every time you play barmaid."

Her tip jar already showed signs of needing to be emptied, and they'd only been serving for thirty minutes. It helped that she wore a breast-hugging top cut high to show off her belly button ring, jeans molded to her hips, and a necklace dangling just above her cleavage. Of course, she loved the looks she got from Brandon and Beau the moment she stepped back inside the tent after she'd changed her clothes. Both men focused entirely on her, much to the chagrin of several other women in the room, and now they continued to sit off to her left at a table by themselves.

In a lull between customers, Becky came over to her side and nodded in the direction of her two men.

"So what's up with you and those two? Are you gonna move to the next step?"

"And what's the next step, Bec?" she asked sarcastically, letting Becky think what she would.

"Sex, of course." Becky's eyes widened and a small, dreamy smile curved her lips. "The thought of being sandwiched between those two hard bodies would make any red-blooded woman horny, and I've seen you shifting your stance over here." Becky laughed, and Emma blushed.

"Well, they did proposition me," she replied, absently wiping down the wooden plank serving as a bar.

Becky's eyebrows almost met her hair when she said, "Really? Wow! What'd you say?"

"Nothing yet. I told them I needed to think about it." She shrugged and glanced their way again, only to find both sets of brown eyes glued to her.

"What the hell is there to think about? I'd take either one, much less both."

"Oh please." Emma put both hands on her hips and snorted. "You're too hot for Seth to even think about being with another guy."

"I think about it, Emma. I think about it a lot, since Seth isn't an option for me."

She shook her head and sighed. "Substituting another man for the one you really want isn't right either."

"Hey! Can I get a beer?"

Both of them turned to face an obnoxious shout of a man at Becky's end of the bar. "Keep your boxers on, Mac. I'll be there in a second," Becky replied.

"Well hurry your sweet ass up. I need me another beer."

"You've probably already had too many, so just chill out a minute. Otherwise I won't serve you."

"The hell you won't, girl. Do I need to beat your ass for you? Maybe you like it a little rough. I bet I can oblige."

Fury and indignation rushed through Emma. Smartass, drunk men pissed her off. "You'd better shut your trap or I'll—"

"You'll what, Emma?" he asked, infuriating her further.

"Enough, Mac," Seth said, stopping next to the tap. "You're done for the night, buddy. No more for you."

"Fuck you, Seth Reardon. My buddies and I keep you in business. Now I want another beer, and I want little miss hoity-toity over there to serve it to me between her breasts. I've got a hankerin' to lick those pretty little tips with the end of my tongue."

The next thing Emma realized, Beau and Brandon stood on either side of the intoxicated man, and the place went silent when Seth pulled back his fist and knocked MacKenzie to the ground.

"If you ever fuckin' talk about my woman like that again, Mac, you won't be walkin' for several weeks, 'cause I'll break your legs for you. And don't bother to come back into my bar. From now on, you can drink somewhere else." Seth motioned for Beau and Brandon to escort MacKenzie from the tent amongst the round of applause from the rest of the people in the place.

"Did you hear that?" Emma whispered in Becky's ear. "He called you his woman."

Tears welled in her friend's gaze, and before Emma couldn't say anything more, Becky turned and fled the tent.

Seth watched from several feet away until Emma went over to him and said, "If you want her, you need to go after her. Enough of this crap. Tell her how you feel, Seth, otherwise you might as well give up right now."

After a moment he nodded and followed Becky outside.

"Damn stubborn men," Emma grumbled, taking her place at the tap again and started serving customers.

The line grew to unbelievable lengths until she noticed the women shifting to the other end of the bar. She glanced to her right and about dropped the cup in her hand when she saw Brandon serving beer after beer. He looked her way, winked and smiled.

"Hey folks! I've got an idea," Beau shouted from the raised stage at the other end of the bar. "How about a friendly competition between Emma and Brandon?"

The roar of approval made her ears ring, but she wasn't sure she wanted anything to do with a competition Beau might come up with. It appeared she didn't have a choice when his voice rose above the crowd.

"On one end of the bar we have local beauty Emma Weston. Dark haired, big blue eyes and cleavage deep enough to make any man's mouth water. On the other end we have Brandon Tucker, country crooner, handsome devil in disguise—so be careful ladies—an all-around ladies' man. We're gonna put up tip jars for both on the table there, and for the next hour while the band plays, all tips will go to Charlene Campbell's folks for her hospital bills. The two contestants can do whatever it takes to make the tips. Kiss, touch... What do you say?"

Is he serious? All eyes focused on her and Brandon.

A wickedly sexy grin lifted the corners of Brandon's mouth, and he took the several steps between them to close the gap. One arm slipped around her waist, and he pulled her toward him. "What do you say, honey? You game?"

"Uh, sure. I guess. It's to help out Charlene, so I'll do whatever."

Fire danced in the brown depths of his eyes, and she had a bad feeling about how this would play out. Somehow, she got the idea that whether she won or lost, Brandon Tucker was about to turn her world upside down.

"How about we make our own little side bet?"

Shivers rolled down her spine, and she took a deep breath to calm her racing heart. "What do you have in mind?" she whispered in a choked voice.

"Let's see," he murmured. "If I win, Beau and I get your company exclusively whenever we want it, to do with as we please—including you naked and at our mercy—for the rest of the time we're in town."

She swallowed hard. "And what if I win?"

"Name your poison, honey."

Did she dare ask for what she wanted? If she lost, she'd still get this gnawing ache inside her filled by two heavenly looking guys, one of whom she'd lusted after for way too long and the other, his identical twin.

The need to see if the real Brandon Tucker could drop the mega-star attitude and be the man any girl would love to fall for spurred her on. Beau would do what she asked without a second thought—with his caring personality, he could do no less—but Brandon?

Leaning toward him so only he could hear her words, she whispered, "You'll give half of everything you make over the next year to charity."

5

"You drive a hard bargain, baby, but you're on," Brandon replied and then kissed her hard on the mouth.

Her whole body tingled under the pressure of his kiss. She arched into his embrace and wrapped her arms around his neck, giving in to the heat of his mouth and the longing inside her. Slowly the wolf whistles and catcalls penetrated her foggy brain enough for her to push against his chest.

"Let the games begin," she whispered and then stepped back to take her place at the tap. "You do know how to handle that thing, right, big man?"

"A beer tap? I'm a cowboy, honey. I've been handlin' beer since before you were born."

"I doubt it." She let her gaze run from the top of his Stetson to the toes of his boots. "Besides, I got somethin' you ain't got, hot man."

"Oh?" he asked, splaying his fingers and cracking his knuckles as he prepared to start pouring.

"Yeah. These," she said, wiggling her breasts and tugging her top down far enough only the nipples and the bottom of her breasts were covered. Then she tucked the hem of her shirt into the elastic bottom of the built in bra. "Bring it on boys!"

The band tuned up and let rip a saucy beer drinking song, and the race was on. Men drooled on her, kissed her, and she even let a few feel a little, but the tip jar on Brandon's side stayed pretty much neck and neck with hers. She watched as he passed out tongue-melting kisses in exchange for lots and lots of cash in his tip jar. The burning ache in her chest from watching him fondle practically every woman in the place never went away. Beau soothed her a little with kisses and touches of his own, but she felt like a third of her was missing.

At the end of the hour, Beau pulled both tip jars and took them up on the stage to be counted.

"Any last bits of change or bills anyone wants to add to either jar? They look pretty close, and I know every little bit will go to help Charlene get better."

The crowd groaned, and one guy yelled, "Hell, I'm already flat damn broke, but all the touches and kisses I got from Emma was worth every dime."

"Chill out, John," she shouted from her spot at the taps. She nervously watched while Beau and Becky counted the money, not sure if she wanted to win or lose.

"This unbelievable, folks. I think someone was keeping count while the whole thing went on. The totals are so close, it's amazing. The grand total of both jars together comes out to four hundred twenty-three dollars and fourteen cents."

The crowd erupted in shouts, high-fives, and wild hugs.

"Now for the winner. Brandon and Emma, you two need to come up here for this."

"Come on, honey. Take your punishment like a lady," Brandon said with a wicked grin.

Emma let Brandon take her hand as they made their way to the stage. When they stood side-by-side in front of the crowd, butterflies erupted in her stomach, and she silently prayed she'd lose. The thought of being at their mercy for the entire time they were in town tied her insides into knots.

Beau stood between her and Brandon and worked the crowd into a frenzy before he calmed them with a raised hand. "All right, all right. We have a winner. Drum roll, please." After several moments and complete silence from the crowd, he said, "The winner is..." He shifted his glance from her to Brandon and back. "Brandon! By thirty-five cents."

"It was my thirty-five cents!" a blonde in the front shouted. "I should get an extra kiss."

"Come on up here, sweet thing," Brandon said, and the blonde jumped up on stage. It took him all of two seconds to plant a wet kiss on her painted lips and her to stick her tongue down his throat, much to the delight of the crowd around them.

Emma couldn't stand to watch it.

As she jumped down from the stage and headed back to the beer taps, she could feel the tears behind her eyes. *I will not cry. I will not cry. What do I care if he kisses someone else?*

"Whoa, honey. Where are you runnin' off to?" Brandon asked, grabbing her hand before she reached the back of the tent.

"I need some air," she whispered, pulling her hand out of his grasp and dashing outside.

"Emma!"

She rounded the back of the stock barn and slipped into the shadows, hoping he wouldn't find her until she'd had a chance to come to terms with the green-eyed monster rearing its ugly head. Neither Brandon nor Beau belonged to her, so why these crazy thoughts and feelings bombarded her heart, she didn't know.

"Come on, baby. I know you're back here."

Refusing to let him comfort her, she stayed silent, hoping he would give up and go back to the tent. The thought of giving herself to the two of them made her pussy ache and throb with need so strong, it almost brought her to her knees, but she had to keep her heart out of the fray, otherwise she'd never survive.

"I'll leave you alone for a bit, Emma, but don't stay out here long. If you aren't back inside the tent in ten minutes, I'm coming out here looking for you."

His silhouette disappeared back around the front of the barn, and she sighed in relief. She couldn't get involved with these two past the few days they'd be in Red Rock. If she did, she'd be left brokenhearted and alone.

Shoring up her pride and building the wall back up around her heart, she headed for the tent, knowing if she didn't make an appearance shortly, he would come after her. She reached it only to find him and Beau both standing just inside the flap.

"You okay, darlin'?" Beau asked, wiping a lingering tear from her cheek.

"I'm fine. I needed a minute. That's all." She glanced at Brandon and then back to Beau. "Did he tell you the contents of our side bet?"

"Yeah, but don't worry, Emma. You don't have to do anythin' you don't want to."

"I made the bet. I'll live up to it," she answered, pulling back her shoulders. "But we still have a few hours left here. Everyone will wander home about midnight."

"Will you dance with me?" Brandon asked, taking her hand and bringing it to his lips. "I want to feel your body pressed to mine."

She took a deep breath and nodded. Moments later, she found herself held tightly to his broad chest, his palm at the small of her back scorching the bare skin above her waistband and his hot breath on her ear.

"Why did you run off?"

"I told you. I needed some air."

"You know the girl meant nothin'. It was just a kiss."

"With her tongue down your throat."

"Ah. I see."

"You see what, Brandon?" she asked, moving back far enough she could look into his eyes. "You don't belong to me, so I can't tell you what to do with other women. You can kiss or fondle whoever you want."

"But Beau and I belong to you like you belong to us...for now."

"For now is all I want. I don't need any kind of relationship. I've got school, my horse, and my family. Men come and go."

"You sound pretty hard-hearted, honey."

"I've seen my share of heartbreak, Brandon, and I refuse to let anyone get that close to me again. Short-term affairs, one-night stands, and no commitment is the way to go." Her heart cracked at the lie. She knew the life-style Brandon and Beau led, with the constant touring and driving from one side of the country to the other, left no time for any kind of real relationship.

"Do you want to tell me about it?"

"No."

"Maybe after some time you'll trust me enough to tell me," he whispered, his hot lips against the side of her neck.

"It's over and done with, and it doesn't matter anymore. I'm not goin' into this thing with you and Beau with my heart on my sleeve. It's gonna be a few days of raunchy sex, good times, and hard lovin'. Nothing more. You're a fantasy come to life for me, times two, but that's it."

It sounded all good and strong, but her heart wasn't swayed, especially when Brandon slid his lips to the spot right below her ear and sucked on it. Her knees wobbled and blood rushed in her ears, but she convinced herself it was all a physical reaction to his nearness.

"Mind if I cut in?" Beau asked from behind her.

"Of course I mind," Brandon growled. "But since we're bound to share her, we might as well start now." He stepped back, brushed his lips over hers, and then headed for the bar.

"What's up, darlin'?"

"Nothin', why?"

"You seemed in an awful big hurry to get out of here a little bit ago."

"Not you too," she snapped, rolling her eyes. "It's nothin'. I told Brandon the same thing. It's nothin'."

"Then why the tears when you came back in?"

"All right. You want the truth? I'll give it to you. It bothered me when he kissed that girl, and it shouldn't have. Neither of you mean anythin' to me except some fun sex for the next several days, so it shouldn't bug me."

Beau ran a finger down her cheek and across her bottom lip. "You don't sound so convinced, Emma."

"Well I am." She saw Becky, waved to her, and said, "Sorry. I have to go finish manning the beer taps until everyone goes home."

"Okay," he replied, letting her go.

She could feel both sets of brown eyes watching her every step as she made her way back to the bar, never letting up until things wound down and everyone started going home. Beau and Brandon helped Seth, Becky, and her clean up the area and put everything away while the band cleared out.

Seth got up on the stage and whistled to get everyone's attention.

"Let's call it a night, folks. Beau. Brandon. Thank you both for all your help tonight and I'm sure the extra money we raised will be very much appreciated by Charlene's family. We'll get the word out about tomorrow's acoustic set, and hopefully we can rake is a lot more."

"Let's hope so," Brandon replied, tucking both hands into the front pockets of his jeans. "I can only imagine what Charlene and her family are going through."

"How long are you guys going to be in town?" Seth asked, stepping off the stage.

"We aren't sure. The mechanic couldn't tell us how long it would be before the parts got here. Could be a few days or a couple of weeks."

"Weeks?" Emma squeaked and then cleared her throat. *Weeks? This isn't good. How in the hell am I going to be at their beck and call for weeks and still keep my heart intact?*

Beau's sexy smile had her squeezing her thighs together to ease the ache in her pussy. Soon. She just had to get away from Becky and Seth.

"Can you give me a ride home, Emma?" Becky asked.

"Um, no. I have an errand to run. Seth can run you home, can't he?"

"Sure. No problem," Seth replied and Becky gave her a nasty look.

She'd been so wrapped up in everything going on between her, Brandon, and Beau, she hadn't gotten a chance to talk to Becky about what had happened earlier when Seth followed her outside. Unfortunately, when the two of them had returned, nothing appeared to have changed. They still managed to avoid being close together, but Emma thought there might be subtle changes no one else noticed. She knew her friends, and it seemed Becky spent a little more time close to Seth, touching his sleeve when they talked and smiling a little more. She really hoped the two of them could work things out.

After Seth and Becky drove off, Emma stood next to her mother's old car. With her truck in the shop, she had to have something to drive, and her dad had insisted she use the old car since it just sat at the house, unused. It felt kind of weird driving it, though, since her mother's death two years earlier.

Silence enveloped the three of them as they stood there looking at each other, each waiting for someone else to make the first move.

"So. What exactly is this bet going to entail?" she asked, her stomach knotting up nervously like a wad of tissue.

"You'll see. Do you want to follow us back to the hotel so you have your car there?" Brandon asked, wrapping a lock of her hair around his finger.

"I guess," she replied, pulling her hair out of his grasp and opening the door to the car. "Lead the way, gentlemen."

Beau flashed her a wicked grin and opened the rental car. "Let's go, Brandon. I got me a hard-on screaming for a sweet pussy."

Emma shook her head, wondering if she was losing her mind, letting these two anywhere near her. How she would be able to come out of this without losing her heart, she didn't know.

Fifteen minutes later, she pulled into the nicest hotel in Red Rock—which really wasn't saying much, but Cade had money invested in it, so she knew the inside could rival some of the nicest hotels in the big cities like Los Angeles and New York. Cade and his big money investors had converted a large old stone building in town and renovated it to the hilt. They could charge an arm and a leg for rooms, since Red Rock wasn't far from the interstate and the huge recreation lake sat mere feet from the back of the building. She figured Brandon could afford one of the suites if he wanted to. It would be interesting to see what room they'd chosen.

Gilded mirrors lined the lobby. Soft deep red brocade covered all the chairs, and marble slabs made up the floor. Crystal chandeliers hung every so many feet along the ceiling, bouncing multi-colored shards of light around the room. Large ferns graced the corners, and a huge black marble counter separated the check-in people from the guests.

Hopefully she wouldn't run into anyone she knew going through the lobby. If word got back to her dad, he'd kill her. It didn't matter that she had passed the age of consent at least six years ago. At the age of twenty-four, she knew what she wanted, and right now it came in the very enticing package of Beau and Brandon Tucker.

"Miss Emma, to what do we owe this surprise visit?"

Emma froze at the voice and slowly turned to face Aiden, the night manager of the hotel and a long-time friend of Cade's, walking toward where she stood in the middle of the lobby. Lucky for her, Beau and Brandon hadn't made an appearance behind her—yet.

"Hey Aiden. How's business?"

"Not bad. I'm sure the rodeo will be bringing in a ton of people starting tomorrow. We're already almost full. Are you meeting someone here?"

"Um...yeah. A friend."

"Ah," he replied, nodding. "Are they coming in for the rodeo?"

"No. Not necessarily." She pulled her bottom lip between her teeth and tried to think of the easiest explanation for her appearance at the hotel without giving away her plans for a threesome rendezvous.

"There are you, darlin'," Beau said, coming up behind her and putting his arm around her waist. "We thought we'd lost you."

"I'm right here," she replied, her overly bright tone grating on her nerves. *Damn it! Do I have to sound so high-schoolish?*

"Evening, sir." Aiden stuck out his hand for Beau to shake. "I'm Aiden Moss. Night manager."

"Nice to meet you Mr. Moss."

"Um, we should go, Beau."

"We need to wait for Brandon. He's parkin' the rental car."

Aiden's eyebrow shot up as he glanced at her and then back to Beau. "Brandon Tucker? I saw his name on the guest roster. It's nice to have you and your brother with us, Mr. Tucker."

"You know, there is one thing you can do for me." Beau tapped his finger to his lip and narrowed his eyes.

"Just name it, sir."

"Send up a bottle of champagne, some strawberries, and whipped cream from the kitchen."

Emma's whole body hummed when she heard Beau's request. Did they plan to eat off her? Or eat her, period? *God, I hope so.*

"Certainly, sir. I'll take care of it right now. Any particular brand of champagne?"

"No. Just somethin' nice and smooth. Brandon and I don't want our lady friend here to think we're some backwoods country boys."

"Of course not," Aiden replied. "Nice to see you again, Emma. I'll mention it to Cade when I see him."

"No!" Emma yelled as Aiden turned to head toward the desk.

He spun back to face her with a quizzical look.

"I mean, I'll tell him I saw you, Aiden. I'm sure he'll be pleased at how well you're running your shift here at the hotel, but don't bother calling him. I'm sure I'll see him tomorrow."

"All right. Enjoy your evening."

As she watched Aiden disappear toward the kitchen, Brandon came through the doors and joined them.

"I figured you two would have already gone upstairs and gotten started strippin'," Brandon said, taking her hand and kissing the palm. "Not changin' your mind, are you, Emma?"

"Uh, no."

"We ran into someone who knows Cade and Emma. The night manager here. I have him sending up some fun items to try."

"Wonderful. Shall we?" Brandon asked, pulling her along toward the elevators. "I can't wait to get you alone." He glanced at his brother and grinned. "Or should I say I can't wait to get you between us?"

Shivers raced down her spine, and goose bumps pimpled her skin as a picture of her sandwiched between Beau and Brandon raced across her mind. Heat spread through her body, centered low in her belly, and her pussy throbbed with need.

Within moments, they stood outside of a suite on the upper floor of the hotel. Even though Cade was a partner in the hotel, she'd never seen the inside of one of these rooms. They were expensive and luxurious. After Brandon opened the door, she caught her breath in a gasp. The room screamed money. Gold and crystal chandeliers hung from the ceiling and smaller versions hung as sconces on the walls. A kitchen big enough to put her mom's to shame sat to her left, and a doorway to the right revealed two of the biggest beds she'd ever seen.

"Wow," she whispered.

"You've never been up here?" Beau asked, wrapping his arms around her from behind.

"No. Cade invests in this place, but I've never seen the suites. This is amazing. I wonder what the bathroom looks like."

"Come on. I'll show you," Brandon said, taking her hands and pulling her out of Beau's embrace.

The bathroom took her breath away. A huge shower took up one whole wall, with adjustable heads to make water spray in several directions at once. The tile squares were black with gold swirled through each one. The vanity had two sinks and ran almost the entire length of the opposite wall, and she couldn't stop staring at the bathtub.

"Oh my God! Look at the size of the tub!"

"I know. Cool, huh," Brandon replied, slipping in behind her. "I would love to put tons of bubbles in there and slide under the water with you, caressing every inch of your skin with my hands and sliding my palms over your breasts until your nipples turn to diamond-hard points just begging for my mouth."

She leaned back against his chest and let his words float to her ears as her eyes closed.

"I'd lift you up on the side of the tub there and bury my face in your pussy. I can't wait to see how you taste, Emma. Salty goodness or sweet like candy? I bet you're so sweet, I'll be hard pressed not to gorge myself on you."

The moment his palm touched bare skin, her pussy flooded with need so strong, blood seemed to hum through her veins. Within seconds, he had her bare breast in his hand, caressing the flesh, but avoiding her aching nipple.

"That's it, baby, relax."

The hand not already occupied flicked open the button on her jeans, and she heard the low rasp of the zipper as he pulled it down.

"God, you're so hot, Emma," he whispered as his free hand slipped down under the elastic of her thong to dive between her thighs. "You're wet for me—for us. So slick and blistering hot. Your pussy is on fire."

Her whole body trembled with each pass of his fingers.

"Hey bro, save some for me," Beau said from the doorway.

"Just gettin' her warmed up," Brandon replied, pulling his hands away and stepping back.

When she opened her eyes, the drop-dead gorgeous come-kiss-me smile on Brandon's lips reminded her of some of the pictures she'd seen of him on the web and in magazines. He'd always had a pretty blonde on his arm, and suddenly she felt a bit self-conscious. Although she considered herself fairly pretty, she knew she couldn't hold a candle to some of the model-thin and big-boobed women she'd seen him with. "Um. I'll be right out, guys. I need to use the facilities."

"Sure, darlin'," Beau said, leaving her alone.

"Don't take too long, baby. My cock is so hard right now, I'll be hard pressed to keep from coming before I'm even inside your hot pussy," Brandon added and then stepped out.

The moment the door closed behind them, Emma took a deep breath and closed her eyes.

I'm crazy. How can I possibly satisfy two men? Hell, I don't even know if I'll be able to satisfy one of them. When she opened her eyes again, the woman in the mirror stared back with a look of terror in her eyes. She'd never thought of herself as gorgeous or anything. Pretty, yeah, but plain. How could she possibly think to hold not one, but two gorgeous men's attention? *Brandon is so hot, he has a different woman every night, I imagine. And Beau? He's sweet, funny, and ohmigod sizzling.*

"Well, the only way I'll find out is to jump in with both feet." After she used the toilet, she quickly rinsed her mouth, checked her teeth for anything funky stuck between them, fluffed her hair a little, and smoothed down her shirt. *Silly. Your clothes will be off two seconds after you walk back into that room.*

After a fortifying breath, she opened the door, only to be met by bookend men with their arms crossed over their chests and wicked gleams in their eyes.

Beau frowned and stepped next to her. "You okay, darlin'? You looked scared to death."

"I'm fine, Beau. Just nervous, I guess. I've never done anythin' like this before."

"Had sex?"

She playfully punched him in the ribs. "No, silly. Been with two guys at once. I'm not sure what to do."

"We'll take care of everythin', honey," Brandon said, sliding in on her other side and wrapping his arm around her waist.

The two of them led her to the side of the bed, sandwiching her between them with Beau in front and Brandon warming her from the back. A nervous flutter started in her stomach when Brandon inched her tank top up from inside the waistband of her jeans. The warmth of his fingers on the bare flesh of her waist sent the butterflies she harbored in her belly up to take flight. His lips caressed her shoulder, inching their way in a slow, delicious slide from the curve of shoulder to a spot on her neck she didn't realize had such luscious consequences.

"She likes that, Brandon," Beau said, sliding the straps down with his thumbs. "No bra, huh?"

"Built into my top," she murmured, wanting him to hurry so she could feel his mouth on her breast.

"Convenient. Do you want my mouth, Emma, darlin'? Your nipples are poking out, begging for me to lick on them."

A soft moan escaped her lips as she tipped her head to the side and back onto Brandon's shoulder, giving him better access to her neck. The moment the top eased off her breasts and exposed her taut nipples to the cool air, they bunched tight. Beau licked the tip of the right one, making her whole body tremble.

"Nice," Beau whispered, before sucking the tip into his mouth.

Her knees wobbled, and one of the twins' arms went around her waist to steady her, although she couldn't have said whose if her life depended on it. Blood rushed in her ears, and she could have sworn that at the very moment Beau sucked on her nipple, the tip of her breast and her clit were somehow connected. The tingling and throbbing she felt exploded into heart-thumping, pulsating need as cream spilled out of her pussy, wetting the silky thong between her thighs. "Please."

"Tell us what you want, honey," Brandon murmured against her neck.

"Suck harder, Beau."

"My pleasure, darlin'."

The pull of his mouth on her nipple and the nip of Brandon's teeth on her earlobe had her body screaming to move, but she couldn't decide which direction to go to get more stimulation.

"Please. I need..." Beau's mouth left her breast, and she groaned in frustration. "No, don't stop."

His lips nibbled at the corners of her mouth right before his tongue slid inside to tangle with hers. Brandon did his own exploration of her spine, shoulders, arms and waist as he reached around, unsnapped her jeans, and lowered the zipper. Cool air hit her skin as the pants and panties pooled at her ankles, and Brandon nudged her to step out by lifting her foot and removing one boot at a time. The moment she stood completely bare from the waist down, Brandon's hands crawled up the insides of her calves as his lips danced over the flesh of her butt, nipping softly at each cheek.

Beau lifted his head and growled, "Damn, woman. You burn me up with those lips, but we need to get the rest of this off." He lifted the tank top over her head and tossed it aside. "Now where were we?"

"On the bed, honey," Brandon instructed, walking her backward until her knees hit the mattress.

Her breath caught in her throat as she watched both Beau and Brandon do a little striptease for her. Each had a smattering of hair trailing from one nipple to the other across a broad chest and then in a sexy path down until it disappeared into the waistband of his jeans. The bulge each sported threatened to rip the seams apart. Hot damn!

"You like what you see, darlin'?"

"Oh, hell yeah," she whispered, capturing her bottom lip between her teeth. "More, please."

Beau unbuttoned his jeans and slowly drew the zipper down as her heart rate seemed to triple with each inch of his cock revealed. Long and thick, with deep veins running from base to head, the sight of it made her mouth water to taste the pearly essence of his desire clinging to the top.

When the denim fell to the floor, she took a ragged breath, glancing at Brandon to see how far he'd undressed before looking back at Beau.

"You keep lookin' at me like that, and I won't be able to wait," Beau said, his eyes blazing with passion and need.

She licked her suddenly dry lips. "Like what?"

"With those big blue eyes and come-kiss-me lips. I want to lick you all over."

"Then do it cowboy," she murmured, holding out her hand and waiting for him to take it before drawing him down on top of her.

Moments later, Brandon crawled onto the bed beside them. The warmth of his skin heated every spot it touched. With his left leg tossed over hers, he effectively spread her thighs open for whatever came next, and what came next was Beau's feathery touch on the insides of her legs. Goosebumps followed the light skimming of his fingers from ankle to thigh, but he avoided the places she needed him most. Her thighs quivered and her pussy throbbed, waiting for him to touch it. She almost screamed when he avoided her pussy in favor of running his fingers over her stomach.

"You have magnificent tits, honey. Nice rosy nipples just begging for attention," Brandon whispered, running his lips over her shoulder.

She cupped both breasts and lifted them in invitation—to which man, she didn't care. "I want your tongue, both of you." A purr escaped her lips when first Brandon and then Beau each took a nipple into his mouth and sucked. "Yes." Beau flicked her right nipple with the tip of his tongue, bringing a tortured moan to her lips as Brandon encircled the left. "So good."

Beau released her breast and blew a cool stream of air over the nipple, humming his appreciation when the peak stiffened and beaded into a hard point.

Unable to stop the emotions and desires flooding her body, she begged for more with soft whimpers and tortured groans until she felt one of the twins nudge her thighs apart.

"Ah, God!" she screamed as the first lick touched her pussy. Her back arched when a wet mouth closed over a nipple and pulled it deep into the warm cavern. The wicked tongue between her pussy lips flicked, swirled, and speared, changing the pace so she couldn't zero in on any one thing to drive her over the edge of climax. Sensations swamped her, bombarding her from every direction. Soft nips of teeth on one nipple, the pinch of fingers on the opposite one, and the warm flick of the torturous tongue built the desire inside her to a fever pitch. Her body wasn't her own. They controlled the craving, spiraling want until she quivered uncontrollably. The tingling started in her toes, rushing up her legs to center low in her belly.

"Please," she begged. "I need—"

"We know what you need, honey," Brandon whispered against her lips, leaving the cooling wet spot on her nipple open to the sensations of his chest hair sliding across the tip.

"She's so sweet, Brandon. Wait until you taste this," Beau said from between her thighs. "I could eat her all day."

"Stop talking, Beau, and do it. Make me come. God, I can't stand this. Please."

"Demanding little thing, aren't you?" Brandon pinched her nipple between his thumb and first finger.

The sharpness of the tug sent heat spiraling through her system and straight to her clit.

"Yes, yes, yes," she panted, tossing her head from side to side.

He slid his tongue over the peak and then bit it at the same time Beau flicked her clit in a quick figure eight, sending her climax washing over her in a huge wave of sensation. Tingles raced up her legs. A sharp burst of heat slammed through her belly, and she screamed as her body convulsed in a mind-numbing climax.

"Oh God! Beau!"

When the whooshing sound cleared her ears, she heard a chuckle from between her legs. Beau continued to slowly lick her clit, holding her desire at a steady pull until she came completely down from her first climax. She slowly opened her eyes to see Brandon staring down at her with a frown.

"What? Did I do somethin' wrong?" she asked, afraid she'd caused a major issue for some reason.

"Nothin'," he snapped, rolling away from her.

"It's not nothin', Brandon." She grabbed his bicep to stop him from moving further away as Beau sat up and crossed his arms over his chest. "Talk to me. You can't frown at me like that—like I screwed up bad—and then hold it in."

"He hates losing," Beau replied with a smirk on his sexy lips.

"Losing at what? I didn't think we had a contest going on here."

"Promise you won't get mad?" Beau asked.

Fear made her stomach clench. What weren't they telling her? "I don't like when sentences start that way, but fine, I promise not to get mad."

"We made a little side bet between the two of us after you almost broke my nose outside the beer tent."

"And?"

"Whoever's name you screamed when you came would get one whole day alone with you," Brandon explained.

"And I won," Beau said.

Irritation cleared the remaining desire from her body for the moment. The way these two made everything a game between them was really beginning to piss her off. "Is this always a game between you two? Because you know, I'm not really into this competition shit. I'm here with both of you. I want to be with both of you, not just you, Beau, and not just you, Brandon." She stretched out on the bed and spread her thighs. "Your turn to make me scream your name, Brandon."

The wicked gleam in his eyes and the sexy smile on his lips told her she had handled the situation correctly, but what would happen later on, when they got around to the fucking part? Which one would actually penetrate her body with his impressive cock? Or would she take both?

6

It was like Brandon couldn't move fast enough to get between her thighs. She smothered a giggle with her hand when he dove over her leg to wiggle into position, but with the first thrust of his tongue into her vagina, she closed her eyes and moaned. Having two men focused on her needs drove her to the brink of a mind-blowing orgasm the minute Brandon touched her with his tongue.

"Open your eyes, darlin'," Beau coaxed, sliding onto the bed near her head. "I wanna see those baby blues when he makes you come."

The wide head of his cock bobbed against his stomach, looking hard enough to be uncomfortable. She reached out and encircled the engorged rod with her hand, stroking up and down a few times.

"Don't stop, darlin'. It feels awesome."

A low growl brought her glance to his face. Strains of concentration crinkled his eyebrows, and he licked his lips several times, as if fighting to hold himself together.

With a small tug on his cock, she managed to convey what she wanted, encouraging him to scoot close enough to line up his rigid shaft with her mouth. She slowly licked up the length and smiled when goose bumps sprung up on his thighs. After several swirls around the purple head, she swiped at the pre-cum with her tongue, tasting the salty, musky essence of Beau.

"Oh yeah. That's it. Suck me," he groaned, shifting his hips closer.

The length of flesh disappeared between her lips, and she felt the vibration of his moan when she whirled her tongue around him. Concentration grew difficult with Brandon between her thighs, licking and sucking her clit between his lips and spearing her vagina with his tongue.

Suck swallow. Suck swallow. *Make it good for Beau.* Each pass of his cock between her lips and into her mouth met with her hand coming up from the bottom to give him the most pleasure she could. She palmed his balls, rolling them between her fingers.

Releasing Beau's cock from her mouth, she moaned, "God, Brandon. Make me come. I need to come so bad."

"In a bit, honey. I'm enjoying this," Brandon replied, slipping two fingers inside her pussy while another finger played with her back hole, not quite penetrating the virgin space. Round and round he went, teasing the puckered ring until she relaxed and pushed her butt back against his finger, begging him to slip it inside.

"Do you want this?" he asked, spreading her juices from her pussy to her asshole. He pushed one digit slowly past the ring of muscle, and then two.

"*Yes.*"

The slow pump of his fingers burned at first, but within moments the pain turned to the most incredible pleasure she'd ever felt. Different sensations bombarded her from both holes. The tingling in her in ass spread to her pussy, igniting the fire quickly spreading through her body. More juice dripped from her vagina to coat his fingers, lubricating the slide.

"Mmm," she hummed, not letting Beau's cock leave her mouth now that she'd engulfed his rock-hard flesh again.

Beau's breathing sped up, matching her own as she fought her impending climax, not wanting the wicked sensations to stop yet. Hot spurts of cum coated her tongue and spilled down her throat with each thrust of Beau's hips and every groan he released. Brandon nipped at her clit, causing her own orgasm to scream through her body so unexpectedly, she barely had time to breathe and remember not to bite down on Beau before she released his softening cock and screamed Brandon's name.

"Beautiful, honey. Absolutely, beautiful," Brandon said, scooping up some of her cream and licking his fingers clean. He glanced up at Beau. "Grab me a condom, brother."

Beau grabbed a foil wrapped package from the nightstand and tossed it to Brandon. "Give me a second to catch my breath, honey, and we'll get this party started."

"I plan to start without you, Beau," Brandon said as he flipped her over on her stomach, brought her up on her knees, and slowly pushed his cock into her pussy. "Oh, hell yeah."

The glide of his cock felt like heaven and hell. She wanted everything —every inch deep inside.

Pushing her butt up and back, she heard him hiss, and she smiled. "Fuck me, Brandon. Give it to me. All of it."

With a hard snap of his hips, he drove the full length into her, hitting the special spot that made her purr like a kitten.

"Yes, yes! Right there."

"You have such a sweet, sweet pussy. You feel amazin', Emma. Tight, hot and wet."

"Brandon?"

"Yeah?"

"Shut up."

He chuckled and picked up the pace of his thrusts. "Better, honey?"

"Oh yeah. Fuck me hard."

She glanced to her side to see Beau stroking his returning erection with his palm and watching Brandon screw her brains out. Her whole body hummed with the knowledge both men wanted her like this, even if it turned into a short term thing. "Your turn next, Beau, so don't stroke it too hard."

"Not on your life, darlin'. I can't wait to get inside you."

"Squeeze those pussy muscles around me, baby. Yeah, just like that," Brandon said, shoving his cock in and out of her so hard, she had to spread her hands apart so she wouldn't scoot across the mattress.

Brandon slipped his hand around her stomach and rubbed her clit with his thumb, spiking her desire to boiling as he continued to pound into her until the orgasm rolled over her like a tidal wave. Two more body-slamming thrusts and Brandon climaxed with a tortured groan.

When Brandon withdrew from her pussy she collapsed onto her stomach and then rolled over onto her back. Her whole body hummed from the mind-numbing climaxes she'd had over the last hour, and they weren't through with her yet. Beau sported a hard-on worth drooling over, and she wanted all the yummy length deep inside her.

"You wouldn't believe how hot it is watching him fuck you, Emma. God, you're beautiful when you come," Beau whispered, brushing the sweaty hair from her face as her breathing slowed. "You ready for me, darlin'?"

She skimmed her fingers over his handsome face. "More than ready, Beau. I've wanted this from the moment you brushed your thumb over my lip at the accident. But can I ask somethin'?"

"Anythin'."

"I want you to make love to me. Slow and easy, face to face."

The smile spreading across his lips lit up the room. "My pleasure."

* * * *

Beau felt like a fist squeezed his heart. Make love to her? He would. Savor the time they had together? He would. Hold them close to his heart when they drove away? He would. Get over Emma Weston? Probably not in this lifetime.

The moment he slipped his cock into her welcoming warmth, he knew he'd found home. Tears glistened on her lashes, and one slipped from her eye into her hair.

"Am I hurtin' you, darlin'?"

"No," she whispered, taking a sharp breath. "It feels fantastic. Don't stop."

Her whole body shuddered when she clamped her pussy muscles around his throbbing cock. Holding still wasn't an option anymore when she lifted her hips and wrapped those magnificent legs around him. The slow glide of his cock in and out of her heat had him on the verge of climax within seconds, but he shoved it back down. He wasn't some randy teenager without any control.

The temptation of her lips drew him. He pressed his mouth against hers and ran his tongue over the surface of her lips, coaxing the response he wanted from her. Her sigh sent shivers down his spine. The brush of her tongue along his drew his balls up tight against his groin. If he didn't hurry her along, he'd blow long before she did—and that wasn't acceptable to him. With a swivel of his hips and a faster pace, she started to whimper into his mouth. He reached between them and raked his fingernail over her clit. Her pussy quivered as her climax built and he could feel every clasp of her pussy and every quiver of the walls of her vagina. When her orgasm hit, he careened over the edge right along with her.

Beau shuddered several times while their mutual climax cooled. Realization hit him square in the chest. He'd forgotten the condom. "Shit, Emma. God, I'm sorry. I've never ever lost control like that before," he said, dropping his forehead to her shoulder.

"What?" she asked, running her fingers through his hair and down his back.

"I forgot the condom." He rolled off of her and threw his arm across his eyes. "Damn it!"

"What's wrong, Beau?" Brandon asked from the bathroom doorway.

He'd completely forgotten his brother was even in the room while he made love to Emma, but now he felt like shit. How in the hell had he forgotten to put on the condom?

"Beau?"

"Yeah?" he replied, not meeting her gaze. Guilt and remorse clouded the excitement of making love to Emma.

"I'm clean, and I'm on the pill."

Leave it to her to make him feel better. He should be the one comforting her—insisting he didn't have any kind of diseases she would need to worry about, and if by some odd stroke of luck he got her pregnant, he'd do the right thing by her. Glancing across the room, he noticed Brandon had disappeared back inside the bathroom and shut the door. *Coward.*

He reached over, wrapping an arm around her shoulders and pulling her up against his side. "I should be comfortin' you. Not the other way around."

With her head resting on his chest and her fingers slipping through the hair scattered over his skin, he could almost lose himself in her and the odd notion of a future with her. He'd never thought about a future with a bed partner before, and the thought of having Emma for more than a few nights confused him.

"We all make mistakes, Beau. You're human, just like me."

"No, you're perfect." *How could Emma think she was anything, but ideal?* From everything he'd seen of her with her friends and family, she cared with her whole heart—taking on things most people would have let others deal with.

She propped herself up on her elbow and stared down at him. "Yeah—whatever. I'm not perfect. Not even close. I make mistakes all the time."

"Like what?"

Her bottom lip disappeared between her teeth, and he had the insane urge to bite it and pull it into his mouth.

"Well, even though I ride barrels during the rodeo events, I don't practice like I should."

He almost rolled his eyes, but he couldn't stop the small smile on his lips.

"I'm a terrible sister."

"How so?"

"I know my sister Elizabeth told someone about you and Brandon being out at our house. When I saw her this afternoon, I chewed her out for blabbing."

"I'm sure she's worried about you," he said, wondering why she wanted to hide their relationship. *Relationship? This isn't a relationship. It's a few fun filled nights with a hot woman.*

Emma slipped her fingers down his side and back up, and his body couldn't help but respond to the intimate touch.

"I know, but I didn't have to jump all over her for it." She glanced up and stared right into his eyes. "How many women have you and Brandon shared?"

I think my world narrowed to a small shaft of light I should be runnin' for to save my ass. The last thing she needs to know is how many women Brandon and I have shared.

"Um, I don't know. Why?" he croaked.

Most people looked stupid doing the one-shoulder shrug, but on Emma, it looked cute. Everything about her screamed 'keeper.' *No, not after only knowing her two days.*

"I'm curious, I guess. It's not like I do this sort of thing all the time," she replied, swirling her finger through his chest hair. "You two seem to have the whole thing down to a science." She sat up and pulled her knees to her chest. "I don't really know anything about you."

"Sure you do. You're a Brandon Tucker fan. Take all his information and multiple it times two."

"Not true, Beau. You two may look alike, but you're nothin' like him." Tucking a piece of hair behind her ear, she continued. "Tell me about Beau Tucker. Tell me the things you like to do, things *you* enjoy."

She can see that? No one's ever figured that out before.

"Okay. I don't know how much you know about Brandon outside of what the media gives you, so I'll start from the beginning." He scooted up and leaned back against the headboard. "I'm ten minutes older than Brandon. I guess you could say that's why I feel obligated to take care of him. Our parents own some ranch land up near Sun Prairie."

"Go on," she whispered, lying down next to him and putting her head on his chest again.

He loved having her this close, her breasts pressed against his side, the warmth of her skin scorching him like a branding iron.

"We did the cattle thing during high school and for a little while afterwards, but Brandon always had talent. He could sing the hell out of any country tune he heard, and he did. Rodeos, festivals, weddings— you name it, he sang at it. Then, one day, he got this bright idea to start playing in a couple of bars as their house band. A couple of his buddies played instruments, so they started up a band and got a few gigs around home. After a while, he branched out and started getting dates all over the country. One night, when he was doing a show in Nashville at one of the dive honky-tonks, a record guy came up to him after his show and told him he wanted to see him in his office the next day. Brandon almost blew the guy off."

"Seriously? He could have killed his career."

"Yeah. He told me about the guy later that night and I convinced him to go see him the next day. Brandon always wanted to be a country star, and now he is. I told him I'd be there with him, for however long the ride lasted."

"What about you? I'm sure you have dreams of your own."

Silence stretched between them for some time while he argued with himself about telling her his heart's desire. The words he'd refused to utter for the last six years hovered on the tip of his tongue. *Would it be safe to tell her and expose all my hopes and dreams—things I couldn't even share with Brandon earlier when he asked?*

"I..."

Brandon opened the bathroom door and said, "Are you two done shootin' the shit out here? I'm tired of hangin' out in the bathroom. I need some sleep if I'm going to keep up my energy for Emma's tutelage in threesomes."

"There *is* another bed, Brandon," she replied, glaring daggers at him. "Maybe Beau and I would like to talk for a while."

Brandon snorted. "Fine. I would have rather curled up behind you while I slept, but since you two seem to have this need to yak, I'll grab the other bed."

"He can be such an ass," she murmured.

"Yes, he can."

"As you were saying," she said, encouraging him to take up where their conversation had lagged when Brandon came out of the bathroom.

"It's not important. We should really get some sleep too." He circled her nipple with one finger, watching in fascination as it hardened.

"You keep doin' that and sleep is the last thing gonna happen."

"You'd have sex with me without Brandon here?"

Her eyes widened in shock. "Are you serious? Of course, I would. We pretty much did it without him here a little while ago—and I'm sure you know exactly how hot you are, so I don't have to tell you."

"Tell me anyway," he replied, wanting to hear her voice more than anything. The moment she'd screamed his name when she climaxed the first time, he'd wanted to hear it over and over.

She licked her lips and draped herself over his chest. "You have the most amazing eyes. Did I ever tell you how much I love brown eyes?"

"No."

"Well, I do. Yours remind me of milk chocolate. Smooth and appealing, with all the sweetness wrapped up inside them. And when they sparkle? Mmm. You could get me to do anythin' you want."

"Anythin'? Could get interesting. Go on."

"And you have a smile that could melt any woman's heart into a puddle."

"Yours?"

"Maybe." She shifted and slid her body down his chest, letting her nipples rub against every inch of him until she stopped with her mouth hovering over his nipple, stirring his cock to life.

"And your chest looks good enough to nibble on." She grazed her teeth over his left nipple. "Just the right amount of chest hair—and it's so soft, it tickles my breasts when I do this..."

He fought the groan in his chest as she lifted up so only her nipples slipped through his chest hair before moving up more and dangling them close to his mouth. If he moved toward her, he could capture one between his lips. *God! The woman could tempt Saint Peter himself—and being only a lowly mortal, I can't resist.*

"And your cock—did I talk about your cock yet?" she asked, sliding back down to straddle his hips.

"No," he whispered, his cock beginning to ache with the need to be inside her.

"When you were inside me, you filled me up so completely." Emma scooted back further and bent low over his cock. "Silk over a steel rod." She wrapped her hand around him and squeezed.

"Fuck, Emma. You're killin' me here, darlin'."

The wet slide of her tongue against his aching flesh about did him in. "You taste fantastic, Beau. A little salty, but not bitter or anything. I loved swallowing all of your cum. Wanna do it again?"

Torn between wanting her to suck him off or fuck her until she came, milking his cock for every drop of cum, he hesitated.

"Somethin' wrong?"

"God, no. I can't decide." Grabbing her under her arms, he pulled her up so she lay on top of him. "I want you, Emma."

"I want you too, Beau. The two of us together could light this bed on fire."

"What about Brandon?"

"I don't want Brandon right now. I want you and only you." With her knees up by his sides, his cock head brushed against her open and waiting pussy lips. "I need your cock. Every magnificent inch."

A fine layer of sweat coated his body as he fought the need rushing through him. Blood roared in his ears. His balls ached and his cock screamed for release.

"What's it gonna be boy?"

"Ride me, darlin'," he growled, pushing her hips down and shoving his cock deep inside her.

"Oh yeah. Perfect," she purred, widening her legs even further and giving him an inch or two more room.

She started to rock her hips, riding him like she would a wild stallion or an untamed bull at the rodeo. Her breasts bounced with each thrust of his hips, until he cradled them in both hands and let her take the reins of their ride. "So good."

"You're so fuckin' tight, Emma. Hot. Scorching hot. Burn me, baby."

Leaning on her hands, she thrust her breasts further into his palms, tossed her head back so her hair tickled his thighs, and squeezed her pussy muscles around him.

"Fuck me, Beau. God, yes. Cram that cock deep. Hit my sweet spot. You know where it is. You hit it earlier."

He pulled his feet up to brace himself on the bed and shoved his cock so deep the air rushed from her lungs on a moan.

"Right there. Hard. Oh yes, hard."

The bed banged against the wall as he shoved every inch of his cock into her squeezing, milking, burning pussy. When she climaxed, his name came from her mouth like a prayer and her pussy held him tight, refusing to let him go until he'd spilled every last drop of cum deep inside her scorching pussy.

"Sweet baby Jesus," he murmured, feeling like he'd shot every ounce of his energy out the end of his cock.

Emma crawled up beside and collapsed next to him on the bed. "Damn, you're good."

"Why thank you, ma'am."

With the last bit of energy he possessed, he curled an arm around her shoulder and pulled her next to him. Sleep tickled the edges of his consciousness even as she grabbed the sheet and pulled it up over them, curling into his embrace with a contented sigh.

"Night, Beau."

"Night, darlin'."

7

Morning light tickled her eyelids, spearing them with brightness and forcing Emma to open them. She groaned and rolled away, only to come up against a hard body. Shoving her hair out of her face, she sat up, holding the sheet to her breasts and staring at the man next to her. *Beau or Brandon?* Without cologne or a single visual clue, she couldn't tell the difference. The light coming through the windows wasn't much, and it made it hard to see.

Bits and pieces of the night before flashed across her mind, bringing with them the memory of Beau making love to her before they fell into exhausted sleep. Even without the slight difference in eye color to tell them apart, she knew Beau lay snoring softly next to her. Given a moment to study him, she propped herself up on her hand so she could let her gaze roam over his features, taking in everything about him. His hair looked so soft, reminding her of the ticklish brush of those locks against the skin of her thighs when he'd eaten her pussy until she screamed his name. It carried a wave, and her fingers itched to run through those silky strands.

She knew his brown eyes had gold flecks in them where Brandon's didn't, and right now, she longed to see them smiling at her with a little twinkle of mischief. The slope of his nose looked regal and straight except for a bump at the bridge where he'd broken it at some point. She frowned, hoping her impromptu head-butt the night before hadn't caused any permanent damage. A bruise had formed near the bridge, but nothing giving her any indication she'd broken it again, thank goodness.

The width of his shoulders and the muscles of his chest displayed strong, work toughened power where the sheet had slipped down his body, and she wondered what he did besides take care of things for Brandon to have such an exceptional physique. The sheet covered his hips, cock and legs, but her memory brought into sharp clarity the length and thickness of his impressive shaft and the firmness with which he'd taken control of their lovemaking the night before.

"Do I meet with your mornin' approval, darlin'?"

Her gaze ricocheted back to his face and heat flushed her cheeks. The appreciation in his gaze warmed her whole body, and she relaxed back against the sheets as they switched positions and he loomed over her.

"My turn," he whispered, slowly pulling the sheet down to expose her breasts. "Mmm. Nice." He licked his finger and circled her left nipple until it stood up, hard and begging for his touch. "You have beautiful skin. So soft and smooth. I love touching you."

Her nipple ached for the heat of mouth against it. Unable to stop, she shoved her breast further into his touch and whimpered low in her throat when the warm wetness closed over the tip. Continuing to pull the sheet down, he exposed first her belly button ring and then the springy curls guarding her pussy. The brush of his lips as he worked his way down tickled her skin, causing it to quiver and jump.

He dipped his tongue into her belly button, flicking the jewel dangling there. "I love these things. They are so damned sexy."

The moment his hand slipped through the curls and skimmed over her clit, her whole body shuddered. She spread her thighs, begging in a whisper, wanting his hands, his mouth, his cock—something to fill the empty void. With her eyes closed, every sensation, every touch brought her desire to an explosive level. The calluses on his hands felt rough and erotic, scraping over her sensitive skin. His fingers left her pussy, and his mouth moved back up to her breast to suck and nip at the tip.

Her eyes flew open when, seconds later, she felt the wet slide of a tongue over her clit.

Brandon winked from between her spread thighs. "Mornin', honey. Wakin' up like this...mmm...a man could get used to it real easy."

Beau's moist mouth moved from her breast to say, "Are you up for ridin' double this mornin', darlin'?"

Ridin' double? Are they serious?

"You mean—"

"One of us in your ass and the other in your pussy," Beau explained, still circling her nipple with his finger.

Her heart hammered, and her ears rang. Just the thought of having both of them at once flushed her body with desire so strong, it made her shiver.

"Don't worry, Emma. We'll make sure you're good and ready before anythin' happens, and if you don't like it, we'll stop. We don't want to hurt you."

Staring into Beau's eyes, she knew he spoke the truth. No matter what, he wouldn't allow her to be hurt. The small nod of her head gave them the answer they sought.

Brandon's wicked tongue danced over her clit, flicking and circling until it throbbed with the beat of her heart. When he slipped two fingers into her pussy, she spread her thighs more and moaned into Beau's mouth as he took possession of her lips. Having two men focused on her needs seemed almost selfish, but with Brandon between her legs and Beau eating at her mouth, she relaxed and let them do whatever they wanted.

The tip of a finger gathered some of her juices and then probed at her back hole, making her stiffen again.

"Easy, honey," Brandon purred, pushing it through the grasping muscles of her anus.

She hissed at the small burn, but it soon turned into a different type of pleasure as he added another finger, stretching her by scissoring those tempting digits. The unmistakable urge to press back against his hand overwhelmed her and tore a moan from deep inside, only to be swallowed up by Beau's mouth. Brandon finger fucked both holes and ate at her clit, sucking it into his mouth until her whole body hummed and quivered. Both her legs trembled as she clung to the edge of climax by her fingernails, trying to get to the other side, but not having quite the right sensation. Beau had relinquished her mouth for her breast, flicking and circling the nipple until it stood up, begging for him to suck until it turned a bright rosy red.

A high keen exploded from her lips when her climax crashed through her, stealing her breath and making her heart hammer so hard she thought it would burst through her chest. Her men continued their assault on her senses until she exploded into a second climax before the first one even finished.

"Think she's ready?" Brandon asked, pulling himself up to sit between her thighs.

"More than ready." Beau tossed him a condom and slipped one on himself before he pulled the tube of lube from the nightstand drawer and laid it on the bed. "Okay, darlin'. This is what we're gonna do." He slipped one arm around her and hauled her over his chest so she straddled his waist. "Open your hot little pussy for me."

The nudge of his cock at her opening awakened all the nerve endings in her pussy again as he slowly entered her body. A soft moan escaped her lips, and she leaned into him. With both hands on her hips, he pushed her down onto his cock, impaling her clear to the root.

"God, you're so tight, Emma. It's gonna be even tighter with Brandon in your ass."

She'd almost forgotten Brandon kneeling behind her until he nudged at her back hole. Beau reached up and flipped him the tube of lube. The next thing she felt was the cold smear of wet lubrication on her asshole. Brandon pushed some into her hole and massaged it around her in passage with his fingers.

"Relax, honey."

Beau shifted and eased his cock in and out of her pussy in shallow, slow strokes, while Brandon slicked her up and then bumped the head of his dick against her. She sucked in a ragged breath as the full head speared through her sphincter in a small pop.

"Goddamn, you're tight," Brandon hissed.

She could feel his hands trembling where they gripped her hips as he fought not to fuck her hard. God love both of them. The initial burn of his penetration eased into the most amazing feeling. Her pussy thrummed and spasmed with each inch of Brandon's cock easing into her hole and stretching her until she felt completely full.

"You okay, darlin'?" Beau asked as his lips brushed her hair.

"Yeah. Incredible."

"Fuck, yeah," Brandon replied.

A small wiggle of her hips brought a hiss from both men—her men...for tonight anyway. "You need to move. Both of you. Now."

With practiced ease, the two of them fell into a steady alternating rhythm, Beau penetrating her pussy and Brandon's dick in her ass. A whimper escaped her lip and her whole body trembled with the need to come, but something held her off. She grasped at the motions of their bodies, hoping she could pluck the elusive climax from the air.

"Somethin's not right, Brandon." They both stopped, and tears burned her eyelids.

"God, please don't stop," Emma whimpered.

"Tell me what to do, baby," Beau whispered, kissing her eyelids.

"My clit. Rub it."

His hand snaked down between their bodies, swirled through the lubrication caused by their joining, and rasped over her clit. At first his touch was soft, until she whimpered and moved her hips. Both men began to fuck her in earnest, and Beau's finger pressed hard against her clit, doing a little figure eight move and then flicking it back and forth.

Her high pitched scream of release bounced off the walls of the room. "Oh God!"

Several moments later, she collapsed on Beau's chest, but the pounding of their hips never lessened. Desire speared through her again, and she huffed an exhausted burst of air over the sweaty skin beneath her cheek. A smaller climax rushed through her, holding her body in its grasp. Within seconds Brandon growled his release behind her, and then Beau groaned as his climax hit him too.

The three of them stayed together, locked in passionate embrace, until Emma heard her cell phone ring. "Shit! Move!"

"What the hell?" Brandon grumbled, sliding his soft cock from her ass.

"Emma?" Beau asked.

"It's my dad. If I don't answer it, he'll freak!" She scrambled from the bed, grabbed her pants from the floor, and flipped open her phone with a winded 'hello.'

"Emma? Where are you honey? You didn't come home last night."

The question made her spin around and hush the two men in the room with her. "I'm fine, Dad. I spent the night with Becky."

"Oh really?"

"Yeah. We helped Seth set up the beer tent and stuff last night. It was late when we left so I just crashed at her place. No biggie."

"Mmm. Want to tell me why you're lying to me, daughter?"

"But Daddy, I'm not—"

"Emma Leanne Weston. Don't you dare lie to me again. Becky called this morning looking for you, so I know you did spend the night at her house. Now where are you?"

"I'm sorry." She chewed her bottom lip and glanced at Beau and Brandon. "I'm at the hotel in town."

"Why?"

"I stayed with Beau and Brandon last night."

"Excuse me? I thought you weren't even talking to those two after you kicked them out of our house the other night."

"I know, but things changed, and I spent the night here."

"I'm sad you felt the need to lie to me, Emma, but I'm not going to lecture you. I just hope you aren't getting into somethin' that will hurt you in the end."

The disappointment in his voice tore at her heart. "But Daddy..."

"I'll see you when you get home, Emma." The silence had her biting her lip. "No matter what, sweetie, I love you."

"Thanks Dad. I love you too," she choked out as the phone clicked in her ear. "God, I'm so stupid!"

"Emma," Beau whispered in her ear, wrapping his arms around her. "You aren't stupid, darlin'. You have needs."

She quickly stepped out of his embrace and spun around. "Needs that can't be satisfied by one man, Beau? This kind of thing isn't normal. I heard the talk around town when Natalie, Cade, and Kale were dating. It was ugly. Do you think I want people to talk about me like that?"

"Honey, no one has to know what happens between the three of us. Beau and I wouldn't talk," Brandon said, stopping next to Beau.

"It doesn't matter. People saw me come in here with you two. I'd be surprised if the whole fuckin' town isn't talkin' already." She crumpled into the chair in the corner and dropped her face into her hands. "What the hell was I thinkin?" A moment later she jumped to her feet and grabbed her clothes from the floor, pulling them on. "I wasn't. The whole thing was impetuous. My mom always said I didn't think things through. Boy, was she right."

"Emma, wait," Beau said, pulling on his own clothes. "Don't leave like this."

"Like what, Beau? This whole thing was a huge mistake. I can't keep one man satisfied, much less two. And you two?" She shook her head and grabbed her keys. "Look at you. Either of you could have whoever you want. I'm a girl from a dinky town in the middle of nowhere, Montana. I couldn't hang onto a man for any length of time if I tried. I'm too tomboy. I've got a big mouth, and I talk tough. Men don't like those traits in a woman. I'm not sophisticated. I'm not beautiful."

"Don't insult yourself, Emma," Brandon said, grabbing her hand and pulling her down on the edge of the bed before she could make her escape. "You're a beautiful woman."

"I hate when people patronize me, Brandon, so please don't."

"I'm not. You are beautiful and sexy." His finger traced along her cheek.

"I need to go," she whispered, not really wanting to leave. Her head warred with her heart.

"Stay."

"No." She jumped to her feet and headed for the door. "Thanks for a good time, guys." After a quick glance behind her, she left without another word.

* * * *

"What the hell just happened?" Beau growled, running his hands through his hair. "Everything was going great."

"I know, Beau," Brandon replied, mimicking his brother's frustrated gesture as he watched the door slam behind Emma's departure. "We'll talk to her again later, at the rodeo. Maybe she'll be ready to listen there."

"Yeah—with a thousand people around, including her family? Are you nuts?"

"Maybe, but I know one thing. I'm not done with little Miss Emma Weston. Not by a long shot." He got to his feet and headed for the bathroom. "I'm taking a shower, and then you can have the bathroom if you want. We need to make sure everything is set for the show this evening anyway. We've got some work to do. I want to be out there around the people today. The more I can interact with them, the more we'll have at the show, and the more money we'll make for Charlene."

"All right. I'll make some phone calls while you're in the shower. We'll need to stop at the garage so we can get your amps off the bus and some of the light setups out of the trailer."

After a quick shower, Brandon picked out the standard cowboy attire. *Damn, I haven't worn the whole outfit in a while.* Fastening each snap on the front and at his wrists, he thought of Emma. Would she be the type to love flinging those snaps open with a quick tug? His cock hardened behind the fly of his jeans just thinking about her. Being inside her ass earlier was heaven. He'd never felt anyone so tight and so perfect. Double penetration with her wasn't like anything he'd experienced before, and he and Beau had done it with a few. Her whimpers, moans, and ultimately her scream of climax had burned through his balls and made him ache to have her again. *Enough. You don't need any kind of entanglements, no matter how enticing the woman.*

Brandon returned to the living room area of the suite, where Beau sat on the couch with a pad of paper on his lap and his phone to his ear.

"Hey, Brandon. I've got things situated. Are you planning on hanging out by the bleachers and around the concession stands? Do we need to alert the local police for security?" Beau asked, shutting his phone and laying it on the table.

"It probably wouldn't be a bad idea to have a couple of cops on standby in case. I don't think it'll be a big deal once the announcement is made why we're doing this." He glanced at his brother and cocked his head to the side. "Are you gonna ride?"

Beau ran his hand over his stubbled cheek and jaw. "I think so. If I win, I can donate the money to Charlene."

"You haven't ridden bulls in a while, Beau. I don't want you gettin' hurt."

"I'll be fine. It hasn't been more than a year or so."

"Since when?" He sometimes forgot Beau had a life outside of the one they had together, but it shocked him to think his brother had ridden bulls while he'd been busy elsewhere.

"I hit a couple of rodeos last year when you went on vacation to the Bahamas with Anita."

Brandon thought back to mistake upon mistake with Anita. He'd thought himself in love with her, until he'd realized she'd liked the fame and recognition of being Brandon Tucker's woman—not him. Sex between them was hot at first, but when he'd started getting into a little kink with her—nothing major, just swatting her butt, wanting to tie her hands to the headboard so he could eat her out until she couldn't move, those kinds of things—she'd absolutely refused to discuss it. He'd even thought about marrying her at one time. Thank God he'd come to his senses without asking. Manipulation came naturally to her, but once he'd realized what she really wanted, he'd dumped her like a hot rock.

No woman could hold his attention long enough even to think about permanent anymore—well, maybe one, and he didn't know whether anything might come of this intoxicating attraction to her. "Well, just make sure you wear your vest and helmet. I don't need you ending up in the hospital."

"Worried about me, brother, or just worried no one else will be able to keep you out of trouble?"

"We fight. Brothers do those kinds of things, Beau, but you know you mean everything to me. If I didn't have you, I'd lose my mind and probably drown myself in a bottle." He laid a hand on Beau's shoulder. "If I haven't told you lately how much I appreciate all you do for me, then I've been an ass."

"You *are* an ass, Brandon. I don't think you've uttered *thank you* since this whole party began."

Brandon frowned and thought about that. He hadn't ever said thank you, and looking back now, he realized just how badly he'd acted the spoiled country star. Everything was about what Brandon wanted, and Beau always made it happen for him, but he'd never understood the sacrifices Beau made to be by his side. The whole idea felt like a punch to the gut. "I'm sorry. I've come to realize in the several days or so, I've been completely selfish, taking up your time and energy to keep everything running for me. You gave up all your dreams, and I don't know how I'd be able to handle this whole star thing without you."

Beau shot him a thoughtful look and said, "Fine. I need a raise."

"A raise?"

"Yep."

"How can you get a raise from nothin'?" Brandon asked with a chuckle.

"You'd be surprised how much you pay me, brother."

"Maybe I need to take a better look at my finances."

"Maybe you do, but trust me, I haven't done anything illegal or unethical. You also donate to several charities, by the way, and you're still a very rich man. You couldn't spend all your money in this lifetime."

He glanced at his brother, realizing he really had no clue how much money he had or where even a third of it might be located. When he needed money, Beau made sure he had it. Beau kept the accounting, booked his shows, made sure he got there on time, and kept him out of trouble. About the only thing Beau didn't do was screw his women for him, but since they shared Emma, he couldn't even say that. What a wakeup call this trip into small-town Montana had been. It was time for Brandon Tucker to take his life and his career into his own hands.

"We'll talk about this more, Beau. Right now, we need to get the equipment and get out to the fairgrounds. If we want to corner Emma, we need to make sure we keep a good eye on her."

"Yes, we do. I'll be out in a minute," Beau replied, heading for the bathroom.

Brandon walked to the window and stared out at the people moving up and down the sidewalk and the trucks zipping past on their way to God only knew where, while he waited for Beau to get ready. All this thinking about how Beau handled everything had gotten him to realize he didn't have any say in what he did anymore. He needed to take more control over his own life. He loved Beau, but his brother needed to follow his own dreams for a change, and he knew Beau's dreams included bull riding, even if the stubborn asshole got himself killed.

8

The crowd in the stands and milling around the fairgrounds always amazed Emma. People came in from miles around to attend the Founder's Day events—the rodeo, the picnic on Sunday, and the fireworks display at the end of the weekend over the lake. Usually, she mingled with her friends, hung out with some of the cowboys, served beer in the tent for Seth, and flirted here and there. Cowboys of every creed and color lined up for their shot at bull riding, calf roping, steer wrestling, and picking up the ladies. Stetson, Resistol, and straw hats adorned every cowboy and most cowgirls as they moved in and out of the crowd, talking, laughing, and making new friends.

She hadn't seen Beau or Brandon since she arrived, and she hoped she didn't. Staying away from those two would be her best choice, since fallin' into bed with them had turned into a mistake—a mistake because her heart seemed drawn to the two men, even when her head said the whole situation was wrong. The chance of running into one or both kept her from doing too much mingling. If she could avoid them for the rest of the weekend, she might make it out of this predicament without making a fool of herself.

Right after her event, Emma rode straight for the livestock barn to put her horse away. The last place she figured she'd run into either of the Tucker boys would be in the stable and it gave her a few minutes to think. She'd only known them a few days, never mind the five years of following Brandon's career and eking out every bit of information on him she could find. She must keep herself separated from the temptation the two of them placed in front of her. *I'll just have to avoid them.* Once she finished brushing her horse, she walked him into his stall and locked the door. She took a deep breath and shored up her resolve before she headed for the beer tent.

A deep, sexy laugh floated to her on the breeze and made her turn toward the sound, goose bumps pimpling the skin of her arms. She knew the sound—she'd heard it a few times last night along with the whispers, groans, whimpers, and sighs of satisfied lovers. *Damn it!* Sure enough, Brandon Tucker stood surrounded by five women near the bottom steps of the spectator stands. Each girl took turns taking pictures with him, wrapping her arms around him and hugging him so tight you couldn't squeeze a piece of newspaper between their bodies. Jealousy burned in Emma's gut. *I have no right to be jealous. He's not mine.* Her head warred with her heart. She wanted to tear each of those women away from his side and plaster herself between him and Beau.

Unable to stop herself from drifting closer, she moved around the back of the stands. From here, she could hear and see everything going on, even though she wanted to kick her own ass for caring.

"Well now, honey. I'd love to dance with you later. I have a show to do first, and then I'll be free. We're raisin' money for Charlene at the concert, so make sure you're real generous."

Damn that Betty Carter. The slut.

"I'm sure I could show you a real good time, Brandon. I've been in love with your singin' since I first heard you."

"Thank you. You know, I sing every song to a beautiful woman durin' a show?"

"Really? I'd love for you to sing to me."

"I'll see what I can do, honey. Just make sure you leave some money in the collection barrel for Charlene, and I'll sing one just for you."

"Done deal, Brandon." Betty locked her lips with his, and he sure didn't look like he minded as he put his hands on her waist.

"Bastard," Emma grumbled quietly.

Once the kiss finally ended, the five women walked away—but not without wiggling their fingers at him and blowing kisses.

"You know I sing to a beautiful woman during a show?" Emma

mimicked in a singsong voice. "Yeah, and you sleep with whoever you can get to drop her underwear."

"Jealous, darlin'?" Beau whispered next to her ear.

She squeaked as she jumped back, banging her head on a low bar on the stands. "Ouch!"

"Serves you right for eavesdroppin', Emma." His warm hand rubbed the spot on her head.

"I wasn't eavesdroppin', and why did you sneak up on me?"

"You've been avoidin' me and Brandon all afternoon, and when I saw you over here watchin' Brandon with those girls, I wanted to corner you."

"Why?"

"For this." He grabbed her around the waist and pulled her to him, his intent clear in his eyes. The brush of his lips against hers made need shoot straight to her pussy. How he managed to crank her up so damned fast, she didn't know—and right now, she didn't care. Having his lips on hers brought back every feeling, every thought, and every raunchy thing they did last night and this morning as vivid pictures in her mind.

After he'd kissed her thoroughly, she sighed and opened her eyes.

"There's a look worth findin', darlin'."

Brandon came around the edge of the bleachers and stopped next to them. "Caught her listenin', Beau?"

"Yep, and she wasn't too happy with your little scene, brother."

"I didn't figure she would be. Why'd you think I did it?"

"Wait, what? You knew I was back here?" She spun around and stepped away, jamming her fists on her hips and then tapping her boot on the hard dirt.

Brandon slipped one fingertip down her cheek, and she could feel her traitorous nipples bead into hard nubs.

"Of course, honey." The finger moved to skim over her bottom lip. "Otherwise, I wouldn't have let that woman kiss me."

The smirk on his sexy lips made her want to smack him and lick him all over at the same time. "I... Damn it!"

"Nothin' to be jealous of, honey."

Beau slipped his arm back around her waist, tugging her to his side. "Brandon is makin' the rounds, darlin'."

"I see that, Beau. Apparently, he's makin' the rounds with several willin' women."

"I didn't mean it like that," Beau said.

"I have to mingle with the crowd, Emma. We need them to be at the show and drop lots of cash in the barrel for Charlene. The more I move in and out of the crowd, huggin', kissin', and shakin' hands, the more money they'll drop during my performance."

The logic of their words hit her like a ton of bricks. "You mean you didn't want to kiss her?"

Brandon moved in close enough she could feel the warmth of his breath on her lips and see the heat of desire in his eyes. "The only woman I want to kiss is you. To feel your soft lips under mine. To slip my tongue between them and tangle it with yours until we're both breathin' hard."

Sandwiched between the two of them like this, her heart and her mind went spinning out of control with need so strong she moaned. Her body betrayed her to both men, and she could see the understanding pass between them when their eyes met.

Brandon licked her lips slowly, and she moaned and closed her eyes.

The need spiraling through her scared her—this wasn't like her at all. What kind of power did these two devastatingly handsome cowboys hold? How did they make her forget everything but the heat of their bodies around her?

"You'll meet us later?" Beau whispered, the tip of his tongue teasing her earlobe. "After the show and everything is over with?"

"Yes," she murmured, unable to stay away from their intoxicating presence.

"I can't wait to see you spread out on the bed again, Emma, breasts begging for the wetness of a tongue, pussy dripping with cream and glistening in the soft lamp light as your body quivers with desire," Beau continued, while Brandon teased her nipple with his finger.

How the hell he'd gotten under her shirt without her realizing it, she didn't know, but the calluses on his fingers played hell with her need. A quick glance over his shoulder confirmed the two men blocked anyone else from seeing what they were doing to her.

"I—I have to go," she stammered, backing up and pushing her shirt back into the waistband of her jeans.

She sidestepped away from them, sighing heavily. *Get a fuckin' grip, Emma. Jesus.* A look over her shoulder showed her twin bulges in their jeans and sexy grins on their lips.

* * * *

The masses coming into the beer tent blew her mind. Where in hell did all these people come from? She didn't know, but her feet were killing her. "Hey, Seth, I need a break."

"Sure, Emma. Go get some air. I hear the bullridin' is starting soon, and I know how much you like to watch it."

"Thanks," she replied, giving him a small smile. He really was a nice guy.

Warm air hit her like a furnace blast when she stepped outside the tent. Sweat trickled down between her breasts, tickling her skin, but she paid it no mind. She needed to get her mind off Brandon and Beau. For the last two hours, they'd been in and out of the beer tent several times. Once or twice with women on their arms, and sometimes alone, but they always managed to get in her line for their beers. Her jaw hurt from grinding her teeth together while they paraded women through the tent. They'd said it helped with the charity event. She wasn't so sure.

Emma heard the announcer begin his speech. "Welcome, ladies and gentlemen, to this year's Founder's Day Rodeo."

The crowd let out a huge cheer.

"Unlike previous years where the bull-riding came last, we are going to run a few riders through on the bulls first, since we have so many contestants. After the first five riders have gone, we'll move onto some calf-ropin', barrel racin', steer wrestlin', and some kids' events. So hang onto your hats, folks—grab a beer and pull up a seat, 'cause we've got a show for you."

Emma made her way toward the split rail fencing and climbed up on the bottom rung. The bull chute stood on the far end of the circular arena from where she took up a spot, but she'd have a good view once the ride began.

"One more thing, folks. We are pleased to let you all know one of country music's hottest talents is spendin' a few days with us here in Red Rock, and he's graciously donated his time to put on a benefit show this evening for our own Charlene Campbell. Brandon Tucker will be putting on an acoustic show at three in the beer tent. Now, folks, admission is free, but we do expect everyone to drop a few bucks in the barrel we'll have near the door. Give generously—this is to help Charlene parents with her monstrous hospital bills."

Another loud cheer went up, with a few feet stomping in the stands. Emma smiled. Brandon's generosity amazed her. A free concert would bring in tons of cash, she hoped.

Three riders did their turns on the bull, two of them missing the buzzer by at least a second or two. The bulls seemed unnaturally ornery today—or it seemed that way to her anyway. Dust swirled in the air, coating everything within twenty feet of the railing with a thin layer, including her.

She hopped down and brushed the dirt from her jeans and shirt until the announcer's words penetrated her brain, chilling her to the bone.

"Next up is... Wow. Folks, this is a special treat. Right now, we have Beau Tucker, former top ten ranked rider, up to try his luck on the bulls. Now, Beau's been ridin' off and on for a few years, but this is the first time he's been on a bull in over a year. Give it up for Beau Tucker, ladies and gentlemen. Beau has also said he will donate any winnin's to Charlene's folks."

Emma spun around with her heart in her throat. She watched the chute spring open, and the biggest, scariest bull she'd ever seen whipped Beau around like a rag doll. His arm, lifted high and to the right, waved back and forth with each twist and turn the bull tried. The muscles of his back bunched and rolled, and his biceps rippled as he held onto the bull-rope and concentrated on staying on the huge animal.

"Come on Beau. Come on," she whispered, almost as a mantra, her eyes glued to his body. If he got hurt, she wouldn't be able to handle it.

She'd seen dozens of men hurt riding bulls, but this was Beau! One of the men who'd wormed their way into her heart, whether she wanted him to or not, and damn it, she had plans for this evening that included him buck-assed naked and not broken into painful pieces. Time seemed to stand still. Her fingers gripped the rail beneath her until her nails dug into the wood. The clock slowly ticked off eight seconds, and he stayed on the bull. When the buzzer sounded, he unwrapped his hand and jumped clear before racing for the railing right in front of her.

"Are you fuckin' crazy?" she yelled as he vaulted over the rail and landed at her feet. "You could have been killed, Beau."

A sexy grin flashed across his face, and he bent down and kissed her soundly on the mouth. "I didn't know you cared, darlin'."

"Of course I care. Damn it!"

"Easy, Emma. I've done this before. Piece of cake. That bull wasn't even tryin' hard."

"You really are crazy," she snapped, and spun on her heels to return to the beer tent.

"Emma, wait," he said, grabbing her elbow and spinning her around to face him. "I'm fine." He brushed his hands over his jeans, patted his chest where the safety vest encased his body and stomped his feet to prove he hadn't been hurt. "See. Nothin' broken, nothin' bruised. All in one piece."

"This time. What about next time? What happens when one of those crazy animals throws you off and charges you? Huh? Then what, Beau?"

"It's not a big deal, Emma."

"Yes it is!"

"What's goin' on over here?" Brandon asked, stopping at her side.

"And you!" She poked her finger into the middle of Brandon's chest. "Ouch."

"How in the hell can you let him ride bulls? Are you crazy, too?"

"Whoa, what brought this on?"

"She got a little hysterical when she saw me ride," Beau answered, crossing his arms over his chest.

"You had a good ride. Eight seconds and all."

"I am not hysterical." She paced back and forth for a moment and then faced them. "You know what? Fuck you. Both of you. Do whatever the hell you want to do. I don't care. Not a whit. Do you hear me? Not one little bit!"

With agitated steps, she headed back to the beer tent. Anger raced through her, but by the time she stepped behind the taps again, she wasn't sure what the hell she was angry about. She glanced at the growing crowd and sighed. Most of the patrons were still out in the stands watching the events, giving her a few moments to contemplate what had just happened out there between her, Beau, and Brandon, but not many. The tent would be overflowing soon. Yes, Beau could have gotten killed, but didn't the announcer say he'd been doing this for a while? Blowing up in front of both of them probably wasn't the smartest thing she could have done. Hell, it probably told them how much she cared, even though she'd spouted off that she didn't.

"You okay?" Becky asked as she poured another beer. "You look upset."

"I'm fine," she snapped at her friend, and then murmured a quick, "Sorry."

"I heard them announce Beau was riding. How did he do?"

"You know, I don't even know. I jumped all in his shit about ridin', I didn't even look at his score."

Becky shook her head and grabbed another cup.

"What?"

"You are in so deep, you don't know which way is up. I hope you don't get your heart broken."

"Am not."

"Yes you are, Emma. Those two are so deep in your heart already, and you're upset because one of them could have been hurt. What does that tell you?"

Emma pulled her bottom lip between her teeth and bit down until it hurt. "What am I gonna do, Becky? They'll be gone soon, and I'll probably never see either of them again."

"Do you want both of them? And I mean *want* as in a forever kind of thing."

"I've known them all of a couple of days. How can I know?"

"Seriously? You've been a Brandon Tucker groupie for the last five years. You know the man's shoe size, his brand of shampoo, and whether he wears boxers or briefs. The only thing I'm not sure whether you've figured out yet is whether he lays his cock to the left or right."

"Size twelve, Axe shampoo, boxers, and he's a lefty."

"See?"

"It doesn't matter, Becky. Those are facts, nothing more. I bet every hardcore fan knows them."

Becky's eyebrow met her hairline as she gave Emma an I-don't-believe-you-said-that look. "You can't be serious."

"Well, I only recently figured out the boxers thing and which side his cock lays on." She glanced left and right before she dropped her voice low and said, "By the way, they're both hung."

"And you would know this how?"

Emma squeezed her eyes shut and grimaced. *Fucking big mouth.*

"You slept with them, didn't you? Both of them."

"Yes."

"Damn," Becky whispered. "Brave girl." Becky glanced around and then dropped her voice further. "How was it?"

"Becky!"

"What? Not like half the women around here haven't fantasized about having two men at once. I mean when all the talk of Natalie, Cade, and Kale flew from mouth to ear, I know I thought about it. Not that I would try it, but you know."

"Promise not to say anything."

"Cross my heart."

She spun them both so their backs were to taps and said, "I want it again and again. Having both cocks—"

"You didn't?"

"We did."

"Wow," Becky whispered.

The crowd started cheering when Brandon came through the tent flap and headed for the stage. Was it time for the show already? She glanced at her watch, and sure enough, almost three.

Once he hit the stage, he plugged in his guitar and pulled up the stool they'd set up. He calmed the crowd with a smile and a wave. Beau stood off to the side to watch and make sure the equipment didn't malfunction, and to possibly adjust sound levels during the show.

"Afternoon folks."

Another loud cheer.

"Where's my girl, Charlene?" He glanced to the left of the stage, where Charlene sat in a special chair next to her parents. Chemotherapy had caused her to lose most of her pretty brown hair, so she wore a cute pink hat with white pokadots, a white blouse, pink jeans, and matching pink cowboy boots. "Ah, there she is. Welcome, darlin'. This is for you and your parents for everything you've gone through and all you still have to endure. You see, I haven't been in your shoes bein' sick and all, but my brother and I lost a baby sister a long time ago to cancer. She only lived to the age of six, and I know I speak for both of us when I say we miss her every day."

You could have heard a pin drop in the dirt while the crowd absorbed Brandon's words and Emma almost cried for him. Her throat burned, and she swallowed, fighting the tears. This tidbit of information was probably the one thing she hadn't known about Brandon—well, other than having an identical twin. That little tidbit of information never leaked out either.

"So, let's get this party started, shall we? We're here to raise some serious cash for these folks. Loosen up those wallets and purses, ladies and gents, while I sit here and do a few songs for you."

For the next hour, Brandon sang almost every song he'd ever put out to radio and a few they hadn't released as singles. Emma sang along and danced behind the beer taps. Every once in a while she'd glance at Beau, and he'd smile and give her a sexy wink.

The crowds enjoyed the show immensely, if she could judge at all. Several people danced together at the back of the tent, and more clapped and sang along to the songs they knew.

"Last song, folks."

The crowd groaned and Brandon laughed. "I'd love to sit up here all night and play for y'all, but my fingers haven't played this much in a long time. I do want to do one more song for you. It's a ballad and one of my favorites, so grab yourself a pretty gal, couple up, and sway to the music."

Emma held her breath. His fingers plucked the first few chords of the song, and her heart tripped over itself when he started singing "The Love of My Life."

The soft brush of fingers on her arm brought her attention around, and she came face-to-face with Beau. "Will you dance with me, Emma?"

The only answer she could give was the small nod of her head.

Beau wrapped one arm around her waist, taking her right palm in his left as he tugged her close. "I've been dreamin' about holding you like this from the moment I saw you," he murmured into her ear.

Shivers rolled down her spine, and the hair on her arms stood up. She had Brandon Tucker singing her favorite song and his twin holding her close—dreams didn't come close to this moment. Well, maybe one. Making love last night to both of them outshone any dream she could have thought up. The reality of making love with Beau and Brandon couldn't have been more perfect.

As the last chords of the song drifted off into the night, silence filled the tent for a few seconds. Ear-splitting cheers, shouts, and clapping broke the quiet, and the crowd went wild. Emma broke the embrace and turned to watch Brandon step off the stage. Charlene had tears running down her cheeks when he stopped in front of her, gave her a kiss, and handed her his guitar.

"He gave her his guitar?" she murmured.

"Yeah. He figured since she was a fan, it would mean a lot to her," Beau answered in a low voice.

"Wow. I'm sure she's thrilled." *This whole situation makes Brandon the kind of guy I've always hoped he would be in person. Kind, caring, considerate, although he's arrogant and selfish sometimes, too.* "I should get back to the taps. Thanks for the dance, Beau."

"You're welcome, darlin'. I love holdin' you. I hope I get a chance to do it again." He gave her a small smile before walking back to his brother's side.

"Can I get a beer please?"

Emma spun around to meet the gaze of the one man she wished would disappear, Joshua Spence.

9

Joshua was a player. He liked his money, he liked his booze, and he figured any woman in the country would drop her underwear and spread her thighs for him if he asked. Emma hadn't been any different in the beginning. His blond hair, blue eyes, lithe body, and hard muscles turned several heads whenever he walked into a room, but his heart belonged to one person and one alone—himself. Joshua Spence was in love with himself. Arrogant, conceited, mean, and selfish, he'd never quite understood why Emma broke off their engagement.

"Well, well. If it isn't Miss Emma. How are ya doin', darlin'? I ain't seen you in a while."

"Josh." She rolled her eyes and grimaced. "What can I get you?"

"Besides you?" he asked, in his usual snarky tone.

She really did hate the man. "I'm not on the menu. Regular or light beer?"

"Come on, Emma. We had some good times together."

"Yeah, until I caught you with Betty while we were engaged."

Josh shrugged his shoulders and smiled like he hadn't done a thing wrong. "It was a mistake, and I've tried explainin' it to you, but you wouldn't listen."

"Nothin' to explain. You cheated, and I don't like cheaters. Get a life, Josh. I've moved on. You should, too."

"Moved on with who?"

His tone told her his own green-eyed monster had reared its ugly head, and she debated whether to tell him the truth or blow him off. "None of your business. You lost the ability to tell me what to do when I took off your ring and threw it at you."

"It's those two out-of-towners? The country guy and his brother? I saw you with them behind the stands." Josh's lips had pulled back into almost a snarl, giving Emma a little satisfaction that he'd seen her with Beau and Brandon. "When did you turn into such a slut—or did Cade rub off on you? You know, fuckin' his wife and his best friend and all."

Fury made her see red. The crack of her hand against his cheek echoed in a room gone suddenly silent at his words.

"What I do is none of your fuckin' business, Josh, and if you say one more word about Cade, Natalie, or Kale, you'll find out just what a bitch I can be." Rage raced down her back at his audacity. "And if I did fuck both Brandon and Beau, it's between the three of us." The sharp inhalation of air brought her attention to her dad standing off in the corner of the tent. "Shit." She glanced back at Josh and said, "Go find Betty. I'm sure she's free, since Brandon turned her down flat."

She walked to her dad's side and said, "Daddy, let me explain." Grasping his hand, she led him out behind the tent where they could talk in semi-privacy.

"You know how badly the town talked after what Cade did came out," her father said, once they'd stopped their hurried rush out of the beer tent.

"I know, Dad, but listen. This is different."

"How so, Emma? Did you or did you not sleep with those two men?" The disillusionment in his eyes broke her heart.

"Yes, I did, and if they'll have me, I plan to do it again. I care about them."

"You've only known them a few days."

"I know, but they've come to mean a lot to me in a short time. Will this work into something more permanent? I don't know, but I want to hold onto what we have—even if it's only for a few days."

A sigh of resignation left his mouth as he asked, "Are you sure?"

"Daddy, I'm twenty-four years old, and I know what I want."

"All grown up, huh," he said, brushing her hair back off her cheek and tucking the strands behind her ear.

"Sometimes you act like I'm still twelve," she said, sadness lacing her words. "I'm a woman, even though you seem to want me to stay a child."

He pulled her into a hug and then let her retreat a few inches. "I wish you would, Emma. You're my youngest. I hate to see you growing up so fast and furious, and I'm terrified you'll be making a huge mistake with those two."

"I can chose who I want in my bed."

"Whether it be one man or two?"

She dropped her gaze to the middle of his chest. "I'm sorry I've disappointed you."

With his fingers under her chin, he tipped her face up so he could see her eyes. "Aw, honey. You never could disappoint me. I'm afraid you'll get hurt in the long run with this whole thing, and I want nothing more than to protect you from it—but I can't, can I? You have to make your own mistakes in this life." He pulled her close and hugged her again. "I love you, Emma, and you'll always be my little girl, no matter how old you get. You do what makes you happy, honey. That's all I ask."

"Thanks, Dad. I love you, too." After a tight hug, she returned to the beer taps. Thankfully, Josh had disappeared into the crowd. God, she hated him with every fiber of her being.

Two years ago, they'd been one of the hottest items in Red Rock. Josh's daddy owned a good-sized spread outside of town, and he'd be set to inherit when his daddy passed on. Trouble was, Josh didn't care for ranching. All he wanted was the prestige of being a land owner, not the work involved in running cattle or anything else. Believing she could change his mind, she'd jumped into their relationship with both feet and huge blinders on. When he'd gotten down on one knee and asked her to marry him, the thrill of what she'd thought was love had driven her to say yes.

Then the rumors had started flying. His excuses had become disturbingly frequent. First he was working late, then he'd wanted to go out with the guys, or he'd had to make a trip into Billings for his dad. The last trip he'd made, she'd decided to surprise him—but *she* had gotten the bombshell when she'd walked into his hotel room to find him with Betty, buck-ass naked and tangled in the sheets. After she'd flung her engagement ring at him, she'd stormed out of the hotel and driven at breakneck speed to cry on her daddy's shoulder. Once she'd cried the hurt out, she'd proceeded to get stinking drunk. The next morning, the sun had crested over the mountains in a bright ray of light, wiping the misery and pain from her heart, leaving the headache of a hangover behind.

Since then, there hadn't been any serious relationship for her. Nope, the moment she'd heard Brandon's voice and gazed into those big brown eyes, she'd been hooked. Every show within a hundred miles found her there, in whatever seat she could get up close to the stage. Of course, Brandon had a gorgeous woman on his arm every moment, and Emma knew she could never compete with them. How she'd managed to snag both Beau and Brandon's attention, she wasn't sure, but she planned to ride it until they moved on.

"Emma?" Charlene's voice broke through her thoughts.

"Hi, honey. How are you feeling?" she asked, taking in the pale skin, dark circles under the little girl's eyes, and gaunt body. "You look fabulous. I bet Brandon could hardly talk, lookin' into those big green eyes of yours." Charlene held Brandon's guitar in her hands like she'd never let go.

Charlene giggled and shook her head. "He's so cute."

"I know, huh," Emma answered, wrapping her arm around Charlene's shoulders.

"He gave me his guitar."

"That is so cool. Are you gonna sell it? 'Cause if you are, I'm buying, honey."

Her eyes widened and she grasped the neck of the guitar harder. "No way! He signed it for me and everything." The little girl traced Brandon's signature and sighed. "I need to learn to play it, so someday when I see him again, I can play for him."

"I bet he'd love to hear you sing. You sing like an angel," Emma whispered, wiping the stray tear forming at the corner of her eye. If the rumors she heard were true, this poor little girl probably wouldn't even make it to her next birthday. The tumor in her brain continued to grow, killing more tissue every day, and they couldn't operate.

"I wanted to say thank you like my mom told me to."

"Thank you? For what, honey?"

"You made it possible for today to happen—for Brandon to be here to sing and all."

"Charlene, I think God had a hand in bringing Brandon and Beau here for you and for me."

The little girl hugged her waist, and Emma fought the tears she knew were just under the surface. "You love them, don't you?"

Shocked by Charlene's statement, Emma started to protest before realizing her little friend probably had more insight than she'd given Charlene credit for. "I'm not sure it's love, Charlene, but I sure like them a whole lot."

"Don't let the busybodies tell you who to love."

Emma couldn't help but smile at Charlene's words. The little girl had a valid point. "When did you get so grown up and so smart?"

Charlene shrugged and said, "I saw you dancin' with Brandon's brother when he sang. You looked happy."

"You're one special girl, Charlene, and I'm glad I know you."

"I love you, Emma, and I just know someday you'll wear the smile you had on earlier every day of your life." Charlene motioned for Emma to bend down and she kissed Emma on the cheek before rushing back to her parents' side.

The crowd in the beer tent thinned out after Brandon's concert, only a few patrons still lingered. Most wandered back out to the stands to watch the rest of the day's rodeo events. Beau and Brandon continued to break down the equipment and haul it outside while she watched.

Each man had his own style. Yes, they were identical, but the more she watched them, the more she realized how different they were. Beau's physique had a little more bulk across his back and shoulders, probably from riding bulls or working out, whereas Brandon seemed leaner. She knew they'd grown up in a small town in Montana, and their parents had cattle, too, like hers—but she didn't know exactly where. Beau seemed to be the epitome of a Montana cowboy. She had no doubt he would be a force to be reckoned with if he had rope to play with.

Rope? "Hmmm."

"What are you thinking, Emma? I see the sparkle in your eyes." Becky glanced to where Emma's gaze seemed glued. "Ah. That explains it. Those two seem to garner a lot of your attention."

"Look at them, Becky. The two of them are perfection—sexy in cowboy boots or out of them and so damned drool-worthy—who wouldn't want them?"

"Very true—even if they aren't my type, I have to agree with you." They both watched for a bit before Becky said, "You never did finish telling me about being with both of them."

"Not much else to tell. Having both men attuned to my needs? What else could a woman ask for?"

"So what happens now? I mean, they travel all the time. It's just a quick fling, right?"

Emma chewed the inside of her mouth for a second before she answered. "Yeah."

"You don't sound convinced, Emma Leanne."

"It doesn't matter. It's not like they went into this thing with me intending to make it a permanent threesome." A heavy sigh rushed from between her lips. "I can imagine the town gossips having a field day with that little tidbit."

"You know what? To hell with them, Emma. You need to do what's right for you. If being with those two gorgeous hunks of man flesh is what you want, then I say go for it."

"Really?" Emma asked, surprised Becky would support her being with two men. "I thought you would be totally not for this."

"Why?"

"Hello? Your daddy is a preacher, Becky. Hell, he didn't even want us to be friends since my parents weren't God-fearing churchgoers."

"I know, but *he's* the preacher, not me. I'm open to new things and trying to live my life the way I see fit, even if it means making him mad," Becky said, a small smile lighting her face and taking away the sadness Emma had seen there for so long.

Shock raced through her at Becky's words. "Are you going to date Seth?"

"Yes."

Emma squealed and hugged her friend tight. "I'm so happy for you! I think you two will make a great couple. Did this come about when he followed you outside?"

"Yeah. We finally talked heart to heart and I realized I was letting my father's beliefs ruin my chance to be with the man I wanted. Will it work into a long-term relationship? I don't know, but I'm willing to give it a try."

"Thank you, God!" Emma hugged Becky again. "I wondered when you would come to your senses."

* * * *

Beau watched Emma and her friend from his position near the stage. "The concert went great," Beau said, putting his hands behind his back and stretching. "Damn, I'm gonna be sore tomorrow. Ridin' the bull and hauling equipment—I haven't done this much manual labor in a while. I can tell I need to do some pushin' horns to get my strength back. At least I placed in the bull ridin' so I could donate it to Charlene."

"Yeah, I know the feeling. I got kinda used to havin' the road crew doin' all this. It's too bad they took a different route since we wanted to visit with Mom and Dad." Brandon glanced at the crates of equipment and sighed. "So how long are we plannin' on stayin' here, Beau?"

"As long as it takes."

"For what?"

"To convince Miss Emma she wants to be with us."

Brandon frowned. "I didn't think that was such a problem. She seemed into it enough when we were behind the stands."

Beau held his breath for a few seconds and then let it out slowly. His brother wasn't going to believe what he was about to say. "I don't mean be with us for the time we are here, Brandon, I mean permanently."

With Brandon's wide eyes and his mouth hanging open far enough he could catch flies, Beau had to work hard not to laugh. Brandon said, "No way. You, thinkin' seriously about a woman? Since when?"

"Since Emma."

"I don't know, Beau. A permanent triad?"

"We can work out the details another time. Right now, we need to convince her being with us is what she wants."

"I'm game. I'd love to have her with us all the time."

"Are you sure? I mean, Brandon Tucker with one woman?"

"If it's Emma, sure. Why not?" Brandon's nonchalant shrug didn't fool Beau. He knew his brother had feelings for Emma, too. Thoughts and feelings were one of those things being a twin came with. They could sense each other's thoughts and feelings, and Beau knew exactly Brandon's feelings on the matter of Emma Weston.

"Then we need a plan. I want tonight with her alone."

"Why you? Why not me?"

"Remember our bet? She screamed my name first."

"Oh all right, fine." The scowl on Brandon's face almost made Beau laugh. He knew his brother didn't like being pushed aside, even by him. "But I get her tomorrow then."

"What are you two plannin' over here?" Emma asked, walking up behind them.

"Us? Nothin', darlin'," Beau said, sliding an arm around her waist. "You did agree to some more time with us tonight, remember?"

Her fingers did a little dance down the front of his chest, playing with the buttons on his shirt. "Yes I did, and since most of the festivities are over with for tonight, except for some rowdy party crowd drinkin' too much beer, I'm ready to go."

"I tell you what, sweetheart, I'm going to stay here and mingle some more while you and Beau have some time alone."

"Seriously?" she asked, her eyes widening into almost saucers. "Why?"

"I asked Brandon to let me have some one-on-one time with you," Beau replied. "He'll join us after while. How about we have a nice dinner somewhere, and then we can do whatever you want."

"Whatever I want?"

"Yep."

"This could be exciting." She stepped out of his embrace and leaned over to kiss Brandon on the cheek. "We'll try not to have too much fun without you." When she turned back toward Beau, she asked, "Just out of curiosity, do you happen to have some rope?"

Rope? "Now, what would I be needin' rope for, darlin'?"

"Oh, I don't know. Maybe I want you to tie me up and have your way with me," she said, wrapping her arms around his neck and pressing her lips to the base of his throat where his heart pounded.

Brandon hissed through his teeth at Emma's words. Beau knew his brother had a kinky side, and he'd never found anyone he could connect with on that level. For both their sakes, he prayed Emma would be the one.

"I think I can find some," he growled. Need spiked hard at her saucy words. He'd like nothing better than to tie her spread-eagle on the bed and do anything he wanted to with her delectable body.

"Let's get this party started then." With her hand in his, they left Brandon in the beer tent and walked to where a truck was parked. "How about we take mine, but you can drive?"

"You got it fixed already?"

"Not exactly. It's my dad's. He doesn't like me out drivin' late at night in the car. The truck is bigger. "

"Great! Where's a good place for dinner?"

"Depends on how much money you want to spend wining and dining me, handsome."

"Your choice, darlin'. Whatever you want."

"Hmm." She tapped her fingers to her lips as thoughts zipped across her eyes in a pattern he could almost interpret. "How about we drive a little ways? There's a town about twenty minutes from here with a really nice restaurant."

"Sounds good to me."

"I want to run by my Dad's place and take a quick shower. I smell like beer and cigarettes."

"Sure, darlin'," he replied, although he wasn't sure he wanted to be cornered by her pa and her brother. "How about after you shower and change, we head back to the hotel so I can do the same? I smell like cattle.

I hope this place isn't too fancy. I don't think I brought anything with me to fit in somewhere like that."

Ten minutes later he sat in her daddy's living room while she showered and changed upstairs.

"You're takin' Emma out for dinner?" her father asked, tapping his fingers on the arm of the leather chair.

"Yes, sir. She mentioned a place in a town about twenty minutes away."

"Probably Red's in Watertown. It's the best steak house around."

"Yes, sir." Damn, he sounded like a teenager being grilled by his date's father.

The older man's eyes narrowed and the tapping on the arm of the chair increased in tempo.

"If there is somethin' you want to say, sir, please do."

"All right then, I will. My daughter means the world to me, Mr. Tucker, and I hope you treat her with respect. She can be impetuous."

"Yeah, she mentioned it."

"What I'm trying to say is, I know about her having sex with both you and your brother."

Beau felt like something sat on his chest. *Aw, hell.*

"And I don't approve of her relationship with you. But, it appears you and Brandon will only be in town a short time, so I will tolerate your presence until you leave. Do I make myself clear?"

"Yes, sir."

"Good."

"Can I say one thing, Mr. Weston?"

"Certainly."

"I care about Emma and wouldn't do anything to hurt her."

"But you will, Mr. Tucker. I've seen your type before. You roll into town like a tumbleweed with no place to anchor itself. You flash your money and your smile, expecting the women to fall at your feet—and they do. Women in these small towns don't have a ton of men to choose from when they seek out a partner for life. But you are not *husband* material."

"I respect your opinion, but you don't know me at all. I travel with my brother because he's my brother, and I promised him I would be by his side while he builds his career. I don't plan to live the way I do for the rest of my life."

"What are your plans then?"

"I bought a piece of property, and within the next couple of years I want to raise buckin' bulls for the rodeo on it. My parents raised us on a ranch, and pushin' horns is what I know."

"I heard your rode bulls." Mitchell Weston's eyebrows drew together and he frowned.

"Sometimes. It's more of a hobby than a career for me."

"Good to know." The frown on her father's face loosened a bit, and Beau breathed a little easier. "Rodeoin' isn't quite the glamorous life it's made out to be, especially if there's a woman involved right along with the rider."

"No, it's not, Mr. Weston."

"Dad, quit grillin' Beau. It's only a dinner date," Emma said as she walked into the living room.

The black strapless dress hugged her curves in all the right places and made his mouth water. It brushed her legs at mid-thigh, tempting him almost beyond his control to taste, touch, and explore.

A raging hard-on in front of her dad is not the way to impress the man.

"Maybe," her father replied, rubbing the stubble on his chin. "I just like to know somethin' about the men my daughter dates. Is it a crime to care these days?"

She leaned down and kissed him on the cheek. "No, Dad, it's not." A quick wink in Beau's direction revealed her impish nature. "I'll be home late, so don't wait up."

"You're coming home?" he asked, clearly not believing she didn't plan to stay out all night.

"I don't know for sure, but I don't want you waiting and then me not showing up at all."

"All right, Emma, but be careful, huh?" he said, hugging her, but staring Beau down over the top of her head.

"I will, Dad. I love you."

"I love you, too, Emma."

Beau scrambled to his feet, relieved the interrogation was over for now. Somehow he knew he wasn't out of the woods yet with her father. Mr. Weston seemed the type to expect a ring on his little girl's finger before things got hot and heavy again. *How would he feel about Emma being with both me and Brandon as a permanent triad?*

Protectiveness, mistrust, and suspicion swirled in her father's gaze when it met Beau's again, and Beau swallowed hard.

10

The lights of Watertown twinkled in the distance as Beau drove Emma's truck down the highway. Tires hummed against the blacktop, lulling her and relaxing her tense shoulders. Catching her Dad grilling Beau made her worry. The last thing she wanted was her father messing up this little rendezvous with Beau and Brandon. If she only had a few days to store away memories, she'd take what she could get.

She'd picked this restaurant for two reasons. One, the food would make anyone's mouth water, and two, there wouldn't be too many folks from Red Rock around—she hoped.

"What are you thinkin' about, darlin'?" Beau asked, grasping her fingers and then entwining them with his own.

"I hope my dad's question and answer session didn't piss you off."

"Nah. He's worried about you. I can't blame him." He glanced her way and then back out the windshield. "How did he find out about our threesome?"

"My big mouth."

"Huh?"

"My ex-fiancé cornered me at the beer taps, and he said some things about you and Brandon. I informed him whether we'd slept together or not was none of his business. My dad overheard the conversation and asked me point blank if we'd slept together. I couldn't lie, so I told him yes." The concerned look on Beau's face sent apprehension down her spine. "It's okay though. He understood."

"To a point, I think he does, but he definitely thinks the less time you spend with us, the better for you."

"He just wants to protect me."

"I know," he murmured, bringing her fingers to his lips and nibbling on the tips. "It's what fathers do."

"Brothers too."

"True. Cade is protective of you."

Several moments of silence passed while she thought about Brandon's story in relation to her own siblings. A sister. She smiled at the thought of them protecting a cute little girl with features similar to theirs. Having brothers herself, she knew how they could be with their siblings—teasing them one moment and ready to punch anyone who hurt them, the next. "I'm sorry about your sister."

"Thanks. It happened a long time ago, but Bailey's always in our thoughts."

"She had cancer?"

"Yeah. Acute Lymphoblastic Leukemia. She'd been sick since she turned a year old and we always knew she probably wouldn't make it to adulthood. The outcome for her type of cancer didn't bode well."

"Was she older than you?"

A heavy sigh escaped his lips, bringing her attention to their fullness and her need to taste him. "We were actually triplets. She was the third born, a few minutes after Brandon."

"Wow."

"Bailey had chromosomal problems from the beginning. She had Down's Syndrome, too, but she was our third." He inhaled a deep cleansing breath and continued. "Our mother had a real hard time with it—always blaming herself."

"She couldn't control those things."

"I know, and so do you, but when it's something like that..."

The need to take away some of his pain enveloped her heart. Even though she fought with her siblings, she couldn't imagine her life without one of them in it. Cade took care of all of them, and Sharon, the oldest girl, took over the motherly duties when their mom died a few years ago, but she had her own family. Elizabeth was the nosy one—always in everyone's business, but she meant well. Being the youngest sister, Emma got the brunt of their protectiveness, but then they had Jarrod. He got all of it, being the baby of the family. Spoiled, mothered by the sisters, and so handsome women came easy to him, he could have any woman he wanted. Emma knew someday he'd run into a girl who would throw him for a loop, and he wouldn't know what hit him.

All the thoughts of siblings and family made Emma feel closer to Beau than she had before. She laid her head on his shoulder and silently tried to absorb all his hurt and pain. He'd suffered so much loss. Losing a sibling probably hurt as much, if not more, than losing a parent. "I can't even imagine the pain you went through, Beau."

"You lost your mom not long ago, didn't you?" he asked, unlacing their fingers and wrapping his arm around her shoulders to pull her closer.

Emma sniffed and tried to hold back the tears burning her throat and choking her words. She missed her mom every day, but today seemed worse. The mention of Beau and Brandon's sister brought home the pain and loss she felt. "Yeah. She was hit by a drunk driver and killed."

"I'm sorry."

"It's okay," she whispered and then cleared her throat. After a moment, she went on. "It still hurts. She'll never see me marry. She'll never see her grandchildren or great-grandchildren, and I know she looked forward to bouncing them on her knee. Cade's little boy, Alan, hadn't been born yet. Only one of my sisters is already married. Elizabeth and I aren't, and right now, there isn't any prospect of a husband anywhere within several hundred miles. Red Rock isn't a beehive of eligible bachelors, if you hadn't noticed."

"True, but I'm sure there's someone you might think would make good husband material, right?"

"Yeah, but the last thing on their minds...uh...his mind...is marriage, or even a steady girlfriend, I'm sure." The lights of Watertown came into sharp view as they reached the city limits. "Turn right at the stop sign. The restaurant is on the next block." Emma, growing uncomfortable with the conversation, was glad of a change of subject. Thinking long-term with Beau and Brandon wasn't the wisest thing to do.

Beau parked the truck, hopped out, and then came around to open her door. *Such a gentleman.*

She stepped out of the truck, and he wrapped an arm around her shoulders as he pushed the door shut.

"Have I told you how nice you look?"

"No, you haven't, Mr. Tucker," she quipped, glancing up at him through her lashes.

"I could eat you up. You look fabulous in that pretty, figuring-hugging black dress," he murmured by her ear and then nipped at the lobe. "I can't wait to get you alone."

"Promise?"

"I'll promise anything if you keep lookin' at me with those sexy eyes."

"Be careful. You never know the things I might force you to promise if you give me the chance."

"Bring it on, babe."

The warm chuckle he punctuated his words with had desire sizzling across her skin. *Was it only this morning we made love?* Made love? No, had sex. She must think of it as having sex.

"What's the pretty blush for?" he asked, guiding her toward the hostess.

"Mmm. Wouldn't you like to know?"

The restaurant boasted a western motif, including old lanterns, antique washboards, signs, wagon wheels, and western tack hung from the walls and ceiling. Country music played softly from the overhead speakers and she absently wondered if they'd hear one of Brandon's songs while they were there.

Beau's lips brushed her neck, and he whispered, "I *will* extract payment for that little smartass comment, Miss Emma."

A thrill of fear followed by the zing of desire had her pussy throbbing to the increased rate of her heart. "I can't wait." *Holy hell! Did I just say that? And what if Beau actually ties me to the bed? Or better, pulls me over his knee and spanks me?*

He cleared his throat as they reached their booth, and he let her slide in before sitting down himself. Together, they only took up a small portion of the horseshoe-shaped bench. A quick glance at his cock before he took his seat revealed his erection pressing against the front of his jeans, and she had to hide her smile.

The waitress introduced herself and gave Beau several bold looks. Emma seethed with frustration and jealousy, although Beau acted the perfect gentleman, never once giving the waitress any encouragement. *I can't believe we ran into her. I can't catch a break here. The one woman who hates me more than anything on this earth, and she has to be our waitress. I hope she doesn't poison my food or something, but I wouldn't put it past her to dump it into my lap—and all over a guy in high school.*

Emma busied herself looking at the menu and pouted while she listened to Beau order a bottle of wine and an appetizer.

"Are you hungry?" he asked, sliding his fingers along the top of her hand.

"Yes, actually. I'm starvin'. I didn't get to eat much after breakfast at the diner, and there usually isn't time while we're servin' folks during the rodeo," she replied, folding the menu and placing it on the table.

"So what are you going to order? At your dad's the other night, you were a hearty eater."

"You noticed how I ate?"

"Sure. I like women who eat normal and don't pick at their food."

She laughed and picked up a peanut from the bucket on the table. Cracking it open with a loud pop, she stuffed the insides into her mouth and tossed the shell on the floor. "I don't think anyone ever said I picked at my food. I eat whatever is put in front of me usually. There isn't much I don't like."

He leaned in from his position next to her and whispered against her ear, "We didn't get to use the strawberries and whipped cream the kitchen sent up. I'd love to lick them off your breasts."

Her nipples drew into hard nubs, tingling and throbbing at his words.

"You like the sound of that, huh? Your nipples are hard just thinking about it."

His hard body blocked anyone from seeing what he did as his fingers plucked at the tip pressing against her dress. The ache of need grew to desperate proportions. The need to have his mouth on her exploded into heart-pounding, pussy creaming desire, and if he didn't knock it off, she'd ride his hips right here.

"Have you ever been tied spread-eagle on a bed?"

"No," she squeaked, imaging herself stretched out and open to his every whim. The mere thought ramped up her desire as she shifted on the seat.

"Open for me. Unable to stop me from doing anything to you I want to. Bringing you to orgasm multiple times with my mouth and tongue." The low growl of his sexy voice, punctuated by several small licks on her skin, and she was ready to do anything he wanted—anything.

Shit! He's killin' me here.

"Licking every inch of your incredible skin. Sucking on your nipples until they're pebble-hard. My cock is so hard for you, it's killin' me." The warm wetness of his tongue played with her earlobe. "Are you hot and wet, Emma?"

The answer eluded her. Her brain turned to mush the moment he'd mentioned *spread-eagle on a bed*. She couldn't think—could barely breathe beyond short gasps.

His hand snaked beneath the tablecloth and shimmied up her skirt to find her naked thigh. The urge to spread her legs and give him unbridled access rushed through her body, taking away any thoughts of denying him.

"Oh God." Her words came out in small pants as she struggled to pull enough air into her lungs to keep from passing out.

"Such a naughty girl, you are. No panties."

One finger brushed her clit, and she almost sank beneath the table.

"Do you want me to touch you, Emma?" he asked in a low purr that reverberated along her nerve-endings.

She whimpered and closed her eyes.

"I'll take that as a yes." Two fingers slid into her pussy. "You're so wet. God, you're driving me crazy."

Her head fell back against his shoulder, and she spread her thighs farther apart.

"Do you want me to make you come?"

"Here?" she whispered, while her pussy sucked at his fingers. A quick glance at the tables nearby revealed their seclusion and the sides of the booth were high enough, no one could see what naughtiness was transpiring within their little world.

"Do you think you can be quiet?"

"I don't..."

His thumb circled her clit, and his fingers continued to push in and out of her pussy. "Come for me, darlin'."

He covered her mouth as she came apart in his arms, stifling her cry of climax with his lips. Public exhibitionism wasn't her thing, but right now, she couldn't care less who knew she'd just climaxed because this gorgeous man had finger fucked her until she couldn't hold back.

Beau finally lifted his head, staring down at her with those fathomless brown eyes. "Better?"

With her breath still coming in sharp pants, she couldn't answer except to nod her head, eliciting a wicked smile from the man responsible.

"There's more where that came from."

"Can we leave now?"

"Impatient?"

"Hell yeah. Appetizers are great, but I'm lookin' for the whole meal."

His roar of laughter brought stares and frowns from some of the other patrons of the restaurant, but Emma frowned right back at them and then kissed Beau on the lips.

"I hope I don't have a wet spot on the back of my dress," she said, sneaking one of the napkins beneath the table to wipe the cream from her thighs and pussy.

"I'll walk behind you, just in case."

A quick glance revealed his wicked smirk had returned. "Right. You want to walk behind me to check out my ass."

"Somethin' wrong with lookin' at your fine ass?"

The waitress returned with their appetizer and all but threw the plate on the table with a loud bang. She shot Emma a scathing look, turned on her heel, and stomped away.

"I think she's a little pissed," Emma said, snagging a deep fried mushroom and dipping it into the ranch dressing. "God, I love these." She licked her fingers very slowly, teasing Beau. Two could fool around at this foreplay thing.

One dark masculine eyebrow shot up, and his eyes darkened to almost black.

"Horny, honey?"

"My dick is so hard, it would shatter if you put too much pressure on my zipper."

"Oh...let's see." She pressed her palm to his cock and sighed.

"Emma," he growled, grabbing her hand and pressing it harder against his dick.

"You made me come. I should give you the same consideration, Beau," she murmured, unbuttoning and unzipping his jeans. His cock sprang free, and he groaned low in his throat. "My, my. All this for me?"

"You know it is. I want to be buried in your sweet heat right now, not coming in your hand."

"How about if I play a little?" she asked, running her fingernail down the length of his cock and back up.

"You're gonna pay for this later, Emma. I'm gonna torture you until you beg," he growled. The quick flick of his tongue over his lips gave away the tight rein of control he must be hoping to hold onto while she tortured him.

"Another promise? I'm likin' this." Wrapping her fingers around his cock, she did a slow slide up and down. "So smooth and hard at the same time." Her thumb spread the pre-cum from the tip of his penis around and around the head as she watched his face flush. She wanted to lick the thick salty liquid, but unless she ducked under the table, it would be impossible. The thought intrigued her.

The small lift of his hips toward her hand told her he barely hung onto his self-control, and she wanted to take it away from him so badly, she could taste it—and taste it she would.

* * * *

The little witch was going to kill him. Her warm palm caressed his cock slowly, rubbing, encircling, and grasping it until he thought he might die. He knew he probably deserved her torture after forcing her to climax in the middle of the restaurant, and he could tell she planned to pay him back in spades.

A wicked grin spread across her lips, and he knew he didn't stand a chance. One beautifully arched eyebrow cocked saucily at him before she disappeared beneath the table.

Aw, fuck!

Her warm mouth closed over the head of his cock, and he almost shot his load right there. Oh, she would pay for this later—no doubt about it—but right now, he savored her tongue swirling around his cock and the tight confines of her mouth when she sucked.

"Sir, can I get you anything else at the moment? Your dinner should be ready soon," the waitress said, glancing at the now empty booth.

"N-no." The high pitch squeak of his voice made him cringe. He cleared his throat to try again. "No. We're doin' fine, thanks." Emma sucked the head of his cock into her mouth and deep throated him. He fought the need to close his eyes while the waitress stood there staring at him. "Water. Yeah, water would be great."

"Of course," she replied and cocked her head to the side like she wanted to say something more before she walked away.

He fought for breath while Emma continued to torment him. His balls were on fire. His dick ached with the need to come. The soft slide of her tongue had his legs trembling. As his climax drew closer, he grabbed a napkin off the table and shoved it beneath the tablecloth, unsure whether she planned to swallow or not.

The little napkin popped back up his stomach and waved like a white flag. Beau looked around to see if anyone watched the goings-on in their booth, and thankfully, everyone seemed occupied with their own conversations.

Unable to fight her loving care anymore, he gripped the tabletop and bit the inside of his cheek as cum shot out of the end of his dick, Emma's eager mouth swallowing every drop.

Several moments later, Emma returned to her seat with a cheeky grin on her lips while he tried to discreetly zip up his pants.

"Emma Leanne Weston. How the hell are you, honey?"

A stout older woman, probably in her eighties, stopped at their table. Her pure white hair, styled into a fashionable bun at the back of her head, gave away her age, but the mischievous twinkle in her blue eyes and the smile on her lips said she lived life to the fullest. "Gram!" Emma slid out of the booth and hugged the old woman tight enough, Beau heard her bones creak. Beau sighed in relief when he managed to get his zipper up without giving too much away—he hoped.

"Easy, Emma, honey. These old bones can't handle all the huggin'." She glanced at him and grinned. "Who's the hunk?"

Emma laughed and sat back down. "Gram, this is Beau Tucker. Beau this is Gram. No, she's not my real grandmother, but she adopted the Weston bunch when Natalie married Cade. She's actually Natalie's grandmother."

"Nice to meet you, ma'am." He jumped to his feet, indicating she could sit. "Would you like to join us?"

"I'd love to, you sexy man, you, but I have a date." The cheeky grin on the old woman's face was priceless.

"A date?" Emma asked, her eyes the size of saucers.

"Yes. I'm meeting Samuel Johnson for dinner."

"Isn't he your attorney?"

"Yes he is, you nosy girl," Gram replied, although the twinkle in her eyes belied her words.

Emma laughed.

"No matchmakin', do you hear me, Emma?"

"I didn't say anythin'."

"I know you didn't, but I can see the sparkle in your eyes—or did your handsome escort put it there?"

Beau couldn't believe his ears. It appeared the old woman had a huge sense of humor, and she obviously had no qualms about saying what came to mind.

"I'd have to say Beau put it there, Gram."

"I'll tell you the same thing I told Natalie when she started datin' Cade. I hope you have condoms in your purse, because it doesn't appear to me your young man will be keepin' his hands to himself for very long."

Beau choked on his water. If she only knew where both of their hands had been in the last half an hour, she'd probably have a stroke right then.

Gram smacked him on the back several times between the shoulder blades.

"You gonna live, young man? 'Cause if you aren't, you best pay the tab right now."

Emma rolled her eyes and giggled.

"I'm okay. Thanks," he choked out and then coughed again.

"Good. You look like a strappin' lad. What do you do for a livin'?" Gram asked, apparently deciding to join them for a few moments after all as she scooted in next to Emma.

"I currently work as a road manager for my brother."

"Your brother?" Gram asked.

"Yes, ma'am. My brother is Brandon Tucker, the country music artist."

"I thought you looked familiar. Isn't he the face you have on your wall, Emma?"

Emma rolled her eyes and sighed. "Yes, Gram, he is. Beau and Brandon are identical twins."

"Well, holy hell on a stick! There are two of them? Hot damn! Two gorgeous hunks like that one there ought to keep you busy for awhile."

Beau laughed and shook his head. He loved Emma's Gram already.

"Gram, please." Emma tried to shush her, looking around. The other diners had begun looking at them curiously.

"Ah, don't worry about them, Emma honey. They're all jealous of the good lookin' couple you make. I'd sure like to see you sandwiched between him and his twin. Wouldn't that be one hell of a sight?"

An elderly gentleman walked up to their table and addressed Gram. "Mrs. Oliver, why don't we take our business to this other table over here?"

"Oh, go on with you, Sam. If you want to go sit, then go sit your ass down. You're an old fuddy-duddy anyway. This here is my granddaughter and her date. I'm talkin' to them for a minute."

"I see. Well, join me then when you're through," he replied, moving off to sit at a table several feet away with an annoyed look on his face.

"Now, where were we?" She tapped her gnarled finger on the table. "Oh yeah, you between him and his brother. I think you'd make a cute threesome. Did I ever tell you how Natalie's mother dated your dad and the idiot she married?"

The waitress arrived with their dinner plates, and Beau hoped Gram might take her leave, but she started talking about her daughter dating two men during high school, and then how Cade, Natalie, and Kale had dated when Natalie arrived in town. It sounded to Beau like the whole place liked threesomes. One could always hope.

"Are you plannin' on settlin' down in Red Rock, son?" Gram asked.

"I'm not sure what my plans are past next month, to tell you the truth. It's important for me to be there for my brother."

Gram nodded and pursed her lips. "I understand the family thing. I sure do—but what about Emma?"

"Gram, I think I can take care—"

"Nonsense. Let me do the negotiatin' here," she said interrupting Emma's words. "Just how do you feel about my granddaughter?"

"Gram, we've only known each other a few days."

"And that means what? Grandpa Oliver told me he loved me the night of our second date. He asked me to marry him one week after we started going steady, and we were married sixty-eight years when he passed on." Gram narrowed her eyes and stared him down. He felt like an insect on a microscope slide while she chewed on whatever she would say next. After several minutes, she nodded and rose to her feet.

"You love her. I can see it in your eyes. You best be makin' an honest woman of my Emma, or you won't want to be anywhere near Red Rock, Montana for the next hundred years or so. See, I plan to haunt people who hurt my family, and Emma is family." Two quick taps of her cane on the floor and she said, "I best get a weddin' invitation." She turned to Emma next. "I want to meet his brother, too. Plan on Sunday dinner at my house, and bring 'em both."

Beau sat with his mouth open watching the feisty old woman walk away. "What the hell just happened?"

"My Gram happened. You have to kind of ignore her. She tends to be very bold and outspoken."

"I really couldn't tell," he replied, chuckling. "She's great."

"I'm glad you think so. Most guys I've dated couldn't handle her."

"I don't know why. She's a breath of fresh air."

Emma frowned and played with her fork, twirling it between her fingers. She apparently had something on her mind and he wondered what as he watched uncertainty and worry, zip across her eyes.

"What's wrong?" Beau asked.

"I love her to death, but I'm sorry she put you on the spot."

He took her hand in his and kissed her fingertips. "Its fine, Emma. I would love havin' her around all the time. She would definitely keep us on our toes."

"She definitely keeps us wonderin'."

A frown settled on his mouth. "What else is bothering you?"

Her bottom lip disappeared between her teeth, and Beau knew she had something on her mind. "Is what she said true?"

"What did she say?"

"She said you love me." Hope and fear laced her words, and he wondered if Emma wanted him to love her or not.

11

His Adam's apple bobbed up and down nervously. "Well, I, uh..."

The inability to answer her question told her he either didn't love her or hadn't even thought about it. Either way, she needed to let him off the hook and bury her disappointment. "Never mind, Beau. It was a stupid thing to ask. I mean, we've only known each other a few days, and people don't fall in love in two days."

Beau took her hands in his and squeezed them. "You are an amazing woman, Emma, and I love spendin' time with you, makin' love to you, and watchin' you take life by the horns, but *in love*? I don't know how to answer you."

"You just did, and it's fine, really."

The caress of his hand against hers almost brought her to tears. She wanted him to love her. She wanted both of them to love her, but she knew their lives held different goals. The road called to the two of them, whereas she needed stability...a home...a family.

"I care about you," he went on. "You've come to mean a lot to me in the few short days we've known each other, and I don't want to hurt you. My life is on the road with Brandon, at least for now."

"I know," she whispered, slowly tugging her hands from his. "When the bus is fixed and you two go on your merry way, I'll miss you." Almost losing her nerve, she caught his gaze with hers and then lowered it to where her clasped hands lay on the tabletop. "Both of you. And every time I see Brandon's face on my wall at home, I'll think of you and him. People may think you two are alike, but I've seen the differences—and I don't mean only intimately, although there's differences there, too."

Grasping her hands again, he brought them to his lips and kissed her knuckles. "Listen, Emma. I don't want to waste our time left together on talk of somethin' only God knows the outcome of. Let's make the most of it. Let me love you."

She inhaled a slow, easy breath and nodded. At least she could show him how much she cared with her body. It didn't matter whether she knew the outcome of their time together. The need for Beau and Brandon simply had to be fulfilled.

The snooty waitress arrived with the bill, and Beau laid out a debit card.

"Are you Brandon Tucker's brother? You look so much like him, it's scary."

"Yes, I am."

"Wow. I mean you two could be twins."

"We are."

"Seriously? I didn't know he had a twin, and I'm like his biggest fan ever. Can you introduce me to him? I'd be forever in your debt," the waitress gushed. "I'd make it worth your while." Her fingers trailed up Beau's arm, and Emma wanted to tear her limb from limb.

"I'm sorry but no. I'm out with my..."

"She doesn't matter."

"Excuse me?" Beau said with a low snarl. "Emma does matter. She's the only one who matters at the moment. Now please, get our tab taken care of so we can leave. And you can be sure I'll report your behavior to the management."

Shock and indignation swept across her face as she planted her hands on her hips. "Well, I never."

"I'm sure you have, actually." He turned to Emma, reached for her hand.

The waitress huffed and narrowed her eyes. Without another word, she headed back toward the kitchen, her shoulders back and her hips swinging as if to entice Beau away from Emma.

"God, I hate her," Emma said.

"Why? She's jealous of you."

"Little town, Beau. She's been a bitch ever since high school. Hatred's run deep between us ever since one of her boyfriends dumped her to go out with me."

The waitress returned with his receipt. "Here you go, handsome," she said, bending over far enough her tits practically spilled out of her top. "Sign right there, honey, and you'll be all set."

Beau grabbed the paper, wrote a big fat zero under the tip, signed his name and handed it back. "Come on, Emma. Let's get out of here before I do somethin' I'm gonna regret."

As they headed for the door, Emma heard behind her, "Can you believe that jerk? He didn't even leave me a tip, and I kissed his ass—or I would have, literally, if Emma the slut wasn't with him."

Emma stiffened, and Beau stopped to whisper in her ear. "Easy, darlin'. I'm leavin' with you, remember?"

"I'll be right back, Beau." He grabbed her hand to stop her from leaving, but she needed to do this. "It's fine." After a quick kiss to his lips, she pulled away and walked back toward the waitress. "Stacey, can I talk to you a moment?"

The other woman's eyebrow rose, and she flipped her hair over her shoulder. "What do you want?"

"I need to set the record straight. The only reason you're pissed off at me is because Greg left you for me back in high school. Don't you think it's time to get over this petty jealousy?" Emma asked sweetly. Kill 'em with kindness, her momma always said, although she wouldn't mind raking her nails down the bitch's face.

"Whatever, Emma. I could care less about Greg the loser," Stacey said with a bored, I-don't-give-a-shit look.

Emma lifted her chin and stared right into Stacey's eyes. "All right. I'm gonna share a little secret with you. Brandon wouldn't be interested in you anyway."

"Why not?" Stacey asked, placing her hands on her hips.

"Because he has me."

"What? You're datin' both of them?" Stacey looked like she could spit nails.

Emma nodded and smiled. "And you know what else? I've had sex with both of them...together."

"See, I knew you were a slut! Screwing both of them? God, what a whore!"

"Might be, Stacey, but I'm theirs. You aren't, and you'll never be." She spun around, presenting the still-sputtering Stacey with her back as she walked back to Beau. "I'm ready."

"What did you say to her?" he asked, placing his hand at the small of her back and escorting her out of the door.

"I belong to you and Brandon, and she never will."

"You don't care whether people know you're datin' both of us?"

After the visit with her Gram, Emma's feelings and thoughts on the matter had changed. Beau and Brandon were gorgeous, single and attracted to her. She wanted them, and she didn't care who knew it. Gossipmongers would have a field day, but eventually something else would happen, and the talk about her, Beau, and Brandon would disappear. "Nope, not anymore. I'm not going to hide and pretend it didn't happen. I'm proud you and Brandon want me. If the biddies and gossips in Red Rock don't like it, too bad."

A smile spread across his lips, and he bent down to brush them over hers. "I'm glad I'm on your side, Emma." They walked to where her truck sat parked in the lot. "Why don't you drive back?"

His request brought her to a stop, and she glanced at him, wondering whether he might be up to somethin'. The plan she'd had for the drive back would be ruined if she drove. "Are you sure? It's fine if you want to drive."

"No, you go ahead."

With a shrug, she walked around to the driver's side and slipped inside the cab. The truck started with a grumble as Beau buckled his belt and relaxed against the seat. "Where are we headed?"

"I'm sure there's a back way to get to Red Rock."

"There is, but why?"

A sexy-as-sin grin spread across his mouth, and she began to wonder if he didn't have a plan of his own. Damn, the man could make her hot with a simple look. After she squirmed and squeezed her pussy muscles together to try to relieve some of the pressure building in her groin, she reversed out of the parking lot.

When the lights of Watertown had faded in the rearview mirror, Beau unhooked his seat belt and slid to the center of the truck. The warmth of his palm caressed her bare thigh as he pushed up the hem of her dress, sending goose bumps from her toes to her scalp. The lump clogging her throat threatened to strangle her as her palms gripped the steering wheel.

Beau dropped his cowboy hat on the seat next to him and leaned toward her. "Are you hot, Emma?"

She couldn't say a word, only whimper.

His fingers stroked higher up her thigh, and she spread her legs to give him access to her pussy if he wanted to go all the way. God, she hoped he went all the way.

"Do you want me to touch you?" he whispered into her ear.

His breath ruffled the fine hairs near her temple, and shivers raced down her spine.

"Pleeeaase..."

"Oh, I love when you beg, babe."

His fingertips brushed the curls guarding her pussy. Seconds later, one found her clit and brushed it lightly.

"Find somewhere to pull off, Emma."

"I can't. It's ranch property," she whispered, desperately looking for a turn off. "Wait! There." An aluminum livestock gate blocked the entrance to the field.

"I'll open the gate. Pull behind the stand of trees to the left there."

"Someone might see us if they drive by."

"The truck will hide us from prying eyes. I want you, Emma, right now—and darlin', I plan on takin' you." As she stopped the truck, Beau slid out of the cab and slammed the door. The echo of the sound bounced around the cab, but the hard thump of her heart almost drowned out any other noise. Once the gate was open, she pulled through, and Beau closed it behind them.

She stopped the truck next to the trees and cut the engine. Beau stood outside by the passenger side and motioned with his finger for her to come around to his side. The twinkle in his brown eyes and the I-gonna-fuck-you smile on his lips had her pussy creaming before she ever got out of the truck. A quick shaky inhalation and then a long sigh helped a little, but the moment he touched her, the calm would disappear like a cloud of smoke.

When she rounded the back of the truck and the passenger side came into view, Beau stood with his arm propped on the now-open door and one booted foot crossed over the other. He held out his hand, and when she placed her palm in his, he slowly drew her closer.

"This is gonna be fun."

"What do you plan to do?" she asked, nervously glancing over her shoulder at the road and then back to him. Even if no one could see them, anyone passing from Red Rock would know this truck.

"You'll see."

The anticipation would kill her if he drew this out too long. She could already feel cream dripping down the inside of her thigh.

"Sit on the seat with your butt on the edge and spread those gorgeous thighs for me."

The warmth of the evening air on her wet, bare pussy made her breath catch in her throat. Cool leather felt strange against her butt when she sat down and spread her legs. He knelt on the running board and leaned forward. The seat height lined him up perfectly to eat her pussy until she came all over his face. The moment Beau's tongue touched her clit, she bit back a scream of ecstasy.

"So wet," he murmured, kissing the inside of her thigh as he shoved a finger deep into her vagina. "All for me."

The wet slide of his tongue from vagina to clit felt like heaven—Beau's kind of heavenly torture. "You're killin' me, Beau."

"Relax, darlin'."

His tongue did several figure eights on her clit before he sucked it between his lips and shoved two fingers into her pussy.

Her breathing came in small pants as she tried desperately to forestall the rising climax he pulled from deep inside her, but it was no use. He had her in the palm of his hand, ready to beg for what she wanted.

"God, Beau, please. I need to come so bad."

The speed of his fingers and tongue stoked her climax and held her on the edge by her fingernails. She whimpered and begged, but every time she got there, he'd slow his strokes until she calmed, and then he'd bring her right back up.

Unable to stand his fantastic torture any longer, she grabbed both of his ears in her fingers and pinched.

"Ouch!"

"If...you...don't...make...me...come...I'm going to torture you by staking your ass out in the hot sun and leaving you to the fire ants."

"A little on edge, darlin'?"

"A lot on edge, Beau. Stop teasing me. I can't stand it anymore."

He stood up and reached into his back pocket for his wallet. With a wicked grin, he tore open the condom he'd retrieved and rolled it over his erection.

"Hurry." Both hands grasped her hips as she reclined on the seat. One hard thrust and he was buried balls-deep inside her pussy. "Ah!"

After Beau released a sharp hiss, his hips started the steady rhythm she knew would throw her over in half a second. When he drew his thumb over her clit and then pressed down hard, she flew apart with a shattering scream that echoed in the silence around them.

"One," he whispered, the hard thrust of his hips never stopping, until she hung on the edge a second time. "Come for me again, darlin'. Squeeze my cock like a vice, Emma. I need to feel you milkin' me for everythin' I've got."

His sexy talk and pounding rhythm threw her into a second climax big enough to rival anything she'd had before. Stars danced behind her eyelids, her chest hurt from breathing so fast, and her whole body tingled as Beau groaned her name and came right along with her.

* * * *

They returned to Beau and Brandon's suite after their torrid romp in the middle of God only knew whose pasture, only to find Brandon still out. Burying the feelings of jealousy deep inside, she dragged Beau into the bathroom, turned on the huge bathtub, and ripped his shirt off with one quick tug.

After they made love in the bathtub, Beau swept her up in his arms and carried her to the bed. "Now, darlin', you're gonna pay for your disobedience."

Anticipation sent shivers down her back while she faked like she didn't understand what he meant. "Disobedience? When did I disobey you?

"Maybe I should say 'impertinence'," he replied, laying her face up on the bed and then pulling out his bull rope—from where, she didn't know.

"What are you gonna do with that?" she asked, her body humming with the images flashing through her mind.

Without answering, he wrapped it around her wrists in a knot he knew she couldn't pull free from. The next loop secured her to the headboard. "I'm not gonna tie this too tight. It's rough rope, so it will chafe your beautiful wrists if I do." He glanced down and met her gaze with his own scorching look. "Do you trust me?"

She bit her lip for a moment and then nodded.

"I think you'll like this, but you'll have to leave your hands there. You could probably pull free if you wanted to."

The soft slide of his lips from her mouth to her breasts and then lower made her whimper. Breathing got more difficult the closer he got to her pussy. Unable to stop herself, she spread her thighs, begging for his tongue in soft sighs. "Please, Beau."

"I'll take care of you, darlin'."

His shoulders kept her spread as he settled himself between her legs and started licking every inch of her pussy—from her slit up and over her clit, down the outside lips of her pussy.

The torture continued until she'd climaxed at least six times. "I can't stand it anymore, Beau. Pleaseeee. I need you inside me."

The word no more than left her lips and he was there, buried inside her to the hilt.

"Beau!" she screamed, climaxing again.

"Easy, darlin'," he soothed, starting the slow glide of his cock in and out. His lips danced over her face, along her jaw, to her ear, and then across her shoulder. "God, I love bein' inside you. One day soon though, I want your ass. I need to feel those slick muscles tighten around me."

"Fuck me, Beau. I need it hard."

He lifted his chest from hers, braced his arms on the bed next to her, and snapped his hips, driving his cock into her depths until she thought for sure he'd stolen her heart. The fast pace of his thrusts threw her into another climax as he tipped his hips up and slammed into her sweet spot with every plunge.

"Ah, God!"

The low growl and hefty grunts signaled his own climax as he followed her over the precipice of sensual release and into the relaxation of both mind and body.

Their bathtub escapades and being tied to the bed thoroughly exhausted her—to the point she never heard Brandon return and slept like a dead person for the rest of the night, curled into Beau's warm body with her head on his chest.

Morning light streamed through the blinds on the window of the hotel room, dragging Emma from the most delicious dreams of Brandon and Beau making love to her. She rolled onto her side and stretched her hand out across the bed only to find it cold and empty. Her eyes flew open and she sat bolt upright in the bed, glancing around to find Beau. Now the room was quiet—too quiet. Wrapping the sheet around her body, she slid out of the bed and walked into the living room of the suite. Brandon sat sipping coffee while he read the paper. Beau was nowhere to be found.

Brandon glanced up and smiled. "Mornin', honey."

"Where's Beau?"

"Gone for the day." He patted the seat on the couch next to him. "Sit with me. Would you like coffee?"

"Yes, please," she replied, tugging the sheet higher. Why, she didn't know. It wasn't like Brandon hadn't already seen everything she had to offer.

"Cream and sugar?"

"Yeah, thanks"

He handed her the cup, and she took two healthy swallows before she set it back on the table.

"I'm assuming since you're here and he's not, it's your day to spend with me."

"Yes." His eyes twinkled with mischief, and she squirmed on the seat wondering what he planned. It would be nice to get to know Brandon a little more outside of his country music star persona.

"So what's the plan?"

"Nothin' too huge. I want you to show me your life."

Her heart began to pound and her palms started to sweat at his suggestion. *This is so personal. I wonder what brought this on.* "My life? I don't understand."

With both of his hands grasping hers, he said, "Show me Emma Weston. I want to know everything about you. Show me where you went to school, show me your parents' place on horseback, introduce me to some of your friends—things like that."

"Why?" she asked, her thoughts skipping off into unknown territory. Why he wanted to know so much about her made her nervous and excited at the same time.

"Because you're special. You're bright, funny, sexy, charming, sexy—"

A small laugh spilled from her lips. "You said that twice."

"I know, but what can I say? You're a very beautiful woman."

"Okay, Mr. Charm-The-Panties-Off-A-Girl stud muffin. I'm sure you say those words to every woman you meet."

A frown wrinkled the skin between his dark eyebrows. "Not really."

She snorted and covered her mouth.

"I confess to charming the ladies, yes, but I don't say things if I don't mean them." He lifted her hands to his mouth and sucked her index finger between his lips.

Desire zinged straight to her pussy, and her body went from cool and collected to hot and needy in a flash.

When he finally released her from his spell, he said, "I see you brought a change of clothes."

"Yes."

"Why don't you take a shower, and I'll call for room service to bring us something to eat." With her hand in his, he helped her to her feet and turned her toward the bathroom. "I may join you in a few moments." The heat of his whispered words against her ear sent shivers down her spine. His small laugh warmed her skin, and his lips did amazing things to her neck as he slid them over her bare shoulder.

A gentle push to her backside propelled her toward the bathroom, while the heat in his eyes when she glanced over her shoulder promised delights to come. The thought of shower sex with Brandon had her pressing her thighs together, hoping to relieve even a little of the pressure building.

After she closed the door, she dropped the sheet to the floor and moved toward the handles. The massive stall had several jets and a rain-type head, and when she turned the tap on, water shot from every direction. The hot spray pounded into her flesh in a rhythmic cadence, relaxing the bunched muscles of her shoulders and back. Tension uncoiled slowly as she dropped her head forward, closed her eyes and sighed. Really, she didn't have a reason to be so tense, especially after the mind-blowing sex with Beau the night before.

Today Brandon had the chance to wine and dine her, and she couldn't wait to see what he planned. He wanted to know her—the real her—and the thought intrigued her.

Her surprised squeak echoed in the tile stall when Brandon took her left nipple in his mouth. She hadn't heard him come into the bathroom. "You scared me."

The wicked lap of his tongue over the aroused tip made her moan softly and clasp his head harder against her chest. The slow crawl of his fingers up the inside of her leg felt deliciously sexy, and she widened her stance, silently begging for more, but he avoided her needy core. His warm mouth closed over the right nipple and she whimpered. One fingertip brushed her clit, bringing her body to the edge of climax in seconds. God, these two know exactly what to do to push her to the top and hold her there.

"Please, Brandon. Touch me," she begged, thrusting her hips forward encouraging him to spear his fingers into her pussy.

"I'm gonna do more than touch you, honey. I plan to fuck you against the wall in this stall. I want to pound into your pussy until we're both screaming loud enough to rattle the windows." Without any other preamble, he grabbed her by the waist, braced her back against the cold tile shower, and lifted her legs around his waist. "Sorry, honey. I know the tile's cold."

"Damn," she hissed and then groaned. "I love when you're forceful. It's hotter than hell."

The tip of his bare cock nudged at her opening, seeking entrance into her needy, pulsating pussy. "Fuck me, Brandon. I want it all."

"No condom?"

Her gaze caught his, searching for anything to tell her if she could trust him with her body like she trusted him with her heart. "I'm clean and on the pill."

He braced his forehead against hers and said, "I've always insisted on a condom, but with you, I need to feel your pussy without anything between us. I want to feel every ripple, every spasm, every greedy squeeze."

"Such a sexy, smooth talker." She pushed her bottom down, teasing herself with the initial penetration of the head of his cock. "All the way, Brandon. Every inch, baby."

With one deep thrust, he buried himself inside her to the balls. "Oh yeah," he moaned. "Perfect."

"Yes, yes, yes."

The slow, rhythmic push of his cock felt fantastic, but she wanted more—so much more. A soft whimper escaped her mouth as she buried her face against his neck. "Harder."

"I can't, Emma. I'll explode."

"We can do it again. Harder, Brandon. Fuck me hard."

He inhaled sharply and picked up his pace until he was pounding away at her flesh. Every thrust of his hips brought her closer to ignition. She dug her fingernails into his shoulders and nipped at the side of his neck.

"Next time I want your ass, honey. God, you have such a fantastic ass."

His dirty talk and the anticipation of feeling his cock deep in her ass again had her screaming his name as her climax washed over her like a rogue wave against the sand. Her whole body tingled and flushed with heat while Brandon continued stroking his cock in and out of her pussy.

His rapid, harsh panting and clenched jaw told her he hung on the edge.

"Come for me, Brandon. I want to feel all that luscious cream you're hiding splash the inside of my pussy."

"Holy hell," he growled, losing the hold on his pleasure and squirting cum deep inside her.

12

Montana summer heat beat down on their heads as they rode east across the plains of her father's land. Wildflowers bloomed around them in a multitude of colors ranging from reds to purples and oranges. The mountains looming in the distance looked close enough to touch as the mid-day sun heated the entire area. Montana could go from hotter than Hades to cool and inviting during the summer months.

"Your dad owns all this?" he asked, glancing at the beauty riding next to him. God, she looked fantastic with the wind blowing in her hair, the twinkle in her blue eyes, and the wide smile on her lips.

"Yep. He has fifteen thousand acres, give or take. This land has been in my family for generations. My great-great-grandfather settled here back when there wasn't much in the state except for wide open spaces."

"I love Montana," he replied, thinking about the many summers he'd spent on his parents' place riding alongside Beau, the power of the horse beneath him and the wind ruffling his hair. Lately he'd realized how much he'd missed being able to kick back and forget the country star thing for a while. The horses moved along at a slow, steady pace, making it easy to talk.

"You are technically from here, right?" Emma asked. "Montana, I mean."

"Yeah. My parents still have a place out east of the mountains. They breed horses and cattle."

"Sweet."

He didn't discuss his youth much, especially with women. Most of the time, he fucked 'em and disappeared so fast, they never knew what had hit them...but not Emma. He wanted to share his life—his past with the one woman who'd penetrated the shell he'd erected around his heart.

"Beau told me about your sister. I'm sorry. I can't imagine what it's like to lose a sibling."

He didn't reply right away. Anger rushed through him for a moment when he thought about Beau sharing Bailey like that. They'd agreed years ago to keep her to themselves, so they could cherish her memory without revealing her problems to the world. Yeah, he'd told the crowd about her during the concert, but he didn't want to share the other medical issues she had. Bailey was special, and he'd wanted to continue to hold her close to his heart without hearing the pity in people's words.

"What's wrong?"

"Nothin'."

Reining her horse to a stop, she waited for him to follow suit. "Are you angry he told me?"

The compassion and sorrow shining in her eyes broke down the barriers of his emotions. "At first, yeah, but not now. It seems natural to share her with you. Did he tell you she was a triplet?"

"Yeah. I can tell she meant a lot to both of you, and I'm sure you wished you could have protected her from everything."

"I did. I do." He raked his fingers through his hair and stared off into the distance. "She meant everything to us."

Emma took his hand and squeezed his fingers.

"Thanks for listening. It's hard for me to talk about it."

She glanced around and nodded to some shade trees in the distance. "How about we get our picnic set up over there?"

"Sounds good." He cocked his head to the side. "Race you!"

The pounding of hooves drifted off into the vast grassy prairie as he pushed his horse into a faster pace. *Damn, the girl can ride.* Neck in neck, they sped across the prairie toward the grove of trees. Her laugher reached his ears and he couldn't help but smile. This was Emma in her element, and he couldn't help loving this woman who met life head on, grabbed it by the horns, and rode it like a bucking bull.

As they skidded to a halt, their horses breathing hard, he jumped off and swept her up in a tight hug, swinging her around in a circle. Her laughter made every worry disappear, and he wanted to hear it day after day for the rest of their lives. *God, I'm pathetic.*

"I'm hungry. How about we break out our lunch and sit under the tree?"

She kissed his lips quickly and said, "Good plan, but you'll have to let me go so I can get the stuff out of the pack."

Her lips called to him to taste, long and slow, exploring her mouth with his tongue and revving up the heat. Their tongues danced from her mouth to his and back, sliding over each other as he savored her soft sighs and whispered moans.

"Lordy, Emma. I could kiss you all day," he murmured, resting his forehead against hers.

"Me, too, Brandon. You're one damned good kisser."

"Who's better? Me or Beau?"

She stepped back and laughed. "Oh, I'm so not goin' there, mister. You don't need any more ego stroking and I refuse to play into the natural competition you two seem to have over everythin'."

Minutes later, the blanket lay across the soft grass, and Emma retrieved the picnic from her saddle bag.

"We have ham sandwiches, potato salad, sweet tea, and chips," she said, handing him a paper plate with all the various ingredients of their picnic. "I made the sandwiches, but my dad's kitchen helper, Gabrielle, made the potato salad. She's more of a cook, housekeeper, and all around keep-everyone-in-line kind of person.

"Do you cook much?"

"Sometimes," she replied, sliding the fork between her lips. "I have the basics down, I think, but I'm not much of a cookin' from scratch sort of gal. My mom, and then Gabrielle, tried to teach me, but I can't seem to get it right."

"More practice, maybe?"

She shrugged and stared at her plate. "Maybe. I never seem to have time to spend hours in the kitchen. I'd rather be out in the barn with the animals, ridin' across the fields out here, mendin' fences—you know."

"Cowboy stuff," they said in unison and laughed.

"I know the feeling, Emma. Sometimes I wish I could go back to the simpler days before all the craziness of tourin' and singin'."

"Don't you like singin'?"

"I love it, but it would be nice to be able to go to the store without someone I don't know recognizing me. You can't imagine how hard it is to take a lady out on a date and get interrupted a dozen times for pictures and autographs. Privacy would be great. Sometimes this star stuff isn't all it's cracked up to be. I'm sure Beau gets it, too."

"But you've been singin' since you were small."

He glanced across the fields they'd ridden through and sighed. "Do you have any idea what it's like never to know if a woman is after you or your money?"

"Can't say that I do, since I don't do women," she replied with a little grin.

His laugh came out as a small snort.

"How do you know I'm not after your money, Brandon?" she asked, lying on her side on the blanket and propping herself up on her hand. "What if I'm some money-crazed fangirl who wants to trap you and Beau into a relationship?"

"Because for some unknown reason, I trust you, Emma." He stretched out beside her and tugged her over so she lay completely on top of him. "Mmm. I like this position. Ready for a ride, cowgirl?"

"I thought you said the next time you were gonna take my ass, big boy."

Need speared right to his cock the moment her words left her mouth. He loved anal sex, and when he'd been in her ass before, it felt perfect—better than anything he'd experienced before. Unable to stop himself, the flat of his palm came down on her ass. "Saucy wench. Strip."

Jumping to her feet, she whipped her shirt over her head, taking her sports bra with it, and then pushed her jeans and underwear off her feet. "You're still dressed."

"Yep, and I'm gonna stay that way," he replied, sitting up to crouch on his knees.

"Then how are you gonna fuck me?"

"You'll see. On your hands and knees, baby doll, and spread your ass cheeks for me." When she'd done what he asked, he sucked in a ragged breath and leaned over to kiss her butt cheeks. "What a sight you are, Emma, honey. I could fuck you until the end of time, just like this." The rasp of his zipper in the afternoon air sounded loud to him, and he glanced around to make sure they were alone. The last thing he wanted on this earth was for Emma to be embarrassed about being with him. He shoved his jeans and boxers down around his knees, releasing his cock and balls from their confines. Grabbing the condom from his front pocket and the small tube of lube he'd brought, he made everything—including her puckered hole—slick and ready.

"Hurry, Brandon," she whispered, wiggling her butt, encouraging him with every movement.

God, she made him hotter than hell with her begging words. He penetrated her hole with two fingers and stretched her well before he did anything else. The last thing he wanted was pain for his girl. His girl. He liked the sound of that.

"Ready?"

"Oh yeah," she whispered, pushing back against his fingers. "Fill me up, cowboy."

The slow penetration of his cock into her ass felt like heaven and hell. The slick walls of her ass gripped him tight as he slowly pushed into her tight passage. "Relax and let me in, Emma."

"I'm trying. It burns a bit."

"I know, honey. Inhale and then exhale slowly."

Doing what he asked, her whole body relaxed on the exhale, and he pushed the rest of his cock deep inside her. "Fuck, you're amazing."

"Oh yeah. Perfect. You feel so good," she whispered, dropping her head down on her folded arms, which raised her ass higher.

A groan left his mouth when she pushed back and squeezed him with her muscles. "You okay?" he asked.

"Fantastic, but Brandon?"

"Yeah?"

"You need to move. I can't stand it anymore. I need you to fuck me hard."

"With pleasure," he growled, pulling his cock almost all the way out before slowly sliding it back in. "I wish I had a toy here. I'd shove it inside your pretty pussy and fuck your ass at the same time."

"Next time we'll play with toys."

"Next time," he repeated, shoving his cock in and out of her, loving her willingness to experiment.

Her anal muscles held him tight enough, he wasn't sure he could hold off his climax if she didn't hurry and come along. Needing to make her lose control, he found her clit with his fingers and started stroking until it hardened more under his touch. High-pitched whimpers left her mouth, and her hips bucked while he continued to pound into her, increasing the pace of his thrusts until he felt her climax building.

"Come for me, sweetheart. Come for me."

An explosive climax shook her frame, and she screamed loud enough, they probably heard her in the next county, but he didn't care. He'd made Emma feel good, and nothing else mattered. With her muscles spasming around his cock, he couldn't forestall his own climax any longer. The blood roared in his ears, and his body trembled from the force of it.

When his vision cleared and he could move again, he pulled out of her ass and collapsed on the ground beside her. "God, you're amazing."

"Glad you liked it," she said with a small giggle. "I aim to please, and believe me, you aren't easy to please."

"Why do you say that?" he asked, worried she felt she couldn't continue to please him as he tugged his boxers and jeans back up.

"How many women have you slept with in the last year?"

He frowned and thought back to the mindless, nameless hoard of women he'd slept with. "To tell you the truth, I don't know."

"And if you'd found one who pleased you outside of ridin' your dick, don't you think you might have wanted to see her again?"

"Maybe, but I haven't really...until now. I did have one serious relationship, or what I thought was serious until I realized she only wanted the money." Her hair felt like spun silk between his fingers as he brushed the curls back behind her ear. "I can't seem to get enough of you."

"What happens after you leave? I mean, the bus should be fixed soon, and you and Beau will be off to God only knows where."

"I don't know, Emma. I wish I did. I'm sure we can work out somethin'. I haven't gotten my fill of you yet." The thought of leaving Emma behind soured his stomach.

The jingle of his cell phone cut through the tight atmosphere developing between them. He cussed out loud when he saw Beau's name on the caller ID.

"What?" he snapped when he opened his phone. "This is my time with Emma. What's so important—"

"Brandon you need to come to the room. We have a problem."

"Can't it wait? We're out ridin'."

"No. It's your management company. You need to be here to hear this. I won't go into it on the phone." The tone of Beau's voice and the evasive answers worried Brandon. It wasn't like Beau to get upset about anything.

"All right. We'll ride back to Emma's dad's place, but it's going to be a couple of hours before we get back and drive into town."

"Its fine, but we need to take care of this soon."

Brandon snapped the phone shut and stood. "We need to get back. Beau says there's a problem of some sort, and I need to be there."

"Okay," she replied, pulling her clothes back on.

Their picnic lunch ended up stuffed back into the saddle bags.

* * * *

They made the ride back to the house in complete and stifling silence. Emma didn't know what to make of Brandon's mood. He'd been so playful and loving out on their picnic, she could almost believe he cared about her.

Deciding to broach the subject once they'd returned to the barn, she said, "Brandon?"

"Yeah?"

"I hope it's nothin' serious."

He glanced over at her from where he stood brushing down his horse. "Me, too, honey, but Beau sounded worried."

"Don't you two have the twin thing where you can feel each others' moods and stuff? I've heard of it before between twins."

"Sometimes, but we usually have to be fairly close to each other. Not like it works miles apart," he replied, finishing up and leading the gelding into his stall. "Are you about ready to go?"

"Yeah. Just let me put Missy away. Can you drop her tack in the storeroom for me along with yours?"

"Sure, honey."

Several moments later, they bounced down the dirt driveway of her dad's place, heading back to town in her truck. A bad feeling sat like a lump of coal in her belly. For some reason, she knew somethin' bad was gonna happen, and she tried to brace herself for it.

The front of the hotel came into view about fifteen minutes later, and she steeled her heart for whatever news Beau had to share. The walk up to their suite felt like what she thought it might be like to walk death row. Trepidation rolled down her spine and made her tremble with uncertainty.

"It'll be fine, honey," Brandon said, taking her hand in his and kissing her fingertips.

"I don't know, Brandon. I have a bad feelin' about this."

Brandon slipped his key card into the door and pushed it open. "Beau?"

"In here," Beau replied from the direction of the dining room area. "You might as well grab a drink, brother, you aren't gonna like this."

When they rounded the corner of the living room and Brandon headed for the bar, Beau looked surprised to see her. "Emma?"

"Hey."

"Hi. I didn't realize Brandon was bringing you along," he replied, brushing her lips with his. "Did you enjoy your day?"

"Yeah. We went ridin' and had a picnic."

"Sounds like fun." The look in his eyes worried her. He looked tired, torn and pissed off.

Deciding she'd rather not hear this now that she was faced with whatever bad news this entailed, she said, "I need to use the little girls' room, guys. I'll be back in a minute." She pushed the bathroom door open and then shut it behind her. It only took seconds for the raised tones to penetrate the door. Even though they shouted, she couldn't make out the words clearly, but anger and irritation rang in their voices.

Moments later silence filled the suite, and she figured she needed to go back out there. Hopefully everything had blown over. When she walked back into the living room, she could see Beau standing by the bay windows, looking out over the wildflowers and the mountains in the distance, and Brandon sitting in the chair, tapping his fingers against the leather.

"Guys?"

"Emma, honey," Brandon said, getting to his feet. "Come here."

She moved into his embrace and let him hug her tight. The trembling of his body as he held her scared her more than anything. "What's wrong? What's happened?"

"Nothin' for you to worry your pretty head about," Brandon answered.

"Bullshit, Brandon. She has the right to know," Beau snapped.

"Know what? You're scaring me."

Brandon glared at Beau for a moment and then sighed. "Sit down, Emma. We need to talk to you."

The ending of their little love affair had always loomed in the dark corners, just waiting to rear its ugly head and force her to face the fact of their departure. The tightness around Beau's mouth and the anger floating in Brandon's eyes made her realize the end was closer than she'd thought.

"Now, what's this all about?"

"God, I hate this!" Beau shouted. "Tell them no, Brandon. Tell them we have something we need to finish here."

"We've been over this, Beau. I can't and neither can you. They could cancel my contract, and I'd be out on my ear. There's no room for a difficult-to-deal-with performer in country music. You know that! You've been pounding it into my head for the last five years."

"Damn it! This isn't fair."

"Uh...would someone please explain?" Emma asked.

Brandon dropped onto the couch next to her and took her hand in his. "We have to leave."

"I know. When the bus is finished being repaired—"

"No, honey, now. Today."

"What? No, you can't leave yet." *I'm not ready for them to leave.*

"I know, Emma. God, I know," he said, raking his fingers through his hair. "Neither of us wants to leave, but we have to. My management company called earlier, while we were out. They're sending a private jet to pick us up to fly us back to Nashville. They've set up another bus to get us around until ours is fixed."

"I thought you'd cancelled the shows you had coming up," she said, her gaze meeting Brandon's, hoping beyond hope this wasn't real. They couldn't be leaving so soon.

"I called them and told them to," Beau interjected, his own despair and disbelief written on his face as he sat down on her other side and gathered her into his arms. "But apparently they didn't. They've decided to make other arrangements for Brandon to be there, and I have to go with him."

Tears burned her eyes, and one trickled down her cheek. This couldn't be happening. They can't leave yet.

"I'm sorry, Emma," Beau whispered, wiping the tear from her cheek. "I wish we had more time."

Brandon rose to his feet and began to pace back and forth. "I know. Come with us, Emma."

"What?" she asked, pulling away from Beau. "I can't. I have a life here. School. My family."

"You can leave that. This would be us. You, me and Beau. We'll take care of you. I have more than enough money. Beau can tell you."

"It's not about the money, Brandon. It's not about you and Beau. This is me. I can't up and leave everything I know."

Beau's eyes were shadowed with hurt and indecision. "Brandon, we can't do this to her. It's not fair to make her chose."

"I care about you, both of you, but I won't leave my family, my friends, or my life here." She got to her feet and backed up.

"Emma, please," Brandon said, taking her hands. "I think I'm falling in love with you. I need you with me—with both of us. I know Beau feels the same."

Disbelief, elation, and then disappointment tore at her heart. "Don't, Brandon. I can't handle it. Please." She pulled away and glanced at Beau, then back to Brandon. "I guess this is good-bye then." Unable to stop herself from one last touch, she pressed her lips to Brandon's and then to Beau's. "Please don't hate me."

"I could never hate you, darlin'," Beau said, running his hand down her back.

"Me either. You know how to get in touch with us if you want to, right?" Brandon added.

"No, but it's probably best." She closed her eyes and bit her lip. "I...need to move on. It's been great, and I'll never forget either of you, but—" With her knuckle pressed against her lips to stop the choking sobs, she grabbed her purse and rushed out the door.

13

Four months. Four fucking months since either of them had seen or talked to Emma and it was driving Beau absolutely insane. At the moment, they sat in one of the houses Brandon owned, in a suburb of Nashville. When he'd made it big, Brandon had said he wanted to own a home with some acreage. Nashville seemed the logical place, with all the time he had to spend in the studios. Right now, all Beau wanted to do was see Emma. She refused to answer their phone calls, and every avenue they'd tried got shut down by those around her.

Beau paced the living room, stopping every so often to glance out at the barren landscape. The pastures behind the house stretched for miles over the gentle slope of the terrain. Horses moved in and out of the corrals, hunting for morsels of hay left from this morning's feeding. "I need to see her, Brandon. I can't stop thinkin' about her."

"I know, Beau. I feel the same way, but we're booked solid on this tour for another month. You know traveling to Montana in the fuckin' dead of winter is a bad idea."

"I know." He slammed his fist down on the tabletop under the window and cussed when the skin on his knuckles broke and bled. "Son of a bitch! I can't sleep. I can't eat. I sure as hell can't fuck another woman, and I'm about to lose my mind." Grabbing a paper towel from the kitchen, he wrapped his knuckles to stop the bleeding and glanced at his brother. "Where's the number you found? I'm gonna try callin' her again."

"She's not takin' our calls, Beau. We've tried this how many times now?"

"I don't care. I need to hear her voice, even if it's just the voicemail." He sank down on the couch, laying his head against the back. "I never thought I'd find the woman I want to spend the rest of my life with by gettin' into a car accident. How in the hell did I fall in love with her?"

"I wish I knew," Brandon whispered, his voice soft and in awe. "If I had the answer to that, I wouldn't be feelin' the same way. I love her too, and it's drivin' me nuts not talking to her or being near her. We should never have left Red Rock without telling her how we felt."

"If those assholes from Nelson and Britchert hadn't corralled us onto the plane so damned fast, I would have. Hell, we were going after her when they caught us in the lobby. This is such a fuckin' mess. Callin' her house didn't work—her dad refused to tell her we called. Cade won't talk to us either."

"Do you blame them? They think we left her high and dry. Have you tried callin' her friend Becky? Maybe she can tell us how Emma is, at least."

Beau snapped his fingers and sat up. He grabbed his phone and dialed information for Red Rock. When he had Becky's number, he crossed his fingers and dialed.

"Hello?"

"Becky?"

"Yes, who is this?"

"It's Beau Tucker. Don't hang up please. I need to talk to you."

"Well, I don't want to talk to you, you asshole, or your brother, either. How in the hell could you leave Emma like that?" she snarled into the phone. "You're both fucking worthless pieces of shit, and I hope your nuts fall off."

The phone clicked in his ear. "Damn it! Is the whole goddamn town pissed at us?" Frustration and fear raced through his mind. What if they never got to see her again? What if he never held her again?

"Probably," Brandon replied. "But I have one more idea. Didn't you say you met Emma's gram when you went out to dinner with her?"

"Yeah, but she basically threatened to haunt us for the next hundred years if we hurt Emma. She's probably put a spell or something on us already."

"Call her. I think she'll listen," Brandon said. He lifted a beer bottle to his lips.

"You didn't even meet her, Brandon. How would you know?"

"Just a gut feeling."

"Fine," Beau growled, dialing information again. Thank goodness Emma had mentioned her grandmother's real name after their conversation at the restaurant. His gut felt like a rock as he punched in the phone number.

"Hello?"

"Mrs. Oliver?" he asked, hope filling his heart.

"Yes? Who is this?"

"It's Beau Tucker. I met you at the restaurant in Watertown, the night Emma and I went to dinner. Do you remember me?"

"I'd say so son. I hope you aren't back in Red Rock. I wouldn't be surprised if there wasn't a bounty on your head for leavin' the way you did. Want to explain it to me before I come after you with my shotgun?"

His heart started to hammer for the first time since they'd left Red Rock. "Yes ma'am, I do. You see, I had called Brandon's management company and cancelled the shows he had coming up for a few weeks in order to have time with Emma and give the garage time to fix his bus. His management company took matters into their own hands and sent someone out to Red Rock to fetch us home like a couple of wayward children. We didn't have much choice but to leave, or they could have cancelled Brandon's recording contract."

"You know you hurt her, right?"

"Yes ma'am, and we aim to make it right."

"Oh? How do you plan to do that?"

Beau's heart sank. Her gram was their only hope, and she didn't sound too forgiving either. "We aren't sure, really. She won't take our calls, Becky hung up on us, her dad and Cade won't talk to us..."

"Do you blame them?" the woman asked. "She's been a mess since you two skipped town."

"No, I sure don't, but we can't explain if no one will talk to us."

"I'm listening, son, so spill it. I ain't got all day." Silence enveloped the phone line as he tried to think of what else to say. "Do you love her?"

"Yes ma'am, and so does my brother." Hope raced through him. At least her gram had given him a chance to explain. "He's standing here next to me, nodding like a crazy fool."

A bubbly chuckle met his ear, and he smiled for the first time since Emma had run out the door, taking his heart with her.

"Did you tell her?"

"No ma'am, but we want to rectify the situation."

"Then I suggest you high-tail your asses back out here and tell her."

"It's not quite so simple. Brandon has another month of touring to do before he can take any time off and—"

"I'll ask this again, son. Do you love her?"

Beau sat in silence for several moments until the light bulb went on in his head. "We'll be there tomorrow mornin' ma'am."

"That's what I wanted to hear, son." Mrs. Oliver rattled off her address and said, "Come by here when you get off the plane. I'll get her over here where you can talk to her privately, without her family and friends hovering. She hasn't spent much time alone the last couple of months, I'll warn you of that now. She's even been datin', although no one I want her tied to. You boys are special, and even though I never got a chance to meet your twin, if he's like you, you'll both make a damned nice addition to the family."

"Thank you, Mrs. Oliver. You're a doll!"

"No thankin' me until you get things situated with Emma. I'm not guaranteein' she'll listen when she does see you both, but I know she's been miserable since you left. Now I'll let you go, since you've got plans to make, and I'll see you tomorrow."

The phone clicked in his ear, and he turned to Brandon with a smile he knew about split his face.

"So, what did she say?"

"We're goin' to Red Rock tomorrow."

"What the fuck?" Brandon's eyes were wide and disbelieving as he turned back toward Beau from his pacing of the living room. "We can't get there from here in one day, Beau. Are you nuts?"

"No. We're using some of your hard-earned money, Brandon. We're flying there, and I don't care if we have to rent a private plane—we are going to Red Rock to see Emma."

* * * *

Emma drove down the snow-covered streets of Red Rock toward Gram Oliver's house. Christmas was fast approaching, and Gram had asked for help with the baking and decorating she did for the local hospital every year. Today they planned to bake cookies and make candy.

Her radio blared country music, and she tapped her fingers to the beat of a new song. She hadn't heard it before, but she knew the voice—she listened to it every night on her cell phone before she went to bed. She still had every message they'd ever left her on her voicemail. No, she couldn't talk to them, but she could listen to their words and pretend they loved her like she loved them. It helped—God knew why, but it did. She knew they'd had to go, and she really couldn't blame them for how everything went down during the last day she'd seen them this summer.

Her friends and family, however, blamed them for everything, and she hoped they'd never set foot in Red Rock again—they might not leave here alive. Kale and Laurel had threatened to lock them up and throw away the key. Cade and Natalie wanted them dead. Becky and Seth wanted to castrate them both. And her dad? Oh, Lord. If he ever got hold of them, not only would they not leave here alive, he'd bury them somewhere in the middle of his pasture, and no one would ever find the bodies.

But Gram, God bless her soul, understood. She never said a word about Beau and Brandon the day Emma came over and cried until her heart felt lighter and she could actually say their names without breaking down. Gram understood she loved the two stubborn men, but she also knew Emma couldn't leave Red Rock.

Or so she'd thought. Since Beau and Brandon left, she'd done some thinkin'. Being with them meant everything to her. They were her other two-thirds. The two of them together completed her, and she'd made plans to fly out to Nashville next week and get the whole thing out in the open. She had to. She couldn't continue this way. Her plan had holes, yes, but she didn't know what else to do except talk to them and find out their true feelings. Did they love her like she loved them? Did they want her to be a permanent part of their lives? Those questions needed answers, and the only way she knew how to get them was to be in their faces.

Gram's house came into view, and Emma smiled. Grandmother Oliver always went all-out when it came to Christmas, and this year was no exception. She had various inflatable ornaments scattered across her lawn. Twinkling lights surrounded every window and the eaves of the house, and Emma wondered who'd put them up there. "Probably Cade." A huge Christmas tree filled the whole front window of the house with its colored lights and accoutrement of ornaments from sixty-eight years of marriage to Doctor Oliver.

Emma pulled into the driveway and shut the engine on her truck off as she stared at the brightly lit house. Someday she wanted her own house, with a loving husband and a passel of kids. Unfortunately, at the moment, there were only two men she could imagine her life with, and she still needed to work things out with them. "Soon. Next week I'll get this all straightened out one way or another. Either they'll declare their love for me, or I'll never see them again." Her heart cracked at the thought. It had only been four months, and she could barely function from day to day. The emptiness and loneliness wouldn't go away.

She grabbed her groceries and struggled out of the truck, slamming the door shut with her leg and almost losing her footing on the slippery driveway. "Cade needs to get over here and shovel this driveway before Gram breaks a hip or somethin'."

Emma looked up to find Gram standing on the covered porch, her shawl around her frail shoulders, calling out, "Emma, quit talking to yourself, child, and get in here where it's warm. Damn, I'd swear it's fifty below out there."

After she stepped up onto the porch, Gram ushered her through the front door and quickly closed it behind them.

"Not quite, Gram, but close." Emma set the bags on the dining room table and leaned down slightly to kiss Gram's cheeks. "At least it's warm in the house."

"Did you bring everything I asked you to bring?"

"Yes'm, but I'm a bit confused why you wanted the duct tape?"

"Oh, somethin' I think might require it. Nothing huge, but I wanted to make sure I had some in case."

Emma shrugged and started unloading the bags of groceries. "We're having dinner here, right Gram? I thought since we'd be baking all day, we could order some pizza for dinner."

"Fine by me, honey, but make sure you order, like, four larges."

"You and I can't eat that much pizza." Emma looked at Gram and wondered what was going on. *Has Gram lost her mind? Maybe a little dementia going on here?*

"Uh...well, I want some for leftovers. You know I love cold pizza. And Cade will be bringing Alan over tomorrow afternoon so he and Natalie can go Christmas shopping for him." Gram pulled out her recipe cards and spread them out on the countertop. "Why don't you do the fudge and divinity, and I'll work on the cookie dough."

Emma chuckled and grabbed the two cards she needed. The ingredients were simple enough, but she wasn't much of a baker. "You just want to eat the dough."

The two of them worked side by side for two hours, but Emma noticed how Gram kept watching the clock, sometimes walking to the front of the house to peer outside. "Are you expecting someone, Gram? You seem awful nervous."

"Nope. Not me. I wasn't sure whether Cade and Natalie might come over. I invited Natalie to help us bake this afternoon, but she wasn't sure if she'd have time. She had a fundraiser to go to this afternoon."

The sun began to set behind the mountains as evening approached. It always got dark so early during the winter, it got depressing sometimes. Christmas music played softly in the background while they baked and chatted.

"Have you ever had a chance to talk to those two men you were seeing this summer?"

"Beau and Brandon Tucker?"

"Yes."

Emma bit her lip and sighed. "No, Gram, I haven't. In fact, I've been avoiding their calls since they left."

"Why, Emma? I thought you had feelin's for them?"

"I do, but I know they did what they had to do this past summer, and I wasn't sure if they cared about me enough to want me in their lives. Neither of them ever said they loved me," she said, stirring the batter for brownies.

"Do you love either of them?"

Emma set the bowl down and stretched her back. "Yes, Gram. In fact, I'm in love with both of them. Don't tell Dad or Cade, but I'm going to fly out to Nashville next week so I can talk to them. We need to clear the air, and the only way I can do that is to see them."

A quirky little smile lifted the corners of Gram's mouth, and her eyes twinkled mischievously. "I think you're doing the right thing, honey."

"Thanks." She hugged Gram and then went back to stirring the batter.

The doorbell rang, and Gram said she'd get it, while Emma spread the chocolate batter into the baking dish. Low voices reached her ear as whoever was at the door walked closer to the kitchen with her grandmother.

"Emma, honey. Can you come into the living room, please?"

She shrugged and said, "Be right there, Gram. I'm putting the brownies in."

Once the oven was set and the timer on, she washed her sticky hands and dried them on the spare dish towel sitting on the counter. The black apron she'd put on over her clothes had flour and batter all over it, so she slipped it off and laid it on the table.

The murmur of voices got louder, and she slowed her steps when she heard her name. Could it be Cade and Natalie? Gram had said they might be coming by. When she cleared the corner and saw who sat on the couch with Gram, her breath caught in her throat. She closed her eyes tightly and reopened them. Nope, nothing changed.

Beau and Brandon flanked Gram, who sat between them wearing a shit-eating grin. *No, no, no! I'm not ready for this.*

She spun on her heels and raced for the back door, stepping out onto Gram's patio. Snow swirled and blew across her face. Shivers rolled over her arms, but she wasn't sure if they were from the cold or Beau and Brandon's appearance.

The door slid open behind her, and she tried to decide what to do, her gaze darting back and forth.

"Emma? Come inside, darlin'. It's too fuckin' cold out there, and you don't even have a coat on," Beau said, taking a couple of steps toward her.

"I..." She shook her head and took two more steps into the blowing snow, but he was right there with her.

"Come inside," he whispered, taking her hand and drawing her toward the door.

Taking a fortifying breath, she allowed Beau to lead her into the house and toward the living room. Gram had disappeared, and Brandon stood near the fireplace, which crackled and popped with a cheery fire.

Beau pulled her down on the couch next to him, and Brandon took the other side. Each held one of her hands and stroked her knuckles.

"What are you doin' here?" she asked, not sure if she wanted to know. *What if they don't love me like I love them?*

Beau said, "We needed to talk to you, darlin', and we both felt the best thing would be to come here and see you."

"Why didn't you answer our calls, Emma?" Brandon asked, pain clearly etched on his face. "We tried several times."

"I know. I have all the voicemails."

"You know? Why didn't you call back or answer?"

Faced with her avoidance over the last several months, uncertainty bloomed in her mind. She didn't know what she'd do if they only wanted her for a few nights of wild sex again. "I...uh...I needed some time to sort everythin' out."

"Is it sorted now?" Beau asked.

"To some degree, yes, I think so—but how did you get time to come here? You had a month left on this tour."

"I still do," Brandon replied, bringing her hand to his mouth and kissing her fingers. "But this is more important. *You're* more important."

Her stomach rolled over, and her heart skipped a beat. "More important than your career?"

"Yes."

Emma sat back against the floral sofa and looked at Brandon and then Beau. "I don't understand."

"We're here because we love you, Emma. You mean everythin' to us, and we don't want to live without you anymore," Beau stated, his eyes serious and pleading.

"You, too?" she said, looking at Brandon.

"Yeah. I love you too, and I want you with me and Beau."

"But your career. What about that?"

"We've got it all worked out, Emma. You'll marry Brandon, and then we'll have a separate ceremony for all three of us. That way all of his assets and money will belong to you should anything ever happen to him."

She looked from one brother to the other twice and then got to her feet. She needed to maintain some distance so she could absorb what was going on here. "Did you just propose to me for Brandon?" she asked Beau.

His warm chuckle sent shivers down her back. God, she'd missed them—everything about them. The easy smiles, the twinkling eyes, the wicked lips. The torturous hands, and especially the daring way they made love to her. "I proposed to you from both of us...but wait, we need to do this right."

Both men got to their feet and walked over to her. Beau went down on his left knee and Brandon went down on his right. Each man pulled a diamond ring from his pocket and held it up in front of her.

"I love you more than life itself, Emma, and I'm askin' you to do me the honor of becomin' my wife." Beau took her left hand. "Please?"

Tears streamed down her cheeks. Never in a million years would she have imagined these two gorgeous men fallin' in love with her, much less askin' her to marry him. "How is it gonna work? We're going to live in a ménage relationship?"

"No one needs to know except our families, Em. It's our business and no one else's," Brandon replied. "No more excuses. Will you marry me?"

"And me?" Beau added.

"Yes, I'll marry you. Both of you," she replied, dropping to her knees in front of them.

Beau slipped his ring on her left ring finger, and then Brandon slipped his onto her right hand. "It'll stay there until we get the wedding ring on. Then we'll move mine to your left hand, too."

"So is there gonna be a weddin' or not?" Gram asked from the doorway to the kitchen. "Or do I need to get the duct tape?"

All three of them laughed, getting to their feet and wrapping Gram in their arms.

"Yes, Gram, there's gonna be a weddin'. Not sure when yet, but there will be," Emma said, kissing her grandmother's cheek and whispering, 'Thank you,' in her ear.

Epilogue

Flashbulbs blinked like streaks of lightning during a summer storm when they stepped from the limousine and out onto the red carpet stretched in front of them. Brandon held her hand and Beau placed his palm on her lower back. Whispers of gossip had surrounded them ever since they brought Emma back to Nashville after the wedding a little over a year ago, and they were rarely seen apart. No one knew for sure they'd made themselves a triad, but the rumor mill always speculated. Tonight, she didn't care what anyone said. She had her men at her sides, and the evening belonged to Brandon. He'd worked his ass off touring, promoting, and changing his image from the happy-go-lucky, partying, spoiled country star to a hard-working family man. The last two singles off his new CD had hit number one, and tonight he was up for several Country Music Association awards, including Entertainer of the Year.

"Brandon!"

Several people yelled, and girls screamed his name over and over. He flashed his million dollar smile and tucked Emma against his side.

A reporter from *Entertainment Tonight* stopped them. "Brandon, can we talk to you for a moment, please?" she asked.

"Sure."

"You've done so well this year. Two number ones already, and this album hasn't even been out six months. It debuted at number two on *Billboard*'s top 200. You've got a beautiful wife and you seem to be riding the golden rainbow. How does it feel?"

"I've been blessed."

Emma's heart swelled with pride at her husband and his accomplishments, but mostly at the love in his eyes.

"What's on the horizon?"

"You mean besides the birth of my child?"

Everyone around them chuckled.

"Well, yes. You've been a busy man lately."

"Yes, I have. Both my brother and I have been extremely busy. He has a successful buckin' bull business goin' on, I've had phenomenal success with this CD, and my beautiful wife is having my child. What more could I ask for?"

"Brandon!" someone yelled, and when Emma glanced toward the railing separating them from the hoards of fans, a smile spread across her face.

"It's Charlene," she whispered against Brandon's ear.

"Get her over here," he snapped to a security guard to his left.

The guard brought Charlene from behind the barricade, and Emma hugged her even though her very pregnant stomach got in the way of a real hug. "You look fabulous, honey. How are you?"

"Good. Momma says the new medicine they have me on is working."

"I hate that you had to move here to be treated."

"It's okay. I kinda like it here."

"Where's your parents, Charlene?" Brandon asked.

The little girl pointed to the right and her parents waved frantically. Brandon and Beau glanced at each other and Beau nodded.

The reporter had moved onto someone else behind them, and the next thing Emma knew, Charlene and her parents stood next to them.

"Tickets?" Brandon asked, in the twin-to-twin thing Emma couldn't possibly understand, even though she lived with these two.

"Right here," Beau replied, pulling them from inside his jacket pocket. "They aren't the best."

"It's fine, son," Charlene's dad said. "We're pleased as punch to be here tonight."

Emma glanced at Brandon and then Beau. "I knew you two were up to somethin', when we were getting dressed."

"Not us," Brandon replied with a wicked grin and a quick kiss to her lips. "I wish your family could come, Emma."

"Its fine, honey," she replied, placing her palm against his cheek. "They support us from afar with our relationship and your career."

"Yes, they do. They've been fabulous."

They made their way inside with the wave of people. Charlene and her parents went toward the stairs leading to the balcony, and she, Brandon, and Beau took the aisle down toward the front, where their seats were. She knew they'd be close, but wow. She never would have imagined being here with all the stars she'd listened to over the years. George Strait, Reba McIntyre, Carrie Underwood, and several others mingled and talked.

Once the festivities got going, everyone took their seats, and the show began. Watching this on television couldn't compare to the long program while you sat in the seats. Brandon's first single from the new album received Song of the Year, and the video, which they'd filmed on their ranch, won Video of the Year, but the big prize still hung in the balance. Emma wanted him to win Entertainer of the Year. It meant everything to him, and now the moment had come. The names were read, the cameras focused on each artist's face, and the presenters arrived at the podium. Emma thought she'd be sick from the nervous butterflies in her stomach. She glanced at Beau, and his warm smile and reassuring presence calmed her jittery nerves. The presenters cut up and laughed, making jokes and dragging out the moment until she wanted to scream for them to hurry up.

When the moment came, they said, "And this year's Entertainer of the Year goes to...Brandon Tucker!" The crowd erupted in ear-shattering screams, claps, and whistles. Brandon leaned over and kissed Emma on the lips before making his way to the stage in front of his peers and fans.

With his award held aloft, he said, "Thank you so much for this. You have no idea how much it means to me to the have the respect and love of all my fans and family." He stopped for a moment like he needed gather himself, and Emma wanted to hug him. This past year of touring had taken its toll on him, her, and Beau, but they'd made it.

Beau took her hand and squeezed her fingers between his. "He'll be fine. Give him a minute."

"Sorry folks," he choked out as a tear escaped and slid down his cheek.

He brushed it away with his fingers and motioned for her and Beau to come up to the stage.

"What's he doin'?"

"I don't know, darlin'," Beau replied, taking her hand and helping her waddle up the stage stairs.

Being seven months pregnant with their first child made it hard for her to get around these days, but she wouldn't have missed tonight for anything. Tonight belonged to Brandon. He'd spent months and months traveling back and forth from shows while she and Beau kept the home fires burning. Beau had stayed home with her, holding her every night, working the cattle they had, breaking horses, raising the bulls Beau wanted, and being ranch owners, while Brandon toured. Sometimes she and Beau flew to where he was playing so they could spend some time together as a trio, but it had been hard on Brandon. When she'd realized she would be having their child, she hadn't been able to hold back. She'd told Beau first, since Brandon was doing a show in San Antonio that night. Beau took matters into his own hands and flew them both out to be with Brandon when she told him about the coming birth of their child. They'd laughed, cried, kissed, and made love while they'd wrapped her in their loving arms.

"Brandon?" she asked when they made it to his side.

"Hush, wife," he scolded and a twittering of laughter echoed through the hall. "I'm sorry to take so long, but I need to say this in front of everyone. This award goes to all three of us. Emma has been my rock over the last year and a half, and Beau—God, Beau. You've been one of the most important people in my life since I started this crazy circus ride."

The crowd laughed again.

"We all know being a country music artist isn't all fun, games, and money. It's hard work. You're gone for days, weeks, or months at a time while your family stays home and keeps things normal. Beau and Emma have been keeping my life stable for the last eighteen months while I pursued my dream of being a singer. Today, with my wife," he moved his hand over her protruding belly, "my child, and my twin brother by my side, I thank you from the bottom of my heart for this award." He held the award up with one hand and wrapped his arm around her waist. "Here's to all of you, my fans. The best is yet to come!"

The End

1

DIFFICULT CHOICES
Montana Cowboys 4

Sandy Sullivan

The distinctive low growl of the Harley vibrated through Delaney Dunn as she pulled the drain plug to change the oil on Mr. Abraham's truck. When she glanced out the open bay doors of the shop, her heart tripped over itself for a moment. The soft curve of the fenders, the sleek black paint job with the specialized accents of a custom spread made her sigh and press her thighs together. Strange how one of those bikes could make her hot, but they did. The sound of the engine, the smoothness of the ride and, oh yeah, a certain rider could do it too. God, she loved Harleys. Shiny chrome tailpipe, handle-bars and mirrors sparkled in the late summer sun, almost blinding her to the rider. Night Rod Special. *Sweet.*

Black leather chaps encased long, lean, muscular legs. One dark boot-covered foot shoved the kickstand down to brace the bike. A nicely emphasized ass met her view for a moment when he swung his right leg over the back to stand next to it. How she knew the rider was a man she wasn't sure, except most women couldn't handle a bike like that. Well, except maybe her.

Long slender fingers pulled the zipper down on the black leather jacket before yanking it off his shoulders, revealing bulging biceps ripped with strong muscles hard enough to absorb a touch of a finger or the punch of a fist.

Breathe, Del, breathe.

A white wife-beater tank top molded to an impressive chest, and a flat, oh-so-lickable abdomen. The man leaned slightly, giving her another drool-worthy view of his ass when he unsnapped the chin strap on his helmet and pulled it off. Shoulder-length jet-black hair settled around his shoulders, making Delaney's mouth go dry.

The man turned toward the gas pumps as he pulled his wallet from his back pocket. A small stud diamond twinkled in his earlobe. His straight nose, full lips and long eyelashes were all too familiar.

It can't be! God, please no. I can't handle this right now.

Delaney didn't realize her steps took her outside the shop's bay doors until she'd already moved halfway to where he stood. As he turned toward her, one side of those fantastic lips tilted up in a smile. Her heart sped up right before it slammed to a stop.

"Delaney," he said in the low-pitched voice that still sent shivers down her back.

"Jake." His name on her lips felt foreign and unwelcome.

"Still doing what you do best, I see."

The amusement in his gaze rankled her nerves. Everyone knew she worked on engines—any engine since she'd been old enough to crawl up and get her hands under the hood of a car, truck or tractor.

Her gaze locked with his and the heat wavering between them still burned scorching hot. "The years have been kind to you, Jake. Hot as ever, I see." She brushed a piece of hair off her cheek. "What are you doing back in Red Rock? When you hightailed it out of here, I really thought you'd never darken the streets of this hole-in-the-wall town again."

"I've got some business to take care of. Personal business."

"Really. Hmm."

She glanced across the street noticing several people milling about near the diner, while she tried to get her wayward body under control again. Her sister-in-law, Laurel, stood talking with Emma Weston near the curb. The vague thought of what her police officer in-law was giving Emma grief over crossed her mind.

Everyone knew everyone in Red Rock, but Del and Emma had grown up together. Since their brothers were best friends, it would have been difficult for them not to know each other fairly well. The two women were total opposites though. Tomboy to the core, Delaney worked on cars, played with trucks and constantly had dirt under her fingernails. Emma, on the other hand, did the cowgirl thing, the cheerleader thing and the boyfriend thing—not necessarily in that specific order.

With her bottom lip between her teeth, she chewed nervously. The unease Jake's presence caused her pissed her off. She never could hide her emotions very well, but the last thing Jake needed to know was how uncomfortable he made her.

When she looked at him again, she said, "Well, I hope you get things taken care of quickly so you can be on your way again. I know Red Rock isn't your speed or your home anymore. I, for one, don't want you here any longer than you have to be."

She spun on her booted heels and headed back for the open shop bay, but she knew he couldn't just let her walk away. Jake would never let her get in the last word.

"Delaney!"

Slowly, she came to a halt, never turning around. She buried her shaking hands in her coverall pockets, clenching her fists into tight balls.

"We're not done," he growled. "Not by a long shot."

Unable to stop herself, she glanced back over her shoulder. "Yes we are, Jake. We were done a long time ago."

Delaney stepped inside the cooler interior of the shop bay and moved to her workbench. Her hands trembled as she tried to grab the wrench she needed to change the filter on the truck. The growl of the bike starting rumbled low in her stomach, spreading heat through her veins like molten lava. Harleys had a distinctive sound and the hum ramped up the desire seeing Jake started. After the sound of his bike faded in the distance, she finally let loose the breath she'd been holding and threw the wrench clutched in her fist across the garage.

"Damn it!" She pressed the heels of her hands against her eyes to stop the tears. *I will not cry. Tears don't help—never have. I'm not going to let him get to me again.* "Son of a bitch!" she yelled, as she sank to the concrete floor. Heart-wrenching sobs shook her shoulders as scenes of their past came back in full force.

The first day of shop class her freshman year.

"All right kids. I'm Mr. Long. I'll be your shop class teacher. During this semester we'll be learning some basics about working with tools and equipment. I know several of you are already advanced in these areas, but we have to treat everyone like they've never touched a power tool." The kids chuckled. Delaney looked from one boy to the next, taking in the scene around her. Most of them she'd known since grade school, but one stood out. Jake Monroe. Yes, she knew who he was. The two of them had been in several classes together over the years. Friends they weren't. He always seemed standoffish. Didn't smile much. Kept to himself. She knew he didn't have a father around and his mother worked as a waitress at the diner. They lived in a small house on the edge of town—him, his two brothers and two sisters.

"Delaney? Are you sure you're supposed to be in this class?" Mr. Long asked.

"Yes, sir."

"I don't think I've ever had a girl want to be in shop." He shrugged, glancing at the papers in his hands. "Has your father or anyone showed you anything about this kind of thing?"

A couple of the boys chuckled again. Obviously, Mr. Long hadn't heard about her. Her gaze shifted from the teacher and locked on the sexy hazel eyes of Jake. The skin between his eyebrows crinkled when he frowned.

"Yes, sir. I help out a lot at home."

"With what? I'm assuming you mean something besides baking and housework."

Embarrassment swept through her, heating her cheeks as she glanced at the floor. It wasn't normal for girls to want to work on cars, but Delaney did. She'd torn apart a carburetor by the time she'd hit age ten, completely rebuilding it for her father, all by reading a book.

"No sir. I like working on engines. I want to learn more about rebuilding one."

Mr. Long laughed and her embarrassment deepened. "You...want to learn about rebuilding an engine? Women don't work on cars, Delaney."

"Well, I do and my name is Del. Everyone calls me Del." From that moment on, she'd hated Mr. Long. Luckily for her, he didn't last long.

"I still think you're in the wrong class...Del. I'll be discussing this with your counselor later this afternoon. Until then, stand in the corner over there out of the way so you don't get hurt."

Several boys snickered and she shot them a scathing glance, but when she looked at Jake, the understanding in his eyes almost did her in. Kindred spirits—that's what they were.

After the class was over, she walked out with the boys to head for her locker. She knew what she wanted and she planned to get it, one way or another.

"Sorry, Del. I know you want in the class, but it sounds like Mr. Long ain't gonna let you," Marty said, holding the door open.

"It'll be okay, Marty. I'll learn like I've learned everything else. I'll find a manual and do it myself."

Jake walked by, glanced her way for a moment and she followed his stride with her gaze as he kept walking. Her budding female body reacted to his in ways she wasn't familiar with. She needed to talk to her mother or one of her older sisters. Oh, she knew about sex just like every other teenage girl. Every guy in high school had one thing on their minds—sex. Well, she wasn't interested. Or was she? Lately, she didn't know. Thoughts of Jake's lips on hers, of his arms holding her tight, of his body pressing hers down on a bed, seemed to occupy her mind more and more. It wasn't right. Jake's reputation for being a bad boy would put him out of any kind of acceptance for her family. Maybe talking to Rhonda would be better. She'd understand—hopefully.

The dinging of the bell indicating another customer brought Del back to the present and the work at hand. She needed to finish this job. There were a few more requiring her attention before she could quit for the day, sink into a tub of hot water with lots of bubbles and wash Jake Monroe from her mind.

Two hours later, she closed up the shop, locking the doors on her way out. *Thank God this day is over.* Her classic Ford pickup sat in the back of the gas station—the pride and joy of her high school years. Unfortunately, it was also a constant reminder of her mistakes with Jake.

She started the truck, popped it into gear and pulled out of the parking lot. Pickup trucks lined the road, some with stock trailers attached, others with bags of livestock feed or bales of hay. More trucks pulled into the local honky-tonk as the Friday crowd gathered to wet their whistle with a beer or two. Loud country music ebbed and flowed with the swing of the doors. She actually contemplated getting cleaned up and joining them, but decided against it. Red Rock, Montana didn't have a ton of choices for entertainment. The locals did what they had to do to spice up their lives, which included a bar fight or two.

The moment she cleared Red Rock, she pointed her truck toward home. The huge tub in her apartment over the barn called her name. With every intention of taking advantage of the deep, soothing water with a glass of wine and some classical music, she'd be damned if she'd think of Jake. Her parents had converted the loft into an apartment for their children's use. Her brother Kale didn't need it since he'd built his own home several miles outside of town, living there with his wife and their kids. The love she felt for her brother knew no bounds and she'd never been happier the day he'd married Laurel.

The long road to the ranch house came into view, making Del sigh. The need to be alone drove her onward until she pulled into her spot next to the stairs leading up to her apartment. Seeing Jake today shook her to her soul.

As she opened the door to her place, her cell phone rang in her pocket. After she glanced at the screen, she flipped it open. "Hey, Rhonda. What's up?"

"Are you home?"

"Just walking in the door."

A pause of silence swept across the line, before Rhonda said, "What's wrong? You sound...I don't know...tired, upset—something."

Delaney sighed. She never could hide anything from Rhonda. "Jake's in town."

"What? Seriously? Jake Monroe?"

"Yes, Jake Monroe. He came by the gas station," she replied, dropping her keys on the bar before she unzipped her coveralls. Her boots came next as she toed them off and set them near the couch.

"Did you talk to him?"

"Like I had a choice. I own the gas station."

"I know, honey, but God. Jake." Rhonda cussed under her breath, making Delaney smile for a moment. "What did he say? What does he want?"

She shimmied out of her overalls, stripping down to panties and bra. "He said he had some personal business to take care of. That's all." She shifted the phone to her other ear. "I told him I didn't want him here."

"There's more to it. Spill it, Del."

A weary sigh escaped her lips as she tipped her head back on her shoulders. "He also said we're not done."

"Not done? How can you not be done? You haven't seen him in five years."

"I know all this, Rhonda. He made his choice when he left. I've made mine. I'm with Colby now."

"Speaking of Colby..."

Thank you for changing the subject. I really don't want to explore the wounds I thought were closed.

"What about him?" she said, heading for the bathroom to turn on the water and pour in some bubble bath.

"Isn't he out of town this weekend?"

"Yeah. He's riding in Billings at the rodeo over there."

"How come he didn't stay in town for the Founder's Day one here? You know there's usually a pretty good purse for bullriding."

"I know, but he's ridden against everyone from here. He wanted some new talent to challenge himself with." Del walked back in the kitchen, heading for the refrigerator. The half-full bottle of red wine in the door would do the trick. Mind-numbing would commence shortly.

"This isn't good, Del. Jake's in town and Colby isn't."

"It doesn't matter. I'm not going there with Jake again. The bridge is burned, buried, stomped into dust. I refuse to resurrect it." She grabbed a hefty wine glass from the cupboard, poured the wine until it reached almost the brim, and then took a big swallow.

"You're drinking."

"Damned right I'm drinking and I plan to get drunk."

"Are you sure you don't need me to come over?"

"No, Rhonda. It's fine. I'm going to climb into a tub of bubbles, drink some wine, curl up with a good book and go to bed early. I have someone manning the station this weekend so I can be out at the rodeo. I'm taking some time off for a change, even if it's only a couple of days."

"All right. I'll leave you alone, but if you need me, call me. Okay?"

"Okay. Thanks. You're a great friend."

"Yeah, I know. I'll catch you tomorrow sometime."

After saying their goodbyes, Delaney walked into the bathroom and shut off the water. She set her glass of wine on the edge of the tub, dropped the rest of her clothes on the floor and then sank into the heavenly bubbles with a soft sigh.

With her head back against the rear of the tub, she closed her eyes, letting the memories take her. Thinking about him and allowing all those feelings of betrayal, loneliness and hurt to swell inside her would be the only way she'd be able to keep things in perspective while Jake was in town.

"Jake!" she yelled, laughing as he chased her around the inside of the barn.

"You can't get away from me that easy, Delaney. My legs are longer and I'm faster than you are."

"Maybe, but I know the inside of this barn better than you do." She ran around the edge of the hay stack, her laughter ringing in the rafters of the huge space when Jake jumped over some of the bales. A quick dart to the left and she ran for the loft ladder. If she could make it up, she could hide in the corner...until she let him find her. She hit the second rung with her right foot and scrambled up three slats before his hand closed over her ankle and yanked her down. Her loud screech echoed around them as she twisted around before tumbling backward. Jake's strong arms wrapped around her, cushioning her from the fall with his hard chest.

"Not quick enough," he murmured, a huge smile on his face. "Now, you'll pay for denying me." He grabbed both her hands, holding them above her head. "A kiss will do...for now."

His eyes sparkled with mischief. With his body over hers, she could feel the full length of his cock nestled between her spread thighs. God, she wanted him inside her. They'd been lovers for six months now and she couldn't seem to get enough of him. They'd been side-by-side for months working on the classic vehicle, polishing it, messing with the engine until it purred. In the process, they'd become best friends. Ever since the final touches had been put on her truck, their friendship had bloomed into love.

The softness of his lips closed over hers, making her moan in response. His free hand slipped up her side to cup her breast in his palm. Heat streaked from where he thumbed her nipple through her top, straight to her clit. He knew exactly what to do to bring her straight up to oh-my-God-I-need-you-inside-me-now.

"Jake, please," she whispered when his mouth moved across her jaw to her ear.

"I want you so much, Delaney."

"I need you, Jake. God, please. I need you inside me."

"No. Not this time," he murmured, lifting his head.

What the hell does not this time mean?

"Slow and easy, baby. I'm gonna make you scream for me."

"Next time. Please."

The wicked grin on his lips told her he was in control. He'd give her what she wanted, but on his timeframe not hers. She loved when he made her wait, but there seemed to be an urgency in her today she couldn't quite understand. The last couple of weeks Jake had been pulling away and it terrified her. She loved him. Surely, he knew that.

He trailed his lips down her neck and across her collarbone as his fingers worked at the button on her jeans. When he finally got it free, she lifted her hips, helping him pull the pants and her underwear off in one fell swoop.

"You're gorgeous." One finger swept from her belly button to her mound. "Soft and glistening wet for me already." Her breath caught in her throat with the brush of his callused fingers over her clit. Her inside coiled tighter and her belly quivered with need. She wanted his mouth on her...now. He must have read her mind. With a sexy wink and a twinkle in his hazel eyes, he bent his head. The sweep of his tongue against her clit had her eyes rolling back in her head.

"Ahhh..."

"That's a start, but you can do better, babe."

Several quick flicks of his tongue on her clit sent her spinning out of control with a burst of colors behind her eyelids. Her scream of climax startled the chickens in the coop outside as they squawked their unhappiness loud enough to wake the dead.

He kissed his way up her stomach until her shirt stopped his movements. Undeterred by her clothing, he skipped over them until he could reach her lips. "Better. I love when you scream."

"It's a good thing no one is home, Jake Monroe. My daddy would have your hide if he knew what we were doing out here while you're supposed to be working."

Jake's eyebrows dipped as he frowned.

"What?"

"Nothing, babe," he said, the frown disappearing a moment later. "Spread those thighs for me. I'm not feeling very patient anymore. I need to feel you wrapped around me." After he quickly fumbled with the button on his jeans, he pushed them down around his legs, swirled the head of his cock in her juices and then plunged in with one swift thrust of his hips. "God, you're incredible, Delaney. You feel so perfect. I'm so glad we aren't using condoms anymore. I love to feel every ripple of your sweet pussy."

Her pussy twitched at his dirty words, but she loved every one. He made her feel special...loved. Every stroke of his cock inside her sent her desire spiraling again. With both legs wrapped around his hips, she rode the wave of pleasure he created with his body until she couldn't hold back anymore, her climax washing over her in a crashing wave of sensation. Jake followed closely behind her with a deep groan.

The low rumble of her daddy's pickup sounded in the distance, startling her back to reality.

"Shit. Jake, Daddy's home."

They both jumped to their feet, scrambling to pull their clothes back into place before they were caught literally with their pants down.

"Do I have straw in my hair?"

"Of course you do, Delaney. We just fucked in the hay."

"Help me get it out. He'll know the minute he sees me." She quickly picked at her braid, attempting to pull the bits and pieces from her hair.

"I'm sure he has an idea we've been having sex."

"I don't care if he thinks he knows. I don't want him to be disappointed in me. If he thinks I'm having sex with..." *Oh shit.* She quickly tried to apologize as her words sank in. Jake's face flushed red with his anger. "I'm sorry, Jake. I didn't mean..."

"With who, Delaney? The local bad boy? The ranch hand? The guy not good enough for the precious daughter of The Double D's owner because he barely graduated high school in June and now doesn't have a clue what he wants to do?"

"Don't. That's not it at all. You know it."

"No, I don't. We've been sneaking around and hiding every time we go out. We go two towns over so people don't see us when we want to go to a movie or something. As friends it's fine, but being lovers isn't."

Tears welled up in her eyes and she stepped closer. "Please, Jake. I care about you."

"Not enough to tell your daddy we've been having sex for months though, right?" He raked his fingers through his hair as he spun around. "I'm done, Del. I'm outta here."

His words sliced through her heart with quite efficiency. He never called her Del. She'd always been Delaney to him—his Delaney. "Where are you going?"

"I don't know. Frankly right now, I don't care. Somewhere away from here. I'm not going to be your mistake anymore, Del."

His footsteps never faltered as he headed for the door of the barn, disappearing around the corner. Moments later, she heard the low rumble of his motorcycle when he hit the ignition. Gravel sprayed the side of the barn, pinging against the metal like a rain of nails piercing her and drawing blood. She'd shored up her heart that day, never forgetting but always loving the man who'd walked away.

Tears rolled down her cheeks as she sat straight up in the bath tub. Five years. Five fucking years since the day he walked out of her life. Choking sobs broke from her lips and she buried her face in her hands. She hated him with every fiber of her being for leaving her like he did. He never called—never came back. He'd just disappeared. Now he was here. Back in Red Rock, but why?

The bath wasn't helping anymore so she climbed out and quickly toweled off. *More wine.* She grabbed the half-full glass, downing the rest in one gulp. A good buzz would be required to get through tonight.

A loud knock on her door made her frown. *Who in the hell could that be?* Dad and Mom were gone for a week on a long-needed vacation. The ranch hands should all be at the bar unless an emergency cropped up. "Shit." The knock sounded again. "I'll be right there." She grabbed her fluffy bathrobe off the end of her bed and slipped it on. It would have to do. "Maybe Rhonda decided to come by after all," she said, tying the belt on the robe before she headed for the door. Another impatient knock had her cussing under her breath.

"What?" she snapped as she ripped open the door only to have her heart stop. "Jake."

2

Easy, Jake.

God, she looked gorgeous. Even more so than the last time he'd seen her with sunlight lighting her hair like a halo, pieces of hay sticking out of her braid, and her blue eyes sparkling with tears. He'd missed her terribly over the last five years, but he was back to settle some things between them.

The door rushed toward his face as she tried to slam it, but he quickly blocked it with his boot.

"Leave me alone," she yelled, trying to get the door shut past his foot.

"No. Not until we talk."

"I don't want to talk to you. I want you to leave—leave Red Rock. Go back to whatever hole you crawled out of."

With a hand against the door, he forced her back so he could get inside. He'd come to make some decisions about his life, starting with her.

"I'll call the cops."

"What are you going to tell them, Delaney? Your ex-lover is back in town and forced his way into your apartment?"

"My sister-in-law is a cop. She'll make you leave."

Jake pulled out his cell phone and handed it to her. "Here. Call them."

Her hands shook when she reached for the phone. With a sigh of resignation, she dropped her hand to tug the robe she wore tighter around her. "Fine." She moved toward the couch and plopped down on one end. "Talk, so we can get this over with."

"Damn it woman."

"Don't cuss at me, Jake Monroe. You're the one who walked out."

He raked his fingers through his hair before he sank down on the leather armchair across from her. "Yes, I did and I kicked my own ass for it every day since I left." Dropping his hands between his knees, he sighed. "Everything happened so fast, I didn't know what to do anymore. You got to me, Delaney. It wasn't supposed to be like that. I started thinking of what happens next and it scared the hell out of me. We were only eighteen."

"You could have stayed. We could have talked then, Jake."

"I know, but you would have wanted to fix everything like you always do. I couldn't handle my life like that. I worked on your daddy's ranch. I barely kept myself fed and everything I earned went to help my mom. Thoughts of anything beyond the here and now wasn't in the cards. I had nothing."

"You had me."

"I know, but it wasn't enough."

"Where did you go?"

"Los Angeles."

"Doing what?"

A rueful laugh escaped his lips. "Worked on cars and bikes. I got pretty good at sheet metal. I customize Harleys."

She ran her hands over her arms, before she tucked her palms between her knees. The bathrobe rode up on her leg, exposing the soft skin beneath. He knew she wasn't wearing much under it, if anything. His cock hardened at the thought of her nakedness. Everything centered on Delaney, how soft her skin had been, how tight her pussy wrapped around him, how blue her eyes were at the precise moment of climax. He'd give anything to kiss her, feel those petal-soft lips under his again.

"You never gave up on your love of Harleys though."

"Neither did you. I saw the bike by the stairs. I assume it's yours."

"Yeah."

Silence stretched between them for several moments.

"I hear you're dating Colby Mason," he said, feeling his heart rip in two. If she only knew the other reason he felt the need to run.

She nodded. "We've been dating a couple of years."

"No wedding plans?"

The small snort from her lips made him smile.

"I don't think Colby will ever settle down. He's too busy chasing bulls on the PBR circuit." She shrugged and chewed her fingernail for a moment, a habit he knew signaled her uneasiness. "It works for us. I don't need a permanent fixture in my life either. I've got too much to do with the gas station."

The pride he'd felt the day he heard about her buying and taking over the local gas station rushed through him again. His little businesswoman and kickass mechanic. *No, not mine. Colby's—at least for now.* "I'd heard you bought it."

Her expressive blue eyes widened in shock. "You checked up on me?"

He focused on the carpet under his boots. "Yeah."

"You know you could have told me all of this five years ago, Jake. If you felt the need to sow your oats, make a name for yourself or whatever, I would have understood."

She got to her feet and walked to the window with her back to him. The curve of her butt reminded him how he'd wanted to take her ass so bad, his balls ached, but he'd never gotten the chance. Sex between them had been explosive. The pleasure he'd felt the day she'd given him her virginity had stayed with him for all these years.

Unable to stop himself, he stood and moved up behind her, placing his hands on her shoulders. They'd always been perfect for each other, at least in his mind, from the moment she'd smiled at him their freshman year of high school in shop class. The day Mr. Long refused to let her stay in class until her father had raised hell at the school board meeting. Something about equality in education. When she'd come back to class the next week, she had her shoulders back and a bright smile on her lips.

A sigh slipped from between her lips as she leaned back against his chest. He ran his hands up and down her arms, inhaling the sweet scent of Delaney. Her head reached to just above his shoulder, making her fit against him like a glove.

"I've missed you," he whispered against her hair. "More than you'll ever know."

She turned in his arms and glanced up so their gazes locked. Desire sizzled, crackling in the air around them. He couldn't stop himself from tasting her—one time—one kiss. Her lips parted as if she knew this would happen, and her eyes drifted shut. The moment his mouth found hers, all the years slipped away and once again he stood with her in the dusty barn, their playfulness and laughter echoing through the empty rafters above them. Her body molded to his, her breasts pressing against his chest and a soft moans escaping her mouth only to be caught by his. He cupped her face with his hands, holding her steady so he could devour her mouth. While their tongues dueled, their hands explored, familiarizing themselves with each other after so many years.

"Jake. God, Jake." She gasped as his lips moved to her neck.

"I need you, Delaney," he whispered in her ear, loving the shivers rolling down her body with each brush of his lips.

The ring of her cell phone cut through the tension rushing between them like a knife through butter.

"Fuck. Colby," she snapped, pushing Jake away. "That's Colby." In the process of her answering, she'd hit speaker as she flipped the phone open and answered with a breathless hello.

"Hey, babe. What were you doing? You sound out of breath."

She shot a nervous glance at Jake and tucked a piece of hair behind her ear, saying, "I just got out of the bathtub and had to rush for the phone. I thought you were riding tonight."

"I am, but I'm between rides so I thought I'd call you." They could hear the cheers of the crowd in the background. "I missed you." Jake felt like shit. He'd been kissing all over another man's girl. "Are you going out to the rodeo in town this weekend?"

"Yeah. I figured I'd hang around with Rhonda since you weren't going to be here."

"Cool." Another cheer roared as they heard the announcer in the background say his name. "I gotta go, babe. I love you and I'll call you later if I can." The phone clicked off, but Jake heard Delaney whisper, "I love you too."

She'd never said those words to him.

Without waiting for her to say anything else, he pulled his keys out and headed for the door. He couldn't stay. Knowing she loved Colby felt like she'd grabbed his heart, torn it from his chest and stomped on it with her combat boots. He whipped open the door and rushed down the stairs to his bike.

"Jake, wait!" she called from the doorway. "Don't leave like this. Not again."

He stopped for a moment, looking up. Her hair blew around her head as the wind caught it. The bathrobe molded to every curve. His body screamed for release—a release from the tormenting desire rushing through him with every breath. She'd felt it too. He knew she did by the way she sighed. The desire between them burned brightly and there would be no putting it out this time without some serious emotional breakdown on both their parts. They needed to put some things to rest and it wasn't going to happen overnight.

"I need to think, Delaney. I'll see you tomorrow at the rodeo." He hit the ignition on his bike, slipped on his helmet and lifted the kickstand with his foot. After one quick glance at the woman who'd stolen his heart, he turned the bike and slowly rode down the long driveway. This time he wasn't leaving in a rush or a cloud of dust. This time he would fight for the woman he loved or he'd put an end to them forever. Either way, the running and fighting his feelings would be over. But he had one more thing to do before he could come to terms with his relationship with Delaney. He had to face Colby.

* * * *

Sleep came with difficulty for Delaney. She tossed and turned feeling Jake's hands on her—Jake's lips on hers. Even after a cold shower, she couldn't sleep without dreaming of Jake. *Damn him.* The sun peeked over the horizon, cutting through the blinds like a razor against her gritty eyelids. Might as well get started on the day. She had a lot of thinking to do.

All her best thinking came on horseback so she saddled up her favorite mare and headed out along the fence line. Not that it needed checking, but it gave her a reason for being out here at daybreak rather than just because she had men on the brain. Men as in plural. *What the hell am I going to do? I love Colby, but it's a safe kind of love—not the intense, mind-blowing feelings I have for Jake. I never got to tell Jake I loved him before he took off, but I sure don't want to give in to those feelings now, not knowing what the hell is going on in his brain. Besides, I'm not sure I still love him.*

Her horse snorted, plodding along like they had all the time in the world to contemplate life.

"Yeah, right," she said out loud. "Not still in love with him, my ass."

In her sophomore year of high school, she and Jake had become friends. He'd come out to work for her dad on the ranch, rustling steer, branding cattle and doing all the other things cowboys do. It caught her as funny in the beginning because she couldn't fathom Jake as a cowboy, but he buckled down and learned everything he needed to know. Respect came hard on a ranch, but Jake managed to gain the high opinion of many.

One day, she'd been working on her truck in the barn when he'd come in from the fields to put his horse away.

"What'cha doing?" he'd asked, stopping next to her.

"Fixing my truck."

"Your truck? Really?" He scuffed his boot in the dirt. "I suppose your daddy bought it for you so you could try your hand at rebuilding an engine."

"Sort of. I'm doing all the restoration on it. The engine is just the start. It didn't run when he bought it last year, but I've replaced everything from the cylinders to the transmission. She purrs like a kitten now. Want to hear it?"

His eyes opened wide. "Yeah." When she started the truck and let it idle, he'd whistled softly in appreciation. "Nice."

"Thanks."

"You doing the body work too?"

"Eventually. I'm not good with sheet metal though. I may have to hire someone to do it for me, but I want it perfect. I've even bought some fenders off another old one without so much rust."

"I'll do it."

She shook her head and smiled. "You know sheet metal?"

"Yeah. It's what I do in shop if you hadn't noticed. I don't go in for all the woodworking stuff."

From that day forward whenever someone wanted to find Delaney or Jake, all they had to do was look in the barn near the old Ford. Hour after hour they'd work side-by-side, laughing at jokes, telling each other stories and dreams—building a friendship she thought would last a lifetime. It did, until the friendship turned to love.

Jake had come into the barn one day after school of their senior year. Instead of finding her in overalls with her hair in a dirty ball cap, she stood near the truck in cut off shorts, tank top and her hair in a braid.

"You planning on working in that get up, Delaney? You'll get grease all over it."

"I wasn't going to work on the truck today, Jake. I thought maybe we could go for a ride," she said, looking at the dirty barn floor beneath her boots. Her fingers nervously played with the braid, flicking the end with her finger.

"A ride. Why would we want to go for a ride?"

"I don't know." She threw up her hands, stomping to the fence surrounding the arena. "I thought maybe you'd like to get to know more about me, Jake."

"Like what? I thought I knew all your secrets. I mean, you told me about how you didn't like the frilly stuff your sisters did with their hair yet here you are with yours in a braid. You told me about how you liked playing in the mud with the pigs when you were little." He twirled the wrench he'd picked up from the tool box between his fingers. "We're buddies, Delaney, so what's this all about?"

"What if I said I didn't want to be your buddy anymore?"

Silence.

"Well, I guess if that's the way it is, then I'll go," he said after a moment, dropping the wrench back in the box. He turned and started walking toward the door when she grabbed his arm to swing him back around.

"What the hell is wrong with me, Jake?"

"Nothing. Why?"

"Why don't you look at me like a girl?"

He swallowed hard, staring right at her like he didn't know who she was. "I can't look at you like a girl, Delaney. If I did, I'd want to do things I shouldn't do with you."

"Like what?"

"Like this." He slid his arm around her waist and hauled her up against his chest. His mouth came down on hers, crushing her lips beneath his until she whimpered. He softened the kiss, sliding his lips along hers, coaxing her to open for him by flicking his tongue over her bottom lip. At the first brush of his tongue, she'd been lost—lost in the feelings her body didn't know how to handle. She tangled her fingers in his shoulder-length hair while pressing her body against his for everything it was worth. Her breasts tingled and her nipples hardened under her top. The dampness of her panties startled her. In her uncertainty, she pushed him away. They stood there in the middle of the barn staring at each other as their harsh breathing surrounded them.

"I'm sorry. I shouldn't have done that."

"I wanted you to, Jake."

"You did?"

"Yes. I..."

"Del? Where are you?" her father yelled from the porch of the house.

"Out in the barn with Jake, Daddy."

"Your mother needs you in the house for a minute. She's working on your prom dress."

"Prom dress?" Jake asked, his eyes wide and uncertain. "You're going to the prom?"

"Yeah. Colby asked me. I said yes."

"But, you just kissed me."

"I know, but the prom is just a dance, Jake. Not a big deal."

"Del?"

"Coming, Daddy." She glanced at him, and then walked toward the door. "Will you wait?"

He'd waited. They'd talked more as they both came to realize their relationship was developing into something more than friendship.

The night of prom came. Jake stood by the barn watching when

Delaney slid into Colby's truck and they drove off down the driveway. She'd wished it had been Jake taking her to the dance in his black tux, but she wouldn't back out on Colby either. Feeling like a fairy princess, she'd danced the night away in the arms of one of the best looking guys in her high school class—next to Jake of course, but when Colby had taken her home, kissed her sweetly on the cheek, and then left without a backward glance, she felt like crying.

"Delaney?"

"Jake," she whispered, jumping to her feet. "What are you doing here?"

"I've been here since you left."

"Why?"

"I wanted to make sure you got home okay," he replied, stepping up onto the porch with her. "You looked so beautiful, I wanted to sweep you up and carry you off somewhere so no one could see you but me."

She pressed her lips together as she laid her hand on his cheek. "Thank you. You have no idea how much that means to me."

"Would you dance with me?"

A small giggle left her lips. "Here? There's no music."

"I can hum."

"Okay."

Jake swept her up in his arms, slowly waltzing her around the big porch. Her dress swirled around their legs and she became the princess she always wanted to be in the arms of the man she'd dreamed of since she turned fourteen.

The ring of her cell phone in her pocket brought her back to her ride along the fence. She sighed when she read the screen. Colby.

"Hey."

"Hi, babe. Where are you?"

"Out riding. How did you do with your ride?"

"Great. I came in second. I have to compete again today."

"Awesome. Are you coming home tomorrow? I miss you."

"I hadn't planned on it. There's another rodeo not far from here starting the middle of next week, but if you need me to come home, I will."

"No. It's okay."

"What's wrong, Del? You sound funny."

Her relationship with Colby had grown over time. After Jake left, she'd been heartbroken and torn by what she felt for him. Not being able to talk about it with anyone, she'd turned to Colby. Rhonda knew, but she didn't know how much she'd blamed herself for what happened. All of what he said had been true. She'd hidden her relationship and her feelings for Jake from her family. No one knew they'd even been seeing each other. Her parents wouldn't have understood at the time. Hell, at eighteen she wasn't even sure what they had, much less how to explain it to her parents.

Colby knew something wasn't right shortly after Jake took off. He'd asked her one day in the barn what the problem was and the whole thing came pouring out. Everything from being friends with Jake to their relationship turning into lovers and not being able to tell her parents, to him leaving because he thought he wasn't good enough for her. Colby held her in the comfort of his arms while she talked. Three years after Jake disappeared, Colby asked her out on a date. They'd been inseparable ever since.

"Nothing."

"It's not nothing. I can hear it in your voice. I haven't heard you sound like this since—"

"Jake's here."

A string of cuss words exploded across the phone line. "I'm coming home this afternoon, Del. Don't do anything, okay? Please? Promise me you won't do anything until I get there."

"Colby, it's fine. Really."

"No, it's not. You've already seen him, haven't you? I mean, in private. Just the two of you."

She sighed, rubbing her forehead. "Yes. He was in my apartment when you called yesterday."

"Son of a bitch! Tell him to keep his fucking hands off my girl!"

"Colby, please." He sounded so hurt it ate at her soul. Hurting him like this wasn't in her plans, but then again, neither was coming face to face with Jake.

"No. He left you. Remember that."

"I know. It'll be fine. I promise. I'm not running off with Jake." Her horse had turned itself back toward home, trotting along at a fast clip.

"Okay. Good. But I'll still be there this afternoon. In fact, I'm leaving now. The drive doesn't take too long."

"You need to stay and ride."

"No, I need to be with my girl. I'll see you in a few hours. I should be there by one so I'll meet you at the rodeo since I know you're going there with Rhonda."

"Fine, but please be careful, Colby. You drive like a maniac anyway."

The chuckle on the other end told her he'd calmed a little. "I love you, babe. Please, remember."

"I love you, too, Colby."

"We'll talk when I get there. Stay away from him."

"I will. See you soon."

The phone clicked in her ear as the weight of the world settled on her shoulders. Love for Jake burned in her soul, but her love for Colby warmed her like a blanket in the winter sitting in front of the fireplace. She needed both of them to be whole, but loving two men wasn't possible, was it?

3

Jake pulled his bike into the rodeo grounds parking lot. Row after row of trucks and cars lined every available space. He'd forgotten how popular the Founder's Day rodeo was in Red Rock.

Word around town talked of a major country music artist doing a benefit concert at the rodeo this afternoon. Funny. No one of any popularity sang in Red Rock. It would be interesting to find out how this whole thing came about.

His palms itched as he brushed them over his jean-clad thighs to wipe the sweat clinging to them. He needed to calm down. Jumping Delaney now would be a bad thing, but damn, he wanted to hold her, kiss her and make love to her more than anything in the world. Taking it slow didn't seem to be an option, especially with Colby in the picture. Things were going to get very intense, he feared.

A brunette with huge boobs threw herself into his arms the moment he stepped off his bike. "Oh, my God! Is it really you? Jake Monroe?"

"Uh...yeah."

She stepped back with a huge grin. "You don't remember me. I'm crushed, Jake." The woman swung her finger between them. "Betty Carter. From high school?"

"Oh. Yeah. I didn't recognize you."

"I know. I kind of went back to my natural brunette color a couple of years ago." The woman pushed her hair up, tossing it off her shoulder. "How do you like it?"

"Nice, Betty. Real nice, but listen, I have to go. I'm meeting someone."

"Oh? I didn't know you had been back in town long enough to hook up with anyone, Jake, but then again, Del Dunn and you were good friends way back when, huh."

"Yeah. I *really* need to find her right now. Have you seen her?"

"She's in the beer tent, I think, talking to Emma Weston and her sister-in-law, Natalie. Did you hear about Natalie dating Emma's brother, Cade and Del's brother, Kale?"

"No."

"Yeah. Happened a couple of years ago, but you were gone then. Natalie is married to Cade Weston now. Kale is married to Laurel Hayes. She's one of the local cops."

Ah. The sister-in-law Delaney mentioned. "Delaney mentioned her yesterday."

"Oh? You've already seen Del? Then you must know all about her and Colby. They've been seein' each other for a while now. Gettin' right cozy, from what I hear. You know, back in high school I wasn't so sure Colby wasn't gay. I knew he did the football stuff, but I even came onto him a few times. He didn't look interested at all. Not like you, Jake. You had the bad-boy thing down to a T." She leaned over and whispered rather loudly, "But, I think Colby is gonna ask Delaney to marry him. 'Course, he's never home. Off doin' rodeo stuff all the time. I have no idea how a marriage like that would even work. I mean..."

Her voice trailed off as Jake left her standing near the stands. The last thing he wanted to hear was how Colby might ask Delaney to marry him. Hell, she'd probably say yes, and then he'd have to kill Colby.

Jake glanced at his watch. One o'clock. He'd told Delaney he'd meet her here, so hopefully he'd be able to find her easily enough. He needed to convince her to leave with him. Spending some quality time with her to convince her they belonged together held top priority. The relationship she had with Colby wasn't going to be easy to get around. Lucky for him, Colby wasn't in town.

Jake walked toward the beer tent and slipped under the open flap. Waiting for his eyes to adjust to the dimmer light, he saw the make-shift bar off to the back corner with several beer taps. Emma, and if he remembered right, her friend, Becky, were chatting up a storm as they poured beer after beer, but no sign of Delaney. A platform stood off to the left of the beer taps. Several speakers were being lined up, for what he assumed would be the benefit concert in a little while. He'd have to make sure he came back to listen. Country music always hit a home chord with him and he knew the family of the girl they were raising money for. The father went to school with him even though he'd been a couple years ahead of Jake.

Heading toward the taps, he figured he'd grab a beer so he could ask Emma if she knew which way Delaney went.

"Well, well. If it isn't Jake Monroe," Emma said, with her hand on her hip.

Even though they were all in the same grade in high school, he hadn't paid much attention to Emma. She had a cute model look with her thin frame, high cheekbones, long dark hair and abundant breasts, but she'd been the cheerleader type. So not up his alley at all. He liked them with pillowy breasts, soft, round curves and enough meat on them he wouldn't feel like he'd break them in half if he squeezed too tightly.

"Hey, Emma. How are things with you?"

"Good. I'm keepin' busy. Want a beer?"

"Please."

"Regular?"

"Yeah." He glanced around before resting his gaze on Emma again. "Someone told me Delaney was in here talking to you. Do you know where she might have gone?"

"Um, I think she might have headed toward the parking lot. She mentioned meeting someone," she replied, handing him his beer. "Three fifty."

After he handed her the money, he said thanks and walked back toward the front of the tent. Hopefully, he'd run into Delaney shortly if she'd been headed out to meet him.

The arena for the rodeo events sat off to the right as the crowd poured into the wooden bleachers getting ready to watch when everything got started. The announcer's voice cut through his thoughts.

"Welcome ladies and gentlemen to this year's Founder's Day Rodeo."

The crowd let out a huge cheer.

"Unlike previous years, we are going to run a few riders through on the bulls first since we have so many contestants. After five riders have gone, we'll move onto some calf-ropin', barrel racin', steer wrestlin' and even some kids' events so hang onto your hats folks, grab a beer, pull up a seat 'cause we've got a show for you." More loud cheering and stomping feet. Jake grinned like a fool. The people of Red Rock really loved their rodeo. "One more thing, folks. We are pleased to let you all know one of country music's hottest talents is spendin' a few days with us here in Red Rock. He's graciously donated his time to put on a benefit show this afternoon for our very own Charlene. Brandon Tucker will be putting on an acoustic show at three in the beer tent. Now, folks, admission is free, but we do expect everyone to drop a few bucks in the barrel we'll have near the door. Give generously. This is to help little Charlene's parents with her monstrous hospital bills."

"Brandon Tucker, huh? Interesting." Jake took a sip of his beer and glanced around. Where in the hell was Delaney? He headed back for the parking lot in search of her. With a crowd this size, the two of them could be looking for each other for hours. *Damn it. I should have got her cell number. Maybe I'll go back in the beer tent to see if Emma has it.*

He turned around and walked back toward the huge tent in the distance, sipping his beer as he walked. His thoughts raced back to yesterday and the kiss they'd shared in her apartment. Nothing had changed. The sparks between them still stole his breath. If her damned phone hadn't rung, who knows where they would have ended up. Between the sheets? Maybe, but Delaney wouldn't cheat. It wasn't part of her personality. She loved Colby. She'd said so to him on the phone. The pain Jake felt when he'd heard her sliced through him again.

What about Colby's feelings in all of this?

"Doesn't matter. She's mine. I had her first."

And you walked away.

"Shut the hell up," he growled, earning him a frown from a couple walking past. "Sorry. Talking to myself here."

When Jake reached the beer tent again, he stepped through the flaps only to glance toward the taps and find Emma wasn't there. "Shit. Now what?"

After another sip of his beer, he swept the interior of the tent with his gaze on the outside chance Delaney came back here. Not expecting to find her, he almost missed the woman standing in the corner with her hair back in a braid, a wispy floral blouse over a white tank top, and hip-hugging jeans molding to her enticing looking thighs. He still couldn't get over the changes in Delaney. She'd been beautiful all cleaned up five years ago, but now, she took his breath away. Jake took several steps in her direction until she turned to her right as a smile lit up her face. Seconds later, a big blond guy swept her up in his arms only to spin her around. Once he set her back on her feet, his mouth came crashing down on hers and he molded her to his body.

As the two people separated, Jake got a good look at the man holding his woman. *Fuck. Colby.*

* * * *

"Hey, babe. God, you look gorgeous," Colby said, sweeping Delaney up in his arms and spinning her around.

She laughed, swatting his shoulder. "Put me down, Colby."

Back on her feet, Colby lip-locked her like he hadn't kissed her in months instead of a few days. His mouth fused to hers, chasing all thoughts of any other man from her mind except him. Right now, she needed his steadying presence to right her world and chase away the temptation of Jake Monroe.

"Mmm," she murmured, pushing against his shoulders.

"I told you I'd be here at one."

"I know, but I wasn't sure," she replied, running her hands over his shoulders and down his arms. "Did you even stop to pee?"

"Nope. I needed to be here," he said, his eyes intense. "You needed me, Delaney."

"You're my rock." She brushed his lips with hers, before she glanced over his shoulder, stiffening in his embrace. "Jake."

Not aware she'd said his name out loud, she jumped when Colby dropped his hands and spun around. Jake stood several feet away, his passionate stare jumping between the two of them. She kept her hand on Colby's arm, saying, "Wait. Don't do this here. Please?"

Colby shook her off, not looking back. With a low growl, he swung, hitting Jake square in the jaw, knocking him to the ground. "Get up, you son of a bitch!"

"You got one shot, Colby." Jake stumbled to his feet. "You won't get another one."

A small crowd started to gather and Delaney stepped between the two men. "You aren't doing this here. Stop it. Both of you."

"Get out of the way, Delaney. This is between the two of us," Jake snarled, pushing her to the side and rushing at Colby.

The two men toppled over tables, fists swinging. Grunts exploded in the air when a hit connected. Blood splattered in several directions. Jake got on top and punched Colby in the eye. Colby rolled them both over, right before he got off a punch into Jake's ribs. Jake groaned and wheezed for a moment, giving Colby another chance at him until Seth Reardon, owner of the makeshift bar at the rodeo, grabbed Colby. "Is there a problem here? If so, take it outside."

"No problem," Jake snapped, his eyes sparkling with rage and frustration as he struggled to his feet.

"Yeah, there's a problem. You gonna keep your fucking hands off my girl, Jake, or I'll kill you."

"Try it, Colby. We're pretty evenly matched, I'd say." Jake's hands clenched into fists.

Delaney stepped in front of him and looked into his eyes. "Please, Jake. This isn't the time or place."

"You didn't tell me he was back."

"He drove in just now. I didn't know he would be back until I talked to him this morning."

"Stay away from him, Delaney," Colby said, pulling at her arm, but she tugged it out of his hold.

"Don't tell me what to do, Colby."

"What? You want him?" Colby threw his hands up. "Go then. Let him stomp all over your heart again when he walks, because he will, Delaney. You know it. He's not gonna stay. His kind never does. But don't come cryin' to me when he leaves." He wiped the blood from his lip. "I've been there for you. Every day I watched you wilt away until you finally told me what happened. I helped you pick up the pieces of your heart."

She turned toward Colby and stopped in front of him, placing her hand on his chest. "I know, Colby, please. I love you, but this thing between the two of us isn't over."

"I love you, Del. You know I do. Has he ever said those words to you?"

Her eyes burned as she blinked several times to stay the tears. "No."

"Then how can you even think of going with him?" Colby asked, placing his hands on her shoulders.

"I need closure or something. I'm not sure. This is all too confusing. I need to think."

"Marry me, Delaney," Colby said loud enough she knew Jake heard him when he hissed behind her.

"What?"

"Marry me."

"You can't be serious."

"I'm dead serious. I want you to be my wife," he replied, reaching into his shirt pocket to pull out a diamond ring. "Please?" He reached for her left hand, but she closed her fist.

"I can't do this right now, Colby. Don't ask me to. It's not fair," she said, moving away. "I don't want to think you're only doing this because you feel threatened by Jake."

"I'm not, Delaney. I love you."

"Can we talk about this later?" She glanced around, noticing the growing crowd. The benefit concert would be starting soon. "Alone?"

"Fine." He grabbed her hand. "Come back to my place with me then so we can talk."

"Not right now. I need to talk to Jake."

"Fuck Jake. This is between us."

"He's involved, Colby. I know you don't want to admit it, but he is."

"More than you even know, sweetheart," Jake said, from her side as he grasped her other hand. "Come with me."

Yanking her hands from both of them, she yelled, "Stop it! Both of you! I'm not some goddamn doggy toy you two can pull apart in your war with each other. What the hell is wrong with you?" She looked from one to the other. Something sizzled between the two men. Something she couldn't quite latch onto. She couldn't think with all the hostility. "Jake, we're leaving." She turned to Colby. "I'll call you later tonight and you can come over to my place so we can talk."

"Don't leave with him, Delaney." The fear and love in Colby's gaze almost dropped her to her knees.

"I need to. I have to sort this out. The only way I know how is to spend some time with both of you...separately." The smirk on Jake's lips pissed her off and she almost decked him herself. "Don't think you've won, Jake. This isn't over by a long shot." She left both men standing in the middle of the tent as she headed toward her truck. *God, the two of them! They'll be the death of me at this rate.*

By the time she stopped at her truck, Jake was at her side.

"Where are we going?"

"Back to my place, but meet me there in an hour."

"Why?"

"None of your damned business," she snapped, yanking open the door before she slid inside. She needed to talk to her mother before this all blew up in her face.

Fifteen minutes later, she pulled into her parents' yard, parked her truck next to the barn in her usual spot and cut the engine. *God, this won't be fun.* Bothering them during their vacation wasn't the best option, but she didn't know what else to do. She couldn't keep going on with this charade without them knowing about her past.

She grabbed her bag from the seat, pushed open the door and slammed it shut behind her before she headed up the stairs. The apartment door opened easily under her hand and she let the soothing colors and warmth of her own space surround her. She shut the panel to the outside world, closing herself off from the mayhem and drama of the last couple of hours.

After a deep sigh, she pulled out her cell phone, slid onto the couch cushion and found her mom's number.

Her mom answered with a cheery, "Hello, Delaney. How are you, sweetheart?"

The sound of her mother's voice soothed her shattered nerves. "I'm fine, Mom. How's the vacation?"

"Really nice. We've got a great little cabana all to ourselves right on the beach. Of course, you know your father. He's constantly worrying about things at home."

Delaney grabbed a piece of hair, twirling it around her finger. "Everything is great here. No problems from what I understand. I've talked to Matt and he hasn't mentioned anything."

"He probably wouldn't either, Delaney. You know how men are."

"Yeah. Oh, do I ever."

"What did you say, honey?"

"Just something about knowing men." She bit her lip for a second. "Mom, is Daddy there with you? I need to talk to both of you."

"Of course. Let me put you on speaker phone." Delaney heard a small click. "Hey, sweetie. Is everything okay?"

"Yes, Daddy. I just needed to talk to you two for a minute or two. Something in my personal life has come up and I need to come clean before you hear it from someone else."

A slight hesitation on the phone had her heart pounding. "Go ahead," her mother coaxed.

"You know Jake Monroe and I were really good friends back in high school. He left kind of sudden not long after graduation."

"Yes," her father replied. "He didn't even really give me notice on the ranch. Just called later that day to say he wouldn't be coming back."

Come on. You can say it.

"The reason Jake left was because of me."

"How so, honey?" her mother asked.

She took a deep breath and blew it out slowly. "Jake and I were sleeping together. The day he left, we'd had sex in the barn. When Dad came back from town, he almost caught us. I didn't want to disappoint you two so I told Jake we couldn't let you find out about us. We'd actually been dating for several months, but we kept it quiet. We never went anywhere in town together other than like friends. Jake lost his temper, accusing me of being ashamed of him. How he wasn't good enough for the owner's daughter of The Double D and never would be because he'd barely graduated high school, could hardly feed himself and help his mother at the same time." Tears welled up in her eyes as one slid down her cheek. The pain she'd seen behind the mask of anger on Jake's face that day came back to haunt her again. "I wasn't ashamed of him. I cared about him a lot, but he was the local bad boy, you know, and I don't know. I just—"

"Sweetheart, it's okay. We knew all about the two of you."

4

Delaney's truck sat in its spot when Jake pulled up near the barn. Her hour was up and he damned sure wasn't going to give her any more time. Keeping her off guard with his presence seemed to be the only way he could get below her defenses and to the bottom of what her true feelings for him were.

He cut the engine as he dropped the kickstand on his bike.

Seeing her with Colby and Colby with her about killed him. Torn in half with feelings he wasn't sure he could face, he took the stairs to her apartment two at a time. Two raps on the door with his knuckles left him waiting for her to open it.

The soft patter of feet came closer until the panel swung wide. She stood in front of him, her eyes sparkling with something. Pleasure? Maybe. He hoped.

"You might as well come in," she said, taking a step back and turning toward the center of the room. "Would you like a beer? I have some in the fridge."

"Sure." Nervousness clawed at his belly, making his palms sweat. His fingertips tingled to touch her, but he knew he couldn't—not yet.

She returned a moment later, handing him the beer bottle. When their fingers brushed, the zing of the desire between them about singed his hair. Her eyes widened and she captured her lip between her teeth. With a heavy sigh, she turned away to take a seat on the couch. He returned to the chair he'd occupied yesterday, sipping the beer to calm his shaking hands if nothing else.

The pillow from the corner of the couch found its way into her arms as she hugged it to her chest as if it would protect her from him. "I wish I knew what to say."

"Say what you feel, Delaney."

"I can't, Jake. It's not that easy." She jumped to her feet and started to pace. "I cared about you so much. God, it killed me when you left."

"I'm sorry."

"No! No, you're not! You didn't think about me or anyone else. It all revolved around you and your damned stubborn pride." Her eyes sparkled with unshed tears. "All the time I was worried about my parents finding out we were having sex?" She threw up her hands and burst into a dry, rueful laugh. "They knew, Jake. The whole time—they knew."

"Wow."

"Yeah, wow. You know what else? They didn't care. To them you had the potential to be so much more than you were. Daddy gave you a job because he knew you could do a helluva lot. He saw the hard worker, the stubborn kid, the man beneath all of it that you would become given the chance. He wanted to help mold you."

Now he felt like shit. Her parents believed in him?

"You always thought you weren't good enough for their daughter when all they wanted was for me to be happy. You made me happy, Jake."

He stood and moved toward her with his hands out. "We still can be, Delaney."

A tear slide down her cheek, making his heart hurt with the need to comfort her, hold her, and protect her.

"You can't waltz back into my life and turn it upside down like this."

"Give me a chance. Give us a chance. I want to make it up to you." He cupped her face with his hands, using his thumbs to brush away the tears.

"I moved on, Jake—with Colby," she whispered, her hands grasping his wrists, but not pushing him away like he thought she would. "But why do I still want you so bad?"

"Because Colby can't give you this." All the pent up desire and all the rushing need spiraling through him since he saw her yesterday burst through his defenses. Her mouth called to him like a siren's song. He couldn't stop the kiss even if he tried. Gentle nips at her lips forced her to gasp, allowing him access to the warm cavern he craved. A soft moan escaped her as she allowed her tongue to duel with his, giving into the desires they couldn't deny. He slid his hands into her hair and pulled her against his chest. When he finally broke the kiss, their harsh breath mingled in the air between them.

Would she surrender to the fires burning inside her? Give into the flames he saw raging in her eyes?

He skimmed his palm down the front of her shirt so he could feel whether her body reacted to him like it used to. Her nipple had already pulled into a tight nub when his palm slipped over the crest, drawing a shudder from her.

The buttons on the front of her blouse gave way to his insistent fingers, one by one. Parting the material, he pushed his hand inside to shove her bra out of the way. The need to feel her soft, velvety skin again drove him past rational thought.

"Jake," she whispered, pushing her breast further into his palm.

She grasped the front of his T-shirt bunching it up until it reached his armpits. Forced to let go of her breast, he grabbed the shirt and whipped it over his head.

"God, you're gorgeous. So much more defined," she murmured, running her hands over his shoulders, down his pecs and across his abdomen until she reached the waistband of his jeans. She glanced up, parting her lips as she cupped his straining erection.

"Be careful, babe. It's been primed since I rolled into town."

"For me?"

"There's never been anyone else, Delaney." *You're such a liar, man.*

"Let's see."

She dropped to her knees and unbuttoned his pants. The rasp of his zipper sounded loud in the quiet room, but the moment her lips surrounded his cock, he lost himself in the feel of her mouth. Soft lips closed over the head, pulling a groan from deep inside him. Seconds later, she followed the large veins running from the base to the tip with her tongue. He couldn't stop the slow rock of his hips. Both of his hands fisted in her hair, holding her head just so, loving the feel of her mouth.

"Delaney, stop. I need to be inside you," he growled, pulling her up by her shoulders.

He took her mouth again as he quickly toed off his boots and shoved his jeans down his legs so he could step out of them. Next, he hooked his fingers in her belt loops to pull her in tight. Getting her naked became the priority. Her jeans gave him no trouble when he unbuttoned them and pushed the denim toward her feet, along with her underwear. He trailed his lips over her cheek until he reached her ear. After nipping at her earlobe, he continued down her neck, across her shoulder. The peak of her nipples thrust out from her breasts, begging for his mouth. A low growl left his lips as he closed over a tip, pulling it into his mouth.

"Oh, God." Her fingers tangled in his hair, holding his head firmly in place.

Jake released her breast and lifted her into his arms. Her legs slid behind his back, her feet locking over his butt, leaving her completely open to whatever he wanted to do.

"Where's your room?"

"Back through the doorway."

He walked with her wrapped around him toward the bedroom. The heat from her pussy almost scorched his cock as the tip rubbed her lips with each step.

Her bed sat in the corner under what used to be the barn rafters. The walls and ceiling had been sheet-rocked. It seemed only fitting the last time they made love in the barn and the first time again would be in the same place. Although, he much preferred the bed to the haystack. A skylight shared the night sky with her during her sleep or daydreaming hours. Did she ever think of him while she looked up through the clear plastic dome? Did she ever wonder where he'd gone? She'd said she missed him. How long after he left did she give herself to Colby?

Needing to clear his thoughts, he shook his head as he laid her on the bed. Right now, all that mattered was getting a taste of her.

"What's wrong?"

"Nothing," he answered, pushing her legs apart to slide his fingers through her wetness. "I'm gonna eat you up."

Her thighs quivered as a trickle of sweetness appeared at her opening. With the tip of his tongue, he scooped it up to spread it over her clit.

The stiffening little nub wanted to hide from him, but he wasn't about to allow it. Her pleasure hung on by a thread and he was about to cut it loose. He'd give her one easy orgasm to warm her up before the real lovin' would commence.

Soft moans and quiet whimpers escaped her lips with each swipe of his tongue on her clit. He pushed her desire higher by sliding two fingers into her hot depths and slowly moving them to the rhythm of his licks. Her channel gripped his fingers, sucking at them, sending out sharp spasms while it tried to hold him inside her.

"Jake." She panted in ragged, uneven breaths. "Pleeeasssee."

"I love when you beg."

He stiffened his tongue and made quick figure eights on her clit as he increased the speed of his thrusting fingers. Her body went completely rigid when her high scream of pleasure bounced off the ceiling. Her pussy clamped down like a vice.

God, I can't wait to be inside her.

Impatient to feel her heat, Jake slid up her body and positioned his cock at her entrance. One deep thrust pushed him home.

"Ahhh!"

Her pussy quivered, softening around him. "Easy, baby." He eased in and out, giving her time to adjust, knowing Colby's cock wasn't quite as long or as thick. *Fuck! Colby!* Jake stiffened.

"Jake?"

"I...can't."

"Can't?"

He swallowed hard and closed his eyes. *I'm not going to walk away from her again. I love her no matter what Colby is or was to either of us.*

"Can't wait, Delaney. God, you're so hot. You're killing me."

"Then move. Fuck me hard, Jake. Wash away the years. Make me yours again. Make me whole."

His big brain shut down as his little brain took over. The heat surrounding him pulled until he couldn't help but move his hips to fuck her hard like she asked.

Delaney pulled her knees up, opening herself to his deep thrusts, groaning with every slam of his pelvis against hers. Jake reached between them to thumb her clit. Her pussy clamped down on his cock and it felt like she might break him in two. Moments later, she lost control, her climax sent spasms along her cunt, milking him and dragging his own grunt of pleasure from deep in his gut. Cum shot from the end of his dick like a rocket to bathe her pussy with everything he had.

"God, Delaney. I hope you're on the pill," he mumbled, pulling out of her and rolling to her side. "I didn't use a condom."

"I am. I haven't been with anyone except you...and Colby." She bolted up in the bed and swung her legs off the side. "Shit. How could I have done this?" The glare she shot him would have shriveled a lesser man. "How could I let this happen?"

Jake grabbed her hand to pull her down to his side. "You can't deny the fire between us. It's always been there and always will be. What you have with Colby doesn't come close to this. You know it's true."

"Fuck you, Jake!" she shouted, wiggling to get free from his arms. "What I have with Colby has nothing to do with you. No, it might not be explosive, but it's safe, warm and loving. He loves me."

"And so do I!"

* * * *

All the fight drained right out of her when she heard his words. Did she believe them? Not really, but they warmed her heart anyway.

"Did you hear what I said?"

"Yes."

"And?"

"And nothing. It doesn't change things even if I did believe you," she replied, shoving herself out of his arms.

"I love you, Delaney. I wouldn't say it if I didn't mean it."

He reached for her again, but she moved off the bed to stare at him, wondering if he'd hit his head recently or lost his marbles somewhere along the way to Red Rock. He'd walked out of her life after a huge argument, didn't talk to her, call her or anything for five years and he apparently thought coming back here, spouting off a few words of love would fix everything.

"This isn't going to change anything."

"Making love with me isn't going to change anything?"

"We didn't make love, Jake. Two people have to love each other to make love. We had sex, pure and simple."

"Okay, we had sex. Explosive sex."

"Geezus!" She threw up her hands as she paced the carpeted floor. Every glance at Jake heated her blood so she kept her eyes trained on the wall, ignoring his gorgeous, naked body spread across her quilt. "What is it with men? All you ever think about is sex."

Jake jumped to his feet and stopped her movement with his hands on her shoulders. "I don't only think about sex, but having you standing here in front of me buck-assed naked, sure does short circuit any other thoughts."

"Fine." She grabbed at her bathrobe, but he stopped her with a hand on her breast.

"I like you naked," he murmured, his lips warm against her shoulder.

"This is wrong." Her bones felt like they had nothing left to hold her up. "It feels wrong. I've been dating Colby," she whispered, tipping her head to the side to give him access to her neck.

He cupped her face and stared into her eyes. "You said you wanted to spend time with both of us so you could sort things out. Then do it, Delaney, but do it with your whole heart. Compare us. Weigh how you feel in my arms—when I make love to you, to what you feel with Colby."

Moments later, he helped her slip on her robe, tying it securely at her waist. Confusion raced through her mind. *Doesn't he want me again?* She glanced at his cock. *Oh yes, he does.* Straight up and hard as a rock.

"Yes, I want you. More than anything, but I know you're confused. You told Colby you'd call him so you two could talk. I think it's a good idea even though I hate the thought of you alone with him. I know he doesn't like the thought of us here together either." Callused fingers pushed her hair behind her ear. "I love you, Delaney. I always have, but you have to decide whether we can get back what we had before or if you need to move on."

After a quick kiss to her mouth, Jake turned his back on her to walk into the living room. When she followed seconds later, he'd already pulled on his jeans and was working on the button. God, the man had it all. The jet black hair she remembered still hung to his shoulders in sharp angles. His whole body had filled out since she seen him last with hard muscles, lean planes and ragged edges. The hazel eyes she used to drown in like a pool of ever-changing colors, still sparkled with life. His lips could still melt her into a puddle with the slightest lift of the corner. The whole package of Jake Monroe wound her up in knots like a three-legged calf tie. He knew how to devastate her composure and yep—the look right there. The one eyebrow lift, sexy smirk on his lips, and those come kiss me eyes. Damn it, she was so screwed.

Once he'd completely dressed, he walked to her side. Saliva pooled in her mouth and she fought the urge to drool at the look in his eyes. Want, need, desire and even love reflected back at her as he slid one finger down her cheek.

"I'm gonna go. I'll call you tomorrow." He kissed her softly on the lips. "You do what you need to do."

When he turned to head for the door, she wanted to call him back—make him take her in his arms again and never leave, but she couldn't. She had a choice to make. It wasn't fair to turn her back on Colby. She loved Colby, but she loved Jake too. How could Jake possibly be okay with her dating or even sleeping with Colby after they had sex? She stuck her thumbnail between her teeth and snapped off a piece. Bad habit, she knew, but right now it was either bite her nails or hit something. He glanced over his shoulder, giving her one of his devastating smiles.

The low rumble of his bike going down the driveway made her want to cry.

God, this wasn't going to be easy. How in the hell am I supposed to choose?

With a heavy sigh, she picked up her cell phone and pulled up Colby's number.

"Hey, babe," he said after the first ring.

"Hey." The sounds of the music, clinking glasses and voices could be heard in the background. At the bar? Probably. "Would you like to come over?"

"I'll be there in five."

She laughed. "Make it at least fifteen, Colby. I don't want to find you splattered on the side of the road somewhere."

"Is Jake gone?"

"Of course. I wouldn't have you two in the same room unless there happened to be a doctor around. You two would kill each other." Silence filled the line for a moment. "We'll talk when you get here."

"This doesn't sound good, Del."

"Don't jump to conclusions, Colby. I love you. That hasn't changed."

"I'm glad to hear it. I love you too." She heard his truck start in the background. "I'll be there shortly."

"I'll see you in a few minutes then."

They said goodbye as she started to pace. What would she tell Colby? How would he take the fact of her making love with Jake? There wasn't any way around it. It had been making love. No matter how much she tried to tell herself and Jake it was sex, she knew in her heart they had made love. She wanted to again.

Before she knew it, Colby's soft knock sounded on her door. She blew out a heavy sigh as she opened it. Colby stood leaning against the doorframe with his arms over his chest and she couldn't help but compare the two men. Colby stood six feet three inches with hair the color of wheat cropped short to his head. He'd always kept his short in the back and a little long in front where Jake's brushed his shoulders in the back and hung along the sides of his face. Colby's body had the hard planes of a bullrider. Wide shoulders, trim hips, flat abdomen, firm thighs made up the whole package and then some. He could make any woman drool, including her. How she ended up with two gorgeous guys fighting over her, she wasn't sure, but man!

His intense blue gaze skimmed over her short bathrobe as a wicked grin creased his face, exposing the little dimple in his left cheek. Without a word, he pulled her tight against his chest, his lips crashing down on hers. His tongue swept inside her mouth and she couldn't help but moan as their tongues dueled. Two strong hands gripped her buttocks, lifting her so her legs straddled his waist, opening her for the sweep of his fingers.

"Damn, darlin'," he growled against her neck. "Already hot for me."

"Colby." She panted, pushing her breasts against him.

Without any kind of warm-up, Colby kicked the door shut and headed for the couch. "I'm gonna take you hard, Del. You got a problem with that?" He unhooked her feet from behind him to let her slide down his body.

Hard and fast? "But..."

"What, baby? I'm fucking horny as hell." A quick spin and she lay sprawled over the back of the couch on her stomach with her ass in the air. Two of his fingers pushed into her pussy. "Hot and slick. Don't tell me you don't want this."

"Yeah, I do."

The soft clink of his belt buckle being released and the loud rasp of the zipper had cream spilling down her thigh. Colby never fucked rough —never took her without a long, slow build up. This new side of him ramped up her need to boiling. Her heart skipped a beat when the hard, velvety softness of his cockhead swirled in her juices.

"Brace yourself, babe. I'm comin' home."

One swift thrust had him buried balls-deep in her pussy.

"Ahhh!" she screamed, widening her stance. "Yes!"

"Fuck, yeah. God, you're so hot. Burn me up, darlin'."

Colby set a pounding rhythm with his hips. All she could do was hang on for the ride. The slap of flesh against flesh and the sucking sounds of her pussy grasping at his long, thick rod, sounded primal, powerful.

Seconds later, he stopped to bury his nose in her neck. "I didn't mean to be so rough, but the thought of you with Jake..."

A sharp nip on her shoulder sent shivers down her spine. "It's okay. Don't stop."

"You want it hard?"

"God, yes, pleeaasseee."

Colby lifted himself from her back, grabbed her hips in his callused fingers and slammed himself against her. Each thrust sucked her further in until she couldn't think of anything beyond the spasms of her pussy. The edges of her thoughts blurred until she could do nothing but reach for the elusive edge. He slowed his thrusts, shifted his stance, and then changed the tempo. The new spot he hit threw her into an explosive climax as she screamed his name in a raw voice.

Several more hard thrusts and he shuddered, grunting his own release, flooding the inside of her pussy with a thick coating of cum. Colby draped himself across her back as their ragged breathing sounded loud in the room. After a moment, he lifted off her and slid out of her pussy. She couldn't move. Her muscles felt like rubber bands with absolutely no feeling left in them at all.

"Are you okay? I didn't hurt you, did I?" The rustling of his jeans behind her almost made her lift her head...almost.

"No," she whispered, her face pressed to the rear cushion of the sofa. "I'm fine. I just need a minute. I don't have any energy left to get up."

She heard a deep rumbling laugh seconds before he swept her up in his arms to head for the bedroom. "We're just gettin' started, darlin'."

Before she could stop him, he walked through the door and stopped dead in his tracks. The rumpled sheets and mussed pillows screamed her infidelity loud enough to wake the cattle.

"You fucked Jake?"

5

Colby stared at the long-neck bottle of beer in his hand, trying to decide what the hell to do. Anger and jealousy fed the raw emotions running through him with each breath. *How could she do this to me?* The minute he'd seen the rumpled sheets on her bed, he knew what had happened and hightailed it out of her apartment so fast, he'd left her standing on the stairs calling his name. Now he sat at the Boots 'n' Spurs drowning his sorrows in his beer like some loser.

The sex between them right before all hell broke loose was spectacular! Delaney never responded like a crazy woman before, but damn if he hadn't lost all control when he'd realized she'd met him at the door in her short robe, wearing nothing underneath. Their love making up to this point seemed definitely vanilla. He usually took his time building her up nice and slow—like a lady ought to be treated. The decision to keep his deviant side quiet hadn't been too difficult, until now. He wasn't sure he'd be able to keep his hands off her without revealing things he wanted to do to her, let her do to him.

The label on the bottle came off in a multitude of pieces while he picked at it with his fingernail. Things had been going great with Delaney. They'd been seeing each other for a couple of years and he really did love her. Spending the rest of his life with her would come with a price, yeah, but he'd be willing to pay it. If he had to turn his back on the way he was so Delaney would love him, then he would.

Why the fuck did Jake have to come back, especially now?

Jake.

Images of their past came back to haunt him as he tried to figure out how to handle the man. The two of them had been friends in high school. Both on the football team for a while, until Jake got tired of not being part of the group, or that's originally what Colby thought.

They'd all grown up in Red Rock together, but Jake was the poor kid from the wrong side of the tracks. His mama worked at the local diner, trying to raise her large family by herself after Jake's dad took off years ago. Jake, being the eldest, felt responsible for her and his siblings. Instead of being able to play football, do track or any of the other things in school, Jake went to work at the local gas station for a bit—until he got hired on at Delaney's daddy's place. The two of them worked side-by-side many days since Colby worked there too. Branding cattle, riding and mending fences, days spent skinny dipping in the water trough on the hill—Colby had loved those days. Actually belonging to a group of men who looked out for each other, the camaraderie, the joking and the fun all helped heal him from the hard-handedness of his own father. It sure seemed Delaney's dad took in some messes in those days.

Things went from bad to worse the summer of their senior year when his dad beat his mother again. She'd finally had enough.

The day his parents died came back in vivid detail.

Smoke and flames licked at the wooden beams of the house when he'd come racing into the yard. Their spread wasn't far from Delaney's and the moment he saw the smoke over the horizon, his gut told him something was terribly wrong. He'd jumped into his truck, speeding home only to find the whole thing engulfed. Sirens blared in the distance, getting closer by the minute, but Colby had tried to save his mom by rushing into the inferno over and over. The firemen had to physically restrain him from going back in the last time as the roof caved in.

In the aftermath, Delaney's parents had taken him in. He'd stayed in the bunkhouse at their place, worked the cattle and finished high school. No one ever knew the true extent of his hell on earth. The daily beatings his mother took shook Colby to the core. He could never understand why she didn't leave.

Colby knew Jake and Delaney were inseparable during their senior year. The two could hardly be in the same room without setting the place ablaze. Their attraction crackled the air around them. Jake often talked about her when they rode fence, but never believed he would be good enough for the boss's daughter.

The day after Jake and Delaney made love for the first time, Jake couldn't keep quiet about it. Sun scorched their shoulders as the early spring day bloomed. Cattle mooed in the distance, breaking the silence.

"We did it."

"Did what?" Colby asked, his gaze scanning the horizon for fence breaks.

"Had sex."

"You and Del?"

"Yeah. Yesterday. In an actual bed even. Her bed."

The smile on Jake's face sent a pang of envy through Colby. "Cool."

"That's all you can say, Colby?"

"What the hell do you want me to say, Jake?"

Jake pulled his Stetson down further on his forehead and adjusted his sunglasses. "I don't know. Congratulations. Way to go, man. Awesome."

Unable to fathom the feelings rushing through him, Colby kept quiet, eyeing the building thunderhead in the distance. It would rain soon and he hoped they wouldn't be caught in it. At least the north pasture line shack wasn't too far if need be.

"What's gotten in to you, Colby? Are you jealous or somethin'?"

"No."

"Doesn't sound like it to me. I didn't know you wanted Delaney for yourself."

"I don't."

Jake threw up his hands and kicked his gelding into a trot, not waiting for Colby to catch up. *What is wrong with me anyway? I like Del. I'm happy she and Jake have gotten together.*

"God, I'm such a liar," he mumbled, giving his own horse a nudge to catch up with Jake.

Black clouds rolled over the horizon so fast they hardly had time to make a break for safety.

"We're gonna get wet!" Colby pointed to the line shack with a tip of his head hoping Jake would get the message as he kicked his horse hard, racing for shelter. Both horses slid to a stop at the hitching post just as rain came down in a sheet, soaking both men within moments.

"Fuck!" Jake snapped, jumping down from his horse, tying him quickly and taking a dive at the porch. "Where the hell did that storm come from?"

"Does it matter?" Colby grumbled, stomping his boots to loosen the mud after he got to the porch. "We'll be here for a while if those black clouds mean what I think they mean. They ain't movin' much so it's gonna downpour for a bit." He grabbed the handle on the cabin door and pushed it open.

Jake marched in behind him, dropping his hat on the one table in the room. Not much to these shacks other than a bed, a table, a couple of chairs and supplies to last a day or two at most. The furniture wasn't fancy—basic wooden pieces to sit on. The bed had a thin mattress, a set of sheets and a couple of blankets. The windows were bare of curtains. A hot plate on the small countertop in the makeshift kitchen, and a little fireplace in the corner with a hefty stack of wood beside it completed the picture.

"I'm gonna build a fire so we can dry off some," Jake said, squatting next to the fireplace. Within moments, he had a cheery fire heating up the room nicely. Even early spring could get chilly when these storms moved through. A cold front could whip the temperatures from mid-fifties to freezing in no time.

Jake stripped his long-sleeved western shirt off, revealing a broad muscled chest with a smattering of chest hair. It wasn't like Colby had never seen his friend without a shirt, but for some reason, the planes and valleys of his muscles caught his attention today.

"What?" Jake asked, noticing his stare.

"Nothin'."

"No, it ain't nothin'. You're lookin' at me funny." Jake rubbed his wet hair with his shirt before he laid it out over the back of the chair. "I'm gettin' out of these wet jeans. I hope they dry before we have to ride back. I hate ridin' in wet pants."

Colby's mouth went dry as Jake unbuttoned his Levi's and dropped them to the floor. His friend went commando.

Fuck! Saliva flooded his mouth at the size of Jake's cock. Long, lean and soft, Colby wanted to lick until it stood up straight, begging for more. He closed his eyes and held his breath. *I'm not gay. I'm not gay. I like girls.*

"Are you okay, man? You look pale."

"I'm fine," he squeaked, clenching his fists to keep from reaching for Jake.

"You need out of those clothes too, so they can dry," Jake said, his own voice now a husky, low rumble.

Colby opened his eyes to see Jake standing directly in front of him. Black pupils almost eclipsed the hazel of his eyes. Hot breath fanned his cheek. Colby felt his nipples pebble and his dick harden. They looked at each other for what seemed like hours. Terrified to move lest the spell be broken, they continued to stare at one another as rain pounded on the tin roof of the cabin, tapping out a song.

Could Jake want this too?

"Jake," he whispered, breaking the spell, but not the tension in the room as Jake wrapped his hand behind Colby's head and crushed their mouths together. Their tongues danced from his mouth to Jake's. Breaths mingled, stopped and restarted. Tension built in every muscle and every curve of his body. He had to touch. The need to feel Jake's hard body under his hands drove him past reason straight into blazing need.

The plunk of buttons hitting the wooden floor when Jake ripped the shirt from Colby's shoulders sounded loud in the still room. Nothing would have prepared him for the mutual attraction they felt for each other—something that had been smoldering between them for years. Moments later, he groaned when Jake pushed the jeans around his hips down to rest against the tops of his boots. The next moment, Jake took his dick in his mouth.

"Holy fuck!" Colby hissed. The warmth of the lips surrounding him made him so hot, his skin prickled from the heat. Like a fiery ball of need ready to explode, everything inside him burned. He wanted to shove his cock down Jake's throat to make him swallow every drop of cum. Colby grabbed Jake's head to guide him into a rhythm. Stroke after stroke brought him closer. He'd never felt anything like this. Nothing prepared him for another man sucking his cock. Girls had done it a time or two and he'd enjoyed it, but this—holy hell!

The second Jake released him, his body shook. He needed to come so badly, he hurt.

"Not yet," Jake said, grabbed his jeans from the floor, pulling out a silver packet from his wallet. "I'm gonna fuck you in the ass. Got a problem with that?" Jake rolled the condom over his thick erection. Colby shuddered at the sight of Jake's cock. The person standing in front of him shook him down deep.

"No," Colby whispered, toeing off his boots and pushing his jeans off his feet.

"Good. I want your tight asshole gripping me list a fist." Jake stroked his cock from root to tip. "Ever had a man in your ass, Colby?"

"No."

"I have once or twice. It's incredible, but it's even better having your cock in a tight ass whether it be male or female. I like both."

Colby licked his lips as a tremor raced through him at the heat in Jake's gaze. Could he really let Jake do want he suggested?

"Bend over the bed," Jake growled, continuing to stroke his hard length as he walked into the kitchenette for a second.

Hot and a little intimidated by the person showing himself now, Colby bent over the end of the bed, pressing his chest to the sheets.

The cool slide of some kind of oil hit the crack of his ass, sliding down between the cheeks.

"Lube. Oil from the cupboard," Jake explained, pushing a finger past the ring of muscles.

"Goddamn," Colby hissed at the burn.

"Easy." The finger swirled around several times, stretching him. "Damn, you're tight. This is gonna feel so good."

Two fingers—more oil. *Fuck! The burn!* The fingers slid in and out with a slow, tantalizing rhythm. Colby felt his ass relax.

"That's it. Relax. Let me make this good for you."

Three fingers pressed through the ring of muscles, opening him wider. *God*. The feeling wasn't something he could describe. Pain mixed with pleasure. A small burning sensation eased off with each stroke of Jake's fingers in his ass.

"Ready?"

"Hell, no."

Jake chuckled as he removed his fingers. "Try to relax. When the pressure builds, ease back against me. We'll take it slow."

The broad hard head of Jake's cock pressed against Colby's ass. Pain. Oh fuck, the pain and burn. Colby hissed and moaned as the prickling sensation in his ass turned to a dark pleasure with each inch Jake shoved up his ass. He felt impaled—stretched beyond what he could handle, but Jake continued until the touch of Jake's balls hit his own.

"God, you feel incredible. Tight and hot. So fucking hot."

A small rock of his hips gave Colby the unbelievable urge to push back against Jake. Unable to quite understand this black need between them, Colby demanded, "Fuck me, damn it. I need this!"

The slap of flesh against flesh drowned out the pounding of the rain on the roof and windows. Groans and grunts from Jake as his cock slammed deeper and deeper, only spurred his need to be fucked and fucked hard. Colby grabbed his own dick in his hand, stroking the length at the same blinding pace of Jake's cock.

"Don't you dare come," Jake hissed, grabbing Colby's hips in his hands. "You'll wait for me." Colby ground his teeth together, holding back his climax with everything he had until Jake growled his release. "Come now, Colby. Right now."

The exploding flash of color behind his eyes almost blinded him as his cum shot out the end of his cock and sprayed across the sheets in several spurts. "Fuck!"

Losing his balance, Colby fell forward on the bed effectively pushing Jake out of his ass, his breathing ragged and tortured. He tried dragging air into his lungs, but everything in the room seemed to suck it right out of him. Lead weights would be easier to lift than his arms at this moment.

A hard hand came down on his ass cheek, startling him into a rapid roll onto his back. "What the hell?"

"Just making sure you survived," Jake said with a smile, completely unashamed of his nude body or the fact of their sexual romp into male on male sex.

Heat flushed his cheeks and he threw his arm over his eyes. He'd had sex with another guy. *Oh hell!*

"You okay, Colby?"

"No!" he snapped, jumping to his feet, grabbing his clothes. The wet material made it difficult to dress, but he didn't care. He needed to get the hell out of this line shack—now.

"What's wrong?"

"We had fucking sex, Jake. I don't have sex with guys. I have sex with girls." The button on his wet jeans resisted going into the hole once he got them over his legs. Away from this craziness was where he needed to be. Away from Jake. He shoved his feet into his boots, minus his wet socks. Blisters would form before morning, but right now, he didn't care.

"Yeah, we did, Colby. There's nothing wrong with it."

"The hell there isn't! Guys don't have sex with other guys."

Jake grabbed his shoulder and spun him around so they stood face to face. "Sometimes they do. I like women."

"Then why in the hell did you fuck me in the ass?"

"Because I like guys too, sometimes. Not all the time." Jake raked his fingers through his hair. "This has been building between us for a while, Colby. You know it."

"No, it hasn't. I'm not attracted to guys, Jake."

"You didn't stop me."

He couldn't deny that because he didn't stop Jake when he could have. "It doesn't matter. Stay the fuck away from me. If you want sex find Delaney," he spat, throwing his shirt over his shoulder and heading for the door.

Rain still drizzled from the rafters of the line shack and his horse hung his head as the rain continued. *Fuck this!* Grabbing the reins from the post, he swung up in the saddle and kicked his reluctant gelding. Back to the bunk house. Back to normal.

"You want another one, Colby?" Seth Reardon asked, jerking him back from his thoughts.

"Yeah."

Another beer appeared in front of him as he mumbled thanks.

"You and Del havin' trouble?"

"Nope," he replied, tipping the bottle to his lips.

"Then why the hell are you here and not with her?"

"Fuck if I know."

With a swipe of the towel in his hand, Seth cleaned the bar, waiting for Colby to talk if he wanted to. The hell of it was, he didn't. Talking wouldn't fix this unless the person stood an inch or two taller than him, had jet black hair and hazel eyes the color of an open field of different colored grasses. Even if Jake walked in right now, Colby wouldn't know what to say to him. After that day in the line shack, they stayed away from each other—far away. Jake had Delaney and Colby had no one...again.

Seth shrugged and wandered back to the other end of the bar.

How Colby ended up with the girl, he wasn't sure except the day Jake left, a huge weight lifted from his shoulders. His need to have the other man fuck him again dissipated with Jake's departure. Shortly afterward his friendship with Del turned into more. He'd found her in the barn crying hysterically, but she refused to tell him what the problem was until he found out Jake disappeared. Never giving Delaney a hint he knew how far her relationship with Jake had gone, Colby turned into her best friend.

The day they made love for the first time left him breathless and eager for more. Loving a woman would be enough. He knew it would be. The desire for a man lingered, but he wasn't going to give into it. A woman couldn't fuck him in the ass the way Jake had so he pushed the dark need for it to the back of his mind, praying it stayed there.

* * * *

Jake glanced around the parking lot of the Boots 'n' Spurs and found the vehicle he'd hoped to find. Talking to Colby was the last thing he wanted to do, but it had to be done. They both loved the same girl, but she needed to choose. *What if she didn't? What if she told them both to go to hell?* He scrubbed his hand over his face. *God, what if she found out about him and Colby?* Thinking about that right now would just make him crazy.

Fear rolled across his shoulders. He'd come back to Red Rock to claim the girl he'd loved for so long, he'd forgotten how to be with another woman or man. His time spent in Los Angeles was a learning experience for Jake. Jobs came easy once people saw the skill he had with sheet metal, but the nights were lonely. The need to hold Delaney about broke him on several occasions during their five years apart. He'd been stupid to leave. He knew that now. The door to Delaney's heart which he'd left cracked open the day he walked away made it easy for Colby to take her away and love her like Jake wanted to.

Stroking her body to a fevered pitch wasn't the problem. They still had the explosive fire between them, but could he manage to convince her they had a future together? Did they? He still had his job in Los Angeles when he was ready to go back. Money wasn't an issue anymore since he'd become the premier custom sheet metal worker for classic car restoration. All thanks to Delaney.

The shop wanted to expand outside the market of Los Angeles. Since several members of Hollywood's celebrity crowd were buying up land in Montana, the owner of the shop asked Jake to check out some locations there. They even offered him a part ownership if they expanded.

But settle back in Red Rock?

Did he want to?

If Delaney chose Colby, he'd never be able to stay. Watching them loving and laughing every day would kill him.

Fucking Colby the one time pushed them apart like nothing else could. The attraction to the other man had burned in his gut for a long time before they'd become lovers. *Lovers. Yeah, a one-time fuck didn't constitute lovers.*

The door to the bar swung open as a man stumbled out.

"Shit," the man mumbled. The rest of his words were incoherent from where Jake sat on his bike. The man weaved to where his truck sat and punched the side with his fist. "Goddamn it!" His keys hit the gravel parking lot, skidding under the truck.

Colby.

Jake flipped the kickstand down on his bike and swung his leg over the back. Obviously, Colby was drunk. Jake wasn't about to let him drive.

"Colby."

The other man spun around, swaying back on his heels. "Jake. What the hell do you want?"

"We need to talk."

"Fuck that! I ain't talking to you. I ain't fucking you and I ain't giving you my girl. You can go to hell, *buddy,*" Colby snarled.

Mussed blond curls stuck up in several directions as if Colby had run his hands through his hair repeatedly. Glassy eyes stared back as Jake tried to decide what to do. One thing he knew—he couldn't let Colby go anywhere like this.

Colby dropped to his knees, cussed up a storm, searching the ground for his keys. "Where the hell did they go?"

With a heavy sigh, Jake knelt down and grabbed the keys from under the driver's rear tire.

"Give 'em to me."

"No. You aren't drivin' anywhere. You're drunk, man," Jake said with a sigh.

"I can still drive. I only had six."

"Six what?" Jake wasn't sure Colby even knew what he'd had to drink.

"Six beers and six shots of whiskey."

"Ah, hell." Jake grabbed Colby's arm, ushering him around to the passenger side of the truck.

"Let go," Colby grumbled, ineffectively trying to pull his arm out of Jake's grasp.

"No. I'm driving you home." Jake unlocked the door and pulled it open. "Get in or I'll put you in there myself."

For a moment, Colby looked like he would argue, but then climbed into the truck before he shut the door.

"God, give me strength," Jake said, tipping his head back on his shoulders for a moment and then glanced at his bike. He'd just have to come back for it later.

The moment he slipped inside the truck cab on the driver's side, he knew there would be a problem. Colby snored loudly from the other side.

"Well, shit. Now what the hell am I gonna do with you?"

6

"Oh, fuck!" Colby grabbed his head and screamed like a girl the minute sunlight hit his aching eyelids. "Turn it off! Turn it off!"

"No can do, buddy. Even *I* can't shut off the sun."

The amused voice pissed him off until he realized who it belonged to, then he was furious. "Where the hell am I?"

"My hotel room," Jake replied from somewhere to his left.

Colby peeled open his burning eyelids to find Jake's foot propped up on the edge of the bed. The bare foot led to an equally bare leg before his gaze stopped on Jake's crotch covered by a pair of boxers. He licked his lips as he let his gaze wander further up, taking in the muscled chest, bulging biceps, jet black hair hanging to his shoulders, stopping at the intense hazel eyes of the man he wanted to forget. "How did I get in your hotel room?"

The foot dropped and Jake leaned forward in the chair, drawing Colby's gaze to the powerful body of the man in front of him. "You apparently got pretty drunk at Boots 'n' Spurs. You wandered outside intent on driving home."

"You stopped me."

"Yep. I had planned on taking you home, but by the time I got into your truck on the driver's side, you were sawing logs loud enough to rattle the fender wells."

Desire and anger warred within Colby with the low timbre of the voice he'd thought he'd forgotten. He didn't want Jake. He wanted Delaney. If he told himself that long enough, he might believe it.

"I didn't know where you lived these days, so I figured it would be best to bring you back here so you could sleep it off."

Shit. I feel like an ass. "Sorry. I wasn't thinkin' straight last night."

"Obviously." Jake stood and walked to the dresser. Taut thighs rippled as he pulled on a pair of jeans and buttoned them at the waist. When he turned back toward the bed, he said, "You're drooling."

"Am not!" Colby snapped, jumping to his feet. A groan escaped his lips at the sudden movement, jarring his aching head.

"I don't have anything here for a hangover. I can run to the corner store if you want me to."

He shook his head, instantly regretting the movement. "Fuck."

"Lie down and go back to sleep for a while, Colby. You'll feel better."

"I can't," he groaned, sitting back down on the bed as he cradled his head in his hands.

"Why not?"

"I shouldn't be here with you."

Jake dropped his hand on Colby's shoulder. "I'm not going to jump you. Sleep. We need to talk, but it can wait until later."

Unable to stand the pounding in his head, the roll of his stomach or the pull of his eyelids, Colby drifted onto his side, tucked the pillow beneath his head and drifted off to sleep. Dreams invaded his mind like flashing lights of the past. Riding fence with Jake, laughing at the antics they pulled. The prom with Delaney, kissing her on the cheek when he'd dropped her off at home. Then the freak rainstorm that chased him and Jake to the line shack—into each other's arms like two long lost lovers. How he'd freaked out about it, refusing to even be in the same room with Jake alone. The day he'd found her crying her eyes out in the barn. When they made love for the first time. How he'd fallen in love with her wit, her sassy spirit and her undying loyalty to her family.

Several hours later, he woke to find the room covered in shadows, but quiet. No sound to indicate Jake was there at all. The room wasn't bad as hotel rooms go. He glanced around the room, realizing the décor reminded him of a fancy hotel in downtown Red Rock. Fancy mirrors, brocade bedspread, silk curtains and a huge writing desk spoke of money.

Colby sat up on the bed, smiling. The headache and queasy stomach were gone. Man did he need a shower. *I'm sure I could sneak in the bathroom, take a quick shower and be gone before Jake even comes back.*

The idea intrigued him. Places like this always had extra shampoo and things for their customers. He grabbed his clothes from the floor, vaguely wondering if Jake had undressed him or not. A quick sniff caused a frown. Everything smelled of cigarettes and alcohol. Yuck, but he didn't have a choice. No clean clothes here. The open drawer of the dresser revealed Jake's jeans. He could borrow some, but no. Having anything to do with Jake at this point was a bad idea. Borrowing his clothes—Colby shivered at the thought.

An open door to the right revealed the bathroom. A huge walk-in shower stall with brown travertine tile surrounding the space and multiple showerheads screamed, "Come on in boy. The water's great." The large vanity with double sinks took up one whole wall with its shiny silver fixtures. Small bottles of shampoo and conditioner along with bars of soap sat on the countertop. Larger ones sat in the shower. Colby couldn't help but grab one and open the lid. Yep, Jake's scent. Weird how he could remember exactly how Jake smelled the day the two of them had sex. The feel of Jake's hair as he'd sucked Colby's dick and Jake pounding in his ass when Jake's cock plunged in and out like a jackhammer made his ass pucker. Colby slammed his eyes shut, hoping to block the images in his mind, but it only made it worse.

With a forced exhale, he opened his eyes and grabbed the knob to turn on the shower. Cold. The last thing he needed to be thinking about was Jake's warm mouth around his dick. The cooler water did nothing to curb his raging hard-on as he rubbed shampoo in his hair, scrubbing his scalp until his head hurt. At least he wouldn't smell like the bar when he finished. The bar. God, he'd been such an idiot to get drunk last night. But every time he thought about Delaney and Jake having sex made him nuts, nothing could stop the feelings of jealousy racing through him. Problem being, he wasn't sure if he was jealous because they'd made love together without him or not. What would it be like to have Jake fucking him in the ass and his cock buried in Del at the same time? Or the two of them fucking her—one in her ass while the other takes her pussy? She'd never let him in her ass and he wondered if Jake ever had. Even so, she'd be tighter than a new pair of boots.

"Can I hope all of that lovely hardness is for me?"

Colby's eyes snapped open at the voice to find Jake lounging against the door frame of the bathroom. His lips were tipped up in a sexy grin as a hard-on of his own pushed at the front of his jeans.

"Get the fuck out!"

Jake held up both hands. "Easy, man. One can wish, you know." After one sweeping look from the top of his head to the tips of his toes, Jake grinned again, backing out of the bathroom.

Colby hurried through the rest of his shower before he dried off with one of the fluffy white towels on the wall. Once he slipped on his dirty clothes, he walked out into the main room. Leather upholstered chairs flanked the huge bay window looking out over the main street of Red Rock. Jake stood by the window looking out, a coffee cup in his hands. Damn the man had more muscles and planes than he remembered. The hell of it was, Colby wanted to run his hands over every one of them— very slowly.

With the cup to his lips, Jake turned around as one eyebrow shot up. "Care for some? You could probably use it," he said, nodding toward the cart sitting near the couch.

I guess we're having this talk now. Knowing he needed the fortification, Colby headed for the cart, pouring himself a cup. They might as well get it over with. He took a seat on the couch and brought the cup to his lips. A little bit of heaven in each sip. He glanced at the clock on the wall, choking slightly. The day had pretty much disappeared.

After he poured himself another cup, Jake took one of the leather chairs and set the cup on the table. "We have to let Delaney know what happened between us."

"Oh, hell no!

* * * *

Jake almost burst out laughing at the total shock on Colby's face. His eyes widened as his jaw snapped shut with an audible click. Red Rock would dry up like the Mojave Desert before Colby ever agreed to tell Delaney anything. "We owe her the truth. Neither of us can move forward with her until she knows."

"No way. No fucking way!" Colby jumped to his feet, nearly spilling the coffee in his cup. "I told you then and I'll tell you again now. I'm not gay."

"I didn't say you were." He sat back in the chair, studying the other man. Colby paced the floor like a caged lion. Every muscle in his bullriding conditioned body bunched with each movement. His fists clenched and unclenched with each step. His blue eyes shot irritated sparks Jake's way with every pass around the room.

"I like women. I love Delaney."

"So do I, but I can't deny my attraction to men...to you. I like pussy the same as I like to fuck a guy's ass." Jake noticed Colby's dick pulsed behind the fly of his jeans when he made the next pass. The other man wanted him, but would he give into those needs?

"Did you..."

He studied Colby's face for a moment before he answered, "Did I sleep with guys in Los Angeles? Yes. A time or two, but I couldn't forget Delaney. She's my life. I love her more with every breath I take."

"You left," Colby whispered, taking the chair again. "You walked out on her."

"I know. I couldn't face the lie I thought we were living with. Little did I know, her parents already knew all about me."

"They did?"

Jake raked his fingers through his hair as a sigh escaped his lips. "Yeah. Delaney told me when I went over there yesterday."

"Before or after you fucked her?"

Great. Colby knows. "Before, if you must know. You have to believe me. I never planned for us to do anything. We were only supposed to talk." He glanced at Colby, reading the pain in his gaze. Pain was something he knew well. "She said she still wanted me. After I kissed her, I couldn't stop even if I wanted to."

"I really don't need to hear this."

"Yes, you do, Colby." He leaned forward resting his elbows on his knees. "We both want her. We both love her and she loves us. Both of us."

"What the hell are you saying, Jake?"

"She'll have to decide who she wants. You need to know though, I don't plan on giving up on her again...ever."

Irritation rolled off Colby like waves of heat off the desert floor. With his shoulders set and his hands clenched, Jake could tell battle lines were about to be drawn. "Yet you fucking came onto me again in the goddamn shower? What kind of shit are you trying to pull here, Jake?"

"I'll have to deal with my attraction to men while I'm with her. I always have. Right now, I'm not with her so to speak. It doesn't mean I don't want you."

"Well, I don't want you."

He glanced down at Colby's lap. "You were pretty hard in the shower. Want to tell me what you were thinking about?"

Colby bristled and pulled his shoulders back. "Del sucking me off."

"You're a fucking liar too, Colby. Your dick is as hard as a rock at the thought of me being in your ass. Mine aches at the thought of you sucking my cock." He watched as Colby flushed, but didn't deny it. "There is going to be a problem though depending on who she chooses."

"What kind of a problem?"

"How are we going to function in the same town depending on who she wants to be with?"

Colby's eyes got as round as dinner plates as his jaw dropped. "You're staying?"

"Yes. The company I work for in Los Angeles is making me a partner. They want to open a shop here in Red Rock. And I want Delaney. You'll have a fight on your hands." He leaned back in the chair, crossing his arms over his chest.

"I'm not giving up on her. We've been together for a while now. I asked her to marry me."

"Yeah and I heard her answer." The smile of momentary victory on Colby's mouth disappeared.

"She didn't say no."

"She didn't say yes either."

They stared at each other for several minutes as the clock on the wall slowly ticked away the seconds. Cars whizzed by on the streets outside the hotel room and every once in a while a shout or a horn could be heard.

"Don't you think she has a right to know about us?" Jake asked, finally breaking the silence.

"There is no us."

"We can't deny it, Colby. It happened. Would have again if I had my way, but you weren't willing to admit the attraction. Obviously, you still aren't."

Colby stood up and walked to the window. Sunlight streamed through the glass, lighting the golden streaks in his blond hair. "When did you know?"

"Know?"

"That you liked both guys and girls," he asked, not turning around to face Jake.

"Back in high school. I couldn't help but notice the other guys in the locker room during PE or when we were working out for football practice. I left because of it."

Colby spun around, his eyes wide with shock. "You quit because you were attracted to some of the guys on the team?"

"Yeah. I couldn't handle being around them all the time. High school is a really bad place to come out of the closet, you know."

Colby came back to the chair and sat down, looking bewildered and confused. "I thought you quit because you had to go to work or because you didn't like not being with the in crowd."

"I did have to work. No doubt there, but it wasn't the main motivation. Confused and scared were big parts of who I was back then."

"What about now?"

"I know what I want."

Colby shook his head and leaned back against the chair. "How do you know whether you like guys or girls or both?"

"Did you like me fucking you in the ass before?"

Several moments ticked by before he answered, "Yeah." He sat up straighter and looked Jake in the eye. "But I like girls too. I love being with Delaney. Her pussy is so sweet."

"I know."

Colby chewed his lips as he narrowed his eyes. "Have you..."

"What?"

"Never mind," he said, leaning back against the chair again, staring at the ceiling.

"No, not never mind. Ask me."

"Have you ever thought about sharing her?"

"Sharing her with who?"

"Me?"

Jake stood and paced the floor as he raked his fingers through his hair. This conversation wasn't going at all like he'd planned. Share? Delaney? "What exactly are you suggesting, Colby?"

The blue of Colby's eyes stared into his when he sat forward to lock gazes with Jake. "Lately, I've been thinking about the three of us—ever since you came back to town."

"You seriously want to share her?" A decisive nod was his answer. "What do you think she'd say?"

After a heavy sigh, Colby laid his head back against the chair again. "She'd probably think we're both nuts."

"We'd have to tell her about what happened before. It's the only way she'd ever buy the three of us together. Even then, I'm not sure she'd go for it."

"I know," Colby whispered.

Jake flopped back into the chair. Something would have to give before he'd ever believe the other man wanted to have a threesome with their woman. "Do you want me?"

"As in?"

"Don't act stupid, Colby. You know what I mean. Do you want me to fuck you?"

"Why can't I fuck you?"

His chest tightened with trepidation and arousal. Could he let Colby have his ass? He didn't know. The thought intrigued him, but he'd never been the submissive type. Rarely not being the one on top, usually being the one to bury his cock in the other man's dark tunnel until they both came so hard, they couldn't breathe.

"You've never let another guy have your ass, have you, Jake." It wasn't a question so much as a statement. He figured Colby knew the answer before he even spoke.

The heavy exhale gave away his feelings as Jake squeezed his eyes shut and pinched the bridge of his nose. "Yes, I have, but only a few times and only under specific circumstances."

"Will you let me?"

7

The day after her rendezvous with both Jake and Colby, Delaney slid under the car in the shop. Nothing new, but her thoughts weren't on the job. Two men occupied the space. She wasn't sure what to do about either of them. Lucky for her, fixing cars didn't take much brain power. She could do it in her sleep if she had to. The station was normally closed on Sundays, but today she needed the busy work. Choices needed to be made. Lives were at stake here. Not only hers, but Colby's and Jake's, too.

The cell phone in her pocket rang. The ringtone gave away the caller's identity.

"Hey," she answered, eyeing the bolt she needed to remove, trying to decide what size wrench would fit.

"Hey, babe. Workin' hard?" Colby asked, his voice a low sexy growl.

She rolled out from under the car. "Of course, even though I wasn't going to work today. What are you up to?"

"Nothin' much. Gettin' over a rough hangover. I had a little too much to drink at the bar last night."

Worry laced her voice as she said, "I hope you didn't drive anywhere."

"Uh...no. I had someone take me home."

"Good. I wouldn't want to hear from Laurel about you wrapped around a tree somewhere." After she climbed to her feet, she tossed the wrench on the workbench and headed for the office. For a few seconds Colby didn't say anything. Sounds she couldn't quite make out reached her ear through the phone line. A voice. A deep voice. "Where are you?"

"Uh...nowhere."

She sighed and rolled her eyes even though he couldn't see her. "Don't lie, Colby. I hate when you try to spare my feelings." She bit her lip for a second. "You didn't cheat on me last night, did you? You aren't at some woman's house, are you?"

"Woman's house? No, darlin'. I wouldn't cheat on you. How can you even ask me that?"

"I hear someone's voice in the background. It doesn't sound like a woman though. It sounds like a man."

"All right. Truth." She heard a sharp intake of breath and knew Colby was bracing himself. He always did that when he didn't want to handle something unpleasant. "Jake looked after me when I got too drunk last night."

"Jake?"

"Yes. He found me in the parking lot of the bar, and took my keys. I passed out before I could tell him where I live now so he brought me back to his hotel room."

"Let me talk to him."

"No. You don't need to do that, Del. It's fine."

"I said, let me talk to him."

She heard Colby say, "She wants to talk to you." A moment later, Jake came on the line.

"Hey, babe."

"What is Colby doing at your place?"

"Uh...didn't he tell you? He got drunk—"

"He told me that part, but you two can't stand each other anymore. How are you in the same room without killing each other?" She started to pace. This wasn't good. The two of them together without her to intervene could end in a blood bath.

"We had to talk, Delaney. You knew it was a matter of time before we talked."

"Yeah, I did, but I'm not sure I like you two being buddies again."

Jake sighed. "I wouldn't say we're buddies. We've got more things to work out between us, but at least we're discussing things."

Picking up a pen from the desk, she twirled it between her fingers. They used to be good friends. She knew that part of their history. When she and Jake had been dating, the two guys were almost inseparable until something happened between them. Neither of them ever mentioned what, even though she'd asked several times—begged even.

"Delaney?"

"I'm still here. I'm thinking is all."

"About?"

"Neither of you would ever tell me why you quit being friends back in high school. Did it have to do with a girl?"

"Sort of."

"Are you willing to tell me now?"

"Over the phone? No, but why don't we all three get together tonight for dinner. There are a few things we need to get out into the open anyway."

"I'm not sure I like the sound of this."

"No!" Colby shouted in the background.

"What's wrong with him? He doesn't want to have dinner with me?"

The noises on the phone sounded like the two of them were fighting over it for a moment as rasping and shuffling met her ear.

"I'm not ready for her to know, Jake. Stop pushing me."

"She has to know, Colby. It's not fair to keep her in the dark."

"Listen!" she shouted, hoping to get both of their attention. "Enough!"

Jake got on the phone. "Sorry, babe."

"What in the hell is going on between you? What should I know?"

"I'm not talking about this over the phone, Delaney. I'll pick you up at your place at six. If Colby doesn't want to come, it's up to him, but I'm telling you everything. I'm tired of keeping these damned secrets."

"Tell him if he doesn't come to dinner with us, I'm done. He can find someone else. I won't have secrets between us. I'm sad it comes out now that there are."

"You tell him."

She assumed Jake handed Colby the phone because a moment later she heard Colby's voice.

"Now Del—"

"Don't now Del me, buddy. I'll tell you like I told Jake. I don't want secrets. If you don't come to dinner with the two of us, I'm done. You won't see me again, Colby."

"You can't be serious, darlin'."

"I'm dead serious." Silence met her ear for a moment, so she went on. "The two of you pick me up at my place. Or I can cook and we can talk at my apartment. Either way, I don't care, but we're getting this all out into the open one way or another."

"Your apartment then. At least we can have some privacy."

They said their goodbyes. Colby didn't say he loved her this time.

"I don't think I'm gonna like this one bit," she murmured, putting the pen back down and doing her best to forget the two disturbing men until she finished the job she had to do.

The rest of the day went by in a blur for her. The decision to come to her place for dinner and their talk didn't come easy for Colby. She planned to stand by her statement though, of not seeing him again if they didn't get this out. Something lingered between the two men and she stood smack dab in the middle of it. This much she knew. Come hell or high water, tonight every little detail would be known.

But what could it be? Something about a woman. Her? Did Colby have feelings for her even then? She didn't think so, but images of prom bounced through her mind. He'd been the perfect gentlemen, never once trying anything during the evening. He'd acted like they were merely friends. Maybe they had been.

What would that have to do with Jake? If Colby had tried something, then she could see some kind of conflict between them concerning her. Maybe Colby told Jake he had feelings for her and Jake told him to back off. Her relationship with Jake was new and fragile then. It wasn't until a few months later things with Jake had really heated up. They'd ended up making love for the first time.

Her parents had gone to a stock auction one weekend and her sisters all had dates. Kale lived with his first wife on the other side of town, so Delaney had the house to herself one Saturday. She wanted to surprise Jake with dinner—just the two of them. Candlelight flickered on the walls from the two placed in the center of the table. She used her mom's fine china and wine glasses even though she could only serve sparkling cider. Two fine rib-eye steaks grilled to perfection, baked potatoes, salad and green beans rounded out the menu for her private dinner. Everything turned out perfectly.

Afterward, they sat on the couch in the den and he'd even let her pick the movie knowing a chick flick would be her choice. Ghost, her favorite tearjerker movie, played as she rested her head on his shoulder while he played with the hair at the nape of her neck. They kissed and petted before, but never touched actual private places. Tonight, she wanted more. She wanted him to touch her...everywhere.

"Jake?"

"Hmm?"

"Touch me."

"I am," he said, trailing his work-rough fingers over her shoulder, then down her arm.

"I don't mean my arm." She took his hand and laid it on her breast. "Touch me."

"This isn't a good idea, Delaney."

"Why?" she asked, sitting up so she could look into his eyes. *Dark, so dark.* Passion glowed in the depths of his gaze.

"I'll want more. What we've been doing isn't enough anymore, baby."

"I know it's not, Jake." She took a deep breath and blew it out on a heavy sigh. "I want you to make love to me."

"Oh God. This is such a bad idea," he said, leaning over her to take her mouth with his.

A soft knock at five minutes before six brought her out of her daydream, signaling the arrival of at least one of the men. With sweaty palms and a racing heart, she pulled open the door to find both men standing on the stoop.

"Come on in. It's not like you two haven't been here before," she said, walking toward the kitchen to finish dinner. Something simple was her choice when she stopped at the store after leaving the shop. She'd actually left right after the phone call to get food before they came over. Keeping her wits about her with this conversation seemed of utmost importance.

The looks on the two men's faces when they walked into her apartment told her this talk wasn't going to be easy to take. "Have a seat. Would either of you like a beer?"

"Please," they said in unison.

After retrieving two long-neck bottles from the refrigerator, she handed Jake one before giving Colby the other.

"Dinner will be ready in about ten minutes or so. It's nothing fancy. Spaghetti, garlic bread—you know, something simple."

"Sounds good, babe," Jake replied, sipping his beer. "I'm hungry anyway."

"Yeah, me too," Colby added. "It smells great, Del."

"I think there's a ballgame on if you want to turn on the television until supper is ready," she said, stirring the noodles. The salad already stood ready in the bowl on the countertop, the table was set with three places, a bottle of white wine chilled in the icebox. The garlic bread would go into the oven shortly.

Jake stood and grabbed the remote off the coffee table, bringing her gaze around to study him. His hair hung loose around his face, barely brushing his collar. *He must have gotten a haircut today. It was a little longer the other day when he rode into town.* The black T-shirt he wore clung to the hard muscles of his chest, arms and back. Her mouth watered at the thought of licking his gorgeous body from one side to the other. Black jeans hugged his ass, tempting her to squeeze his butt cheeks with both hands. All she could think about at the moment was riding his hips into tomorrow's sunrise.

The microwave dinged, telling her the garlic spread was warmed and ready to put on the bread. Once she had it in the oven, she checked the noodles again as her gaze fell on Colby. Blond, built rough and tough, he had the muscular body of a bullrider. His arms bulged under the button-down western shirt he wore, straining the stitches with every movement. The slight curl of his hair at the top made her fingers itch to run through the strands. He tapped out a nervous rhythm on the back of her couch as he watched Jake flip through the channels.

Testosterone flowed through the room like a wave against the shore.

The mingling of the two men's cologne bombarded her senses, pulling her nipples into tight buds. Confusion swept through her. Which one did she want? Why was it so hard to choose between them? They were as different as night and day. Colby, with his light coloring brought sunshine and warmth into her life at a point when she'd felt so cold she wasn't sure she could go on. Jake. Dark and mysterious—strong, bold, take charge, no shit Jake. The man who turned her world upside down the moment their gazes met in shop class.

The timer on the oven dinged. "Dinner is ready, guys. If you two want to take a seat, I'll have it on the table in a second."

"Sure, darlin'," Colby answered, getting to his feet.

Colby took one side of the table while Jake took the other, putting her between them at the head. *Now this is kind of weird. Sitting between them with one warm knee pressed against my left and another against my right.* A vision raced across her mind—Jake behind her with his chest to her back with Colby in front of her with her breasts flat against his pecs.

Jake took her hand between his. "You okay, babe?"

With a shake of her head, she dislodged the disturbing image. "Yeah. I'm fine." She poured herself a glass of wine, wiggling the bottle to see if either of them wanted any. They both declined since they still had beer left.

"Shall we toast?" She raised her glass and glanced at both men.

"To what?" Colby asked.

"To truth and no secrets."

Both men looked at each other before they slowly raised their bottles to clink against her glass. "To truth," they repeated.

After each had taken several bites of food, Colby said, "This is really good, darlin'."

"Thanks. I know you both are fond of spaghetti, plus it's easy to make."

"You remembered?" Jake asked, his eyebrows arched in surprise.

"Of course. I remember everything about our time together." Colby cleared his throat. "I'm sorry if that makes you uncomfortable, Colby, but it's part of my past with Jake. We can't act like it never happened."

"I know, Del. I knew all about the two of you back then."

Her forked dropped to her plate with a loud clank. "You did?"

"Guys talk, Delaney," Jake added. "I know I bragged some."

She exhaled loudly and squeezed her eyes shut for a second. "I supposed you two compared notes."

"No. Shortly after we started having sex—"

"Making love, Jake. It was always making love," she said, staring into his eyes. "I loved you."

"You never once told me," Jake replied.

"I know. I wanted to." A tear slid down her cheek. "So many times I wanted to. The day you left, I'd planned on telling you. I wanted to make you understand we should be together." She wiped the tear away with her fingers. "But of course, things didn't go like I planned."

"Wasted years," he murmured, grasping her hand, rubbing his thumb over her knuckles.

"It doesn't matter anymore. Things are different. I'm different."

"No, you aren't, Delaney. You're still my girl."

"Stop already!" Colby snapped. "She's not your girl, she's mine."

"It's fine. I've got choices to make and it's not going to be easy," she said, slowly pulling her hand from Jake's hold. "I love you, Colby. I do, but it's a different kind of love than what I feel for Jake." She picked at her salad with her fork, moving the lettuce around, but never taking a bite. "Can a woman love two men? Is it possible?"

"I think it is," Jake replied. "Just like it's possible for a man to love more than one person."

"You make it sound like you care about more than just me, Jake. Is there someone you fell in love with in Los Angeles? Someone you left behind?"

"No, I love you. I have since we were eighteen, but there is someone I care a great deal about besides you, Delaney." Jake glanced across the table at Colby. "Wanna jump in here sometime, buddy?"

"I tried. You both shut me up."

"You know what I mean," Jake said, reclining against the chair back.

"That's right. Something about lies and secrets? Care to explain, Colby?"

"Don't fuckin' put me on the spot like this, Jake. This whole thing started because you couldn't keep your damned hands to yourself."

"What's that supposed to mean? Did you cheat on me, Jake?" she asked, her gaze stopping on Jake again.

"No, Delaney. I didn't." He frowned as he glanced at his plate for a second. "Actually, I guess you could say I did. It happened not too long after the two of us made love for the first time. I didn't plan it. It just happened."

Her whole world tumbled down around her ears and her heart felt like it lay shattered in her chest. She rubbed her sternum to ease the ache his admission caused. The man she loved admitted he'd cheated on her while they dated. How would she handle this? Did it really matter? They weren't together now, but she was actually contemplating being with him again, so yeah, it mattered. "Who?" she whispered, praying it wasn't someone she knew personally or someone she called friend today.

Jake glanced across the table as Colby flushed.

Did Colby know? All this time Colby knew Jake cheated and never told me.

"Did you know, Colby? Did he tell you he cheated on me and you never said anything?"

"You could say he knew," Jake said, leaning forward, resting his arms on the table.

She jumped to her feet to head for the window. Moonlight spread silver across the pasture, lighting the whole area almost bright enough to be daylight. Stars twinkled in the sky above. A rare clear night for spring, but she couldn't appreciate the beauty with her thoughts in turmoil. Her current boyfriend knew her old boyfriend cheated on her and neither of them ever told her—neither of them could look her in the eye.

"Just tell me who," she whispered, fighting tears. "I have to know."

"Colby," Jake said in a low, tortured voice.

"What?" Colby asked.

"Tell her."

"I..."

Colby wouldn't look her in the eye when she turned around. "Tell me, damn it! I refuse to be in the dark anymore. This isn't fair. You knew all this time he cheated on me and with who, but you won't tell me now?"

"It was me."

"You? What the hell are you talking about?"

"Jake cheated on you with me."

8

"He what?"

"Jake cheated on you with me."

Laughter bubbled from Delaney's lips as tears streaked down her cheeks. *This is a joke. It has to be.* "You're trying to tell me you're gay? Both of you?"

"No! I'm not gay," Colby snapped, jumping to his feet. "I like women. I love you. I love making love with you. I like pussy. Okay?"

"Then explain to me how Jake cheated on me with you."

Colby closed his eyes before he slumped back into the chair.

"Jake? You haven't said a word here. Are you trying to tell me our whole relationship was a lie? That you're gay?"

"No. I'm not gay either, Delaney." He got to his feet and stopped in front of her. "I'm what most people call bi or bi-sexual. I like both men and women. I prefer women most of the time, but there are times when I like being with a guy."

"So when did this cheating occur?"

"The Sunday after we made love for the first time."

"You mean the day after I gave you my virginity?" With her arms folded across her chest, she frowned at Jake.

"Yes."

She threw up her hands. "This is priceless. Did you know all along you like men?"

"I had an idea. It's why I wouldn't stay on the football team during high school. Coming out of the closet during those years is a bad idea, if you know what I mean."

"I guess so." She bit her lip and stepped back out of his reach. "How many guys have you been with? For that matter, how many women have you been with?"

"Does it make a difference, Delaney? I love you. I want you."

"But you want Colby too. Colby is who you said you have feelings for, isn't he."

"Yeah. You have to understand something about what happened the day I left you. Colby and I were only together one time. He couldn't come to grips with what happened between us."

"The real reason you two couldn't be friends anymore. It didn't have anything to do with me."

"It did in a roundabout way. You were my girlfriend. I had deep feelings for you that were growing stronger every day, but after Colby and I had sex, it was like a part of me didn't belong to you anymore. It belonged to him. Back in the line shack." He put both hands on her shoulders as he looked deep into her eyes. "The confusion I felt kept dragging me away from you. When you made it sound like you didn't want your parents to know about us, I blew a gasket. I couldn't handle the pressure of us being a secret. I needed to sort out my feelings for both of you. Everything kept coming back to bite me in the ass."

"Now you have?"

"Sort of. All of the feelings running through me are the reason I came back to Red Rock. I had to come to terms with them before I could move on with my life in any other direction."

He turned to glance over his shoulder at Colby, but the look on Colby's face told her he knew none of what Jake had just said.

"Let's sit down on the couch so we can talk this out," Jake said, taking her hand, and then motioning to Colby to precede them into the living room. "This involves all of us."

The two of them took a seat on the couch as Colby sat in the armchair across from them, but after a moment, Delaney stood and moved to his side. "We're together in this. You need to sit with us."

Colby flushed for a second, and then took her hand.

Once they all sat on the couch with her in the middle, she started to talk. "So let me get this straight. Jake, you're in love with me."

"Yeah."

"But you also have feelings for Colby."

"Yes."

"Colby, you're in love with me too."

"Yes," Colby answered in a mere whisper.

"Do you have feelings for Jake?" she asked, turning to face Colby.

He closed his eyes and ran his fingers through his hair.

Delaney framed his face with her hands and brushed her lips against his. "It's okay," she murmured, placing her forehead against his. "I love him too, but you need to be honest with yourself. We can't go on like we have been if you have feelings for Jake."

The blue of his gaze bore into hers. "I'm not sure what I feel, Del. I'm confused. I have been for years."

"Wow." She sat back, stunned at everything transpiring within the room. "I thought the worst thing I would have to deal with today would be my feelings for the both of you. Now we have all kinds of emotions running around here."

"Don't put words in my mouth," Colby said. "I'm not sure of anything anymore."

"Okay." Delaney tucked her feet beneath her and turned around so she sat backward on the couch. This way she could face both men. "Tell me what has you confused."

"I don't know. I love you. You know I do."

"Yes, but obviously there is unfinished business between you two."

"I can't do this right now." He jumped to his feet. "I need some air."

Before she knew it, Colby had raced out the door and the rumble of his truck engine faded into the night.

"What the hell just happened?" she asked, her gaze locking with Jake's.

"I wish I knew, babe." Jake wrapped his arms around her and pulled her against his chest. "He has to work this out for himself. We can't force him to accept what's going on here, no matter how much we want to."

"What is going on here?"

"I don't know about you, but I'm thinking threesome."

"Seriously?" she whispered, stroking her fingers over the fine muscles beneath her cheek. "Like you and Colby and me?"

"Yeah. I think it would be great."

Yeah, great. Two men and me in bed. Two sets of work-roughed hands stroking my skin. Two cocks pleasuring me before pleasuring each other. Wow.

* * * *

Colby didn't know where he was going except away from those two. Anywhere was better than dealing with the feelings being in the same room with those two brought up. Love. He loved her. Did he love Jake too? Want, need, desire—those things he could deal with in relation to Jake, but love? The big L. Men weren't supposed to fall in love with other men. It was wrong. Men belonged with women.

It didn't matter what Jake wanted. Him and Delaney. They were meant to be together, just the two of them, not with Jake between them. *Damn it!* He sure managed to get himself there though—right smack between them.

Several moments later, Colby found himself pulling down a long familiar driveway. One he hadn't visited in several years. Not since the day his parents died. Darkness surrounded everything. No lights for miles. The shell of a house stood outlined against the night sky. He shut the truck off to stare at the buildings through the windshield. As the sole heir after his parents death, the land and what little of the building still stood belonged to him, but up until now, he didn't want anything to do with the asshole he called father or the legacy.

After he shut his headlights off, he crawled out of the truck and walked closer to the house. *Deep breath, man.*

Screams echoed in his head—the high shrill cries of his mother and his father's laughter as he locked her in the pantry because she disobeyed him again. The shouts of arguing voices, the sounds of flesh slapping flesh— of bone snapping. His mother reassuring Colby from within the pantry, after his father finally left for the day, that everything would be fine after he spent minutes trying to pry the lock off the door. Scenes repeated in front of his eyes. The years of abuse and how she tried to protect Colby from his father's heavy hand weighed hard on his mind. How he'd always been too afraid to stand up to his father. The shame he felt for not helping her and for letting everything continue until she took the matter into her own hands, setting the house on fire with both of them inside.

That day his world ended and began again.

He went from being a scrawny, lanky kid to lifting weights until his muscles begged for mercy and his body could take anything another could dish out. The tough bullrider—the man's man. Quick to get into fights over a woman or easily goaded when someone called another a fag. The bulls became his reason for being a man. Delaney made the reasons worth living for.

"Colby," a whispered voice reached his ear.

"Mama?"

The shadows shifted as he squinted trying to make out where the sound came from.

"Move on, son. Live your life. Don't let him take that away from us too."

The scared little boy surfaced, wanting, no, wishing his mother could hold him again. "If Daddy ever found out about..."

"It doesn't matter, Colby. Daddy can't hurt you anymore. He can't hurt me anymore. The Devil has his soul. Love who you were meant to love."

He dropped to his knees, tipped his head back on his shoulders to stare at the heavens. *Who am I meant to love? Delaney? Jake? Both of them?* The soft brush of fingers pushing the hair back from his forehead eased the ache in his chest. Finally, his gut loosened and the knot began to unravel. Mom would understand—she did understand. From wherever she was now, she watched over him.

The sky to the east began to lighten over the horizon. He didn't know how long he'd sat there in the middle of the yard at his childhood home thinking. Several hours apparently. Delaney would be worried, hell, Jake too for that matter. Decisions needed to be made. Could he accept a relationship with Jake? Would Delaney be open to a relationship between the two of them with or without Jake in it? He didn't know what lay ahead, but he damn sure wouldn't let his father or pain from his past color his future anymore.

He grabbed his cell phone from his pocket to call the one person who had always loved him for who he was, not who his parents were and not because of his background or lack of—Delaney.

A sleepy hello met his ear. It wasn't Delaney.

* * * *

Jake pulled the phone away from his ear and stared at the screen for a minute, trying to figure out who called.

"Colby?"

"What are you doing answering Del's phone?"

"Waiting for you, man. Where are you?"

"In my truck about five miles outside of town."

Visions bounced around in Jake's mind. He knew of the hell Colby went through when they were in high school. It was one of the things Colby had shared with him all those years ago—the frustration, the anger, the shame and the guilt for not helping his mother. Colby had gone home. "You went back to that hell hole."

"Yeah. I don't know why, Jake, but I found myself here after I left you two. Maybe it put things into perspective for me. I wish I knew."

Jake slid out from under Delaney's arm where it lay draped over his chest and sat up on the side of the bed. After Colby had taken off the night before, they talked for several hours about everything. Things that had happened while he'd been in Los Angeles, people they knew in Red Rock, her plans for the future, his possibly opening a shop in town backed by his current employer...and Colby. "What conclusion did you come to?"

"I think that's something I need to discuss with both of you. I'm assuming Delaney is still asleep?"

"Yeah, naked, sedated and snoring like she's sawing logs."

A long pause of silence met his ear.

"I'm kidding, Colby. No more making love to her until something is settled." He let his fingers brush down her arm, watching the goose bumps rise in the wake of his touch. "She is sleeping though. Want me to wake her up?"

"Get some coffee started. I'll be there in a few minutes. We can talk then."

"Got it. Coffee and maybe breakfast. I'll see what I can rustle up around here."

"Tell you what. I'll stop at the store on the way through town to grab some eggs, bacon, bread and orange juice."

"Sounds good. I'll get her up, showered and dressed before you get here."

"See you in a few." The call ended with a click.

"Delaney, baby. Time to get up."

"No. Sleep."

"Honey, Colby will be here in a few and we need to get showered."

"Colby?"

"Yeah. He just called your cell."

She sat up, pushing the hair out of her face, wide awake now at the mention of Colby's name. A sharp pain stabbed Jake's chest. *What if she loves him more than me?*

"You talked to him?"

"Yeah. He's stopping to get some breakfast food and he'll be here in a few minutes." Jake reached over to slap her butt. "Up you go. I'll get the coffee started while you shower."

"Mmm...you don't want to join me?"

"I would love to babe, but we shouldn't," he replied, grabbing her robe from the dresser before helping her slip it on.

"Shouldn't? Why not?"

"It's not fair to Colby for us to make love until we talk this out." It killed him to keep his hands off her tempting curves, but he had to. Until things were out in the open and they all knew where they stood, he wouldn't make love to her again.

"But I want both of you." She ran her fingernail down his chest. "To-gether." Her lips followed the same path. "At the same time." Her tongue flicked his nipple, bringing it to an aching point. "You said you wanted that too."

"Colby isn't here though, babe," he growled, low and tortured as she continued to torment his now fully aroused body. "It's just the two of us."

"So when he gets here, we'll make it a threesome." Her eyes sparkled in the dim light of her room when she looked up through her lashes. "I'm hot thinking about it, Jake."

"Oh, God. Me too," he whispered, curling his hands into fists at his side. His whole body hummed with need. "But we can't. I promised myself."

"Party pooper," she sassed, sashaying her little butt as she turned and headed for the bathroom. "If you change your mind, I'll be right here."

"Bitch."

Delaney laughed and closed the door.

After several deep breaths, he walked toward the kitchen to make coffee. His cock throbbed behind the fly of the jeans he refused to shed last night even in sleep. *God, I want her.* The desire to pound through the door, push her against the wall in the shower and ram into her from behind, almost brought him to his knees. *Do I have enough time to jack off? Coffee first, then raging hard-on.*

He got the coffee brewing in a few short minutes as he tried to decide what to do about the stiff cock in his pants. Relief couldn't come in the form of Delaney and he sure didn't think Colby would be interested helping him with either his mouth or his ass.

"Rosey will have to do if I can make this fast enough." Jake took a seat on the couch, listening for the shower to make sure Delaney wasn't done already and kept an ear out for the door in case Colby showed up.

With images of Delaney's mouth wrapped around his cock, he unzipped his pants to palm his erection, fisting it tight. A soft moan escaped his lips as he rolled his head back on the couch, closing his eyes. The images of her slowly running her tongue around the engorged head, filtered into his brain. She'd lick from root to tip like an ice cream, quickly flicking the tip of her tongue inside the slit to capture his pre-cum. The veins running along the sides would require her attention too, as she would follow them from top to bottom, before totally engulfing the entire thing into her hot, wet mouth. The need to come built to explosive with every flick, every lick, every suck. Jake stroked his cock up and down, faster and faster until he felt his balls draw up closer to his body. *Yes, a little more.* "Suck it, baby," he murmured. The images were so real he could almost feel the slick slide of her tongue around the head of his cock, the warmth close over it.

Jake opened his eyes and squealed.

How had he missed the door? "Shit," he groaned, losing the battle of forestalling his climax as it squirted out the end of his dick and was caught in the half-smiling mouth of...

9

Colby.

"What the hell are you doing, Colby?" Jake watched Colby lick his semen from his lips.

"Making a decision, Jake. I'm tired of running from what I know is the right thing."

Jake lifted his gaze when he heard the bedroom door open to find Del standing there in nothing but a towel.

"What about me?" she asked, leaning against the doorframe.

"I want you too, Del."

She sauntered toward them both as Jake tucked himself back into his jeans. "We need to get some coffee and breakfast before we get moving on this conversation."

"I'm ready to move onto other things," Delaney said, waggling her eyebrows.

"Food, Del. We need to eat before we talk."

"But Colby got to taste..."

"No sex until we talk," Jake snapped, jumping to his feet. "Where's the food?"

"Right here," Colby replied, grabbing the bag and heading into the kitchen. "I'll get this stuff started while you dress, Del."

With an irritated *hrmph,* Delaney disappeared back into the bedroom, slamming the door in her wake.

"Testy, isn't she," Jake murmured.

"She's horny. She always gets wound up and grumpy when she's horny."

Jake laughed. "Yeah, I do remember that about her even from before. Sex relaxes her right out."

"Does it do the same thing to you?" Colby wanted to know.

"Most of the time. I ain't relaxed, even though I got off." Jake glanced at his friend and former lover. "You didn't have to suck me off, you know."

"I know. I couldn't resist when I walked in to see you stretched out and ridin' the rosie train." Colby chuckled as he slapped Jake on the shoulder.

Jake felt heat rush into his cheeks, embarrassed to be caught jacking off.

"Hey, nothin' to be embarrassed about. It's not like we haven't all been there."

"Does that mean you've come to a decision?"

Colby turned back toward the cooking bacon. "Yeah, but I want Delaney around when we talk this out. She's involved more than she knows. She doesn't know about my parents except the fire. The whole abuse thing has never come up."

"Well, it should now, you know."

"Yeah. I have to tell her." He glanced at Jake again. "What if I'm like him, Jake? What if I get angry and hit either of you?"

"You won't."

"How do you know? You haven't been around me when I'm really, really angry. I lose my temper. I'm hot-headed."

"But you wouldn't hurt either of us. Your father did it for fun. He enjoyed hearing your mother's screams, you crying, your fear. He lived on it. It made him feel like a man even though it only proved how much of a coward he really was, because he could only beat up those smaller or weaker."

"I should have protected her."

Jake turned Colby around so he could look into his eyes. "You couldn't, Colby. He was a grown man. You were a kid."

"I couldn't even get her out of the pantry."

"What would it have accomplished if you could? She wouldn't leave and he would have just beaten her again. He probably would have left her in there for days." The blue of Colby's eyes sparkled with unshed tears. Jake couldn't do anything but pull Colby into his arms and let him cry. "Sshh. It's over. He can't hurt you or your mother anymore."

Tears soaked his shirt, wetting the skin beneath. The wracking sobs shaking Colby's shoulders tore at Jake's heart. He'd known the pain and despair Colby felt back then, but he hadn't known the depth of the guilt. Hopefully, letting the tears flow now would help cleanse some of the pain Colby bared.

"I need to get the bacon," Colby mumbled into Jake's shirt.

"I got it," Delaney said from behind Jake. "Grab some coffee for you two, Jake, and I'll finish up breakfast. This sounds like it's going to be an emotional morning."

Colby jumped back when he heard Delaney's voice, flushing red.

"Don't be embarrassed, Colby. I love a guy who can cry." She ran her fingers down his still wet cheek. "It's okay. I knew the hell you went through with your dad."

"You did?"

"The whole town knew what an asshole he was, but no one understood why your mother stayed."

"Because of me. She couldn't afford to raise me on her own."

"I don't understand why she never asked for help though," Delaney said, turning the bacon and starting the eggs. "There were people in this town who wanted to help her."

"Too proud would be my guess," Jake replied as he poured them all coffee from the pot. "I'm sure she didn't want to admit the abuse at the hands of a man who swore to love her. I mean, how could she understand the depth of everything going on inside your dad?"

"She tried. She wanted to get counseling, but he always refused."

"He needed more than counseling, Colby. He needed a serious ass beating by someone bigger so he knew how it felt." Jake set all three cups on the table and pushed Colby down into one of the chairs.

Moments later, Delaney placed a heaping plate of food in front of him. "Eat. You'll need your strength if I get my way. I plan on having both of you as a mid-mornin' snack."

Jake nodded his head indicating Colby better eat before Delaney went all motherly on them and force-fed them the food she'd finished preparing.

"We need to talk, Del," Colby said between bites.

"We will. After we eat."

The next plate landed on the table in front of Jake before she leaned over and kissed him on the lips. "Just a taste. I'm starving and I don't mean for food at the moment. Seeing what happened earlier makes me want to skip the food and talk and get straight to the sex, but I know this conversation needs to happen sooner rather than later."

A short time later, she took the remaining chair, digging into the food in front of her as he and Colby started to clean up the dishes.

"I'll do the dishes," she said between mouthfuls of egg.

With a shake of his head, Jake replied, "You cooked, darlin'. We'll clean up. Right, Colby?"

"Yep."

"I kind of like this—men helping out around the house."

"Good. There'll be a whole lot more of it if things work out."

She stood and walked into the kitchen to place her plate in Colby's soapy hands, then leaned in for a kiss. "Mmm. Bacon."

"Go sit. We'll be done in a second."

"Ah!" she groaned, taking a seat on the couch and putting up her feet. "The lap of luxury, being waited on by two gorgeous men."

Within seconds, Jake took one side of her as Colby took the other.

"Okay. So let's get this out in the open. Colby? Do you want to tell us what's going on?"

"You probably won't believe me, but when I went out to my parents' place, I heard my mother's voice."

"Like you thought you heard her, right?" Delaney asked, her eyes wide with uncertainty. She glanced at Jake, then back at Colby like he'd lost his mind.

Colby shook his head as he grasped Del's fingers in his hand. "No, I heard her. I talked to her and she reassured me I could love who I wanted to. You see, part of my problem with being with Jake came from my father's attitude toward people. He would never have accepted me with another guy. Holy hell, if he found out we wanted to make this a threesome..."

"Do you want both of us?" The tremble in her voice gave away her fear of what Colby might say, even to Jake's ears.

"I love you Del, but things haven't been right between us for a while."

"So you love me like a friend, not a lover and you'd rather be with Jake." Delaney started to scoot off the couch.

Jake grabbed her hand to hold her in place. "Listen and stop jumping to conclusions, baby."

"No, Delaney. I want you, but I want Jake too."

"What are you saying, Colby. You want us to be a threesome?"

"Yes. If the two of you want me."

"Of course I want you," she replied. "I love you. I love Jake too. But how can this work? Are we thinking permanently?"

"I don't know about permanent," Colby said, drawing a confused look from Delaney and Jake knew he had the same look.

"What are you suggestin' then?" Jake asked.

"A temporary thing."

"You asked me to marry you not long ago. Did you change your mind?"

"No. I still want to marry you, but I'm not sure if things with Jake are permanent or temporary."

"I can understand your feelings on the subject," he added. "I'm not sure a permanent threesome would be a good idea either."

Delaney swung around to face him. "What do you want out of this, Jake?"

"A good fuck?" The look on her face made him laugh when she rolled her eyes. "Can't we take this one step at a time? I mean nothing has to be decided tonight. We can play it by ear and see where it goes."

"Your plan has merit." She grabbed his hand, then reached for Colby. "I love both of you. The thought of not having one of you scares the hell out of me, but the type of relationship we're contemplating can have some bad ramifications. What if the town doesn't accept it? I've lived here my whole life. I can't see moving away because the townsfolk can't abide an unconventional relationship between us."

"They might not accept me and Colby together, but they would the two of us."

"Of course they would. Half the town thinks we should have been together anyway, but what happens if they stop using my shop when our threesome becomes common knowledge? I won't have an income. What happens if they won't frequent your new venture, Jake?"

"Won't happen."

"You don't know that. This is a fairly liberal town, but there are those who won't accept it."

"Let's just take this one day at a time, okay?" Colby replied, finally giving his opinion. "Right now is all that matters. We can deal with the consequences later."

"What exactly are you saying, Colby?"

"I want to make love to you, Del and I want to fuck Jake too."

* * * *

Colby's words sent a shiver through Delaney. Her fantasies of having both men and watching the two of them make love to each other had her heart pounding as blood rushed in her ears. Could she throw caution to the wind and make love with both of them at the same time? *Hell yeah!* They could worry about the future later. For now, this would be enough.

"Who's going first?" she asked.

"Why don't you do a little strip tease for us?" Jake replied, his hazel eyes sparkling with lust when she glanced his direction. Colby's gaze held the same raging desire.

She let a half smile lift one corner of her lips as she got to her feet. "I could do that, but I need a little music." The stereo sat on a small corner unit near the window and held all her CDs. Surely, she could find something appropriate in her arsenal of country music. Moments later, Chris Young's voice filled the room with "Gettin' You Home." Each time the chorus about the little black dress hitting the floor came on, she dropped another piece of clothing until she stood in nothing more than her black thong.

"Damn, I love those things," Jake growled.

"Me too. They are so fucking sexy, they make me hard enough to break rock with my dick."

She shimmied and twirled around so her back faced the men. Hooking her panties with her thumbs, she slowly drew the bit of lace down her hips until it was loose enough she could drop it to the floor.

Within seconds, the heat of a naked chest warmed her back as another warmed her front.

"God, you make me horny, Del."

"I want your ass, babe," Jake murmured. "Will you let me?"

"I'd have to let one of you if we're doing this as a threesome."

"Not necessarily. You could suck one of us off if you aren't up to anal," Colby reassured her.

"But I want this. I want both of you."

"You've never had anal sex before though, babe, right?"

"No."

"We'll get a butt plug to ease you into it before we do anything along those lines," Jake said. "We don't want to hurt you. Without preparing you, it would definitely be uncomfortable."

"I can vouch for that. Jake's not a small man," Colby added.

"How about this, one of you in my pussy and the other would be between you two. You choose."

"Jake?" Colby asked. "What do you say?"

"You gonna let me do you?"

"Why don't I fuck you while you fuck her? I'm about to explode just thinking about watching you with Delaney while I'm in your ass. You had mine the first time. It's my turn."

Colby dipped his head and took a nipple into his mouth sucking it as he swirled his tongue around the tip. A deep moan escaped her lips and she tilted her head back on Jake's shoulder.

"I love watching him suck on your nipples, babe."

Jake's lips did a slow glide from her ear, down her neck until his mouth stopped at her collarbone. The tip of his tongue tickled as he licked the indentation while his hands roamed up and down her arms.

One set of fingers dipped between her thighs, spreading her outer lips seconds before two fingers plunged inside her. "Ahhh! God, that feels good."

"I want to eat you until you come so hard you see stars," Jake whispered against her neck.

Colby's tongue flicked down her stomach while his fingers started a slow rhythm of plunging and retreating.

Jake's arm snaked around her waist when Colby finally settled between her thighs, flattening his tongue, licking her clit. Good thing Jake had a hold on her because her knees buckled with the sensations rushing through her.

"I think we need to take this into the bedroom," Jake said. "A bed will be much more comfortable."

The next thing she knew, Jake had her cradled in his arms, heading for the door to her room. When he tossed her in the middle of her bed, she squealed, then scooted toward the top. "I hope you two brought condoms and lube."

"Got it covered," Colby said, pulling the supplies from his jeans pocket. "Bought some at the store when I stopped for food."

"Pretty sure of yourself, weren't you?"

"No, just very hopeful."

The two men stood side by side, both in direct contrast to the other. Where Jake had a few inches in height on Colby, Colby had a little more bulk to his frame. The lean bullrider and the tough biker screamed testosterone as their glittering gazes glued to her.

"My turn at your sweet pussy, babe," Jake said, dropping down between her legs on the bed. "Open for me."

With her thighs spread by his shoulders, Jake's head dipped as two fingers spread her open wider for his penetrating tongue.

"Mmm," she hummed, lying against the pillows, closing her eyes and enjoying the sensation of the rough pad of his tongue on her clit. Colby latched onto her left nipple with his mouth. The awareness of having both men focused on her needs sent her desire skyrocketing. The swirl of their tongues and the hit and miss sucking motion brought her to the brink of climax, holding her there by her fingertips. When Jake slowly inched two fingers into her wet opening, she lost the battle to hold back with a high-pitched cry of ecstasy.

She opened her eyes to find both men grinning.

"That'll do to start with, but I think you can do better. I wished I'd brought toys."

"Toys?"

"I can use my fingers to stretch your ass, babe, but a butt plug works much better. Next time for sure. I'll make sure to find an adult store somewhere before we do this again."

"Ooh, again. I like the sound of that." She stretched her limbs like a languishing cat. "What do we do now?"

"You can watch the two of us for a bit. We'll see if it makes you hot." Jake reached over to pull Colby into a kiss.

The fusing of their mouths and the wandering of their hands had her pussy throbbing with the need to be filled within seconds.

"I'm gonna fuck you in the ass, Colby. Then while I'm buried balls deep in Delaney's pussy, you can bury your thick rod in mine."

"I like your plan, Jake."

Delaney watched as the two men stripped off their jeans, revealing both of their cocks to her riveted gaze. Taking her eyes off them wasn't an option. The thought of not looking never crossed her mind while the two of them kissed again and grasped each other's cocks. Soft moans of satisfaction filled the air making Delaney want to touch herself. The two men were so into each other, she didn't think they'd noticed if she played a little.

Reaching into her nightstand drawer, she pulled out her little bullet vibrator and switched it on.

Two sets of eyes immediately focused on her.

"Damn, baby. Watching you with that and touching Jake like I've wanted to for so long is hotter than hell."

"You ain't kiddin'," Jake replied, continuing to stroke Colby's cock. "Hot, darlin'. Really hot. Now, make yourself come. I wanna watch while I fuck Colby." Jake grabbed the tube of lubrication and pushed Colby chest first onto the bed next to her. "Touch her, Colby, while I get you ready. I'm sure you'll be tighter than a vice around my dick."

Jake squirted some lube down the crack of Colby's ass as he penetrated him with two fingers. The sharp hiss escaping Colby's lips made Delaney apprehensive to let one of them fuck her there. If it hurt Colby with just Jake's fingers, how would it feel to have one of their enormous cocks there?

"Don't worry, sweetheart. Jake will make it good. I want this."

"Does it hurt?"

"A little, but it's the most incredible feeling when he's in there. I can't describe it really." Colby pushed two fingers into her pussy as she pressed the bullet vibrator to her clit.

"Ready, buddy?" Jake asked as he rolled on the condom he'd just opened.

"Go ahead. I've waited a long time to feel this again."

The head of Jake's cock eased into Colby's ass and Delaney creamed as she watched inch by inch disappear.

"Fuck! God, you're incredibly tight." Jake hissed when he finally seated himself balls deep.

When he finally picked up a slow sliding rhythm, Colby matched his pace with his fingers in her cunt. The vibrator against her clit ripped her up the mountain of her climax in half a second, holding her on the precipice as she watched Jake. "I'm gonna come, Jake."

"Let me see it, babe. Come for me."

She lost the last bit of hold on her climax. "Oh God!"

Seconds after she came, she heard Jake grunt and moan his climax. "Don't come, Colby."

"Damn you." Colby groaned.

"Why can't he come?" she asked.

"It'll be better if he waits. Holding off makes it that much intense when it happens." Jake pulled out of Colby and headed for the bathroom. "I'll be right back. Let me clean up."

Colby closed his eyes and clamped his teeth together so hard, she could see his jaw flex with the movement.

"You okay?"

"I will be as soon as I get to come."

"It's cruel, you know."

He opened his eyes and grinned. "It's worth it. Trust me. Try to hold off next time you're ready so you can see how it feels."

Jake returned a moment later and she wondered how quickly he could return to performing size. Obviously, her stare gave away her worry.

"Give me a minute, babe. It won't take long. I'm still horny as hell. I want to be inside your sweet pussy more than anything in the world right now."

Before her very eyes, Jake's cock thickened and lengthened. *Damn he's a sight.* His cock stood straight and proud with its full flaring head, bobbing against his stomach like she'd touched it.

"I want you so bad," she whispered, reaching for him. "I need you inside me, Jake."

He sank down on the bed beside her, gathering her in his arms. "I need you too babe. So much, but more than that, I love you."

"I love you too."

The other side of the bed dipped as Colby crawled in on her other side. "I love you too, Del."

"I love you, Colby." She glanced from one to the other. "I love both of you so much, but I'm terrified this isn't going to work."

"We'll make it work," Jake said, then took her lips in a blinding kiss.

She wanted to believe—needed to believe if even for tonight. If she had to choose between the two of them, she'd never be able to. The only alternative would be letting them both go.

"Love me, Jake." She wrapped her arms around him, pulling him on top of her.

"Condom." Colby flipped one from the nightstand to Jake and he quickly rolled it on.

The moment the head of his cock penetrated her opening, Delaney sighed and closed her eyes.

"Open your eyes, babe. I want you to know who's got you. I'm never letting you go again. Never."

When she looked up, his hazel gaze stared back with a fire of possession she'd never seen before on either man's face. He was right. He wouldn't let her go easily even if it was the best thing for all of them. Thinking about that right now made her want to cry.

"What is it, darlin'? I'm not hurting you, am I?" he asked as he finally seated himself completely inside her.

"No, Jake. You feel like heaven."

"Colby?"

"I'm right there, Jake," Colby said, rolling on a condom and moving behind him. "You ready?"

"Hell yeah. I've been dreaming of this for five years."

Jake spread his knees and lowered his head onto her chest as Colby positioned himself behind Jake.

"Easy. I'm no virgin, Colby, but it's been a while. You're big."

"Fuck, this feels incredible." Colby's voice sounded high-pitched and ragged.

"Tell me what it feels like, Colby," she said, wanting to know.

"Like a fist squeezing. I know it's something you can't compare it to, baby, but *ohmigod*. I'm gonna come before I even get to move at this rate."

"Let's do it this way. I'll pump and you two stay still," Jake said, moving his cock from her pussy and back against Colby.

"Christ!" Colby moaned.

"God, Jake," she murmured. "Fuck me hard. *Please.*"

With a slow snap of his hips, Jake filled her again. The three of them found a rhythm that brought them all to the edge within moments.

"You there, babe?"

"Hell, yes," she whimpered. "God, don't stop." Thick, long and wide, Jake filled her to capacity with each thrust, tapping at her G-spot and pushing her until she begged. "Please."

"Hold on. Don't come."

"I can't, Jake," she cried. "I need to so bad."

"You there, Colby."

"Yeah." Colby sighed behind Jake. "I can't wait much longer."

"We'll come together. Ready?"

"Fuck, yeah," she and Colby said together.

Jake slammed his pelvis against hers several times, riding her G-spot until she exploded on a cry, then shoved back against Colby as he moaned, collapsing onto Jake's back. Seconds later, she felt Jake stiffen as he came too.

10

Later in the afternoon, Delaney awakened to find both men gone. After their lovemaking session, the three of them had fallen asleep with her sandwiched between them. Jake under her cheek with her hand on his chest and Colby curled behind her with her butt against his groin.

Instead of jumping up to find the two men, she rolled onto her stomach, pulling her pillow against her cheek.

How can we make a threesome work? The people of this town won't accept us together, I know they won't. Jake couldn't even let his sexual preferences be known for fear of persecution.

"What the hell am I gonna do? I love them both."

I can stay and fight for the men I love. To hell with what the town says or I can let them both go and hope to find someone to love like I love them. She punched the pillow as a tear slid down her cheek. *I can't hurt my parents. They could be ruined if my relationship comes to light.*

"Jake and Colby together...God! This town just about ran the few gay couples we've had here out on a rail. Only Aaron and Craig managed to stick it out. They didn't grow up here either."

Noises from the living room drifted through the doorway, but she wasn't quite sure what they were. It sounded like the two of them were talking, but not quite. She couldn't make out specific words, only sounds.

Her next thoughts shocked her. Maybe they were having sex without her. She wasn't sure she liked the idea of them making love without her in the room. How would that affect a relationship between the three of them? What would happen if she bowed out? Would they continue to be lovers? Could she just be with one of them? However would she choose who to be with? What if neither wanted her, but they wanted each other?

"Stop it. They both said they loved you. Quit being an idiot."

With her curiosity getting the better of her, she wrapped the top sheet around her still nude body and headed for the door. She quietly opened it to peek out into the living room to find the two of them sitting on the floor. Colby doing sit ups with Jake holding his knees.

"Better," Jake said. "Those crunches you were doing weren't giving you the abs muscles you need for bullriding. You need to work your obliques more and your back muscles. You wouldn't have to work so hard to stay on the bull if you strengthened everything up. Your legs need better tone too."

"Where the hell did you learn this stuff?"

"I've been working with a trainer in Los Angeles. Not for bullriding of course, but for a heavy workout. He's been helping me with my core training doing weightlifting and general workouts."

"Can you help me with mine?" Colby asked between reps of his crunches. "We don't have a gym around here though."

"Maybe you could start one. You know, do some bullriding courses. With the kids around here, surely there are tons who want to do the rodeo stuff. You could help some of the kids, while keeping your strength and tone up."

"Good idea," she said, coming into the room. "With the three different business ventures we would be involved in, surely the town can't boycott all of them."

"The town isn't going to boycott anything, Delaney. You worry too much, darlin'."

"I have to since you two don't seem to be." She chewed her bottom lip with her teeth.

"What's wrong?" Jake asked, coming to her side, sliding a finger down her cheek.

"What if my parents can't accept us?"

"You said they already knew about the two of us five years ago."

She sighed and stepped away. This close to him, she couldn't think clearly and right now thinking fell on her shoulders more and more as they progressed into this threesome relationship. "Yes. They know all about me and Colby. They would accept either of you in my life, but both?"

"Why do they have to know?" Colby stopped his workout and sat up.

"I wouldn't lie to my parents, Colby. Not for anything."

"You sort of lied about the two of you way back when."

"How?"

"You didn't tell them about you until recently, right?"

"He's right, babe."

"Shut up. Both of you." She spun around and flopped down on the couch with all the elegance of an elephant sitting on a barstool. "Fine. Yes, I omitted my relationship with Jake five years ago until recently, but I refuse to do it anymore. They know about it now and they'll know about everything if things progress beyond this room."

"If?"

She didn't like the look in Jake's eyes. Black as midnight and sparkling with the anger she could see coming off his body, he looked ominous. If she didn't know better, she'd almost think he was ready to hit something the way he clenched and unclenched his hands.

"If?" he repeated.

"Yes, if. I've heard nothing but talk from both of you during this little reunion. How do I know you're serious about anything? You took off when talk got beyond what you could handle before, Jake."

"Not fair, Delaney. You know the reason."

"Yeah, you were scared, but what's to tell me you aren't afraid now? How do I know you aren't going to take off again? What kind of reassurance can you give me?"

"I'm not scared," Colby said.

"Shut up, Colby," she and Jake said in unison as she shot him a scathing look.

"I can't, babe. You have to believe me when I say I love you. I'm here for the long haul."

She pressed her lips together and shook her head. "I'm sorry, but I don't think just your reassurance is enough."

"What do you want me to do, Delaney? Tell me. I'll do it." Jake threw up his hands, clearly frustrated. "What? Do you want me to marry you? I will if that's what it takes. Right now. Today."

Tears burned her eyes as she blinked in a vain effort to keep them from falling. "You don't understand, Jake. It's hard for me to trust you with my heart again. I did before and you broke it. You don't have any clue what I went through when you took off."

After he moved to her side, he wiped at the tear she wasn't aware had escaped to drip down her cheek.

"Delaney. God, babe, don't cry. It kills me when you cry." He threaded his hand around her neck to pull her close. "I love you with all my heart, but you'll have to decide whether it's enough. I can't force you to believe me. Hell, I wish I knew what to do to make it all right again. Leaving five years ago was stupid. I know that now. Back then I couldn't describe the terror I felt at thinking about the long term with you. Today, I can completely think about a future without any regrets." He pressed his forehead to hers. "You mean everything to me except for the part Colby owns. You know all about me and him so it's no secret. I came back because of both of you. I couldn't continue to live my life without you both in it in whatever capacity. I didn't know you two were a couple, but it makes everything all the better. We can have our own little thing going on. No one needs to know about it except our families. You can tell whoever you want."

"I don't know, Jake. It all sounds too easy," she whispered, fighting back more tears. *Why can't I believe in him? Maybe it's because Colby isn't into this threesome thing as a permanent fix for our situation.*

"It can be easy. Don't make it harder than it has to be."

"Colby hasn't committed to any kind of a permanent thing, Jake. If I have to choose between you...I'm not sure what I'll do."

"What do you mean choose between us," Colby said coming to stand in front of her. "There's no choice right? You love me."

She glanced up, but the tears made everything swim in her vision until she blinked rapidly several times. "I love both of you. If we don't have this threesome thing, we can't have anything."

"I'm not liking where this is going, Del." Colby shoved his hands into his pockets. "You've been with me for a couple of years now. Jake took off and left you. Remember?"

"We've been over this, Colby," Jake said. "She doesn't have to be reminded."

"Apparently she does, if she thinks leaving me for you is the right choice."

Anger flushed Colby's face bright red. He didn't usually get mad. The thought of her choosing Jake over him didn't sit well. Little did either of them realize if she had to, she wouldn't pick either. "Stop it, Colby. I'm not choosing either of you. You need to decide whether this is a long term thing for you or not. That's what would be holding up any decision making on anyone's part except yours. Jake's already made his intentions clear and so have I. If we're doing this, it will be all three of us together. Yes, there will be a wedding. I'm not living in sin with you two popping out babies every year."

"Babies? No one said anything about babies," Jake snapped.

"I want children. If this is a sticking point, say it now." She wiped the tears from her cheeks, and then folded her arms over her breasts.

"Well, I..."

"I want babies with you, Del," Colby said.

The need to smack the crap out of both of them overwhelmed her. Having had enough of the two of them, she jumped to her feet to move to the window overlooking the back pasture to give her a moment to think. Time and space seemed to be the logical conclusion to this after-noon's talk. "Okay. You know what. We all need some time away from each other where emotions aren't running high, sexual need isn't off the charts and you two can figure things out. My parents will be home from their vacation soon. I want to talk to them about this whole thing. I want their take on it as well as how the town will react."

"What are you saying, babe?"

"I want you two to leave me and each other alone for one week. No seeing each other, no talking to each other—nothing."

"But..." Colby started.

"No buts, Colby. I need to clear my head. I can't do that with you two hovering. I've said what's on my mind, now it's up to the two of you to make peace with what you want from me and each other."

With all the regality of a queen, Delaney swept the sheet over her shoulder like a toga and waltzed back into the bedroom, firmly shutting the door behind her.

* * * *

"Mom, Dad. I need to talk to you about something," Delaney said the day after her parents returned from their vacation. She hadn't wanted to drop this in their lap, but her time seemed to be running out. Her week of solitude was almost up and she'd have to come to some hard decisions based on what the two men had to say.

"Sure, baby. What's up?" her dad asked, folding his paper and sliding it onto the coffee table.

"It's about a relationship issue I'm having."

"Has something happened with Colby, honey?" Her mom never minced words.

"Sort of."

"I think you'd better explain." Her mother sat down next to her dad, grasping his hand between hers.

Delaney sucked her bottom lip between her teeth, wondering how she could tell them everything that had happened since Jake's return.

"I don't think I told you before when I talked to you about Jake and what happened five years ago, but Jake is back in town."

"Yeah, we know. We saw him in town yesterday evening."

"Do you still love him, Delaney?"

"Yeah, Mom, I do, but there's more."

"More?"

"I love Colby too."

"Understandable, sweetheart. Your relationship with Jake was never resolved even though you moved on with someone else. You'll have to come to terms with your feelings for both men." Her mom glanced at her dad, then back at her. "Is this the reason Colby hasn't been over here in several days?"

"How did you know?"

"The men around here talk," her father answered.

"Nosy bunch of...little old ladies."

"They have your best interest at heart, baby. They all care about you like you were a sister or daughter to them. Hell, most of the men have been around here since you were born."

"I know, but I don't need them hovering."

"What's this all about, Delaney. You aren't saying something. I can see it's eating at you," her mother said.

She released a heavy sigh and stared at the ceiling for a moment. "I want a relationship with both Jake and Colby."

"Ookkaayy."

"I guess I have to explain something to you before I expand on this. The two of them had a relationship sort of way back when Jake was here before. It's the reason Jake said he left. He couldn't come to terms with loving me and wanting me, but still wanting Colby."

"So Jake and Colby are gay?"

"Not gay, Mom, bi-sexual is the term. They both want me as well as each other too."

"What do you want or does it matter?"

"I want both of them. I want a threesome relationship. We'll all live together—be together every day of our lives."

"A ménage?" her dad asked, worry clouding his expression.

She nodded. "Yes. My question to you is how do you feel about it?"

Her parents looked at each other. "Whatever makes you happy, sweetheart, is what makes us happy. If you want both men in your life on a permanent basis, then we would accept it as your choice."

"What about the town? How do you think they would react to it?"

"Some would ridicule, of course. If it's your lifestyle, then they would have to recognize it eventually."

"But my shop. They could boycott it, putting me out of business."

"Yes they could and you'll have to ask yourself if the love of the two men in your life are worth it or not. Only you can decide."

Delaney stood and walked to the sliding glass door. The pasture behind the house stretched for miles, the sunshine lighting the blades of grazing grass to a burnt gold. Warm breezes shifted the swaying stalks in a hypnotic motion that soothed her soul.

Home. Everything around her from the white-washed ranch-style house to the huge barn in the distance, had been her home from the time she was born. She couldn't leave it. Red Rock, Montana meant the world to her. Her friends were here—her family—her life.

Did Jake and Colby mean more to her than those things? The answer didn't come easily. Yes, she loved them, but she loved her hometown and all the people in it. The choice wasn't Jake or Colby anymore. The choice was Jake and Colby or Red Rock.

She turned back toward her parents, rubbing her arms. Suddenly, she felt cold and dead inside. "What do I do, Mom?" she asked in a whisper.

"You have to decide, sweetheart. Can you live without those two?"

"I don't know."

"I think it's a good thing you haven't seen them in a few days. A clear head will help you in the long run," her father added. "You know we like those two, even if Jake's leaving did make me mad back then. I hated to see you so hurt."

"I think he's learned his lesson, Daddy."

"I hope so. If he tried something so stupid again, I'd have to hunt him down to hurt him." Her father moved to her side, wrapping his arms around her shoulders, pulling her into a hug. "I love you, baby. You do what feels right in your heart. If people around here don't understand, it's their problem, not yours."

"Thanks, Daddy. I love you."

"We love you too, baby."

* * * *

The next day, Delaney stood inside the shop bay at her garage working on a car as the bell near the gas pumps dinged, telling her a customer had arrived. Her helper wasn't around today, so she headed out to take care of whoever had pulled in. Customers came before her love life no matter how screwed up things had become over the last week. Work wasn't on her mind these days.

When she approached the car, she rolled her eyes, smiling at the little lady behind the wheel. "Mrs. Oliver. What brings you out today?"

Mrs. Oliver was the adopted grandmother of both the Dunn and Weston clans. Her true biological relationship came from Natalie Weston, Cade Weston's wife, but ever since Natalie married Cade, she'd taken in half the town as her family, especially after Natalie had dated both Cade and Delaney's brother Kale at one time.

"Just taking a drive, my dear. How are you?"

Delaney stuck the gas nozzle into the woman's tank, flipping on the pump. "I'm hanging in there, Mrs. Oliver."

"You need to call me Gram like everyone else in your family, Delaney Ann."

She shook her head. "Yes ma'am."

"So what's this I hear you're having man troubles?"

Oh hell! "Not really. I mean..."

"Don't give me that bullshit. I heard all about it or some of it anyway." Gram pushed open her car door, planted her cane on the ground and wiggled her way out of the car. "Let's go inside where it's cooler and you can bring me something to drink. I wish there was a bar close. I could use a belt."

Delaney laughed and shut the door behind Gram. "You're driving though."

"Yes, I am. I probably shouldn't be at my age, but with no one living with me anymore, I have to get out on occasion."

"I thought Natalie's mom moved in with you," she said, taking the older woman's arm.

"I kicked her out last week to get her own place. She's been driving me nuts wanting to do everything for me instead of letting me do for myself. I'm not an invalid, you know."

"No ma'am, you aren't. You're as feisty as they come."

Within moments, she settled Gram into the chair behind the counter off the small store she ran in conjunction with the gas station. Nothing much, just a few staple items, candy, soda and sandwiches took up the shelf space.

"What can I get you to drink? No, I don't have any alcohol in here."

"Well, damn it anyway. I could have used a whiskey sour, but a lemon-lime something or another would be great."

After she retrieved the cold can of soda, she handed it to Gram and took a sip of her own as she sat down in the other chair.

"So tell me what's been going on with you?" Gram asked. "I hear an old boyfriend is back."

"Yes. I dated Jake Monroe in high school."

"Oh, I remember him. Doc used to care for the mother a lot. Saw the kids occasionally when one of them came down sick. Nice kids." Gram squinted her old weathered eyes as she studied Delaney like a bug under a microscope. "Didn't he leave right after high school?"

Delaney snorted. *Why am I not surprised Gram knew Jake's family.* "Leave it to you to know everything about everyone."

"Of course I do. Now quit stalling," Gram said, patting Delaney on the knee. "Tell me what the trouble is."

"I've been dating someone the last couple of years. Things were getting pretty serious between us."

Wise eyes watched her for a moment. "Now the ex-boyfriend is back and wants you again."

Delaney sighed and nodded. "At least that's what he says, but I'm not sure I can trust him."

"Do you still love him?"

"Yes. I never stopped. I love Colby—my current boyfriend—too. I can't choose between them." Delaney took her grease rag between her fingers and twisted it.

"Who says you have to? Why can't you have both?"

"Both?" Delaney asked, unsure if Gram meant what she thought she did.

Gram tapped her cane on the floor. "If they both love you and you love them, why not be a family with both of them?"

"What would the town say to a threesome though?"

The frown on Gram's face made Delaney smile. If anyone had the balls to stand up to what this town thought, it would be her. "Who gives a crap what the old biddies of Red Rock think. You have to live your life the way you see fit."

"They could shut down my station by getting their gas at the Quiki Mart and their car repairs in Smithville."

"If anyone begrudges you the happiness you deserve, then they are a small-minded, self-centered, old-fashioned stick in the mud."

She chewed her bottom lip for a moment. "But a threesome relationship is so out of the normal, Gram."

The multitude of wrinkles on Gram's face deepened and the laugh lines around her eyes crinkled as she smiled. "Yes it is. You'll have to be strong to stand up for what you want with whoever you want be it with Jake or Colby or both. If you love them like I think you do, you won't be the least bit happy if you weren't in this with both of them."

"I'm sure you're right, but..."

"No buts. Now, what do we need to plan to make this work?" she asked, rubbing her gnarled, weathered hands together. Her eyes twinkled with glee at the mere thought of something juicy. Knowing it would be no use fighting her on this even if she wanted to, Delaney rolled her eyes and sighed at the inevitable tornado her life was about to become.

"I've told the guys I didn't want to see them for a week."

"When's the week up?"

"A few more days."

"If they love you, they'll jump at the chance to be with you early," Gram said. "Call them and tell them to meet you at the old cabin on the south side of town."

"How is that going to help, Gram?"

"Sex, my dear. Down and dirty sex."

"But Colby can't decide whether he wants the three of us to be a long term thing or not. More sex isn't the answer."

"More?"

Delaney nodded as heat flushed her cheeks.

"Do you know two other men who might be interested in you?" Gram laughed at the shocked look on her face. "Fight fire with fire, my dear."

"I can't be with anyone else. It's not right."

"I'm not saying actually *be* with them, Delaney. Just make it look like you're moving on without Colby and Jake. A little jealousy never hurt anyone. I had to shock old Doc a few times while we were dating to get his ass in gear and ask me to marry him, otherwise we still wouldn't be married."

A snorted laugh left Delaney's mouth. Old Doc Oliver and Gram were the cutest couple she knew. They always held hands and snuggled at picnics and community events, making everyone around them sigh.

"I think I know exactly who to ask."

11

Colby walked into the Boots 'n' Spurs and found a table in the back corner. He needed a beer with a whiskey chaser to wash away the loneliness and desolation surrounding him since the two people who meant most in his life cut off communication. This had been the longest damned week of his life.

He glanced up when the waitress asked, "What can I get you, cowboy, other than me?"

Pretty—blonde with blue eyes and big boobs. He'd seen her around a time or two, but she wasn't a native of Red Rock. Normally, she'd be someone he might take a second look at, but not tonight. Tonight he needed solitude, not a come-on.

I should have stayed home to drink myself into oblivion. "Long-neck and a whiskey, please."

"Comin' right up."

As she walked away, he couldn't help but notice the rounded ass with a slight jiggle in her tight jeans, until his mind immediately compared her to Delaney. *God, what the hell am I gonna do about her? And Jake?*

Attraction sizzled between the three of them like lightning striking during a thunderstorm. Air snapped with the waves of desire emanating off their skin when they touched. He knew it. He felt it. Every touch, every kiss spoke volumes to his heart, but did he want to listen to it? Could he make a long term commitment to the two of them? He knew he loved Delaney. Did he love Jake?

A high-pitched giggle met his ear and he sat forward to see. Sure enough, on the dance floor stood Delaney with the Lawson twins flanking her, with one at her front and one at her back. Each hand a hand at her waist with a belt loop clasped in their fingers as they swayed to the slow music from the band.

What the hell is she doing?

The smile on her lips and the look in her half closed eyes looked dreamy and satisfied.

Did she sleep with them and move on without me and Jake?

Her voice drifted to Colby and he almost choked on his spit. "Wow. Being sandwiched between you two is a total turn on." She swung her hips slightly, rubbing her gorgeous ass all over the front of Cam's jeans.

"Ever had two guys at once, baby?"

"Mmm...maybe."

"Think you can handle both of us?" Colton asked.

"Easily, boys."

Colby grit his teeth and glanced across the bar as he tried to get his rage and jealousy under control, only to see Jake scowling at Delaney from his seat near the door. Apparently, Jake didn't like her little act either if the tick in his jaw gave anything away.

The moment their gazes met, Jake's eyebrows shot up. Two seconds later he stood in front of Colby. "What the hell is she doing?"

"I wish I knew."

"Well, I'm stopping this bullshit right now," Jake snapped.

Colby grabbed his arm to stop him. "Leave her be."

"You can't be serious. Our girl is out there practically fuckin' them on the dance floor."

"She wanted her space, Jake. We have to give it to her."

"All because you couldn't make up your damned mind whether you wanted what we have permanently."

"Maybe this is her way of saying she doesn't want us."

"She did until you couldn't decide." Jake's rage rippled off him in waves. "Fuck this. I'm leavin'."

Jake spun on his booted heels and disappeared out the door of the bar as Colby stared after him.

The waitress returned a few minutes later with his drinks and the come 'n' get me grin on her lips had him frowning. Forward women always made him think about his parents since his father constantly accused his mother of coming onto other men. After he flipped her some money, he said, "Keep the drinks coming and you'll make some good money. I don't need anything else from you."

The smile slid from her lips. "Are you sure? I could make your night."

"I doubt it. I'm not interested in the least."

"Fine. I don't beg, so find yourself some other girl."

"I already have one. Thanks." He did. He had Delaney, but he needed to decide whether he wanted Jake too on a permanent basis.

The sex was hot—off the charts hot. The thought of spending the rest of my life with both Delaney and Jake scares the hell out of me though. What happens if one of us wants out? He downed half his beer before returning the bottle to the table as he glanced across the room and noticed Delaney had disappeared along with the Lawson twins. *Who would Delaney marry? What about kids? Who would be their father? The town wouldn't accept us. What about fights? There would be disagreements, of course.*

"Maybe I need to talk to Delaney and Jake about all these things instead of trying to reason them out myself," he said, swirling the whiskey in the shot glass before he threw it into the back of his throat. "The last time I got drunk, Jake had to take me home." *Yeah and he got a good look at what he'd been missing all these years. He still came back for me.* He signaled the waitress for another round. "So much for bringing them to me."

Round after round finally started appearing at his table as the other patrons in the bar got blurrier and blurrier.

Getting this drunk probably isn't the answer to my problem, but I don't care. Jake and Delaney can have each other. I'm done! Done! A silly grin spread across his face as the waitress returned to his table again. "You're purdy."

One eyebrow arched as she slid into the booth beside him. "You're cute, drunk or not."

"I ride bulls, ya know."

"Do you? I bet you're good at it too."

"Done okay for myssselfff."

"I'm Rissa."

"Colby," he said, sticking out his hand. When she slipped her palm along his, he planted a wet, slobbery kiss on the back of it. "Nice to meet you. You ain't been here long."

"Nope. I bet you have though."

"All my life." He grinned and she laughed.

"I'm gettin' off right about now. How about I join you for a drink?"

"Sure, baby. We can dance, drink, play pool—whatever you want to do."

She leaned close to his ear. "I wanna ride those bullrider hips into tomorrow, cowboy."

"Sounds like a plan to me. Your place would be good."

"Come on. I'll drive." The woman slid out of the booth, then helped him to his feet. "Damn, you're big."

"All over, baby. All over."

She grinned again. "I can't wait to find out."

With his arm around her waist, they headed past the bar. He got a huge scowl from Seth as they walked through the doors and into the night air.

* * * *

The streets of Red Rock were deserted this time of the morning except for the local diner where the patrons of the town gathered for morning coffee before they went off to their respective jobs. Didn't matter if they were ranchers, farmers, cops, businessman or whatever, they rubbed elbows with each other, gossiping with the best of them.

Jake throttled down his bike and took a parking spot on the street. He had an appointment with Cade Weston about the business proposition of the new custom motorcycle shop his partners in Los Angeles wanted to open. Cade owned the building Jake figured would be the perfect spot for it—right on the main street of town across from the diner. The shop would sit on a prominent corner of downtown Red Rock and anyone who drove through town would see it. They would sell custom bikes but also some of the standard Harleys on their lot. Jake was excited to get started now that things were under control with Colby and Delaney or at least he thought they got everything worked out.

This forced separation of hers had him on edge though. He wondered what each of them had done this past week. He knew Delaney's parents had returned home and she mentioned talking to them about their situation. Her dad hadn't been happy with him five years ago when he'd quit without much word at all. Her parents had always been good people, willing to give a second chance. As long as they knew he loved Delaney, that's all that mattered. They'd support whatever decision she made.

"Hey Jake," Cade said, waving from the door. "Come on inside where it's a little cooler. I swear the summers get hotter every year."

They took a table near the front window where he and Cade could see the building he wanted as well as everything else on Main Street for a couple of blocks. "Things haven't changed much. This place is still where everyone comes in the mornings for coffee."

"Yeah. Been that way ever since I can remember. I doubt it will change much in the coming years either."

"So I hear you're married with a couple of kids now," Jake said, turning over his coffee cup as the waitress approached the table with a pot.

"Happily. I married a girl who grew up here, but moved away for several years. You remember old Doc Oliver, right?"

"Of course. He used to take care of my mom and us kids."

Cade grinned, pulling out his wallet. "I married Natalie, his granddaughter."

Jake took the pictures, scanning the faces of Cade's wedding picture. A little boy and a little girl grinned back from another. "Two kids?"

"Yeah. One of each."

"Nice family. You should be real proud." Jake handed the pictures back.

"I am," Cade replied, sliding his wallet back into his pocket. "Now, about this building. What's your plans?"

"The company I work for out of Los Angeles wants to put in a shop and sales floor for custom Harleys."

The soft high-pitched whistle Cade released through pursed lips, echoed even in the loud talk of the customers around them. "High-end stuff, huh?"

"Yeah. They figure with all the movie stars moving up this way, there's a market for them. When the word gets out we have custom bikes, they'll be all over it." Hot coffee burned his tongue slightly as he shifted his gaze out the window to Seth Reardon's Boots 'n' Spurs bar on the corner.

"I'm sure we can make a deal on the building. I think it would be perfect for what you want to do with it, Jake. There's shops in the back and wide open space in the front with big glass windows that would be perfect for showing off those sweet rides."

"After we're done here, can we take a look? I told them I'd get some pictures with my phone and email them back so they can see it. They trust me, but even as a partner in this venture, they want to know what's going on step by step."

Cade sipped at his own coffee. "Not a problem. I brought the keys with me."

The waitress returned to their table and took their order for breakfast. Once she walked away, Cade said, "So what's going on with you and Kale's sister, Delaney?"

Jake's stomach clenched at the mere mention of her name. Thoughts of their time together before she sent him and Colby packing could still make him hard as a brick. "I love her."

Both of Cade's eyebrows shot up to his hairline. "Wow."

"You know we dated way back when."

"Yeah. I heard Kale would have killed you if he could have caught you."

"I'm sure. Thing were pretty messed up then, but we're sort of back together."

"I thought she was dating Colby Mason."

"That's right." An explanation wasn't going to be forthcoming if Jake had anything to say about it. It wasn't anyone's business what happened between the three of them until things had been straightened out. They weren't anywhere close to being straight yet.

"None of my business. Got it, but be careful. Kale still isn't real fond of you."

"Thanks for the warning." Jake looked outside, noticing a truck sitting in the bar parking lot and he glanced at his watch. *Nine is awfully early for someone to be at the bar unless it's Seth, but the truck parked there looks an awful lot like Colby's.*

Breakfast arrived, drawing his attention away from the suspicious vehicle until after he and Cade finished their food. As they walked outside to take a look at the building across the street, they rounded the outside of his prospective establishment. He got a clear look at the truck in the bar parking lot. It *was* Colby's truck. *What the hell is he doing at the bar this early in the morning, unless he left it there last night? Shit. He probably got drunk again and needed someone to take him home. I really need to talk to him about this getting wasted business.*

A rundown apartment complex sat on the other end of the block and Jake hoped the tenants wouldn't have a problem with the motorcycles during the day. Harleys could be rather loud. Movement near the front of the second apartment caught his attention and he squinted, trying to bring the image of the couple into sharper focus. A woman in a short silky robe braced herself against the doorframe as the man stepped outside.

I'm gonna fuckin' kill him!

"I'll be right back, Cade. I see someone I need to kill right now." With a quick glance in both directions to make sure there weren't any cars about to knock him on his ass, Jake took off across the street, heading straight for Colby.

The woman leaned over and brushed Colby's mouth with hers, then stepped back. "Next time, lover, don't drink so much."

Jake grabbed Colby's shoulder, spun him around, then hit him right in the jaw, knocking him back against the building.

"Jake."

"Yeah, you asshole." Another fist to the jaw and Colby's hat went flying.

"Wait."

His breaths tore at his lungs with the effort to hold in his temper. "Hell no, you fucking bastard! How could you cheat like this?"

"But, I..."

"Just because Delaney made us all back off, you slink around to fuck some chick you picked up in the bar?"

"I didn't."

Jake hit him again.

Colby apparently was done getting punched as he straightened up and landed one to Jake's middle, and then his mouth.

"The hell you didn't." Jake swung.

Colby ducked before landing another blow to Jake's ribs. He took two stumbling steps back and Cade jumped between them.

"Enough, you two. What the hell is this all about?"

He looked at Colby and shook his head. "Nothing."

"Nothing? You're beating the hell out of each other for nothing?" Cade looked at Colby, then at the woman who still stood in the doorway unfazed by the two men fighting. "Who the hell is she?"

"A friend."

"Kale will kill you for this, Colby. You cheated on Delaney and didn't even have the balls to try to hide what you were doing? For Christ's sake, man, you're out here in broad daylight," Cade bellowed, holding the two of them apart as they tried to get at each other again. "Knock it off. Both of you."

Obviously, he'd read Colby all wrong. Care? Hell, he didn't care about anyone except himself. Not Delaney and certainly not him. "Take your fuckin' shit and stuff it up your ass, man. Love—you don't know the meaning of the word." Jake wiped his mouth with the back of his hand. Blood streaked across his knuckles. His or Colby's, he wasn't sure but he didn't care.

A cop car stopped at the curb and Laurel Dunn unfolded herself from the driver's seat. "Problem, Cade?"

"Other than these two trying to beat the shit out of each other, Laurel?"

"Do I need to take them in for disturbing the peace?" she asked, unhooking the cuffs from her belt.

"You might," Cade replied, pushing Jake back when he lunged at Colby again.

Laurel grabbed him by the arm, wrenching it up behind his back. "Chill, cowboy, or I'll have you cuffed and stuffed before you can take your next breath, understood?"

"Yeah," Jake snarled, not the least bit happy about being held by the much smaller woman. At over six feet, he'd never live it down having a five-foot-nothin' woman cuff him without a tussle. Of course, it would be one more nail in his coffin with Kale since the officer is his wife.

"What's this all about anyway?"

"Asshole there is cheating on Delaney," Jake hissed. "With the bimbo at the door."

"Kale's Delaney?" Laurel asked, loosening her grip on his arm.

"Yeah. So don't you think you need to cuff him instead of me? I was defending her honor."

"You'll be in deep shit, Colby, if this is true," Laurel said, pushing her sunglasses up on her head. "Kale will kill you for this."

"It's not," Colby snapped. "Yes, I got drunk last night and planned on fucking the lady here, but I passed out on her bed. I woke up a few minutes ago." He glanced at Jake and frowned. "I swear, Jake."

"Why should anyone believe you? I saw her kiss you."

"What he says is true," the woman added. "I got a bit jealous because he wouldn't this morning when he sobered up, so I kissed him to make sure he knew what he was giving up."

"He's got a girl. I think," Jake said.

"Yeah, I know and a guy. He told me. Someone he loves very much." She wrapped her robe tighter around her middle. "We all make mistakes."

"Not at the cost of the people we love, we don't."

"Fine! You want to hear me say I'm not good enough?" Colby moved so he stood nose-to-nose with Jake. "I'm not good enough. Not for you or Delaney and she made it clear she didn't want either of us last night."

12

A soft knock on the door brought Jake upright in bed with a hefty groan. *God, that hurt.* The punches Colby got off did their damage to his pride as well as his body. His whole body seemed bruised and battered.

The knock came again and he steered himself toward the door. He knew by the sound who stood on the other side.

He opened the door gingerly, wincing at the anger and pain on Delaney's face. "What are you doing here?"

"How could you two beat the shit out of each other, Jake?" she asked, pushing her way past him and shutting the door. "Sit so I can see these cuts."

"How'd you know?"

One perfectly arched eyebrow shot up. "Let's see. Neither of my two boyfriends could call me. No. I had to hear it first from Laurel, then Cade. Oh, but that was after Kale called me and threatened both of your lives if either of you ever touched me again." Shaking her head, she moved toward the sink in the bathroom. A few moments later, he heard the water running. "Is there an ice machine close by?"

"Yeah. Down the hall by the elevators."

"I'll be right back," she said opening the door and propping it so she could get back in without him having to get up from his spot on the bed.

If he didn't hurt so much, the thought of her taking care of him would be cute.

"Damn stubborn men," she mumbled when she returned a few moments later with the ice. "What the hell were you two fighting about anyway?"

"Colby fuckin' around on us."

She stopped fumbling with the ice to stare. "He cheated?"

"Didn't you?" She flushed red and dropped her gaze. "I saw you last night."

"I didn't do anything."

"Sure looked like it to me. I'm surprised you still had clothes on the way you were rubbing all over Colton and Cameron."

"I did it to make Colby think about us."

"What?"

"I wanted to force his hand, Jake. I knew he was there and I knew he watched. The twins were in on it. Nothing happened."

"I believe you."

"I'm glad." She reached up and brushed her lips against his. "What's this about Colby cheating?"

"I don't know for sure, but there's pretty damning evidence." Jake jabbed his hand through his hair. "I caught him coming out of some woman's room at the Sunset Apartments earlier. Cade and I were checking out the building for the new shop. I saw him." The pain knifing through his chest made it hard to breathe. "How could he, babe?" Tears made her eyes sparkle like diamonds, killing Jake to see them.

The ice forgotten, she moved to his side and wrapped her arms around his waist. Pain sliced his side as he gasped. "I'm sorry he hurt you—hurt us."

"I got the best punches." Jake shrugged, wincing at the movement. "He got off a couple good ones though." The scald of her tears burned his skin when they hit his chest. "Don't cry, darlin'. He's not worth it if he can't be faithful to either of us." She lifted her head and he tenderly wiped the tears from her cheeks. "You still have me."

"I love you Jake, but—"

"You love him too." He cupped her face with his palm. "I know, honey."

"I thought he loved me. He told me he did," she whispered. "How could he do this to me—to us? I could have sworn he cared for both of us."

"I knew he wouldn't admit it. Not yet anyway." Jake tucked her in next to his uninjured side to hold her close as he let his own hurt envelop him. Feelings for Colby ran strongly through his heart. It would be difficult to move on without him. Their friend and lover had obviously made his choice. It wasn't either of them. Colby didn't want commitment. "He's scared, babe. Being a threesome is a big step. If we do this, we're bucking everything normal and saying we want to do our own thing. It's not easy to do that."

She sniffed and he reached for a tissue from the nightstand. "If he loved us like he said he did, it wouldn't matter, Jake."

A loud knock sounded on the door and he looked down into Delaney's eyes. "I wonder who that is."

After she struggled to sit up without hurting him, she said, "It could be Kale. He threatened to come over here to finish what Colby started."

"Nothing against your brother, darlin', but I ain't lettin' him beat the shit out of me."

With her hand in his, they approached the door to find out who waited on the other side. "I won't let him hurt you. I promise." She sucked in a ragged breath and blew it out as she reached for the handle to pull open the door. Anger and frustration washed through her when she saw Colby's battered face. If what Jake said was true, how could she trust him? "What do you want?"

"I need to talk to you two," Colby replied, pushing past Delaney, and then turning around to face them again. "I'm going to say my piece so sit down and shut up."

Jake glanced at Delaney, then Colby. "Fine, but if you make her cry again, I'll kick your ass. This time I won't stop until you're bloody and raw."

The bruise on Colby's jaw stood out in stark contrast to his tanned skin. One eye was almost swollen shut.

"On the couch," Colby said with a wave of his hand.

Jake and Delaney sat down side-by-side as he grasped her hand in a death grip. This wouldn't be easy depending on what Colby had to say.

"First of all, I didn't cheat on you, Del, or you, Jake."

"But I saw—"

"Never fucking mind what you saw. You jumped to conclusions and wouldn't listen." Colby pushed his fingers through his hair. "Yes. All right? Yes, I had every intention of wiping you two out of my brain with some unknown woman who came onto me at the bar. This whole situation is driving me nuts. I don't know which way to turn."

"If you'll just—"

"Shut up and listen for a change, Jake."

Delaney squeezed Jake's hand. "Go on, Colby."

"I'm scared. I can ride bulls, rope steer and do all of those other things without feeling any kind of terror, but being in a serious relationship scares me to death." He shoved his hands in his pockets as he rocked back on his heels. "Here you two want us to buck convention and live in a permanent threesome. I'm not sure I can."

"Do you care about us, Colby," Delaney asked, her eyes sparkling with unshed tears.

"Yes," he whispered, dropping his gaze to the carpet. "This last week has been hell. That's part of the reason I ended up at the Boots 'n' Spurs last night. I needed to forget how you both make me feel." He glanced up and Jake could see the worry in his eyes. "I didn't want to fall in love with either of you. Things were so much simpler when Jake wasn't here, Del. We got along great and we had awesome sex regularly."

"But you were holding something back from me. I noticed it when you made love to me after you found out Jake was back. The whole night seemed different."

"Jake brings out something primitive in me. I can't be rough with you, honey. Jake can take the kind of sex I want. With you I have to be gentle and loving—"

"To hell with that, Colby. I like it rough sometimes. I want to explore having one of you up my ass. I want to be tied up spread eagle on the bed. I want someone to eat my pussy until I scream."

Colby stood with his mouth open and Jake smiled, thinking about doing exactly what Delaney described. Eating her out used to be one of his favorite pastimes. "I like the sound of that."

"Shut up, Jake," she snapped, jumping to her feet. She grabbed the front of Colby's shirt in her fist. "I love you and I love Jake. I want both of you in my life. To hell with what people in this town think. My parents know all about our relationship and they told me to do what would make me happy. The two of you make me happy."

"What if one of us wants out, Delaney? Then what?"

"We can cross that bridge if it ever arises. If we love each other, we can make this work. I know we can."

Colby ran one finger down her cheek. "I've been miserable without you." He glanced up and locked gazes with Jake. "Both of you."

"Me too. It killed me not to talk to either of you this week. I laid in bed thinking about making love with you." She ran her now flattened palm down Colby's chest. "Making myself horny as hell wanting you both."

"What did you do about it, babe?" Jake asked, coming up behind her to sandwich her between them.

"I had to give my toy an extra hard workout."

"Wanna show us?"

"I didn't bring it with me." She pouted, wiggling her butt against his groin. "But I'm sure we can make do with one of the hard cocks in this room, don't you think?"

"Witch," Jake growled, cupping her breasts with both hands, pulling her back. "I distinctly remember someone mentioning getting tied spread eagle on the bed."

"Yeah, me too," Colby replied, grabbing her ass with one hand and Jake's cock with the other. "I want in this ass, baby."

Jake moaned and Delaney hissed.

"I've got a butt plug we can use to get her ready," Jake said through clenched teeth. The feel of Colby rubbing his dick through his jeans drove him crazy with lust. "We'll have to be careful though."

"Why?"

"Jake's ribs are bruised because of your fight."

"Sorry, man, but I know how you feel. I won't be sucking or licking anything for a few days. My jaw is killing me."

"How about this? I lick her pussy and make her come while you're fucking me. Then Delaney can ride me while you take her ass."

"I like your plan," Colby said, removing his hands and lifting his T-shirt from his torso to reveal the hard planes of his abs.

The mouthwatering muscles made Jake pant like a dog over a juicy bone. He loved Delaney's curves, but the differences between his two lovers excited him past the point of no return. To make love to both of them was like a dream come true.

Jake whipped Delaney's shirt over her head and reached for the button to rid her of the jeans riding low on her hips. "Get them off."

Within moments, all three of them reached for the others. Hands explored, mouths fused and licked. Bodies came alive with need to love and be loved. Colby lifted Delaney and headed for the bed. "Do you have anything to tie her with?"

"I bought handcuffs and nylon rope the other day, anticipating doing this," Jake replied, pulling out the toys from the adult store he'd found.

"Nice."

"You're going to stick that huge thing in my ass," Delaney asked, her eyes wide with wonder and a little fear as Colby laid her on the bed. "Is it going to hurt?"

"A little at first, babe, but you'll love it by the time we're through. There's nothing like the feeling of being so full there." The packaging came apart in his hands as he withdrew the cone-shaped plug. He squirted lube on it, rubbing it around a bit as her worried expression grew.

She chewed her bottom lip with her teeth, nodded, and rolled onto her stomach. "Okay, but go slowly."

The moment her perfect ass rose to meet the smack of his palm against it, he almost lost his rigid control on his own desire. "Spread her cheeks, Colby."

Staring at her puckered hole, Jake groaned and closed his eyes for a second. To bury his cock there would be a dream come true. Not today. Today Colby would be there in her virgin hole. His time would come...soon. He spread some of the cold liquid around her anus, working it into the tissues until he could slip one finger inside her. The last thing he would ever do was hurt this woman, either physically or emotionally.

"It feels weird."

"Weird?"

"Good, but strange." She pushed her butt back toward him. "I need more, Jake, please."

He pushed two fingers past the ring of muscles and she groaned her pleasure as he scissored them, working them in to spread her more. "Ready for the plug?"

Her breathing hitched as she held it for a moment before she nodded. After he removed his fingers, he pressed the lubricated plug's nose through. Delaney hissed and cried out, "Burns."

"I know, baby," Colby said, kneading the muscles of her stiff shoulders with his hands. "Relax. It will be easier."

"I'm trying."

"Easy, darlin'," Jake whispered, slowly pushing the plug past the resistance until it was fully seated inside her. "Better?"

"God, it feels incredible. I'm stretched beyond belief. I have this full feeling," she murmured, rolling over onto her back.

"Give me your wrists." When she complied, Colby wrapped the fur-lined cuffs on and stuck the Velcro sides together. "Lift your arms up toward the top of the bed." Colby threaded the small chain through the slats in the headboard, snapping it to each cuff.

She pulled slightly against the restraints and shot Jake a worried look.

"Too tight?"

"No, but..."

"You'll be fine. I'm not going to tie your ankles unless you don't keep your legs open." Jake spread her thighs and wiggled into position between them to lick at her pussy. "Nice." The smell of her arousal sent tingles down his spine. The glistening wetness on her pussy told him the whole scenario turned her on to screaming proportions. With a slow lick from slit to clit, her hips rose as a moan escaped her lips.

"Harder, Jake."

"Mmm. Mine to play with. You lie back and enjoy."

"God please," she begged, pulling at the restraints and trying to close her legs.

He reached up to smack the inside of her thigh lightly. "Leave them open. I'm not done yet."

"Don't tease me, Jake. I need this."

The decision to not prolong her desire came with Colby's lubricated fingers against his asshole. They all needed this so badly, he knew denying their pleasure this time wouldn't be wise. "Fuck my ass, Colby." The moment the hard, broad tip of Colby's cock slowly penetrated Jake's ass, Jake sucked Delaney's clit between his lips and flicked the tip with his tongue.

"Oh God, oh God, oh God!"

Cum flooded his mouth as Delaney's pussy quivered against his lips and her whimpers of ecstasy reached his ears.

Colby pounded against his ass as each hard thrust pushed Jake's tongue into Delaney's pussy. The tongue fucking prolonged her climax until she whimpered in another growing orgasm.

The moment Colby stiffened and cum filled Jake's ass, Delaney came again in a screaming orgasm of her own. Jake's own dick throbbed and ached with the need to come himself, but he held off by gritting his teeth. Forcing his orgasm back down wouldn't kill him.

"You didn't come?" she asked, eyeing his stiff erection through sleepy eyes.

"Not yet. I want inside your sweet pussy when I do."

"You two are going to kill me."

"Not quite, baby. You'll be ready for a real nap after we're done," Colby said, withdrawing from behind Jake and heading for the bathroom to clean up.

"I'll be right back, darlin'. I need to wash up too." A quick release latch on the cuffs let her arms go as she rolled over onto her side.

Delaney mumbled something as her eyes closed and Jake smiled. She looked so beautiful lying there curled up in a ball with her hands beneath her cheek. When she drew her knees up to her waist, the edges of the butt plug peeked out. He chuckled to himself.

The second he passed Colby near the bathroom door, he touched the other man's semi-hard erection and cocked an eyebrow. "Ready so soon?"

"Damn right. I can't wait to take her virgin ass."

"You're lucky, man. I wanted the pleasure, but I can't with these bruised ribs. Thrusting would be painful."

"I'm really sorry, Jake."

"Me too, lover." He frowned at the ache in his chest as he looked at the floor for a second. "It killed me when I saw you with that woman. The thought of you cheating on us broke my heart, Colby. I love you and Delaney. I hope if you ever get the urge again—"

Colby grabbed a fistful of his hair and pulled his head closer so their mouths were mere millimeters from each other. "I won't, Jake. I love you. Things just got so crazy last week, I didn't know what to do. Now I do. The three of us are meant to be together."

Their mouths fused in a desperate kiss.

"Hey, save some for me," Delaney said from the bed. "I'm feelin' kind of lonely over here."

Both he and Colby glanced back with a grin. "Keep her occupied. I'll be right there."

"No problem."

The door closed behind him as he sighed. Things had worked out between the three of them and he couldn't believe his good fortune. He had the woman he'd loved from the time he could remember and the man he'd come to care more about than just friends. His job had given him the security to go after what he wanted. Now he had it. Colby and Delaney.

Soft moans reached his ears. It sounded like Delaney might be getting wound up again by Colby before he could get back out there. A quick wash up and he walked back into the room to find Colby between her legs, his ass in the air.

"Fuck, that's about the hottest thing I've ever seen," he said, stopping at the side of the bed, taking one of her nipples in his mouth.

"God, I love when you suck like that, Jake."

"Up, babe. I need your sweet heat wrapped around me," he said, helping her sit up so he could lie down on his back. "Straddle me, tilt your butt up. Colby will take the plug out."

The hiss of her breath against his chest when Colby slid the plug from her ass scorched his skin. Goose bumps rose along his flesh.

"Ride me, darlin'."

The moment her pussy surrounded him, he closed his eyes and sighed. He was home.

With her breasts cushioned against his chest, she took all of Colby into her ass in a slow push that had Jake almost losing the control he had on his desire. Only a thin membrane separated the two cocks.

"Oh my. So full." A soft whimper left her mouth only to be captured by his.

"I love you, babe," he whispered in her ear, then looked up at Colby, whispering the same.

Tears clouded his vision. The love he felt for these two people drove all hurt, mistrust and terror from his heart.

Home. He'd finally found the place where he belonged.

* * * *

Jake softly snored on the other side of Delaney who lay curled up next to Colby, but he knew she didn't sleep. He could feel the soft brush of her eyelashes against his chest every time she blinked. Darkness cloaked the room in soft grays and blacks except for the thin strip of light from the streetlight outside.

"You okay?" he asked softly, running his fingers down the arm sprawled across his chest.

"Yeah. You?"

If she could have seen the smile on his face, she would have laughed. "Yeah. I'm okay. We weren't too rough on you, were we?"

She snuggled deeper. "Just rough enough. I never knew it could feel like that."

"I love you, baby."

"I love you too, Colby. You and Jake mean everything to me. I can't live without either of you."

One tear scalded his chest where it dropped. "Hey. No crying. I'm not going anywhere."

"Thank God." She sniffed, wiping her face with the sheet. "Are you accepting this as meant to be?"

"Yeah. I think I am. I can't picture my life without you two in it."

"We can make this work for the long haul, Colby. If you love us like we love you, it doesn't matter what anyone else thinks."

"Baby, it's okay. You don't have to convince me anymore."

"Which one of you is going to make an honest woman of me to the eyes of the world?"

He frowned as his fingers stopped their trek. "We hadn't really discussed getting married."

"You do want to marry me, don't you?"

"Of course I do."

"Well, I can't marry both of you except in private with just our families, but I want to be legally tied."

"I think you should marry Jake."

"Why?"

"Because with the new shop and everything, he'll have more to offer you should something happen to me while I'm riding. Bullriding is a dangerous business, baby. God forbid, but if something happened to me, Jake would have to take care of you."

Colby felt a shift in the bed as Jake rolled and fitted himself against Delaney's back.

"I think he has a point, darlin'. We can all marry privately, but it would be better financially if you were my wife. If something happened to me, you would inherit my share of the shop."

"All this morbid talk—"

"It's not morbid. It's realistic," Jake replied and Colby could do nothing but nod. "On that note, hang on just a second."

Jake jumped from the bed and headed toward his suitcase in the corner. Several seconds later, he returned and sprawled himself across hers and Colby's legs on his stomach, grinning like the cat who ate the canary.

"What are you up to, Jake?" she asked.

"Yours is the left hand, darlin'. Colby's is the right." Jake opened both hands palms up and asked, "Will you two marry me?"

In his palms lay a diamond engagement ring in platinum with several smaller diamonds surrounding it and a matching man's band with a row of diamonds across the top. He picked up the engagement ring, holding it out for Delaney to take or reject. Colby smiled when she nodded enthusiastically as Jake slipped it on her left hand. Next, he took the band and held it up for Colby. "Will you?"

"I can't think of anything I'd rather do," he said, holding out his left hand for the ring.

"Of course, we'll have a ceremony. This is just the engagement, but you both belong to me now and I belong to you."

"When did you pick this out, Jake? It's beautiful."

"I took a trip into Billings earlier this week and found a neat little shop. I knew as soon as I saw them it would be perfect."

"I don't have one for you," she said, sadly.

"Me either."

"Ah, but I come prepared. If you two had said yes, I bought one for me too," he replied, retrieving a second matching band exactly like Colby's. "I have the matching wedding band for yours, Delaney. You'll get it when we legally marry." He handed her the thicker one to place on his hand. "These will be our official bands. You two can purchase something later if you want, for me to wear and for each other. I figured our matching ones meant our love is a circle of three."

"They're perfect, Jake." She took Colby's hand and they slipped Jake's on his finger together.

Epilogue

The sun rose bright in the eastern sky the morning of their joining ceremony. Delaney stood at the window gazing down at the crowd standing around her parents' back yard waiting for her, Jake and Colby to make their grand entrance.

It seemed the entire town stood below as the sun rose overhead. It still surprised her how supportive and accommodating everyone had been when the news of their threesome made the rounds of the gossips. Oh sure, there were a few who couldn't understand how she could love two men or how the two of them could love each other, but things like that didn't bother her anymore. She'd learned to ignore the stares until the ruckus died down and everyone went on with their lives.

Their joining ceremony would bring up the gossiping again, but this meant everything to her. This meant she finally belonged to both of them for the rest of her life.

They'd taken care of the legal formalities the month before at the courthouse with her, Jake, Colby, her parents and Jake's mother present. Today would be her wedding day.

"You okay, honey," her mother asked, coming to stand behind her, placing her arms around her waist.

"I'm fine, Mom. Just misty-eyed is all."

"You'll ruin your makeup if you cry."

"I know," she whispered, sniffing to hold back the tears.

"Are you happy, sweetheart?"

"I couldn't be happier. I get to be their wife for real today."

"You've always belonged to both of them, you know."

She turned around and hugged her mother. "I love you, Mom."

"I love you too, baby. I'm happy to welcome Jake and Colby into our family. They've always been a part of it from the time they started hanging around here trying to get your attention."

"They did not."

"You might never have noticed, but they sure did. Those two couldn't stop looking at you. It was near impossible to get them to ride fences. They wanted to hang out in the barn with you." She touched Delaney's curls and sighed. "You look so pretty."

"Thank you for lending me your dress."

Her mother laughed and hiccupped. "I never thought I'd see you in this. My little tomboy never wanted to wear dresses. Always the jeans and coveralls."

"I'm still your tomboy, Mom."

"I know, but right now you're a beautiful woman ready to meet her destiny in loving those two downstairs." She wiped a tear from the corner of her eye. "You'd better be making me some grandbabies soon."

"I'm not sure if the guys want any right away. Besides, you have Kale's two."

"Three."

"Laurel's pregnant?"

"So they told us last night. They didn't want to say anything else to the family or ruin your day."

"I guess we'll have close cousins then."

Her mother's eyes widened. "You mean—"

Delaney nodded and pressed her hand to her still flat stomach. "I'm pregnant too, but you can't say a word! Neither of the guys knows yet. You're the first person I've said anything to."

"You know for sure?"

"Pretty sure. I took a home test yesterday morning while the guys were gone to town on errands and it was positive."

"Oh sweetheart!" Her mother pulled her into a hug. "I'm so happy for you. I'm sure the guys will be thrilled."

"I hope so. I hadn't planned on this happening so soon. We didn't really try to prevent it though."

"Then they can't be upset." Her mother gave her a serious look. "You have talked to them about starting a family, right?"

She turned back toward the window and saw Jake standing near the altar with Colby standing in the distance near the barn. The clock on the wall said ten. The ceremony would be starting soon. Her stomach was in knots. Luckily, no morning sickness had started yet, but she didn't hold her breath hoping there wouldn't be any. "We've discussed it, yes. I just thought it would be a little further down the road."

"Everything will be fine. It's not like they can change their minds now. Besides, they love you. It's so obvious, it makes me smile to see and I know you three will be happy together for a long time to come."

"Thanks, Mom," she whispered, turning to hug her mother again.

"When is the house supposed to be ready?"

"Before winter sets in. We can finish the inside after, but the outside will be done in the next couple of months."

"You know, I was surprised to hear you three were building on Colby's parents' foundation. I know he had such a rough time there, the memories could be overwhelming."

"They are sometimes, but we're working through them together. Colby insisted we build a house with love at the center of it to wipe out the horrid memories of what his father did." She glanced back outside and caught Colby looking up at her bedroom window. She knew he could at least see her outline when he lifted his hand to wave. He looked so handsome in his white tux shirt, black jacket with his jeans, black cowboy hat and shiny new boots. His blond hair was a sharp contrast to the darker colors. She lifted her hand and waved back.

Jake turned and looked up. The same attire graced his lean, muscular form. Both men looked so handsome, they took her breath away.

"It's time, honey," her dad said from the doorway.

She took a calming breath and blew it out before she turned to take his arm.

"You're sure about this?"

"More than anything, Daddy. I love those two stubborn men down there and I can't wait to start our life together."

Her mother grabbed the long train of her gown while her dad escorted her down the stairs and out the front door. Soft music played from the DJ's booth in the corner as she stopped in the doorway of her parents' home to face her wedding day.

A late summer breeze cooled the air, rustling the leaves overhead. Jake stood at the altar and turned to face her. Colby took his place at the end of the aisle where he would walk with her to meet Jake. They would take their vows as husbands and wife at the vine-filled trellis.

The moment she locked gazes with Colby, tears welled up in her eyes and she fought to keep them at bay. She loved these two more than anything in the world and she prayed to God, He would see them through their darkest days as well as their brightest mornings with His loving hand to guide them.

"I love you, baby," Colby said, taking her hand from her father, kissing her fingers.

"I love you." She smiled to spite the tears. "Shall we meet our other half?"

"You bet," he replied, threading his fingers with hers as they made their way toward Jake.

The moment they reached Jake's side he leaned over and kissed her and then kissed Colby. "Are you two ready for this?"

"More than you know," she replied.

The two men stood in front of her side by side while they said the vows they'd written for each other.

"Jake—Colby. I take the two of you for my wedded husbands. From this day forward until death do us part, I will love, honor and cherish both of you forever. You've become the sunshine in my days and the warmth in my nights. We might fight from time to time, but we will always find each other in the darkness. I love you."

"Delaney—Colby. I take you, Delaney, as my wife and you, Colby, as my husband from this day forward until death do us part. I will love, honor and cherish both of you forever. The two of you are my world and my life. I didn't know what love was until I found you. Even on our darkest days, we will have the light of our love to guide us. I love you."

"Jake—Delaney. I take you, Delaney, as my wife and you, Jake, as my husband from this day forward until death do us part. I will love, honor and cherish both of you until my dying day. You both became my saviors and my guiding spirits a long time ago when I didn't know what value my life held or how I would escape the hell it had become. The love we share will bind us together forever. I love you."

The minister stepped up. "These three have exchanged their rings previous to this ceremony and now are bound in the eyes of God and their families until the end of time. You may now kiss each other."

The crowd laughed as the three of them exchange passionate kisses and then turned to face their friends.

"Ladies and gentlemen, may I present to you Mr. Jake Monroe, Mr. Colby Mason and their wife, Delaney."

* * * *

Later that night when she lay sedated and well loved in the arms of her two men, she whispered, "You know I love you guys, right?"

Jake lifted his head, glancing her way. "Of course, we do, babe. We got married today and pledged our love forever. Why would you think anything different?"

She shifted around to sit up. "There's something I need to tell you. I should have said something before the ceremony, but I couldn't bring myself to."

"Baby, what's wrong?" Colby asked, worry clouding his expression.

"I know we didn't really discuss it very much beforehand. You know, it's not something we really tried to prevent. I want you to know it's fine with me if it's fine with you two. If not, we can think of something—"

Jake reached up and drew her down into a kiss. "Whatever it is, darlin', we'll work it out."

After a huge sigh, she said, "I'm going to have a baby."

"We know," Colby replied and then kissed her until she couldn't breathe.

"You know?"

"Of course we do. When did you figure it out?"

"Yesterday when I took the home pregnancy test. What about you?"

"A week or so ago when you were complaining how sensitive your breasts were. It almost hurt when I sucked on them." Jake ran one finger over her nipple as she gasped. "See. You're responsive anyway, but overly so now."

"What about you, Colby?"

"I figured it out when you bit my head off after I came back from the rodeo last weekend and didn't kiss you fast enough."

"I'm sorry."

"I know. I figured you were either pregnant or getting ready to go on the rag. When you didn't start a few days later and we still made love, it was obvious you were pregnant."

"How do you guys feel about this?"

The two of them look at each other and grinned. "We love you, babe. We'll love a little bundle of joy whether it's born in nine months or nine years."

"Really?" she sobbed, loving these two more every day.

"Yes really, Delaney," Colby replied. "Baby, our love is not based on just the three of us. We talked about having babies and if we're having one soon, all the better. This just means we'll have to make it a priority to get the house done."

"God, I love you two. I thank the Lord you both made the difficult choice to love me and each other in return."

"Forever," Jake replied.

"Forever," Colby said.

THE END

MASKED STRANGER
Prequel free read to
Montana Cowboys 5

Sandy Sullivan

How in the hell did I let Cade and Natalie talk me into coming home to visit and during the annual masquerade ball for charity event? Elizabeth Weston stood off in the corner fidgeting with the fan in her hand. The Marie Antoinette costume covered all of her essential parts, but left little to the imagination where her boobs were concerned. It barely covered her nipples. The dress required a corset beneath the elaborate ornate stitching, ruffles and wide skirt, to cinch her into it and she fought for every breath. How women wore these things every day, she'd never know nor did she care to find out. One concession with the skirt was the short almost mini length in the front and the long train in the back. At least she could walk without tripping over it and it showed off her legs. Her one attribute even Ari couldn't complain about.

The ballroom at The Millhouse sported extensive Halloween decorations in every corner and on every available space. The crystal chandeliers had fake spider webs hanging from them and several black creepy crawly things wound into the web. The tables were draped with black and orange cloth and fine china settings. Dracula stood in one corner while a large haystack and scarecrow were set in the other. The five hundred dollar a plate dinner brought in tons of money for the local boys and girls club every year.

The only fun of the whole evening so far, was seeing what everyone else wore. Pirates, cowboys, of course, barmaids and even a Little Bo Peep graced the attendees.

"Are you having fun," Natalie asked, coming to her side in her pirate wench costume, a perfect complement to her husband's pirate. Cade made an awesome one with his light brown hair wind tousled, white shirt open to the waist showing off his wide chest and those pants? Where did he get a set of breeches that tight?

"Oh yeah. A blast."

"You need to get out there and mingle, Elizabeth. There are several unattached men here, you know."

"I'm not unattached, Nat. I have a steady guy."

Natalie's eyebrow rose and she gave Elizabeth her I-don't-call-your-asshole-boyfriend-worthy-material look.

"I know you don't care for Ari, but we're getting serious."

"Okay. Sure. Whatever you say." She glanced up and down Elizabeth's dress and said, "I love the outfit, by the way. Very sexy."

"My boobs are about to fall out."

"Yeah and I can only wait to see the attention that brings."

"Bitch."

Natalie laughed and sauntered away to find her husband, no doubt. They made such a cute couple, she couldn't help but love her sister-in-law even if she liked to butt in and get nosy about Elizabeth's love life.

Several moments later, the skin on her arms started to tingle as if someone watched her. She glanced around the room, but didn't notice anyone paying an overly extended amount of attention her way. The feeling wouldn't go away though and it made her a little nervous. Reactions like this usually spelled trouble. Even she'd learned that lesson when she moved to Los Angeles seven years ago, the night she'd been attacked in an alley. *Stupid. Leaving the club and trying to walk home alone. What an idiot thing to do.* Luckily, she hadn't been raped or worse, left for dead.

The tingling turned to goose bumps and shivers down her back. Who watched, she wasn't sure, but the feeling intrigued her more than frightened her.

Sweat beaded between her breasts and heat flushed her cheeks. The punch bowl near the other side of the room called to her parched throat. The fan swishing in front of her face didn't cool her enough. With a heavy sigh, she headed toward the long table with the punch and finger foods set out to hold everyone until dinner was served at nine. She skirted the dancers on the floor, nodded to several people she thought she recognized, but nothing would keep her from reaching the refreshingly cold punch she needed to quench her thirst. The alcoholic drinks would flow in a little while. She didn't want to get too drunk tonight even if she felt a little lost amongst the folks here. Yes, she grew up with most of them, but since she'd moved away, she felt like she didn't belong anymore.

"Can I buy you a drink?" The voice rolled over her like a blanket, warm and fuzzy.

She spun to her left, almost elbowing the man in the ribs. "Uh, I'm sorry."

"Don't be. It's not too often I run into a beautiful woman, literally."

Startling blue eyes stared back from behind his mask. Thick brown hair the color of chestnuts clung to his neck just above his color, and one piece defied placement as it fell over his left eyebrow. Decked out in a tuxedo jacket, black tie and form fitting slacks, the man oozed sex appeal and confidence. The width of his chest and the size of his biceps spoke of a hard laborer—someone used to physical work.

"Do I know you?" she asked, her voice breathless and low. Her nipples pebbled into tight nubs at the mischievous sparkle in his eyes and the wicked smirk on his lips.

"I don't think so. I'm sure I would have remembered someone like you."

"Are you from here?"

"Yes."

"I grew up here. I know everyone."

"Obviously not," he replied, one side of his lips lifted in a half smile. He reached for a glass of punch from the table and handed it to her. "You look parched."

"Thank you."

They sipped the cool liquid in unison, their gazes never leaving each other. Never in her life had someone put her body on high alert like this. Cream slid from her pussy to wet the silky underwear between her thighs. *Damn. Even Ari doesn't do this to me. Ari. Shit.* She glanced away as embarrassed and arousal warred within.

"What was that thought, beautiful?" he asked, one finger sliding down her bare arm.

"Nothing, why?"

"You frowned." He laughed low and sexy. "You could give me a complex with one of those looks."

"Well, we can't have that now, can we?"

"Come." He took her punch from her fingers and set both their glasses on the table. "Dance with me."

Tugging her toward the space set aside for dancing, he quickly swept her up in his strong arms and swung her around the floor. Damn, the man can waltz? What the hell? She didn't know anyone in Red Rock who could waltz.

"You must have moved here recently," she said, inhaling his spicy yet musky male scent. Her dress swirled around their feet, playing peek-a-boo with his dark slacks and cowboy boots.

"What makes you say that?"

"Three things. One, as I said, I know everyone in Red Rock. Two, you waltz and no one here waltzes and three, I'd remember those eyes if I'd seen them before."

"Thank you for the compliment."

"You're welcome." They continued to dance to the slow music, her right hand clutched in his left, and her other hand on his broad shoulder with his warm one at the small of her back. She couldn't seem to look away from those mesmerizing eyes.

"You're correct in your assumption. I moved here about a year ago."

"Ah. That explains it. I moved from here several years ago."

"Yet you return?"

"For a visit, yes. My family is here."

"Where do you live now?"

"Los Angeles."

"Too bad." He swung her in a wide circle and then waltzed her out the side doors onto the balcony of the hotel and off into a semi-dark corner. "It's a pretty night and warm for October."

"Yes, it is. It's usually much colder." Goose bumps rose on her bare shoulders and she rubbed her arms to ward off the chill.

"Cold?" he asked, although he didn't wait for her response before he slipped his jacket off and draped it around her.

"Thank you. It's a little chilly without a wrap of some sort."

He tipped his head in acknowledgement and asked, "What do you do in Los Angeles?"

"I work at an international shipping firm while I pursue my degree."

"Degree in what?"

"Medicine."

"Ah. A doctor, eh?"

"Yes. I plan to specialize in women's care."

"Noble profession. Doctor's, I mean."

"What do you do? You don't look like a rancher." Her gaze swept over him from the top of his thick hair to the tips of his boots. The cowboy boots on his feet almost made her giggle. So typical of someone in Montana, but not in a tuxedo.

"Ranching, no. But, I think I'll keep myself a bit of an enigma to you."

"Why?"

"Mystery is intriguing, is it not?" he whispered, his finger sliding along her jaw.

"True." She couldn't breathe, couldn't think beyond the touch of his skin, the warm of it along her face. Her mouth went dry even though she practically drooled at the look in his eyes. The heat, the need and the desire reflected clearly in his gaze. He wanted her. She had no doubt. Her womanly ego puffed up knowing she affected him. God, she wanted to know who he was. With lips parted, she invited the kiss she knew would rock her world. A small smile made the crease in his cheek more pronounced and she wanted to run her tongue along it.

For several moments, they stared at each other, both lost in the other's eyes, unaware of anything or anyone else around them. When he bent his head and she closed her eyes to take in everything about the kiss, her heart stopped beating and then resumed with a slam against her ribs the moment their lips touched. His softly caressed hers, sliding over them with such care, she wanted to cry and yet she felt the need to grab him and deepen the kiss to mind-blowing. The soft brush of his tongue on her bottom lip opened her mouth on a sigh. Tongues entwined, sliding over each other, both trying to taste the other and absorb the moment of their first kiss. He deepened the kiss, exploring her mouth and tasting everything she had to give with every stroke of his tongue.

Callused fingers found the flesh of her breast above her neckline, rasping softly along the pimpled skin. God, she wanted him to touch her.

His mouth left hers to skim along her jaw until he flicked her earlobe with his tongue. Warm lips found her throat and sharp teeth nipped at her skin as she vaguely wondered if real vampires existed, and whether he might be one. She almost giggled at the thought until those same sharp teeth bite into the muscle where her neck and shoulder met.

"I wish your hair was down. I bet its gorgeous flowing around your shoulders," he murmured, kissing the stinging spot left by his teeth.

The roaring in her ears muffled the sound until the second call of her name. "Elizabeth?"

He lifted his head, smoothed his thumb over her bottom lip and smiled. "Someone looks for you."

"Apparently."

"Thank you for the dance and the kiss. We'll meet again."

"You're welcome," she whispered, as he took two steps back.

A soft smile played on his lips when he winked and turned to go back inside, disappearing into the crowd without a backward glance.

"There you are," Natalie said, coming to her side. "Dinner is being served."

"Did you see the guy who just left?"

"What guy?"

"Tall, brown hair...gorgeous blue eyes?"

"I didn't see anyone," Natalie replied, taking her arm. "Come on. I'm starving."

Dinner went by in a blur for Elizabeth. Her mystery man had disappeared into the night like something out of a movie. No one she asked seemed to know who the stranger might be and it frustrated her beyond belief.

After the ball, she cornered Natalie and Cade at their house. Why she felt the need to know who this guy was, she wasn't sure. His kiss went beyond anything she'd ever experienced before. Warm, liquid heat zipped through her even thinking about his lips on hers. The way the kiss had started soft and gentle and then turned into hard and demanding meant the man knew the passion he aroused. "You have no idea who the guy could have been? He said he lives here. Brown hair, collar-length, big gorgeous blue eyes? Tall? Muscled?"

"Sorry, Elizabeth, but there are several men in Red Rock who might fit that description," Cade answered.

"I can't believe you have no idea!" Cade and Natalie exchanged glances and secretive smiles. Elizabeth wanted to punch them both. "You're going to make me go back to Los Angeles tomorrow without any idea of who this guy could be?"

"I don't understand why you have such a fascination with him. Are you sure you weren't imagining him?" her brother said.

"No, Cade. I didn't imagine a tall, dark, handsome man kissing the living daylights out of me, feeling up my boob and then walking out of my life like he never existed. What? You think I'm nuts?"

* * * *

Doctor Marcus Milton crouched behind the mare laboring in her stall. His brown hair plastered to his head as sweat ran from his scalp. Even though the temperatures were cooler with November here, the heat inside a barn with a sick or hurt animal could be stifling. This particular mare was having a hard time birthing her colt. As the new or not so new veterinarian in Red Rock, it fell on his shoulders to keep the stock healthy, including cats, dogs, rats, snakes or whatever other type of pet the people decided to have this week.

"Will she be all right, Doc?" Natalie Weston asked from near the stall door standing next to her husband, Cade.

Marcus glanced up through his glasses and said, "She'll be fine, Nat. I may have to turn the colt though. It appears like he wants to come out backwards."

Cade and his wife were some of his favorite clients and good friends since he'd moved here over a year ago and taken over Doctor Alexander's practice when he retired.

"You'll have to stay for dinner, Marcus," Cade said, folding his arms over the stall door.

"Wish I could. I've got a couple of other animals I need to check on before it gets dark." Marcus stood and wiped his hands and arms on the towel he grabbed from the ground near his foot.

"We aren't eating until later anyway. If you're back by seven, you'll make it," Natalie replied with a wink.

He stepped out of the stall and shut the door behind him. "I don't want to impose."

"You aren't imposing, Marcus, and you know it so stop. Besides, Elizabeth left this morning to head back to Los Angeles." Natalie's grin told him she knew all about his little secret.

Damn it. Am I that transparent? The visible relaxing of his shoulders gave him away. "Good."

"Good?" Cade asked. "What am I missing?"

"Nothing," he replied, grabbing his bag from the ground. "I'll be back in a couple of hours. Call me immediately if anything changes with the mare and I'll come right back." Heading for his truck, he hoped Natalie didn't tell Cade. When he glanced out the windshield at the pair, he knew his secret had been blown when his friend grinned and waved. *Great! Just fucking great!*

After two hours, two cat calls, one pregnant rat birthing and a Chihuahua puking hair balls, Marcus rolled back into Cade and Natalie's yard. First stop, check the mare—second stop, avoid Cade and Natalie's matchmaking.

"You can't stay out here all night and avoid us, Marcus," Natalie said, finding him in the barn.

"I'm not, Nat. I just got here."

"Thirty minutes ago."

He glanced up and groaned. The twinkle in her eyes gave away her intentions and he knew he'd be screwed the moment he went into the house and not literally either. "I'm checking the colt position one more time."

"Fine. I'll expect you inside in five then," she called over her shoulder as she walked down the dirt aisle of the barn.

"Great," he grumbled, slipping on his gloves and sliding his hand inside the horse. The mare grunted and shifted, but otherwise laid still. "Easy, girl. You'll be fine. I'm hoping your little guy turns himself before he makes his final appearance though." When he finished, he snapped off the gloves and wiped his hands and arms. No use trying to avoid the confrontation. Natalie reminded him of a pitbull with a bone when it came to things like this. He exhaled and headed for the house.

The door swung open the moment his knuckles touched the panel. "No need to knock, Marcus," Cade said, standing aside to let him enter.

"Thanks, Cade. I need to wash up, so I'll be back in a second."

"No hurry. Dinner is still about fifteen minutes from being done," Natalie said, walking in from the kitchen. "Beer?"

"Please," he replied, heading down the hall. He knew Natalie and Cade meant well, but they needed to leave well enough alone.

The minute he returned to the living room, Nat handed him his bottle of beer and he took a seat in the leather chair to the left of the fireplace.

"Did you enjoy yourself at the masquerade ball last night," Natalie asked, taking a seat on the arm of the sofa next to Cade.

"It was...interesting." He took a drink and let the cold, malty liquid slide down his throat.

"I imagine," she replied with a grin. "Nice costume you had on, by the way. Very mysterious and all. I almost laughed at the cowboy boots. Typical man."

"What can I say? I love my boots." He grinned and shrugged. "Country boy at heart. Besides, it's much easier to dance in boots."

"The ball is always a great money maker for the boys and girls club in town."

"It should be at five hundred a plate. Damn man. Expensive, but a good cause."

Cade grinned. "And it's sold out every year."

"Why did you leave so early last night, Marcus?"

How in the hell can I answer that without giving myself away? "My beeper went off on a call."

"Ah," Natalie said with a grin and then a laugh. "You're such a liar!"

"Nat," Cade growled.

"He's lying, Cade. He left because of Elizabeth."

"Natalie, please. We really don't need to go into this, do we?" Marcus asked as he felt the heat of embarrassment flush his cheeks. Bold and brass could never be used to describe him. How he'd been able to be the confident, self-assured man last night with Elizabeth, he didn't know. Maybe it was the mask and the fact of her ignorance to who he really was. The simple country animal doctor and not the mysterious, sexy man.

"You danced with her," she said, folding her arms over her chest.

"Yes, I did, but she doesn't know me and I really don't know her either," he insisted. "It really wasn't more than a dance." He took a drink of his beer and hoped to avoid anymore talk of Elizabeth, but apparently Natalie wasn't going to let it go.

"I saw you watching her from the corner of the room when she didn't realize. The sparks between you two practically lit up the place."

"We danced and talked, Nat. Nothing more." *Forget the kiss. Forget the kiss.* He wiped his mouth and stifled a groan. *Yeah, like that's going to happen. I fucking dreamt of her all damned night after I went home.*

Natalie studied him for a moment and then her eyes lit up. "You didn't tell her who you were, did you?"

"No," he whispered, picking at the label on his beer.

"The mysterious stranger. She'd never met you before so she wouldn't know who you are. You wore your contacts instead of your glasses, you wore a tux and a mask as you played the man of mystery. Brilliant!" Natalie clapped her hands and grinned. "She'll be so intrigued, she won't know what to do."

"Did she mention anything this morning?" he asked and then grimaced. *Damn it! Quit feeding this.*

"No."

"See? It's nothing."

Natalie huffed and slid down the side of the couch until she hit the cushion. "If she'd just leave the jerk she's seeing in Los Angeles."

"She's seeing someone?"

Natalie bit her lip and said, "Yeah. She's been seeing this rich dumbass for a few months now. He's a real piece of work."

But, she kissed me like she wanted to. "She's in college out there, right?"

"Yeah. UCLA for medicine. She's about done with it though. I believe she graduates next June, but then she has residency to do," Cade said, finally adding to the conversation after keeping quiet. "She's applied at the hospital in Billings from what I understand."

"Hmm."

Natalie got up and went back into the kitchen to check on dinner.

"If you're really interested, Marcus, I can introduce you."

"No!" He cleared his throat at Cade's raised eyebrow. "I mean, it's not necessary. We don't even live in the same town, so it's a mute point."

"True, but she does come home to visit frequently and she'll be leaving LA when she's done with school."

"Does she plan to settle back here?"

"I'm not sure what her plans are when she's completely finished," Cade replied, a tolerant grin on his lips. "What would it hurt to introduce you two?"

Marcus sighed and shook his head. "I'm sure she doesn't need anyone fixing her up with dates, Cade. It's better left alone. She's totally out of my league anyway."

"Why would you say that?"

"She's beautiful, smart, and sophisticated. I'm nothing more than a country veterinarian." He shrugged and finished his beer. "Can we drop it please?"

"If you insist, but I doubt Nat will."

Marcus rolled his eyes and groaned. "Yeah, that's what I'm afraid of."

Cade sipped the beer in his hand. "One thing for you to remember about Elizabeth, she's a born and bred country girl herself. She might look sophisticated and everything, but she's a cowgirl at heart."

"It doesn't matter. We're miles apart." He sat forward in the chair and draped his hands between his knees. "I would appreciate it if you and Natalie didn't mention anything to Elizabeth."

"You don't want me to tell her who you are?"

"No."

Cade rubbed the bridge of his nose. "Why, Marcus? Maybe if she knows, she'll want to meet you."

Shaking his head, Marcus stood and moved toward the big bay windows overlooking Cade and Natalie's pasture. "Last night was a fantasy. Two people coming together for a brief moment in time. A shared kiss under a starlit sky." He turned toward Cade. "A fairytale. She has her life in Los Angeles and I have my practice and my life here in Red Rock. Maybe someday we'll meet again and I'll tell her, but it has to be me, Cade. Can you understand that?"

"Yeah. I can. I just hope you aren't making a huge mistake."

The telephone rang and he heard Natalie say, hello.

"Oh, hi Elizabeth," she said, walking back into the living room. "I'm glad you got home all safe and sound."

A pause in the conversation and Natalie's face went white and then red.

"What do you mean Ari is going to propose?"

To be continued...

1

DOCTOR ME UP
Montana Cowboys 5

Sandy Sullivan

An explosion of shattering glass silenced the noisy terminal of Los Angeles International airport. Elizabeth Weston dropped the champagne bottle and fluted glasses she'd brought to celebrate her engagement to Armand Listolini into the large metal trashcan sitting near one of the pillars. Anger, disgust and frustration rolled down her back in a nauseating wave of sensation as she watch him step away from a tall, slender blonde. Never in a million years did she suspect he'd been cheating on her. Apparently he had. For how long? Right now, she didn't care. It was enough to know he cheated once.

"You sorry son of a bitch!" she screamed, grabbing her perfect stiletto heel and throwing it at his head. Unfortunately, he quickly ducked as the heel careened on past him to lodge itself against the wall. *How many women has he been with while he'd been with her?* "Did you take your fuck buddy with you to New York, Ari?"

"Elizabeth, calm down." With his hands stretched out in front of him, he almost looked sorry, whether for being caught or because he'd cheated, she wasn't sure.

The pleading look didn't calm her, only fanned the flames of her anger. "Calm down my ass!"

"Sweetheart, let me explain."

"Explain what? You came down the escalator with your tongue down her throat. What's there to explain?" She laughed hysterically as she hobbled on one heel back and forth in front of the baggage claim. The plan to surprise him was tossed in the trashcan along with the expensive champagne she'd bought to celebrate. "Or maybe you want to explain the receipt to Coleman's on your desk? The one I thought might be for an engagement ring since we've been fucking for over a year." The other heel sailed toward his head. Her aim missed. The shoe bounced off his chest, leaving the imprint of her heel on his expensive suit. "Instead you gave a bauble to *her.*"

His expression screamed boredom at her antics and it did nothing but fuel her fury to raging. "Really, Elizabeth. Hysteria doesn't become you." He absently swiped at the dirt on his jacket.

She flicked a glance to the woman at his side wearing a matching expression. A gorgeous emerald and diamond necklace at her slim throat. *The bitch.* Blonde, stunning and tall, the designer dress hugging her curves to show off each dip and valley to perfection, made Elizabeth hate her all the more.

"Hysteria? You want to see hysteria. I'm just getting started, buddy." With both hands firmly planted on her hips, she pulled her lip back in a snarl. "I'm a redneck girl from Montana, remember? The one apparently not good enough for the likes of you, well guess what? You can have your painted up, botoxed until she explodes, fake boobs and liposuctioned bimbo. I'm done with your ass. Take your pencil dick and shove it up her ass from now on. I do hope he's better in bed with you than with me, honey, because he sure lacked for any imagination."

Not aware of the crowd gathering, she flushed when a round of applause rippled through the group. At this point, she didn't give a shit about the scene she made especially looking back at Ari again. His complexion had turned a ruddy color instead of the even tan he usually sported. Hopefully he'd burn in hell for his cheating ways. Or maybe his dick would fall off. One could always hope for the best.

"You'll be sorry you made such a scene, Elizabeth."

"Sorry? Seriously?" She shook her head as she laughed. "Shall I call a few of my friends from redneckville Montana and have them come out here to kick your ass for you? I'm sure my brother and his friend Kale would love to use you as a punching bag for a few rounds." A sobering thought crossed her mind. "I should have known." Pressing her lips together, she looked up at the ceiling for a moment as tears gathered in her eyes, but she refused to let them fall. Never in a million years would she let him know how much this hurt. "All the time we've been together was a game for you. See how long you can tie up the backwoods girl in a knot while you're fucking your newest investor on the side."

"Did you think I would be interested in something long term with you?" He snorted, making her want to punch him. "You're a nobody from a small ranching community in Montana, Elizabeth. I, on the other hand, own a large international shipping company. I need someone on my arm who can keep up with me in style, poise and mannerisms. You, although you are hot between the sheets, are a country girl to the bone. You wear T-shirts to bed. You insist on doing yard work. You want to own a *horse*!"

She moved so she stood within arm's reach of him. "I may be a country girl, but don't fuck with me." Despite the skimpy black dress, primping all day with hair done just so, makeup perfectly applied, mani and pedi at the salon, she'd stood ready to receive the surprise she knew was coming when Ari returned from New York, not the shock of a lifetime. With her hand clenched in a fist, she pulled back her arm and let the punch fly hoping she connected with something—maybe knock a tooth out.

Pain screamed up her arm as she watched Ari stumble back to land on his butt. "Shit, that hurt." She shook her hand, grimacing. After she spun on her bare feet, she headed for the front door of the airport to retrieve her car. *Let him suck eggs through a straw for the next couple of days. Fucking bastard.* "How dare he use me like this."

Tears streamed down her cheeks, dripping off the end of her chin. She really thought he loved her and she loved him, didn't she? Real passion didn't exist except in fairytales. Men didn't illicit those types of feelings in her. She just figured she couldn't get sexually aroused like most woman. The scrape of a man's hand over her skin, the brush of his kiss on her lips, his tongue lightly flicking against her mouth before taking the kiss he wanted, those things might turn her on if she ever felt them, but so far she just tolerated sex.

Only one man ever got her blood pumping and her skin tingling.

"I imagined the whole thing, I'm sure. Yeah, his kiss was nice, but really..." She shook her head and wiped her face, refusing to cry anymore over Ari-the-asshole or her mysterious masked stranger—the man she met six months ago on her last trip back to Red Rock for that fateful Halloween Ball. If she admitted it to herself, the man had left her with nothing more than a toe-curling kiss before walking out of her life. She'd never learned his name or anything about him other than he stood approximately six feet tall with broad shoulders strikingly emphasized in his tuxedo jacket. Had the most gorgeous blue eyes she'd ever seen on a man and the softest chestnut colored hair she'd ever run her fingers through. No one she'd asked the rest of the evening seemed to know who he was.

"I left there, turning my back on the toe-curling kiss and went home even though it was to a man I thought I loved. I played right into Ari's self-centered attitude by go back to him and his cheating ways."

She'd flown home the next day. Back to her life, school in Los Angeles —back to the man she thought loved her and planned to ask her to marry him soon. *Enough is enough. I'll finish my degree before heading somewhere back toward home to do my residency. When I'm done, I can open my practice anywhere I want.*

Red Rock was home—had been since her family moved there, helping to establish the town. Westons and Dunns were founding families. Everyone knew them and respected their leadership in the community. She'd been the successful daughter. Moving to Los Angeles, getting her medical degree had been her dream from the time she could remember. She wanted the loving husband, white picket fence, two point five kids and a dog.

Hell, who was she kidding? Being a doctor wasn't going to allow for a normal life. There would be long hours, midnight phone calls, extended rotations, but taking care of people was her life passion. She couldn't imagine doing anything else.

The moment her car came into view, she hit the button in her hand to unlock the doors. Once inside, she grabbed a napkin out of the glove compartment to wipe the mascara from under her eyes. "Great. Just fucking great."

She grabbed her cell phone from her purse to dial her sister-in-law. Natalie hated Ari even though they'd met only once when Cade and Nat had come out to California to visit a year ago.

"Hey sis. What's up?"

After a huge, noisy sniffle, she said, "You wouldn't believe me if I told you."

"What happened?"

"Ari came home from New York."

The impatient huff on the other end of the line revealed how much Natalie wanted to hear the news. "So?"

"He's been seeing someone else."

"Oh, Liz. I'm sorry, honey. I know how much you must be hurting."

Incredibly, Natalie actually sounded sorry. "You aren't going to say I told you so?"

"Of course I am, but not right now." After a long bout of silence only broken by her occasional sniffing, Natalie said, "Okay, I told you so, but I'm glad you found out now. Honey, he's not worth your tears."

"I know, Nat, it's just I really thought he was the one. You know? Even if there weren't fireworks."

"There should be. Don't settle for less." A small snort followed as the words left her mouth.

"I've never felt scorched by someone's touch before. It's pleasant, but not something I would write home to mom about."

"If you're with the right man, you'll have the fire, the excitement. Though maybe you wouldn't want to tell your mom even if she were still alive. A girl has to have her secrets."

Should I ask? The two of them seemed so happy and so in love, sometimes they make me sick.

"Go ahead. Ask, Liz. You know you want to."

"All right. Is everything all sparks and light up the night sky between you two?"

"Of course. It's been exciting and fulfilling from the moment I laid eyes on him after so many years. His kiss curls my toes. Everything tingles like an electric charge."

"I wish," she murmured.

"You'll find the right guy, Liz. When you do, it'll be the same for you." Natalie laughed. "I have an idea. Come home for a few days. It'll be nice to catch up. You know, spend some time with you."

"I have two more weeks of classes and graduation."

"Then you can come home with us after graduation. You know we'll be there."

"I knew I could count on you, Nat."

"I love you, Liz. You know I'd do anything for you."

* * * *

Two weeks later Elizabeth stepped out of her car, stretching her back to relieve the kinks from the long drive. The trip from Los Angeles back to Red Rock with all her stuff sucked. Several days with nothing but her own company just wasn't a nice trip. Hot, sticky and sweaty, Elizabeth couldn't wait to stand under the shower to wash the grime from her body in the lovely spray of water calling to her.

The expanse of the Double D Ranch stretched for miles in several different directions, almost reaching the mountains or so it seemed. The question of how much land they actually had crossed her lips one day as she rode in silence next to her mother. The woman was feminine to the core but it never stopped her from being the epitome of a rancher's wife, living her life at her husband's side, raising their children and loving the land. When the answer came, Elizabeth couldn't fathom the miles of land stretched in front of her as belonging to her family.

The one story ranch house with the wraparound porch called her like a mother's lullaby, whispering words of comfort and longing to have her home. Tears pricked the back of her eyelids. Her mother wouldn't be here to greet her this time. Grief still stung at the loss so early in life. It wasn't fair. She'd never get to see her grandchildren, never be able to watch her daughters marry—missing out on all the simple pleasures in life living in God's country.

Sunlight streamed down from the sky, lighting everything in a soft, yellow glow. Blue skies with white puffy clouds rolling lazily by, wiped the sadness away momentarily as she took in the changes since the last time she'd been there. Freshly painted fences gleamed in the sun and new shutters on the house brought the homey feeling in as the old rocking chairs on the porch reminded her she was home. She couldn't wait to gallop across the open fields on a powerful horse again. It had been too long since she felt the bunch of muscles of a horse beneath her, the breeze in her hair and the freedom of racing the wind.

"Elizabeth!" her father yelled from the barn as he walked toward her before he wrapped her in a warm hug.

"Hi, Daddy." The warmth of her father's embrace began to heal the crack in her heart forged by her mother's passing and Ari's betrayal.

"I'm so glad you're home, sweetheart."

"Me too even if it's not permanent." She looped her arm through his as they walked toward the house.

"How long are you staying?"

"I've taken a month to be here with you to enjoy everything before I have to be in Billings for my residency."

"Have I told you lately how proud I am of you? My daughter the doctor."

"Yes, but you can say it a few more times." They laughed as they stepped on the porch and he pushed her into the rocking chair.

"I'll get you some lemonade. You look wiped out."

"I am. It's a long drive with not much else to do but think."

Her father shook a finger at her as his lips turned down in a frown. "Don't even think about that guy. He's not worth the fuss. If I could have gotten my hands on him, I would have ripped him in half."

Her deep sigh had to have revealed her turmoil to her father when he studied her face closely. "I know, Daddy. I just thought he was different, but he turned out to be like all the other men." She giggled. "Besides, Cade took care of him for me when he showed up at my apartment demanding his jewelry back."

He patted her hand, saying, "I'll be right back. I want to hear all about it."

She glanced across the open pastures with another heavy sigh. Home. Everything would be better at least for the month she planned to stay. Soft grass under her toes, warm sunshine on her face, cooling breezes blowing her hair would calm both nerves and heart. *Enough of men. I don't need them. I don't want any of them around. I've got my life and my work. It's enough.* A soft breeze picked up a piece of hair, blowing it across her cheek. As she pulled the strand back to tuck it behind her ear, she noticed a pickup truck she didn't recognize near the barn. Dually wheels and shiny chrome made her whistle through her teeth in a small show of appreciation. She always was a sucker for a guy with a truck.

Did Dad buy a new truck?

The bang of the screen door pulled her from her musings. She whispered thank you when her dad handed her the glass. "Did you get a new pickup, Dad?"

"Oh, you mean the one by the barn."

"Yeah."

"It's not mine. Belongs to the vet. One of the mares is getting ready to foal. He's keeping an eye on her for me. Doc Alexander retired some months back. Doctor Melton took over his practice." Her father took a seat in the empty chair, sipping from his own glass. "Nice guy. Cade and Nat know him pretty well."

"Hmm." She sipped her lemonade, glancing back at the barn. *New vet. Colleague of sorts.* "I should probably introduce myself."

"Sure. He's a few years older than you."

"I'm not looking for a man, Daddy."

He held up his hands. "I didn't mean anything by it, Elizabeth. Just making conversation. Come on, I'll introduce you."

"Should we take him some lemonade too?"

"Good idea. It's pretty warm in the barn."

After she retrieved a big glass for the vet, she headed to the barn with her father at her side. The huge white structure housed their prize horses, the tons of tack required and several stalls for sick cattle. The soft nickering of horses greeted them when they stepped inside.

"Marcus?"

"In here."

"How's the mare?" her father asked as they approached a closed stall to the left.

"She's progressing nicely. The foal should be here soon. Within the next few hours anyway."

Her father pushed her with a hand at the small of her back, toward the stall where the doctor sat crouched in the hay with the heaving mare. She couldn't see much—a black cowboy hat, lean hips and firm thighs. "I'd like you to meet someone."

"Oh?"

"Marcus Melton, this is my daughter, Elizabeth Weston. She's home for a short visit before she heads off to Billings for her residency."

He lifted his head, cocked an eyebrow and smiled. "Nice to meet you. I'd shake your hand, but I'm a bit tied up at the moment."

Her stomach lurched at the sexy grin on his lips. Pretty blue eyes and nice long eyelashes stared back. *Did he just wink at me?* "No problem. I brought you some lemonade. We thought you might be thirsty."

"Thank you. You can leave the glass right there. I'll get it in a minute," he said, going back to his work as he checked the mare again.

"Have you been a vet long?" she asked, thoroughly intrigued by the self-assured man with the firm ass in those Wranglers.

"A few years."

"I just finished medical school. I guess that makes us colleagues of a sort."

The grin appeared again as he looked up. "You can be my colleague anytime, darlin'."

She glanced at her father, but he only shrugged. Was the man really flirting with her? *Why does he remind me of the guy at the ball?* "I guess we'll leave you to your work. I can't imagine being with a laboring mare for hours on end." She cocked her head, squinting as she tried to make out some more of his features. His hair looked thick and dark as the ends brushed his shirt collar. Strong hands, firm arms, broad shoulders— things he would need working with animals, she supposed. The lighting in the building left something to be desired if one thought to get a good look at one thing or another. "It was very nice to meet you. Maybe I'll see you around town. I'll be visiting for a while."

"Sure. Maybe we can have dinner one night. You know, compare notes."

When they left the barn, she looked at her father saying, "Wow. Definitely an alpha-male there."

"Alpha-male?"

"You know. Self-assured, cocky, arrogant."

"He might be those things, Liz, but Marcus is the best vet I've seen in a long time. He knows his stuff. A couple of mares have already seen his expertise. Those aren't the only females following him around. Almost all the single women and half the married ones seem to need him to take care of their pets now more than ever." Her father scratched his chin. "He almost acted as if he knew you."

"I've never met him before today, Daddy."

Her father chuckled, looping his arm over her shoulder. "Well, I'm sure you'll meet him again in town or over at Cade's."

She shrugged, heading for the house. "I suppose. For now, I need to unpack my car. Wanna help?"

* * * *

Marcus leaned back on his haunches as he listened to the fading footsteps. His body screamed for release from the torment of her voice on his libido. Celibacy sucked. He'd been in its clutches for too long now.

Holy hell! I didn't realize she was coming back to town. Sweat trickled from under his cowboy hat, leaving a trail of wetness along his temple until he took off the felt, wiping the moisture away impatiently.

"Gettin' her into bed would solve all my problems. Yep. A nice roll in the hay would get her out of my system so I can get back around to being single and available."

He stumbled to his feet, wiping his palms on the towel lying across the stall gate. The mare was doing fine. He didn't really need to stay here, but if he walked outside and saw her again, he'd probably embarrass himself gawking like a teenager. *Get a grip, man. She's just a woman.*

"Just a woman. Just the woman I've been dreaming about for the last eight months—the woman who can tie me up in knots with one look from those bottomless blue eyes."

The sound of her laughter drifting into the barn on the breeze sent goose bumps down his arms and brought his cock at full attention. *Damn it!* "Why isn't she in Los Angeles? Neither Cade nor Natalie mentioned her coming home." He started to pace across the stall. "She's married or engaged at least, so it doesn't matter. She's off limits." He inhaled sharply, raking his fingers through his hair as the scene from the Halloween Ball came back to haunt him.

"Can I buy you a drink?"

She spun to her left, almost elbowing him in the ribs. "Uh, I'm sorry."

"Don't be. It's not too often I run into a beautiful woman, literally."

The white wig she wore for her costume emphasized her ivory skin, making her almost glow in the ballroom lights. Her gown hugged her shape like she'd been poured into it as the tops of her breasts peeked above the neckline, begging for the touch of his lips. The blue of her eyes reminded him of the Montana sky in the middle of summer—crystal blue and clear as a mountain stream. The faint scent of lilacs reached his nose making him want to bury his nostrils in the curve of her neck to inhale her sweet fragrance.

"Do I know you?"

His cock hardened at the tone of her voice with its breathless, low, sexy sound.

"I don't think so. I'm sure I would have remembered someone like you."

"Are you from here?"

"Yes."

"I grew up here. I know everyone within a hundred miles or at least I used to."

"Obviously not." He reached for a glass of punch from the table, handing her the plastic cup. "You look parched."

"Thank you."

They sipped the cool liquid in unison, as his gaze moved over her face to take in everything about her.

She glanced away as she blushed at his perusal, he assumed.

"What was that thought, beautiful?" he asked, one finger sliding down her bare arm.

"Nothing, why?"

"You frowned." He chuckled. "You could give me a complex with one of those looks."

"Well, we can't have that now, can we?"

"Come." He took her punch from her fingers and set both their glasses on the table. "Dance with me, please?"

Tugging her toward the space set aside for dancing, he quickly swept her up in his arms and swung her around the floor.

"You must have moved here recently," she said. Her dress swirled around their feet, playing peek-a-boo with his dark slacks and cowboy boots.

"What makes you say that?"

"Three things. One, as I said, I know everyone in Red Rock. Two, you waltz. No one here waltzes. Three, I'd remember those eyes if I'd seen them before."

"Thank you for the compliment."

"You're welcome." They continued to dance to the slow music, her right hand clutched in his left, her other hand on his shoulder with his at the small of her back. Her beautiful eyes kept him spellbound.

He tipped his head in a silent acknowledgement. "You're correct in your assumption. I moved here about a year ago."

"Ah. That explains why I don't recognize you. I moved from here several years ago."

"Yet you return?"

"For a visit, yes. My family is here."

"Where do you live now?"

"Los Angeles."

"Too bad." He swung her in a wide circle, waltzing her out the side doors onto the balcony of the hotel, into a semi-dark corner. "It's a pretty night and warm for October, although the air is still crisp."

"Yes, it is. It's usually much colder this time of year." Goose bumps rose on her bare shoulders and she rubbed her arms to ward off the chill.

"Cold?" he asked, although he didn't wait for her response before he slipped his jacket off to drape it around her.

"Thank you. It's a little chilly without a wrap of some sort."

"What do you do in Los Angeles?"

"I work at an international shipping firm while I pursue my degree."

"Degree in what?"

"Medicine."

"Ah. A doctor, eh?"

"Yes. I plan to specialize in family medicine."

"Noble profession. Doctors, I mean."

"What do you do? You don't look like a rancher." Her gaze swept over him from the top of his thick hair to the tips of his boots.

"Ranching, no. But, I think I'll keep myself a bit of an enigma to you."

"Why?"

"Mystery is intriguing, is it not?" he whispered, his finger sliding along her jaw.

"True."

He couldn't breathe, couldn't think beyond the feel of her skin beneath his fingers. The heat, the need, and the desire reflected clearly in her gaze. She wanted him. No doubt. With lips parted, she invited his kiss with an unspoken word.

For several moments, he stared into her eyes, lost and unaware of anything or anyone else around them. When he bent his head, she closed her eyes as if she wanted to take in everything about the kiss, his heart stopped beating, resuming with a slam against his ribs the moment their lips touched. The need to deepen the kiss to mind-blowing consumed him. The soft brush of his tongue on her bottom lip opened her mouth on a sigh. Tongues entwined, sliding over each other, both trying to taste the other and absorb the moment of their first kiss. He deepened it, exploring her mouth, tasting everything she had to give with every stroke of his tongue.

Brushing his fingertips against the flesh of her breast swelling above the neckline of her gown, he thought he'd die to feel the weight of them in his hands.

He left her mouth to skim along her jaw until he flicked her earlobe with his tongue. A soft nip to her shoulder made her sigh as she leaned into him.

"I wish your hair was down. I bet it's gorgeous flowing around your shoulders," he murmured, kissing the stinging spot left by his teeth.

The roaring in his ears muffled all sounds until the second call of her name. "Elizabeth?"

He lifted his head, smoothing his thumb over her bottom lip as he smiled. "Someone looks for you."

"Apparently."

"Thank you for the dance and the kiss. We'll meet again."

"You're welcome," she whispered, as he took two steps back while she shrugged out of his jacket to return the garment to him.

Reliving that moment had tortured him for the last eight months. Her perfume still enveloped his jacket as it hung in his closet. Cade and Natalie wanted to introduce them, but he refused not wanting to break the enchantment of the night with the real world intrusion.

Marcus Melton wasn't a debonair man able to woo a woman off her feet with sweet words and soft kisses. He was a country veterinarian used to being elbows deep inside a horse or a cow, not some rich bastard who wore tuxedos or drove a fancy car. His fancy sports car came in the form of a pickup truck. His tuxedo consisted of a western shirt, jeans and worn cowboy boots.

The night of the ball, his world stopped and started in the beautiful blue eyes of Elizabeth Weston. He hadn't been the same since.

2

Elizabeth made several trips back and forth to her car. All of her worldly goods sat in the back seat, front seat or trunk. When she left Los Angeles, she left for good. To hell with Ari and to hell with that town. Right after the blowup at the airport, she'd gone to his office, quit her job and packed her things. The entire office gasped when she informed them she was leaving, but no one seemed surprised when she told them why.

Fucking asshole. Everyone in the office probably knew all about his infidelity but no one could bother to inform the girlfriend. "Doesn't matter. I'm done with men."

She glanced at the barn squinting to see better as Marcus came out to stop at his truck. After a brief moment, he looked up and their gazes locked. He was taller than she originally thought. Well over six feet of muscle from his bulging biceps to his firm thighs. Wranglers encased his lower half, hugging the curve of his ass, over his legs, down to his feet, molding to each long, lean line of his body.

A shiver rolled through her, pissing her off. Desire was something she didn't want to feel for anyone at the moment. The vet wasn't her type at all. Sure, he seemed to have a nice body, but he wasn't cut for a business suit or tuxedo. She enjoyed a man with the cloth of a jacket molded to his ripped chest. How a dress shirt would sculpt to every plane as if he'd been poured into his clothing. Linen slacks encasing his firm thighs, hiding the body beneath until you unwrapped it like a Christmas present. The last thing she needed to do was get involved with another man so soon after her breakup with Ari.

The kiss of the mysterious masked stranger at the Halloween Ball came back to haunt her. Her nipples beaded into tight nubs. Goose bumps raced across her arms. The man knew how to dress. Boy did he know how to kiss. Her toes curled in her shoes as she crossed her arms over her chest to hide her reaction to the memory.

"Are you leaving, Marcus?" her father asked, walking down the stairs on the front of the house.

"For now. I'll be back later though. I have a couple of patients to see at the office."

Her father moved to Marcus's side, but she could still hear their conversation.

"The mare still has a few hours of laboring left before the foal arrives, but if there is any trouble, call me and I'll be back immediately."

"How about staying for supper?"

The frown on his face made Elizabeth wonder at the cause. "No, I couldn't really. I wouldn't want to impose on your daughter's first night home."

"Nonsense. I'm sure Liz would love to have you." Her father looked her way. "Right, honey?"

"Of course. You're more than welcome, Doctor Melton."

He looked thoughtful for a moment like he wanted to refuse. "How can I turn down such an invitation? Thank you." After he opened the truck door, he glanced back and said, "I'll see you two in a few hours then."

"I'll keep an eye on the mare."

"Thanks."

Elizabeth watched his truck disappear down the driveway, wondering about the strange reaction she had to him.

The phone rang in the house and her father jogged up the porch steps to answer it as she grabbed the last of her things from the car. "Honey, it's Natalie."

"I'll be right there, Daddy. Tell her to hang on."

With her stuff clutched to her body, she headed for the house and the lecture she knew was coming from her sister-in-law. At every turn, Natalie made sure to tell her how much of an asshole Ari was and how he hadn't been good enough for her anyway. Unfortunately, she couldn't dispute any of her reasons and actually agreed with most of Natalie said.

"Hey, Nat."

"How was the drive?"

"Long, tiring, boring, exhausting. What else would you like to know?"

Natalie laughed. "At least you're home. You can sit back, relax, and enjoy your month here, get your bearings back. There are several nice men around Red Rock."

"I'm done with men."

"You can't mean that, Liz. I know you want to find someone worthy of you. I know you want to settle down eventually."

"Not really. I'm tired of always giving and getting nothing in return. Every guy I've been with has been conceited, egotistical and selfish."

"Maybe you're looking at the wrong men."

The thought had occurred to her on more than one occasion, but she really didn't think that was the cause of her inability to find the right man. "What's that supposed to mean?"

"Look at those you've went out with. Most are businessmen, high-powered executive types, thus your self-centered, all about me attitude with them. You need to find a nice cowboy."

"Not my style."

"Please." She could almost see Natalie roll her eyes, even through the phone lines. "Aren't you the least bit attracted to a man in tight jeans with a pair of nice cowboy boots on his feet?"

The image of Marcus popped into her head. She had to admit, even if only to herself, she did find him physically attractive. "Not a bit."

"You're a liar too." Natalie laughed. "I'm sure I could find you a nice guy around here even just to hang out with for a bit while you're home."

"I'm not dating anyone while I'm here, Nat. I want to relax, spend some time with my family and chill out before I hit Billings." Elizabeth twirled the phone cord around her finger, wondering if she should ask Natalie about Doctor Melton. She didn't want to sound overly curious, but the man had piqued her interest even if only for a moment. Surely, she wasn't attracted to him. "Can I ask you a question?"

"Shoot."

"Dad said you're friends with Doctor Melton."

"Marcus? Yes, we are. He treats all the animals in the area since Doc Alexander retired. He's a nice guy and hot if you know what I mean. Why?"

"He was here when I got home working with a laboring mare. I think Dad is playing matchmaker." She shot her father a scathing look, but he grinned. "Doctor Melton seemed, I don't know, rakish?"

"Rakish? Now that's a term I haven't heard in forever. He *is* a ladies' man, but I think it's more the women chasing him than him running after them. What did you think of him besides rakish?"

Giving Natalie any indication she thought of the guy as anything besides being the vet, would be a bad thing. The woman was like a dog with a bone. With something to chew on, she'd growl and snap until you moved on, leaving her alone. She took after her grandmother like that.

"I don't know. He seemed nice I guess. Really flirtatious like he knew me or something."

"Well, I'm sure you two will get along famously once you get to know him."

"I don't want to get to know him."

"If you say so, Liz." She heard a snicker. "What's it hurt to have another friend?"

"A guy friend?"

"Why not? Is there something wrong with having a guy who is nothing more than a friend? I have Kale but I'm also friends with several women too, like Laurel. There something about having a guy you can talk to about male things who'll give you a straight answer when you can't talk to the one you love."

Worry rushed through her, settling low in her gut. Were her two favorite people in the world having problems? "You and Cade are doing okay, right?"

Natalie laughed. "We're fine. Don't worry. I can ask Cade just about anything, but there are times when I want a man's opinion about something other than my husband's. He tends to be a little more cautious with what he tells me where Kale isn't."

"You had me scared there for a minute."

"You need to come over for dinner one night or we need to have a girl's night out so we can talk."

"Talk about what?"

"You and how you're doing."

The breakup with Ari hurt, but her world hadn't stopped spinning. For the last two weeks, she realized how much of herself she'd lost in her relationship with him. She almost forgotten who she was and where she'd come from. When he'd cruelly pointed out her upbringing in the middle of the airport terminal, she'd come to realize she liked being a small town girl from Montana. The morning after, she'd finally been able to look in the mirror and liked the person she saw. Yes, her heart ached for love. She wanted it—needed it with every fiber of her being, but she wasn't willing to give up herself to find love. It would come along when the time was right, not a moment sooner. "I'm so over this whole thing, Natalie. I don't need a man in my life right now."

"Let's make a date then for Saturday. We'll hit Boots 'n' Spurs for a few drinks—some girl talk."

"All right. Until then, I'm staying right here and doing nothing."

"Sure, honey. You keep telling yourself that. We know damned well you'll be out mucking stalls or ridin' fences. You know, all the other cowgirl things you've forgotten you loved while you were hanging out with all the stars in Los Angeles, inside two days."

For the first time in a long time, she laughed. Natalie was right. She missed spending time on horseback, watching the cattle silently graze on the long, swaying grasses of the pasture around her parent's house, missed the moonlight night sky over Montana, the blue skies hugging the tops of the jagged mountains in the distance during the day. A long sigh escaped her lips.

"See? I can hear the longing in the sigh. You'll be on horseback tomorrow, I bet."

"Probably." She glanced at the clock with a frown. Dinner would be soon. Doctor Melton, that disturbing enigma of a man, would be back. Why she felt so curious about him, she wasn't sure. "I better go. Supper will be on soon and we're having company."

"Oh?"

"Yes. Dad invited Doctor Melton for supper. He accepted, although a bit reluctantly." The laughter in Natalie's voice made Elizabeth wonder what was so funny.

"Marcus is coming over for dinner? Boy, I want to be a fly on the wall for that one."

"Why do I get the feeling you're keeping something from me?"

"Who me? Not at all. I think you'll find Marcus a very interesting dinner companion. Bye, Liz. Have fun at dinner."

The line clicked as Elizabeth stopped to stare at the phone. Something was up. She knew Natalie enough to know her sister-in-law had to be plotting some mischievous plan.

* * * *

Marcus sighed as he drove back up to the ranch style house of the Double D. Several excuses had crossed his mind when he thought about the dinner planned for this evening, but he couldn't bring himself to back out. The need to know whether Elizabeth recognized him or not, spurred him on. Could she feel the electrical pull between them? Would she see the need and desire in his eyes? How could he hide his attraction for her? The last thing he wanted in this world would be to do anything to hurt her. If she found out he is the same man who kissed her last October, it might screwed up her marriage.

With a twist of the key, he shut the engine of his truck off to stare at the front of the house. The first time he'd seen the wide porch, plantation shutters and flowers encircling the front, he'd fallen in love with the place. The huge barn in the distance and the open fields of the pasture around the ranch called to his soul. The buffalo grasses swaying gently in the cooling breeze of the evening made him sigh. He'd always wanted a ranch. Playing cowboy was his favorite pastime during his childhood. His brothers and sisters wanted to play space aliens or some other such thing, but not Marcus. He always loved being the cowboy with his horse camping out in the open prairie, shooting bad guys and saving the lady at the end of the day.

No use putting it off. Mitchell Weston walked out of the barn wiping his hands on a towel as Marcus climbed from his truck. "How's the mare?"

"She's doin' fine, Marcus. I think she's about to deliver so I'm glad you're back. I'm hoping the foal isn't turned wrong. She's laboring pretty hard."

"Let me check her." The mare lay in the same position he left her in. Not a good sign. Her sides heaved with each breath as worry laced through him. He slipped on his exam sleeve to protect his shirt and his rubber gloves. "Rest, girl." Kneeling behind the mare, he shifted close to her tail, inserting his hand to the elbow. The horse grunted.

"What's wrong?" Elizabeth said, stopping next to the stall door.

"The foal is trying to come out in the wrong position. I'm going to have to try to turn it." He glanced up, locking gazes with Elizabeth. Her worried eyes touched his heart. Her lips parted as she ran her tongue across the bottom one. His cock went rock hard in an instant. *Great. Turning a foal with a major hard-on. Not my idea of a good time.* He shifted and slipped his other hand inside the animal. The mare tried lifting her head.

Elizabeth slipped inside the stall, dropping on her knees next to the horse's head. "Easy, sweetheart. It'll be okay. Marcus will take good care of you."

His name on her lips sent shivers down his spine. The soft caress of the syllables made him wonder what it would sound like coming from her mouth in the moment of an explosive orgasm. Shaking his head, he concentrated on the work at hand. Exactly as he feared, the foal needed to be turned in order to come out in the correct position. After several tense moments of sweating, pushing and pulling, he had the baby turned. Within seconds the foal slid out of his mother in a gush of fluid.

"He's beautiful, Daddy," Elizabeth said, tears streaming down her cheeks. "I'd forgotten how wonderful these moments are."

"Take the girl out of the country, but you can't take the country out of the girl." Mitchell laughed. Elizabeth beamed, a huge smile on her lips.

The mare struggled to her feet, nudging the colt with her nose. The colt wobbled to a standing position and took several unsteady steps closer to his mother.

Marcus sighed, wiping his forehead on his shirt as he peeled off his protective gear from his arms. In the ruckus, he'd forgotten his rubber apron. He now had fluid from the horse all over his clothes.

"Hmm. I guess I won't be stayin' for dinner after all."

"Why?" Elizabeth asked, rising to her feet too.

He glanced down with a grimace. "I can't be good company with this all over me."

"You and Dad are about the same size. I think you could borrow something to wear. Right, Dad?"

"Sure, Marcus. No need for you to go without dinner. We're having enchiladas. I know how much you love those."

Damn. I thought I could get out of this meal. "I'd appreciate it, Mitchell. I sure do love Mexican food."

"You two follow when you're ready. Dinner is about done. I'll grab you those clothes and leave them by the door. There's a bathroom just inside the back door you can use to change." Mitchell disappeared out the barn doors, leaving the two of them alone. Tension crawled down his back at being this close proximity and not touching her.

"You did fabulous with the mare."

"All in a day's work." Her lips lifted in a radiant smile. He forgot to breathe.

"I hope I have the same bedside manner with my patients."

He chuckled running his hands down his wet thighs, glancing at his damp clothes. "A little different I would think. I know I couldn't handle humans as patients. At least animals can't complain about their treatment."

"Why did you want to become a veterinarian?" she asked, handing him a towel.

"I've always loved animals of any kind, but especially horses. It's one of the reasons I settled in Red Rock. I'd love to have some land someday."

"Have you ever been married?" She blushed, dropping her gaze to his boots. "Never mind. That's really none of my..."

"No, I haven't. Not even close."

"Me either."

"But I thought..."

"Thought what?"

"Never mind. It's nothing."

She grabbed the spare towel from the low stall door as he stepped closer, running the edge of the rough material across his cheek. "You've got some on your face," she whispered. The riot of curls around her face looked so soft. Her blue eyes burned like the center of a flame. Soft looking lashes framed the dilated orbs. The whisper of her breath wafted over his lips. His whole body hummed as her tongue peeked out, wetting the surface in the most erotic gesture he'd ever been privy to witness. After a moment, she cocked her head to the side and frowned. "Have we met before?"

"I...uh."

"Marcus? Elizabeth? Dinner is ready."

She stepped back as she turned toward the door. "Coming, Dad."

Once he shut the stall, he sighed heavily, following behind. Her sweetly shaped ass wiggled slightly as she walked toward the house. He had to fight with his cock not to react to the scent of jasmine or her luscious body. When his feet hit the porch, she held the door for him and pointed to the clothes lying on the bench.

"There are the clothes. The bathroom is through the door there to your left."

"Thank you. You're a very gracious hostess."

The pink color in her cheeks delighted him and made him edgy at the same time now that he knew she hadn't really gotten married. Getting involved with her would be wrong on so many levels. If she didn't get married, it meant she was probably on the rebound from a breakup. Those types of relationships never last. Not that he thought of her on a long-term basis. They were too different. He'd grown up poor whereas he knew by the look of the house and the land surrounding it, she'd grown up fairly well to do. Yes, he had a thriving practice, but at the moment ends barely met. He hardly had time for any type of relationship anyway.

After a moment of uncomfortable silence, she dropped her gaze to the floor and he headed for the bathroom to change. The sooner he could leave the better. The more time in her presence, the more apt she would be to guess his identity.

Mitchell kept up the conversation during dinner as Marcus listened to the two of them tease each other and laugh. The sound of her laughter made him smile. The throaty chuckle drew his balls up tight against his groin as his fingertips tingled to trace her smiling lips.

"Do you have siblings, Marcus," she asked, her attention now on him as she slipped the tines of the fork between her lips.

"Yes, two brothers and one sister."

"Oh, I bet you all tortured her terribly while you were growing up."

"Not so much. We protected her more than anything else. Of course, she says we never let her have any fun."

"Where do they live?"

"Boston."

"I thought I heard a hint of a New England accent. What brought you to Montana?"

He shrugged, focusing on his plate. He hated talking about himself.

"Oh, come on. Something drew you to our fair state," she said, wiping her mouth with the napkin.

"It's kind of embarrassing actually."

"It certainly can't be any more embarrassing than my love of riding fences and branding cattle."

Surprise whipped down his spine. "You brand cattle?" The sexy laugh made him hold his breath waiting for her answer.

"I can brand 'em with the best, huh Dad?"

"You bet, honey. She's one of the best wranglers and ropers I had until she went off to Los Angeles for school." Mitchell patted her on the hand as he took another bite.

"Remind me not to give her any rope."

"You would be in so much trouble."

His cock pulsed behind the fly of his jeans, riding the zipper so hard he imagined the teeth of the fly gouging his engorged flesh. *Fuck. This is getting out of control. Easy man. She's off limits.*

With their plates clean, they all pushed back from the table and moved toward the kitchen.

"Why don't you two grab a beer and head out back? I think you two probably have a lot in common. I've got some work to do on the books, but it's a beautiful night. Might as well enjoy it."

"I would love to be able to talk to someone about doctor stuff. There aren't too many people I can talk to who understand at least a little of what I'm saying. What do you say, Marcus?"

"I really should be getting home. It's been a long day and I—"

"Just for a few minutes?"

He sighed, mentally kicking himself as the words spilled from his lips. "All right."

The moment they stepped outside, she moved toward the swing to sit down. "Dad's right. The night is gorgeous. I'd forgotten how pretty the night sky is here. In L.A., you can't see the stars very well."

"Do you miss California?" he asked, taking a seat next to her even though he knew it was a bad idea.

"No. Things got bad right at the end of my schooling. I'm glad to be out of there."

"Do you want to talk about your situation?" *Stupid Marcus, really stupid.* "I mean you don't have to if you'd rather not..."

She inhaled a sharp breath before saying, "I found out my boyfriend was using me while he fucked around with everything in a skirt between home and Singapore." A quick brush of her fingers across her cheek revealed the wetness that tore at his heartstrings. Her rueful laugh sounded hollow and forlorn. "Sorry. I guess I'm still a little bitter. I found a receipt from one of the jewelry stores on his desk. I thought he was about to ask me to marry him. When I went to meet him at the airport on his return trip from New York, I got a really rude surprise."

Unable to stop himself, he reached over to grab her hand, squeezing it in comfort. "Any man would be a fool to do something so stupid to you."

"Thank you," she replied, turning to look at him full on.

Moonlight spilled across her face as she frowned, pulling her hand from his grasp. *Crap.*

"Are you sure we've never met?"

"I—"

After a sharp inhalation, she said, "You're him. My masked stranger."

3

"I'm not sure what you mean, Elizabeth."

The perplexed look on his face almost made her think she might be wrong, but no. She knew those eyes, the striking blue color had mesmerized her from the moment she'd stared into them. "The guy from the ball last year. In the tux. We danced. *You kissed me!*"

"Elizabeth, I..."

She followed him to the rail, forcing him back around with a hand on his arm. Tingles raced down her spine as her breathing sped up, pushing her straining nipples against the rough fabric of her shirt. *What the hell?* Indignation rushed through her. He'd deliberately kept something from her. The lack of a relationship between them didn't matter. He knew all along who she was and he didn't say a word. "What kind of game are you playing?"

"I'm not."

The sincerity and hurt in his eyes made her flinch. "Then why not tell me who you were?"

"The man from the ball isn't me. The whole thing was a masquerade—a fantasy." He rubbed his hands up and down his arms and then across his chest. "This is me. The simple country veterinarian. My days are filled with caring for animals, having my hands inside of a horse to my elbows, neutering cats and dogs so they don't breed out of control. I don't wear tuxedos on a regular basis. I'm usually in a T-shirt and jeans, not the debonair man you saw at the ball."

The question she wondered about for the last eight months, bounced around in her brain until it finally spilled from her lips. Is what he said true? Is it all a lie? "Why did you kiss me?"

He closed his eyes, pinching the bridge of his nose. "Hell if I know."

"That doesn't help the self-confidence, Marcus."

"I wanted to. All right? Simply the magic of the evening. You looked stunning. I lost my head."

Obviously, the kiss didn't affect him like it did me. "I'm sorry the whole situation was such a letdown for you," she snapped, spinning around to head back into the house.

"Elizabeth, wait. I didn't mean..."

"Never mind, Marcus." She flipped her hair over her shoulder. "You're like the rest of the male population. If a woman shows some interest, he wants to throw her on the bed like a caveman and fuck her brains out without regards to her heart or mind. It doesn't matter to you whether the woman is already in a relationship or not. At the time, I was in a relationship yet you had no regard to the fact. You didn't care."

His gaze held anger. The thought of what made him angry made trepidation roll down her back. "Yes, I did. I didn't know you were seeing someone."

"You didn't bother to ask either. You just swept me up in your arms and kissed the hell out of me whether I wanted you to or not."

"You sure as hell didn't fight me." Fury grew in him until his whole body trembled before her eyes. "Or do you go around kissing strange men all the time."

Crack.

His head snapped with the force of her hand to his cheek. "How dare you. You don't know me so don't assume to judge me by your own behavior." She spun around and slammed through the front door, letting the screen bang behind her. "The audacity of that man!"

"Something wrong, sweetheart?" her father asked, poking his head out of the study. "Where's Marcus?"

"Gone I hope. Good riddance."

"What happened? I thought you two were getting along famously."

"We were, but I found out something about him. It made me realize he's a liar and a con-artist."

"Oh please." Her father's eyes narrowed. "The man is no more a liar than I am. You must have misunderstood. I've known him for almost a year. He's good friends with your brother. You know how Cade is. If the man wasn't worthy of friendship, he wouldn't give him the time of day."

Her anger deflated rapidly as she chewed on her bottom lip. *Maybe I'm wrong. Maybe things did get out of control that night.* The memory of his kiss returned full force. Her body trembled from head to toe. *Damn, the man knew how to kiss.* The feeling of his lips on hers had driven her out of her mind with desire. Even Ari's kiss hadn't affected her the same way Marcus' had. The moment their lips touched, she'd been transported to a world filled with color and feelings. Even making love with Ari had been so black and white she hadn't realized how lacking the entire thing was until now. No finesse. No imagination. She rubbed her arms. "Maybe I did overreact."

"I think so," her father replied, going back to his busy work. "You can go into town to apologize tomorrow. I'm sure Marcus will be glad to see you."

It doesn't matter. I'm not getting involved with anyone anyway even if the feelings he stirs are disturbing yet intriguing. She shook her head and left her father to head upstairs. Thoughts of the toe-curling kiss danced in her mind as she headed to her room to unpack what few things she might need during her stay at home.

The next morning, Elizabeth sped down the dirt driveway as dust billowed out behind her. Apologizing to Marcus wasn't going to be easy. The man disturbed her on a level no one had before. The feelings bothered her. He'd played a huge part of her dreams from the night before, always with shadows of mystery surrounding him even as he kissed her, stroking her body until she burned with need. The attraction between them sizzled like bacon on a griddle while she denied the appeal with her last breath. *Damn it.* She wasn't attracted to him, she wasn't. He totally wasn't her type at all.

Yeah, I keep telling myself that.

After several minutes, the buildings of Red Rock came into view. The diner with all of the local's vehicles parked around it waiting for breakfast or their pals for coffee, the new florist shop sitting on the opposite side of the street. A new upscale motorcycle shop selling custom Harleys and several other stores along the street. She knew exactly where Marcus' clinic sat when her father described the building to her. He'd taken over Doc Alexander's practice, but had his own set up established with state of the art equipment. He'd also rented out part of the back to a local pet groomer from what her father said.

A cop car sat near the front of the diner. She waved at Laurel Dunn, Kale's wife, as she passed by. It seemed like the Dunns and Westons lives were irrevocably connected in one way or another, but more so lately due to Natalie's grandmother adopting both clans. When Natalie dated Cade after her return to Red Rock, Kale had somehow gotten involved in the mix of the dating pool. Her grandmother played matchmaker by pitting the two guys against each other in order for one of them to back off. Then Kale met Laurel after she came to town to rescue her sister from an abusive husband who happened to be one of Kale's ranch hands.

Her own sister Emma got tangled up with a country singer and his identical twin. Now they were happily a triad living in Nashville with their ever growing brood of kids. Not that a triad situation ever crossed her mind. The excitement of being with two men might be something to try once, but she could never be in a threesome on a regular basis. Kale's sister Delaney recently married Jake Monroe. Elizabeth remembered Jake and Delaney hanging out a lot during high school. Shortly afterward, he took off for parts unknown. Last she'd heard, Colby Mason and Delaney were a hot item. Obviously a juicy story seemed hidden in the confines of those three.

"Such exciting lives where mine is boring. I really need to get out more."

Marcus' clinic came into view. Elizabeth pulled into the parking lot. Several cars waited out front and trepidation skittered down her spine. She didn't want to make a scene but by the looks of all the cars, it sure seemed like half the town sat in his waiting room with their animals. "Maybe I should just wait until tomorrow." As she grabbed the gear shift to put the car back into drive, Marcus stepped out the back door of the clinic. A slight breeze picked up the piece of hair falling over his forehead and ruffled it like a set of lover's fingers. The white lab coat molded to his sturdy frame, emphasizing the breath of his chest. Even though he didn't do hard physical labor like a cowboy might, he still had a physique of someone who worked out or did demanding work on a regular basis.

After a moment, he turned and caught her gaze through the windshield of her car. *Great. I can't leave now.* She inhaled a sharp breath as a frown crossed his features. He didn't seem pleased to see her. *What did I expect? I slapped the man last night.*

She pushed open her car door and stepped out. "Marcus?"

"Hello, Elizabeth. What can I do for you?"

Once she shut the door, she approached slowly, her steps faltering at the look on his face. She pressed her lips together for a moment, wishing to be anywhere but here. Apologizing to the man seemed necessary, but it didn't mean she had to like it. The clear blue of his gaze penetrated the iciness in her chest. "I came to apologize for my behavior last night. I was totally out of line and slapping you...well I shouldn't have."

"Apology accepted. Now, if you'll excuse me, I have patients to see."

His quiet dismissal hurt. She wasn't sure why. Wasn't he moved by their kiss at the Halloween Ball? Apparently not if he could just walk away from her without even a goodbye. "Wait, please."

"Is there something else?"

"How about if I buy dinner tonight?" *What the hell? Am I crazy? The last thing I want is to be alone with him.*

"Why?"

"I'm really sorry for how I acted. I want to make it up to you."

"There's no need, Elizabeth, really. It's fine."

The clipped tone of his voice told her of his anger and disappointment in her. It hurt. No one had ever been disappointed in her before. "I want to. Please?"

He tipped his head back, looking up at the sky. At first she didn't think he would go until he finally said, "All right. Where would you like to go?"

"I heard The Millhouse is really good even if Cade has interests in the business."

A soft smile lifted the corners of his mouth. Her heart thumped loudly in her chest. "Don't let him hear you say something like that. He takes pride in his business decisions." He tilted his head to the side. "Do you really want to go back to the scene of the crime?

"Scene of the crime?"

"The ball took place there."

She dropped her gaze to the wide breath of his chest. "True. They have really great food though from what I hear. Cade would have my head if he heard me. I've never eaten there though."

"You haven't?" he asked, moving a step or two closer. "I'm surprised the two of them haven't taken you there when you were home."

"We didn't get the chance."

"It's a date then. What time would you like me to pick you up?"

"Oh no. It's fine. How about if I meet you there? It's not like this is a date or anything." The frown returned and she wondered what she'd done to piss him off now.

"Six o'clock?"

"Great." She turned to head back to her car, but stopped near the front bumper, glancing over her shoulder. "Marcus?"

"Yes?"

"Don't worry about a tux even though I know you have one." She smiled as he grinned.

"Not a problem, Elizabeth. See you at six."

Once she slid back inside her car, she felt like she could breathe again. The way his lip lifted when he grinned and the small dimple that appeared in his cheek reminded her of the sexy, tuxedoed man she'd been dreaming of since she'd met him eight months before. He didn't think he could be that man again, but she had a feeling there were two sides to the very disturbingly different Marcus Melton.

Several hours later, Elizabeth nervously checked her appearance in the rearview mirror for the third time as she fought with herself over why she'd stupidly asked Marcus to dinner. Her father had laughed when she'd told him what she'd done right before she'd left the house.

"Honey, I think it's great. There's nothing wrong with
two headstrong people having dinner and discussions over

a mistake one of you has made. Marcus is a great guy. Even if nothing develops past an association, it doesn't hurt to have another friend on the list."

"Natalie said the same thing."

"Nat is a very wise woman." He patted her shoulder after he helped her pull on her sweater. "Have a nice time and don't worry about your old man. I'll be fine here."

"You could come with me, Daddy. I'm sure Marcus wouldn't mind."

He frowned for a moment. "I'd mind. I'm not tagging along as a third wheel on my daughter's date."

"It's not a date. We're just having dinner and some conversation."

"Sounds like a date to me."

She rolled her eyes as she shook her head. Her father didn't understand how couples could go to a party, dinner or a movie or any other place and only be friends. "I don't have time for a man in my life anyway so quit your matchmaking already. I'm leaving in a month. I won't be back for three years. I'm not doing a long distance relationship. Just so you know, people don't fall in love in a month."

"You never know, sweetheart. Don't close your eyes or your heart to the possibilities. Things happen for a reason. Only God knows what those reasons are."

"You miss Mom, don't you?"

"Of course I do. Every day. I keep reminding myself that God took her from us for a reason although we don't know why. When it's your time, it's your time in my book. It was His wish to have her by his side and even though she's no longer physically here, she'll always be in my heart."

"Can I ask you a question?"

"Shoot."

"Was Mom the only girl you ever really loved?"

Her father dropped his gaze to the floor, shuffling his feet.

"Dad?"

When he lifted his head and stared into her eyes, she knew he'd loved another. "No. There was someone else early on, but she chose another over me."

Elizabeth hugged her father whispering, "I'm sorry. I don't know how any woman could ever give you up for someone else. She obviously wasn't worthy of your love if she could walk away from you so easily."

"It doesn't matter. She has her life and I have mine. I had a beautiful wife for a number of years. One I loved very much. I have great kids who love me. Some awesome grandkids to love. If I could get a few more, I'd die a happy man."

"Someday, Dad."

"I know, honey. I just want you to be happy. I know that asshole in Los Angeles wasn't the man to make you happy."

Now as she sat outside the restaurant trying to get her nerve up to open the door, she chewed her lipstick off for the sixth time. Why she felt jittery and jumpy, she wasn't sure. After all, she didn't think of Marcus as boyfriend material, did she? No. A friend. Nothing more.

She exhaled sharply and pushed open her car door only to have it wrenched out of her hand. A small squeak escaped her mouth until she looked up into the blue eyes of Marcus. His brown sport coat molded to his broad chest while his white linen shirt emphasized the width of the pecs beneath. Brown tailored slacks and boots completed the picture of the gentleman cowboy.

"Sorry. I didn't mean to startle you. I saw you sitting here for several minutes. I thought maybe you'd changed your mind."

"You look nice," she said, locking the door, shutting it behind her.

"Thank you. It's not a tux, but it's not jeans and a T-shirt either." His gaze raked her from the curls on her head to the toes of her heels. "You look fabulous yourself."

She smoothed her black skirt down over her hips and adjusted her sweater around her shoulders. Shivers raced down her back when his hands lifted the edges of the material to help her settle it around her. "Thanks."

"You're welcome. I wouldn't want you to catch cold."

"I'd forgotten how chilly the weather gets here in the evenings sometimes, even in the summer. Los Angeles never cooled off."

"I've been there a time or two," he said, tucking her hand into the crook of his arm to guide her toward the entrance of the restaurant.

"Where did you get your degree?"

"Why don't we wait until we're seated before we talk shop?"

"All right," she replied as they stepped through the double doors of the hotel to make their way toward the restaurant in the corner.

As they approached the gentleman seating people, the man nodded, addressing Marcus by name. "Ah, Doctor Melton. Very nice to see you sir."

"Thank you. We have reservations."

"Yes, sir. It'll be just a moment."

The warmth of his hand over hers where it rested on his arm, made her very aware of the strength he harbored under his clothes. She could only imagine the steely strength it required to wrestle animals all day.

The lights from the chandeliers overhead highlighted the soft browns of his hair. She had to resist the urge to push the errant lock falling over his forehead back in place. He had such a boyish charm about him. The sharp contrast to the cut of his face seemed chiseled in stone but when he smiled, his whole face changed, softening him to the most handsome man she'd ever met. The blue of his eyes reminded her of a clear stream reflecting the sky above. They seemed so clear, she could see herself reflected back. Long sooty lashes framed those perfect orbs, any woman would kill for. The fullness of his lips reminded her of the kiss they'd shared so many months ago. She shivered, almost wanting to feel the pressure of his mouth against hers again.

A quick clearing of her throat brought her attention back to the crowd around them and the inappropriateness of her thoughts. "What types of animals do you treat, Marcus?" she asked as the waiter led them to their table.

"All kinds. If they are pets, I treat them if they're sick."

"Wow. I thought treating the different types, size and diseases of humans seemed tough. I can't imagine keeping all the different animals' heart rates straight, much less all the other stuff." She nodded to the waiter and took the seat Marcus held out for her with a soft "thank you."

"Medicine in general can be a bit overwhelming. It's a good thing there are lots of reference books. If I don't know something, I look it up same as you I assume."

She opened the menu handed to her by the waiter, glancing over the selections. Lots of restaurants in Los Angeles boasted of great steaks, but nothing beat the beef in her home state. Medium rare meat had saliva pooling in her mouth as her taste buds tingled. It had been forever since she'd had a good steak.

"What would you like to eat?"

"I'm going to have a nice piece of red meat. I missed those in Los Angeles." He looked startled as she laughed. "Don't look so surprised, Marcus. I did grow up on a cattle ranch."

"Yes, but I assumed they had really good restaurants in L.A. and knowing you were dating a very wealthy man, you'd probably eaten at some of the best of them."

Indignation zipped along her nerves. How dare he think her a snob. "The man I was dating owned an international shipping firm, so yes, we did wine and dine at some of the best restaurants in L.A., but I'm not a snob, Marcus. I like hometown diners and small restaurants. They seem to have the best staff and the best foods. In no way have I ever considered myself above eating at places like that."

"I'm sorry. I've insulted you." He took her hand in his running his callused thumb over her knuckles. "I never intended for you to take exception to my words. I didn't mean them how you perceived them at all."

The scrape of his thumb on her hand sent shivers up her arm. She had to press her thighs together hoping for a little relief from the throbbing starting low in her belly. "I'm sorry I snapped. It's just one of the reasons my ex told me he didn't want anything long term with me was because I didn't have the social skills he wanted."

"I've already told you my opinion of him. I hope you know I would never think any less of you for being born and raised on a ranch in Montana. It happens to be some of the prettiest country I've ever seen. I'm glad I live here."

She reluctantly pulled her hand from his grasp as the waiter returned to take their order. The moment the waiter disappeared again, they continued their conversation. "You said your family is in Boston?"

"Yes. I was born and raised there."

"Where did you go to school?"

"University of Kentucky."

"Wow. That's a long way from Boston."

The waiter returned with the bottle of wine they'd agreed upon, pouring a small amount in the glass for Marcus to taste. "Delicious. Thank you." After the waiter departed the table, he said, "We didn't have much while I was growing up. A fairly large family didn't make for easy times."

"Where were you in the pecking order?"

"Middle boy. I have an older brother, a younger brother, younger sister."

She swallowed a sip of wine, relishing the bite on her tongue. "I bet it made you feel, um, lost in the shuffle a bit."

"Yes. How did you know?"

"I'm the oldest of the girls in our family, but still a middle child so I know what you went through. We had a big family too." She pressed her lips together before she smiled. "I love my family. Don't get me wrong, but it's hard being a middle child."

"Mitchell is very proud of you," he said, sipping from his own glass. "You should be proud of yourself. It's not easy being a physician of any kind. Where in Billings are you planning to do you residency?"

"Billings Memorial. I have everything set up already for when I arrive. I'll be working a lot of different rotations. Surgery, pediatrics, emergency, you name the specialty, I'll be doing a rotation sometime during my time there. I need to get the most rounded residency I can get so I can practice general medicine back in Red Rock." His choking concerned her as his eyes watered and he gasped for air. "Are you all right?"

"Yes," he croaked. "Wrong pipe." He coughed several more times and wiped his eyes with his napkin. "You're practicing in Red Rock when you're done?"

"Of course. We need a good clinic and physician. It's too far to go to head to Billings for treatment. We don't have a hospital, which I wish we did, but at least a clinic would save people from making the long trek into one of the bigger towns, don't you think?"

"I think you have a great idea. Yes, we need the medical care in Red Rock."

"Why do you seem so shocked I want to practice near home?"

He shrugged as he leaned back in the chair. "After you attended school in Los Angeles, I just assumed you didn't want to live in a small community again. It's hard to go from the fast paced life of California back to the slow, lazy crawl of rural Montana."

"I love the slower pace of home. I can't wait to start treating patients. The little kids with their ear infections, doing women's health and all of that kind of work. It excites me to think about being part of the community like I belong."

"You do belong, Elizabeth. This is home. Why would you think differently?"

"Red Rock hasn't felt like home in several years, Marcus. Going off to Los Angeles was a smart decision. One I had to make for my education, but I never wanted to leave home on a permanent basis."

"What about your engagement to the gentleman there?"

"It doesn't matter now since it's not longer happening. I realize now the life I had there wasn't what I wanted. Yes, the fast paced hustle and bustle of things seemed great for a while, but the whole atmosphere got crazy. I'm ready to slow things down."

Their dinner arrived and they both dug in, letting the conversation lag a bit. The food melted on her tongue as she groaned in ecstasy.

"Good?"

"You have no idea."

The eyebrow over his left eye rose and she wondered what he thought as a small smile lifted the corners of his mouth. *Damn. I almost sound like I'm having an orgasm here.* The meat went down a little rough as heat crept up her chest. Getting into that kind of conversation with Marcus would be a bad idea.

"I'm glad you're enjoying the steak."

"Oh yes. The meat is so tender, I can almost cut it with my fork. I do plan to save room for desert though. The chocolate decedent cake looks sinful. It's been a while since I've had chocolate." Marcus laughed. The rich, deep, sound reverberated along her nerves as if he plucked the strings of a bass. "I love your laugh."

"Thanks, but yours is amazing too. I heard you earlier when I was in the barn. Very light and happy."

"I haven't had much chance to laugh lately so it felt good to let go." She blushed again. "I don't even remember what I was laughing about." The flickering candlelight bounced the deep burgundy color of the wine in her glass around in a prism of rich color.

"I'm sure Mitchell could tell you. I know he liked to hear the sound. He's been worried about you as are Cade and Natalie."

"You've discussed me with my family?"

Marcus dropped his gaze to his plate as a deep flush rushed into his face. "Um...yes. I guess so."

"How long have they known?"

"Known what?"

"About what happened at the ball?"

4

"Things aren't like they appear, Elizabeth." *I'm so screwed. She'll never believe anything I say.*

"Aren't they?"

"No."

"Then answer my question."

He blew out a long sigh. "They've known since the ball. They knew we danced. Natalie and Cade have kept my secret since then."

"Why, Marcus? I don't understand you at all." The napkin landed in a heap on the table top as she leaned back in her chair and crossed her arms over her ample chest. A small wrinkle appeared between her eyebrows. He wanted to smooth the crease away with his thumb. Kissing her until she melted against him would probably be a bad idea right now even if she'd let him.

"I didn't want you to know who I was. The two of them wanted to introduce us, but I refused. I'd heard you were getting married so it wouldn't have been right away."

"Why the secrets?"

"I told you. The man you saw at the ball isn't really me."

"I think it is." She leaned forward resting her arms on the tabletop. "You see, you were too comfortable in your own skin. Something like that can't be faked, Marcus. You might think you aren't dashing and debonair, but in reality the man is a part of your personality whether you wish to admit it or not."

Could it be true? Do I really have it in me to be the man who could sweep her off her feet? Do I want to be? "You're seeing things that aren't there."

"I don't believe so, but if you aren't willing to admit that man exists inside you, then there isn't anything I can do to convince you."

The waiter returned and she ordered dessert. Chocolate cake splashed across her skin and he would lick the succulent treat off one crumb at a time, raced across his thoughts. The last thing he needed tonight were erotic images of his dinner companion. This would probably be the one and only occasion they'd spend time alone together, much less do any kind of touching. Maybe he needed to find a willing substitute. Several of the women in town made it known they wouldn't shun his advances should he choose to pay them some attention. None of them drew him like Elizabeth did.

"Marcus?"

"I'm sorry. Did you say something?"

"I asked if you were ready to leave."

He glanced at her plate realizing she'd already finished her cake and was removing the remaining chocolate from her fork with her tongue. The wicked flick of pink skin over the sterling silver of the fork made him think of her savoring the shaft of his cock. Her sharp gaze would focus on his face as she slowly licked along his length and then swirled around the head. The warm heat of her mouth would surround him as she engulfed the entire head between her lips. His body trembled with need at each passing fantasy. He cleared his throat and sighed heavily. "Yes, I'm ready." *More than ready.*

He reached for his wallet but she stayed his hand. "My treat."

"As you wish." He nodded and smiled. "I'd never turn down dinner with a beautiful woman, especially if she's paying." He wasn't sure, but he figured Elizabeth had an independent streak a mile wide and he wondered if her free spirit took over in the bedroom. Although he didn't think of himself as the strong alpha type, he did enjoy being in control between the sheets. What would she do if she knew about his dominate nature?

"Such flattery."

Once he helped her to her feet, he tucked her hand into the crooked of his arm and led her toward the doors. "Too bad they don't have dancing here. I'd love to waltz with you again."

"You know, I knew you couldn't have been from Red Rock originally since you knew how to waltz at the ball."

"You're a very graceful dancer yourself. Where did you learn to waltz?"

"My father taught me. So I would know for when I married someday."

"If Mitchell knows how to waltz then I'm not the only one in Red Rock."

"Okay, clarification. The only one of our generation. Face it, kids who graduated in the seventies or even eighties didn't waltz. Slow dancing consisted of shuffling your feet back and forth while you hung on."

The soft laugh escaping from her lips did little to calm his aching cock. He'd already fantasized about her to the point of pain and beyond.

"Where did you learn to waltz?"

"My parents were old fashioned in that way. All of us kids learned to dance in the middle of our living room. My mother used to be a dancer some years back so she taught us all."

"How sweet."

"She's a great mom. I miss having them close, but I wouldn't trade living here for the world."

"You really do like Red Rock, don't you?"

"I do. There's nothing like the smell of the wildflowers in bloom in the spring, the gurgle of a mountain stream as the rushing water winds itself around boulders and trees, or the sight of a beautiful woman spread out on a blanket under the stars waiting."

"You've had a woman spread out on a blanket under the stars?" she asked, her voice a mere husky whisper as they approached her car.

"No, but I do have my fantasies." He stopped her beside the driver's door and turned her toward him. "What are your fantasies, Elizabeth?"

"I have a few."

"Care to tell me?"

Her tongue peeked out as she ran the tip over her lips. He had to stifle a groan of pure torture as he fought himself over whether to lean in and brush his mouth over hers. One kiss. One touch. It's all he wanted...for now. Warm, wine-tinged breath wafted over his face. His cock got impossibly hard and he finally decided to give into the torture of having her this close.

The moment his mouth met hers, she sighed, opening herself to him.

Automatically he reached for her hips, bringing her body into the curve of his. There would be no way she wouldn't notice his cock against her belly.

Her lips were soft and yielding beneath his, just like he remembered. Her tongue swept out to slide along the side of his.

Wanting to feel more, he pulled her in tighter, wrapping his arms around her back. Her hands pushed into the hair at the nape of his neck, curling into the strands like she wouldn't let go.

A soft laugh broke the spell as another couple moved past them with a soft, "Excuse us."

"I'm sorry, Elizabeth. I never meant..."

"Don't be sorry, Marcus. It cheapens the kiss. I enjoyed it, but you have to understand, I'm not looking for a relationship. I'm only here for a short time."

The crystal blue of her eyes stared back, although they'd darkened now to a light sapphire color with her increased passion. Her breath sawed in and out, driving her breasts into his chest until he thought he'd lose his mind.

"I'm not looking for a relationship either." She frowned as he stepped back and opened her door. "Goodnight, beautiful lady."

"Goodnight."

* * * *

The next morning found Elizabeth on the back of a horse, riding fence line. She'd slept restlessly throughout the night as the feeling of Marcus' mouth on hers drove her desire to a level she'd not experienced before, except for the last time he'd kissed her. "This is ridiculous. He's just a man and a *cowboy*. I don't do cowboys. Most are egotistical, arrogant, and not the least bit shy about taking their own pleasure. Their thought is to hell with the woman." She should know. She'd been with a few right out of high school. Never mind the fact of their youth or inexperience. *The businessman didn't suit my needs much either if I count Ari.*

She tapped her fingers against her lips as she said, "Maybe a short term fling with Marcus might be all right. I mean, I'm not staying in town after the month is up. We could have a good time together, have some great sex. If the heat we produce when he kisses me is any indicator, we should ignite the sheets." She wanted more. No, he wasn't the business suit type, but he had the sexy cowboy thing down. He sure looked good in the sport jacket and slacks he wore last night though.

Birds circling in the distance caught her eye. *Hmm...I wonder what that's all about?* Moments later, her cell phone rang.

"Hello?"

"Hey, cowgirl. Where are you?"

"Out riding of course."

Natalie laughed on the other end of the line. "Of course! Hey, want to meet me for lunch?"

"Sure, at the diner say elevenish." She glanced at her watch. Nine. She'd have just about enough time to finish her check of the fence and get back to the house to shower if she hurried. Nudging her gelding with her heels, she said, "If we go early, it won't be so crowded."

"Eleven is fine. Cade's going to watch the kids so we can have a nice leisurely lunch."

"How sweet of him. Tell him I love him, would you. I'll see him for dinner one night this week."

"I'll tell him. How did dinner go with Marcus the other night?"

"I'll tell you at lunch since I need to have a discussion with you about that and the ball."

"Uh-oh."

"Yeah. I heard about your part in his secret."

"Elizabeth, I wanted to tell you."

"He told me part of what happened. How you and Cade wanted to say something, but he wouldn't let you, but we'll discuss things more at lunch. I've got a little more to tell you about."

"Sounds intriguing. Me thinks you are attracted to our fair doctor."

"Attracted yes, but looking for anything beyond a short term fling...no." The birds circling in the distance bothered her. She needed to check it out before she headed back. "I need to go, Nat. There's something I want to check out before I meet you for lunch. Talk to you in a couple of hours."

"Sure, hon. See you then."

Elizabeth stuffed her cell phone back in her pocket and leaned in, urging the gelding to a faster clip as they galloped toward the area to her left. A small outcropping of rocks sheltered a nice pool of water where many of the animals gathered in the heat of the Montana summer. She wondered if maybe a late calf didn't survive. "There are an awful lot of birds for one carcass."

As she crested the hill a disturbing sight met her eyes. Several dozen cows along with their calves were being ravaged by the buzzards. The stench just about caused her to lose her breakfast. She clamped her hand over her mouth. What could have taken out so many? "I need to warn Dad."

She reined her gelding around and raced across the open field toward the ranch house in the distance. Nothing had prepared her for the slaughter of so many animals. That's all she could think of it as...slaughter.

Her father stood on the porch looking in her direction as she skidding to a halt in the front yard. "Somethin's wrong."

"Yeah. I just came from there. Several head of cattle have been slaughtered. It's going to be hard to say what did it, Dad. The buzzards have done a pretty good job of picking them clean already."

Removing his hat, he jabbed his fingers through his hair before replacing the felt with the brim down low across his forehead. "Damn it. This is the second time in the two weeks."

"Seriously?" she asked, swinging down from the gelding's back. "You've got a hell of a problem then. From what I saw, it wasn't something natural. Something like a coyote or wolf pack would only take down a few. This was at least a dozen."

"Near the pool?"

"Yes."

"I need to talk to the neighbors or the hands. Someone had to have seen some commotion. Maybe Marcus knows something. He inoculated several head in the last month for me."

"Marcus?" she asked, grabbing the reins to lead her winded gelding in a cool down.

"He's been out here a lot helping me with the horses and cattle," her father said, stepping into an easy rhythm next to her.

"I didn't realize he'd spent so much time here lately." *Maybe Marcus had seen something, but he wasn't aware of it. Being a vet, he'd surely pick up on the animals acting strange.*

"Yes he has. Probably more time than anywhere else. I should just put him on my payroll to call it good." Her father chuckled as he shoved his hands in his pockets. "I'd better call him. He'll need to check the rest of the herd to make sure nothing is wrong with them. I'll also need someone to check the water supply in the pool out there. Someone might have poisoned it."

"I'm headed into town to have lunch with Natalie, Dad, so I won't be home for a couple of hours. Are you okay? Do I need to cancel?"

"I don't think so, honey. Enjoy your lunch. Don't worry about things here." He hugged her, and then stepped back. "Tell Nat hello for me. Let her know I'm still planning dinner out at their place on Sunday."

"Sure," she replied, heading across the yard.

"Tell her to make sure to kiss those grandbabies for me," he yelled from the porch as she stepped into the interior of the musty, hay filled barn.

A quick wave over her shoulder told him she heard him. The tack room sat off to the back of the building with the door ajar. She heard muffle voices coming from the room, piquing her curiosity as the timbre got louder.

"No. I've done what you ask. I want my money."

Elizabeth clipped the lead rope onto the horse's bridle and cocked her head. She didn't recognize the speaker. His agitation seemed clear enough though.

A loud "wait" followed by grumbling and a thud of a boot against the wall floated to her position several feet from the door. She moved closer to peek inside. Wide shoulders, blond hair, black cowboy hat, jeans and boots. Typical cowboy on the ranch. The set of his back and wide legged stance told her of his irritation. "Fucking dumbass! He doesn't have a clue what ranchin's about."

"Hello?" she called, pushing open the door.

The cowboy spun around, a deep scowl lined his face and drew his eyebrows down over his eyes. "Who the hell are you? What are you doin' in here?"

"I'm Elizabeth Weston," she said, hands on her hips. "Can I ask who you are?"

The scowl disappeared as a handsome grin lifted the corners of his mouth. Chocolate brown eyes stared back with a sexy twinkle. "Jackson Leaf. I'm your dad's foreman." He stuck out his hand. "I'd heard his daughter was home for a bit. It's nice to meet you finally. Your dad talks about you a lot."

"Uh, thanks." The warmth of his hand spread up her arm, sending goose bumps flittering along the surface. "Jackson. Did you see anyone around here who shouldn't be recently? I was up on the ridge and there are several cattle dead near the pool. Dad said this is the second time it's happened in the last two weeks."

He scratched his chin with his fingers, making a rasping sound with the five o'clock shadow of whiskers lining his jaw. "Nope. Can't say that I have. Well, except the good doctor doing the shots on them. He was up near there a couple of weeks ago with his truck. Not long before the last batch went down, I'd say."

"Hmm."

"I gotta run. I've got work to do. See you around?"

"Yeah. I'll be here for a month or so anyway."

"Hey, maybe you'd like to have dinner with me one night. We can talk cattle. I hear you're pretty handy with a rope and a branding iron."

"I'm flattered really, but I'm not dating while I'm home."

"It wouldn't be a date, Elizabeth, just dinner and drinks."

She shrugged as she stepped back. He moved toward the door. "Maybe. We'll see. For now, I'm just visiting family."

"Well think on it, pretty lady. I'd love to have a nice time with you."

Not sure if his words had a double meaning or not, Elizabeth moved back out of his reach, grabbing the brushes from the bucket on the other side of the door so she could groom her gelding. Jackson Leaf winked and strolled off, the soft whistle of a tune coming from his mouth as he disappeared out the door of the barn. She wasn't sure why, but the man rubbed her wrong. Cocky came to mind when she thought about him. She didn't like cocky. Her life had been way too full of those types of men lately.

The sound of a truck pulling up caught her attention. She removed the tack from her horse and started brushing his coat wondering who might be visiting. Moments later, men's voices floated on the breeze. She could tell her father spoke with someone near the steps of the house, but she couldn't quite make out the words.

After she finished grooming her horse, she put him in his stall before she put away his tack. *Shower and lunch.*

When she stepped into the sunshine, she shielded her eyes as she made her way toward the house. Marcus' truck sat near the porch. She wondered if her dad had called him to discuss the problem. *Probably. Dad seems impressed with Marcus' knowledge and expertise with the stock.*

The cool interior of the house soothed her overheated body. Low murmurs came from her father's office. Glancing at her watch, she knew she had a few minutes before she needed to get ready to meet Natalie.

The low, sexy rumble of Marcus' voice sent awareness along her nerves like an electric current after a summer storm. "I don't know Mitchell. There are a lot of things that could have happened to them. First thing I'd check is the water supply up there."

"It's always been great water for the cattle though."

"Even a dead animal in it could poison the supply."

"True. We didn't check it after the last bunch went down." Elizabeth cleared the doorway and stopped just inside the room. "Hey, honey. We were discussing the cattle you found up on the ridge."

"Hi, Marcus."

"Elizabeth," he replied with a tip of his head.

He looked good—too good. Jeans molded to his lean thighs, emphasizing the muscles beneath the material. A soft looking chambray shirt the exact color of his eyes stretched over his pecs, showing off the strength and breadth of his shoulders. *Damn the man was mouthwateringly sexy.*

Those lips lifted in a slightly mocking smile, like they shared a secret—the secret of last night's kiss.

"I assume Dad filled you in on the cattle."

"Yes, he did. I'm sitting here trying to figure out what might have happened."

"I talked to the foreman, Dad. He said he hadn't seen anyone around here that shouldn't be."

"You talked to Jackson? When?"

"In the barn a little bit ago. He was on the phone with someone in the tack room. They sounded like they might have been arguing. He wasn't a happy guy when he hung up."

"Hmm."

"You sound like you don't trust him or something, Marcus."

"I don't know the man very well, but he just rubs me the wrong way."

"He said you were the last person not working for this ranch, up on the hill near the pool when you inoculated the cattle."

"I didn't see anything unusual while I was up there."

"Well think about it. Maybe you missed something. Anything." She kissed her father's cheek before headed back for the door. "I'm off to the shower and then lunch with Natalie. I'll talk to you two later."

"Have a good time, sweetheart."

"Enjoy your shower."

His eyebrow shot up over his left eye as a sexy smirked lifted the corners of his mouth, reminding her of the heat of their kiss the night before. "I'm sure I will." Her gaze wandered over his body before it rested briefly on the bulge in the fly of his jeans. Just to tease him, she licked her lips and tilted her head. "I'll see you later."

5

Little witch.

"Marcus?"

"Sorry, Mitchell. I was lost in thought there for a moment. What did you say?"

"Nothing. Maybe you could happen by the diner while Natalie and Liz are having lunch?"

"Playing matchmaker?"

"Not me. Not that I wouldn't mind my daughter living close to home again, but I know she's got a few years of residency to complete before she can settle down again."

"She does plan to practice here, from what she's told me."

"She does?"

"I take it she hadn't told you her plans."

"Not really, no. After her break up with her boyfriend in Los Angeles, she hasn't mentioned much of anything. I don't think she wanted to get our hopes up."

"During our dinner date last night she mentioned returning to Red Rock."

"I'd forgotten you two had a date."

"The whole situation wasn't really much of anything to write home about. We had dinner together. Some good conversation, compared notes —that sort of thing."

"She needs a good man in her life. The idiot she was seeing before didn't appreciate her for her intelligence and her fun nature. She's a great gal. I hope she finds the perfect man for her someday. I think you two would be good for each other, but I'm not pushing."

He laughed at Mitchell's blatant shove in the direction of his daughter.

Yes, the attraction was there in spades, but she wasn't staying and he didn't want a relationship, did he?

Their talk returned to the cattle and the death of so many. He still thought something with the water supply had killed the animals. Testing the pool would need to be done immediately to rule out contamination. Unfortunately, with the buzzards already doing so much damage to the carcasses, he wouldn't be able to tell what had killed them. He could have done some testing had one of them died a little closer to the house.

Several moments later Elizabeth sailed down the stairs, her hair a wild disarray of curls around her face, pink tank top, cut off shorts showing off her gorgeous long legs and sandals on her feet completed the picture. *God, she's stunning.* "You look good enough to eat."

Her face lit up. "Why thank you, Marcus." She grabbed her purse and her car keys. "I'm off to lunch. I probably won't be back for a couple of hours."

"No problem, honey," her father said. "We'll see you when you get back."

The door shut with a soft click behind her. The sound of her car starting made him want to follow her like a lost puppy. He shook his head. Getting involved with her would be a bad idea. She already distracted him to no end from things he needed to do.

"She's a very beautiful woman, isn't she?"

"Yes, she is, Mitchell. I'm sure whoever finds himself in love with her will be one lucky man, even more so if she loves him in return."

* * * *

The diner sat in the middle of town. Everyone ate lunch there which is why she told Natalie eleven. Even then, the place seemed busy when she parked her car. Pickup trucks lined the street along with cars and one cop car. *Maybe Laurel is around.*

Elizabeth shut her car door behind her as she glanced across the street to the Harley shop and the small gas stationed owned by Delaney Dunn —oops, Delaney Monroe now. The Harley shop looked busy too. She noticed a long, lean guy standing near the bay doors. Muscle shirt, black jeans, dark hair to his shoulders and dark sunglasses. Jake Monroe. She remembered him from high school although he graduated a few years behind her. Man, did he turn out yummy.

Blonde hair in a ponytail and coveralls caught her attention next as the woman walked quickly toward Jake. Delaney, Elizabeth assumed. It had been a long time since she'd seen any of these people, but when the two embraced and shared a hot kiss, she couldn't miss the fire between them. *Wow.* Jake grabbed her ass, swung her around and pinned her to the side of the building with his body. *Holy shit!* Cream slid down between Elizabeth's legs at the display. She wanted that. She wanted someone to take control, make her his, fill her up, and leave her wanting more. She quickly blew her bangs off her forehead and spun around. *Damn, I need to get laid.*

Natalie waved from two cars down. "Hey girl!" she squealed as she grabbed Elizabeth in a hug. "Damn those two can heat up the sidewalk, eh?"

"Two?"

"Delaney and Jake. I saw them across the street. Newlyweds, you know."

"Yeah, I'd heard. What I wouldn't give to be in love like that."

"Someday, hon. He's out there. You'll find him soon enough," Natalie replied, looping her arm through Elizabeth's as they walk toward the diner.

Once inside, they found a booth near the back. The place was already crawling with people but Mabel waved them over to seat them in a booth. "Elizabeth, honey, my goodness, how are you? I haven't seen you in ages."

"I'm good. Home for a month or so. Natalie talked me into some of your famous food for lunch."

"Well of course. Nat, where are those babies?"

"At home with Dad today so I could have some girl talk with my sister-in-law. What's the special today, Mabel?"

"Chicken and dumplin's."

"Oh, sounds good to me," Natalie said. "A soda to drink, please. What are you gonna have?"

"The same for me, Mabel."

"Very good. I'll be right back with your drinks."

They both put the menus away. Natalie grabbed her hand. "Now, tell me about things with Marcus."

"There's nothing to tell," Elizabeth said, pulling her hand back, stuffing her napkin down on her lap.

"Bullshit. I see the twinkle in your eye when his name is mentioned."

"It's nothing, Natalie. He's very nice and all, but I don't want any kind of relationship or anything."

"You're attracted to him though, I can tell."

"Yes, I am. Maybe we'll have a quick fling while I'm here. I could definitely use some attention like that for a change. Things with Ari sucked in the making love department."

"Pencil dick?"

Elizabeth burst out laughing. "He wasn't well endowed."

"Well I couldn't tell you about Marcus' but I'm pretty sure he's attracted to you."

"If our kiss says anything, I'd say so."

"Kiss?"

"I didn't tell you, did I?"

"No, spill it girl."

"I went to his office yesterday to apologize for my behavior. The night before when I found out who he really was, I jumped to conclusions I shouldn't have. By the way, I'm pissed at you for not telling me."

"Telling you?"

"About Marcus being the guy from the ball."

"He asked me not to."

"I realize that, but I'm still pissed. Anyway, I asked him to have dinner with so I could grovel appropriately. He agreed. We went to the Millhouse."

"I love their food."

"My steak was excellent, of course. Anyway, he walked me out to the car and kissed me goodnight."

"Nothing else?"

She glanced from her right to her left to make sure no one paid any attention to their conversation before she said, "It curled my toes."

"See! I told you!"

"Sshh."

"Sshh what? You two are perfect for each other."

"We're not perfect for each other. I hardly know anything about him."

"Well, let me tell you—"

"That's not what I meant, Natalie. Yes, he seems to be a nice guy, but I don't have time for any kind of relationship. I'm leaving for Billings in a month. I'll be there for three years. Long distance relationships don't work."

"Just get to know him, Liz. You never know where things will lead."

Mabel returned with their drinks and winked as she stepped back. "Doctor Melton has enough women chasing him, he won't miss you if you don't pursue him, Elizabeth."

"I'm not interested..."

"I'm only giving you my opinion. He has enough of the women in this town panting like their little dogs when he's around. Gorgeous and eligible around here gets noticed rather quickly."

Elizabeth closed her eyes. Everyone seemed to be interested in matching her up with Marcus, not that she didn't think he would be a catch, but she couldn't take the time to formulate anything with anyone, much less Marcus right now. He had his life and she had to finish her residency.

Within moments, their food arrived and they dug in as they talked about her niece and nephew, her schooling, how things actually went down with Ari and what she planned when she got to Billings. She mentioned the cattle. Natalie agreed something suspicious seemed to be going on, especially when she mentioned this was the second time in two weeks.

"Dad is going to have the water tested in the pool. It seems the other incident happened in the same location or close to it. Marcus mentioned the water might have been contaminated by a dead animal or something."

"No one has seen anything weird?"

"No. I talked to Jackson, you know, Dad's foreman. He hasn't seen anyone except Marcus up there." She tapped the fork in her hand against her lips.

"What? You look like you're thinking of something."

"You don't think...no, he can't be involved."

"Who? Marcus?" Natalie slammed her fork down on the table and Elizabeth jumped. "No way Marcus would be involved in something like this. He loves animals. He'd never hurt one. Not even a cow."

"Why would he anyway? It doesn't make sense."

"See? Even you couldn't really believe he would behind something like this. It has to be an accident."

"If Dad didn't know the pool might be contaminated, he wouldn't know to keep the other cattle away." Elizabeth cut off another piece of dumpling. "What do you know about Dad's foreman?"

"Jackson? Not much. He's been there for a few years, I guess."

"I've never seen him before."

"I think he avoided you the last several times you've been home. I doubt you two have much in common. He's a cowboy after all." Natalie laughed. "I know how you are about cowboys."

"Marcus is a cowboy."

"That's why I think it's so funny you're attracted to him. Why such an affinity for them?"

"I went out with a few in high school. They always seemed so egotistical and worried about themselves rather than the woman they're with."

"Lost your virginity to one?"

"Yep and he dumped me the next day."

"That was high school, Liz. Boys are more worried about getting laid than anything else including girls."

"I know, but it still hurt."

"I can imagine so."

"Who did you lose yours to?"

"A guy in California named Jason Grant. Football hero and gorgeous. We went out for about six months before we had sex. We lasted another three before I dumped him."

"You dumped the football star?"

"Yes. He kept pressuring me to get married."

"Married at eighteen? No way!"

"Oh yeah. He wanted a wife on his arm when he went off to college, but when I turned him down, he got mad at me. Smacked me around a bit. I dumped him immediately." Mabel came over and the girls ordered pie. "I wasn't about to put up with being smacked."

"I would have dumped him too."

"See, we're a lot alike you and I."

"In some ways, yeah." The conversation died when Mabel returned with two slices of apple pie and ice cream. "How are the kids?"

"Great! Growing like weeds."

"So when's are you going to have another one?" Elizabeth asked, running her observant gaze over Natalie's form.

"We aren't for awhile. We really don't want anymore this soon."

"If you're on birth control, you should be good."

"Yeah, but I hope it works. I've missed a day here and there."

"Be careful then until you get back on a schedule or you will end up being pregnant before you want to."

Natalie frowned as tears welled up in her eyes. "I hope if something like that happened, Cade would be happy. I don't want to disappoint him. He's my life."

"Oh stop now. He loves you so much you two make me ill." She grabbed Natalie's hand and squeezed. "Besides, he always said he wanted a big family."

"I don't know how I got so lucky."

"I do. Your grandmother."

Natalie laughed. "You aren't kidding. She's got her hands in everyone of the kids who've gotten together lately. She even helped Delaney, Jake and Colby get things straightened out."

"Speaking of. What's the scoop? I know Delaney and Jake got married..."

"Oh, they're in a nice little triad with Colby Mason."

"Seriously?"

"Yes," Natalie said, drying her eyes with the edge of the paper napkin.

"Apparently Jake and Colby had been lovers before. It's the reason Jake took off right after high school even though he was in love with Delaney. They've worked everything out now. They all live together as a happy threesome."

"Those threesome things seem kind of weird to me even though Emma is happy as a pig in shit with Beau and Brandon."

"Isn't she due with another little bundle soon too?"

"Yeah. Last time I talked to her she was feeling like a cow and ready to burst any day, but she still had a month to go."

"I haven't talked to her in a couple of weeks. No one has mentioned her going into labor yet so I figured she was still holding onto her little girl."

"It's a girl?"

Natalie nodded. "The last ultrasound showed a girl. Beau and Brandon are over the moon. They'll have one of each."

"See, I'm not sure I could keep two men happy. One would be plenty for me." She glanced at Natalie and noticed her deep red blush. "I'd forgotten about you, Cade and Kale. I didn't mean..."

"It's fine. It was a onetime thing. Something to try and be done with. We didn't plan to make it a permanent thing. I don't think your brother would handle sharing me anyway. He's pretty possessive."

"To each his own, I guess. I think having two men might be something to try." Natalie's blush deepened. "I could get some pointers from you."

"Can we talk about something else?"

"Oh, come on Nat. You're not embarrassed by what happened, are you?"

Natalie leaned over and whispered, "I don't broadcast it. Enough people in this town know I dated both men, but I really don't want everyone knowing we had a threesome."

"We'll talk in private then one day. Okay?"

"Why are you so interested? Do you really want me to tell you how your brother and his best friend were in bed?"

"Not details...well yeah maybe details just don't mention names." Elizabeth glanced out the front windows, noticing Laurel Dunn standing near her police car as she talked with a gangly young man. "How is Laurel with knowing it happened?"

"We don't discuss it, Liz. She knows. It's not like it happened more than once."

"Did you want it to?"

Natalie sighed. "I'm not talking about this here and no, I didn't. I love your brother. Nothing else mattered. Maybe you should discuss the threesome thing with Emma if you want a permanent take on the whole thing."

"Maybe I will."

Mabel came by with refills on their sodas and the check. "Are you two finished? Can I get you anything else?"

"No. I think we're done, Mabel. Thanks," Elizabeth replied. "The food melted on my tongue as usual. I'll make sure to be back before I leave again."

"You aren't staying, Elizabeth? I thought you were done with school?"

"School yes, residency, no. I have to spend three more years working in the hospital in Billings before I can practice."

"Are you planning on coming back here when you're done?"

"Yes ma'am. I plan on opening a practice here."

"Really, Liz? I didn't know you planned to stay. That's fantastic!" Natalie said, taking out some money and handing everything to Mabel. "Keep the rest for your tip."

"Hopefully it will all work out. I need to get a really rounded education while I'm in Billings so I can do family practice."

"You'll be able to follow the kids and everyone then."

"I know we need a doctor here in Red Rock so people don't have to go all the way into Billings to be treated for minor things. I won't be doing surgery or anything, but I can treat sprains, ear infections and whatnot. I want to put an office right down at the corner where the old grocery store used to sit. It's got plenty of room. I can divide everything up into exam rooms very easily. Maybe Cade would help with the construction for me."

"You know he would, Liz, but that's a few years down the road."

"I know." She sighed. "I wish things would move a little faster. I'm so ready to be done with all of this."

She noticed over Natalie's shoulder, a tall, dark-haired man come into the diner. When he removed his sunglasses and grinned, she couldn't help but smile back. Of course, Natalie noticed. "Marcus, come join us."

"Hello ladies. What are you two gorgeous girls doing sitting alone?"

"We finished our lunch and were just about to leave."

"We can stay a little longer, Liz. Refill our glasses, Mabel, and we'll talk to Marcus while he eats his lunch."

"I really should get back to the house."

"To do what pray tell?" Natalie asked, not moving so Marcus had to slide in the booth next to Liz.

"I'm sure Dad has some kind of work I could be doing."

"I just left there. Everything is fine."

"What about the dead animals?"

"He's having the water tested right now. Until the results come back, he's having the hands put up a temporary fence around the watering hole. He's going to keep the cattle down in the lower pasture."

"I should be helping with the fence then."

"You build fences too?"

"I can. What's it to you?"

"Nothing." He laughed. "You amaze me is all. You definitely aren't the typical woman."

"I was raised a rancher's daughter. We did those things. All of us helped whenever something needed to be done. It didn't matter whether we were male or female and Dad treated us all the same."

"No offense, Liz. I think you'll make a wonderful rancher's wife someday."

"Thank you...I think."

"It was a compliment."

Mabel returned to the table with a plate of the chicken and dumplings for Marcus. He dug right in with gusto.

"Hungry?"

"Starving. I hadn't eaten since last night's dinner which, by the way, thank you for the meal."

"My pleasure. We should do it again before I leave."

"How about tomorrow evening? I'll buy this time."

"Okay, sure."

"Oh, another date," Natalie added, clapping her hands.

"It's not a date," the two said in unison.

"It's just dinner, Natalie," Elizabeth replied. "We aren't dating."

"Nope. No dating," Marcus said between mouthfuls of dumplings. "Casual dinner is all."

"Sure. You two keep telling yourselves that. You might believe it eventually. I'm sure you've been dreaming of Marcus, Liz and I know how he talks about you."

Elizabeth coughed and kicked her under the table as Marcus choked on his lunch.

"Ouch!"

"Shut your mouth, Natalie. What goes on between me and Marcus isn't your concern." She elbowed Marcus who jumped up to let her out. "I'll see you tomorrow night, Marcus."

6

"What did I do?" Natalie asked, as Marcus sputtered and coughed.

"Got involved," he croaked after another couple of coughs to clear his throat. "I told you to stay out of my relationship with Elizabeth, Natalie."

"I only want to see the two of you happy, Marcus."

"She's leaving in a month. A relationship between us is dead before it gets started, but you in the middle of this will only make everything worse."

"But you've been pining after her for months."

"It doesn't matter. Can't you see she's rebounding after her breakup with her guy friend in Los Angeles."

"Asshole, you mean."

"Whatever. She's still not ready to move on to someone else. We'll spend some quiets nights dining together. That will be the end of it."

"I know you don't want things to end though."

"I don't need a woman in my life. I have my practice. It's enough."

"Bullshit."

"It's not bullshit, Nat. Elizabeth is beautiful, charming, sophisticated, and all the things a man could want in a woman, but she's busy—too busy for a love life unless it's a short-term relationship. I'm okay with something along those lines for now. If we get together under those circumstances, then so be it." He finished his dumplings and pushed the plate away. "How are Cade and the kids? I haven't been out to visit in a while."

"They're fine. Why don't you join us for supper on Sunday?"

"I supposed I could. I'm not busy."

"Great. Six?"

"Sounds fine, but I should go now. I've got some patients to see and a dinner date tomorrow to prepare for." He grinned as she rolled her eyes.

"Guys don't prepare."

"This one does, especially if I want to impress said lady."

"You're impossible, Marcus. I hope you know what you're doing."

"I do. We're good. See you Sunday," he said, tossing some bills on the table to cover lunch before he headed for the door. He knew what he wanted and even if he could only have her for a short time, he'd be willing.

When he got back to his office, the lobby was full to the brim with women and their pets. Everything from cats, to dogs, to lizards graced cages, collars and laps.

"There you are Doctor Melton," his receptionist said. "Thank goodness you're back. It's been like this for the last hour. Are you ready for patients?"

"Yes, Cindy. Give me two minutes to get settled. I'll take care of everyone in time."

"Yes, sir. Mandy is already in the back waiting for you."

"Thanks."

A soft wolf-whistle echoed the noisy room, but he chose to ignore it. He had put up with the flirting and random suggestions since taking over the clinic. Unfortunately, he hadn't figured out how to discourage his female clientele.

A primped and cut French poodle waddled in on a studded leash with Mrs. Warber holding tightly to the end.

"Mrs. Warber. What seems to be trouble with Fifi this week?"

"I think she's got a fever. She doesn't seem to be herself the last couple of days."

"Are you sure? She seems fine to me," he said, noting the rapid step, wagging tail and lolling tongue of the large dog.

"She sleeps all the time and doesn't seem to have much energy."

Marcus shook his head, but grinned. Mrs. Warber had been in with Fifi five times in as many weeks, always for some milady or another. The other females in the waiting room were there for the same reason. He let it go and treated the animals, as if they were really sick. Good thing he enjoyed seeing his four-legged patients. "I'll have Mandy get her temp and we'll check her out. How's she been eating?"

"Not very well, Doctor."

He checked her tongue, in her ears and ran his hands over the poodle's entire body. One thing he had to say, animals loved him. Fifi gave him a big lick on his cheek and he laughed. "Mandy, check her temp and I'll be back in a minute."

Once he stepped outside the exam room, he ran his hands through his hair before pinching the bridge of his nose. Not quite understanding the fascination with him, the women of the town kept him in business with the constant visits, but they were getting tiresome.

He wanted a relationship. He wanted a steady woman in his life. None of the women he'd come in contact with so far did anything for him—except Elizabeth Weston. She didn't want him. Well, maybe that wasn't necessarily true. He got the impression the attraction between them was mutual. Her plans to go off to Billings for three years put the breaks on any kind of relationship beyond some hot sex. Somehow he knew making love with her would burn up the sheets.

Back to work. "So Mandy," he said, stepping back into the exam room. "How's our patient?"

* * * *

The next evening rolled around without much hoopla except the nervousness Elizabeth felt every time she thought about dinner with Marcus this evening. Why the man fascinated her so much, she wasn't sure, but he did. Men with broad shoulders, collar-length brown hair, big blue eyes and a killer smile were a dime a dozen, right? Maybe it was the mystery surrounding him. He'd done the tuxedo thing, pulling it off with grace and style, now he did the jeans and western shirt thing with just as much sexiness. *Shesh, the man dries up my self-control.*

Standing in front of the mirror in her room, she twisted left, then right deciding whether she wanted to wear the dress she had on. The soft cotton material swished against her bare legs, the softness caressing her skin. She wore no nylons to stifle her skin from the heat, only flat sandals graced her feet. The thing spaghetti straps of the dress left her shoulders uncovered as she hoped for a sexy look. She'd seen the women around town giving Marcus the eye. Beautiful, sexy, some single, some not, they all made her bristle with what? Jealousy? She had no reason to be jealous. Marcus didn't belong to her.

The doorbell rang and she jumped. The clock on her nightstand read five fifty five. *Damn.*

"Elizabeth? Sweetheart, Marcus is here."

"Thanks, Dad. I'll be right down."

Time had run out. She'd have to wear what she had on unless she made him wait. Grabbing her shawl and purse, she opened the door and headed down the stairs. Marcus stood near the door, cowboy hat in hand. He took her breath away. Black western, button-down shirt graced his shoulders emphasizing the width and size. Wrangler jeans molded to his impressive thighs and black cowboy boots completed the picture. *Damn, if he wasn't a sight.*

"Hi," he said, walking closer. "You look beautiful."

"Thanks. It's nothing special." She beamed at his compliment.

"Shall we?" He held out his arm and she slipped her hand into the crook of his elbow.

So dashing.

"Where would you like to eat?"

"Um, how about Mexican. We had steak the last time."

"Sure. I love Mexican food too."

"Is the Cantina still sitting on the corner of Onion and Spruce?"

"Yep. They have the best around these parts by far."

"Yes, they do."

Marcus opened the door to his truck and helped her slide into the cab. *Such a gentleman.*

After he shut the door, he raced around the front of the truck to get into the driver's seat. "How was your day?" he asked, starting the truck before he pulled out from in front of the house.

"Good. I helped my Dad with moving the cattle away from the pool. He hasn't gotten the results back on the water yet."

"I hope it's not anything major. He's lost a lot of them the last month or so between these two outbreaks. I wish I could help more."

"The foreman said you spent a lot of time up there when you inoculated the cattle. Did you see anything?"

"No, but I wasn't really looking. Several of the hands were up there with me. Did you question them?"

"I haven't questioned anyone really. I thought I'd ask you first since it happened about the time you did the shots."

"I wish I could help."

She shrugged. "It's fine. Let's talk about something else."

"Like what?"

"Oh, I don't know. How about you tell me about your family?"

He pulled into the parking lot of the restaurant and shut off the truck. "Not much to tell. All of my siblings live in Boston near my parents. I'm the only one who's traveled so far from home."

"Did you always want to be a vet?" she asked when he opened her door.

"Yeah. From the time I can remember. I was always bandaging up the dog and cat at home. They finally started running from me by the time I turned ten." He chuckled. "Poor things."

She laughed along with him as they approached the door to the restaurant. Soft Mexican music played from the speakers set into the ceiling.

"Good evening. How many?"

"Two please. May we sit on the veranda?" Marcus asked.

"I would love to sit out in the evening air. Great idea, Marcus."

"Certainly. Follow me please."

The waiter sat them at a table near the wrought iron railing under a fan to keep them cool until the sun went down. The music seemed muted enough they could talk as she looked over the menu for what she wanted to eat.

"What looks good to you?"

"Hmm..." She tapped a finger against her lips. "I'm thinking the fajitas. I love those."

"Good choice."

Someone brought chips and salsa to the table. She dipped a chip into the mixture of tomato and spices before she popped the concoction into her mouth with a soft groan.

"Good?" he asked, watching her mouth.

"Yes. I love the spices. They burst on your tongue in a happy little dance."

He smiled as he grasped her hand. "You have such a way with words."

After he brought her fingers to his lips and kissed each one, he returned her hand to the table top, but didn't let go. The small gesture seemed so intimate yet not. She wasn't sure what he meant by it. Did he want her? He seemed to. Did she want him? Oh yeah. With every breath she inhaled his spicy yet manly scent, letting the fragrance run the gamut of her senses. His eyes twinkled in the fading sunlight, almost as if he knew the war she waged with herself.

"What would you like?" the waitress asked, standing next to their table.

Once their drinks arrived, they went about small talk of various things. How she'd decided to become a physician. How medical school seemed different than veterinarian school, but yet they seemed very similar too. How he'd become friends with Cade and Natalie. What her plans were after residency.

"I've even got the place picked out for my offices."

"Oh?" he asked, taking a bite of his enchilada.

"Yes. The building just on the edge of town across from Delaney's gas station. It used to be a a grocery store years ago. It's too small for most doctors, but not me. I'd love to practice here." She took another bite of her fajita, and then swallowed. "Are you staying busy with your practice?"

"Oh yes. I think half the town has decided their pets are sick at least once a week."

"The women, you mean."

"Well, yes. I'm not sure what the whole thing is about."

"You're a very handsome man, Marcus. Why wouldn't the women be attracted to you and want a little bit of your time?" A flush of red crept up his neck. "You're blushing."

"I don't like to talk about myself."

"It's true, you know. The women around here led pretty boring lives.

If bringing their cats, dogs and every other pet imaginable into your clinic brought them a little closer to you, then they will."

"What about you?"

"Me? I don't have a pet."

"Do you want to be near me?" he asked, grasping her fingers.

"Well, I..."

"I'd like to be closer to you. Out of everyone I've seen walk through my clinic lately, you're the only women within a hundred miles of Red Rock who I'm attracted to."

She swallowed hard and exhaled. "I'm attracted to you, Marcus...a lot, but you know I won't be here beyond a month."

"I know, but what says we can't spend some quality time together while you're here?"

"Nothing, I guess. I just wanted to make sure you knew where things stood."

"I'm aware, but I still want you."

As the waitress dropped the check at their table, she removed her hand from his and sipped at her drink. The tequila went straight to her head, making her brain a bit fuzzy. At least she hoped it was the tequila and not Marcus, but she wasn't sure anymore. He made her hot with nothing more than a look.

"How would you like to go back to my house to watch a movie?"

Watch a movie when I want to do nothing more than jump him? I need to feel those arms around me, those hands on me and those lips doing wicked, wicked things to me. "Sure. Sounds like a good idea."

He laid his plastic on the table as they waited for the waitress to return to get their check. The sun had already set, leaving them bathed in the muted lights of the restaurant's veranda.

"Would you rather go dancing? I'd love to hold you in my arms again."

"I think the movie is a better plan tonight. We can always do the dancing thing another time."

He grinned like a boy who'd just been given his favorite toy for his birthday. "I'd love to take you out again."

"Me too."

Once the waitress returned, he helped her to her feet, kissed the palm of her hand and tucked it into the crook of his elbow. "You're beautiful."

"Thank you, but you don't need to say that, Marcus. I still plan on sleeping with you."

The shocked look on his face was priceless.

"What?"

"I really didn't expect you to say something like that."

"After my last disastrous relationship, I've decided to go for what I want." She reached up and pulled his mouth down to hers. "I want you," she whispered against his lips as her gaze met his. The moment their mouths fused, she lost the battle to keep herself from falling under the man's spell. Every woman in town wanted him. She knew why, but it didn't help her keep her sanity around him. He would be deadly to her heart if she let him get too close. Right now though, every cell in her body screamed for his touch.

"Let's go," he murmured, lifting his head.

Within moments, she stood in front of Marcus' house, amazed at the architectural of the home. It wasn't a ranch house like most of the others in the area, but something more like a Mexican abode with sandstone walls and native Montana plants. The big front door had to be made from oak and the surrounding pastures supported buffalo grass swaying in the breeze. Several cattle mooed in the distance.

"You have cattle?"

"Sure. I've always wanted a ranch although it's not very big. I only have a few head. Less than a hundred."

"It's still impressive, Marcus." They walked inside the moment he opened the front doors. Wide windows filled the front of the house, reflecting the moon outside onto the shiny black tile floor of the hall. A gourmet kitchen graced the space to her left and a large open living room took up everything to her right. More huge windows opened to a back deck. She glided to the sliding glass door as if her feet carried her without conscious thought. She opened the door and stepped out onto the patio. Her breath caught in her throat at the view. The mountains glowed in the distance with the moonlight shining over the peaks igniting the tip top like diamonds on the water. A small fountain trickled water in the corner, splashing lightly into the pool beneath. She couldn't help but step closer. Carp swam in the water like colorful flowers blowing in a summer breeze. "It's beautiful out here."

"I'm glad you like it. I don't usually bring women home with me, but I still like to have a pretty setting for barbeques and whatnot."

"I'm sure people you've entertained have been impressed. Your view is breathtaking. How did you manage to snag such a magnificent home?"

"I didn't. I had the house built," he replied, sliding his hands around her waist and drawing her back against his chest.

"Seriously?"

"Yes. I knew what I wanted. I helped design the plans. I planned on making Red Rock my home, the moment I stepped foot in this town. The views are beautiful, the people are warm and welcoming. Who could ask for more?"

She relaxed as Marcus' hands came around to rest on her stomach. His warm breath tickled the hair near her ear. She tilted her head slightly to give him access to the sensitive spot if he so chose.

A moment later, she closed her eyes and sighed when his lips slid down the column of her neck, stopping to nip at the curve of her shoulder.

"You have no idea how much I want you."

"I think I do otherwise you've got one hell of something hard in your pocket."

He spun her around and slid his hands into her hair. "You have no idea what you're doing to me."

"Yes, I do. Kiss me."

"With pleasure," he said, right before his mouth crushed hers in a desperate, lip-locking kiss.

Desire pooled low in her belly as his hands worked their way from her neck, down her arms and around her waist again to draw her closer still. Her breasts were already crushed against his chest. Her nipples pulled into hard nubs, begging for the touch of his hand or his mouth. A moment later, his palm skimmed over the peak. She moaned into his mouth. Their tongues danced from his mouth to hers. She wanted this man with something so deep she couldn't comprehend how far he touched her soul.

"Please, Marcus," she whispered as their mouths separated. "I need you."

"Come." He grasped her hand to lead her back into the house. The hall to the left of the living room yawned in front of her with its dark corridor and impressive paneling. "My bedroom is this way." He led her up the stairs and down a thick, padded hallway to a large door. His room reminded her of him—darkly masculine with its massive furniture.

She nervously wiped her now sweaty palms on the front of her dress as he shut and locked the door.

"Nervous?"

"A bit."

"Why?"

"Because I've wanted this since I met you at the ball and I can't believe I'm here."

"You have no idea, Elizabeth," he said, cupping her face as he took her mouth again. The tip of his tongue slipped along the seam of her lips before he took what he wanted by diving into her mouth. She wanted this, needed this with something deep inside. To have her control taken away seemed like a dream. Not worrying about what she needed to do to please him raced across her mind and she wondered if he could be the man she needed.

The moment his mouth released her, he said, "Strip. I want you naked."

With shaking hands, she slipped the spaghetti straps of her dress down her arms, letting the silky material pool at her feet. Black lacy bra and panties seemed almost too much as she stood in front of him waiting for some sign of what he thought. Did he think her pretty? She wasn't necessarily fat, but she had curves. Maybe too many curves. Her butt always seemed a little big and her boobs seemed too small.

He stepped in front of her, cupping her face in his hands. "Stop!"

She dropped her gaze to the middle of his chest and laced her hands in front of her stomach, like she tried to hold herself together.

"You're a very beautiful woman, Elizabeth. I like curves. Most women are too thin. You aren't. Everything about you is gorgeous. I want you so bad, I ache with need for you."

She trembled, raising her eyes to see the truth of his words in his gaze. Blue eyes sparkled with appreciation and warmth. He wasn't lying to her. He really did think she was beautiful.

"On your knees. I want you to suck my cock."

Damn! Where did the nice, non-demanding Marcus go?

Her pussy throbbed as she immediately dropped to her knees and began to work the belt buckle at this waist. His impressive length strained the front of his pants, tenting the material until she freed him.

"Easy, honey. Go slow. We have all night," he coaxed when she finally freed and licked him like an ice cream cone.

Around the head she licked, earning a soft groan from him. Goose bumps flittered across his legs. She palmed his heavy balls, squeezing lightly. He tasted a little salty, but good...so good. The large vein running up the back caught her attention. She tongued the pulse, following along as if it was a lifeline. The purple tip of his dick strained toward her.

"Suck me."

She took the head into her mouth and slowly slid him along her tongue until he reached the back of her throat. Her eyes watered when she gagged slightly.

"Breathe through your nose. Relax your throat. You can take me."

Dropping her head back, she opened her jaws wider and let him in. A quick swallow earned her a hiss from his mouth as his fingers tightened in her hair. His smell surrounded her. Everything about him brought her senses on high alert. His voice sent chills down her arms. His whispers play havoc with her mind. His body made her want him more than anything on the earth.

"Enough. I want inside you when I come." He laid her across the quilt on his bed before quickly kicking off his shoes, then shedding his pants.

Two fingers popped the catch on the front of her bra, releasing the globes of her breasts to his hot gaze. The rough pad of his tongue circled her left nipple, before leaving her shivering as he moved to the other breast. The moment his hand dipped between her legs, she released a soft moan.

She cracked her eyelids open to see him kissing down her chest, across her abdomen and then settling between her spread thighs. Her pussy clenched wanting something to fill the depths.

"I can smell you." He took one finger, skimming down her pussy even though her underwear hid her skin from his touch. "So sweet."

A quick squeak revealed her sensitivity to his touch as he wet her underwear with his tongue just over her clit. The need to feel his mouth overwhelmed her. Her pussy wept with cream for the flick of his tongue. She quivered as she begged, "Please, Marcus."

"I like when you beg."

"Plleeeease..."

"Hmm."

His finger slipped along the lacy edge of her underwear between her pussy and her thigh, making her shiver with need. He hooked the edges of her panties, moving them so he could slide them down her thighs. Her whole body shook with desire when he settled between her legs. Ari never ate her out. She almost didn't believe Marcus was about to until the tip of his tongue touched her clit.

"Oh God."

"You like your pussy eaten."

"Oh yes. Please, touch me."

"My pleasure, sweetheart." His tongue delved between her pussy lips, making her sigh.

He's eating me out. He's really eating me out.

The quick figure eights on her clit brought her straight up to *oh my God* screaming need within moments as he gripped her ass cheeks in his hands and held her to his mouth. The scratch of his beard against her sensitive flesh only made her whole pussy more sensitive to the touch of his tongue. She needed this...wanted this with everything inside her. The want to have a man believe she had it in her to be sexy and alluring, drove her to this point in her life. No one before Marcus had made her feel like she might actually be woman enough for him until now. Desire spiked hard as she trembled with the need to come. Just a little more, a few more swipes right there and she'd...

Her whole body tensed as heat flooded from her toes through her abdomen and settled between her legs right at the spot Marcus' tongue played.

"Ohgod, ohgod, ohgod," she screamed, tossing her head from side to side.

Marcus continued to slowly lick her pussy until she came down from her orgasm. Before she could open her eyes, she felt the latex covered head of his cock at her entrance. *When had he put on a condom? Who cares!*

"Easy, babe. I'm comin' home," he murmured, swirling the head in her juices before pushing slowly into her quivering pussy.

"God, you feel good. So good."

"Such a hot pussy. All for me."

"Fuck me, Marcus. Hard, please. Oh God, hard."

With a snap of his hips, he shoved his cock to the hilt inside her, hitting her G spot on the inside slide.

"You're so hot."

"Please." She wanted more. She wanted all of him.

A clench of her muscles was rewarded by a hiss and several jerky motions of his body. Each demanding plunge of his cock brought his pelvis hard against her clit. She speared her hand down between them and rubbed her ever hardening nub with her finger, shooting her straight to oh-my-god-I'm-going-to-come.

"Come for me, Elizabeth. Make yourself come around me. Milk me dry, baby."

She screamed his name as she came hard enough she saw stars behind her eyelids.

A moment later, he groaned and she felt his cock jerk as he exploded in his own orgasm, spraying his seed into the latex reservoir.

"You are magnificent," he whispered, burying his nose in her neck.

"I bet you say that to all the girls."

"No I don't," he replied, propping himself up on his elbows. "Believe it or not, it's been a long time since I've had sex with anyone. I'm usually not into one night stands, but a man has needs."

"I know. I was kidding, Marcus," she said, smoothing his hair back from his forehead. "I didn't think you were the promiscuous type."

He slipped from between her legs and lay down on the quilt besides her. "I want to keep seeing you."

She slid her hand through the hair on his chest. "I'd like that."

"I mean see you. Make love to you. Have sex with you. Go on dates together."

"Okay."

"Okay? That's it? No arguments?"

"No. I like you. We're good together inside and outside of bed although I think inside bed was pretty amazing."

"Oh, I do too," he replied, skimming his hand over her breast and bringing the nipple back to an aching point. He cleared his throat. "I wasn't too rough on you, was I?"

"Too rough? No way. I loved the forceful nature of sex with you."

"I like being in control if you hadn't noticed."

"Yeah, I kind of did. It worked for me if you couldn't tell. I got very turned on by everything you did."

"Have you ever had someone tie you up spread-eagle on the bed?"

"I can't say that I have, but it sounds intriguing."

"Next time I'll get out some of my toys."

"Toys?"

"Yep. Vibrators, handcuffs...you'll enjoy yourself, I promise."

"Why not now? The night is still young."

The grin on his face let her know the idea tripped his trigger too. "You are in so much trouble."

The next morning, Elizabeth woke with a warm brown arm draped across her stomach and the feeling of hot breath on the back of her neck. Marcus.

She let a small smile drift across her mouth as she moved slightly to check the time. Good thing it was Saturday. She assumed he didn't need to be at the office this morning. Contentment filled her soul. Why she wasn't sure, but it felt right to be here with him like this. Their encounter from the night before seemed almost surreal. He took control like she'd always hoped to find a man to do. He was a complete enigma. The personality she thought he had seemed nice, calm and non-assuming. In the bedroom, the real Marcus came out in spades, dominating her from the moment he ordered her to strip.

"You okay?" he whispered, brushing his lips against the nape of her neck.

"Oh yeah." She rolled over to her back and found his gorgeous blue eyes staring down into hers. "You...wow."

His lips lifted in a crooked half smile. "Wow, huh?"

"I don't know what else to say. That was something I've wanted for a long time, but never found."

"Sorry if I came on too strong. It's just who I am in the bedroom."

She cupped his cheek with her hand. "No. Don't be sorry. I wanted someone to take control."

"How did you like being tied so you couldn't do anything?"

"I loved it."

His gaze dropped to her chin, then raised again. "I liked having access to this beautiful body of yours to do anything I wanted."

"How did you know?"

"Know what?"

"The control thing. You seemed to know immediately what I needed."

"I know what I wanted. I saw the reaction to my words in your body. Your eyes dilated, your skin flushed, you shifted under my stare and dropped your gaze to the floor...all of those are signs of submission, at least in the bedroom. I just took things from there."

"I'm glad you did."

"What about anal sex?"

Heat flushed her cheeks as she bit her bottom lip a moment before answering, "Again, intriguing. I've never tried it though."

"Maybe later." He rolled over on top of her and pressed her into the mattress. "Right now, I want to taste you all over."

"Taste?"

"Uh-huh. Lick, nip, bite. I love the taste of your skin. I want to find all the crevices your smell lingers like the crease of your thigh, the top of your pussy right above your clit and the underside of your breast."

"God, I love your sexy talk."

"Quiet now. The only words I want out of your mouth are yes, sir."

"Yes, Sir."

"Lovely. You'll make a master very happy someday with your total submission. For now you're mine." The moment his mouth found hers, she sighed, leaning into his kiss as his tongue swept along her bottom lip, demanding entrance. Denying this man anything wasn't in her immediate plans. She could do nothing except hold on for the ride.

The palm of his hand found the curve of her breast, kneading the aching flesh until her nipple pulled into a tight nub begging for a harder touch, a rougher stroke. His tongue swept into her mouth demanding she submit to him, to his desires thus finding the satisfaction of her own. Less than a week ago, she never in her life would have imagined herself here with him.

Her skin flushed with desire. Need spiraled out of control as her pussy throbbed and her clit thrummed with every beat of her heart. Cream slipped out of her pussy, wetting the entrance in preparation for his penetration. Keeping her heart from becoming attached to this man seemed a distant thought in the back of her mind. One she had to pull forward every few moments to remind herself of. Falling in love with Marcus would be the cap to how out of control her life seemed to twist these days.

His lips skimmed over her jaw, sending goose bumps down her arms. He nipped at her earlobe, drawing a shudder from somewhere deep inside her. The moment his lips closed over her aching nipple, she pushed her head back into the pillow and groaned in complete sexual satisfaction. *God, the man was good.* He knew exactly what to do to her to draw out each sensation.

"Elizabeth," he whispered in a low growl.

"Hmmm?"

"Stay in the moment with me. Feel what you do to me." His cock pressed insistently against her thigh. "My cock begs for the warmth of your pussy. It wants to push inside you and take what you sublimely offer to me with the arch of your neck." He nipped at her throat. "The animal inside us knows your mine. Your body gives itself to me even though you try to hold back a part of yourself."

How does he know?

"You are female. I am male. It's in our genetic code. Your surrender means the world to me even if it's only for a short time. I will take what you beg me to take with each sigh from your lips." He pushed his cock into her slowly but demanding her surrender with each short stroke. "I haven't been with another woman in months. I get tested regularly. Are you on birth control?"

"Yes and I'm clean. I want to feel you bare deep inside me."

With one final plunge, he buried himself to the hilt, his balls nestled against her ass.

"God, you feel like heaven, Marcus. Fuck me hard. Take everything. I'm yours."

"For now."

He slammed his pelvis against her, grinding the bone against her clit to stimulate the sensations he had to know would bring her to the brink in seconds. She was his even if she didn't want to admit the feelings stirring inside.

Heat built in her abdomen. The tingling started in her toes as she wrapped her legs around his hips. "Yes, yes, yes."

He grabbed her legs, pushing her knees to her chest, opening her to his thrusts, but at the same time, pinning her to the bed to do as he pleased. "Leave them there."

She used one finger to find her clit, rubbing the little button until she hung onto the abyss by her fingertips.

"Don't come."

What? Seriously? "But..."

"What do you say to me?"

"Yes, Sir," she murmured between clenched teeth. *Damn it! I'm going to...oh God!* Stroke after stroke, he pounded into her pussy. The walls of her vagina quivered under the need to come, but she wouldn't. He said not to and giving him control was what she wanted. "Plllleeeease, Marcus. I need to come. Please."

"You beg so pretty, Elizabeth." His words came out in a tortured pant of need. "Come for me now, darlin'."

Her world exploded in a kaleidoscope of color as her whole body shook from the force of her climax. Never in her entire life had she come so hard. Heat spread through her, making even her scalp and fingertips tingle. "Oh God!" she screamed as the last of her conscious thought lost itself in the spiral of sensations.

When he stiffened and groaned his own climax, she felt his cock expand before he lost the battle to hold himself on his arms above her.

* * * *

His body went limp. His legs shook and his arms wouldn't hold his weight anymore as he lost the fight to hold his orgasm back. Everything about Elizabeth fit him like a glove and it scared the hell out of him. Falling in love with her would be easy...too easy.

Her fingertip played with the bumps on his spine as he tried to catch his breath. The scent of jasmine surrounded him, winding its way into his senses until he couldn't breathe without the fragrance becoming a part of him.

"Wow."

"You said that before."

"Yeah, but I mean really...wow."

He chuckled and rolled to his side, bringing her with him until she rested her head on his chest. Her scent lingered in her hair setting his libido off again, making his cock begin to stir.

"Again?" she asked, a giggle in her voice.

"I can't help myself around you. You smell delicious," he said, burying his nose in her tresses. "Your scent makes me want to eat you up."

"You didn't eat anything this last time."

"Getting spoiled are we?"

"No. I'm happy to let you do whatever you want with me."

"Good because I'm not through with you. Did you have plans today?"

"No."

"Will you stay here and play with me?"

"What did you have in mind?"

"Have you ever been flogged?"

"No." She shivered in his arms as her breathing sped up. Even if she'd never had it done, she seemed intrigued by the idea.

"You know, I've read about this kind of stuff a little."

"And?"

"I always thought all of the BDSM sounded sexy as hell."

He ran his fingertips down the back of her arm and back up to her shoulder, watching goose bumps form on her flesh. "You're very trusting toward me even though we've just met."

"I can't trust you?"

"Of course you can. I would never do anything to hurt you or take you beyond something you can't handle, but for someone new to any kind of playing within this realm, you are handing a lot of control to me."

"Two of the most important people in my life trust you so I'm sure I can too."

"They don't know about this side of my personality."

"I bet a lot of people don't."

"Very true."

"Where do you normally engage in this kind of behavior?"

"At a club in Billings."

"Interesting thought. I'll be there doing my residency."

"I know," he replied, brushing the hair back from her face before he circled her ear with his finger.

"Maybe we could hook up while you're there."

"Maybe."

He felt her stiffen at his noncommittal answer and start to pull away, but he held on until she quit squirming. "I didn't say you could move."

"But..."

"Who is in charge here, Elizabeth?"

"You are, Sir."

"Good. Now I want you to roll over on your back and spread your legs."

After a moment's hesitation, she did what he told her. The second she parted her thighs, he positioned himself between them, spearing his tongue into her pussy. Cream coated his tongue—a bit salty with a tang of her taste. A lot of men didn't like eating a woman out, but he did. There was something inherently trusting about a woman when she climaxed under his tongue. The give and take of a relationship like this soothed the restlessness in his soul.

"Ah!"

He could hear the short pants of her breathing, feel the restless quivering of her muscles as she fought against the need to come since he hadn't given her permission.

"Please Marcus."

"Please what?" he murmured against her pussy, sliding his tongue around the outside, but not giving her what she needed to climax.

"Can I come? I need to so badly."

"Since you asked so pretty, you may come now." With the flat of his tongue pressed to her clit, he pushed hard to give her just enough pressure to explode.

Her breaths stop for a split second before she groaned and flooded his mouth.

"Sweet baby Jesus," she whispered.

He pushed two fingers into her pussy, curling them up against her sweet spot. The echo of her cry bounced off the wall as she climaxed again although not near as forcibly as the first time.

"I can't...take it anymore, Marcus. I couldn't possibly have another orgasm. Just do what you will while I lay here."

"No way, babe. You've got more in you," he said, pushing his rock hard, aching cock into her pussy. The quivering flesh expanded and sucked at him, pulling him deeper into her depths until his balls rested against her ass. "You will come for me again, Elizabeth."

"Please. I don't think I can."

"Oh yes, you can."

Her eyes dilated and she moaned as he began to slowly slide his cock into her scorching flesh. Each pass of his shaft into her sucked more from his soul. He'd wanted her from the first moment he'd seen her at the ball. He'd lost his heart the second their lips touched and there would be no getting it back. She had him by the heartstrings. He was more the fool for letting her in. But how would he survive when she left? Trips to Billings even every weekend would be difficult. Her schedule would be erratic and he had his demanding practice here. Any relationship between them would be precarious at best.

"Fuck me, Marcus. God, please fuck me."

Lost in the blue of her gaze, he picked up the pace of his thrusts until she wrapped her arms and legs around him, pushing him beyond control. Her pussy squeezed his cock, milking him until he couldn't hold back his own climax. As he pumped his seed into her hot depths, she climaxed along with him in a blaze of desire strong enough to shatter his heart.

8

Spread eagle, bound hands and feet on something he called a St. Andrews cross, Elizabeth felt helpless. Trepidation raced down her back. *What do I really know about this man? Yes, we've had amazing sex for the last two days, but should I really let him do this? What if I don't like it? What if I can't handle the sensations?*

"You're thinking too much, Elizabeth."

"I can't help it."

"Talk to me."

"What if I get overwhelmed?"

"We discussed a safe word. Do you remember?"

"Yes. It's pink because I hate pink."

He chuckled and she smiled as the tenseness inside her evaporated. She wanted him to take control. The need to have him dominated her unleashed a desire in her so strong, she felt like she would shatter if he didn't complete what he'd promised.

"I'm going to flog you and then I'm going to fuck you in the ass over the spanking bench because I can. You want me to, don't you."

"Yes, Sir."

"Good girl. You look fabulous tied like this. Your body primed and your pussy wet just from being unable to move."

He ran his fingers down the crack of her ass and through her folds. When his fingers came away moist, she groaned as he sucked the juices from his fingertips. *God, he's sexy.*

"You taste wonderful."

"You like the way I taste?"

"Yes. There's nothing like an aroused woman."

When his mouth founds hers, she took him inside her, playing and sliding her tongue along his until he groaned too.

"You're such a temptation I can hardly keep myself from taking you right now."

"Do it."

"No. We do this on my terms," he replied, moving around behind her until she could no longer see him.

"What are you doing?"

"No more questions. No more talk or there will be punishment rather than excitement. Of course, you may like my bare hand on your ass."

Pain zipped from her left butt cheek, and then her right. He was spanking her!

"Your ass reddens nicely, Elizabeth."

She laid her head against the crossbeams, sighing softly. Why did she have this need for pain? She shouldn't. *It's wrong to feel this way.*

Trails of something soft moved over her calves and up the inside of her thighs. Her body quivered at the sensations. She fought the sounds in her throat. Something *whooshed*, and then slapped against her buttocks. Not hard enough to sting but just so she knew it landed. He did this several more times without force behind the blows. The next lash to her upper back landed harder, stinging like the slight snap of a rubber band.

His rhythm traveled along her back although careful to not get near her kidneys, down her buttocks and thighs he went, each swing just a little harder than the last until every lash held the bite of the leather against her flesh like a wasp sting.

Her mind drifted until the slap of the flogger melted into a combination of pain mixed with pleasure. Each time the leather bit into her flesh, she drifted further from herself. Marcus stopped and moved in front of her to cup her breasts.

"Are you all right?"

"Yes, Sir."

Warm lips closed around her left nipple and sucked. Desire zinged straight to her clit with each pull of his mouth.

"You'll come for me now, Elizabeth."

"Mmm."

He dropped to the floor in front of her to place his mouth on her clit. His hot tongue licked from back to front, stopping on the throbbing nub to suck.

"Oh God!" she screamed as her climax washed over her so quickly she felt like she crashed against jagged rocks on the shoreline. Hot then cold. Her body shivered at the force of her orgasm.

"I think you're ready for me now," he said, standing behind her and unhooking first her legs, then her arms.

She sagged like a ragdoll, but he was there to catch her in his arms as he swept her up and walked to the spanking bench.

"Since you've never had a man in your ass, I need to prepare you."

The bench was wrapped in leather and very padded so when he draped her over the contraption, rebuckling her so her legs were spread, she couldn't move if she wanted to.

"I'm not going to strap your arms since they are probably sore from the cross, but don't move them from move your head."

"Yes, Sir."

"Good girl."

Something cold hit her anus, drawing a moan from deep inside her. She'd never had a man fully penetrate her there, but she had fingers ream her ass from time to time. The sensations got her so hot, she climaxed just from a touch and it had been a while since anyone wanted to.

"You are very sensitive there," he said, rubbing the warming lubricant into the muscles.

"Yes, Sir."

"You've never had a man in your ass, correct?"

"No, Sir, but I've had others touch me there."

"Ah. So you are no stranger to anal play."

"No, Sir."

The tip of his finger penetrated the tight ring of muscles, drawing a deep sigh from her lips.

"Ready for two?"

"Yes, Sir."

"Good girl," he said, pushing two fingers into her ass and scissoring them to stretch the muscles.

"Oh God, yes."

The flat palm of his hand came down on her right butt cheek. "Silence."

"But..."

His fingers disappeared and she groaned again when he smacked the left cheek. "I said silence or I won't continue."

She pressed her lips together and sagged against the spanking bench. The need for him had grown to the point she ached for him to be inside her. In her ass, in her pussy or in her mouth. She didn't care at this point which orifice he used.

Something crinkled behind her, making her wonder what he planned now. A cold hard object pressed against her anus, slowly penetrating until she felt full and the wider base stopped at her hole. *A butt plug?* She read about them but never used one. The stretching was uncomfortable. She squirmed slightly earning another smack on the butt.

"I didn't say you could move."

Damn!

Two fingers plunged into her pussy.

Ah fuck!

"You may whimper, moan, groan or make any other sexy noise, but do not speak unless I ask you a question. Only then answer with yes, sir or no, sir."

A high whine escaped her mouth followed by a whimper.

"Very nice."

He continued to work his fingers in and out of her pussy until she hung onto her climax by her fingernails, not daring to let herself plunge over the edge until he said she could.

"Do not come, Elizabeth."

The fingers in her pussy disappeared before she felt the butt plug being removed. *Maybe now he'll fuck me.*

Again, the cold sensation at her asshole and something probed at her opening.

"Relax."

She closed her eyes, trying desperately to loosen up everything below her waist as the broad head of his cock penetrated her anal muscles.

"Are you okay?"

"Yes, Sir."

The sensations bordered on pain—burning pain, but she knew there wasn't anything she wanted more than to have Marcus possess her fully. Every part of her wanted him. Every crevice and piece craved his touch.

When his balls stopped to rest against her pussy lips, she knew he had seated himself completely inside her. The burning turned into an overwhelming need to push back against him. She couldn't move. If she did, he would punish her. She could do nothing except take what he gave her and only what he allowed her to have.

After a moment, he began to move. The slow glide of his cock into her ass drove her passion to new heights. She'd never felt these sensations and didn't know what to do. He controlled everything. A groan escaped her lips. She fought the urge to climax as heat crawled over her skin, washing over her in a heady sensation. Her pussy throbbed and spasmed with the need for something, anything to fill it.

He wrapped one hand around her hip and slid his finger over her clit.

White hot need shot straight through her body.

"Come for me now, Elizabeth," he whispered against her ear as he pounded into her ass with a blinding rhythm. "Shout out your pleasure for me."

"Ah God!"

"Yes, oh God, yes." She heard behind her as he slammed his cock into her and shouted with his own orgasm.

When he collapsed across her back, she felt a shudder roll through him while he tried to regain some control over his breathing.

"You were magnificent. I couldn't have asked for a better sub."

"Thank you, Sir."

A minute later, she felt him withdraw his softening cock from her. "I'll be right back."

He returned seconds later with something warm that he slipped over her backside and between her thighs. *A washcloth?* After he finished a very thorough job, he unbuckled her legs and helped her draw them back together slowly.

"Easy. You might be a bit sore," he said, bringing her back into an upright position.

The look on her face must have told him she wanted to speak, but was afraid of saying anything out of turn. Spanking might be fun although full-blown punishment might not be.

"You can speak freely now, Elizabeth. I'm not the twenty four seven type of Dom."

"Thank you."

"How did you like anal sex?" he asked, running his hands over her shoulders and arms.

"Everything was intense. I don't think I've come so hard in my life."

"Good. The feeling is indescribable to me."

"Do you enjoy anal more than vaginal?"

"Not always. It depends. It's a different type of feeling." His lips settled over hers in an all too brief kiss. "Shall we get something to eat? It's going on dinner time."

"I can rustle us up something if you like."

"Not necessary. I'd like to take you out for a simple meal. Burgers?"

"At Jack's?"

His eyes twinkled with mirth. "You are the connoisseur of the best burgers in Red Rock. Jack's it is."

They moved into his room and redressed although his eyes never left her body. Her gaze seemed to drift to his maleness almost as much. The hard muscles and delicious plains of his sculpted body called to her to touch, to explore with her mouth. Her palms itched to stroke him, feel the hair-roughened skin.

"Stop looking at me like that or we won't be going anywhere."

"I can't help it. I want to feel you under my hands."

"I'll let you explore later. Deal?"

"Oh yeah. I can do whatever I want?"

"Maybe. It would be difficult for me to give up total control, but I may allow you to explore my body at will. Actually, it sounds fun."

She allowed a small smile to drift over her lips and one of his eyebrows arched over his eye as an answering grin lifted the corners of his mouth.

She moved to stand in front of him, lifting her hands to smooth over his chest until he grabbed them in his palms. "Not now or we'll never get food."

"Spoiled sport." This earned her a swat on the butt. "Ouch!"

"Behave yourself, sub. Backtalk will not be tolerated although I think you would enjoy me reddening your ass."

She gave him a saucy wink. "Maybe."

Once they were both dressed, he took her hand in his and headed back toward the living room. "I really should go home to change. I didn't bring clean clothes."

"I'll run you home. You can meet me back here in about an hour?"

"That would be great. I could shower, slip into something sexy and come back."

He wrapped his arms around her and pulled her to his chest. "You're sexy in anything or nothing at all."

"Sweet talker." She kissed him quickly.

"Let's get going before I change my mind and keep you here tied to my bed."

After she slipped on her shoes, they walked outside. He held open the door to his truck so she could slide inside. *Such a gentleman.*

Silence enveloped them in a warm cocoon of intimacy as they drove out to her dad's place. Marcus took her hand and held it in his on the drive out there. Something so small but very significant to her. *I hope he's not getting too wrapped up in this relationship. I don't want to hurt him.* "Marcus, don't forget I'm leaving in less than a month."

"I know, Elizabeth," he said, squeezing her hand. "I'll keep my heart intact. I promise. You are a very tempting woman though."

She sighed and pressed her lips together. *I can do this. I can keep this simple and non-assuming. I can keep my own heart from becoming emotionally involved with him. It would be a rebound relationship anyway.*

I was in love with Ari. Her heart vehemently objected to her internal observation. She knew the feelings she thought she had for Ari didn't compare to the budding feelings stirring for the man beside her. Nothing had prepared her for what he stirred.

They pulled into the driveway of her childhood home. She squinted as the setting sun painted the white house with an orange glow. White lace curtains blew in the breeze through the windows and cattle shuffled around the pen on the side of the house. Obviously, her father had decided keeping them closer would be better until they found out what had killed the group.

"Hi Dad," she said, stepping out of Marcus' truck to find her father with his foot braced on the fence.

"Hi, baby. Are you just getting home?" he asked, his perceptive gaze stopping on Marcus.

"Actually, I'm only home to shower and change. I'm going out for burgers with Marcus."

"Again? You've been gone since yesterday."

"Dad, I'm spending time with him. Didn't you want us together?"

"Well yes, but you said you didn't want a steady guy."

"We're okay. We both know how this is working. Don't worry."

"I don't want to see either of you get hurt, Elizabeth. That's all."

"We aren't. Right, Marcus?" she asked as he slid his arm around her waist.

"True, Mitchell. I hope you don't mind me seeing Elizabeth."

"Not at all. I think you two are good together. Just be careful, eh?"

"Of course." She turned to Marcus and brushed her lips against his. "I'll meet you back at your place in an hour."

"Sure. See you there."

She glanced behind her as she stepped onto the porch, noticing her father's glance and Marcus' gaze. Her father's words echoed in her head. Was she getting in too deep? Would she lose her heart to Marcus before the month concluded or would she be able to walk away unscathed? Somehow, she didn't think so.

About fifteen minutes later, her father tapped on her door. When she opened it, she didn't like the new lines on his face or the worry in his eyes.

"What's wrong?"

"I got the test results back on the water."

"And?"

"It's been poisoned."

"By what?"

"Nitrate. There were toxic levels found."

"What the hell could have contaminated the water with nitrate? The pool looked fine. No decaying animals or plants in it."

"I'm not sure. I don't know whether it's a combination of high levels in the water or possibly the extra feed they've been getting to fatten them up before we take them to auction."

"It's crazy, Dad. Are you sure?"

"Yes. I intended to talk to Marcus about the situation, but he seemed in a hurry to get back to his place. I really need to ask him what other sources of contamination could have occurred and if he saw anything up there when he inoculated the herd. They are specific symptoms of nitrate poisoning he might have observed."

"When I asked him about it, he said he didn't see anything."

"You two have talked about our situation?"

"We did do other things besides have sex, Dad."

"Too much information, Elizabeth."

She laughed and kissed his cheek. "Well, you asked. I'm sure you had to be aware we've been sleeping together."

"I doubt sleep had anything to do with it," he said, brushing her hair off her forehead. "Please be careful, sweetheart."

"I am. We aren't getting serious or anything. Hell, I barely know the man."

"Yet, you're having sex with him?"

"Who is Elizabeth having sex with?" her sister Caroline asked, stepping out of her room down the hall.

"None of your business, sister dear. Are you just now getting up? It's almost dinner time."

"I was out all night working at the bar."

"Working or playing?"

"Including the Lawson twins? Playing a little and working a lot."

"I'm going to work in my office. I really don't need to hear about my daughters' exploits."

"We're adults, Dad."

"Yes, but you'll still be my little girls even if you are over eighteen," he replied, kissing Elizabeth first, and then Caroline before he disappeared back down the hall.

"So, the Lawson twins, eh?"

"Yep. If one is good, two is better."

"I wouldn't know, but I'm sure Emma could tell you."

"She has. Why do you think I'm doing the twin thing? Sounded intriguing to me."

Elizabeth grabbed Caroline's hand and pulled her into the bedroom. "Tell me."

"What?' Sweet, innocent Elizabeth wants to know the down and dirty with two guys?"

"Yes, damn it. Not that I would try it myself. One is enough for me if it's the right guy, but two..."

"It's hot, let me tell you."

"Really? How does it work? I mean they go at separate times, right?"

"Nope. Been with one and with both together."

She pulled Caroline down on the side of the bed. "What's two men like?"

"Intense. To have two men focused on my needs is incredibly hot."

"Care to give me deats?"

"No. Just know where there are two, it's double the pleasure." Caroline stood and headed for the door.

"You're rotten, you know."

She grinned as she waggled her eyebrows. "I know, but it sounds like you're hot and heavy with the incredibly handsome Doctor Melton."

"Yeah." The heat from a blush crept up Elizabeth's cheeks. Although she wasn't ashamed of being with Marcus, just a little self-conscious of how he had half the women in town wrapped around his little finger, yet he wanted her.

"I hope you don't get in over your head though, sis. He doesn't seem like the settling down type."

"Neither am I."

"You thought you were marrying Ari and didn't have a problem with it."

"I do now. I want my life on my terms. I want to get my practice going, and then worry about settling down with one man. Marcus is just a diversion until I go to Billings."

"Yeah, but Billings is only a two hour drive. It's not like it's half-way across the country." Caroline returned to the bedside and kissed her cheek. "Think about it. If he hints he wants more than a month-long fling, I say go for it."

9

"You seem distracted. Did something happen at your father's?" Marcus asked as they sat down at the picnic table outside of Jack's Burgers.

"Not really although Dad said he got the water sample report back and he wanted to talk to you about it."

"What did they find?"

"Toxic levels of nitrates."

"Damn. Seeing any animal suffer kills me, but nitrate poisoning is horrid."

"You've seen that type of death before?"

"Yeah, a time or two. The animal basically suffocates."

"Shit." She chewed her bottom lip for a second, then popped a French fry into her mouth. "How do you think high levels of Nitrate might have gotten into the pool?"

"Decomposing animal, fecal matter…there are a number of ways," he replied, taking a bite of his hamburger. "Does your dad suspect foul play?"

"Why would he? He doesn't have any enemies that I'm aware of."

"It seems odd to have high levels of nitrates in the water supply without contamination of some sort. You said you didn't see anything right?"

"No. The pool looked clear."

"I'm sure they tested for fecal matter to rule it out as the source. *Hmm*…this really seems strange to me." He wiped his mouth with a napkin before he stuck a fry in his mouth. "You aren't hungry?"

"Not for food."

"Naughty girl." He reached over and took her hand in his, which garnered a few raised eyebrows from the surrounding patrons. Their mouths drops opened when he brought her fingers to his mouth to suck one between his lips.

"Marcus." The word came out in a breathless pant. "People are staring."

"I don't care," he said after he nipped at the tip. "I like being with you. If this town is too uptight to see me with you, then it's their problem."

"I don't think they are uptight, Marcus. After all they've accepted some pretty unconventional relationships from my family and the Dunns in the last few years."

He returned her hand to the tabletop but didn't release it. "Like?"

"My sister is living with and enjoying a triad with two men in Nashville. Their bond started here though. No one really got upset about it. Delaney Dunn is in a triad relationship with two men who are also together from what I understand. She's married legally to one but the three are together."

"What would they think if they knew I spank your ass until it's bright red under my hand or they saw the bench I fucked you on last night? In the ass, no less," he asked, his voice dropping to a whisper of conspiracy.

"You might ruin your reputation or you might be the most sought after single man in Red Rock."

"I only want you so it doesn't matter what my reputation is as a single man in this town."

"Marcus, I..."

A smile creased his lips as he tried to lighten the mood. "Don't get hung up on what's going on between us, Elizabeth. I'm okay with a temporary relationship. It's fine. Really."

"Are you sure?" *What the hell am I saying? I'm not even sure I'm okay with it.*

"Yes, I'm sure. You'll go off to Billings at the end of the month. I'll be left right here. We can see each other occasionally if we so desire to and continue to see other people if we want. Right?"

She dropped her gaze to the tabletop and shrugged. Somehow when he sounded so nonchalant about the whole thing, she didn't care for the idea. Him seeing another woman or many women didn't sit well with her. Sharing him seemed wrong all of the sudden. "Sure. Sounds good to me."

With one finger under her chin, he forced her gaze up to his. "Why don't I believe you?"

"I'm okay with it. I mean getting attached to you right now would be totally stupid." She pulled her face from his fingers and sipped her soda for something to keep her occupied. Hopefully he wouldn't see the lie in her eyes.

"Would it?"

"Yes. We've only known each other a short time. I really don't know very much about you and even though we've been together in the biblical sense of the word, the whole thing is just two people having fun."

"We've discussed seeing each other after you leave."

"Not really discussed. You've mentioned the possibility."

"Billings isn't so far away to be unreasonable."

"No, it's not. Are you sure you want to continue this?"

"I do. Do you?"

"Let's see how things go while I'm here and we'll go from there."

Silence stretched between them for several moments before he changed the subject. "The Fourth of July picnic is coming up. Will you go with me?" he asked, finishing off his food.

"I'd love to, but I'll have to come back to town for the celebration. I hope I have the day off. I'll pack the lunch if you bring the blanket."

"Sounds good to me. What about until then? The fourth is still a couple of weeks away."

"We can still see each other unless you'd rather cool things off."

"I'd rather heat them up if you know what I mean." He brought her hand to his mouth to kiss her palm. "I like you hot and wet."

"You don't have to do much to get me there."

"No?" he asked, his eyes turning a sapphire blue.

"Not at all."

"Are you there now?"

"Hell yes." Her blood rushed in her ears as desire pooled in her belly. She wanted this man with everything inside of her. How he'd tied her up into knots, she wasn't sure, but she didn't care either.

"Shall we go back to my place?"

"Please."

"Oh, I love how you beg, Elizabeth. So pretty. I love to see you on your hands and knees sucking my cock," he whispered, tonguing her palm, sending shivers down her arms. "Look. Goose bumps. Are you excited?"

"More than excited. My blood in thrumming for you."

"Good. Let's go then. I have a need to feel your lips wrapped around me again."

They tossed their wrappers and remaining food into the trash receptacle before they rushed to his truck like two giddy school kids, laughing at their antics as she glanced over at the others eating with their shocked expressions. She continued to giggle when they pulled out of the drive-in.

"What's so funny?"

"The faces of some of the others at the burger place just cracked me up. Nothing huge. They need to lighten up a little."

They drove off down Main Street, past the diner, Jake's Harley Store and Delaney's Gas Station as they headed out of town. Several moments later, they pulled up in front of his house and he jumped out to come around to her side of the truck. She squealed as he scooped her up in his arms before he walked up to the door.

"Where are your keys?"

"In my pocket. Care to retrieve them for me?"

"Sounds like fun, but you'll have to put me down."

"Reach between us. They're in the front right pocket. You should be able to reach them."

"Is that what's poking me in the butt?"

"No. My cock is searching for its home."

"Ah, well then. We'll have to make sure he finds it now won't we."

"Oh hell yes." She reached between their bodies only to hear Marcus hiss when she grazed his cock with her hand.

"To the right, Elizabeth."

"Sorry." She giggled.

"No you aren't. You'll be getting ten swats for your little wandering hands."

"Only ten?"

"Shall we make it fifteen? I could always get out the crop I have. You might not find the swats so pleasurable."

"Let's not."

"All right, fifteen with my hand. We'll see how red I can make your ass," he said in a tortured whisper as she finally retrieved his keys and opened the door.

The moment he set her on her feet, she dropped to her knees, glancing up through her lashes. "Shall I suck you now?"

"I'll do the directing. You may not speak."

She dropped her gaze to the floor. Would she ever figure this stuff out? She wanted to be a good sub for him, but the mechanics of when and how to do things kept evading her. Hopefully, Marcus would instruct her or give her some kind of reference material. *Maybe I should ask him?*

He put his finger under her chin to bring her gaze up to his. "In this type of relationship, Elizabeth, you do not have to worry about if you'll please me. You already do. I will tell you everything you need to do and say. You do not have to guess at what I want. If I don't tell you to do something, then don't do it. Is that understood? Say yes sir or no sir."

"Yes, Sir." The relief she felt at his words lightened her mood. She'd always worried with other lovers if she should pump her hips with him, suck his cock or not. Lick it or suck it. Caress his balls or don't touch them. Did he want her on top or not?

"You will not have to worry about anything. I'll do what I want with your body. You'll have no choice but to allow me to. While we are playing, you'll not speak unless I ask you a direct question." He released her face. "You may unzip my jeans and lower them to free my cock."

With his direction clear, she lowered the zipper and pulled the jeans down around his knees. He wore no underwear. The musky scent of his cock called to her. She moved to take him into her mouth.

"Did I say suck my cock?"

"No, Sir." *Damn!*

"Grasp my cock in your hand, but don't do anything else."

When she did what he told her, she earned herself a groan and the tightening of his fingers in her hair.

"Cup my balls with your other hand. Roll them in your palm."

She massaged the egg-shaped sac she now held.

"Yes. Perfect."

She continued to lick and swirl her tongue around his shaft.

"Take just the head into your mouth. I want to feel you suck it." The moment she surrounded the head of his cock with her mouth, the slightly salty taste of his pre-cum exploded on her tongue. "Swirl your tongue in the slit. Oh, fuck yes."

The dirty words coming from his mouth almost made her giggle. He was so different when they played than his steadfast persona of country veterinarian.

A low whine escaped his mouth and she knew she pleased him as his hips pumped toward her face.

"Take all of me into your mouth. I want to feel the back of your throat."

Breathing through her nose, she inhaled and took the length of him. She gagged slightly, but worked through it by tipping her head back to open her jaws for his penetration. Would she ever get over that? She wasn't sure, but for Marcus she was willing to try.

"Okay, stop now. I don't want to come in your mouth," he said, lifting her by her arms. "On the bed on your stomach."

Now what the hell was he planning?

"I'll do what I want, Elizabeth. Remember that." She lie spread out on the bed with her legs and butt over the side. "You'll now get your swats."

He reached around, unbuttoned her jeans, yanking them along with her underwear down to mid-thigh. The burn of his palm on her ass cheek startled her and she yelped.

"You'll count for me."

"One, Sir." The count continued until tears burned her cheeks. She sobbed openly.

"I don't like punishing you, Elizabeth. There is a difference between erotic spanking and punishment. This was the later. Sometime we'll try the other." He grabbed some balm and spread it over her flaming cheeks.

She didn't think she liked being spanked anymore and she sure didn't want to find out the difference when her ass stung like a thousand bees had attacked her.

"Up we go," he said lifting her and placing her onto his bare thighs. She squeaked as her tender butt hit his legs.

The gentle feel of his fingers brushing the tears off her cheeks tugged at her heart. She didn't want to care about this man, but he'd torn down the walls around her heart like a construction worker with a jackhammer. Now her insides lay bare and open for him to do with as he wished.

* * * *

Did she know how a tear-stained face could pull at the heart of a Dom? Was she manipulating him like the other women he known? He didn't think so. Elizabeth had an open and honest face. She had the need to please that went deep into the soul of a natural submissive even if she also had the personality of a highly intelligent and decisive woman who knew her mind.

"All better now."

"May I speak, Sir?"

"You have a question, Elizabeth?"

"Yes, Sir. Even though I didn't like the punishment of the hard spanking, I don't see how something so painful can be erotic?"

"Remember the flogger?"

"Yes, Sir."

"It stung when I used it on you, but after awhile, the pain turned into a pleasure so strong you couldn't help but float with the feelings. An erotic spanking does very much the same thing."

"I don't think I want to find out."

"You don't have a choice in the matter, sweetheart, but we won't be trying it tonight. Your bottom will be very sore for a day or two." He lifted her off his legs and lay down spread out on the coverlet. "Ride me, Elizabeth. I want your pussy wrapped around me."

She crawled up to straddle his hips and lowered her pussy down onto his shaft. The length of him slid into her quivering depths in a slow glide. *God, It feels good.*

"Fuck me like you love me." *Where the hell did that come from?*

"I do Marcus. God, help me I do."

Oh, hell. This isn't good. She's not supposed to fall in love with me. "Elizabeth?"

"Forget I said that. I didn't mean it the way it sounded. I love being with you. Nothing more."

"All right."

After a moment, she rocked her hips, rubbing her clit across his pelvic bone. He reached down between them to thumb the hardening little nub, earning a low moan from her lips. Her hands did a little danced over his nipples, pulling a groan from his lips. "I love when you play with my nipples. They are sensitive like yours. You can suck them." She leaned down and ran her tongue over his left one. His cock pulsed inside her. "Bite them." Her teeth nipped at one and then the other. "God, you're so sexy."

When she sat back up, he palmed her breasts and pulled down so he could suck on hers. He loved her breasts. A good handful was the best size for him. She continued to ride him in shallow strokes as he sucked first one, then the other. He released her breasts to grasp her butt cheeks in his hands, earning a squeak when he lightly smacked her sore butt.

"Mmm."

"Like some pain with your pleasure, do you?"

"Yes, Sir."

"Good. Lean back and brace your hands on my thighs."

With her hands back, her whole pussy and clit were open to his touch. A sharp slap of his fingers against her engorged clit would bring her the pain he felt she craved even if she wasn't aware of it. Two quick whacks ramped her up to a quivering mass of energy surrounding his aching cock. Her pussy fluttered around him, squeezing to almost painful proportions.

"Your pussy is grasping me so hard, it feels like you're going to snap me in two."

"I'm sorry, Sir."

"Don't be. I love it. Clamp down on me again."

He groaned when she squeezed her muscles around him so tight he thought the top would blow off his cock. With his feet under him, he met her downward thrusts, bringing her to the brink, her body was coated with a fine sheen of sweat as she tried desperately to hold back her orgasm. He reached for her clit, rubbing one side like he realized she liked it best. "Come for me, Elizabeth." Her hair brushed his thighs when she threw back her head to scream out with her orgasm. Her pussy milked him to the point his own orgasm washed over him like the backward flow of water during a tsunami without any regard to the destruction the water would cause. The drowning sensation clouded his mind and heart while he tried to keep her from becoming such a part of him, he couldn't function without her near. Falling in love wouldn't do. He couldn't get involved with her on the level of love. It just wouldn't work. Seeing each other for a weekend romp was one thing. But relationships where two people didn't see each other for long periods of time were doomed. He knew this from experience.

10

"I have to go home, Marcus. Dad has work for me to do at the ranch," Elizabeth said, stroking the hair on his chest between her fingers.

"You can stay until tomorrow can't you?"

"No. I really can't. I'm sure Dad is already planning a wedding between us with how much time we've spent together the last couple of days."

"Well, we can't have that now, can we?" They both laughed but it sounded hollow even to him.

She sighed and sat up to pull on her clothes. "We can get together again before I leave, right?"

"Sure. I think my schedule will be free although I can't say for sure. Sick animals are sick animals."

"I know. Your practice comes first. I hope Dad can figure out what's killing his cattle soon. He can't afford to lose anymore."

"He really should send a tissue sample from one of them to a lab if he can. Something doesn't smell right with this whole thing."

"How about coming out to the house for dinner one night?"

"I would love to."

"Good. What about tomorrow evening?"

"You've got a date, darlin'."

She shivered and he smiled. "I love when you call me that. It's such a cowboy thing. Did I ever tell you I'm not into cowboys?"

He laughed and pulled her back down next to him. "No. Why don't you tell me why you don't like us cowpokes."

"It's not you. You aren't a hardcore cowboy, but I've usually been attracted to men in business suits."

"Ah. This is why the tuxedo thing turned you on."

"Well, yes and no. I'm attracted to the man in the tuxedo, which you'll need to put on sometime so I can take it off you." She leaned in to kiss him.

So, my little minx is forceful at times too.

"I've realized the men in business suits are a cover for what I really want."

"Oh?"

"Yes, a man who takes control but still allows me to be me."

"Ah."

"You're that man, Marcus."

"Don't get tied up with me, Elizabeth. What you're feeling is gratefulness to a Dom who introduced you what the lifestyle means to a submissive. Nothing more."

"No, it's more. I want you in my life, but we can't really have this conversation now. I need to get moving."

"Think about this before you say something or do something you'll regret later. What if you meet someone in Billings?"

"I know what I want. I want you." She jumped to her feet to finish dressing. "I'm not talking about love, Marcus, just getting to know you better when we can get together," she said, snapping her blouse while he watched from the bed. "We can see where things go from here. I'm tired of waiting for what I need. You give me what I desire. I think there could be something more between us, but I don't want to push you. If you don't feel the same, say so now."

"I like you a lot, Elizabeth. You're beautiful, smart, funny, sexy-as-hell and you do for me what many women haven't been able to. You let me be me. You're open to what I can teach you in your sexuality. I think it's gorgeous. We can continue to explore this D/s relatoinship until we're both satisfied, but I don't want you to think there will be anything beyond that."

She looked up and smiled, her eyes twinkling in the light of the room. "Good. We're on the same page then. If I don't see you before, I'll see you at Dad's tomorrow evening for dinner."

"You bet!" Her eyes wandered over his body as he stood from the side of the bed.

"Such temptation."

"For you, but you must go, remember?"

"I know, but I want to touch."

"No touching. Off you go," he said swatting her on the jean-clad butt.

"Spoiled-sport."

"You've earned ten swats for your smart remark, young lady."

"Damn it!"

"Shall I make it fifteen?"

"No, Sir. My lips are sealed, Sir."

She snapped off a smart salute and disappeared quickly around the corner of his room before he could swat her behind again. Her mouth would get her into trouble, but he wasn't quite sure if she was looking for ways to get spanked.

* * * *

Hot, tired and thirsty, Elizabeth dismounted from her horse with a groan. She hadn't sat on a horse for hours on end in years. Her poor thighs were screaming at her for the tortured they'd endured today. *Poor Marcus. I won't be able to spread my legs for him.* She giggled at the thought.

"What are you laughing about?" her father asked with a grin. "You look like you're walking bowlegged and you're laughing about it?"

"I think it's funny, Dad. I'm so sore I can hardly walk."

They shared their laughter as he helped her walk to the porch and slide into the rocker. "I'll get the horses put away. You rest cowgirl."

"Thanks, Dad."

Marcus' truck rumbled up the driveway right on time and she rolled her eyes. She hadn't even had a chance to shower yet. The smell of sweat, horses and dirt permeated every part of her body. Lord, would she be attractive to him right now.

"Hey, darlin'," he said, leaning over to give her a kiss. "Been out all day?"

"Yes, and I hate to burst your bubble, but there won't be any sex tonight. I can't spread my legs."

"Oh, poor baby. How about if I rub some great liniment I have at my place into those sore muscles?"

He rubbed his palm on her thigh and she groaned in pain. "I don't think I can move from this chair to even shower. I smell awful."

"You smell like hard work, woman. There's nothing wrong with that. Besides, I happen to think sweat, animals and dirt is sexy."

She laughed. "You would."

"I can help you shower," he said, waggling his eyebrows.

"I'm sure you'd love to do it too."

"You bet!"

"Hey Marcus. I didn't realize you were coming over," her father said, stepping up onto the porch.

"Elizabeth didn't tell you she invited me to dinner?"

"Oops."

"No problem. We can set another plate."

The spray of gravel announced the arrival of Cade and Natalie.

"We've got a houseful tonight."

"Are you sure it's not problem?" Marcus asked.

"Not at all. We always have tons of leftovers anyway," she replied, waving to Natalie coming up the stairs behind him.

"Marcus. It's nice to see you. We've missed you coming over for dinner," Natalie said, giving him a hug.

"Elizabeth has been keeping me busy when I'm not at the office."

"Has she now? Interesting."

"Shut up, Nat," Elizabeth snapped. "Don't butt in."

"I'm not! Geez."

"Heya brother. How are things with you? I haven't seen you since I've been home and it's almost time for me to leave."

"You've been busy, sister-dear and you haven't been over for dinner either."

"Yeah, well I've been working the cattle with Dad and entertaining Marcus."

"So I hear." Cade's gaze shifted between her and Marcus before stopping on their father. "So what's this I hear there were toxic levels of nitrates in the water sample?"

"Yes. I wish I knew how they got there."

"I asked Elizabeth if you had any enemies who might want to poison your herd, but she said no," Marcus said. "Can you think of anyone?"

"Not me," Mitchell replied.

"What if they were out to hurt someone close to you through you?"

"I'm not sure I know what are you getting at, Natalie."

"What if they weren't after you at all, Dad, but someone close to you like Cade, Elizabeth, Caroline or one of the other girls?"

"If they were after Cade, wouldn't they just hurt you at your house?" Elizabeth asked.

"Probably so we can rule out Cade. You made an enemy in Ari, Elizabeth, when you made a fool of him at the airport, true?"

"Possibly, but I don't think he would go to these lengths to get back at me. Besides, he's not around here. Trust me, he would stick out like a sore thumb."

"Maybe he's using someone on the ranch?"

"This is all pretty farfetched, don't you think?" Marcus said, adding his opinion.

"Without someone physically poisoning the water supply, I can't see how the nitrates would get in there."

"I'll have to think about this. Surely there is another explanation," Mitchell said, moving toward the door as they heard the housekeeper say dinner was ready.

Dinner turned into a laughing, telling stories affair for all. She and Cade tried out doing each other with tales of their childhood, telling stories of things they got into trouble for. Marcus and Natalie smiled through the teasing.

"But remember the night you snuck out the window after the parental unit had fallen asleep to go to Jenny Bain's party?" Elizabeth asked.

"You weren't supposed to tell."

"Come on, Cade. How old are you now? I don't think Dad is going to punish you now for it although Natalie might."

"I might at that. Jenny Bain still tries to come onto him every chance she gets when we go to town. She doesn't care if I'm standing right there either."

"Jealous, baby?" Cade asked, wrapping his arm around his wife.

"Nope. I've got your ring on my finger and your babies in our home. I've got you by the balls mister. Funny thing is? You don't want to get away."

Cade burst out laughing. "No way. I love you, wife."

"I love you too Cade. My big, handsome husband."

"Oh my God! Mushy, mushy." Elizabeth giggled, sitting back in her chair.

"Oh like you're one to talk there little sister. I saw you two at Jack's the other day. You didn't even notice me. All the finger licking going on."

"What?" Embarrassment flushed her cheeks red with heat.

"I like the way her fingers taste," Marcus said, pulling her hand closer and taking one of her fingers in his mouth.

A low hiss escaped her lips as she clenched her thighs together only to be reminded of her all day trip on horseback when her legs screamed in agony. "Oh shit."

"What?"

"My legs."

"I'll rub them and make them feel better. I did promise."

"All right you two. Knock it off," Cade said.

She groaned as she stood. "I need to run up to take a shower before I fall asleep at the table. I'll see you all in a bit."

"Sure, darlin'. Take your time." Marcus winked.

* * * *

"Are you serious about Elizabeth, Marcus?" Natalie asked the moment the bathroom door closed down the hall.

"What do you mean by serious?"

"I mean like seeing her more serious? She is leaving in a couple of weeks."

"I know this, Nat. We've discussed it, but what is between us is just that, between us."

"Spill buddy."

"Nope."

"Do you love her?"

"I can't say one way or another, Nat, but I care about her and I like the way things are going between us. Can we talk about something else, please? This isn't open for discussion."

"What is your take on the water situation, Marcus?" Mitchell questioned.

"I'm with Natalie. I think there is foul play involved here although I don't have a clue from where. The levels they found in the water suggest a large contamination."

"See?" Natalie sat back in her chair with a smug look on her face.

"Fecal matter might do this, but no one found large amounts of it in the water supply. Do you have any new hands on your place, Mitchell? Someone who might be suspicious?"

"Nope. I trust all the men on my place."

"Enough money might persuade someone to jump sides though," Natalie said.

"It's true, Dad. I could see a couple of your guys doing something like this for enough money. Not that you don't pay them well."

"I guess you're right, Cade. I could see it as well. There are a few who've been kind of jumpy lately. Jackson seems to have some extra cash these days. He drove home in a brand new larger pickup truck the other day and I don't think I pay him enough to afford one. A couple of the hands said he was flashing some cash at the bar this past weekend, too."

"Sounds suspicious to me," Cade said. "You'd better have the law talk to him."

"I don't want to jump to conclusions though. He's been a good man on this place for many years. He kind of got screwed when his wife left him a few years ago. I know their divorce hurt him financially pretty badly."

"He'd be kind of desperate for money then wouldn't he?" Marcus asked.

"Possibly. I hate to think he'd turn his back on me though after I've kept him on the place for so many years." Mitchell scratched his chin. "But, I'll talk to the sheriff tomorrow so he can question him."

The ringing of a phone caught their attention. Marcus noticed a cell phone on the floor. "It must be Elizabeth's. She must have dropped it before she went upstairs." He laid it on the table. "Should we answer?"

Natalie grabbed the phone and flipped open the lid. "Hello?" Her eyes widened. "No. This is her sister-in-law. She's in the shower. Can I take a message?" Her face turned beat red. "I'll tell her." She snapped the phone shut and growled, "That was her ex-asshole boyfriend."

"Ari?" Cade asked. "The bastard has the gall to call her?"

"Apparently. He wanted me to tell her to call him so he could apologize and beg for her forgiveness. There is no way in hell I'll tell her he even called."

"You can't keep this from her, Natalie. It's not fair. She has to make her own decisions on who she wants to be with. If she chooses him, we must abide by her decision."

"You can't be serious, Marcus? She doesn't want him, she wants you."

"I hope this is true, but it's up to her."

"What's up to her?" Elizabeth asked, walking back into the room, her hair mussed and wet. She slid onto his lap as she looped her arms around his neck. Her warm body heated his blood to boiling the moment her warm thigh touched his.

"Your phone rang. You must have dropped it before you went upstairs."

"Oh. Who called?"

He looked at Natalie, Cade and then her father. "Your ex-boyfriend."

"Ari?"

"Yes, darlin'."

"Who talked to him?"

"Nat."

"What did he say he wanted?"

"He wanted you to call him so he could apologize for his behavior apparently."

"Seriously?" she asked, sliding off his lap and back into the chair she'd occupied earlier. "Wow."

He didn't like the look on her face. Not one bit.

"You aren't considering calling him are you, Elizabeth?" Natalie asked, her eyes wide with shock.

"Well..."

"No you can't possibly! The man is an asshole. He cheated on you. You never loved him. He just used you for a plaything while he fucked around with anything with female parts. Come on, Elizabeth!"

"Enough Nat. It's her life," Cade answered. "She can be with whomever she thinks is the right person for her, although I happen to agree with you on the asshole part."

"Don't you think everyone deserves the benefit of the doubt?"

"You saw him kissing the woman coming down the escalator, right?"

"Yes."

"I don't think there is a benefit of the doubt then."

"True." She turned to him. "What do you think I should do, Marcus?"

"For me to answer that would be selfish on my part. I know what I want you to do and say, but I can't make the decision for you, Elizabeth. You have to decide on your own." He climbed to his feet. "I'm going to head for home now. You don't need me around to complicate matters."

"Don't leave, Marcus. She needs you here," Natalie said.

"No, she doesn't. She must make up her own mind." He leaned down, kissing her cheek. "Remember how it felt to be in my arms and then remember how you felt in his. Your choice," he whispered in her ear. "Thank you for dinner, Mitchell. Cade. Nat. I'll see you two around. Maybe for dinner on Sunday if I'm still invited."

"Of course," Cade replied, standing as well. "I'll walk you out. I'd like to ask you something."

"Sure." He looked down at Elizabeth, noting the tears glistening in her eyes. "Call me when you've decided."

When he turned to glance at Elizabeth before he walked out, he almost laughed at the shocked look in her eyes. She apparently thought he would go all Dom on her and tell her she must be with him. Well, she didn't know him very well then because having a sub who didn't want to be with you could be much worse than being in a relationship with a woman who hated you. He'd done both.

"I think you did the right thing in there, Marcus."

"Thanks, Cade. I can't make her decision for her. She either wants to be with me or she doesn't."

"She's confused."

"I'm sure. She thought she loved this other man. But what choice does she have? She's facing a relationship with him knowing he cheated on her or a non-existent relationship with me."

Cade put his hand on Marcus' shoulder. "Yours isn't non-existent, Marcus. I saw the way you two were together."

"We haven't known each other long enough to establish a relationship. We've spent some time together, yes, but that doesn't make a relationship."

"Don't let her think too long before you make another move. I'm afraid she'll decide to give asshole another chance."

"If she does, it's her choice, although I hope she doesn't. I care for her a great deal."

"Have you told her that?"

"No. It has no place in what's currently between us. She and I established we might pursue something after she leaves on a long distance type basis. We haven't discussed anything beyond those terms though."

"Going back to him would cause the same issues. She's already committed to doing her residency in Billings."

"I know. It's closer to Red Rock than Los Angeles."

"True. I believe what you two have is genuine. What she had with him was based on lies and misconceptions. She wanted to be in love. The major flaw in her plan was he wasn't in love with her. I believe the man cheated on her several times. She just didn't catch him until the last time at the airport."

"I hope she remembers how she felt to see him in a compromising situation. It would help her decide."

"You would be good for her, Marcus. I'm sure of it."

"I'm counting on her coming to the same conclusion, Cade."

11

Elizabeth watched in surprise as Marcus glanced back before he walked out the door. Did he care at all? It didn't appear to her like he did. "What the hell?"

"You can't expect him to decide for you. And let me tell you one thing sister dear, if you even seriously consider calling that asshole, I'll personally kick your butt."

"I will, too, Elizabeth. I can't believe your behavior with this," her father chimed in.

"I'm just shocked he called. I don't want anything to do with him. The man cheated on me God only knows how many times. I wanted to see what Marcus would do. He doesn't seem to want to commit to anything between us."

"Maybe he's testing you to see how you'll react to this and him."

"Maybe. I don't like this at all."

Moments later, Cade came back into the house and plopped down into his chair.

"So what happened out there?" she asked, not liking the concern on Cade's face.

"Are you really going to call Armand back?"

"No."

"Good. Then Marcus did the right thing by letting you chose. Be careful. He cares about you, but he's not going to let you run roughshod over him."

"I don't want to. Things are very different between me and Marcus."

"How so?"

"I can't talk about it. It's private. Let's say he does something for me no man has done before."

"Then what was all the discussion like you were seriously contemplating getting back together with Armand?"

"I wanted to see if Marcus would react."

"Not a good game to by playing, Elizabeth. Not with a man like Marcus. What if he doesn't want to play your games? You might have just cost yourself the love of your life."

"Don't say things like that, Cade. Marcus understands me or at least I hope he does."

"I don't think he understands this. The gut punched look on his face when you slid off his lap hurt my heart to see," Natalie said. "He cares about you."

"I care about him too, but I can't get tied up with a man right now, Nat. I'm leaving in a week or so. I really should probably cool things off with Marcus anyway."

"Whatever! I'm about tired of you playing your games. If you hurt him, I'll never speak to you again, Elizabeth. He's a nice guy," Natalie snapped, jumping to her feet.

"Nat, calm down."

"I will not. I didn't think she played games but apparently she learned well from her ex-boyfriend because now she's pulling the same kind of shit."

"I did not cheat on anyone!"

"You're playing head games, Liz." Natalie began to pace the kitchen floor. "If you hadn't made it sound like you planned to call the asshole back, Marcus wouldn't have left. You'd better fix this."

"I will. I'll call him right now."

"Call him hell. You'd better go over there and apologize. He's hurt for Christ's sake."

"Fine!" Elizabeth slapped her hand on the table. "I'll go over there. You are such a hardass, Nat. I don't believe you," she said, throwing up her arms.

"I don't like seeing my friends hurt. You upset him with all of this. Was it really necessary?" Natalie asked, taking her seat again next to Cade.

"I guess not, but maybe I wanted him to declare himself. If he really wants something with me, he needs to let me know instead of playing so nonchalant." Elizabeth's hands flew back and forth as she talked. She'd always been an animated talker.

"Have you told him you're in love with him?"

"I'm not in lo—"

Natalie interrupted with a sharp, "Bullshit. It's written all over your face."

"I haven't known him long enough to be in love with him."

"Then you care deeply. Whatever you have going on between you is something special. You're a damned fool if you walk away from it."

She threw up her hands. "All right, yes, I care deeply. I shouldn't because I hardly know him. This is ridiculous, you know. The feelings I had for Ari didn't even come close to what Marcus already makes me feel."

"You weren't in love with Ari."

"I thought I was, but apparently I wasn't in love with him. Maybe I was more in love with what he could give me. Could I have been that shallow?"

"He's shallow. Why do you think he kept sleeping with his investors, their daughters, wives and anyone with big boobs?"

"True. I'm not huge," she said, plumping up both breasts in her hands as they all laughed, breaking the tension in the room.

"You're a beautiful woman, Elizabeth. I don't see why Ari couldn't see that."

"You're only saying so because you're my brother."

"Not so. I know several men in this town who enjoyed your company."

"Before I went to Los Angeles? I was eighteen, Cade."

"And beautiful even then."

"Oh, psh." Her face heated. "I didn't have all the football players chasing me like you had the cheerleaders, Cade."

"Um...cheerleaders? As in plural?" Natalie folded her arms across her chest, glaring at her husband.

"He had all of them hot after him, but you snagged him the minute you came back to town."

"I didn't stand a chance when she crawled out of her wrecked car and flashed those eyes at me."

"Such a cute love story," Elizabeth said. "Now, I'm off to apologize to Marcus. Should I dress sexy?"

"I don't think he'll care." Natalie crawled into her husband's lap and wrapped her arms around his shoulders. "Shall we go home, husband?"

"Only if you..." He whispered in her ear as Elizabeth watched her smile get bigger.

The love the two of them had for each other was something Elizabeth strived for. She wanted that type of give and take relationship, each partner being the other half of a whole. *Can I have something like that with Marcus? He seems to only want playtime, not anything permanent. Do I? I'm leaving in a short time and we might not see each other much. Maybe we can work something out.*

"I'll see you two later."

"Probably not. We're headed home."

"Okay. Lunch in a couple of days, Nat? You can buy for chewing me out."

"Lunch is good, but you're buying for me having to chew you out."

Elizabeth laughed. "Okay, fine. I'll buy." She glanced at Cade. "You've got a wife who should have been a Wall Street executive or a lawyer. She's vicious."

"Only to protect those she loves. Remember that."

Elizabeth kissed them both on the cheek before she headed upstairs. Her recent shower took care of the stink from the animals, sweat and riding, but she wanted to put on some sexy underwear for Marcus. Groveling wasn't something she really wanted to do. She did realize now though she shouldn't have made it sound like she really wanted to get back with Ari. If he would have done something similar, she would have been hurt too. "Crushed probably, which doesn't bode well for my heart." She stopped and tapped her fingers to her lips. *Am I in love with Marcus? I thought I knew what love was with Ari. This is totally different. He makes me want to be near him all the time and especially when we aren't together.*

I think about him constantly. I can't wait to be in his arms. I want to please him all the time. "Sounds like love to me, but what happens now?"

The door to her closet stood open. A short black dress hung near the end of the stack of colorful clothing lining the rail. She grabbed the hangar, pulling out the dress, turning it this way and that to examine her pick closer. Soft cotton material caressed her fingertips as she slipped her hand over the bodice. She really did love this dress. Marcus would too, she mused. The hem hung to mid-thigh on her and emphasized her mediocre bustline. The sweetheart neckline looked fabulous on her. With a simple string of pearls, she'd look like she dressed especially for him. Nude legs and strappy black sandals would complete the picture of seduction. Unknown to Marcus Melton, seduce him she would, one way or another. This would also give him an eyeful when she knelt at his feet, if she managed not to cringe from pain on the way down.

Once she slipped into the dress and shoes, she wound her hair up in a messy bun on the back of her head, slicked on some kiss-me-red lipstick and nixed any idea of underwear. She almost wore the black thong in her drawer, but she figured no panties would make it so much easier. Regardless of the ache in her thighs, a small cat-got-the-canary-grin spread across her lips. "I'm so getting laid tonight."

Twenty minutes later, she pulled into Marcus' driveway, noting no lights on in his house. *What if he isn't home? What if he got really pissed off and found someone else to play with?*

She swallowed hard as she opened the car door. With heels clicking softly on the concrete walk, she made her way up to the door, glancing at the watch on her left arm. He'd only left her dad's place an hour ago. Surely he isn't in bed. It's only nine.

A rhythmic crack caught her attention. Loud enough she could hear the noise through the front door, but muffled, giving her the impression the sound wasn't nearby. Curious, she opened the door, softly calling, "Marcus?"

The cracks continued, so she decided to shut the door and follow the sound down the long hallway toward where they'd played on his cross. She peeked around the edge of the door where he'd left it open. Marcus stood in the middle of the room with a long coiled bullwhip at his feet. Large sections of butcher paper hung on the wall in front of him. Sweat glistened off his bare back, running in streams down the taut muscles emphasized by the track lighting over his head. He pulled back his arm and let the whip fly. The tip struck a red X placed in the middle of the paper, with precise precision so accurate, she flinched.

"Come in, Elizabeth," he said, never turning around.

How the hell does he know I'm here much less it's me?

"I can smell you."

"Damn you're eerie sometimes."

Not turning around, he said, "Observation is one of the keys to being a good Dom. If I don't know what you're feeling or how you're reacting to something I'm doing, how can I know what you need?'

"I guess."

"Why have you come?"

"You don't know? I thought you knew everything?"

"You've earned yourself ten swats for your smartass comment."

"Not if you don't want me to be your sub anymore."

He turned and let his gaze wander from her eyes to the tips of her toes. "I never said I didn't want you to be my sub. The question is, do you want to continue or are you going back to your ex?"

"No, I'm not."

"Not what?"

"Going back to Ari. I'm sorry if I gave you that impression."

"No you aren't. You wanted to make me jealous. You did your job well." His appreciative gaze raked over her again. "I do believe you're dressed to impress especially since you're not wearing underwear."

"How do you know I'm not wearing panties?"

"No panty lines, darlin'."

"Oh," she replied, dropping her gaze to the floor and slid to her knees.

"Very pretty, Elizabeth."

"Thank you, Sir."

"What have you come here for?"

"To apologize, Sir."

"And?"

"I'm not sure what you mean, Sir."

"What do you want from this relationship, Elizabeth? Do you want us to be nothing more than master and sub? Play together every so often? Or do you want something more?"

She licked her lips as she closed her eyes. *It's now or never.*

"I want more...Sir."

"How much more?" he asked, stroking her hair with his hand.

She never heard him move and it startled her to realize he could be very quiet if he so chose. "I..."

"Be truthful. I don't like liars."

"I'm trying."

"What do you call me?"

"I'm trying, Sir," she snapped, unable to keep her temper from showing. "I'm confused."

"Confusion is a sign of something more than friendship."

"I don't think of you as a friend."

"No?"

"No, Sir. You're more to me than that."

"I'm glad." He lifted her chin with his fingers.

"You are?"

"Yes because you mean a great deal to me too," he whispered, bringing her to her feet. His lips came crashing down on hers in a bone-melting, panty-wetting kiss. The whip fell to the floor with a thump as he wrapped his arms around her, crushing her to his chest. Lips mashed against lips. Tongues dueled from his mouth to hers. She moaned low in her throat, pulling him to her, wanting to absorb everything about him before she had to leave. Pushing the disturbing thought from her mind, she kissed him back with everything she had.

With apparent reluctance, he pulled back and looked down into her eyes. "Strip."

"Yes, Sir," she answered enthusiastically as she stepped back and unzipped her dress, letting the fall to the floor. Standing in nothing but her bra and shoes, she wondered what he thought. Did he like her body?

Now is a hell of a time to worry about my body. He's already seen the whole shebang.

"You're beautiful, Elizabeth."

"Thank you, Sir."

"I love everything about you from the rich almost alive bounce to your hair to the tips of your painted toenails. Those fuck-me heels are a major turn-on."

She bit her lips to keep from continuing to talk, knowing he wasn't a talker when they were about to play.

"You like a little pain with your pleasure I've noticed."

Her eyes widened and she fought to shake her head no. Pain didn't please her. Or at least she didn't think so, right? The spanking was bad enough. He said he still owed her swats, but anything else he could think of like the nasty looking bullwhip he'd been using before, made her shake with apprehension.

"Easy, darlin'. I won't do anything I don't think you can handle. Tonight, you aren't ready for the bullwhip but maybe soon." She sighed in relief as he chuckled. "But I do owe you spankings. I know you enjoyed the flogger."

"Yes, Sir." The flogger wasn't something she couldn't handle. She'd actually enjoyed the soft flicks of the suede ends on her flesh.

"We can play with some toys too."

"Toys, Sir?"

"Dildo, vibrator, nipple clamps...I'd love to show you what I have. It's been a while since I've had the chance to play with someone on my own turf," he replied, walking to the cabinet in the corner to open the doors. Several rows of *toys* lined the cabinet. Everything from dick-shaped vibrators, to handcuffs, to bejeweled nipple clamps sat in every nook and cranny of the shelves.

"These will do." He grabbed a set of nipple clamps and walked toward her. She took a hesitant step back, shaking her head. "What do you say to me?"

"Yes, Sir."

"Good girl." With an arm around her waist, he dropped his head to her chest, sucking her left nipple deep into his mouth. She moaned as he sucked hard, bringing the nipple to an aching point. When he lifted his head to take in his handiwork, the aching bud cooled in the evening air of the room as he let it dry. The pincher-type contraption bit into her nipple as he tightened the device until she winced, then made the teeth clamp down just a hair tighter. After he secured the second one, he stepped back to admire his handiwork, the bastard. "Very pretty, Elizabeth."

"But..."

"Do you want to use your safe word?"

"No, Sir."

"Then be silent." He returned to the cupboard to retrieve several more implements...a vibrator, a butt plug and a smaller item that looked like a flogger, but with much shorter strings. At her curious look, he said, "A pussy whip." One more thing she noticed in his hand...a paddle about the size of an overly large ping pong paddle.

She didn't like the idea of that last item at all and released a whimper.

"Don't worry. It'll be fun."

For who?

"Across the spanking bench, Elizabeth. I owe you twenty swats."

Fuck! Twenty? She exhaled sharply and lay stomach down on the bench while he secured her limbs even though her thighs screamed in pain.

"Comfortable?"

"Yes, Sir."

"You'll count for me and thank me for the lesson when we're through." The paddle came down fairly easy on the first swat across her left butt cheek.

"One, Sir." Each subsequent swat got harder until tears rolled down her cheeks and she sobbed with each swat. "Twenty, Sir. Thank you for the lesson, you bastard," the last two words were said under her breath.

"I heard you. Do we need to start over?"

"Fuck."

"I'll let it go this time. Now, let me hold you."

"You want to cuddle after you hit me?"

"Punishment is as hard on me as it is on you, darlin'. I don't like hitting you in such a manner. There is a difference between erotic spanking and spanking for punishment. You've only had the punishment kind. Soon, I'll show you the erotic kind." He ran his hands over her hot ass, mixing the pain of the spanking with the pleasure of his touch. After he unhooked her from the bench, he wrapped her in his arms and sat down in the chair next to the wall. "I need this cuddle time too."

"This is all so strange."

"You'll learn, sweetheart. For now, let me hold you. We'll get to the fun part of the spanking bench. You did notice it's the perfect height for me to fuck you, didn't you."

"Yeah, I kind of noticed, Sir."

"I want your ass tonight, Elizabeth," he said, smoothing his hand over her hair as he tucked her into his arms, rocking her slightly.

"Only my ass, Master?" She loved the way his title rolled off her tongue. Never in her life did she ever think she'd call anyone Master, but it fit Marcus.

She'd done some research on BDSM since they begun to play together. Some of what she'd learned was scary, but other stuff intrigued her. Rope bondage called shibari looked fascinating. Wax play looked scary and so did fire-play. The bullwhip Marcus had in his hand when she'd come through the door scared the shit out of her. The thing looked like it would seriously hurt. She wasn't into pain that much or at least she didn't think she would be. She seemed to be learning things about herself every time she played with Marcus like this.

"Oh, I plan to take all of your holes soon. We'll see how much you are up to tonight and we'll go from there."

"Yes, Master."

"Better?" he asked, shifting her on his legs and chuckling when she squeaked.

"Yes, Master."

"Then back across the bench with you. My cock aches for your warm hole whichever I chose to use tonight."

12

"I'm done being your pansy," the cowboy snapped as he paced the floor of the barn on Mitchell's ranch.

"You'll do as you're told or there won't be any pay."

The clipped voice on the other end of the phone pissed him off. No one told him what to do. "You're fucking with my livelihood here too, asshole. If I get caught, I won't be able to work anywhere in the cattle business."

"I don't care what you're risking. I want that ranch destroyed. Elizabeth will rue the day she turned her back on me. No one walks out on me."

"You're crazy, dude. She's just a woman."

"She's my woman. I'll kill anyone who touches her."

"You'd better get in line then. She's fucking the country vet who works here." The animalistic growl from the other end of the phone sent shivers down his back.

"I want more nitrates in the water supply. Kill every animal that moves."

"You're a real bastard, you know it?"

"Of course, I am. Why do you think I'm on top of my game?"

"Why do you have to destroy this ranch though? Not man enough to get Elizabeth without it?"

"She won't give me the time of day anymore and I'll not have it. Women come to me, I don't go to them. If she doesn't come crawling back to me, I'll destroy her entire family."

"Dude, you need to get a life. She isn't the only woman in the world." He stepped across the handle of a rake lying on the floor and moved into a stall. "I'll admit, she's got a nice rack on her, but my world wouldn't stop if she didn't give me the time of day."

"I'm not discussing my love life with you. Do as you're told and you'll get your money."

"Fine." The cowboy snapped his phone shut and grumbled under his breath as he pulled the bottle of poison from his pocket. Killing animals wasn't something he would be proud to say he'd done for money, but he needed the funds to pay off a gambling debt before the man he owed killed him. Fifty thousand dollars was a lot of money. Way more than he'd ever earn working as a lowly cowboy. He moved steadily toward the water tank. Poison in the main water supply would kill off anything living from the horses to the cattle in one swoop. It would be done...the job. The moment he finished, he'd pack his stuff so he could disappear. He couldn't afford to be caught.

A crack of thunder could be heard as he moved closer. A mid-summer storm was brewing, kicking up dust and making the animals nervous. No one seemed to be around tonight. Most of the cowboys if not all, had already headed into town for the regular pool game.

When he got closer, several of the cattle stomped their feet and shifted nervously like they knew he wasn't supposed to be there. A couple of the horses snorted when a flash of lightning exploded in the night air. "Wow. That was too close."

He moved next to the tank as he prepared to drop the whole vial of nitrates into the water when a flash of lightning lit up the night sky, hitting the lightning rod attached to the top of the tower. The cattle and horses spooked into a frenzy. He screamed and dropped the vial as one of the horses reared up, pawing at the air, kicking him in the skull with both front feet.

* * * *

Elizabeth drove into the front yard and squinted through the windshield. Rain pelted the front of her car with fat droplets in the mid-summer storm. She'd spent the night in Marcus' arms praying she would come to some conclusion about where their relationship would go from here, but awoke this morning with more questions than answers.

Cattle and horses braced themselves against the rain in a large group near the water trough. This wasn't usually something she'd notice, but a flash of red on the ground drew her attention as the animals shifted.

"Are you coming in or are you going to sit out there all day?" her father asked with a chuckle, standing on the front porch.

She didn't want to walk across the muddy yard in her heels but she hadn't brought any other shoes to wear. "Stupid, Liz. Really stupid." Her short, tight black dress would probably be ruined by the time she got to the porch, but there wasn't any way around it. She had to run for it. Once she got the door open, she jumped out, slammed the door and sprinted as fast as she could in three inch heels toward the front door.

"You didn't come home last night."

"No, I stayed at Marcus'."

"I assume you two made up?"

"Yes. I really wasn't serious about calling Ari back, Dad."

"It sounded like it to me. I'm sure to Marcus too, otherwise he wouldn't have left the way he did. Games like that will get you into trouble in a relationship, Elizabeth. I thought your mother and I taught you well enough to avoid those."

"I already apologized so forget it. Okay?" She glanced back at the pasture. "What's out there in the middle of the mud? There is something red on the ground."

"Probably a bandana one of the cowboys lost, I 'spect."

"It looks larger than a bandana, Dad. Don't you think you should check it out?"

"I will when the rain lets up some. They said this storm should move off in about an hour."

"Good. I guess I should have waited to come home. I would have saved my shoes," she said, lifting her waterlogged and muddy heel up for his inspection.

Her father laughed and hugged her. "Let's get some coffee."

"I'm going to run up to change back into some ranch like clothing. Jeans and a T-shirt?" She giggled as she pulled off her heels and pushed her wet hair back off her forehead.

"I'll make sure the coffee is hot."

They walked into the house together and she headed up the hall to change her clothes. Grabbing a dry towel out of the bathroom, she walked into her room only to find a dozen red roses sitting on her dresser. "What the...Where did these come from?" A small white card sat nestled in the buds. When she opened it, she smiled and shook her head. "When did he have time to do this?"

"They came early this morning," Caroline said from the hallway. "Pop left them in here figuring this would be the first place you'd go when you got home."

"They're beautiful."

"Marcus?"

"I assume so. The card just says 'All my love.' But why didn't he say something last night?"

"I don't know. Maybe he wanted to surprise you?"

"I guess. I'll have to call him to thank him."

"You could thank him properly by going back to his house."

"Yeah. But he has to work today."

"You can go back over there tonight then?"

"I really need to start getting my stuff together to head to Billings. I'm leaving in a few days."

"True." Caroline cocked her head and smiled. "Have you told him you love him?"

"Why is everyone convinced I'm in love with Marcus?"

"Because you are. You smile when his name is mentioned, you have the little twinkle in your eyes plus you get the dreamy look on your face."

"Maybe it's someone else."

"Yeah, right. Who else are you doing the horizontal mambo with?"

"No one."

"See. Besides, I think you two look cute together."

Elizabeth peeled off her damp dress and slipped on her bathrobe. A shower would feel heavenly before she got redressed.

"What the hell happened to your butt?"

"Marcus."

"Is the man crazy? Your ass is splotchy like he spanked you."

"He did."

"Seriously? What the fuck for?"

"I smarted off. I don't expect you to understand, Caroline."

"I want the deats, but I'm not going to push now and I can't believe you went to his house with no panties?"

"I planned on getting some, didn't I? Makes things easier."

"True. I'll have to try it next time I'm wanting to get laid." Caroline laughed as she headed down the hall, leaving Elizabeth to finish getting dressed.

Hot water sprayed out of the nozzle as she turned the handle. Steam rose inside the bathroom, obliterating her reflection in the mirror, thank goodness. She really didn't want to see how red her ass probably was after Marcus' spanking. She knew she deserved the swats, but keeping her wayward tongue under control wasn't usually her first concern.

Dropping the robe to the floor, she stepped into the stream of water with a sigh. *Damn, the heat felt good.*

Images from the night before zipped across her mind. After he'd held her for several moments, he'd ordered her back across the spanking bench. A semi-large butt plug passed the muscles of her anus as Marcus slipped it in. Even the thought of the plug made her clench her muscles. Once he had the plastic in place he proceeded to fuck her senseless with the plug in her ass and his cock in her pussy. She'd never felt so full in her entire life. Holy hell, the sensation wasn't like anything she experienced before. *Did it feel like that with two cocks? I might need to clarify the feeling and ask Emma.* Would her little sister even tell her? Who knew, but it might be worth it to ask. This fascination she had with having two men needed to get out of her head. She didn't want two men, really she didn't. The thought was there. Maybe Marcus would...nah. Well maybe just once?

She quickly finished her shower and redressed in comfortable work clothes. Coffee and breakfast would be good. She hadn't eaten before she left Marcus'.

"Thanks for putting the flowers in my room, Dad."

"You're welcome, honey. Here's your coffee," her father said, sitting a cup down in front of her. "Who are they from?"

"Marcus, I guess. Although I don't know when he would have ordered them unless it was before I went over there to apologize."

"There wasn't a card?"

"Yes, but there wasn't a signature on it."

"Well, I'm sure you'll thank Marcus properly when you see him again."

"Of course, she will, Dad." Caroline laughed and Elizabeth smiled behind her cup.

"Did you go outside to find out what's in the pasture?"

"The rain is slowing down so I figured the moment the downpour stops, I'll go out there. It isn't very far of a walk anyway. It's right by the water trough."

"Maybe whatever is out there will give us a clue to who's messing with the water supply."

Her father shook his head. "Surely it won't be such an easy fix. Besides, we still don't know if someone is or it's a natural cause."

"You never know, Dad." She paused and took a sip of her coffee. "Do you really think it's natural? Marcus said the nitrate level is well beyond what would normally occur even with fecal contamination."

"True, but I don't want to be pointing fingers until we know something more concrete."

"All right, but we need to put guards up or something."

"Elizabeth, we can't guard this large of a ranch. The manpower involved would be astronomical."

"But if something happens to the rest of the herd, it would kill this place, Dad. You can't afford that either."

"I know, sweetheart. I wish I knew the answer to this whole thing," he replied, scratching the five o'clock shadow of whiskers forming on his chin.

He looked worried and haggard. The whole situation had taken its toll on him. Dark circles under his eyes told her he wasn't sleeping well. The almost gaunt appearance to his cheeks told her he wasn't eating like he should either.

A quick look out the window assured her the rain had stopped, giving them a chance to check by the water trough. She grabbed her boots from near the back door to trudge out in the mud as her father picked up the coffee cups and put them in the sink.

"Thanks for getting those, Dad. I was going to do it when I got my boots on."

"I'm used to it, Elizabeth. Your mother, God rest her soul, always left her coffee cup on the table."

"I guess I get it naturally then."

"Yep." He put his cowboy hat on his head, motioning for her to precede him through the back screen door out into the filtered sunlight. Now that the clouds were breaking up, blue sky shone between the wispy puffs of white again.

"It's going to be fun getting out there in this mud."

"Yeah, it's the joys of living on a ranch with cattle and horses. There is always a mud pit around somewhere."

"True," she said, opening the gate to the pasture as her father followed behind.

The closer she got to the red material in the mud, the more worried she became. First a red shirt, blue jean, and then boots made her gasp as they got to what lie on the ground near the trough.

"Shit, Dad. It's a man."

Mitchell bent down next to the body to touch his neck. "He's dead."

"What the hell happened here?"

"I'm not sure, but we need to call the sheriff."

"I have my cell in my pocket," she replied, pulling it out to dial.

Within several minutes, the house buzzed with a few sheriff's deputies as they took notes and the paramedics moved the body onto a stretcher.

"Appears like one of the animals kicked him in the head," Sheriff Monteau said, scribbling in his notebook.

"An accident?" her father asked.

"Looks like it. The animal probably spooked during the storm."

"What the hell was he doing out near the trough in a storm? Its nuts," Elizabeth said, adding her two cents into the equation.

"I wouldn't know. We'll contact the state investigators' office to make sure they don't want to go through a full investigation before we close this, but I'm ruling the death accidental."

"Thanks, Sheriff."

"You're welcome, Mitchell. I'll call you if I need anything else."

Once the police cars left, Elizabeth and her father stood near where the body had lain. "I'm still suspicious, Dad. Why would he be out here in the middle of a storm? This whole scenario doesn't make sense."

"I haven't the foggiest idea. Maybe one of the gates got left open and he closed it?"

"There aren't any gates close to the trough." She glanced around the area and noticed something next to the base of the metal watering hole. "What's this?" A small plastic vial sat propped up against the tank on the opposite side of where they found the body. The sheriff and his deputy's must have missed it buried in the grass around the trough.

"I don't know. Why would there be something like this out here?"

"You should have the contents analyzed, Dad," she said, handing him the vial. "It could be important. You don't have any of the hands treating the water with anything, do you?"

"No. The cattle get the extra nutrients they need in their feed, not the water supply."

"I don't like this."

"Me either, honey. I'll get this back to the house and have the lab who did the water testing, get right on it."

"Great. I'm going to poke around here a little to see if I find anything else out of the ordinary. Maybe in the barn?"

Her father glanced at the large structure in the distance and shrugged. "Maybe. You never know."

As he trudged off toward the house, Elizabeth checked out the area. Layers upon layers of hoof prints in the mud obliterated much of the vicinity, making it difficult to see anything. Horses and cattle milled about in the distance. A brown mare wandered close, searching for a scratching. She reached her hand to the animal's ears to itch behind the left one. "Are you gonna help me look, sweetheart, because you're in the way right now." The horse shook her head. Elizabeth giggled and pushed the mare away. "Go on with you then."

Sloshing through the mud wasn't her idea of a good time. Unfortunately, it came with the territory of being on a ranch. She couldn't remember how many times her mother yelled at her for tracking mud into the house. *Oh Mom, I wish you were here. It sucks not having you to talk to.*

A soft breeze blew hair across her cheek and she smiled even though tears gathered in her eyes. Losing a mother at any age hurt like the devil. When hers died tragically in a car accident a few years ago, the pain went heart deep.

She sniffed back the tears and looked down. Something shiny silver winked in the morning sunlight. She bent down to push the mud back. *A cell phone? What the hell is a cell phone doing out here in the mud? Maybe it belonged to the guy we found.* She brushed the dirt away. "Huh. What a weird thing to find out here. Of course, you don't find dead bodies in the mud very often either." The screen flashed missed call so she flipped open the top and gasped as the number registered in her brain. "Why in the hell would he be calling one of the guys on Dad's ranch?"

* * * *

Marcus stepped outside his office to take a breath of fresh air. The storm from earlier had finally moved off. He hoped it would stay away for a bit. Thunder and lightning were great for cuddle time with someone, but they played hell on his sinuses. The pressure from the high humidity always clogged him up. He sniffed to try to clear his nostrils, which didn't help. But the rotting food stench coming from the diner down the block that shared the same alleyway he did seemed to do the trick. *Great. Just what I need to smell when my nose opens up a little.*

To erase the disgusting odor, he let his mind drift back to Elizabeth and how their night progressed after she arrived to apologize. With her kneeling at his feet so beautifully, her hair glinting red in the lights of the room, the smell of her perfume drifting to his nose, he remembered the excitement radiating off her skin when he draped her back over the spanking bench. She wanted to be fucked hard. Being taken turned her on. The scent of her arousal stimulated his own sense of fulfillment at having a sub available to him—one who wanted to be there unlike Marie, his ex-wife.

Two women in his life had broken him down, Marie and Julia. Marie wanted him to give up his dominate traits to become the vanilla lover she wanted. He'd tried for a while, but it became apparent early on he wouldn't be able to maintain that way of life. Domination was part of him—something he couldn't turn off like a faucet. The breakup of their marriage some ten years earlier still hurt. Loving a woman who wouldn't even contemplate some excitement in their bedroom life became a burden he couldn't shake.

Then he found Julia. He'd met her at a club one night as a sub looking for a Dom. Beautiful, curvy and blonde, she screamed total submission from her bent head to her kneeling position in the roped off area for the unattached subs. They negotiated to play several times together over six months, but the more he tried with her, the more he realized she wanted a twenty-four/seven slave relationship. He couldn't do it. He wanted a partner in life, not someone he would be required to make all the decisions for. A submissive in the bedroom, but not in their every day life would be the perfect sub for him. Unfortunately, he hadn't found a woman to fit the description in his mind...until now. Elizabeth.

"Love? Is that what this is?"

Everything points to the description of love. You want her. She fulfills everything you need in the bedroom.

"Can I trust her?"

You already do.

"True."

She compliments you in every aspect of your life. She's strong and independent, but submissive in her sexual needs. Her world doesn't revolve around you.

"But how can I say I'm in love with her?"

Listen to your heart.

After he thought about it like that, he realized love came in many different packages. The feelings he had for Elizabeth went far beyond anything he felt for other women in his life. The love he'd felt for Marie didn't come close to what his heart held for Elizabeth. He wanted her, yes, but in many different ways. By his side, cooking with him, cleaning his house, enjoying the sunshine, picnics, long walks...babies.

"I do love her."

Seconds later, a sharp crack split the air like the snap of a bullwhip. He grunted and staggered back as a bright red splotch formed on the front of his lab coat. *What the fuck?* Pain seared through his chest as he dropped to his knees. *Please God, don't let me die before I have a chance to tell Elizabeth I love her.*

Darkness surrounded him as he collapsed against the warm pavement.

13

"I need to see him now. Get me a supervisor," Elizabeth snapped at the nurse guarding the curtained off area where Marcus lay helplessly. The two hour drive to Billings was torture, not knowing what had happened or whether he would live or not. Thank goodness the fire department paramedics knew enough to call for Life Flight.

"I'm sorry, ma'am. The doctor is with him and we're prepping him for surgery."

"Surgery?"

"Yes. He needs surgery now. They have to stop the bleeding."

"Marcus? Ah, hell, Marcus!"

Seconds later, she heard a squeaky, "Elizabeth?"

"See. He wants to see me."

"Let her in nurse, if it will make the patient more comfortable."

Elizabeth dashed around the woman and parted the curtains. *Holy shit!* Marcus' skin looked milky white except for the large stain on the bandage over his shoulder. "What happened?"

"Apparently, I was shot."

"Why would someone want to shoot you?"

"I wish I knew. I don't think I've pissed off any of my patients lately." He coughed, making the blood seep from the wound.

"Don't coughing. No moving. You have to be okay."

He grasped her hand in his, squeezing her fingers. "I will. They have to stop the bleeding and clean up the wound. The bullet hit some big veins. I'll be fine."

"You'd better be. I don't want the man I love dying on me," she said with tears in her eyes.

"You love me?" he asked, his eyes wide with wonder.

"Yes, I do. I'd planned on telling you tonight with a romantic dinner with all the trimmings, but now you'll be in here for at least a few days."

"We'll put off the romantic dinner, but not the other. I love you too."

"Seriously?"

"Yes." He brought her fingers to his mouth to kiss each one.

"Enough. We need to get this man to surgery."

"I'll be at your bedside when you come out of surgery. You can count on it, so no running off," she said, sniffing in between sentences. She couldn't lose him. Not now. "Take good care of him, will you?"

"We'll do our best, ma'am."

She watched with a heavy heart as they wheeled him out of the curtained off area and down the hall, silently praying he would be all right. The love she felt for this man couldn't be compared to anything she'd felt before. The feelings were all encompassing. Her heart ached and she hugged herself trying to hold in the sobs.

"Liz?"

She sighed before she wiped her face with the back of her hand.

"Liz, where are you?"

Knowing she had no choice but to face Natalie and Cade, she walked out into the long hallway.

"There you are. Where is Marcus?"

"Headed to surgery."

"What the hell happened?" Natalie asked, hugging her. "I heard he was shot? Who the hell shoots people in Red Rock?"

"He took a bullet to his upper chest on the left side right above his heart from what I could tell. It hit some major veins so they are going in to close things up. They have to stop the bleeding." Her entire body started to shake from the shock of finding him like this. "What if he doesn't make it, Nat? I can't lose him now. I love him."

"Does he know this?" she asked, stepping back to link her arm with Elizabeth's.

"Yes. I told him before they took him away and he said he loves me too. God..." She scrubbed her face with her left hand, laughing. "What a way to declare your love for someone, huh?"

"It'll be fine. You've given him something to look forward to now. You'll have the rest of your lives to figure things out."

"Being in love with someone doesn't make everything hunky-dory, Nat. I'm going to be working in this hospital next week. I'll be here for three years."

"Billings isn't far. You'll make things work."

"He needs to get through this before I worry about making anything work or not."

The cell phone in her pocket vibrated and she jumped. She'd forgotten she had put it there after she found it in the mud. Pulling the phone out, she glanced at the screen, recognizing the number. *The rat bastard!* She flipped the phone open and said, "Hello Ari."

Click.

"The fucking asshole!"

"Who?"

"Armand." She slid the phone back in her pocket. "You know about the dead cowboy we found near the water trough this morning, right?"

"Yeah, Dad told us."

"Well, Dad took the vial of whatever we found back into the house, but I stayed out there to look around the mud for some clues. I found a cell phone. Guess whose number showed up as a missed call?" Natalie's wide eyes confirmed she suspected the same asshole. "Yep, you guessed is...Ari."

"What's he got to do with a dead cowboy?"

"I wish I knew. Whatever it is, it can't be good."

When they reached the waiting room, Cade sat in one of the chairs with Mitchell next to him. They both stood as she and Natalie reached their side.

"How is he?" her father asked.

"They just took him to surgery. There's some bleeding they need to stop and I don't know if the bullet is still in there."

"Who would want to shoot, Marcus?" Cade stuffed his hands in his pockets. "What kind of enemies could a veterinarian have?"

"I wish I knew."

Sheriff Monteau walked in through the doors, approaching the group with a frown on his face. "How is Doctor Melton?"

"In surgery, but they expect him to recover, I think. Have you found out anything about who shot him?"

"We caught the guy."

"You did?"

"Yeah. Someone from the diner saw a car speed away shortly after the crack of the shot. They're the ones who found Marcus in the alley behind his office. The guy is singing like a bird. Appears as if someone paid him to shoot Marcus, although the original plan failed when Marcus turned to go back into the office. They guy caught him in the shoulder instead of the heart."

"The guy meant to kill him?"

"Apparently."

"Did he say who paid him?"

"Some guy from Los Angeles is all I can tell you. We've put out an APB on the guy for attempted murder."

"I hope they get him before he tries again."

"We will. He's some big shot out there. Business owner of some sort. We hope he hasn't skipped the country."

Rage ripped through her. She knew in her gut who was behind all of this, but she didn't know why. "Somehow, I don't think so. If it's who I think it is, he thinks he's untouchable."

"Oh?"

"Yes. He's an ex-boyfriend of mine, but why he'd want to kill Marcus, I don't know."

"Jealousy?" Nat suggested. "He was pretty adamant he wanted you to call him. When you didn't, all of the sudden people are dying or being hurt around you."

"Why? He doesn't know I'm seeing anyone."

"Maybe he does."

"Sheriff Monteau, I know you're investigating the death of the cowboy at our ranch also. I found this," she pulled the cell phone from her pocket, "in the dirt out there. We heard about Marcus right after I found it so I didn't have time to call you to tell you. One of the phone calls to-day was from a familiar number to me. Armand Listolini. Why he would be calling a cowboy on my father's ranch, I don't know. If he's behind Marcus being shot, I'll kill him myself if you don't arrest him and put his ass away for a long time."

"We'll do our best, Ms. Weston."

"Good. If you need anything from me, let me know. I could probably tell you where he'd hide out if he tries to disappear. I was his personal assistant before I left his ass."

"We'll be in touch then if we don't get him under arrest inside the next twenty four hours."

"Thanks, Sheriff." After the Sheriff left, the group decided to get coffee and something to eat from the cafeteria at the hospital while they waited for Marcus to come out of surgery. All of the prayers Elizabeth had said as a child went through her brain, while she silently talked to God on Marcus' behalf. He just had to be okay. She couldn't lose him now.

Two hours later, the doctor came out into the surgery waiting room. "Are you with Doctor Melton?"

"Yes, Sir," she said, coming to her feet. "Is he okay?"

"He's fine. The bullet didn't hit anything major but it was still lodged in the fleshy part of his shoulder. It did chip part of his collarbone so he will be sore for some time until the bone heals. We've cauterized, sorry that means burned the ends of the veins so they don't bleed anymore..."

"It's fine, Doctor. I'm a physician. In fact I'm doing my residency here starting next week."

"Oh good. Then you understand. We sealed everything off and stopped the bleeding. There is a hairline fracture in the collarbone. It'll heal in time. He's in recovery now. You can go back to see him if you like. He's been asking for Elizabeth, although he's not fully awake, yet."

"I'm Elizabeth."

"I assumed as much." He motioned to the nurse. "Take this woman back to curtain four, please."

"I'll be back in a couple of minutes."

"You take your time, sweetheart. We know you need to be back there," her father said, kissing her cheek.

"Thanks, Dad."

When the nurse left her at the curtain of the room where Marcus lay, she inhaled sharply and pushed her way through. His skin had more color rather than the pasty white he'd been before. The bandage on his shoulder was clean and dry now. His dark lashes lay against his cheeks, covering up the beautiful blue eyes she'd come to love so much. She moved to the side of his bed to pick up his hand. "Marcus?"

"Elizabeth," he croaked through dry lips.

"Hi, handsome. You look like shit."

"Thanks. You look beautiful," he said. "I guess this means you get to play doctor with me?"

"You bet. I'll baby you all I can. I plan on talking to the hospital's medical director to see if I can postpone my start date."

"No you don't. You need this. I'll be fine."

"I love you. I'm going to be there to help you recover."

"I love you too, but there wasn't anything major hit except a hairline fracture in my collarbone from what the doctor said. It's more of a flesh wound. It'll heal just fine as long as I don't do too much. I'll have to close the office for a few weeks, but I'm sure my patients will understand."

"You *will* take it easy, mister. If I have to tie your ass down, I will."

"A bit bossy for a sub aren't you?"

"When I have to be." She frowned before she dropped a quick kiss to his lips. "Seriously, Marcus. You won't be able to do some things around your house. I'll be there to cook and clean."

"You'll do your residency. I won't hear anymore about it."

"Then I'll drive back and forth on my days off. Natalie and Cade will help too. There are plenty of people in Red Rock who will help do things for you, I'm sure. You're a popular guy."

"Don't send the women over. There's only one woman I want waiting on me. You."

"You'll move into my house then."

"You want me to move in with you?"

"Yes...I mean it only make sense to..."

"Okay."

"Okay? No arguments?"

"Nope. I want to be with you even though this isn't the best of circumstances."

"As long as I get to hold you when we sleep, I'll be a happy man," he said softly, drifting off to sleep.

She shifted to remove her hand from his, wanting to let him sleep now that he was on the mend, until his eyes popped open again. "I'm going to let you rest."

"I'll rest better with you by my side."

"I know, but they won't let me sleep here no matter how much clout you think you might have."

"Which is none around here."

"I'll be back when they move you upstairs, okay? I want to give Cade, Natalie and my father a progress update."

"They're all here?"

"Of course they are, Marcus. They care about you."

"Did they catch the guy who shot me?"

"Yes, but we'll talk more about it when you've recovered a bit more."

"All right. I love you, Elizabeth, but I think I'll sleep now for a bit. I'm kind of tired."

"I love you too, Marcus. I'll see you in a little while."

As he drifted off to sleep, she heard a soft snoring sound. Slipping her hand out of his, she went back out into the waiting room to fill everyone in on his progress.

* * * *

Two days later, Elizabeth stood at the side of his bed with her hands on her hips. "You need to get up and move around more, Marcus. You can't be letting these nurses wait on you anymore. I know with your charming disposition, you have to be making it difficult for them to do their job."

"I've been a grump, haven't I?"

"Yes, now let's go for a walk."

"I want out of here."

"Tomorrow," she said, sliding his slippers onto his feet.

"I hate these gowns. Couldn't I have some scrub pants? What about my underwear?"

"I'll ask the nurses, but if you treated them better, they probably would have given you scrub pants to wear, you know."

"Maybe."

"No maybe's about it." She grabbed his hand, tucking it around her waist so she could steady him on his non-injured side. "Easy now."

They stepped out into the hall, walking toward the nurses' station. Several eyebrows shot up as they walked nearby and down the other hallway. The nurses seemed shocked as they walked past. He really hadn't been that bad of a patient, had he?

"So what's the progress on the shooter?" he asked, turning back toward his room.

"He's in jail for attempted murder."

"What about the man who paid him?"

"I wish I'd never told you about that."

"He can't hide forever."

"I've given them all the information I can recall from his offshore accounts to his estates out of the country. They've located him at one of them. Now they have to get extradition papers to have him arrested. I'm sure they'll have him in custody soon."

"I hope so. The man sounds crazy. I don't want him anywhere near you."

"Did you hear what Dad found out about the vial?"

"No."

"It was sodium nitrate concentrated. Enough to kill the whole herd."

"How in the world did it get there and why would one of your dad's own hands want to put him out of business?"

"I'm not sure, but I have a good idea. I didn't tell you about the cell phone I found."

"Cell phone?"

"Yes, in the mud near where the body was. There were all kinds of calls from Ari's number on the phone. Apparently, Ari's been paying the guy to poison my dad's herd ever since our blow up at the airport."

"He must really have loved you." Marcus didn't like the thought of another man touching his woman, much less loving her like he did.

"No, I wasn't anything more than a possession to him. When I walked, he didn't like it."

"Now I know the man is crazy. Any thoughts on why he tried to have me killed?"

"I don't know. I don't think he knew about the two of us, but you never know." When they returned to his room, she helped him get back into the bed, tucking in the covers around him.

"Thanks, Mom."

She blew him raspberries as she continued fussing with the blankets. When she made it around the other side, she gave him a quick, unsatisfying peck on the lips.

"More."

"No."

"Spoilsport. You'll pay for your answer when I can wield the paddle again."

"Promises, promises."

"You're really asking for it now," he threatened good-naturedly.

"Yes, Sir." She grabbed her purse. "I really need to get back to Dad's. I need to pack since my Master insists I come back here in a few days to start my residency."

"Yes, he does. You'll be great."

"Thanks." She kissed him again. "I love you."

"I love you too. Be careful driving home."

"I will. You have your cell so I'll call you when I get there."

"All right."

Quiet surrounded him the moment she left. He leaned back in the bed and smiled. She belonged to him. Thank God!

14

Elizabeth sang to the country tunes on the radio as she pulled into her dad's driveway. A car she didn't recognize sat pulled up to the porch with a rental tag. *That's weird. I wonder who is visiting.*

After she grabbed her purse, she slid out of her car, walking by the sedan. A briefcase and overcoat sat on the front seat. *Who wears an overcoat in Montana in the middle of summer?*

"Dad?" she called, walking through the door. "I'm home."

"Welcome home, Elizabeth."

The hair stood up on her arms. "Ari. What are you doing here?"

"I came to retrieve my fiancé."

"You never asked me to marry you."

"No, but you assumed I would so now I've come to rectify the situation."

"I'm not going anywhere with you." She glanced around to see her father sitting in one of wing chairs. His gaze shifted from her to Ari and back.

"He's fine. For now..."

"Why do you insist on this? You don't love me. I've realized I don't love you."

"Oh, but I always get what I want. You walked out on me. No one walks out on Armand Listolini."

"You can have whomever you want. Any of the women you've fucked while you were with me would love to be with you, I'm sure. Take one of them."

He sighed, shifted and pointed the gun she hadn't noticed before, at her father. "I'll kill him and your boyfriend. You see, no one fucks me over."

"You cheated on me, but it's not right if someone doesn't play by your rules anymore? You're crazy, Ari."

Before she could blink, he lifted his left hand and slapped her hard across the cheek. Finding herself on the floor by the end table, she touched where the ring on his finger cut her face.

Her father started to move, but sat back down when Ari lifted the gun in his direction.

"I would stay put if I were you. What I do with my fiancé isn't any of your business, old man."

"The hell it's not, you fucking bastard," her father growled. "I may be thirty years older than you, you son of a bitch, but if I get the chance, I'll beat the hell out of you."

"You won't get the chance."

The butt of her father's .45 stuck out from under the end table. She inched her hand closer, trying desperately to reach the gun without Ari seeing her. One thing her father had taught her and her siblings...how to shoot.

Her cell phone jingled a saucy tune from her purse. She wasn't about to retrieve it, but she knew by the ringtone who was on the other end. Marcus. He would have expected her to call already. Once her cell phone quit ringing, the home phone started. All three of them stared at each other until the answering machine picked up.

"Elizabeth, sweetheart, are you there?"

"How touching," Ari grumbled.

"Honey, pick up the phone." A long pause accompanied the silence. "I called your cell but you didn't answer and you've got me worried. You should be home by now."

"I need to pick it up, Ari. If I don't he'll send the law out here."

"Fine, grab the phone, but no funny business. Just tell lover boy you're fine and he can go about his business."

She grabbed the phone. "Hello?"

"Baby, where were you?"

"I'm sorry, Marcus. I didn't hear the cell and I was talking to my dad. I wasn't going to call you because I didn't want to disturb you."

"Something's wrong."

"No, it's fine. I'm fine, really. We're waiting on the results from the vial. That's all."

"He's there, isn't he?"

"Yes, I know you want to know the results, but the lab is supposed to call the sheriff with them."

"I'll call them the moment we hang up. Be safe, honey. Help is on the way. I wish I could be there."

"I love you."

"I love you too."

She hung up the phone. Ari made a gagging sound as he waved the gun around. His eyes looked wild. Sanity dimmed in his gaze the longer she looked. He'd really lost his grip on reality.

"You'll never see him again."

"Listen Ari, I'll go with you if you leave Marcus and my father alone. They haven't done anything to you. You want me. I get it. Let's go away, just the two of us. We'll leave this mess behind."

"You'd leave with me?"

"Of course. I don't want my family hurt."

Sirens could be heard faintly in the distance. She cussed under her breath. Surely they weren't stupid enough to come up to the house with sirens blaring. Her hope died as they came closer.

"You called the cops?"

"How could I have called them, Ari? They're probably going next door."

He jumped up and glanced out the front windows as the sheriff pulled up in front of the house. With his back turned to her, but still able to keep her father in his sights, he didn't realize she had the .45 in her hands until she pulled it out.

"Put the gun down, Ari so we can let the police handle this."

"No!" he screamed, swinging around to point the gun at her. "If I can't have you, no one will. You're mine!"

The gun exploded with a loud pop.

* * * *

Expecting her life to flash before her eyes, she wasn't prepared to open them and see a large stain of red spreading across Ari's chest. She shot him? With her eyes closed? Her dad always told her to keep them open when she shot at targets as a kid.

His eyes were wide as he looked down at his chest, dropped his gun, and then slid to the floor.

Her hands started to shake, causing her to drop the gun on the floor beside her. The quake spread to her whole body. She started to fight when strong arms pulled her in.

Her father whispered, "It's all right, now. Everything is over with. He can't hurt anyone again."

"Daddy?"

"It's me, sweetheart."

"I shot him."

"No, you didn't. The sheriff did when he came in the room behind Armand. You didn't shoot anyone."

"Thank God. I couldn't live with myself if I'd taken a life."

He pushed her back and looked into her eyes. "You would have done what had to be done to protect your family. You didn't have to though."

She grabbed his arms and hung on tight. "Help me outside, Dad. I need the air on my face."

"Sure, honey."

Together, they made their way toward the door.

"I'll need statements," the sheriff said.

"We aren't going anywhere. Just outside."

"Okay."

She couldn't look—didn't want to look at the body sprawled out on their living room floor. That could have been her or her father. Why did Ari have to go to this? Why was he so insistent? Nothing made sense. *Crazy doesn't make sense.*

"I need to call Marcus. He'll be worried sick or on his way home to find out what's going on."

"Here is my cell phone."

"You had it in your pocket?"

"Yes, but I couldn't get to it without alerting Ari."

"I know, Dad. Thanks for being there."

"I didn't do anything, sweetheart. I wish I would have been able to protect you."

"You couldn't with a gun on you." She took the cell phone and punch in Marcus' number with shaking hands.

"Hello? Mitchell?"

"It's Elizabeth."

"Oh thank God. Are you all right?"

"I'm fine. Ari is dead. The sheriff shot him before I had to."

A heavy sigh reached her ear. "You're safe. Everything else can be worked out."

"I'm a little shaky. I wish you were here to hold me."

"I'm getting dressed right now."

"You can't leave the hospital, Marcus. You need to stay there."

"No, you need me. I'm taking a cab from here."

"It's a two hour cab ride."

"I don't care, baby. I need to be there with you."

"All right, you stubborn man."

"You know it. I'll be there in a few hours. Until then, remember, I love you."

"I love you too. See you soon." She clicked the phone shut and handed it back to her father. "He's leaving the hospital and coming home."

"Why am I not surprised."

"He shouldn't be, Dad. He should stay there."

"He's a man in love, sweetie. He needs to reassure himself that you're all right."

They sat in the rockers on the porch. She took several large breathes to remove the smell of gunpowder and blood from her nose. Blood shouldn't bother her. After all, she's a physician, but she had to fight with her need to help Ari or let him die like the dog he was.

"You couldn't have helped him. The sheriff's bullet killed him in-stantly."

"Thanks, Dad. How did you know I had a conflict going on inside of me?"

"I'm your father. I know you well. I know you want to fix things. It's why you became a doctor. Even if the sheriff hadn't killed him, I think the man was beyond help, except for psychiatric help."

"The look in his eyes..." She shivered again. "I'll never forget the look. He truly had lost his grasp on reality."

The sheriff came out onto the porch. "We'll remove the body when the coroner gets here. I need to ask you two a few questions."

For the next hour, they went over step-by-step how things went down. She gave detail after detail of her relationship with Ari, how his phone number showed up on the cell phone belonging to the cowboy, what his expressions and words were during the time he held the two of them at gunpoint and his demands.

"We won't have to do any kind of investigation since you didn't shoot him. Your bullet went wide and hit the wall. I shot him."

"Thank you for helping us."

"Make sure you thank Doctor Melton. Without his call from the hospital in Billings, we wouldn't have known to be out here."

"I plan to."

The coroner's van pulled up. Within several moments they removed the body.

"You two are free to go back inside if you like."

"Thank you. I need to get the blood out of the carpet before it dries," she said, thankful for having something to keep her mind occupied until Marcus arrived.

"You don't have to clean up, Elizabeth."

"I need to, Dad."

She grabbed a bucket and filled it with cleaning solution and water. The carpet he landed on was a throw rug so they could get rid of it if the blood wouldn't come out. She wanted the rug clean though. It was one of her mother's favorite woven Indian rugs. No way would she let the crazy man ruin something so dear to her mother. Pass after pass with the brush, little by little the blood slowly came out. She didn't realize tears streamed down her cheeks until someone took her arm and lifted her to her feet.

"It's okay, darlin'."

"Marcus. Oh God, Marcus," she sobbed into his uninjured shoulder.

"It's okay. It's over. You're safe. Your father is safe and he can't hurt anyone again."

"I should have protected Dad. I had the gun. I closed my eyes. If the sheriff hadn't shot him, he would have killed me or Dad."

"You aren't a killer, Elizabeth. You're a healer."

"But it's my fault."

"It's not your fault. He was crazy. Stop blaming yourself."

"I...I can't. If I would have never got involved..."

"Come with me." He took her hand and led her to her bedroom. "Across my knees."

"What? You can't be serious."

"I said across my knees, sub. What do you say to me?"

"Yes, Sir." She dropped her pants and underwear to her ankles before lay across his knees, balancing herself on her hands so her ass pointed in the air.

"I can't hold you down so you'll leave your hands on the floor until I'm done."

"Yes, Sir."

The slap of his hand on her ass stung, but the self-loathing she felt wouldn't dissipate.

"I'm going to do this until you realize none of this was your fault. Your ass will burn long before my hand tires."

His hand rained down on her until pain sizzled from her butt cheeks. Still she couldn't let go.

"Let go, darlin'. It wasn't your fault."

"But..."

"I can do this all night."

Tears burned her eyes and dripped onto the floor. Her heart finally opened up for her to realize she couldn't control what Ari did. Yes, she got involved with him, but she couldn't have known how possessive he would become when she walked out. He cheated on her. The light in her head clicked on and she sobbed uncontrollably.

"There you go. Let it out."

The rain of blows stopped but still she cried. She cried for losing control of her life. She cried for Marcus being hurt. She cried for losing her mother even though she felt her presence on a regular basis. She cried for all the things in her life she felt she'd dropped the ball on. When the firestorm subsided, she felt cleaner. "Thank you, Sir."

"You're welcome, darlin'," he said, helping her stand so she could pull up her jeans.

"How did you know?" she asked, taking a seat next to him on the bed.

"Sometimes a sub must let go of the feelings bottled up inside. A good spanking can be a trigger to help you release those emotions you wouldn't normally show. A Dom takes that control out of your hands and allows you to face those issues. You now realize you needed to release those things to heal."

She sniffed, wiping her face until he pushed her hands out of the way, doing it for her. "I hadn't even really cried over the death of my mother. I just stepped in and tried to be the woman of the house after she died. Hard to do hundreds of miles away."

"But you realize now those emotions were crippling you."

"Yes."

He kissed her lips as he tucked a bit of hair behind her ear. "I'm sorry. I should have picked up on those earlier."

"Everything okay in there?" her father asked through the door.

"We're fine, Dad. I needed a firm hand is all."

"In more ways than one," Marcus whispered, raking a thumb over her left nipple.

"Good thing Marcus was close by," came from behind the closed door. "I'll get lunch started."

"I want to make you come so bad." He grabbed a tissue from the bedside table. "Do you know what those tears do to me?"

"What?"

"They make me hard as a rock for you. I want to comfort you, but I also want to lick your pussy until you scream for me."

"Spanking makes you horny?"

"It makes you horny too. Shall I dip my fingers into your pussy so I can find out?"

"I can tell you what it does to me, but you'd want to find out for yourself."

"Take your boots off. Drop your jeans and panties. I want to see your pussy."

"Can I suck your cock?"

"Did I tell you to?"

"No, Sir."

"Then do what I told you. I don't like repeating myself."

With a huge grin on her face, she stood and unbuttoned her pants, dropping everything to the floor. She toed off her boots so she could shimmy the rest of the way out of her clothes.

"Lie down on the bed."

On her back with her legs together, she waited for his next instruction.

"Spread your legs and hold open those sweet lips."

He dropped down on his knees between her thighs, his mouth level with her pussy. A squeak left her lips at the first touch of his tongue. God, she wanted this—needed this—needed him to make her feel alive again after the events of the morning.

With a kiss to the insides of both thighs, he swiped his tongue from slit to clit. A deep moan escaped her mouth as he began quick figure eights right on her clit. He wasn't going to bring her up slowly. It would be fast and furious from horny to climax. The moment he sucked her clit between his lips, she exploded in shards of light as her climax washed over her like a wave crashing against the shore.

He shoved two fingers into her pussy and then curled them up to reach the soft, spongy spot behind her pelvic bone.

"You'll come again for me, darlin'."

"I can't, Marcus, please. Fuck me." The tips of his fingers rubbed over her G spot. She shot straight up to immediate arousal. "Oh God." Her breath came out in short, agonizing pants.

"Come for me, babe. You can do it." He sucked her clit into his mouth before biting down on the little nub slightly causing her body to go bow tight. She lost her grip, spinning out of control as another climax blindsided her.

She quickly grabbed the pillow from beside her head and screamed into it, muffling the sound as he chuckled. "Bastard."

A quick slap to her inner thigh told her he heard her.

Trying to catch her breath, she lay boneless on the bed. She vaguely heard him unbuckle his belt and drop his jeans to the floor before the head of his cock pushed at her opening. *Finally!* She tossed the pillow aside to look up into his eyes as he stood over her.

"I love you."

"I love you too," she said.

"Play with your nipples for me." She reached up, pinching both nipples. "Roll them between your fingers. Pull them until they are hard. I want to lick them."

With his arm in a sling, he couldn't do these things for himself as he pounded into her flesh. One hand braced on her hip, he slid in and out bringing them both to clawing need within seconds. His cock rode her G spot, drawing out the desire to oh-my-God proportions. Her own fingers pulling at nipples seemed wrong, but so sexy, she couldn't help but feel a little naughty.

"You feel heavenly," he growled.

"Fuck me hard, Marcus. Make me yours."

"You're mine. All of you. Every inch belongs to me and only to me."

"Yes, Sir."

Epilogue

"No. The dresser needs to go in the other bedroom, Jonathan." Elizabeth said, supervising the move of her things to Marcus' house. "Just because you're my brother doesn't mean you get out of work."

"I love when you're bossy," Marcus said from his spot near the doorway.

"Yeah right, Mister. We know who is the boss in this house."

"Yeah, me," he replied, stopping in front of her. The kiss he laid on her lips quickly turned into a bone-melting duel of tongues.

"All right you two. Save it for when the guests go home," Cade said, balancing one end of the dresser Jonathan held. "Spare room?"

"Yes. I'm using half of Marcus' dresser so my things will go in the other bedroom."

"I'm going to go start the barbeque so we can feed this hungry bunch and get them some alcohol for their help."

"Okay. I'm going to help Natalie put away the kitchen items I bought and those I brought with me. Plus we have to get the salads out of the refrigerator."

"Alcohol?" Jonathan piped in as he and Cade made their way back toward the living room.

"Beer is in the trashcan with the ice. Wine coolers and other mixers are in the cooler." She turned toward the kitchen. "Cade? Can you bring me and Natalie a wine cooler, please?"

"None for me, thanks," Natalie said, winking at Cade.

"Water, babe?" he asked.

"Great. I'd appreciate it."

"What's with you and water lately? You aren't drinking? I bought all of this alcohol and I'm going to have to drink every bit with Caroline?"

"What's wrong with me drinking," Caroline asked.

"Nothing, sis."

"I can't drink for the next several months."

"You're pregnant?" Elizabeth asked, pulling her into a hug.

"Yep. Baby number three is on the way and will be here by spring."

"Cool! Congratulations." Elizabeth hugged her again as Cade handed two wine coolers over, and gave Natalie a bottle of water.

"Unfortunately, my sister the doctor hasn't finished her residency in time to follow me."

"I can do your minor check-ups if you want. I'm doing a prenatal rotation for the next several months at the hospital anyway."

"Great!"

"How is the residency going anyway? I haven't seen you much." Natalie mixed the ingredients for the potato salad while she talked.

"Neither has Marcus," she said, folding her arms over her chest. "The only way we'll see each other is on my off days and if I live here. I think it's the only reason he asked me to move in. He doesn't like not getting sex on a regular basis."

"I doubt that's all it is. He loves you."

"I know. I love him too, but it was getting really hard to see him working five days a week. Tired doesn't begin to tell you how I feel on my days off."

Marcus poked his head through the crack of the sliding glass door. "Are you ladies joining us? The burgers are almost done."

"Sure. We'll be right out."

The three ladies walked outside only to be surrounded by the others at the party. Marcus had invited Kale, Laurel, Emma, Brandon, Beau, Delaney, Jake, Colby, and everyone else in both the Dunn and Weston clans. The huge group laughed and hugged as news of Natalie's pregnancy made its way around the party. Several minutes later Marcus announced the food was ready and everyone grabbed a plate. Tables of other condiments, pickles, desserts and salads lined the walkway. Everyone piled their plates high and then settled down to eat.

Marcus leaned over and kissed her on the lips. "Yum, potato salad."

"You're so bad."

"You love it."

"How is your shoulder?"

"Good as new." She gave him her best 'I don't believe you' look and he laughed. "All right, Doctor, it's still sore, but I don't need the sling anymore. I just try not to move my shoulder around too much."

"Good."

Gram beamed from her spot next to the pool, her own sexy pool-boy at her feet in the form of Mr. Johansson from in town. They'd been seeing each other regularly these days and it made Elizabeth happy to know Natalie's grandmother might find someone to spend time with since her husband passed away.

"Get the smirk off your lips, Elizabeth. I'll have no matchmaking around me anytime soon."

"You didn't get a chance to be in on my little lovefest like you have with my siblings and a few of the Dunn clan."

"Who do you think told Marcus to send you those flowers the other day?"

Elizabeth shook her head and laughed. A quick kiss to Mrs. Oliver's cheek and she was off to locate the love of her life.

After everyone had finished eating, Marcus took her plate and set it on the floor. He slid from the chair to kneel at her feet.

"You know I love you."

"Yes. I love you too."

"I wanted to do this with our friends and family here. I know you still have a long way to go in your residency, but we can work together to make our lives the happiest we can. You've made the first step in that come true with moving in here. Now, it's time to take the second step. Elizabeth, will you do me the honor of becoming my wife?"

"What?"

"Didn't I make myself clear?" he asked, laughing. "I want you to marry me."

"Seriously?"

"Damn women. I didn't think the words were that mumbled." He grabbed her hand and kissed her fingers before he produced a beautiful square cut diamond solitaire. "Marry me, Elizabeth."

"Yes!" she screamed, throwing herself into his arms.

The End

About the Author

Sandy Sullivan is a romance author, who, when not writing, spends her time with her husband Shaun on their farm in middle Tennessee. She loves to ride her horses, play with their dogs and relax on the porch, enjoying the rolling hills of her home south of Nashville. Country music is a passion of hers and she loves to listen to it while she writes, although when she writes sex scenes, it has to be completely quiet.

She is an avid reader of romance novels and enjoys reading Nora Roberts, Jude Deveraux and Susan Wiggs. Finding new authors and delving into something different helps feed the need for literature. A registered nurse by education, she loves to help people and spread the enjoyment of romance to those around her with her novels. She loves cowboys so you'll find many of her novels have sexy men in tight jeans and cowboy boots.